Foreword

I am a Bodacious Woman,
Never an Old Lady.

I will grow leaner
And keener
And meaner.

I will begin to blend
With all the colors
Of the Earth

Until the day
I fade away
From Pure Joy.

Colette Dugas
(My Mantra)

I wish I could claim it. A cursive handmade sign with this poem on it hangs on the outside wall of my workshop as you open the door. It is surrounded by joyous flowers blooming and hanging purple Wandering Jew on the porch that leads to the yellow brick path at 106 Fairy Land.

It's a small building that my husband purchased for me to create in, and I turned the building into my own haven so it has always welcomed me, and I have been comforted.

Don't confuse it with a "she shed." It's always been a workplace and without all the frivolous things (well, some of my friends would disagree) you think goes along with being a she shed. I always felt it was an offensive thing to say, "she shed." I guess it's because my husband had a man cave.

As if.

On the other side of the entrance is a large frame with a smaller frame in it. The words written by me on the sign in the smaller frame, in big letters, say, Eve was framed!

That's one of my beliefs in my fey world. And trust me, we ain't going there.

The Wandering Jew has wandered with me throughout my life, starting with a cutting from my mama's house more than fifty years ago. Sometimes, there's been just a cutting left. It always comes back with me, moving on down the road.

∞ ∞ ∞

MY life has been one of wandering, totally lost. Being led to the demise of my innocence. It's has definitely been one of the good, the bad, and the very ugly.

At sixteen years old, I had no idea who I was going to be when I grew up.

Very shortly, which seemed as though it was forever, I was left with three children to take care of, it being he thought my mama and daddy would take of us. He considered my family wealthy.

Let's put it this way: he was hit with bad karma!

I raised three children, and they raised me. The oldest was almost my peer. It was a "good time had by all," and I write about it in my first book, Madam C's Beliefs and Make-Believes, the chapter about Mama and the Trio.

But, at times it was harsh, and real reality knocked on the door.

What did a twenty-two-year-old, bipolar, forsaken artist-writer, working menial jobs to feed the chirren, with absentee papas, KNOW? So, we all made it anyway, in spite of negativity surrounding me and them. They became wonderful people, raising good, normal children and successful.

Now, I know there's no such thing as normal. We all became well acquainted with the word dysfunction. I like this term better, but I know I gave them all a touch of batshit crazy!

It's all cuz of Minou and Joe

AN ANTHOLOGY OF MAYHEM DOWN THE BAYOU

Madame C

Edited by Dani J. Caile
Cover Design by Thomas Lamkin Jr.

For more information, email www.linebylionpublications.com

I had a late-in-life baby, with my daughter already having a year-old daughter. Nine months later, I had a grandson from my eldest son.

I knew that the Higher Beings gave me another trio to do over again. They are the new Trio.

∞ ∞ ∞

I find it hard to write about myself. Ah don' like dat!

I want to get to the shortcut that leads to Madam C coming out of the closet she lived in. I just couldn't keep the door opened, and I was the one keeping the windows rolled up.

I had a bookstore. Can you believe it? I, with a little help from my friends, turned the old store that stunk into a place of magical mystery every day, burning mulberry candles all day and sometimes through the night.

I absolutely loved it.

The Lamppost Emporium.

New books came in with so much excitement in the boxes. The new ones in front and then a trade center for used books all the way to the back of the store.

So many new ideas leaning on New Age and self-help books. Each type of book had its own section. Book readers came in looking for a particular novel. I would go right to it, knowing where every book was located.

The store had been a clothing store. They left many neat things that I could use in decorations. Western section had a huge sign nailed to the wall advertising Wrangler Jeans, with a cowboy sitting on a horse and a huge picture of John Wayne.

The romance books were behind red-painted shutters, with a play area for kids built in where they laid on pillows with books to read. It was the old dressing rooms I used. I had painted a sign that said "Bodice Rippers!" Leading into that section, I had a big poster of Brad Pitt from Legends of The Fall on the outside wall. I put on every color of lipstick I had and kissed him all over his face.

One day, this woman walked in, asking me if I had a small place for her to do massages and ear candling and healing people of nasty chakras. I said, "It just so happens I have your room in the back waiting on you." (Not quite, but pretty close to the truth.) Her business took off and led to a remarkable career.

I had to decorate two huge bay windows that used to have mannequins standing in them, posed for the next dress or shoes on sale. I did this every week, having to climb up in the windows through a small door. It was hot! I dressed both windows, trying to make the windows shine out with books and related items.

This store was located in a town where a hometown boy made good. This man had an inauguration and ball coming up for governor. I was given the tickets for both ceremonies by a valued customer.

I dug through all articles about this famous man and found a book written by his mother. Everything I could find was put into both windows about his journey to the governorship. Books, articles, and pictures, leaning on other books in the windows, showing how proud the town was of him.

I wasn't from there, so I found it very disconcerting that the Main Street stores didn't have any congratulations for the man that had done good.

I wasn't there at the bookstore the day of all the happenings, and my friend who had taken my place said it was full of all the TV stations filming his hometown, with newspaper people too.

Shit, Ah don' like dat!

There was a three-sided mirror in an alcove where people were able to see themselves trying on clothes, and that's where my Cockatiel named Sugar lived in a huge cage, looking at herself in the mirrors. I taught her how to whistle a tune, and when I opened in the morning, she would sing her little tune, greeting me.

One of my closest friends came in and asked if I wanted a cypress tree. What? Here he came with a styrofoam cypress tree from the casino that was throwing out old decorations. It was very light to carry, full of real moss dripping down over an honest-to-goodness look-alike cypress. It stayed in the middle of the store, with a sitting area surrounding it to read your books or hang out conversing.

Another idea I had came out of nowhere. Woke up one morning to a vision about fairies. I began to put a doll together in the bookstore where there was ample room to create things. Crazy little women fairy dolls from the swamps. I still make them and have sold hundreds all over the world.

My many friends threw me a birthday party unlike any I had before, and it was so fun and filled with friends that loved me and were celebrating me. We were all discussing what the dolls would be called as well as what would be my creative AKA.

One of those there said, "Madam C and the Louisiana swamp fairies."

As they say, the rest is history.

All my grandchildren and my son had political meetings in the back room, wanting to solve the problems of the world. They put a newspaper together for their schools using the school's old copying method. My son eventually had the newspaper in town putting the paper together and delivering them. Never, ever did he receive any recognition for this professional job.

I'm not naming the place, but it still has caused me to ride through this town and shudder.

∞ ∞ ∞

MANY things – good, bad, and ugly – have happened along the way. I am free at last, God Almighty, I'm free at last. Finally, since I was sixteen.

I have been given a new lease on life, first time with real money and bills being paid by my banker granddaughter. All I have to do, other than household chores, is write.

Word after word, wondering where the hell I came up with that.

I truly believe a Higher Power wouldn't give me a new life and then cut me off by killing me. I am healthy and wise. I ain't old, but

I've been around a long time. I've got another twenty-five years, or so I've been told.

This book has been chaotic, cathartic, cleansing, and calming from what was going on around me.

I dedicate this book to my magician, my desperado, my enigma who was there encouraging me to write. He left lasting memories of the good, the bad, and the ugly. It carried me until I became, truly, Madam C.

From now until I pass, I will be Colette Dugas.

Colette Dugas Sanders Canty

Part One

Chapter One

Loup-Garou

HERE she comes, leaving dusty clouds in her wake, a combination of gravel and oyster shells caused by her skipping barefooted.

Minou. That's who she is. In her bare feet and tattered overalls, kicking at the gravel and shells, heading for Mrs. Flavia's store.

Minou's mama calls her that because it's short for Minna Sue, and she favors the little kitty cat. Bertha doesn't let her out the house looking like that. She'll grab her and pop the brush off the top of her head, trying to tame the beast to be beautiful.

Her mama is Bertha, and she doesn't catch her this time because she gets away early, before Bertha can even make the coffee.

∞ ∞ ∞

MINOU Peltier comes from a Cajun family that settled this area with the Houmas Indians a long time ago. Strong survivors with work ethics, well known up and down the Parish.

Jake Peltier was her papa, and he was killed when she was an infant. Minou and Bertha live in their own house that her papa had bought from his papa, Irby Peltier. Irby was well-known and thought highly of until the day he quit talking and became a hermit in the house he lives in with Minou and Bertha. He has been an invalid for years and doesn't talk anymore. He has lived with Minou's family since before her papa was killed and is Alcide's daddy too.

Alcide is Jake's last brother out of seven; no sisters. Pawpaw Irby was a seventh son too. Several brothers have passed already, but the rest have moved from the bayou for greener pastures. It's just the four of them now.

Being he's her papa's youngest brother, Alcide comes in and out the house. He isn't married yet and not looking. He's kind of different. Do you know what they say about the seventh son? They have peculiar things in their lineage.

Alcide lives next door to Minou, her mama, Bertha, and her Pawpaw Irby. Alcide lives in the house where Pawpaw Irby raised his seven sons, because his wife was killed by an alligator trying to get the baby, Alcide. The two houses did belong to Pawpaw Irby, but he lives with Bertha because he needs special care, and he's the only pawpaw Minou's got. They love the little man even though he just one day quit talking and wants to stay inside on his recliner.

The two big houses clear about an acre, with front porches screened against those mosquitoes and flying wasps. Both houses have seen better days, but there's not enough money to fix either one.

Minou's papa, Jake, was killed on an offshore drilling rig. A young man who died way before he was supposed to, leaving Bertha and Minou in one of the houses with his daddy. Never has Bertha felt they aren't wanted or needed in the family.

The oil company has never sent any money to the widow and her daughter. Sometimes those people aren't very sympathetic and too greedy. They think that it was just his bad luck.

Bertha knows all about hard work and is a hunter who brings deer to the table.

Bertha is a hardworking widow who has never been thought about by the oil company that is responsible for her husband's death. That doesn't happen anymore, the sleazy bastards.

Her family, the Dardars, have a strong connection to the Houmas and Atakapa tribes that have lived along the coastline of Louisiana for centuries.

∞ ∞ ∞

THIS little girl who just made ten has a strong sense of competition between her and the owner of the store, Mrs. Flavia's General Store. Who can find out first, the gossip going around the village. This is because Minou and Mrs. Flavia are way too nosy for their own good.

She runs into the large old wooden store that has a big front porch, slamming the screen door advertising RC Cola on its handles. Her big collie dog, Couyon, is running into the store behind her, sliding into whatever display is being put up by Mrs. Flavia for the day.

Flavia picks up her large straw broom and whacks the dog, pushing him back through the door he has just run through, cussing and yelling at him. She likes Couyon but not in her store.

This happens every day, kind of a habit with those two, in Larose, Louisiana. Down the bayou there are big shrimp boats coming and going under the drawbridge that Huey P. Long built. Larose is a small village that sits on the side of the road that comes all the way from Shreveport on the way to the Gulf on Highway One. It's one village after the other until you get to Grand Isle. And it's a one-sided road on the bayou because the other side is swamp.

News is passed from one house to another, then another until it reaches the person the news is for. Before the horse with a rider bringing the message from up the bayou can get to the destination.

Minou is well known in Larose. She is very bossy and commands attention wherever she goes. It's not because of how she looks. It's because she is straight up questioning everything and is always thinking.

Minou Peltier comes to spend her money with Mrs. Flavia for drinks and sandwiches for her and her friend Joe before going fishing. She gets up early to do her chores, and then she can fish the day away.

Mrs. Flavia tells her what not to do in the big swamp that borders her yard and the store.

She says yes, ma'am but has no intention to follow the orders or even let the thought cross her mind when she's out of sight of the store.

Minou is not but 10 years old but is quick to tell you, she knows everything. Her mama has given up on the idea that there is a girl under that wild curly hair with a cap on it and overalls getting too tight for a growing girl. She never gets any taller than five feet three inches. But she has a small Napoleonic complex. So, she brings fresh fish every day and sells what her mama doesn't use.

∞ ∞ ∞

MINOU has been hearing about the loup-garou for a long time, long as she can remember. Her mama and Mrs. Flavia have been warning her about that monster since she's been old enough to walk. She doesn't think she wants to believe that. Minou is that kind of girl, you better show it to her, for her to believe it. Minou has to see it for herself.

Minou ain't scared of nothing and is quick to tell you that.

Her parrain is the worst in telling her. He knows for sure it's true because he's seen one. A loup-garou! He had to run for his life. Parrain Alcide won't tell her when, but it's been a long time ago. He makes a necklace for her to wear with a little bag of protection against the loup-garou. Minou thinks the damn thing stinks bad but catches a bad fussing when she takes it off. No telling what's in that bag.

Anyway, Minou loves her parrain so much she follows him, along with the dog, Couyon. He doesn't mind.

Alcide is a strong Cajun man. He is dark-complected, with a wiry frame and tight curls on his head. He's not what you call a big man, but he is the one you call on for help with whatever needs doing. He's quick and dependable to get the job done. He speaks good English most times because he has a 10th grade education and loves to read anything he can find.

Alcide has found out all he can about the loup-garou, like the history of all the monsters that someone wrote about. They have been here a long time, back to when the Cajuns got kicked out by the English in Nova Scotia.

Alcide makes sure he's gone on the night of a full moon. Bertha tells Minou Alcide is going to a house of ill repute. Minou of course knows what it is by now, but she doesn't question anymore, after Alcide tells her that's not true.

Minou is after her parrain to answer her questions.

"Parrain, how can ya be so scared? Ah ain't scared none, me! Why ya can't stay to protect us if dere's such a t'ing? Shit, Ah'll just shoot tha bastard!"

Minou is now a short and feisty little woman of fifteen. He says to her, "Lil girl, if ya don't go to ya house, Ah swear Ah'm gonna slap dat smart mouth. Ah been tellin' Bertha dat ya got no business out dere in tha swamp!

"Yeah, you right. Ah'm scared as merde every month 'cause Ah know what dey can do to ya. Once was enough for me!"

Minou knows this, but she does it to him every full moon, and he always says the same thing over and over.

She knows she's smarter than her parrain, but she doesn't tell him.

Bertha doesn't let Minou out the house after dark any night. Minou got a bad spanking one time when she was little. That's all it took at that time but now, she's antsy and feeling her hormones. Her mama doesn't know, since she is older, Minou goes out at night.

Well, mostly every night now, you have to say.

Her mama is asleep by nine o'clock, while the TV is playing Dragnet. She works hard and gets up at 5 every morning. Bertha is a large woman that shows in her face all the hard living and work she has had to do since she was made a widow. It is obvious to everybody that she is a beauty but not to herself. She has a smile that can light up a room, and she is natural with her laugh, a wonderful one that comes from her gut. You learn how to laugh at whatever comes down the road.

Minou's childhood companion and always boyfriend, Joe, is meeting her out in the swamps. Joe Thibeau has fished with Minou, fought with Minou, protected Minou from ugly people, and loves her with his huge, big heart. He's a mama's boy out of necessity since his dad has been gone to the other side of the dirt. His mama, Ethel, depends on him too much.

His mama would be upset to know he's in the swamps at night, just like Bertha would be. Ethel Thibeau would be upset more if she knew he is out there with Minou Peltier.

Joe's mama knows Minou isn't daughter-in-law material. She won't be controlled and doesn't listen to nobody. Non, not for her daughter-inlaw. Something could happen.

After all, they both old enough, being fifteen together.

The next time there's a full moon, Minou waits for Bertha to fall asleep in front of the TV watching Jerry Springer. Pawpaw Irby has been asleep on the recliner. She slips out the back door, heading for the swamps. She's not worried about her pawpaw because he doesn't hear a thing!

Joe is waiting in their spot under the big oak tree where they have worn the palmettos down until it is matted on the ground. Their chosen spot for years. They fish together where the moss hangs from trees that are centuries old. They have put together a makeshift wharf where they can see everything on the bayou. They keep the area clean because it's a place for them to go to talk and do whatever comes into their minds.

Since they are both older, their feelings are what most teenagers begin to be aware of: sex.

These two little fools don't pay attention to the moon. The dark of the night becomes light, and they have enough in any phase to see each other. If not, they bring some candles. They prefer it if it's full, but they forget about the old loup-garou that's supposed to be roaming in the swamps.

On the fullest of the moon, the monster comes out. Many of the people that live up and down the bayou have claimed to see the French werewolf. Some have not come back to tell the tale.

Minou and Joe are quiet, busy making out. They take a break from their kissing and hugging when they both hear a growl and something moving in the swamps. They hide in the standing palmettos to see him, but they are out of view of the loup-garou.

The monster looks like a dirty, hairy, big-headed man loping on four big-ass paws through the swamps and cypress trees. A skinny-looking wolf with long hair all over his body, he stands straight up on his two hind legs. His face is long like a wolf, and his teeth are bloody, and he is snarling and howling.

Well, he starts running to the bayou, and he's making guttural sounds like a wolf would do if he's in heat!

They are silent in their fear watching this, but Minou is way too nosy and watches everything the loup-garou is doing.

The monster doesn't see them or smell them. That loup-garou has more pressing matters to deal with, because he is crossing the bayou to where another hairy creature is waiting. Holy merde!

That isn't a male on the other side of the bayou waiting, because they could see she is really hairy with giant tetons, and when that creature across the bayou starts howling like another wolf looking for a mate, they decide to run.

They take off running when Joe trips on a cypress knee poking out the water and falls face first in the muddy bayou and is covered in lily pads, like he is some creature from the Black Lagoon!

The next morning they meet at Mrs. Flavia's store and each get an RC Cola and two cigarettes. Flavia charges 50¢ for one of her cigarettes, tight as she is.

But they both need one. It is so serious what's taken place in the swamps.

Flavia doesn't say anything about the cigarettes but slips some Trojans to Joe, free of charge!

∞ ∞ ∞

FLAVIA has had her store since Minou could remember. Generations of storekeepers hand down the mercantile business to the next of kin, going on since before the Civil War. Bertha tells Minou one time that Flavia had a Jewish pawpaw way back in her family. Don't ask her because she is kinda close-mouthed when it comes to her business and her religion.

She is a tall, muscular woman with hair like a helmet on her head. A tight curl only a home permanent would do. She isn't friendly most days and quick to tell you what you should do and not do.

She is every bit as nosy as Minou and hollers behind them, "Where tha hell are y'all runnin' to dis early? Y'all didn't get no worms, so ya sure ain't fishin'! Ya bettah behave, you two."

Joe and Minou get to their spot they have carved out of the swamp.

"Mais, Minou, who we gonna tell dis to? We bot' in some deep merde! Lawd, don't tell Alcide, or he'll slap ya and then make y'all move! Ah t'ink it was tha loup-garou, and now we know dere's two of dem! What we gonna say? Ah feel haunt 'cause we can't warn nobody!"

Minou hugs Joe real tight and then says, "We ain't gonna tell one livin' soul. T'ink about it. Den tha sheriff and his posse be tramplin' t'rough our spot and want to know where we saw dem. Mais, it would be in tha newspaper in Golden Meadow and bunches of people will be lookin'. And then da sheriff will ask what the merde we doin' back dere. Lawd, we gonna be on the Channel Six news too if dey find out. Ah'm not gonna tell one damn person."

Of course, she is lying because she goes back to the house to tell her parrain, Alcide, just to be a smart aleck and to tell him it is for true.

She wants to see them again.

When she tells Alcide, he screams real loud and grabs Minou by the arm. "What tha hell Ah been tellin' ya, ya stupid, foolish lil girl? Ya coulda been bit, and Joe coulda been his next meal. Don't ya know what happens if ya bit? Den ya got tha curse! Ooh, Minou, ya don't want dat just to be some brave girl who is too nosy for her own good. Ah'm gonna tell Bertha on ya!"

And he does just that.

Bertha is frying catfish when Alcide comes through the door, dragging Minou by the arm. She turns from the hot stove so fast that Minou kinda jumps.

Bertha wails and throws a dish at Minou's head. "Sumbitch, Ah t'ought Ah was raisin' ya right, and ya sneakin' behind my back wit'

Joe! Ya know he's a mama's boy, and his mama gonna come kill ya. Dey ain't no tellin' what y'all saw! Dat's good for ya lil asses. What's wrong wit' ya? Haven't we told ya all ya life not to go out at night in tha swamps? Are ya dat cuckoo to t'ink ya could go out dere and somet'in' not happen to ya? Merde, ya could be comin' home wit' a baby if ya don't listen!"

Minou takes her chastisement because she knows her mama is right. She promises she will listen and not go back in the swamps at night. She just leaves out "except for the full moon."

If Minou has something in her head, it's not in her foot, so she plans carefully for the next full moon. She is determined to see those two loup-garous again. She's talked Joe into going with her, in spite of him being scared to death of the monsters and his mama.

Alcide and Bertha are keeping their eyes on her every move. Bertha has already got a call from Joe's mama, and boy, do they have words! His mama wants nothing to do with Minou, worrying about them getting married or worse, coming home with a baby.

Bertha doesn't like Ethel even for a little bit. She doesn't like a woman that plays the victim all the time because she knows what it is to struggle with life. Ethel is this whiny-ass old lady that will tell you every detail of a minor surgery or how much she has suffered throughout her life. Bertha isn't one to suffer fools, and they've never found any common ground until Minou and Joe give them one.

Minou's parrrain and her mama have been very secretive, the two of them always whispering and conniving. Pawpaw Irby never says anything.

Bertha tells Minou to ask her pawpaw about the monster, and Minou wonders what the hell she's talking about. He doesn't talk! So, she sits by his legs propped up on the recliner and says, "Pawpaw, ya know about tha loup-garou? Ya believe in dat?"

She falls over backwards as he stands straight up and makes eerie, scary noises like he can't breathe.

"Mon Dieu! Mon Dieu! Mon Dieu! Have mercy, have mercy! Tha loup-garou's gonna get me, gonna get me, gonna get me! Oh, my sweet Jesus! Mon Dieu!" He is screaming with his arms straight up, reaching for relief.

Pawpaw falls back and starts crying like a little baby, trying to get in a fetal position and reaching for the glass of water that's always on his side table. He is gulping and spills a lot, but Bertha is there to fill up the glass again. She gives him a shot glass full of cherry bounce Alcide has made.

Bertha makes sure he has calmed down after drinking the shot glass empty, in one gulp too. She brings him to his bed and says prayers with him.

Minou is crying, waiting on some kind of explanation. "Why ya made me do dat? He don't talk no more, but he sure spoke some words, and he was scared shitless. Ah feel so shame, Mama! What tha hell happened for him to act so crazy, Mama? Tell me! Ah gotta know tha truth, Mama! Gimme some of dat cherry bounce. Merde! Merde! Merde!"

Minou doesn't know what to do with herself, and she is walking round and round the table while Alcide watches her from a kitchen chair. She gets what you call a temper, so he knows when not to pick. Bertha comes and makes Minou sit at the kitchen table with her and Alcide. The two of them have prepared the whole quemas, and Minou is some pissed off!

"Why tha hell ya ain't told me somet'in'? Ah don't know merde 'bout Pawpaw Irby. Tha only t'ing Ah remember is him holdin' me when Ah was lil and smilin' at me. Tell me, goddammit!"

Bertha reaches in the cabinet where the potent stuff sits on its own shelf. She pours drinks for all of them from the bottle of Johnny Walker Red. She lights a cigarette and starts talking.

"We never told ya why Pawpaw Irby don't talk no more. Ya never asked! He hasn't talked since Alcide was a teenager. One night, he and his pal Clifton go bull-froggin', and dey come upon tha monster. Dey start runnin', but tha loup-garou catches Clifton and shreds him into dog meat. Pawpaw sees it all and blames it on hisself. Ya didn't know 'cause ya papa makes us promise not to ever tell ya. But nooo, ya so damn nosy and know everyt'in', you t'ink, ya foolish little twat! Dere's a lot ya don't know, and it's better dat ya don't."

Bertha tells her there's many people right here in Larose that have seen and heard the loup-garou at night. Others have gone missing; Clifton is not the only one that's lost his life over this monster. There are others. She says Mrs. Flavia's papa went into the swamps and was never seen again. Some say he's run off with the mechanic's wife, but others know better.

Minou has never asked why her pawpaw quit talking. It never comes up as a thought in her head. She feels sorry that she upset him.

She goes to meet Joe at Mrs. Flavia's store. Minou politely asks Flavia about her papa and is told straight up it is none of her business. Flavia fusses at Minou, saying they been telling her all her life and what she does is the opposite of what she is told! Of course, the tale has reached Flavia, probably by Bertha.

She fusses at Joe the same way; except she tells him to keep his dinga-ling in his pants around Minou.

They sure as hell don't tell her everything because she would be the first one on the phone calling the sheriff!

They leave, heading for their spot where they have been during the last full moon. Joe, throwing his line out with a big worm on the end of his pole, says, "Ooh, baby, now what we gonna do? We got e'rybody pissed off at us, and dey gonna be watchin' us like hawks. Not to hold ya and kiss ya like we been doin' for so long. Ah don't know if Ah can do dis no more. Why don't we just run off and get married?"

Minou laughs and shakes Joe by the arms, saying, "Mais, we not old enough! Not even tha justice of tha peace would marry us wit'out some kind of okay from my mama and yours. Are ya a couyon? We love each other enough to be married, but what we gonna do? Shack up? Ya mama don't like me even a little bit, and she would have a heart attack! What we gonna do now is make our plans for tha next full moon."

Minow has been sneaking around Alcide's house to read all the books he has on the subject of the monster. She finds a shelf full of books on all kinda scary topics, reading what she could. She knows what to do as always, because now she knows everything!

She begins to tell Joe what they need to be prepared for the next time, as she is determined to lay a trap for the loup-garou. Nobody ever, she thinks, has ever tried this before! Lawd, this girl thinks very highly of herself.

They have begun to save all their dollars and change to pay for the stuff on the list that Minou has made. They can't use the charge account the family has at Flavia's. She's gonna ask enough questions as to why they need the unusual supplies.

The day before the full moon, Alcide is leaving to get away from the swamps and the monster. The same old, same old words are spoken, except Minou isn't fooling around with him. She wants him to go but doesn't tell him that, for sure. He would know they have something afoot.

Bertha seems to be more alert in watching her, pacing the floors with Minou and not sitting still, both of them. It's very tense in the house, and Minou is being stifled, but they act like not a thing is wrong. They are both sneaky and conniving together but not on the same canaille!

Little does Bertha know that everything is in place and ready for the round, white, large circle of the moon to appear and bring the loup-garou to their swamp.

Minou and Joe have this huge trap ready, along with some big flashlights and nets. They've built a huge rabbit snare, tying it to the massive oak for strength. They've brought the boat back there in case they have to run and take off in the little putt-putt to escape.

The trip to Flavia's is the biggest obstacle and they go together, slamming the RC Cola advertising screen door. They give her the list that she looks at, and you could tell the questions are coming.

"Minou Peltier and Joe Thibeau, what tha hell ya need this for? Ya mama knows ya buyin' all dis? Why ya need dis big hat? Y'all not runnin' away, huh? Joe, ya been doin' what Ah said? Look, don't tell ya mama, but Ah'm gonna give y'all some rubbers. Shoo, shoo, hush, don't make me say it loud! Don't say nuttin'! Ya hear me?"

Flavia has it all figured out, and she is gonna give them the next morning before she calls Bertha.

Minou is watching her Mama's nervine, and she is acting like she won't ever go to bed. She's taken care of the situation by fixing her mama's Dr Pepper full of ice with a couple of sleeping pills Pawpaw has to have.

Minou says she is going to bed and watches as her mama falls to the sofa. Minou climbs out the big window in her room, hightailing it to Joe.

Joe is waiting by the back of Flavia's for Minou to come out. As agreed, he's put the same medicine in his mama's RC Cola. He's feeling so guilty about that until Minou tells him to shut up because there's more serious business to worry about.

They finally make it out to the palmettos, where everything has been set up to catch at least one of those loup-garous!

Minou is scared but more curious. Joe is more scared, and he shows it. He'll be a pushover for Minou if they marry.

They hide among the palmetto and proceed to wait for the monsters.

It is about an hour later 'til they hear the screeching howl!

Minou thinks it's a whole damn pack of wolves!

Walking upright, it is slowly moving into the swamps to reach the bayou, where there is a large female loup-garou howling back at him.

Joe almost faints but instead soils his pants. Minou thinks it's time for them to move out in view for the monsters to see them.

Minou hollers, "Hey, you! Ugly big-ass loup-garou! Come over here, ya nasty creature!"

She is wearing the big hat and all her winter clothes for protection against the monster's bite. She has the mosquito spray in one hand and a huge stick with her silver rosary beads wrapped around it. She got that for her first Communion when her daddy was alive, but now her and Bertha don't go to Mass. Her mama got pissed off when the priest told her to put money in the envelope every week. Bertha coulda used help from the church, instead of the other way around.

Joe is in the clearing, flashing both of the beams into the beast's eyes, daring him to come over there! He's in the camouflage overalls he uses for hunting and some netting over his head. He looks ferocious himself as the monster. He's jumping up and down, making sure the loup-garou sees his antics, to move him away from Minou.

The loup-garou turns at the hollering commotion and screams like he's just found his next meal! That fiend starts running toward them, and Minou is steadily spraying him with the Off! She runs toward the trap and shakes the stick at him, with the rosary beads flapping in the wind. That just irritates the creature, and he howls and screams with his big mouth and stands there.

The loup-garou is snarling with his mouth open. Minou sees the blood in his mouth foaming and says, "What big teeth dis fuckin' wolf has!"

She is leading him down to the bayou edge where the snare is waiting and the dog, Couyon, is making like he is so brave with his barking and growling at the loup-garou. He would run like crazy if the monster just looked his way.

The snare catches the loup-garou, and the net comes tumbling down on him. That large stick with the rosary is swinging, hitting the monster!

A massive fishing net they borrowed is extra strong, and it flips over, covering the beast, with his left hind leg caught in the snare.

Minou throws the other can of spray to Joe; he sprays across the bayou, hoping it will reach the female waiting for her man.

The other loup-garou runs back into the swamps on the other side of the bayou, screaming out her howling. They have managed to ensnare the creature from the Black Lagoon!

It is truly caught in the rabbit trap and is attempting to get to them from under the heavy netting and scratching at his eyes. This has got to be the biggest fish those nets have caught!

Joe lights this huge fire they have prepared, so the whole area is lit up. They have made it out of logs and old cypress boards piled so high, it looks like a pyramid! They use three containers of kerosene.

Joe worries it will cause a call into the fire trucks, but it doesn't seem anyone is looking out their windows to see the flames.

They are really waiting on Bertha to come screaming and put out the fire. Nobody comes.

They sit in silence, watching that monster try to untangle itself to get to both of them. Minou and Joe don't taunt the loup-garou because they think he will really find the strength to tear the net and eat them. They watch his foaming, bloody jaws and teeth gnawing the ropes that hold him by his hind leg, trying to kill them.

They sit and wait until the sun dawns and watch that loup-garou change back into a man, with the trap folding around him. They go to untangle the man from the nets and snare. They both fall back, tumbling on the ground, seeing who it was.

None other than Parrain Alcide!

He stands up in horror and is so haunt because he is naked! He falls on the ground crying, knowing he could have killed his beloved godchild.

Joe takes his overalls off and hands them to Alcide to put on his naked body. Everyone is silent because they are lost for words, even Minou.

They all walk back to the house without saying a word where Bertha is waiting, all of them stinking from Off! spray and kerosene and wet dogs!

Minou's heart is broken because she has to tell her mama just who was under the trap. She knows that it'll be her, Minou, to tell who it is.

Minou and Joe already said they thought he was shacked up with some barmaid.

Minou is feeling guilty with her nosy self. She knows if she hadn't been so busy trying to find out something that was none of her business, this wouldn't have happened. She says to her mama, "How tha hell are we gonna keep dis from Flavia, Mama? She's already sniffin' around, knowing somet'in' was happenin'. She t'ought we was runnin' away to get married!"

Minou and Joe are looking hard at Bertha because she doesn't have on her housedress like she wears every morning, fixing her Mello

Joy coffee and lighting her Pall Mall menthol cigarette. She and Alcide have their coffee every morning together. Both get up with the chickens.

Bertha looks like she has been looking for them because her clothes are muddy and disheveled and her long hair is looking like a rat's nest. They all look at each other, waiting for someone to get up from the chair and give some kind of explanation of the serious thing that has happened to their family.

Bertha speaks as Alcide pours the coffee for everybody sitting at the table and reaches for the Johnny Walker at the same time. These people don't care what time of the day it is when they feel like taking a little sip of whatever is in the cabinet. They don't know a thing about five o'clock somewhere!

"Well, you lil nosy shit, what ya gonna do now? Ya made me so dizzy Ah couldn't do nuttin' but walk and growl. Ah'm just a dazed and confused werewolf! Ya had to find out, in spite of us warnin' ya!

Well, if ya haven't figured it out yet, ya don't know nuttin'!

"It's me, Minou, waitin' for him to cross tha bayou and come to me! And dat mosquito spray stung tha hell out my eyes, ya lil bastard, Joe!

"Ya both stay where ya at and don't make no sudden moves 'cause y'all messed up my night, being so gaga Ah couldn't t'ink! Ah don't know if it's tha drug or tha loup-garou callin' me. Now Ah'm fixin' to tell y'all tha trut' of it all and no more damn secrets in dis family from nobody!

"Ah know more 'bout ya two dan ya two t'ink! You too, Joe. Ya ain't goin' nowhere else 'til we settled dis quemas! Joe, call ya mama 'fore she busts up in here and sees dis. Y'all for sure ain't gonna get married if she does. Tell her ya fell asleep on the sofa, and Ah will talk wit' her if she wants."

Alcide fixes the cups of coffee but still hasn't said one word. He doesn't dare leave because there's no telling what will happen.

Bertha will tell for true the rest of the story.

"Me and Alcide been in love for a long time. He's been a loup-garou for many years, but he had ya papa to take care of him. Ya papa used to help him not kill people and run all cuckoo and mean through tha swamps.

"When ya papa was killed and before we fell in love, Alcide had no help to deal wit' tha curse. When we found out we loved each other, we felt dat tha match could never happen.

"So one day, Ah let Alcide bite me on tha neck before he changed into dat monster. Ohh, Ah can still feel dat bite! Mais, we don't know if it would take 'cause he was Alcide and not tha loup-garou. But it caught, and now we worse off dan before!

"Dat's all he could figure out, tha dumbass. Ah t'ink he went to kiss my neck and got carried away! Alcide can't help hisself sometimes, but me, Ah always eat tha deer. How come ya t'ink we got deer meat all tha time? Mais, merde! Before ya lil ass gets up, Ah bring it home.

"Alcide done some terrible deeds, and it's hard for him to live wit'. No one ever bit Alcide but wit' dis seventh son shit, he became one. If we could just bite someone and not kill 'em, tha curse would be given to dem, and we could be free of dis damned-to-hell curse.

"So, now ya know tha start of what has happened. Ah don't feel ya need to know nuttin' else, so don't start askin' ya damn questions. Now

Ah want to know, are y'all gonna call tha sheriff?"

Minou figures her parrain will tell her more when she starts questioning him. Lawd have mercy, he doesn't stand a chance. Minou gets irate thinking her mama would even think that!

"As if! As if, Mama, Ah'm gonna call tha sheriff. And you, Joe, ya ain't gonna say nuttin', neither. Ah sure as hell didn't t'ink it would be my mama and my parrain as tha loup-garous!

"What we gonna do, Mama? Ah'm just fifteen years old and don't know what to do 'bout dis horrible t'ing!"

Lawd, the little-know-it-all admits she doesn't know everything! Probably won't hear that out her mouth again.

"Me, Ah'm gonna take dis to my grave," Joe says as he stands on the side of Minou. "Ah vow on my love for Minou and dat's a life-livin' love. We want to be married right now so dat we're dere for bot' of you. Dat's how Ah feel about dis quemas, and my mama will never know from me. Ah'm part of dis family already!"

Alcide stands up from the table and reaches for the hands of Minou and Joe. Grabbing them, he is mournfully crying. He's on his third handkerchief and probably his third drink.

"Ooh, ooh, Mon Dieu, what have Ah done! Ah'm so shamed y'all saw me naked as a egret! Minou, my big-big love for ya woulda been over wit' just one bite! Instead of protectin' you, Ah let ya catch me with a goddamn rabbit snare and a silver rosary and a can of Off! Ah'm so shamed dat ya could catch my hairy ol' ass!

"Ya know how long Ah've been loup-garou? Aww, my bébé, Ah just wanna put a gun to my chest and hit my cursed heart! Ya don't know either dat my love for Bertha is as big as yours and Joe! Ah hate to be tha one to tell ya, ya don't know shit from Shinola. Ah don't know how ya missed tha love between ya mama and me.

"Ya so la-la-la, being nosy e'rywhere else, and ya don't see what's been in front of ya all dese years! Dat's a sad sad tale to t'ink we could only be lovers as loup-garous. Well, dat ain't true. If dis is 'bout tellin' no lies, Ah'm sorry.

"Now Ah want to shoot me and Bertha and put us out of misery, like ya would do to a dog. Couyon, he was so brave he was tryin' to bite me, not scared of nuttin', just like you!"

Couyon would have shit if Alcide would have made a move in his direction.

Minou and Joe just sit there, waiting on some answers, until Bertha speaks up. "We just gonna keep dis to ourselves, and Joe was right in what he said. You two can get married. Ah'll give my permission.

"Joe, go tell you mama dat Minou got a baby comin', and Ah know her, she'll consent 'cause she don't want tha gossip to fall on ya head.

"Minou, we was waitin' on you to get married before we told ya we was gettin' married too. Ah have a hard time keepin' Alcide from killin' people, so maybe ya and Joe can help dat way when we change into tha monsters.

"Not no big affair wit' tha marriage, and y'all can live here after. What y'all say?"

Bertha knows she isn't saying one damn thing to Flavia. You don't tell what's going on behind your bedroom door. In their case, what's happening in the swamps.

Minow and Joe grab her mama and Alcide, and they all hug and cry like babies. Minou is still crying when she says, "What tha hell, Mama? Why ya t'ink Ah woulda been upset at ya gettin' married? Mais, y'all don't t'ink better than dat from me? Parrain has been wit' us and helpin' us for so long, he just as soon be my new papa. Ah have wished dat for a long time, a new papa.

"Ah can understand 'bout not tellin' me ya was tha loup-garou, keepin' dat a secret. Ah see how ya two look at each other, and Ah would be glad dat me and Joe would be dere to help y'all.

"Mais, it seemed like maybe ya wouldn't be so damn mad as tha monsters if ya didn't have to wait for each other one day a month! Dat's what Ah t'ought, but now Ah know ya been shackin' up! Ah mean, now come on, dis is tha perfect solution.

"But Ah will spray ya wit' tha Off! and keep tha silver rosary wit' me all tha time.

"It sure don't make no never mind to Pawpaw Irby as long as he don't see nuttin', and he hasn't yet. E'rybody dat lives in Larose has some kinda trouble in dere family, and we ain't no different.

"We gonna get busy for tha weddin'. Mais, let's bot' of us get married together in tha Catholic church so Ethel don't get too mad and cry tha whole time."

Before the month is over, Betha and Alcide with Minou and Joe stand at the altar of the old church, and all of them get married at the same time in a big double wedding with the priest giving the marriage sacraments.

Flavia holds a big fais do-do for the two couples where they have huge pots of seafood gumbo, homemade bread, and lots of cakes. Everybody dances to the live band of The Bayou Folses. In the true tradition of the fais do-do, the children are sleeping on the pallets that are brought.

Liquor is flowing, and the priest, who is a different one Bertha has put in his place, is enjoying the reception and the booze, dancing with the old mawmaws sitting eating the wedding cake. Lawd, if he only knew who he has married.

Mrs. Flavia and Joe's mama cry through the whole thing, Flavia because she is glad it isn't a shotgun wedding and Joe's mama because she has Minou as the daughter-in-law. She doesn't say a thing about the baby she thinks is coming to Larose, Louisiana.

Chapter Two

Gaspar, The Not-So-Friendly Ghost

MINOU and Joe have been together for four years as man and wife. Joe's mama, Ethel, is still looking for that baby she knows for sure is coming when they get married so young. She thinks Minou tricked her Joe with that story!

They don't have time for a baby right now.

Ethel makes her feelings about Minou known, but it rolls off Minou's back like a wet pouldeau.

Minou is still fast with everything she does. Joe has to tag along most of the time because she doesn't wait on anybody. They're always together, so when you see Minou, Joe isn't too far behind.

He sure is no mama's boy anymore because all of his time is with Minou, and he won't go over there to his mama's house if she doesn't go. When they do go, Ethel tries to make like she likes Minou, but Minou can tell she doesn't. She will go with Joe, but if it's too much, Minou will go home. Not too much merde will she take.

They both fish and trap for their livelihood in the swamps behind their houses. They have a secondhand boat that takes them down the bayou. She makes pretty what-nots out of the banked driftwood in the basin. She sells them at Flavia's, and they sell quick.

So they want for nothing. Minou is good with the money.

You already know that Minou and Joe take care of those two loup-garous when they come out in the full moon. It's their duty. Minou regrets she is so nosy when she catches the two of them in their full werewolf get-up, one her mama, and her parrain the other one. Gawd have mercy.

They don't share that burden with anyone, so Flavia doesn't even know.

∞ ∞ ∞

"MINOU, where ya at?" Joe says, comin' in the house after washing his boat. They keep everything neat and clean because they are proud of what they have.

The Thibeaus are saving up their money to buy a double-wide trailer. They would love to have a brand-new house. It seems the old Acadianstyle houses are falling down and need extensive work to fix them. Even the little shotgun house they rent has problems.

"Bébé, Ah just found out where dey some pecan trees, and nobody is gettin' tha pecans. Tha people who own dat land don't pick dem up. So ya wanna go tomorrow mornin'? We have to go wit' tha boat. Ah'm gonna go get some gas for in tha mornin' at Mrs. Flavia's."

Flavia says hell yes to the pecans. She can sell them here and split it with them.

Minou is all about picking pecans. She loves it when they are all over the ground, waiting to be picked up, and she gets excited trying to see how many she can get in her hands at one time.

Everybody will help in cracking and saving the nuts for all the delicious pies and fudge and whatever else you can put them in to eat. They pick up more than they can use because Mrs. Flavia and Ethel need some too.

They prepare to go early in the morning. Minou gathers up the empty burlap sacks from the lean-to Joe has built so she can tote the pecans back home.

They leave out of the landing while the sun is just peeking on the rise and stop out on the bayou to drink their Mello Joy and share a cigarette. They've left all the chores undone, like there was a mess. Minou can find one little grain of rice on her floor, keeping everything so spotless.

She doesn't know about Fabulosa yet.

She is surprised at how far out in the swamps they have to go, at least five miles!

The oaks are huge, with their growth reaching so high, you get dizzy trying to see the tops, so very old with the Spanish moss drooping, looping, and twirling, reaching from one branch to another branch of an oak or cypress tree going down the length of the bayou. Cypress trees stand in the mix of the oak, producing cypress knees in between.

It is the Church of Nature they slowly go by, saying nothing at all to each other. Minou and Joe feel like they are in a spiritual awareness, one of the beliefs they share.

Along the banks they can see beautiful wild flowers blooming deep into the swamps where all kinds of wild animals jump around with no fear in their world. Palmetto bushes are everywhere, like an island off the coast of anywhere tropical. Huge, spiky fans open wide and create shade along with the thickness of the trees as they pull into the dock of the property.

It smells so good here because of the two big magnolia trees greeting them where they pull up. The pecan trees are mixed up between the cypress and the live oaks in the back of the property.

Someone cares because the property is kept mowed where there had been a large house at one time and a yard still blooming with flowers planted all those years ago. Pecan trees are planted in what's left of an orchard.

They see traces of people who have lived here at one time because the foundation of a huge plantation house stands, left to abandonment and ruin on the land and a chimney still standing, red with handmade bricks. Antique roses climb up it and down to the ground with a perfumed smell that could gag you, it's so strong.

Minou thinks she could probably sell some of those vines to Flavia because she loves roses. Every little bit of money counts because Flavia charges full price without blinking an eye. She does let them charge at her store, but they pay it weekly. They do a lot of bartering too, always have.

It is dark in the swamps with all the foliage, with huge rabbits and fat squirrels jumping around in there like it is their playground. It sure is a happy place for all the little creatures.

Minou has brought the shotgun just in case, for either shooting game or protection from what's out there. She might catch a few rabbits for supper tonight. She thinks about the game that's abundant on this property and changes her mind after seeing the millions of pecans on the ground.

Minou thinks she won't have time to hunt with all the pecans that cover the ground everywhere. They're going to have hot dog spaghetti instead.

Minou and Joe finish their baloney sandwiches and the RC Colas to wash them down with. Slices of the purple onions fall over the side of the Evangeline Maid bread. The tomatoes are cut thick, and there's lots of mayonnaise. Oh, is that good!

They are smoking a cigarette and finishing the colas when Minou spies something out the corner of her eye in the trees, kinda glowing and moving fast through the trees.

"Mais, Joe. Ah saw somet'in' movin' t'rough tha trees! Ah got tha frissons just now tellin' ya dat. Ah know what Ah saw! Get up, Joe. Let's go see!"

Joe gets up slowly and looks at Minou, thinking about the last time she saw something in the swamps. "Hellfire, Minou. Dat don't make me want to go look and see! It might be tha goddamn Bigfoot dis time! We got all tha monsters we can handle, just me and you! Merde, Minou. Ah'm too scared to look! Forget 'bout tha damn pecans!"

You think that is going to stop Minou? He should know better than to say that, because that's like a green light to go fast-fast.

Minou grabs the burlap sacks to go pick the pecans in spite of what she sees, and Joe follows behind, cussing all the way.

Minou says it glimmered and moved real fast, but the big-ass pecans on the ground are calling to her. Big, big pecans! Come pick us, come pick us, Minou!

They are on their second sack when she sees it again, and it's bigger this time, about the size of the two full sacks of pecans.

She just knows it's a ghost.

Minou has seen ghosts before in her Mawmaw Dardar's house down by Golden Meadow. Her mawmaw has told her it was a long-ago relative that didn't want to die. He has some unfinished business he never got the chance to do this side of the dirt hill.

Bertha has seen the ghost as a lil petite, and it scared her for the rest of her life. Now even being with the loup-garou hasn't changed that fear. The family has a strong belief in supernatural things.

It appears as an old man with tattered clothes and a hat that only a pirate would wear. A dirty eye patch covers what is an empty socket, and a gray bunch of wild hair in a long, twisted braid falls down his back.

A big-ass, mean-looking parrot ghost sits on his ghostly shoulder, looking like he could pick them to death! The pirates must have shot the bird too. Why didn't it just fly away before they could shoot him?

She's thinking maybe he didn't even know that!

The ghost has a bandana tied under his hat, and the poor ghost has a wooden leg! This is a very unlucky pirate, just too cursed to live. Big, gold loop earring in his ears, he looks like he's been rode hard and put up wet!

It speaks in a mournful and angry voice.

"You two thieves! Many have come before you, you madam of a whorehouse with your big slave. I kept them from finding my treasure. They ran because of their great fear of me! I have cursed this place. You, little petite heathen, show up to claim what's mine! Begone from here, and never come back! You're not escaping with Lafitte's treasure! Leave while you can!"

Minou hollers loud because she sure isn't expecting that and stumbles into Joe. The two big sacks of pecans spill back all over the ground. They take off running for the boat, and Joe throws the motor into high gear, taking off in the direction of their house.

That boat motor makes so much noise in high gear they can't hear each other talk. That keeps them quiet, but Minou is already pondering the situation.

∞ ∞ ∞

"WHAT we gonna do? Ah'm still shakin', and Ah have to run for da baffroom again! A real live ghost we saw, and no one will believe dat!" says Minou as she pours stiff drinks in the jelly glasses. Those glasses have held more Johnny Walker drinks than jelly!

Joe stands by Minou, and he holds on to her for dear life. He is some scared too.

Both are shaky and smoking shaky cigarettes. They have gotten old enough to buy a pack of cigarettes instead of one for 50¢ at Flavia's.

Joe says to Minou while they are holding each other, "Minou, we told e'rybody we was bringin' home sacks of pecans, and we come home empty-handed. Mais, hell. Ah'm too scared to go back."

With that being said by Joe, Minou gets mad-mad. No ghost is gonna keep her from getting her pecans.

"Joe, we gonna go talk with Mama and Parrain about tha ghost. Dey might know some stuff wit' all dat history Parrain knows about, like a legend or somet'in'. Come on. Dey got some supper. We can eat wit' dem." Minou walks into her mama's house and fixes her and Joe some white beans with some tasso and homemade bread. Joe and Minou have rented the little shotgun house next door. They find out they like privacy!

She looks at the hairy duo and tells them what's happened.

"Minou, ya know dere ain't no such thing as a ghost! Ya know better dan dat!" says Parrain while dipping his bread into the Steen's syrup, not taking them seriously.

"Merde, Parrain! Why ya said dat? A lot of people don't believe in no loup-garou, and we bot' know ya da real thang! Dat was stupid to say! Couyon! Be ashamed!

"With all da books ya read, ya never heard 'bout ghosts? Mais, ya musta skipped some pages! Ya ain't heard no stories 'bout a ghost dat looks like a pirate? Never no tale of tha Ghostly Pecan Protector?"

Minou makes him think twice about what he's said, and he is shamed. She does that quite often to her parrain.

Bertha, Minou's mama, speaks up while pouring some Jack Daniels in everybody's jelly glasses. Mais, they make some good glasses when the jelly is gone.

"Minou, Ah remember my great-great-pawpaw tellin' us ghost stories he swore was tha trut'. Jean Lafitte and his pirates hid some of his gold and silver somewhere way back in tha swamps on an old plantation wit' slaves and sugar cane. Dem people dat had tha place always had some bad luck, and dey was mean and ugly. Dey was so mean dat tha slaves revolted and killed tha old man! Now what's left of dat family is pretty much levee rats and always in trouble.

"My people, tha Houmas, use to feed dem bastard pirates, and dey still raped tha pretty young maidens! Merde, mais. We might be kin to him or one of tha other bastards he had with dem!

"He killed a pirate named Gaspar to make sure his ghost guarded his treasure. Pawpaw told us he even had a name. It must be Gaspar y'all saw.

"Mais, Ah believe in ghosts. Just don't show dem to me 'cause Ah already saw one when Ah was petite by my mawmaw's house where Ah lived at. Scared me so bad-bad, but Ah don't t'ink it was Gaspar."

Minou is getting madder and madder just thinking that Gaspar, the not-so-friendly ghost, was gonna keep her from getting her pecans. She can't believe that her parrain is so stupid in believing there ain't no such thing as real-life ghosts. As if! It must be he pays no attention to the other supernaturals, because he's too busy keeping track of his monthly period.

She thinks about the ghost and the spilled pecans and knows that it will take more than Gaspar to keep her from going back to the hollering pecans!

∞ ∞ ∞

IT takes three days before she convinces Joe to go back with her. He is terrified, but Minou gets over being scared and is okay with leading them back to the land.

She wants the pecans.

They land the boat, and Minou jumps out with her rosary beads on a stick and a bottle of holy water. She used all kinds of things when they trapped the loup-garous that turned out to be Bertha and Parrain! She adds the holy water because she had forgotten it the first time.

Joe is slowly getting out the boat because he is pissed! Minou just drags him into all kinds of stuff. And he just follows like an old cur dog!

He sure as hell is scared of all this he'd rather not know about. He says that the priest has told him to "cleave to each other and you got to stay until one of ya passes on. For better or the worse." Joe thinks you have to take that better or that worst when you get married, but why the worst all the time?

Minou is steadily heading for the big-ass pecans on the ground, which are calling her name. Minou! Oh, Minou!

While she is stuffing the sacks again, the ghost makes another appearance, and she hears Gaspar the unfriendly ghost say to her again to leave.

The parrot is screeching a not-of-this-world scream and snapping his jaws with his beak. Joe says, standing behind Minou, "Like tha ghost wasn't bad enough. Ya got to t'row a bird in tha mess!" Minou tells him to go pick some more pecans.

The ghost, in its fineness, tells Minou floating right up next to her, "Begone from here and never come back! Don't take anything, you whore's wicked girl child! Take that slave you've got that's worthless and begone, I tell you!"

Minou is steadily picking pecans and filling another sack. She stands up and looks the ghost right straight in his one eye, "My name is Minou, and dat's Joe over dere by some trees. Look, he's peekin' at ya! He ain't my slave. We been married, and he's a good man wit' all his legs and eyes, not like ya! Tha pecans are gonna rot on tha ground. Dat's a real shame to leave dem all for tha squirrels. We can fix ya a piece of pecan pie if ya can eat some. And Ah ain't no goddamn whore's daughter. Ya need to say ya sorry!"

The spirit begins to wail like an Irish banshee! Minou just stands there, looking at old Gaspar.

"Ah ain't scared of ya, ya foolish old trampy ghost. How come ya still stuck over here? Dat Jean Lafitte made a big couyon outta ya. Ah'd be hauntin' his ass! We came to get all dese pecans. Ah don't even know if dat's what ya been protectin'!"

Minou grabs the sacks of pecans and has Joe picking more nuts, filling another burlap sack. He's looking at the ground so he doesn't see Gaspar the unfriendly ghost. Right now, he's more scared of Minou if he doesn't. This whole bunch of merde is too much for him. He's been sorry ever since they caught the loup-garous and Minou dragged him into that damn-to-hell crap!

He's gotta get much better in telling Minou no. Non! Hasta la vista, baby! Joe figures it's between Minou and Gaspar, not him in the middle of those two well-matched fighters.

Gaspar is continuing with his ghostly warnings, and Minou is toe-totoe with him. He's using his loud, scary voice. "You sassy, devious wench, no one has ever been brave enough to speak to me in over two hundred years, much less tell me you are taking one of my treasures! And a female that doesn't know her place! I've been haunting this place to save Lafitte's bounty. I'm still very angry that he killed me. I don't care about these nuts! His treasure is why he turned me into this haunting, lonely spirit! Begone from here, you woman! Whoever told you that you can EVEN talk back to a man or ghost, much less me?"

By now Gaspar is a real-live pirate standing there in the dark swamp, with a big sword and an old, old gun. He is in color too, showing bright garments with a green pirate's hat, the kind that Peter Pan wears. Neither one has a chance to grow up.

The parrot is awesome in color, displaying all his colorful feathers and still squawking at them.

Gaspar must be starved for any kind of conversation. He's talking to this woman because her man is weak – but man enough to listen to the warnings.

He's out in his full regalia, daring Minou to say anything else to the pissed-off apparition.

Well, we all know that Minou is not one to mind her tongue and is nosy enough to ask where the treasure is. "Mais, all ya gotta do is tell me! Ah won't tell nobody else. Mais, me and ya could be kin! Dat's what my mama told me. Ya remember all dem pretty little Houmas girls ya use to fool around wit'?"

Joe has picked all the pecans he could find, and now he's running back to the boat, looking straight ahead with half his weight in pecans!

"How dare you! You, you bossy female wench who thinks she is a man, to ask about the bounty I've been guarding for centuries! Big men have tried and run away screaming. You better find some courage and run for your life while you still can! Don't tell me about anything concerning my offspring!"

The bird is steadily saying his choice words, squawking, Fuck you, fuck you, fuck you!

Minou is getting real nosy about what he is hiding and wants to know what's he been guarded all these years. But that's for another day, another time.

Minou and Joe get in the boat with the nuts and race full throttle from the pecan grove. Minou looks back and sees Gaspar pitching a screaming hissy fit!

∞ ∞ ∞

WELL, you know by now that Minou can't stop thinking about the treasure that's still hidden and persuades Joe to go back with her the next day.

Joe's cussing and fussing, saying he "ain't talkin' wit' no ghost!"

They get out the boat on the dock, and Minou goes running to the back where trees are not thick and down a beaten path where Gaspar must be wandering, dragging his gun and sword on the ground through the back trees.

It's not long before the ghost comes back with new warnings. Minou is truly not afraid and wants to find what else is there.

"Well, Gaspar, Ah found out ya name! Why do ya still want to haunt dis place? Ya know by now Lafitte just bamboozled ya, and ya pissed off at him anyways. Why protect it? Please, oh kind and lovin'-

women ghost, show me what it is? Ya could be gone from here searchin' for ya sleazy captain in tha hereafter. Let's see what ya got."

Gaspar the unfriendly ghost is now covered in hazy fog, and sparks are flying from him. He flies to the back trees, two that stand alone. The parrot flies, and sparks are flying from his plumage of bright colors as he goes to meet Gaspar.

Gaspar is just moaning and moaning at Minou, but she isn't scared any more. She stands her ground while the wind blows and lightning strikes.

"You sassy, sneaky wench female! Go while you still can! Don't come back here by the two trees! I'll strike you dead!"

Well, guess what Minou does? She runs to the back trees standing side by side.

The ghost is twirling like a dervish! The parrot named Pedro continues with his nasty mouth.

Minou hollers at Joe to bring the shovel that's in the boat. Joe comes running with two shovels, one for each of them, and runs through all the fog to get to the trees!

He sure doesn't have to be told twice!

He's excited to find out himself what it is! Maybe it will be enough to buy that riding lawnmower he saw at Theriot's Hardware Store!

"Come on, Gaspar! Show me what ya been protectin' all dem years. Ya been such a lonely ghost. Don't ya want to be free to go wherever ya can? Ya don't even know what he buried in dose trees 'cause he shot ya dead before ya could even bat ya good eye! Mais, why tha hell did dey shoot ya parrot?

"Ah'm comin' to claim dat treasure! Ya gotta give it up, and Ah'll guard it for ya now."

Minou and Joe begin to dig in between the two trees, and the ghost is throwing all its powers to prevent them finding it, screaming at the two, while lightning is striking close to them and pelts of hail hitting them! The ghostly bird is trying to peck them, but just little puffs come out his mouth! None of the animals are to be seen, hiding because they see the terrifying ghost pitching a fit like he is some little baby. Everything is so bright when it's usually dark. The animals are seeing way too much of their surroundings and looking at their mates, wondering why they hooked up with such an ugly creature!

All this is to no avail because Minou and Joe are slinging the dirt all around! They each pick a tree, but Minou is the first to hit the chest buried under the live oak, a huge wooden pirate's trunk.

Gaspar finally stops with all his tricks and stands watching while Minou and Joe pull the massive trunk out the dirt. He is curious to see what is in it too, because he was dead before Lafitte buried it!

They have also dug up Gaspar's grave, and he sees himself, a skeleton still in the same clothes he haunts in. The parrot is buried in there with him. Pedro is visibly upset too, seeing his bones.

He starts moaning and sparkling like he can't believe what he sees. Minou and Joe stand by the ghost, like they are praying with him over his grave.

The couple are sad watching Gaspar, very somber looking at his resting place that hasn't been too restful!

Joe knocks the trunk's big lock away, it being so rotten, and Minou reaches down all the way to her toes and grabs a large satin bag that is rotten too. The trunk just falls apart at their feet. Can't sell the chest at Flavia's looking like that.

Gaspar is hovering over them to see what comes out of the rotten satin bag. The bird is screeching out his obscenity, and Gaspar tells him to shut up!

In the bag are two long, heavy, solid gold chains with jewels encrusted into the large chain and five golden rings covered in jewels. One of the rings is a ruby, the other a massive opal. The other three rings are large diamonds in clusters around the bands.

The bag also holds a huge crucifix covered with emeralds and pearls. A huge silver cross holds the heavy rocks that don't have any cuts, just as it comes out of the ground. It's very heavy because it takes Minou and Joe to carry it to the boat.

Probably a Catholic Church on some island got robbed of their crucifix and their virgins!

Gaspar roars at the remnants of the supernatural show. "This is all the cheesy bastard killed me for? That's what he thought of me, a loyal pirate that sailed the heavy seas and robbed the Spanish with him for twenty years? That no-good, treacherous scallywag son of a whore! I will find him in the afterworld and taunt him for eternity for killing me.

"Poor Pedro. They shot him just because he was my bird! Lafitte's already dead so I can't kill him! I will leave this godforsaken place and search for him."

With just a puff of smoke Gaspar the unfriendly ghost and Pedro the parrot leave the swamps, leaving Minou and Joe holding the heavy rotten bag. They leave with some more pecans and their buried treasure, going as fast as the boat will go.

Minou can't pass up the pecans on the dirt. You just gotta pick them up!

∞ ∞ ∞

MINOU and Joe run into Bertha and Parrain's house, hollering at Bertha and Alcide to get the whiskey down out the cabinet because they've got something to show them that they aren't gonna believe!

Alcide and Bertha start jumping around. The excitement is contagious.

They are hugging each other and hitting each other, showing them the treasure and pecans and laughing so loud that Flavia hears the commotion from the store. For some reason, she has a headache so she doesn't come to the house to see what's going on. What a time for her to not be nosy. She will come to regret that.

Minou and Joe, trying to talk at the same time, show them what's in the red satin bag that is all muddy, and the crucifix falls, denting the linoleum on the floor.

Minou hushes Joe and proceeds with the tale so unbelievable.

"Mais, if y'all coulda seen dat! Gaspar just went up in tha smoke, still cussin' dat damn Lafitte, and left for wherever ghosts can go. Tha bird he called Pedro flew off wit' him! Ah figure to New Orleans if he can. He probably hung out dere when he was live.

"When we saw what was in here we knew we could buy somet'in' we need."

Everybody is so excited, even Pawpaw Irby turns his head, watching, and smiles. Alcide hollers, laughing, and Bertha goes to look for her smelling salts and her glass of Jack Daniels! They pull one thing after the other out, and each time they take big gulps of their mixed drinks.

Then Parrain begins to tell them how they will handle this. You know? The Godfather?

"We'll take dis bag all the way to New Orleans to find out how much we can get for all dis beautiful stuff. Maybe a priest over dere knows 'bout some church missin' tha big cross? All tha antique shops ya can shake a stick at 'cause dey so many! We gonna go to tha one all of us feel we can trust. Dis could be at least two hunnerd thousand dollars, Ah bet y'all! He can tell us how much money we can get! We gonna be rich!"

Parrain says this as he's dancing all over the kitchen with his partner, Bertha. Everybody starts dancing as they get ready to take the trip in the morning.

All get pie-eyed that night, but no one is worried about hangovers the next morning, after having two pots of coffee. And they still get up early.

∞ ∞ ∞

THEY pile up in the old station wagon and roll down the windows because the air-conditioner isn't working. The radio plays real good, and they are singing loud to the music on station KVPI, with the wind blowing through the windows. Good thing it's in October, a week before Minou's birthday. And what a birthday gift!

It's the first time for Minou and Joe to go to the city of New Orleans.

All four of them are going up and down Magazine Street, searching for the right antique shop. They stop at Babineaux's Fine Antiques where a Monsieur Babineaux sits waiting for the next customer. He is short and bald on the top of his head and doesn't look like he's missed too many plates of red beans!

He greets them in a quiet, French-speaking voice, just knowing they come from the country. They wonder why, because they got their good clothes on! Maybe the old station wagon with the chank-a-chank music blaring as they pull up in front of the shop clues him in.

In French, Minou tells the monsieur the truth. "Comment ça va. We are Mr. and Mrs. Joseph Thibeau from Larose, Louisiana. Dis is my mama, Bertha, and my parrain, Alcide Peltier. We come to tell ya that we found a true-to-life pirate's chest under some big old oak trees out in the swamps. Ah could tell ya a bunch more if ya want.

"Well, it all started with some pecans and a ghost named Gaspar...." Monsieur is amazed at what they have brought in for him and laughing to tell them what this treasure is worth! He has never seen anything like it and knows it is museum quality. The cross belongs in the Vatican!

Monsieur Babineaux even hears the tale about how they got the treasure. He looks like he is dubious about the story, but he picks up each individual piece of jewelry, saying how much each item is worth.

Monsieur tallies up the total and convinces Minou and Joe it's worth a half of a million dollars!

Minou and Bertha keep the two rings with the opals and rubies. Mrs. Flavia tells Minou that the opal is her birthstone, and Bertha loves anything that's ruby!

Monsieur Babineaux leaves to go to his bank to get the money, while Minou watches the antique shop in case a customer comes in while he is at the bank.

The family looks at everything in the shop, amazed at some of the furniture that is there with prices in the thousands of dollars! Two pieces are just like the dresser and the armoire in Bertha's house. That furniture has never left the Cajun cottages, never having been taken out of the house, just handed down from one family to the next, where it sits forever in the same spot.

Flavia thinks the armoire was made centuries ago by a carpenter named Mallard out of New Orleans and tries to buy it. She buys antiques up and down the bayou, and she gets them cheap. The people saying, Mais, ya want dat old t'ing? We gonna go get some new furniture at tha Walmart!

Monsieur Babineaux comes back finally, huffing and puffing like he has run the whole way and back. He did run, carrying all that cash money on the streets of New Orleans because that's how the family asked for it. All of those dollars that they want to see and hold!

Monsieur locks the door and puts the Closed sign up, pulling the shades as he does so. He tells them as he sits down, "Here is the money coming to all of you like you said, in cash. It took all the money from the bank, and they had to close early because there wasn't a dollar left in the whole place! I want you to know I thoroughly enjoyed meeting all of you. It's such a pleasure to be with people so refreshing and honest.

"With this much money passing from me to you, well, we won't ever forget each other. What better people to have such wonderful luck! I can't think of more deserving people than your family. I would enjoy visiting with all of you again. Me and the wife have a camp on Grand Isle down there close to you. She comes from the Callaises down in Golden Meadow, so we will stop and visit y'all."

When Parrain tells him about the pieces that they have at the house, Monsieur gets the address and the phone number of Alcide and Bertha's house right away and says he's coming to the bayou soon. He checks his appointment book for a place to come the following week.

He must have a lot of money to give them the half a million in hundreds and still have more to spend. He's coming to Larose on Highway One to try and convince Bertha and Alcide that they should part with the family antiques in their two houses.

Good luck with that.

Alcide tells him that people are always trying to get rid of their junk furniture that comes from a long-dead relative.

Put dat to tha road! Ya want dat ugly t'ing? Mais, dat was my long-ago pawpaw's chifforobe. Look at da drawer. It's got a crack in tha wood. Ya can have dat, cher, if ya haul dat from da road!

They get three duffle bags with locks given by Monsieur to put all the money in the back part of the station wagon. Monsieur Babineaux gives them all a glass of Champagne to toast their good luck. For sure, lock all the doors, and get the hell out of Dodge!

They hug and kiss, with Monsieur inviting them to the camp for the weekend on the fabulous Grand Isle.

They stop for a mechanic to check the AC, and he says it only needs freon. Alcide fills up the car with gasoline that's a dollar a gallon.

He says, "Mais, tha gas is some expensive in New Orleans, and dey don't even wash tha windows for ya!"

Behind the windows locked, they're all saying, "Go faster, go faster!"

Minou gets an idea in her head about New Orleans when she reads a brochure in the antique shop. She's tucked it in her purse. Minou knows they are coming back, but not with all this cash.

They are already discussing before they get home what they will do with the massive amount of money. Everybody is saying what they want, not what they need! Joe will get that lawnmower he can ride on the street. Minou and Joe will purchase 400 acres of land and then decide to buy three double-wide mobile homes to put on the land.

They also will buy the land where the pecan grove is located. The owners think the land is haunted, so they will sell the land for cheap. The remaining relatives are delirious with the amount of money they are given for the land but are already fighting as to who is going to get the money. If they wouldn't be so lazy, not caring about the land and not putting shovels in their hands, think about what they've lost. Again.

Land isn't that expensive at this time, and they all look for bargains, like they've done all their lives. One of the large homes is for Minou and Joe. One trailer is for Bertha and Alcide and the third for Joe's mama, Ethel. They all get new vehicles. Just what they desire, even if it is a Cadillac!

Minou and Joe still have a lot of money left over, so they put the rest in Parrain Alcide's large old-time safe. They trust themselves with the money, much better than banks. Well, we don't know if they heard of the IRS.

∞ ∞ ∞

THE people in the town of Larose are wondering where all this money has come from, but Minou and Joe are completely silent on the mystery. They know they are now the richest people around Lafourche Parish, besides Flavia. They are proud of that.

Mrs. Flavia is still trying to find out where the money is from, and she thinks she knows where.

Minou finally tells her, and she says Minou is a lil ass for telling her that made-up tale.

Oh, but she thinks she knows the truth. But that's for another story.

Minou and Joe are set up for a long time so they don't have to hunt and fish if they don't want to.

All of them will never quit working. That's how Cajun people are.

Old hateful Ethel thinks her son has struck oil, and Minou is gonna spend it all!

They feel blessed, and no one else has heard the story about the dead pirate Gaspar and Pedro the mean parrot, who fought them for the treasure.

Chapter Three

Minou and Voodoo

ONE morning over their cups of Mello Joy and pain perdu piled high on a plate with some Steen's syrup, Minou tells Joe it's time for them to take a honeymoon!

They've been married for six years but with so much quemas going on, they haven't even thought about that. They've been honeymooning since they were fifteen years old but still young enough, at twenty-one, to want to go someplace exciting and try different stuff.

Minou tells Joe, after she grabs the little Larose Gazette out his hands and makes him look at her, "Dis business is for sure more important dan tha Gulf tides ya check every week. Mais, don't treat me like some old mawmaw who don't dance no more and don't t'ink nuttin's funny! Like tha women at tha fais-do-do sittin' in tha corner, eatin' demselves into dat diabeetus crap. Mais, ya could crack an egg on dere faces!"

She goes right back into the original idea for talking about this to Joe and goes into sweet-talking Minou, but Joe knows all about that with her, like the brand-new nozzles in their trailer that turn on hot water the minute you touch the damn faucets. Minou's charms run like water.

"Joe, my lil tootoo, don't ya t'ink it's time we went somewhere by ourselves instead of always goin' with tha old people?"

Oh, Lawd! thinks Joe while finishing his breakfast of eggs and grits. Minou never calls him that unless she's got some cuckoo thing in her head or she wants him to clean their double-wide.

Minou says, "Ah been lookin' at some magazines where dey only talk 'bout New Orleans. And Ah saved tha brochure from Monsieur Babineaux's in my chest-a-drawers for a long time. We got plenty of money 'cause we never go nowhere! We can go for four days and four nights for about a thousand dollars, and ya know we got dat, huh? We just got dat old Couyon to worry about, and he's always down dere by Mama's house anyway. Mais, baby, what ya t'ink 'bout dat?"

Joe knows it's already a done deal. Minou is just getting around to tell him.

He jumps right into this adventure because he wants to do another trip to the Big Easy. Joe has always been the one dragged into merde, but this idea has got him wanting to do the whole quemas in the big city, with the Mississippi River winding around, pushing to the Big Gulf. He's only been to New Orleans once in his life and Minou the same.

Joe has been getting ideas of his own and talking to Alcide about being podnahs for a big boat. Oh, yeah, Joe is digging the feeling right now in his kitchen!

"Ah bet, Minou, we could go get some new clothes at dat Walmart, and ya could go buy somet'in' dat's in tha back corner of Mrs. Flavia's." Flavia keeps an adults-only section at the back of her store.

"Mais, Ah would get so haunt to talk wit' Mrs. Flavia 'bout dat merde. You! Ya talk to her 'bout anyt'in', and ya ain't shamed! Ya know, for all dem men comin' home off tha Gulf? Dey closed tha famous store all tha way in Leeville, and now Flavia's tha spot where ya go for tha real nasty stuff! Non, not all dat, just somet'in' we gonna know what to do wit' it! Go see, baby, what she got! Mais, we bot' twenty-one, and dat's old enough.

"Ah know ya already got the days picked out for when we goin', so tell me."

∞ ∞ ∞

THEIR one trip to New Orleans was two years ago, when they got the treasure chest from the ghost Gaspar. From Jean Lafitte's buried pirate's loot has come enough money to buy three double-wides and 400 acres, with plenty left over in the big black safe that Parrain has at their house.

They buy the whole swamp back of Mrs. Flavia's store and their old houses. They repair the Cajun cottages and now rent them out to people they know and trust. The property with all the pecan trees they buy real cheap! The people think the land is still haunted and cursed. Not any more.

Minou and Joe buy one double-wide for themselves, one for Bertha with Pawpaw Irby and Alcide, and one for Joe's mama, Ethel, on her property.

Minou doesn't want her next door; too close for comfort, as they say.

The people in Larose are still trying to find out where they got that money all at one time.

All of them have long-lost cousins coming to visit and acting like they are their new best friends. Their sudden abundance is big news up and down Lafourche. The family is kinda strange to everybody!

Minou gets tired of Mrs Flavia asking, so she tells her where, when, and how! Flavia gets so MAD MAD MAD because she thinks Minou is bald-faced lying and acting like a smart-ass and not telling her the truth! They both of them can claim all the titles mentioned!

So Flavia quits asking and starts pondering. Then she knows she's figured it out by herself. Joe and Minou must be growing that marijuana all up in the swamp they just bought and selling it too! She's gonna get the surprise of her life for being so Nosy Rosy up in everybody's business!

∞ ∞ ∞

THE dates that Minou picks are for the last four days of October. They will spend Halloween in New Orleans.

They leave for New Orleans early in the morning, before anybody is up at the trailers. Their new Chevrolet SUV is humming, with three seats and a back area to haul whatever they find to buy or take off the side of the road. The car has air-conditioning, and the radio is blasting out Cookie and His Cupcakes!

Minou and Joe get up the road to Raceland, DesAllmonds, Paradis and Boutte, straight up over the Huey P. Long Bridge, looking for the hotel around the French Quarter.

The hotel doesn't look like the place they show in the brochure, but it still delights them both. On the brochure that Minou got at Monsieur Babineaux's Antique Shop couple of years back that she's kept in the top drawer of her chest-a-drawers shows a place different from what they are looking at.

It's got to be twenty years ago that the picture was taken. It shows a small hotel with trees secluding the place and an iron lattice fence surrounding it, with the same lattice on the balconies, and tropical plants growing with abandonment. It used to be a townhouse of a plantation owner coming to New Orleans for business or definitely pleasure. Now the place has seen better days.

The Caldonia.

Neither Minou nor Joe has ever stayed at a hotel before, but the ice machine and the swimming pool have them dazzled at first sight. The water in the oval pool is a pretty blue, and they have some nice little tables with umbrellas over them, placed all around the cement laid to surround the watering hole.

Joe says he will get a swimming pool for them when they get back home, he loves it so much. They only swim in the bayou, not knowing what the hell is swimming with them! Maybe tha creature from the Black Lagoon!

And he's definitely getting an ice machine!

After they're through with the honeymooning, Minou and Joe are having a well-earned cigarette. Minou says after her puff, "Mais, Joe, ya turned tha loup-garou loose on me! Ay yai yai! Mais, Ah liked some of dat stuff we bought by Flavia's, but all dat shakin' goin' on, Ah couldn't take dat every day!"

They've never ever felt this kind of privacy before, in a darkened room with this new bed, for sure not thinking about the people who probably did their own honeymooning in that same new bed. You could even put a quarter in the bed, and it vibrates like you in some carnival ride! Joe puts in $3 worth of quarters but stops because it's making him dizzy!

"Mais, Minou, Ah feel like my legs are hose pipes, and my ding-aling feels like a blister on it! Mais, ya want to do it again, chér?"

They use all the stuff from Mrs Flavia's store and Minou's lil sexy outfit from the Walmart with her hollering not to tear her good outfit!

Minou says to Joe that it's dark outside. "Bae, we gonna go see about tha Quarters tonight. Non, Ah ain't goin' ask for more quarters! Ah'm haunt! Put ya good clothes on 'cause dey dress fancy down dere, and we don't want to look like we from tha country!

"Poo-eeee! Ya some stinky! Go turn dat shower on for us! And change dem draws!

"We gonna drink dat Hurricane, and we gonna listen to some good honky-tonk music. Maybe we can look for somebody dat looks like he sells dat marijuana. Whatcha say?

"Ah just want to be able to strut my stuff! Bae, we gonna have us a damn good time!"

∞ ∞ ∞

AS usual, Joe is following Minou as she gets into the taxi the lady at the desk called for them.

That's a first time too, and Joe wants to catch a heart attack, so he can get out the crazy-ass cab with its crazy-assed driver, who's going fast, passing up everything and singing some song. "I want to walk you home." Well, Joe thinks he would walk home, dragging this city man through the swamp!

He can't understand what the taxi driver is saying to him. All he understands is, "Where ya at?"

Joe says, "Bro, you tha one dat's supposed to know where ya at."

They eat their supper at the Commander's Palace restaurant where they order Oysters Bienville. They need two plates of those oysters after today.

They take off walking until a yellow taxi passes, stops, looks at the two definitely from out of town. The cabbie hollers out the window, "Mais, Ah know where ya bought dem shoes at! At Mrs. Flavia's, dat's where! Ay yai yai!"

The driver is a hometown Cajun from Galliano, much older than them, and takes them right to Bourbon Street.

Joe hands him a dollar for his tip, and the driver, Laurence Michel Jr., just falls out laughing.

Minou and Joe go looking for Hurricane drinks, and it doesn't take long to find them. They start walking down Bourbon Street, where they are seeing tourists out in the streets.

One woman raises her fancy blouse up, showing some big, old, saggy tetons with no brassiere! Poor, poor old lady. Minou shouts, "Mais, baby, put ya shirt down. Tha police is gonna come!"

The local characters are going about their business, talking about their business with no one but themselves. People are walking all over with big dogs on fancy ropes and don't even glance at you. The dog either. Some stuck up.

You could tell who is from here and who are the drunk tourists. They tend to move in groups with nasty stuff on their T-shirts.

Minou and Joe are holding hands for comfort and some protection because the sights are very strange to them. Boy! Some people's children.

Their mouths are wide open when they see all those almost-naked women dancing in the windows and a man trying to talk you into coming in and buying you a drink.

Minou tells Joe, "Bébé, ya know Ah can dance like dat, but Ah don't want no man to look at me naked! As if Ah'm gonna do dat? Ah betcha dey make plenty money!"

Drinking drink after drink after drink until they are hanging on to each other to stand on the streets, Minou and Joe dance to all kinds of music for most of the night. Them oysters must be helping! Their limbs look like Bony Maroni has taken over. Joe goes to find a phone to call Larry Michel to come pick them up. They are ready to find their bed at the Caldonia now.

They cross over Bourbon looking for Larry Michel's taxi where he's told Joe to meet him. The streets are darker, with not as many people on them. They don't want the people to see them looking as bad as they are, swaying, holding their Hurricanes in to-go cups.

Joe has laughed all night, pointing his finger for Minou to look, while he laughs at the other people! He sure doesn't want them laughing back at them. They forget about that other cigarette for this night because they're trying to bring their drunk asses to the hotel.

Minou is still holding her last Hurricane, looking down the dark street, when she stands still and drops her drink, splashing that sweet mixture all over both of them.

"Joe, Joe, Joe. Ah saw someone lurkin' in tha shadows down dat street under tha light, and Ah swear Joe, it was a vampire! Ah saw him holdin' a lady under dat lamppost, and he was bendin' over her with his cape around dem, just like tha movies! Joe, let's go see what he's doin'! Ah want a better look."

Minou can hardly stand, and she is swaying, trying to walk down the street to see what she believes is a bloodsucker. Joe is standing there, doing his own swaying. He says loud enough to alert whoever is down the road, "Not no, but hell no! We ain't goin' down dere! Dere's no tellin' what you saw, and we don't need more supernatural merde in our lives! Ya drunk and Ah'm drunk, so what good would we do, and Ah'm scared shitless! He may not be finished wit' his meal and come after us! Hold on to me and don't look no more. Ah'm tellin' ya, Minou, we ain't goin'! Non!"

Joe never says no to Minou. If she wasn't so drunk, she'd notice.

Larry Michel Jr. pulls up, and Joe shoves Minou inside the car. He stumbles into the back seat. Joe doesn't care about the crazy driving. The faster, the better!

Minou has passed out, and he carries her into their rooms. They don't wake up until the sun is high in the sky.

∞ ∞ ∞

"BAE, we gonna go see tha New Orleans Aquarium where dey have all kinds of fish we ain't never seen before! Then we gonna go to tha Audubon Zoo where dey all axe for you! Ha, dat's what tha song says. Tha monkeys axed, and tha elephant axed. Oh, hell! Ah gotta go t'row up again!"

Both of them are hung over, and nothing sounds good to Joe. He wants to go lay back down.

Minou and Joe find a little café where they drink three cups of strong coffee and have biscuits with lots of butter dripping down. They can't handle the eggs that they have every morning at home.

They walk up the street from the café and the hotel. Minou has found the Caldonia is within walking distance of many of the tourists' favorite things to see in New Orleans.

After walking in the cold air with the sun beating down and the many cups of coffee, they feel ready for the day.

Joe gets so excited when he sees the fish, wondering where the hell they come from. He never sees those fish in the bayou!

"Minou, look at all tha different catfish over dere in dat big-ass tank! Man, Ah feel like Ah'm under da water wit' tha fish! Ya can't see t'rough tha mud in tha bayou so no tellin' what's in dere wit' tha alligators and snakes! Look at dem piranhas comin' to eat us like on dem scary movies! Aww, baby, look tha fish over our heads! For sure it feels like we swimmin' wit' tha fish!"

To Minou it makes the turmoil in her stomach begin to feel like a motorboat, and she passes the fumes.

"Oh, Joe, ya heard dat? Mais, Ah know for sure ya smelled dat! Ah'm so haunt up in here! Ah'm gettin' real dizzy too. Look, dey got some benches. Let me sit down for a lil while. We can still see tha fish. Look, dey comin' to stare at us!"

They are sitting down and enjoying the ice-cold Cokes Joe has bought. That's good for Minou's ailments.

Never having seen the wonders in the Aquarium, they are awed once again. Being both avid fishermen, they're wondering which fish could be fried. Minou is sitting, being calm, and is fascinated, watching the fish and all the people. She is watching the fish swimming over Joe's head when she catches something in the distance coming toward them. She screams and grabs for Joe.

"Dere's a goddamn shark comin' dis way!"

Minou is screaming to all the other people to run and is grabbing Joe by the arms, trying to make him go fast-fast! Both are standing holding each for protection while everyone is staring at them like they aren't dealing with a full deck. The duo is fascinated with everything, but the people are quite fascinated with them two!

Minou screams loudly when the shark passes over their heads. She says to Joe where everyone can hear, "Joe, ya can forget about goin' fishin' in tha goddamn Gulf!"

She has had enough of the fish, and she is dragging Joe because he is still looking. Maybe she will buy her own fish tank, and Joe can still look at fishes.

They walk out into the bright sun. It feels blinding to them as they reach for their new sunglasses.

Minou puts her new sunglasses on that she has bought at Flavia's. They are bright green with rhinestones all over. She is glad for the glasses because she knows her eyes are bloodshot from last night.

Joe has bought some old-timey frames with rose-colored lenses. He says he wants to sing that song, Rose Colored Glasses.

They call Larry Michel to bring them to the zoo. Audubon Park is too far to walk, and they are tired of their mouths hurting, wide open all the time.

Larry is talking to them about all kind of things in New Orleans. He tells them, "Mais, y'all, Ah'm takin' ya on Saint Charles Avenue, and ya ain't gonna believe how some people live! Dey say dat's old-old money dat live on dis street. Like a pawpaw had a plantation on tha Mississippi, but tha family would have two homes. One for livin' in down tha Mississippi River and tha other one for all the pleasure New Orleans has to offer. Maybe another little house on Esplanade for his mulatto wife and chil'ren. Ya know, on tha other side of the blanket! Anyway, it's still tha same family livin' dere. Can y'all imagine dat kind of money?"

Minou and Joe keep their mouths shut. They don't know him that good or his family on the bayou.

Larry pulls up in front of the zoo and tells them he's gonna try and come back to go in the zoo but for sure come back and get them.

∞ ∞ ∞

JOE wants to go see the big cats like the tigers and lions, so they head that way. Minou and Joe see some of the same people that were at the Aquarium and on Bourbon. Those two holler at them, waving and causing an uneasy feeling among the crowd.

Oh, my God, Diane. It's those two again!

They see the animals that can be found in the swamps of Louisiana, like the black panther and the coyotes and cougars that are yellow. Minou has a black panther rug on her floor that's real old, skinned by some ancestors.

"We sure can't bring Bertha and Alcide to see dese big-assed beasts! Dey might turn into loup-garous if dey saw all tha wild animals! Don't even ask! We ain't bringin' dem!" Joe says to Minou while they eat cotton candy for the first time. A mess they make trying to get the candy off their fingers. They have it on their faces too, and they laugh at each other. Now they decide it's time to go see the monkeys that are "axing" for Joe!

Everywhere the other visitors are laughing at them, and some are standing with their mouths wide open, looking at them instead of the animals. Minou and Joe are laughing back at them, thinking they are being friendly. They are funny just to look at, Minou being five foot three and Joe, a massive man that stands six foot three inches and muscular, with a beard black as his hair.

Minou is a wild-haired beauty but doesn't realize or care about that. Minou has never cut her dark brown hair. She wears it in a high ponytail and it's to the ankles of her tiny feet. Bertha cuts just enough of it to stay off the floor. Her mama used to pull it real tight, and Minou would holler. Bertha would say, "Shut up, you. Ya gotta suffer to be beautiful!" Minou would say, "Ah don't want to know nuttin' 'bout bein' beautiful! Turn loose of my hair!"

She's tried some makeup she bought at Mrs. Flavia's from the Avon book. She knows what to do, watching her mama do it, but that's been a long time ago.

The lighting at the Caldonia is not the best, for sure not in the bathroom. Minou sees one thing and in the daylight, everybody else sees this little woman with big old patches of rouge on her high cheekbones and Flaming Red on her full lips.

Joe tells her she looks so pretty, and he doesn't lie.

So you could imagine this little woman looking like an Indian and her big burly man like he is the trapper!

Think about those two country mirlitons who wear bright clothing because Minou loves the colors. When she can, she dresses Joe the same. Laughing, saying they could be twins!

And it just so happens, this is one of those days.

Their accents make you want to stop and listen at the strangeness of their words, sounding like they are French. Cajun patois is archaic French with added words, each different up and down all the bayous where they settled. Can't understand what they are saying, but they aren't shy!

I know you can see them, plus they must have the tribe's costumes, being both dressed alike.

Larry Michel shows up to join them there.

They are walking up to see the many different species of monkeys there at the zoo, and Joe is laughing so hard he starts coughing, so Minou has to hit him in his back.

The other people are laughing too, at the monkeys or at Joe and Minou. They stick out like sore thumbs, the monkeys and Minou and Joe. They are in front of the huge monkeys now, the gorillas. Joe and Larry are watching this red-faced, mean-looking, nasty ape coming to the guard posts that keep the monsters on the other side from the people looking at them.

Joe says to Larry, "Boy! Mais, if dat bar cracked and dey could escape over tha railin's, it would be a damn massacre!"

The trio is watching this big hairy monster meander over to where they are standing. Minou points for Joe to look, "Mais, baby, look at his big red ass! It's worse dan his face! Oh, Gawd! He's turnin' himself wit' that ass lookin' straight at us! Mais, it's even more scary than the loup-garous! Ah know. Ah know. Ah didn't say it loud, but anyway, Larry wasn't listenin'."

All three are wide-eyed and staring and still laughing! They watch while the gorilla gets close to the rail, staring at the trio laughing at him. He craps in his hand and turns around to look at them while holding the steaming, stinking pile of crap!

The gorilla looks like he's going to aim it straight at Joe, and he isn't off his aim. The nasty stuff lands on Joe and Larry, and they both go to hollering.

Joe says, "Why he did dat? All over my new clothes! We goin' to tha hotel, Larry, to get my shotgun Ah brought! We gonna come back and shoot tha bastard! Sumbitch! Merde! Shit all over me!"

One of the workers goes to calm them down and bring wet towels for their faces and clothes.

Larry said he's so sorry, but he can't get in his cab with all that crap on him and leaves. It's bad enough with just him. He has to go home and change his clothes and loses the rest of the day in making his fares!

He's afraid for the cops to come and arrest them.

A supervisor comes and asks politely for them to leave the zoo. You can't talk about guns anywhere in public!

Minou tells them she wants her money back.

They have to ride the streetcar back, so Joe is in the open air. Joe still stinks so bad, the conductor asks them to sit way in the back.

Joe runs into the hotel room and shucks off his clothes, leaving them outside the door.

"Mais, we gonna have to wash my clothes 'cause dis merde will stain my brand-new clothes from tha Walmart! We gotta ask tha people at tha front desk where to go to wash dat filthy mess! Dat sumbitch! Why he did dat to me? Ah wasn't doin' him nuttin'!"

Minou is trying hard not to laugh, but it is killing her! "Mais, he musta t'ought ya was somebody else. Maybe his cousin! Ha, dat's why dey all axe for ya!"

Minou can't help herself anymore and starts rolling around the bed, laughing so hard that Joe can't help himself either!

After Joe strips down to nakedness, they do some more honeymooning.

∞ ∞ ∞

THE staff at the hotel offers to wash his clothes, so they go swimming until it gets dark and they are off to bed. Both are exhausted from the day and the night before.

They both dream all night, and Joe lets out a couple of goddamns and sumbitches in his sleep.

Minou and Joe spend the next day swimming in the pool until the sun sets. They love the little tables and the diving board where Joe makes double flips off of it. He learned that in the bayou, with long ropes tied up on an oak leaning over the banks. Joe and Minou both love to swing out into the water and let go.

Minou has brought what she thinks is a good thing to put on your skin, a mixture of baby oil and iodine. They rub this on each other all day.

The Caldonia has a young Black man named Henri Aucoin serving them mint juleps all day because that is the specialty of the day in their bar. Like two for one, they say. Henri and Joe are talking and laughing, Henri trying not to wet his nice, starched and ironed white shirt and black pants.

Henri has a bowtie and a nametag telling you his name. Joe's gonna have one made for himself; he is impressed with this.

They can't believe Henri's long hair in twirly braids coming down his back. Minou is gonna try that when she gets home.

Joe keeps trying to pay Henri, and he can't understand why he won't take his money. "Mistah Joe, we gonna put it on a tab that ya pay when ya leave the Caldonia. No, sir. I don't want ya money. Now ya sure can tip me, if ya want."

It is Henri that brings them the sunburn medication, along with some Popeyes Fried Chicken. He tells them that his great-aunt has a patented lotion for sunburns, but he can't go get any. It's all the way in the Quarter. He tells them his great-aunt has a small place down there, and she is Madam Aucoin. She sells Voodoo potions and charms and even the Voodoo dolls. She is a priestess in her religion that is truly Voodoo.

Minou is so excited the next morning to go buy souvenirs for everybody and to go meet Madam Aucoin. They drink some strong black coffee and have beignets in the Café du Monde before they go in search of the Voodoo shop. Larry has never come back for them. He is kinda afraid of the cops, being he's a little shady.

"Ah feel like a damn crawfish! Ah'm so burnt! Ah wish Ah could take dese clothes off right now and get a job down tha street, but we ain't stayin' dat long!" Minou cries to Joe as they still search for Madam Aucoin. They have already bought T-shirts for everybody and a little music box each for the mamas and Flavia back home.

They saw the sign first, and they come up on this small shotgun house painted gold with black shutters, a lot of hanging baskets with long strands of ivy twisting around the porch, and an old dog lying in the doorway. People come and go out the two wooden doors like they have some serious business up behind those doors. They don't look like tourists.

A brass bell announces them to the working staff there.

Minou walks up to a beautiful woman with skin that shines a shade of golden brown. Her hair is exploding down her back under the turban she wears, smelling so good. Later, Minou will know all about patchouli.

She smiles big at this woman and gets another smile, showing a big gold tooth.

"How ya do? Can we please talk to Madam Aucoin? We friends of her nephew Henri. He told us to come and visit her. He said she has tha best lotion for bad sunburns."

Minou is shocked when the woman breaks out in a larger smile and says she is Madam Aucoin. Minou doesn't see any sign of a great-aunt. This woman looks so young!

Madam Aucoin is looking at Minou like she knows something about her, and Minou just stares back. They smile at each other like they have already met and are friends.

Joe isn't comfortable watching this, and he goes off to look at everything in the shop. He feels the attraction between the two women and doesn't like it one bit.

"I am so pleased that Henri told you about me. That's a wonderful name you have, Minou. That's the big black cat sitting in the window.

Her name is Minou. She's been with me for a long time."

Madam then takes Minou's hands and says quietly, "You have the Second Sight, don't you? I could tell the minute I saw you. Minou, I know you have knowledge of the supernatural world, and your awareness of this, you take it nonchalantly every day. You are a very powerful young lady and have no idea what you're capable of doing. You are a breath of freshness I don't feel much in this old city.

"First thing I will do for you is give you the potion for the sunburn you both suffer with. Then we'll talk about your abilities you don't know about. Are there any traiteurs in your family or something that goes way back to your ancestors?"

Minou is trying to keep her mouth closed because one of her old uncles was a traiteur. Bertha, being mostly a native coastal Indian with a little Cajun thrown in the pot, had a great-grandfather that was a shaman, a medicine man in the Chitimacha tribe.

Minou begins to tell Madam Aucoin about what life has brought to her. She thinks she's brought it on herself because she's so nosy and has to have her way about everything.

Madam starts to laugh hard after Minou tells her about the trap they built and the big cans of Off! mosquito spray they bought to capture the loup-garou. Minou tells Madam that the loup-garous are her mama and her parrain. She has never told that to anyone, but she trusts the Voodoo queen. Madam really laughs out loud when Minou tells her who they turn out to be.

She isn't surprised when Minou tells her about Gaspar the unfriendly ghost. And Pedro.

The potion she gives for the sunburn is definitely working on Minou and Joe.

After talking for an hour while Joe is speaking French with some older Black man, Madam Aucoin begins to show Minou all the elixirs and potions she has in the store. She begins telling her of spells and how they work, and Minou is following the instructions like she is in school. Minou's mind is quick to remember things as she wants to know about everything. Nosy to a fault, Minou is going to ask questions.

They stay in the shop for three hours. Joe is completely freaked out! Joe has listened to some of their conversations, and he doesn't ever want to see how you raise a dead man that becomes a zombie!

Madam Aucoin makes sure she has the address and phone number of this lovely little woman. She for sure is coming to visit! She's coming next week.

Damn, they are bringing more people to their house without even trying!

Minou and Joe leave the shop just in time to go to the Caldonia, change clothes, and come back to the Quarter for Halloween night celebrations. They don't bother with Larry anymore because first thing you know, he'll be knocking on the door.

Joe is very concerned about Minou now because she hasn't talked about the Voodoo shop at all.

A quiet Minou only happens when she's sleeping. Joe tries to make her laugh and hugs her to put some spunk in her silence, but it doesn't work. She is as serious as a heart attack.

Minou sees a sign outside one of the shops advertising a ghost tour of the Quarter, and that sparks something in her demeanor. She grabs Joe's arm and pulls him to where the tickets are being sold.

"Baby, Ah want us to go on dis! Madam Aucoin told me 'bout it. She said Ah would make contact wit' tha spirits tonight! Ah want to see if she knows dis for true. Joe, it ain't 'bout no vampire!"

Their tour guide is dressed in the costume of a witch, and she leads the group down avenues and small cobblestone alleys. Everyone taking the tour has dressed for the occasion, and Minou is in fairyland with monsters and one vampire!

All of the mansions are lit up and decorated in Halloween colors with skeletons holding skulls and leading on the path into the homes, laughing and carrying on like they really didn't believe all this stuff.

She doesn't tell Joe about seeing the vampire again. He is at the first mansion. While there, the gentleman looks straight into her eyes, bows and lowers his hat to Minou. Wearing a cape, he disappears down the street.

Time after time, house after house, Minou doesn't see one damn ghost! She feels like she is in another world. New Orleans has that effect on people.

Minou has given up on seeing a spirit when the group comes to the last mansion. This house is one of the known places that Jean Lafitte lived in when he was a pirate walking the streets of old New Orleans with his crew of motley bandits. Operating on the Gulf Coast and the Caribbean, Lafitte hid many treasures and gold-filled chests in the bayous. They know that for sure because Minou and Joe have found one in a pecan tree grove and bought the land it's located on.

Poor Joe's feet are hurting. "Bae, Ah'm ready to sit down somewhere in dis house. My feet hurt like Ah got a big old blister! Ah'm gonna go barefoot if we don't!"

They both are looking for a place to sit down, and they hang back from the group to find a bench outside the kitchen. Minou is rubbing Joe's feet when she looks up and sees an unfriendly ghost by the name of Gaspar. He speaks out to Minou and Joe with a loud whisper.

"Oh, Bejesus, not you two scallywags again! You crafty wench, I will never tell you about the treasures I guard again. I came here looking for Lafitte because he's nowhere to be found in the heavens. He must be drinking the devil's ale with the devil himself! I don't belong there so I haunt this house waiting for him to come here.

"Now leave this abode before I start wailing like a banshee and frighten all the people here! Go now!"

Pedro the parrot is still screeching at them like he remembers them too. He speaks, "Laissez-nous tranquille!"

Minou and Joe stumble out the kitchen door, when they hear blood-curdling screams and see the witchy tour guide running out the front door with the group of monsters, fairies, and a couple of Lil BoPeeps screaming behind her!

They look at each other and at the group running fast-fast up the street. Minou and Joe just bust out laughing so hard she nearly pees her pants. She is no longer under a dreamy New Orleans spell.

They sleep a good night's sleep with no dreams after making love in a very dreamy atmosphere.

∞ ∞ ∞

BACK home, they talk nonstop about their honeymoon. Everyone gets their gifts and is amazed at pictures Minou has taken with her camera from Mrs. Flavia's.

One picture is of Joe with the gorilla throwing the crap all over him.

It is circulated at Mrs. Flavia's store like a postcard.

Minou is still quiet about the Voodoo shop, although she brings both the mamas and Flavia some cream that will remove wrinkles and make you look young. Madam Aucoin uses it daily, and it sure works on her.

She hides the Voodoo doll she's gotten from Madam Aucoin's shop. She takes it out secretly and laughs when she puts a pin in it and Joe starts scratching his butt!

The spell she casts to make Joe's mama like her is so successful that Minou runs from all the kissing and hugging his mama wants to do when she sees her!

The honeymoon in New Orleans is so great that Minou and Joe are having a baby in nine months.

Chapter Four

Minou and T-June

WELL you know, Minou and Joe come home from their honeymoon in New Orleans with a baby coming. Everybody is so happy about the news, and Joe's mama, Ethel, will finally have the baby she's been looking for since before they got married.

Ethel knows for sure Minou already has had one in the oven, being they were just fifteen when they got married. That's the first trick from Minou toward Joe's mama.

Now Ethel loves her insanely because Minou has used a spell on Joe's mama to just like her a little bit, and the spell works too well.

Mrs. Flavia treats Minou differently now. She's always wanting to stuff Minou with food and junk.

Flavia is already ordering baby supplies like this child is the only one in Larose being born.

Mrs. Flavia's store has been there since her great-grandpa opened the mercantile. Flavia's papa disappeared one night, and no one has seen him since. She and her mama ran the store after the mystery of a husband gone. Flavia changed the name of the store after her mama passed on.

The villagers think two things about her papa. He ran away with the mechanic's wife, or he was a meal for the loup-garou.

Flavia is a divorcee and proud of it. She doesn't need a man telling her what to do. Mrs. Flavia was married long enough to have two hellbent boys who struck terror wherever they went. So her husband just walked up the road in broad daylight in Larose, so people know he hasn't disappeared into the swamps.

Her two grown sons have both moved to the North, and she has two grandchildren she has never met. It's bothered Flavia for more than twenty years.

It's been Flavia's store since Minou was a baby in Bertha's arms. Minou has been raised with Flavia's advice, and still she's gotta listen to Mrs. Flavia. But y'all know Minou by now.

Everybody treats Minou like she's a princess. Only when she's in the mood will she let them. She acts like royalty since she's come back from New Orleans anyway, for sure after she met Madam Aucoin.

Madam comes to the country every week to see Minou and her family. She is still a teacher of Voodoo and also the correct way to say a word.

When she meets Bertha, they're like two sisters. Each is an older and wiser Minou! They talk on the phone almost every day.

∞ ∞ ∞

MINOU insists on working with Joe up until the morning of her labor. It's a Saturday afternoon during the LSU football game that Minou's water breaks and goes all over the floor.

She hollers out some cuss words as it happens. "Aw, hellfire! Ah'm gonna clean it up! Ah'm so haunt!"

It won't be the last time she cusses on this day!

Bertha and Madam come running in from the kitchen where they are making pralines and see the mess. They are laughing with glee that Minou is having her baby.

Minou doesn't think anything is funny. She's so tired, carrying this big-ass basketball around. All you see is the big belly because Minou is short, like five foot three inches, and scrawny most of the time.

Bertha calls Flavia at the store, and she closes early to come.

Minou isn't going to the hospital. Her mama, Bertha, has been a midwife for a long time. All three of the women know about birthing babies, so Minou is okay with this because she is feeling pains and wants it over with. Now!

Joe and Alcide are chased out the house in the middle of the football game. They aren't worried about the game. They can hear Minou yelling cuss words, so they are beating a path in the front yard and lighting cigarette after cigarette.

The women are amazed at how fast Minou gives birth. She yells a few choice words, and the massive boy comes out yelling!

The baby is covered in hair. He also has a membrane covering him like a blanket. The hair on his body is light and a bit fuzzy. His head has a shock of black hair that looks like a Mohawk from some distant ancestor.

The baby even has a tooth in the front of his mouth!

He weighs 11 pounds. He looks like he is a month old. Everybody is in awe of that! Minou, being so short, feels like the baby was in her throat.

Madam Aucoin smiles at everybody and says, "Minou, the baby is born with a veil over him! That means he will have the Second Sight, just like you. He may be many things because of this veil, like being a traiteur or can see future things or even be a loup-garou! He is special and will be magnificent as a man! You carry Bertha and Alcide's genes."

Bertha goes to crying while Mrs. Flavia tries to comfort her.

Flavia's knows about the werewolves after she stalks Minou's family one night because she wants to see the marijuana bushes she just knows they're growing. You would think this would be enough to cure being nosy!

It takes a while for Flavia to come around to talking to them again, but she never says a word about it to anybody. She can be very tightlipped when it involves her best friends.

Now she helps when she can with her two friends that turn into monsters once a month.

Bertha is still crying at Minou's bedside. "Ah'm so sorry, so sorry, Minou. Ya didn't have all dis hair when ya was born, and now we might have to shave him! But ya did have tha veil, and my mama said what it was."

Madam Aucoin laughs and tells them, "My beautiful people, this hair will continue to lighten on his body as he gets older and will be thinner. He will be a beautiful man with a beard he'll shave when he needs to. Don't worry about that. That's the least thing you will worry about!"

Mrs. Flavia is quiet, holding the baby even before Minou gets to hold him. She hands the child to Minou with tears dripping down her face. She asks Minou if she can be the nanan, the godmother. Minou smiles at Flavia and says she and Joe would be honored.

Minou looks into the face of her baby boy and sees he is in a quiet stare, looking straight at her. His round light green eyes are so clear, looking at his mama's eyes. Then he smiles with his front tooth shining.

She pets his fuzzy arms and laughs at his Mohawk. Their faces are together, and Minou kisses his mouth, nose, and those eyes wide open.

"Hello, lil boy. Ya want to see ya daddy?"

Joe grabs the baby and laughs and cries! He holds him high and says,

"Oh, my beautiful Minou! Ah could just kiss ya all over!" She passes him a look that says Ya better not even try!

"Bébé, he come here almost grown! Mais, Bae, how ya got dat big baby t'rough ya… Okay! Okay! Ah so sorry to be even t'inkin' 'bout dat! Ah'm not gonna say no more!"

Joe's attention goes to his son. "Ah'm ya papa, my lil boy. Look at me, baby, let me see dose big round eyes!"

Of course, everyone holds and kisses the beautiful baby boy. It's wonderful to hold a chubby baby and not be afraid of holding a teeny tiny one.

Nobody except Madam Aucoin has seen a baby in years. Minou and Joe see their friends' children, but that's all. They stick together and don't need other people than family, because of the quemas every month.

Minou doesn't take her eyes off her son, and strangely, his little eyes search and find his mama, no matter who is holding him.

He starts crying, but when she grabs him, he's a silent baby. It will be that way his whole life.

Minou gets up and walks into the living room where her grandfather is sitting in his recliner. She bends to give him the baby.

He looks seriously hard at the baby like he isn't sure if he wants to hold him. Pawpaw Irby starts grinning at the baby boy, then he proceeds with belly laughs to talk to him. "Atakapa! You gonna be my podnah! Chér, bébé, Chér, bébé! Atakapa!"

Minou knows about all the different tribes of blood racing down the generations of their family, but she is as shocked as everyone that he speaks!

Pawpaw Iby sits holding the baby, crooning to him and holding him while the family sits around him.

Joe's mama, Ethel, comes running in to see the baby. Minou hasn't wanted her at the birthing because Ethel loves Minou so much she would have been in the way, trying to smother her with kisses.

She says, "Mais, Joe, we got us a lil Injun! Mais, Ah want to hold him!" Ethel is trying to take the baby from Pawpaw Irby, so there is a commotion between the two, with Minou stepping in to take the infant from both!

Ethel is trying to get to Minou to kiss her, and her son and asks, "Minou, what we gonna call him? He's gonna be a Junior, huh? Just call him Joe Junior after his papa."

Minou takes the baby because he's hungry and leaves the room with him still looking at his mama's eyes. He latches on to her breast like he is starving.

"Ay yai yai! Lawd, these tetons full of milk hurt bad, so don't pull so hard, ya lil turd! Ya hurtin' Mama! Dat's gonna be tough tittie, said tha kitty!

"My lil man, ya gonna be some loved! Look how big ya are! My lil tootoo, ya gonna be a big man like ya papa, and Mama will hold ya like the treasure ya are!

"We gonna call ya T-June. But ya gotta start lookin' at everybody else instead of Mama all tha time."

Joe and Minou have already decided what they will call him. Minou doesn't like Junior so they shorten it to June and of course the "T" is short for "Tee," or petite. So, his name means Little Joe Junior!

Joe is so happy having a son it doesn't matter to him. If it had been a girl, Minou wanted to name her Caldonia!

Bertha and Alcide want him to be Joey, Flavia wants Alan, Madam Aucoin will have her own special names for the beautiful boy.

Minou comes back with her son.

"Let me tell y'all who dis is. Dis is our Joseph Alan Thibeau Junior. We gonna call him T-June. Dat's short for all of it. So who wants to hold T-June, this big old boy?"

Madam Aucoin hasn't held T-June yet, so she reaches for him.

"My wondrous boy! My JoeJoe Star. You will know Madam for as long as she lives. Try not to startle your mama and papa with what you're going to do. Chér, Madam is baffled by you. You are such an old soul."

T-June is listening intently to Madam Aucoin's words while she pulls a tiny sterling silver chain out of the pocket of her housedress she has on over her gauze shirt and long skirt. It's a Voodoo symbol that is for protection against all evil.

The chain settles on the gold links with a crucifix Flavia has already placed hanging to his chest. T-June will have a third when Alcide finishes with his tiny leather strap and a potion pouch on the strand, the same potion he has made Minou wear. Lot of good that does!

All of the neck jewelry is worn at the same time. T-June's chubby little neck will carry all this weight forever.

∞ ∞ ∞

T-JUNE has been fishing with his mama and papa every day since he was three weeks old, laying on the palmetto while they fish.

All the midwives have raised hell with them for not waiting at least six weeks. That's what they used to say to do, but some mamas can't refrain because they have another baby in diapers with three more toddlers needing her.

That's the rhythm method the Catholic Church tells you to follow with your husband.

As if!

Minou knows she isn't the first little woman on Bayou Lafourche to have a baby, and she knows that half the women on the bayou don't follow that rhythm either.

Minou carries him in an old-fashioned way of bundling. He is always in a position where he can look at Minou's eyes and not far from her tetons, hurting like they do!

T-June insists on looking at no one but her. He's always searching for Mama.

Joe and Minou are lying on the old palmetto leaves that flattened so long ago, right next to the bayou. It's where they caught the loup-garous years ago. They have the fishing poles in the bayou, waiting on bites from a choupic. That's good eating.

T-June is sitting on the blanket. He's six months old today. He's got a bunch of toys that Madam has brought from New Orleans on the pallet. Minou glances at him and sees what looks like he has arranged all the toys in some pattern.

She thinks he is some smart!

Minou sees her cane pole line go under, and it's bobbing around. Good! Now she knows they're biting! She goes to check for a fish, but when she gets there, there is no sign of a fish, and the worm is still wriggling.

Minou puts it back in the bayou, and before she turns around, it does it again.

This business with the cane fishing pole happens three times more. She is scratching her head!

She walks back up to where Joe is holding T-June and sees his little fingers reaching for her. Minou thinks he's reaching for her so he can stare at her eyes and eat until he's slap happy!

She grabs T-June, and he's looking at her with his hand still pointing. The fishing line goes under again. She looks hard at T-June pointing and tells Joe to go stop the bobbing of the line.

"Stay dere, Joe, and make sure it don't move. Now watch, Joe, watch T-June. Ah be damned if he ain't making dat line do dat, dat bobbin'!

"Mais, hot damn! Joe, what we got with dis baby? Ah don't know if we should tell e'rybody! Ah mean, he ain't but six months old! Make him do it again. Go and fix tha line!"

They tell no one like it's a handicap of some kind. Well, they shouldn't be worried.

∞ ∞ ∞

IN the kitchen where everybody is standing getting ready to fix their plates, T-June makes a wooden spoon land right next to Bertha. She drops her favorite iron skillet, hitting her bare feet. Bertha goes to screaming.

"Minou, you saw what T-June did! Oh, my Gawd! Oh, my Gawd! Mais, Ah got at least two, two broken toes!" Bertha begins to tell them while they're tending to her toes.

"Ah been seein' my dishrags lyin' on tha floor and knowin' damn well Ah didn't leave dat dere!

Blamin' it on y'all! All dis time it mighta been him. Oh, my Gawd!

Let me go call on tha phone Madam and see if she can come tonight."

T-June is handed to Pawpaw Irby, with him saying, "Atakapa!"

Bertha is telling Madam what is happening on the bayou, arms flying in the air and hands just shaking! Madam is driving down from New Orleans tonight and will spend the rest of the week watching T-June do his thing! She has a long word for what he's doing.

Joe and Minou take T-June to see his nanan, Flavia, that afternoon when it's closing time, and he points his fat fist toward a sucker on the counter. Sure enough, that sucker comes bobbing to his little hand reaching for it.

Flavia goes to hollering and scares T-June, so he goes to hollering too!

It takes some time to calm them both down, and Joe has already pulled the doors shut and the Closed sign.

After she gets over her fit, Flavia makes them promise her they will not show that to nobody else!

She tells them again what she thinks of the government. Mrs. Flavia is all about those conspiracies and the wars and the spies. Again, she tells them.

She thinks the people in Larose will try and put him in the circus. And the government will want to make him into some kind of war machine, making him a freak. Flavia gets so wound up in her blaming the government and protecting T-June that she sounds like she will put him in some kind of gated place away from everybody! Shotguns being held by the guards. The big-ass dogs too!

Now Mrs. Flavia isn't all that happy concerning Madam Aucoin either. The Voodoo scares her, and she doesn't trust a thing Madam Aucoin has to say.

Both ladies just stay in their own lanes, away from each other. Neither one is going anywhere.

Madam Aucoin arrives at dusk with satchels full of magic and Voodoo. Everybody is sitting in the living room at Bertha and Alcide's house with Pawpaw Irby, while T-June sits in his lap.

Minou moves the remote control and puts it on a small table. T-June has that remote just a-bobbing toward Pawpaw and back on his blanket. Pawpaw just breaks out laughing and calling, "Atakapas! Atakapas! My lil podnah!"

Madam Aucoin says that the baby has telekinesis. It's when you can move objects with your mind. She says proudly, "JoeJoe Star is the youngest I have heard about having this capability! I say it's best you don't let him use these powers in front of other people. They wouldn't understand this and would be frightened if he did this in the public.

"I said to you when he was born, there's no telling what he will be as he grows, but you need to be very vigilant in watching him. Don't censor him. We will be able to guide him, teaching him about this ability and how to use it.

"My family, I know there are other things coming with JoeJoe Star, but I don't know what they are. We will take the paths given us, and do the best we can. We will have more chosen people along the way, and we will need them, whoever they are."

∞ ∞ ∞

T-JUNE is a year old today. He has a mouth full of teeth and the Mohawk has turned to black curls around his chubby face. When he is teething and his little mouth is hurting, things just move out of his way, like he's throwing them. At 10 months he is walking, talks like a two-year-old and can put words in Minou's head. She begins hearing them and thinks she is going cuckoo ma choo! She would hear words his mind would say to her. He knows, as every baby does, that Mama will get it for you instead of making the effort of reaching for it.

He likes to watch Minou as she moves fast around everything.

He will be on his pallet in the living room, Minou will hear noonie – that's what they call the pacifier he loves to suck with a passion – and of course he will be looking at her eyes.

T-June has the prettiest, fullest red lips; it's hard not to kiss him on his mouth! Big, round, light green eyes and eyelashes all the women wish they had, and hair that is black as night beginning to curl.

The first time he speaks, Minou jumps and looks straight into his round eyes. "What ya told Mama with ya lil mind? I heard ya. Ah'm gonna get ya noonie for you, but ya can say tha word noonie out loud wit' ya mouth!

"Stay out my head, my lil man, unless it's somet'in' important for Mama to hear by herself! Ya bettah look at my eyes! Mais, ya coulda got up ya-self to get it! Don't be lazy, ya lil turd!"

T-June just laughs with his big belly and hollers like he's grown up! Can you imagine that with a toddler that looks like he's three when he isn't?

Minou is so glad when he starts walking! He walks fast-fast-fast, just like his mama, always beside her.

T-June is sitting next to Minou, eating his scrambled eggs early in the morning when she hears, Mama, Nanan is coming. She sad, Mama, sad, sad.

Of course, he's steadily eating his eggs while he is putting thoughts into Minou's mind.

Minou gets up and goes for the door, looking for Flavia. Minou trusts his gifts without asking and because she's used to it.

Poor Minou. A baby, mind you, a baby that can do all this quemas. What the Terrible Twos will bring, Oh, my Gawd!

Mrs. Flavia walks through a heavy rain to stumble into the living room where the iron stove is steadily warming everyone. In tears, she grabs T-June; he goes into her arms, reaching for her. He is holding her as tight as he can.

Quietly crying she says, holding the baby as tight as she can, "Minou, Ah just got a phone call dat my oldest son Stephen was killed in a car accident. Ah haven't seen him in twenty-five years. He would call me on my birthday, on Mother's Day, and at Christmas. Never any long talking between us, just short phone calls a coupla times a year.

"Oh, Lawd, it used to hurt me so bad, and Ah'm crying now 'cause Ah'm sad. He never married and lives wit' another man. Ah never said nuttin' 'bout dat, so Ah don't know why Ah'm not close to either of my boys. Maybe 'cause Ah'm so bossy and used to have to whip deir asses 'cause dey was bad.

"But dat's a mama's job. Maybe Ah didn't love on dem like we do wit' T-June."

Flavia goes to sit down next to Pawpaw Irby. He is looking at her with sorrow in his eyes and says, "Ah'm sorry for ya loss, bébé."

He reaches for the baby, who he still calls Atakapa, and Flavia gladly gives him T-June.

Pawpaw Irby has been much better since T-June arrived. It's like he's coming back to life! It's almost like the baby is helping him. Maybe T-June talks to his mind!

Bertha is coming out the kitchen with hot coffee and toast. She grabs her friend, crying and holding her so tight.

Mrs. Flavia continues talking while sipping her coffee. "My other son is tha one to call me. Ah haven't seen him in twenty-five years either! He tells me it's time to meet his two chil'ren, who are teenagers. Dey call me Grandmother! Just always too busy, bot' of them, to visit me one time!

"Horace, my other son, tells me he's bought an airplane ticket for me to fly up for tha memorial service for Stephen. He's gonna be cremated. His boyfriend, Ah might as well say, is Chinese, and my son went by his religion.

"They want me to go for three weeks to visit wit' dem and go see the sights of Philadelphia! Ah mean, it's like Ah don't know dese people, even though Ah'm deir mama."

Minou and Bertha tell her not to worry about a thing. They will take her to the Louis Armstrong Airport in New Orleans tomorrow morning. Of course, Alcide will drive them.

Mrs. Flavia says, "Minou, will ya and Joe run the store while Ah'm gone? Y'all been watchin' me in tha store since ya was little. Ah'll pay ya real good 'cause Ah don't want the store closed all dat time. Y'all can have anyt'in' in tha store, and for sure T-June can come wit' you.

"What y'all say? Ah don't know what else to do!"

Of course Joe and Minou say yes, indeed. They've both been in that store forever and know how everything is run. Maybe not as smooth as Flavia, but they will get the job done.

∞ ∞ ∞

MINOU and Joe open the store the next day, and T-June is placed in the huge playpen his nanan has bought for him to keep there.

He has to stay in the playpen because he's fast-fast in the store, with things flying all around him. Minou prays he doesn't do that when there are customers! You can't use paregoric on babies no more, you know.

T-June is standing in his pen watching people as they walk in and out. His curiosity is beyond belief so he might be using the trait he got from his mama, being nosy watching everybody walking around. He's not doing his tricks, so Minou and Joe are thankful for that.

T-June has taken an interest in this young boy who comes in every day to the store. He watches him in silence, even though the boy talks to him and tries to make him laugh. T-June lets the boy hold him, and he cuddles into the boy's arms.

Mixed messages, as they say.

He is sucking his noonie, watching his mama. The store traffic is slow.

Minou hears him in her mind. The boy is hungry, Mama. He takes food, Mama. Don't fuss, Mama, don't fuss him.

The boy just shows up at the store every day but buys things most of the time.

She pays him no mind because it's busy when he shows up, and Minou remembers when she and Joe did the same and Flavia would chase them out.

She's on alert now because her nosiness kicks in. Minou watches the next day for the boy to come.

As he walks in, he goes to T-June, and T-June reaches for him with a smile!

Go figure, the mixed messages again!

Minou, watching these two, says, "Hey, lil man, ya got a name? My name is Minou, and that's lil T-June over dere. Ya came a lil early dis mornin'. Wait, Ah'll give ya a baloney sandwich wit' a root beer if ya watch the baby for a few minutes. The Lunch Bunch is comin', and dey leave wit' dere sandwiches. Can ya do dat for me?"

Minou is glad to see the boy light up. He says, "Yes, ma'am, Ah can do dat for ya. Ah love me some June! Ah got dis, Ah got this, Miss Minou!"

He plays with the baby for another 40 minutes, walking him outside until the crowd goes back to work. He eats every crumb of his sandwich and drinks the can of soda empty.

Minou sits down next to the boy and asks him his name and where he comes from. He looks her in the eyes. "Miss Minou, Ah belong to Old Man Guidry down the road in dat nasty houseboat on tha bayou. He's my pawpaw. My mama left me wit' him 'bout six months ago. Ah miss her. She took a boyfriend that don't like kids. He don't even like his own, my mama says. So Ah came here.

"My daddy is dead. He was killed offshore when tha rig blew up wit' no survivors. My mama got a lotta money. Ah'm stayin' wit' her daddy."

"My name is Matthew Miller Junior. That's what my mama named me after my daddy who died. My mama always calls me Butch, and you can call me dat too. Pawpaw calls me other things. Ah don't wanna tell you.

"But ya know, Miss Minou, Ah could do dis every day for ya, and tha sandwich and pop would be good for me."

Minou asks him to be truthful and tell her if he's been taking food from the store. Butch says right away that he has. He tells her his pawpaw stays drunk most nights and doesn't think to buy food for them. The refrigerator in the houseboat is full of dead bloody things Pawpaw caught.

He has to wait until the old man is sleeping so he can get money out his pockets.

Butch's clothes are stained and ripped in many places, but you could tell they were quality at one time. Butch tries to wash them, leaning over the side of the houseboat.

Minou's mind is in overload, and she starts pacing. T-June starts crying, reaching out to Butch to be held. The baby is holding him tight.

Minou asked if he has been taking things from Mrs. Flavia.

He says no, ma'am, because she watches him like a hawk and goes to pick up a broom after him. Minou laughs at that. That's Flavia!

After she tells him to go wash his face, which is covered in tears and dust, Minou says to him, "Butch, here's what we gonna do. Ya come every mornin' at eight o'clock. Ya can do tha sweepin' and dustin' and takin' care of T-June. Ah will pay ya eight dollars an hour and wit' whatever ya see to eat. Butch, why ya not in school?"

He tells her he hasn't been since he came to Larose. His pawpaw doesn't like schools, but Butch loves school and misses it. He makes straight As, and he is just 11 years old. The most favorite pastime for him is coming to the store.

He tells Minou he will follow them home but stays in the bushes. Minou is some mad! She's telling Butch he's coming home with her today.

"Ya don't have to go back dere again, Butch, if ya don't want. Ah don't want ya bringin' dat old stuff ya been wearin'! Me and Joe are gonna buy whatever ya need, and Ah sure as hell don't care 'bout Old Man Guidry! Alcide and Joe will deal wit' his nasty ass!

"Go pick out right now whatever you want, ya hear me? Startin' wit' ya drawers and a toothbrush!"

Joe has been hunting with Alcide, so he's been out of the store, knowing Minou will holler for help if she needs him to do something. And that she does!

She tells Joe and Alcide about Butch and how she has hired him to help in the store with T-June.

Then she tells them how Butch is coming home to live with them.

Joe and Alcide know the dirty old bastard Guidry, and they don't like him not one bit. Alcide had punched the old paiyan one night at Tee Man's Bar and Fish Dock down the bayou.

Minou will cast a spell to make Mrs. Flavia like the boy when she comes back.

Minou is fired up and wants Butch's mama's phone number so she can tell her what is going to take place and to get her ass down there to see what she's left her child in. Over some goddamn man.

"Joe, ya and Alcide are gonna go talk wit' Old Man Guidry. Ya'll gonna convince him to let Butch live wit' us. If he says no, we gonna tell tha law on him for keepin' tha boy outta school. Threaten him, 'cause Butch is havin' a miserable time with his Pawpaw Guidry.

"We will deal with his mama when she comes back from wherever she's been shackin' up. She betta stay on tha porch in dis dogfight!

"He's gonna live wit' us. Ah already asked Mama if it's all right, and she said okay. We just gonna be more vigilant when it's a full moon. He don't need to know about tha loup-garous!"

Joe and Alcide and Minou go down to the houseboat where Old Man Guidry is skinning catfish right off his dock.

He sneers at them, saying, "What da hell ya want?"

Alcide tells him, "To tell ya how tha cow ate tha cabbage!"

He stands to raise his fist at Alcide, and overboard off the dock he goes, with a punch to his jaw. "Dat's what da hell Ah want!" Alcide says.

They all walk back up the road, while behind them, Old Man Guidry is cussing and trying to get out the bayou.

∞ ∞ ∞

BUTCH goes to the store every morning with Minou and T-June and has found all kind of things to help with in the mercantile. He is very strong because he totes T-June all over the store. He cleans the windows until they sparkle, makes sandwiches for the work crews when they come for their meal, and keeps T-June occupied!

Now Bertha's been making gumbo and jambalaya to add to the menu that's only been ham and baloney and olive loaf.

They are making a killing in the store for Flavia. The money has been way over what she brings in.

Maybe if Mrs. Flavia would smile and be nicer to the customers, she would have more people buying her groceries!

Butch is sitting down, holding the baby when he tells Minou, "Miss Minou, Ah got somet'in' to tell ya. Ah know T-June has got some tricks. He makes t'ings come to him, and sometimes Ah hear him tellin' me somet'in', and it's not talkin' he does. He puts it in my head."

T-June only does that with Minou right now and maybe Pawpaw Irby!

Butch goes on. "Ah've never seen nobody do what T-June does. Shucks, he's just a lil baby! Ya gonna need some help wit' him! He can't be doin' dat in front of the customers! Ah live wit' y'all now, and Ah'm so grateful. Ah can go to school next mont', and Ah'll work part time if

Mrs Flavia wants me to. But what ya think about dis other idea instead?" Butch takes a drink of his pop and stands up, handing the baby to Minou. "Ah get a lot of money on the t'ird of every month. Pawpaw Guidry has been keepin' it for hisself. Ah get dat from the oil company dat killed my daddy. Mama makes sure dat Ah get it, but she don't know what Pawpaw's been doin'.

"Ah got a savin's account at tha bank in Thibodaux. My mama would take me every mont' to put my money in tha bank and leave out enough for me to have to spend for tha rest of tha mont'. Ah'm savin' to go to college 'cause Ah wanna be a history teacher.

"Ah got money to help wit', and Ah can come straight home and take care of T-June every afternoon 'stead of workin' at Flavia's. Ah don't need to work ever. Payin' me for workin', Ah wouldn't have needed it if Pawpaw would have given me my money, and Ah had to steal it back from him. Ah'm goin' to live wit' y'all as long as you'll have me. Ah always wanted a brother to play wit'.

"Ah've been lonely 'cause my mama takes her money and goes shoppin' for another outfit to wear for tha night comin'. She likes to hang out in tha bars where she finds a man for him to be another daddy. Ah never knew who is in my house. Ah don't blame her, poor t'ing. Don't t'ink she isn't a good mama. We do take care of each other, and Ah know she loves me. But now Ah get to be a big brother, and T-June will need me 'cause he's so different. How ya like dis idea? T-June and his big brother, Butch."

∞ ∞ ∞

MINOU and Joe have agreed to Butch's idea, and there's plenty room for Butch in their double-wide. Pawpaw Irby calls him "my son."

Alcide and Bertha love him like he's theirs, and Bertha makes peanut butter fudge for him every week.

Flavia takes a liking to him in spite of the spell but is glad he doesn't work there anymore. She thinks it was a good idea adding plate lunches to her menu. Her and Bertha split the money.

Truth is, Flavia likes to work by herself. She is self-reliant and doesn't need help. Time will come when she does.

She makes out her will after she comes back from staying with her family. T-June will inherit all that is Flavia's.

∞ ∞ ∞

MADAM Aucoin laughs all the time with Butch. He is hilarious when Madam comes to visit.

Butch wears a chain identical to T-June's that Madam brings him. Butch already wears the leather chain that Alcide made with the pouch attached to it for protection from the two Cajun werewolves! The silver charm protects from everything else.

Mrs. Flavia brings him a gold chain with a crucifix hanging down his chest. She tells him, "Ah t'ink ya are a good boy and savin' ya money to become a teacher. Ah can tell ya a lot of history from around here. Ya can call me Nanan if ya want."

Chapter Five

Minou, T-June and the Coon

MINOU is a busy mama, tending to T-June with all of his abilities, staying in constant awareness of what her little black-haired boy magician will do next.

Alcide and Bertha are watching T-June like some hawks waiting for a squirrel. Bertha has a slight fear of him because she isn't a woman that likes surprises.

June just looks at her and smiles, so she doesn't ever know what the hell is going on in his little mind. T-June can't talk with the hairy pair in their heads, and Bertha just doesn't trust him.

Minou is so thankful that Butch is living with them because he helps so much with the baby's antics. He keeps T-June in line and protects him from other people in the village finding out about the strangeness of the child.

Minou tells Butch about her papa dying on an oil rig too and how she and Bertha don't receive any checks at all. Bertha has had to do what she can in any situation they find themselves in, but Alcide has been buying the groceries since her Jake went to his grave.

All of them keep his white tomb so clean and fresh flowers on his grave. That is a must in the family, especially for All Saints Day. That's when everyone on the bayou cleans and paints all the white tombs and visits with other families and their dead.

Butch's mama, Irene, comes to see him regularly. He tells her that he wants to stay with Minou and Joe. She sighs heavily but seems relieved.

Irene has gotten in a big brawl with her daddy, Old Man Guidry, and the police have to come down the bayou and arrest the bastard because Irene presses charges and pushes him in the bayou again after Alcide and Joe did the same thing. Irene comes up a couple of notches on Minou's belt right then.

It is "Good night, Irene" after that!

She still picks up Butch every month to deposit his money in the savings account. They go shopping together for more clothes for Butch; he's growing fast too. He is happy, and so is Irene.

Minou finds that she likes Irene, in spite of the rocky start when they first meet. She has known her most of her life, a young girl watching while Irene walked the levee going to the dance.

She can tell that Irene dearly loves Butch, but some women are not cut out to raise babies. Some women think they need a man to take care of them, and Minou knows nothing about that need because she is surrounded by strong women who can survive without being under some man's thumb. For sure, Irene needs to sit down with Mrs. Flavia because she would get an earful about men!

Minou tries to trap and hunt with Joe whenever she can leave T-June in the custody of the family. They have to keep their eyes on the baby and make sure he's not finding a new trick to display without supervision.

Bertha tries to keep him out the kitchen because he will make everything in her cabinets fly out, and then she's got to pick up behind his busy butt!

∞ ∞ ∞

MINOU wants to go fishing bad. It's her favorite thing because it's where she does most of her pondering about what life has brought to her and Joe. They can't take the baby fishing any more because he still finds the bobbing of the cork funny, so they never know if a catfish has taken the bait or T-June is laughing while he makes it bob.

It's been a couple of weeks since they been fishing, so it doesn't take long for them to get their stuff ready to go. They're just waiting on Butch to get off the school bus.

June, as Butch calls him, gets so excited when he sees the children on the bus. He'll take off fast-fast toward the highway to get to Butch. Who the hell knows if he's capable of stopping a car, and they don't want to find out!

Butch is getting ready to go fishing with Minou and Joe. He'll keep the baby from messing with their cane poles and the catfish that are dangling on the line. T-June will start swinging that fish, and the mess will be all over them!

Butch grabs the sandwiches for everybody that Minou has prepared while Butch is in school. She makes olive loaf po'boys with thick slices of tomatoes and leaves of lettuce, with thin slices of purple onions hanging over the Evangeline bread and plenty of mayonnaise. Of course, their soda pops are in a big ice chest. They love their Cokes and RCs!

The palmetto leaves are still in their spot right by the bayou. They've added over the years the huge leaves on top of each other until the palmetto makes a large mattress on the well-worn ground.

The cane poles' lines are in the bayou, waiting on a true for-sure bob. Minou and Joe are laughing and enjoying the time together.

Butch has taken June walking around the cleared areas and on the path through the swamp. They both are laughing, watching the little magician throw flowers he can make float in the air!

June is talking with his mouth, telling Butch what this is and that is. He remembers everything that is told to him, even as an infant.

He is talking in Butch's head, but it's like he doesn't hear too good. That trick is what you call having a brain too big for your head!

The boys sit down on the path and are eating their po'boys because the two are sharing that big sandwich. June looks at Butch with a serious face and says with his little voice, "Butch, mais, dere is a big coon hurtin' somewhere over in tha swamp. Butch, bring me, bring me, bring me!"

June wants to do everything for himself. He knows when he's just too little, so he will ask for some kind of help. Or put the thought in your mind! So he knows he has to be carried through this thick part of the swamp, searching for the coon.

He tells Butch to go look for it. Butch has him up in his arms and asks his little brother, "June, Ah don't hear no cryin' from no coon! How ya know that? Ya mama and papa don't know where we are, so we gotta hurry up. Come on. Let's go see."

In the back of two cypress trees leaning over the bayou, they see a large coon caught in a trap, laying still, trying not to move. Butch bends over to look at the animal and sees she's alive, but he knows he can't open that heavy trap because June is steadily hollering, "Get her out! Get her out!"

Minou and Joe come running to where the boys stand, and June is steadily crying and has raised both his arms.

The trap comes flying open, with the raccoon standing still, looking at them instead of running fast into the swamps.

The family stands there with their mouths wide open. Minou can barely open the traps, and there is T-June just waving his arms and the trap opens!

Joe says, "Mais, damn. He's some kind of Superman!"

Minou notices the raccoon just looking at them and says, "Look, Joe! Dat coon ain't movin'! Mais, Ah never saw dat in my life unless dey was babies.

"T-June, how ya know dat coon was dere, huh? Tell me wit' ya mouth, how ya know dat? Butch said he didn't hear nuttin'! And how de hell ya sprung dat trap? Tell me, bébé. Ah ain't mad at ya. Ah just need to know what ya did."

Butch is still holding June when he looks at his mama. That big old coon is still just standing there, watching.

"Mama, 'cause she was tellin' me! She was cryin' for some help. She just talks to me. She said no other people can hear her. Me, just me. She wants me to go over dere where she's waitin' for me. Put me down, Butch."

∞ ∞ ∞

MADAM Aucoin works hard to teach all the family the correct words to use instead of the family's Cajun concoctions. Minou is trying to speak proper, but Bertha's a lost cause. June does well most of the time, but he's excited and reverts back to what he hears at home.

Lawd! They're gonna have to call Madam to come. She's more in the country now instead of her Voodoo shop. Every time he does something else that baffles his family, she comes running!

T-June walks on his fat little legs down by the bayou and sits next to the raccoon that is standing on her back legs. There's an injury on her hands where she has been caught in the trap.

He sits quietly and seems to be talking to her, the coon. T-June gets up after talking – or not talking – to the racoon to go to Minou and Joe.

He speaks to both of them because Butch is down there petting the coon! "She said dat y'all need to stop huntin' all tha animals, and she's comin' to live wit' us to make sure y'all don't catch no more."

Minou and Joe should have listened more to that statement.

"She says dat she lived wit' people before, and dey called her Ruby. She says she's gettin' too old, or she woulda seen tha trap. She says she's gonna be my pet. Me, Ah told her, Mais, sure. She could come to our house."

Butch gets excited to hear T-June saying that. He's gotten kind of used to T-June's powers, but this is like Dr. Dolittle, and he loves those movies! He's over there talking to the coon and asking June what Ruby said.

Minou and Joe said okay reluctantly but have no idea what is coming down the road for them and that smart-ass coon.

Joe builds a cage for Ruby. She supervises, and T-June gives the instructions.

People will be thinking that the whole bunch is as crazy as the pouledoux!

Minou takes care of Ruby's injuries, so now there's a few scars on Ruby's little hands. She does have the run of the house, picking at Couyon, their old dog, stealing his food and washing her hands in his water bowl.

Of course, Madam Aucoin comes that evening to see these amazing traits blossom out. She wants to see Ruby because she had a pet raccoon as a little girl.

She sits down where T-June is lying awake in his pawpaw's lap. Madam speaks seriously to him when Alcide and Bertha and of course Flavia come to listen with Minou and Joe.

"My little JoeJoe Star, what else can you possibly do? We are all worried, and now you can talk to the animals. Like Butch says, a regular old Dr. Dolittle!

"Then you opened the trap with your little hands flying in the air, pointing at it. You did that in anger, didn't you? You were really mad!"

Madam leaves him sleeping on Pawpaw, both going to sleep. Madam drinks coffee and smokes her ganja pipe. (Minou and Joe know about that Wacky Tobacky now, but only Minou and Bertha have ever wanted to try it.)

Then Madam says, "Look at me! Talking to a child that hasn't seen his second birthday yet! My family knows something is up in the bayou, and I dare not tell them about our Monsieur Mayhem! They would be telling the neighbors sitting on their porches and going from one porch to another all the way down Esplanade Avenue and into the Quarter!

"We have to take care of this. It's almost out of control! Minou, get Alcide to help you find out all you can about your two families. This would have been thought to come from the devil. A relative that was locked up in the attic or sent to an insane asylum? Do this right away so maybe you can find out if this is all inherited in T-June.

"If not, some spirit visited you in my shop! I don't think I've got that much power in my religion of Voodoo. I prayed many, many prayers for this Monsieur Mayhem. I've burned so many candles for him because I always sensed something about your child, Minou. I still burn those candles all day!

"All of this is too much for us to handle. We don't understand the fullness of these powers he's been given. We need help. I would like to bring with me someone who lives in the city. If you give me permission, I will bring Bishop Laurant Toussaint from my church. He's like a king; you could think that when seeing him. He used to be known as Dr. Manly Tall, because he stands in a frame of six feet nine inches. He's very important in the city."

Flavia gets up in a defensive stance and goes to walk out the house but changes her mind and sits back down. She doesn't want a Voodoo doctor talking to T-June.

That nanan is some mad! She says, "Ah'll be goddamned dat happens! Ah'm gonna get Father Becnel at St. Luke's to come if ya let another witch doctor come up in here! Father Becnel is what ya call a liberal, and ya know how dey behave. So, tha more help we need, we'll take it in tha name of Jesus!"

Madam Aucoin speaks up quietly and says, "I call him Yahweh. He is our prophet from long ago Africa and came with us on the ships used for bringing all of us to this land of opportunity for White people to climb on our backs to achieve their wealth. He is who we cried out for! He is the same but much blacker than your statues of Jesus. I mean, Flavia, think about how we looked, coming from that part of Africa." Aww, merde!

Flavia means to say some more when Minou says, "Please, Flavia and Madam. Quit dis right now! We have to make some decisions now!"

Joe says, "Hell, yeah! Let dem all come to my house! If dey can all help with T-June, Ah say let dem all come! But, one at a time, ya hear me? Me and Alcide taught T-June some good t'ings. Even Pawpaw Irby is talkin' to my son in French! So has his mama and Bertha and his nanan taught him! Ah don't want dat touched, to go away from his mind. Tha minute Ah see dis, e'rybody will get da hell out!"

∞ ∞ ∞

MADAM Aucoin comes back the following Friday with Bishop Laurant Toussaint, AKA Dr. Manly Tall. He is a very tall man, very Black, and as slim as he is tall. He wears a black suit with the coat hanging down to his knees. A man wearing a shirt so white while he is pitch Black. A gold tooth shining among the very white teeth and a smile that lights up the room.

Dr. Manly Tall, AKA Bishop Laurant Toussaint.

He has been given enough information to make him interested about T-June but is amazed when the baby starts making a dishrag twirl in the air.

June takes to him and is allowing the bishop to hold him while he gives him the biggest kiss right on the mouth! Then he says in the bishop's head, Ah so glad ya got here. Ah been waitin' on ya.

Toussaint is completely captivated.

The bishop has had dealings with those who show signs of abilities that normal people don't display. He takes June's hand and begins to lead him out the back door into the large yard bordering the swamps.

They stay together all morning, and the bishop is carrying T-June in his arms when the two come in the back door. T-June goes for Pawpaw Irby to hold him, and he climbs in his lap for a nice nap.

Bishop Toussaint sits down for a cup of Mello Joy but turns down the plate of smothered pork chops with white beans and Bertha's homemade bread. He says he just can't eat right now.

The bishop says, "Madam Minou and Monsieur Joe, I've never seen another human being with all the gifts he has been bestowed with. I'm seventy-seven years of age, and I have been doing my doctoring since I was twenty-five.

"I am struck with a large fear for this family. A baby using all of his gifts now as an infant, what will he continue to show as he grows? This family is going to need much help from now on.

"Minou, you and Joe are going to have to look deep in your family history because this didn't start with you. Your line of ancestors has been very powerful, just as Acadians had to be to survive. We all know about the Chitimachas and the Houmas surviving, so that is a strong lineage also.

"I see in you, Minou, the features of your native blood as well as Bertha. Joe, I see the strong backbone of a Cajun man who has been taught to live off the land. Alcide too, but it's off-kilter for him at times.

"Joe, the only thing that even slows you down is your Madam Minou, am I right?

"I have to sit down and eat now for some strength I know I'm going to need in the coming months. I have to ponder on what I need to say to all of you."

The old man, who looks like he's 60, sits at the table next to Madam Aucoin. They are talking to each other in a patois whisper, but the rest sitting at the table at Minou's house don't know what they are saying. So being Minou, she says, "Come on, y'all. Ya know we don't understand what ya sayin'. We don't talk Cajun 'round y'all! So tell us what y'all were sayin'."

Madam and the bishop stop and turn to where everybody else is sitting and listening. She speaks up with a haughty look on her face. "Oh, well, Miss Nosy, since you insist! We were discussing as to how to tell you that we have lived together for fifty years as man and wife. Shacked up, like you refer to the situation. But we jumped the broom, and that was a ceremony for everybody and as good as a marriage contract.

"I never told you about Bishop Toussaint because I sensed disapproval from some of you. Bertha has been knowing, but she keeps a secret well. I never know about Flavia. You never know what's coming out of her mouth! Sorry, Flavia, but it's the truth, and I know you don't trust me."

Flavia stands up and hugs Madam, telling her she's sorry for making her feel like she isn't welcome. She says to both of them, Madam and the bishop, who stand up too, "Aww, hell, dat's just tha way Ah am. Ah don't trust many people, and ya come here so strange to me. Ah ain't never met no Voodoo queen before! Ah heard 'bout Voodoo 'cause my mama used to scare me, tellin' me dat tha Voodoo was goin' to get me. She was really mean to me. She sure as hell didn't trust nobody!

"Me, Ah was raised a strict Catholic, and Ah got excommunicated from dat same church 'cause of my divorce. Ah don't trust tha other religions, for sure not dem holy rollers down the road.

"Ah don't care about no shackin' up! A lot of people do dat so dey don't lose deir Social Security. Come on, let's be friends. Ah don't want to fuss wit' ya! Ah do have trust wit' what ya do, and it's a big help."

Madam Aucoin and Mrs. Flavia hug each other again, and everyone sighs in relief. Everyone wants to hear what the bishop will tell them, and he does.

"T-June is a tremendous gift to all of us here. Thank Yahweh! He is also a tremendous force to be reckoned with. He is an old soul who's been here many times before. We have beliefs in reincarnation with our religion.

"This child has a huge, loving heart and He does not know fear. This is what we have to teach him. How to curb his gifts, so they can be managed by all of us. To learn who the people are that mean him harm. I think he can already tell that. There's going to be people who will not like him because they will be afraid. Children are the most cruel.

"We will prepare him to live with us normal people. I know there is more to come, my family; he's only going to be two, and this will be a lifelong endeavor to bring him to manhood. He's just so wide open with everything, but that will get better the older he is. It's really too much for him also, because he is so very young.

"We have to try to keep his life as normal as we can. Well, this family is not the run-of-the-mill type of family anyway. You agree?" He pauses, smiling to himself.

"The coon named Ruby was with us the whole time today, running along on the side of Monsieur Mayhem. I haven't laughed so hard in years, watching him talk to Raccoon Ruby and repeating for me what she said. Ha! I got to tell you this. That coon is up to no good!

"You can forget that it's only Ruby he can talk with. I know you were hoping it was just her. I heard him say out loud as some large serpent came close – I never saw anything – he says, 'Thank you for moving fast to the water.' Of course, I asked what the snake said, and he said the snake was telling him that he was moving through the swamp. And have a nice day!

"Mon Dieu! I wish I could do that! There's a movie I love to watch, and it's about a doctor that talks to the animals!"

Butch comes in the kitchen and hears what Bishop Toussaint says about Dr. Doolittle. They begin to talk about other movies, finding out they are both avid movie watchers.

Butch and the bishop begin talking about the vampire movies they love, like Interview with a Vampire. The bishop tells him that he knew the author, Anne Rice, very well. She was a good customer of Madam Aucoin for years.

Bishop Toussaint has been told about the two loup-garous by Madam Aucoin. Bertha has shared that with Madam because she has the feeling that she knows already. He wants to be with them the next full moon.

Flavia wants to go now to help. The night she decides it is time to catch them pulling up the marijuana, she comes full face to the loup-garou growling at her.

She screams and falls into a deep faint.

She wakes up with all of them standing over her, waving some palmetto branches at her face. She won't talk with them for several weeks.

Minou looks at Joe and sees he's getting nervous while they are talking about vampires. She has seen the creature when they were on that magical honeymoon in New Orleans. Joe doesn't even like to hear the word!

Minou thinks that wouldn't be that bad, this beautiful undead man reaching for her lily-white neck, while her nightgown falls to the floor!

Chér, Bon Dieu!

Bertha is finally sitting down after fixing the large meal and the dessert tarte a la bouillié, which is a creamy pudding in a sweet crust. She sells the treat at Mrs. Flavia's and makes even more money when she brings fudge and pralines. Alcide is sitting next to her when she speaks.

"Ah heard talk of tha old days from my great-uncles and my great-pawpaw when Ah was a lil petite. Sometimes, Ah would hear 'bout a traiteur who was kin to me or tha tales about tha loup-garou. Dey would all turn over in dere graves if dey knew 'bout me!

"Ah know my old aunt used to make potions and used Voodoo. Dat must be close to what ya do, my friend. And on my mama's side, dere were all kind of holy men famous in tha tribes.

"Ah wasn't born no loup-garou, but Ah let my beloved Alcide take a bite of me. He bit me before de mont'ly moon when he changes into tha monster. Lawd, Ah get haunt just t'inkin' 'bout it!

"Minou and Joe take care of both of us when tha curse is on us. Lawd, have mercy on all of us when T-June finds out! Shit, like he don't know already what happens. Ah don't trust tha lil booger! He don't ask me nothin 'bout dat.

"He can't make me hear him in my brain. Alcide, him neither. He says 'cause we loup-garou! Ah got some strange people in my family Ah heard 'bout over dose years. Alcide can speak for hisself. He's tha real deal! A seventh son."

Alcide starts talking after Bertha hands him some more tarte a la bouillié, and he wolfs it down! He knows all about wolfing. His belly is satisfied, and he lights his pipe made of cypress carved out by him.

"Ah was born with tha genes dat makes me into a monster every full moon. Ah was born tha seventh son of a seventh son, and Ah had tha veil too over my face. My papa didn't have dat, but he's seen one dat rocked his world!

"Ah've read all tha books Ah could get my hands on 'bout my fate. Ah read 'bout tha seventh son, but dere's a lot of books 'bout tha veil over a baby's body when dey are born too.

"The seventh son beliefs come from tha Gypsies, and it's through dem that tha werewolf came to be. It musta been from tha French Gypsy, to be called loup-garou. Ah believe we tha same werewolves. Some kind of ancient curse done to us. Ya stuck with dis even if ya bite somebody and dey turn into loup-garou too! But it's still dere wit' you. Look at Bertha.

"Ah know for sure Bigfoot is out dere too! Ah got in a fight one time with tha hairy beast, and he was runnin' so fast, after he grabbed my neck and t'rew me into a tree. Of course, Ah was tha loup-garou at the time, and Ah stayed dizzy for three days after. Mais, Ah musta caught dat concussion!

"No tellin' what dis earth keeps hidden from sight. Hellfire! Ah believe in everyt'in' now dat ya hear about! T-June is tha top of tha line! Ah would bet ya he knows already about us being loup-garou."

Jumping up from the table, Joe laughs and says, "Goddamn if it ain't so! Ah saw dat Bigfoot in tha swamps one time, me too. Ah never said nothin' 'bout it 'cause Minou said Ah was crazy seeing t'ings!

"As if, Minou. As if! Dat happened before T-June was born, and now everyt'in' and e'rybody is crazy!"

Joe sits back down and puts his head down on the table.

Madame Aucoin sits and smokes her ganja while Butch and the doctor are watching Doctor Doolittle again on the TV.

Flavia is in the rocking chair, saying her rosary while everyone else goes to take naps. She still takes Communion every Sunday and dares anyone to say anything. She has made an appointment for Father Becnel to come visit during the week. Flavia gives plenty of money to St. Luke's, even though she's supposed to be kicked out!

∞ ∞ ∞

FATHER Becnel comes to meet the family on a Monday morning. He is a young man, with his hair tied back on a leather strap. Kinda looks like Jesus but more Cajun handsome.

He greets them, talking in Cajun French. Father Becnel says he comes from Ville Platte.

He is taken back by what he sees June do after Minou asks her little boy to show him.

He plays with T-June until noon and then stays for the gumbo and potato salad. Bertha's bread comes out the oven that morning, and Father can't resist the smell.

He says, after eating his meal and blessing everyone there, "God creates everything in this wonderful world. Who are we not to accept his plan? I would be so honored if you allow me to be part of his upbringing. I am a priest who listens to everybody's secrets and shame, and I am sworn to not reveal anything I have heard. June will be our secret if you allow me.

"I know this whole family is in St. Luke's Parish because I went into all the old documents to find y'all's families.

"I have never met any of you, but it wouldn't hurt any of you to bring T-June to Mass. I want him to know both Jesus and Yahweh. Yes, Mrs. Flavia told me about that. I made it top priority to come this morning."

∞ ∞ ∞

T-JUNE now sees both Bishop Toussaint on the weekends and Father Becnel on Mondays. Bishop Toussaint and Madam Aucoin come every Friday and stay until late Sunday night. Father Becnel comes every Monday to see what Bishop Toussaint has told him over the weekend!

June loves all of them, and they love him dearly. They have a calming effect on him, but none has any intentions of stifling his gifts.

Things seem to be calming for everyone now, because T-June is delighted and fascinated with talking to Ruby. He has already found out he can talk with all the animals! Ruby knows that, because she wants the other animals to talk to T-June about the dangerous traps.

Ruby is what you call a bonafide shit-stirrer! A rabble-rouser. And she has T-June's full attention.

Not Minou's or Joe's or Butch's or Bertha's or Alcide's. For sure not Mrs. Flavia!

Flavia doesn't like Ruby. The coon has jumped on her head and run off with her glasses!

Madam and Bishop Toussaint love her. Madam has conversations with Ruby while June is steadily relaying what she's saying.

Butch and the bishop have become great pals. The bishop goes to June first, because that's why he's here, but shortly after, he goes to Butch to watch movies.

Minou and Joe have decided to go back hunting and trapping. Plenty help with T-June, so they can visit with each other again without all the disruptions and people they not used to being around all the time. They set the traps and go to pick pecans in their pecan grove. They even catch two big catfish for supper.

They go back to their traps the next day to see if they have caught game. All of them are sprung and empty!

They set them again and come back the next morning to check. Same thing, and they are wondering what the hell is going on.

They look at each other and both say at the same time, "T-June."

They can't wait to get to Bertha's and Alcide's because everyone is there watching the toddler. Butch is doing his homework, and supper is on the stove.

This is a big problem, and they are going to get to the bottom of this!

Butch is asked to go put Ruby in her cage and leave her there. He is coming back from Minou's and Joe's double-wide and comes upon a heated conversation in Bertha's kitchen. Everybody wants to know what the hell T-June is doing now.

Minou talks to T-June, and he knows she is pissed!

"Lil boy! What ya been doin' to ya papa and ya Pawpaw Alcide's traps? Ya messin' wit' deir livelihoods! Dat's a job we do to put meat on tha table. Ya wanna starve? Joseph Alan Thibeau Junior! Ya betta tell me right now!"

T-June has never heard his mama talk this way, and he starts tearing up.

Minou tells him, "Lil man, ya can stop dat cryin' and fess up like a big man!"

He's just a child dealing with what he can do, and on top of that, he is trusting someone he shouldn't. Big Fat Ruby, who lives with them in luxury!

Minou calms down with the help of Joe. He knows to stay away when she gets mad-mad, but he has been doing this calming of Minou for a long time.

T-June stops crying, with everybody tata-ing him. He climbs up on Joe's lap and begins to tell his tale about him and that troublesome coon.

"Ah went down to tha swamps with Ruby, and she told me to free tha animals dat were caught. After doin' dat we kept tha traps open every time we saw one. Ruby told me to get mad and me, Ah just got real red in my face and pushed as hard as Ah could and t'rew my hands up, and den tha trap would open!

"Mama, Ah'm strong like tha Superman!

"Ah was just listenin' to Ruby. Maybe she don't know dat ya cook what ya catch. Me sorry, Mama, for doin' dat. Me real sorry. Don't be mad at me no more. Ya scared me 'cause ya don't never fuss me.

"Mama, me can talk to all tha animals. Dey said to go somewhere else, not in tha swamp by our house to hunt. Ruby said tha pecan grove has plenty animals. She don't know dem."

That coon sure has some nerve and doesn't care about the other animals on down the bayou!

Minou and Joe ask Butch to go fetch Ruby and bring her here.

Minou tells T-June to go over there where the coon is sitting, being still. She must know the jig is up and she's in trouble. June tells the coon to talk to him when he sits down by her. He listens to her in his mind.

He gets up and goes to where everyone is sitting at the table. Alcide and Bertha are mad too! He climbs back up on Joe and asks for his noonie.

He is so young, and it's hard for him to understand what he is capable of. He stops sucking but holds the pacifier in his little hands.

"Mama, she says she was protectin' her friends. Sometimes, tha trap kills dem, and it's really terrible to watch 'cause dey can't get demselves free. Ah saw dat too and how happy dey were when dey were freed. Their lil families were waitin' on tha side to help.

"Ruby told me cryin' dat she watched as her mate died in a trap. Ruby had a nest full of babies she raised by herself. Dey still come to visit her. She musta been a good mama, huh, Mama? She says a lot of her friends are ready to leave tha swamp dey lived in all deir life. Dey said tha same t'ing to me, and it makes me cry.

"Mama, Ruby says please don't send her away. She's old and won't live out dere in tha cold and wet winter days. She says she's t'rough wit' bein' bad to us. Please, Mama, don't send her away!"

T-June is steadily sucking his noonie because it comforts him with all the turmoil he and Ruby have caused.

Minou doesn't trust the old conniving coon but says Ruby can stay as long as she doesn't put ideas into June's mind. They all are watching her seriously, Alcide said they ought to throw her in the pot!

∞ ∞ ∞

THE family, along with Mrs. Flavia and Madam Aucoin and Bishop Toussaint and Father Becnel, continues to watch T-June and guide him to learn how to live with his abilities.

Butch is truly his big brother and teaches him all about what boys do. He wants to prepare June for what lies for him when he begins school.

Minou and Joe are satisfied with the help that has been given with the amazing boy who continues to surprise them the older he gets.

Joe and Alcide take their traps down the bayou to where their pecan grove waits with plenty of wild game. All this mess has gotten them thinking about the trapped animals. It's taken all the fun out of trapping!

Minou has to change her mind about Joe fishing in the Gulf. Joe and Alcide go to hire on with fishing boats that go out into the Gulf every day and bring in large fish they enjoy catching.

They don't know if T-June talks with the fish.

They all have money left from the treasure that Minou and Joe found, so they are not worrying about doing without or starving.

Minou goes to work at Mrs. Flavia's store, where she learns about the business of running the store. Mrs. Flavia is getting older, though she won't admit that. She thinks Minou should learn about everything because T-June will inherit all of Flavia's wealth.

That's if she doesn't give it all away to St. Luke's.

Chapter Six

T-June and Pieyan

T-JUNE has made it to five years old without any incidents that alerted the public. He has been trained by everyone involved in his upbringing, and he takes instructions like a grownup would. He has shown maturity well past his age, and he is very intelligent, already can read and write like a 10-year-old.

June is way bigger than other children his age. Minou and Joe have considered homeschooling him because they are afraid of what he might do when he starts to be around other children. Minou feels like he would get the best education from all the family members, but he has to know the world, not just their little bubble of security.

Bishop Toussaint and Father Becnel disagree with that idea of homeschooling. The priest thinks he ought to go to the Catholic school on the side of the church. The bishop says that would be excellent because there aren't that many children that can afford the tuition.

Father Becnel wants June to have the knowledge that Catholicism would bring. The teachers at the Catholic school are all nuns from the Academy of Lafayette. The smaller school will be much better than the public schools that have a large attendance and many more disruptive kids to excite him into doing his tricks.

Bishop Toussaint wants to pay for Butch to go there too. Butch loves going to Mass with the family. Butch is excited to go to the Catholic school so he can keep an eye on what his little brother will do with all his gifts being hidden. Butch's mama, Irene, says she could well afford to send him herself and pay for him to start the coming year. T-June will start first grade this year as well.

∞ ∞ ∞

IT'S still summer on the bayou, so T-June is getting prepared for what is coming.

T-June is large enough to go to the swamps now without somebody following him.

Ruby is his constant shadow, showing off to the animals. She tries telling him the difference between talking to friendly animals and those he should stay away from. That's because Ruby has gotten in fights with the ones she is saying he must stay away from, the trashy critters!

The swamps are cleared of the traps because Joe and Alcide have learned the trade of deepwater fishing. They have bought their own boat because they don't like working for somebody else.

T-June walks into the part of the swamp that is thick with cypress trees and moss hanging to the ground. Ruby is following, fussing the whole time. She tells him, "It's too dangerous back in the trees! There are animals in there I don't know and don't want to. Come back, Lil June, from there! I wish I could tell your mama and papa where you going, but you won't tell them for me!"

Ruby is getting real nervous, but she tags along anyway to help with whatever the swamps will reveal.

June is steadily going deeper into the trees where the sunlight doesn't shine in the swamps. It's dark and very quiet among the trees, and the cypress trees are everywhere, coming out the damp ground and growing in the water that covers the back of the swamp.

This child has no fear and continues walking, with the coon warning him to come back. June is watching all the rabbits running everywhere and the squirrels on the ground talking to him. They are warning him too. They know what is hiding in the swamps, and they are afraid.

The animals know about the loup-garous, but they know who those two are. The animals watch when Bertha and Alcide change back to human. They know Minou and Joe help them, and Flavia once in a while comes too. They stay away from her because she is mean and hollers at them.

T-June has found out about Bertha and Alcide by accident when his mawmaw comes in the back door, muddy with her hair all messed up. It gets him nosy, because Bertha wouldn't say anything to him. He can't talk to her in her mind, and she just tells him to go play.

So June goes to his coon, Ruby, and she proceeds to tell him what happens during the full moon. June says he always feels a different feeling around them, but he doesn't want to see them like that ever! He says he would cry, feeling really bad for his grandparents. He never questions his mama about this, although he hears them leaving the house late at night.

June doesn't ask anybody else about it. A secret in their family. Nobody needs to know what he thinks, but he and Butch are the ones who don't know about the loup-garous.

June doesn't know if he should tell Butch.

The animals know there is something else that roams the swamp and run clear of this monster because they might get eaten.

T-June walks into a clearing among the trees and becomes aware of all the bones of dead animals that surround the area. Even the graveyard of bones doesn't frighten him; he is curious instead.

He sees the trees start to move as though there is a strong wind, like a hurricane is blowing. He hears a strange howl that makes his hair stand up, and he begins to shiver with the sound.

All of the animals are hiding, and T-June thinks twice about being back there. He doesn't see anything, but the blood-curdling howl is enough to make him leave fast with Ruby in his arms. She can't run as fast anymore because she is full of arthritis like people get. She is old, too old to be chasing after June.

He gets back to the house, where Butch is waiting for him. Butch sees that T-June is upset like he's never seen before in the young child.

"Mais, Butch, dere's somethin' out in tha swamps dat made all tha animals hide, and its howlin' was enough to make me run fast-fast out of dere! Ruby was hollerin' for me to run away before it was too late.

She said Ah might be tha next meal for dis t'ing. Mais, what ya t'ink is back dere?"

Butch is telling him not to go back because he has no idea what this thing is. Butch is scared just hearing about this. But that is like turning on the green light for June to go.

Butch tells on June, and everyone begins to fuss at him, telling him not to go deep in the swamps and leave alone what's back there! Alcide and Joe already know what's back there, having seen up close the Bigfoot. They both tell June not to go back there; he's gonna catch a whipping if he doesn't listen.

Yeah, like that scares him plenty.

∞ ∞ ∞

JUNE is already planning to go back and without Ruby. He gets up while everyone is still sleeping. He brings a couple of sandwiches for him to eat and two RC Colas in his knapsack.

June is planning to stay until he sees for himself what makes that awful sound. He leaves Ruby in her cage with her screaming not to go.

T-June is sitting on a fallen tree and he's eating his baloney sandwich, drinking his last sip of the RC Cola. Everything is quiet, no rabbits or squirrels around the clearing, and he feels alone with no animals to talk to him.

He starts his whistling until he hears something moving through the trees. June hears loud thumping, making the ground shake.

He sees a white face, kinda of what Old Man Bergeron looks like, peeking at him. But when he goes to look further in the trees, this huge creature comes barreling out toward him.

T-June feels a large amount of fear, thinking he's going to be eaten and wishing he had listened to the grownups! The fear he is not used to in any way. This thing runs past him going fast-fast into the swamps!

The boy can't run as fast as the creature and watches him disappear into the trees. T -June has his curiosity back, and the fear goes away. He is so nosy, just like his mama, Minou.

He is walking back to his house when he hears everybody calling his name! June knows he's got some explaining to do when they see him.

T-June isn't capable of lying and tells them where he has gone. Minou starts her yelling and tells him to get his little ass in the house!

"Lil boy, ya t'ink ya too big for ya drawers! Ya t'ink ya don't have to listen anymore to tha grownups? Sit ya ass down on dis chair, and ya not gettin' up 'til you tell me why ya t'ink ya big enough not to listen. Why tha hell ya went back when we all tellin' ya don't go?"

Minou is riled up and hot as a Tabasco pepper, so nobody else dares to speak. When she is on a roll, everybody gets out the way.

She suddenly gets up and goes with June into his bedroom.

T-June's mama is looking hard at him, expecting him to talk inside her head. He does that better when he gets nervous around his mama.

He's telling Minou inside her mind, Dere's a large, large creature livin' in tha swamp, and all tha animals are scared to death of it. Ah saw it, but it ran in front of me so fast Ah couldn't catch up. Ah ain't scared no more 'cause he coulda eaten me for a meal. He eats tha animals so he can live. Just like we do, huh, Mama?

Minou wonders if she's gotta go call Madam Aucoin. Maybe she and Bishop Toussaint can conjure up a spell to run the thing off of their property!

She asks June, talking to him while he squirms on the bed, looking for one of his noonies because he's got one in every room.

"T-June, ya gotta promise me, bébé, you'll stay out tha swamps and leave dat creature be! We kinda know what it is, but ya papa and Pawpaw Alcide swear dey know, bein' dey both saw tha t'ing too. It's what we call da Bigfoot."

T-June's mama is holding him and trying to ease his discomfort. He has no intentions of giving up in finding the creature and tells his mama that. "Mama, Ah can't make no promise. Ah'm a brave boy, and Ah ain't scared no more. Ah gonna go find him and ask why he's here on our land.

"Please don't make me stop! Ah gotta look for him! Dis Mistah Bigfoot is fast, and he don't like tha animals or people! He's got a lot of bones back dere on tha ground of all tha animals he's eaten, but Mama, dere ain't no people bones, so he don't eat us.

"He's gonna be hard to find 'cause he hides in tha swamp. Me, Ah'll bring him somet'in' to eat so he don't want to eat me.

"Mama, Ah just can't make no promises, Mama."

Minou gets up to go and calls Madam Aucoin and Bishop Toussaint. This is too serious and very scary. Maybe they can come up with something to convince June not to search for the Bigfoot.

Butch is too scared to go and begs June not to go.

Pawpaw Alcide says he will follow him and shoot the damn thing! He remembers when he got into a fight with the Bigfoot, even though he was loup-garou. Alcide remembers the terrible headaches he got and thinks he might have caught a concussion!

Madam Aucoin and Bishop Toussaint come that night from New Orleans. They think this is very serious and begin to conjure up a spell to make the Bigfoot go away so that he goes before June can look for him.

They are thinking about buying a house in the Larose community. Madam and the bishop are here all the time anyway. They are even thinking about retiring so they can be here instead of running down from the city every time they have to rush to the swamps from New Orleans.

Madam's daughters can run her business. All three were babies at her feet, watching and learning everything about her shop of wonders. They are insisting on coming down the bayou and meeting this JoeJoe Star and his family because they think their mama and their papa have joined some kind of Christian cult!

Bishop Toussaint has figured out how he can protect T-June if the beast acts like he will do harm to the boy.

"I will follow you, June, but I'll stay far enough away from the Bigfoot that he doesn't know I'm there. I won't wear any scents either, just be there in the swamps so I can hear if you holler for help. You need an adult sometimes, even though you think you're a grownup, because you're too smart for your own britches. You won't see me, but I'll be there, watching."

The family doesn't trust this idea, but it's better than trying to keep June out of the swamp. Butch decides he will go with them because both him and June trust the man with all their hearts. This way Butch can protect his little brother if he needs help.

The trio going deep into all the cypress trees doesn't know it, but Joe, Minou, and Alcide plan to hide in the swamp too when T-June goes on his search.

Mais, they must think Bigfoot can't smell them!

T-June is going into the swamp with Ruby. She has made a hole in her wired cage and escapes to follow him. She isn't going to miss this for anything! Something else she can brag about to her followers in the swamp.

Bishop Toussaint and Butch are far behind him, moving quietly through the cypress trees.

T-June isn't aware of the others hiding too. His mind is on the Bigfoot, so he isn't thinking about anything else.

June comes upon the clearing, sitting down to drink his soda and wait. The animals are all out and enjoying their day. They don't feel or see any signs that the creature is nearby.

All the rabbits and squirrels are talking at the same time to T-June. They are excited because they think T-June will scare the monster out of the swamp and away from them. The animals are always telling T-June what they need.

Some of the rabbits are still warning him not to go look for the Bigfoot. The squirrels can climb up the cypress trees so high that the creature can't get them. They can watch the whole thing if June comes across the Bigfoot.

Suddenly, the animals are all gone, with one rabbit saying with his big ears flapping in the wind, "He's comin'! He's comin'!"

T-June sits quietly, waiting for something to happen. And it does.

He sees the white face hiding behind the trees, and then the Bigfoot goes fast, running in front of June and disappearing so quickly that the boy can only watch as it passes in front of him.

June knows he can't run that fast to try and catch up with him. He also knows that part of the swamps have deep water and evil snakes that won't warn him, being such mean-ass serpents!

They all go home, Minou and Joe with Alcide beating them back to the house. They are at the table in Minou's kitchen drinking coffee when the rest of the safari comes into the house.

T-June starts talking so fast he stumbles on his words. "Mama, me saw him good dis time! He's so fast dat when Ah stood up, he already had gone deeper in da swamps. Mais, he is some big, Ah tell ya! He's got hair dic-dic all over him, not like Ah have on my arms and back. He's almost all white so he's gotta be old.

"Mama, can you fix a big deer roast for me to bring next time? He sure can't pass by dat smell! He's way taller dan tha bishop and must weigh a ton! He shakes all tha trees when he passes. Please, Mama, please, please." Minou does just what T-June asks of his mama.

∞ ∞ ∞

BERTHA and Madam are waiting at the house for them to return. Bertha's afraid of turning into the loup-garou if she sees the other monster. She's worried about Alcide doing the same thing.

Madam has fear too, and Flavia is busy saying her rosary because she's scared to death of what's out there with the spies and G-men and aliens.

Flavia is thinking that the Bigfoot may have killed her papa instead of the loup-garous who are her friends. She doesn't want to think that Alcide might've done it!

Everybody else is hiding in the swamps, knowing that T-June doesn't suspect them in their sneaking ways.

Well, the same thing happens again. The Bigfoot runs away, leaving T-June holding the roast. This time the creature howls his displeasure at T-June, and everybody else hears the godawful scream.

June takes off running with everybody else in the swamps! This time he knows that the swamp is full of his family.

They all make it back to the house at the same time. Lawd, have mercy! They have never heard anything like the howl before!

"Dere's too many people out dere! Dat's why he runs away, maybe he can smell y'all! Ya told me it would be just tha bishop and Butch. Ya lied to me!" June says with big tears running down his face. He finds it hard to believe that Minou would do him that way.

June is very hurt, and he runs into his bedroom and slams the door.

The family is in the living room at Minou and Joe's house.

Flavia is over there tapping lightly on his door, saying, "It's Nanan, baby. Ah didn't do nuttin'. Let me come in!" To no avail, because he won't open the locked door to anyone. Flavia says she is calling Father Becnel to come over there.

Well, why not?

Father Becnel comes the next morning, which is of course Monday. He begins talking in his Cajun French because everyone there can speak the language of their ancestors except for Madam and the bishop. They have listened to the Cajun patois enough in their lives to have picked up most of what's being said.

Father Becnel can't believe what they are telling him. He reaches into his satchel he carries everywhere and lights up a marijuana joint, with everyone staring. They can't believe what they're seeing!

Everybody has to adjust their belief systems.

"It's for my nerves because I am shaken to the core. My brother grows a small patch, and we share it.

"June, do you know how many people have searched for this elusive creature? They call it Sasquatch, among other names, because he's been seen all over the world. No one has ever gotten close enough to prove he really exists.

"I am so afraid for you to continue this hunt! You are just a boy, and the people who search for him are grown men. I know you are so special that you think you can do anything, but you can't. What if Bigfoot tries to make a meal of you?

"I don't want you to continue on this path, and neither does your family. Jesus would be mad-mad and would cry his eyes out!

"I noticed all of you missed Mass yesterday."

Minou and the whole family get up and go to Mass every Sunday. T-June loves going, and it sure doesn't hurt anybody. They have been too busy stalking the Bigfoot to get to Mass.

T-June is in the swamps every day now and is not listening to anybody. Even the threat of an ass-whipping doesn't stop him.

T-June stands there waiting, like he would take the belt but would still continue with his search. He has about as much fear of that happening as the fear he doesn't have anyway.

They have to make him come home to eat and take his bath. He is some stinky, coming in from the swamp. His Pawpaw Alcide makes him sit down and tries to make him listen.

"T-June, we all scared for ya chasin' tha Bigfoot. He beat me up one time when Ah was in tha swamps! Don't act like ya don't know 'bout me and ya mawmaw. We can't keep nuttin' from ya nosy lil ass!

"Anyway, he grabbed me by tha t'roat and t'rew me into tha trees. Ah was tha loup-garou den, and Ah get plenty big and scary, but he's t'ree times bigger! If Ah had just been myself, he woulda killed me. Dat monster don't like nobody, and dere's no tellin' what he will do to get away from ya! Ah'm gonna shoot his hairy ass if Ah see him!

June is listening politely to what his Pawpaw Alcide tells him, but his intentions are still the same.

He is gonna find Bigfoot, come hell or high swamp water!

T-June gets up real early while the family is still sleeping and heads for the swamp. June leaves way before the sun comes up. He knows his mama gets up at 5:30 every morning of her life, and it's dark outside when he leaves, sneaking out the back door.

He has his papa's big flashlight.

Minou opens his bedroom door and sees that he is already gone. She tells this to Joe while he is pouring two cups of Mello Joy. "Mais, he's gone already! Just like you, Joe! He's just like you! He don't listen to nobody!"

Joe stands with his mouth agape. Talk about the pot calling the kettle!

June has brought his knapsack with the deer roast in a separate bag, dripping with the juices leaking down the sides. He is sitting in his usual spot and drinking one of his RC Colas when he hears the beast roar with that horrible sound.

June almost runs, but he is determined to talk with the Bigfoot.

The beast comes running through the trees, and June is steadily running after it. Both are running fast into the thick trees where there is swamp water standing over the land.

T-June has run as far as his little legs will carry him when suddenly the Bigfoot stops, and June runs right into him! June stands with his mouth wide open, looking up into the creature's mouth.

Bigfoot is tremendous, and June is way too short to look into his eyes. He looks around and sees this large tree that has fallen to the ground, and he climbs up on the tallest branch that will hold him.

Now June can see the monster's eyes, and they are looking severely into his big, round, green eyes. Eye to eye!

When June sees Bigfoot open his mouth, he thinks, He's gettin' ready to eat my ass!

Bigfoot looks at him and says with his voice that sounds normal like

Father Becnel's, "What the hell do you want, kid?"

June is at a loss of words, and all he can say is, "My mama made dis roast! Ah saved ya some pop for ya to drink."

Bigfoot sits down on the bottom of the tree where June is still standing in the top branches. Bigfoot takes the bag with the roast in it, throws the bag, eating the deer meat in one bite. The RC Cola in one sip! June's hands are trembling like Couyon does after his bath. Now he knows how the old dog feels!

"Your mama can cook real good. Now you're gonna tell me why, lil boy, you trying to chase me down. Big, grown men chase us using all kinds of tricks to lure us but have never been able to capture any of us. Here you come along, a mere slip of a child! What the hell do you want, since you were so persistent in getting my attention? I know you won't leave me alone."

T-June calms down his shaking body and begins to talk with his mind to the Bigfoot, who is still sitting. Bigfoot makes a sound that T-June can compare to Pawpaw Irby's laugh.

"I never met any other animal, human or otherwise, that can do what you just did. We've always been able to speak the human language, but we don't want them to know that. You don't have to talk with your mind, though it's way-way cool," says Bigfoot with a huge smile on his face.

June is content where he is on the branch but allows the creature to reach for him, taking the boy into his arms where they are face to face.

Bigfoot's face changes after the laugh, and he looks so kind and interested in T-June.

"Mistah Bigfoot, Ah can talk wit' all tha animals in dis swamp. Ah got a pet racoon named Ruby, and she tells me about everyt'in' dat goes on here. She and all the little animals are scared of ya 'cause ya eat dem. Me, Ah'm nosy just like my mama. Ah just wanted to talk wit' ya and learn things dat ya could show me."

Bigfoot says to June, "You can call me Pieyan. Tell me your name, little boy. I know your 'coon, Ruby, and she stirs up quite the mess in the swamp. She had the squirrels up in the trees where they were throwing all kinds of things, pelting me until I had to run. Don't bring her back here. I might step on her on purpose. She is somewhat messy with her business."

Ruby has never told T-June what she's been up to!

Pieyan and June continue to sit, with June in the Bigfoot's arms. They sit there together, talking until June is lulled into sleep. Pieyan lays the little boy in the branches lower to the ground and leaves him sleeping.

T-June wakes up late in the afternoon and runs back to his house.

Ruby is in the repaired cage, fortified to make sure she stays there when it's needed. She is hollering at T-June to let her out, but he walks right by her, saying nothing.

Minou has baked chocolate chip cookies for the boys and Joe. While she is hugging June and messing up his hair, she says, "Where ya been? Mais, ya some stinky! Bébé, ya caught ya Bigfoot yet? Ya t'ink ya so big, goin' out dere in tha dark!

"Now tha summer is almost over, and we need to get ya ready for tha first grade. Whatcha say, my big beautiful T-June?

"Ya must be starvin' 'cause ya lil ass been out dere all day. But ya stink like a skunk! Oh, yeah! Ya some stinky. Shit, go throw ya clothes in tha washin' machine right now!

June smiles and shakes his head no to his mama's question. He thinks that's better than a bald-face lie!

He tells no one about his encounter.

∞ ∞ ∞

WHEN Madam Aucoin and the bishop come for the weekend, he goes to the swamp with June to search for Pieyan. Of course, the Bigfoot stays hidden, and T-June acts like he is really looking and plays like he is serious. What a little sneak June is learning how to be!

He continues with his silence because Pieyan tells him not to tell his people anything.

Pieyan watches all June's family in the swamp, knowing they are all looking for the elusive Bigfoot.

He recognizes Alcide's smell and remembers him from the time they tangled up.

He wonders about the scene that takes place every full moon and feels sorry for the two, but that's their business what they do. He watches Bertha and Alcide turn every month into the loup-garous from his hidden spot in the trees. It's a family affair now, with all of them showing up and making noises to guide the two werewolves.

Pieyan thinks Flavia is the funniest of the bunch, with her flapping her arms up and hollering at all the creatures and slapping at the mosquitoes!

June continues his secret meetings with Pieyan. Pieyan and June are regular podnahs. He talks a lot to the boy, more than T-June thinks he will.

The Bigfoot is long-winded and mostly one-sided when talking to June, figuring he knows all he wants to know about humans. June hangs on his every word, he being so awed by Pieyan.

T-June is secretly taking meat from the large freezer outside in the shed. Pieyan doesn't care if the meat is frozen or not. He will let the meat defrost some because he says he's got a bad tooth.

It is on the Saturday before June starts school. Minou sends Joe to get a large roast from the freezer outside. Joe comes back empty-handed, and she questions him, did he look good, real good?

Minou huffs out there, muttering cuss words to look for herself if the roast can be found. She finds there are several large packages of meat gone!

She is cooking tonight for everybody and doesn't find anything but ground meat left that she bought at Flavia's store!

Oh, Gawd, does she get pissed!

Minou knows it's nobody else but T-June. Minou goes to looking for Bishop Toussaint and Madam Aucoin. She wants them to help her in her search for the lil bastard that stole her meat!

After walking far into the darker part of the swamp, Minou and the bishop come up on T-June and Pieyan sitting, eating the muffaletta sandwiches that Madam has brought from Central Grocery in New Orleans.

They are so intent on eating and drinking RC Colas that they don't hear his mama and the bishop walk up.

Pieyan stands up, dropping his muffaletta and howling the loudest that T-June has ever heard. He is frightened too.

Then Bigfoot runs away so fast that Minou isn't sure of what she's seeing.

Bishop Toussaint sits down hard on the tree and is holding his chest, telling Minou to find his pills in his pocket of his coat he has just taken off. T-June reaches for the bishop's hands and holds them until Minou finds the pills. They aren't necessary because T-June's touch and using his mind causes the bishop to sit up with no pain at all.

These are more gifts that T-June has shown, to the continuing bafflement of his poor family.

Minou and Joe are growing old with all the worries, and each new thing that he shows is all hard work for everybody. She says, "Bon Dieu, help us all, Lawd! My blessed Jesus! Pick someone else for a change instead of T-June, would ya?"

Minou forgets the meat for a while, asking June, "Oh, my blessed child, was dat tha Bigfoot we saw? Dat gave tha bishop his heart attack, but den ya touched him and he got better? Aww, merde! Ah don't know what to say to ya first. Ah need some of Madam's marijuana!"

They are all walking back in silence to the house. Minou can't take any more, and she and T-June go to her bedroom, asking someone to find Joe.

Minou and Joe and T-June come out of the bedroom several hours later. She is composed now, and Joe follows her into the kitchen where everyone is sitting, waiting for them to appear.

Madam Aucoin is the first one to ask questions of T-June.

"My gifted, blessed child! I have to ask you if you cured Bishop Toussaint of a heart attack. This is something so tremendous and seriously so important that you have to tell me.

"This is very frightening, and you are way too young to have this gift. Nobody on this earth can do that! We can't let you do this anymore. Have you done this before?"

June is holding his noonie, although he is five years old. Minou has never thought about taking it from him. June needs something to comfort him. He takes it from his mouth to answer Madam.

"Yes, Madam, Ah t'ink it worked on Pawpaw Irby. Ah just kept tellin' him he could get better. Me, Ah can talk wit' him in my mind. He got much better, Ah t'ink. Ah never touched nobody 'til Bishop Toussaint fell down sick. Is it wrong to do dat to people?"

Minou and Joe are worried about this new development that T-June is capable of, almost forgetting about seeing him and the Bigfoot talking in the swamp.

Joe can't talk right now because he's thinking about all of T-June's abilities. How can they hide this new gift? How someone, probably the government, would come to get him if this was known. Everybody will have to start carrying their guns, not letting anyone come on their land.

Minou stands while Joe keeps his head down on the kitchen table. He says that helps him so he can think of what to say and do next. Joe knows Minou would never cheat on him, but he's had this thought before. What in the world did he and Minou bring back from the honeymoon? He also wonders if T-June isn't the next Jesus!

Minou starts talking, and the whole kitchen with everyone there is silent like the tomb. Flavia is going to wear out the rosary.

"Ah figure it's dis way. June might be tha next traiteur, and he will have to listen to dis callin'. JESUS WEPT! Why did he get a triple dose of dat gene, like Bishop explained to us?" Minou says, crying the whole time.

Minou is weeping on the table. Joe and Alcide and Bertha and Flavia and Madam Aucoin and Bishop Toussaint and Father Becnel are all doing the same.

Butch has gone to spend the day with his mama, Irene. The coon is in her cage. None of them want Ruby in there because she will blather her mouth off to the swamps!

They all need a good cry to soothe their hearts and souls. All of them have been in some kind of defensive stand for five years to protect the child. Their nerves are shattered, even though all have been praying to their gods more than they ever have. The tears flowing in that kitchen could fill two buckets!

Madam is asking if anybody wants to smoke.

T-June is in his bedroom, thinking hard about all the gifts he has shown, worried about Pieyan and Ruby, and wondering why this new gift is so frightening to everybody and not to him.

He worries himself into a deep sleep. He's probably needing the sleep as much as everyone needing to cry. He dreams of going to school and smiles in his sleep like he has just been told something.

Everybody is feeling so much better since the deluge. Flavia is over by Pawpaw Irby's recliner and laughing at what he has told her in French. He is now walking into the kitchen with Flavia and joins the group at the table. He talks in broken English but is perfect in talking in the language he was brought up with.

T-June has told them he has helped Pawpaw get better, talking to him in his head. June has been talking the Cajun way since he first started making sentences.

Now the question has been answered. They have been thinking Pawpaw Irby has been better seeing his great-grandchild. June must have started talking to him when Pawpaw Irby first held him.

Pawpaw says he remembers when the change came over him. "God bless tha lil saint dat took away my misery. Ah say my prayers every day for tha love and tha gifts he has been given," Pawpaw tells the group, crying again.

Joe stands up and tells everyone he has something to say. Being the man of the house, it's his every right to do.

Minou decides it's better for him to make the stand. She hasn't been feeling that good. There's another baby coming for Minou and Joe.

"Dis is what Ah got to say about all of dat! We handle tha healin' gift like everyt'in' he's shown us.

He probably will become traiteur early in his life, and we have to show him how not to heal everyt'in'.

Leave some for Jesus! Dat is, if you still in tha family wit' us?

"He starts school on tha next Wednesday of dis week. We decided we won't talk 'bout dis Bigfoot Pieyan right now 'cause his mind needs to be on his schoolwork. Who knows if he's goin' to tha first grade? He might be promoted to tha t'ird! What we gonna do if dat happens?

"Listen, tha night is callin' me and Minou to bed. Y'all need to go to ya houses. We feel like we had enough company for a while.

"Y'all be good, or ya can name the baby after me! Ha ha! Good night, and be careful."

T-June comes out of his room to say good night to his mama and papa and tells them about his dream. "In my dream, Mama, Ah saw the prettiest lil girl. She's waitin' for me at school."

Good Lawd!

Chapter Seven

T-June and the Saint

JOE and Minou are drinking their coffee at the table before it's time to take the boys to school for their first day. Butch will start the seventh grade, but the nuns think June is prepared to go into the third grade already.

Minou and Joe agree to the second grade because they don't want him to skip being with children his age, even though he will be the biggest child in the classroom. Even the second grade children are small compared to this big bruiser.

Joe says, "Ma stomach is cuttin' up 'bout T-June goin' to school. Dere's just too much for him to keep hidden and quiet 'bout! He ain't never listened to us, and we just let him run wild! What if he starts showin' off for tha children? He sure as hell can't say nuttin 'bout talkin' to tha animals, and for Gawd's sake, not Pieyan! Lawd, Ah need some of Madam's stuff dat's like tha Hadacol!"

Butch gets dressed by himself, but Minou is going over T-June with a fine-tooth comb, tucking his uniform shirt into his little khaki pants. The shirt is red, with an emblem of the school's title, SLCS, right over the pocket. She is trying to tame his hair down under the little red cap that's part of the uniform.

Minou is telling him this and that, what not to do this or that, and T-June is wanting to cover his ears while she drives them to school.

June is so tired of everyone telling him not to do this or not to do that. He thinks he's learned to behave by himself with no more instructions from the grownups.

Aww, what's going to happen as he gets older? There's just no telling!

Minou takes Butch and T-June to their first day of school. At St. Luke's Catholic Elementary on the side of the church, Father Becnel is waiting nervously for the boys to come.

They walk up the hall where a beautiful young nun waits on them by her door. Sister Lydia is her name, and she will be Butch's teacher. She has the face of a brown angel and speaks softly in an accent foreign to the boys and Minou. She tells them she is from the southern border of Peru, where there are tall mountains and it's very cold.

Sister Lydia is dressed in the black robes of a habit, with a wimple covering her braided hair. Minou can see the long black braid moving under her headpiece.

Sister Lydia says it has taken a long time to get used to South Louisiana, but she has been here for 10 years. She speaks English with an accent so pleasing, but it has taken her some time to understand the patois of the Cajun children.

She is delightful, and Minou is so glad Butch will have her for his teacher.

Butch wants to be a Catholic priest and teach history to the little children. Butch wants to become an altar boy for Father Becnel. He doesn't remember ever being in any church before.

Irene says it is her fault, her being a very lapsed Catholic. He is baptized, Irene tells them, but no First Communion. He's just getting old enough for his Confirmation. So, she will make sure he has everything he wants or needs. Of course, the best of everything, buying for him what she couldn't give him.

Butch's classmates are all admiring his fancy tennis shoes. Flavia's store for sure doesn't carry that shoe. They cost $150! Irene will spare no expense in getting him all name-brand clothes and shoes, for sure. Her guilt is in shacking up with a man who doesn't like kids!

Minou sees the receipt for $150 and says to Joe, "What tha hell is dis world comin' to? Dey got some crazy people out dere who waste some money! Irene, her, is da worst! Poor t'ing! All dem cuckoos out dere would be glad to have dem tennis shoes wit' dere last dollar! Dey some cuckoo ma choo, huh?"

Can you think of anybody crazier than Minou and Joe's family?

Minou is holding T-June's hand as they go to his classroom to meet the sister waiting at the door.

Minou's heart is fluttering, and she worries about her soul when she sees the formidable woman in black from head to toe. She is Sister Bridget from around the Carencro area, close to where Father Becnel comes from, Ville Platte.

There is quite a difference in the two nuns. Sister Bridget is a large woman, with big shoulders and a belly that she seems to be proud of. Closest she will get to pregnancy!

Her posture is straight, and her stern face is very intimidating. She's an older woman who looks like she doesn't suffer fools and would be quick to slap your sassy mouth. She would make you kneel on rice in the corner!

She wears the traditional black garments too. Around her neck is a large gold crucifix that hangs past her stomach. Biggest one Minou ever saw!

Sister Bridget looks down at T-June. He looks up and is staring hard in her eyes too. He's too scared to talk to her in his little head.

She has a ruler in her hands and has already hit a boy being bad. The other children are sitting quiet, and a few are crying softly.

This is not good.

Sister Bridget says to T-June as he and Minou stand almost at attention to this horrifying nun, "I have heard a lot about you and couldn't wait to meet, after the Father put you into the second grade. I don't remember how long it's been since I've had a student skipping any grade. That means you are very smart, and I will expect your work to prove that.

"If you give me no trouble, there won't be any trouble with me. Do you understand?

"I know your nickname is T-June, but we will have no such foolishness in this class. Your given name is Joseph, and that's what I'll call you as long as you are in my class.

"Go sit down with your classmates while I talk to your mama."

T-June is walking up to the front of the class, saying hello to all the children, and it makes all of them less afraid. He's asking all the children their names and telling them his. T-June is so friendly, glad he sees so many friends in the making. Just talking in his Cajun accent has them smiling. Oh, boy!

Minou is worried she will answer all of Sister's questions with a yes, ma'am! She can't imagine why Father Becnel would put T-June with this horrid woman!

Sister Bridget begins to talk with Minou, while the Sister is standing with the door partially closed. Not a sound comes from the classroom with twenty small children sitting frozen in their seats. T-June is already talking and clowning. Oh, Lawd!

"Madam Minou, from what I have heard, your boy is super intelligent and could have been ready for the third grade if you would have consented to. He even speaks fluent Cajun French! Congratulations on the raising of this young boy! Sometimes it takes a village to raise a child, as they say. Is the rest of your family involved with doing just that?"

∞ ∞ ∞

"IS she t'inkin' Ah don't look dat smart? She's twice as bad as Flavia can be! Ah wanted to tell her, 'Woman, ya don't know nuttin'!' Shit, she made me as scared as tha kids! Ah'm callin' Father to see why he gave T-June to dis witch from Carencro! Mais, yeah, Carencro means buzzard, so dat's it! The Buzzard Witch! Just 'cause dey might be related, who knows?" Minou is telling Joe when she gets back from Flavia's store and St. Luke's School.

"Flavia says she's been at dis school for a long time and shoulda retired long ago. Sister Bridget flunked bot' Flavia's boys! In' tha second grade! Flavia had many bad words with dis teacher, but ya know her boys were tha terror of dis town.

"Dat nun bettah be nice to him 'cause Ah'm gonna knock her lights out if she don't! Tha nerve! She says she will call him Joseph instead of

T-June! He ain't going to answer tha nun if she calls him dat!"

Of course, Minou has to call everybody to tell them what the beginning of June's first day is like. Alcide and Bertha say they see her up front in the pews all the sisters sit in church. She always has a nasty look on her face. They're afraid if she looks at them, she's gonna know about them!

T-June gets home and carefully puts his school bag down and sits slowly down at the table with his head hung down. Poor baby. He says, "Mama, Ah got into trouble in our class today. Sister Bridget moved me to tha back of tha class."

Minou gets up from the table across from June and goes to where he sits eating the chocolate chip cookies his mama has baked. The first day?

"My bébé, what happened? Tell Mama in my head. Ya not in trouble here."

June goes and sits in his mama's lap. He is still just a baby and looks for his noonie.

Mama, Sister Bridget asked us if we had any questions, and my hand was the first to go up! So, Ah stood up and asked her why all tha nuns wear dose black ugly dresses? Ah said dey could wear some pretty red dresses or some turbans like Madam Aucoin instead of dat long scary veil? Ah told her she could knock herself out with dat big crucifix. She told me Ah was a heathen. What's dat? Like tha Indians on tha TV?

She got red faced and mad at me. She made me go sit in tha back 'cause all da children started laughin', and she didn't like dat.

Minou is furious with what he's telling her and goes to find Joe. She finds him out in the shed, where he is mending his fishing nets with Alcide. They are having some Miller beers. They are making a good living fishing out in the Gulf, and the shrimp they catch and the crab they catch and the fish they catch, well, they sure are treated like they're the catch of the day!

Minou says to Joe while Alcide leans over his shoulder, "Mais, Joe, T-June already got in trouble wit' dat Sister Bridget today! Mais, his first day! Ah'm gonna call Father Becnel and tell him to get his ass over here right now! Shit! She told dem to ask questions, and ya know T-June! He just like ya!

"We gonna take care of dis today. Mais, June ain't a sumbitchin' heathen. He goes to her church all tha time! Ah know she sees us dere every Sunday, and if she don't, she's blind as dat bat!"

Father Becnel is already at their house before she makes her call. He comes in through the living room and sits down hard on the sofa. He waits on Minou to talk, and boy, does she give him two ears full.

He says, "I've already heard everything from Sister Bridget. She was appalled at his behavior and told me she didn't know if she could teach him anymore! She hesitated when I said he would remain in her classroom and to move him back to the front of her class. She is the best teacher for him, and y'all will see that in the coming days."

Minou jumps up and says to Father Becnel, "Why tha hell did ya put him in her class? Ah don't like her. She acts like she is bettah dan me! Shit, she's tha one who told him to ask questions, and innocent like he is, he was curious!"

Oh, that's a better way of saying nosy, don't you think?

"She said she will call him Joseph 'cause T-June ain't no proper name. Dat's really rude how she said dat. Ah mean now, come on. Why tha hell, Father?"

Father sits in the kitchen where he is offered a Mello Joy cup of coffee and says, "You must hear what I have to say. It's very important, and then you will understand.

Minou goes and makes sure T-June is nowhere around. It is only Bertha, Alcide, Joe, and her at the table talking with Father.

Butch has gotten off the school bus, an hour after T-June. They have gone to the swamps with Ruby and Couyon, the old dog. Couyon loves to go with Butch and June, but Ruby hates the dog, and she can't stand not to be the center of attention. She tells June that Couyon is just too messy for her.

Talk about nerve!

∞ ∞ ∞

THE family sits around the kitchen table as usual. Father is sopping up homemade bread, reaching for the can of Steen's syrup sitting on the table. Sometimes, Minou will fry the bread dough, and boy, if that's not good!

Bertha reaches for the Crown Royal in the cabinet and gets her new glasses down. Now that they have some money big time, they don't buy the cheap stuff.

After eating, Father Becnel begins to tell them why June needs to be in that class.

"There was a small girl that lived not far from where I grew up. They swore on the Catholic Bible that this sickly child had healed many people. Her name was Charleen Richard. She cured others but couldn't heal herself. She died a very painful death, at thirteen years old.

"Down there in the prairies where there are horse ranches. The cowboys are Cajun-speaking Black men that listen to Zydeco. Black or white, they came to see her and pray with her. Sometimes, there were lines outside her house waiting to be blessed.

"Some people believe the young girl is already a saint. The Catholic Church in Rome is deciding on whether or not she will be canonized and enter the sainthood. Now, the people started praying to her as if she was already a saint and saying Charleen is still performing miracles to this day.

"People from the small town of Basile, Louisiana, where she lived with her family, and from parishes all around came to see her before she passed. It was the biggest funeral ever seen outside of Lafayette.

"Charleen was the daughter of the youngest brother of Sister Bridget. She was Sister's little niece."

"Sister Bridget has been teaching for forty years, and I'm sure she has seen many things hard to explain. She has much empathy for the little children because her upbringing was harsh, and they were poor.

Sister does love the children, but her act of being stern and uppity has worked for forty years!

"She is the most spiritual nun I have at the school, a true believer of the Trinity. She carries her rosary around her neck. She uses the beads every chance she gets.

"What I'm trying to tell you is that she deeply believes in miracles! She isn't the woman who would run screaming if, well, if Joseph did something unexpected. She would stand up with him, protecting him.

"No nonsense from her ever, and she is calm around any situation of chaos! My lovely people, I knew Joseph had to be under her care.

"She was anxious after today, but no way will she not have him in her class. We even had her laughing after a while.

"Sister Lydia was giggling about the red dress. She was used to wearing the many colors that her people wore. She did ask about Madam's turban! I would not DARE tell her about Madam Aucoin and Bishop Toussaint. How are we going to keep him from talking about them?"

∞ ∞ ∞

MINOU waits nervously for June to get home the next day from school and every day since. She refuses to call him Joseph.

Most days are regular with T-June/Joseph. He's gotten comfortable with both labels. He comes in running with a happy smile, showing his parents all the stars and A's he has earned that day. He gets a huge star for behaving in his class. He talks like he likes Sister Bridget, but he's very leery of her. T-June doesn't want to get in trouble again.

June tells them he makes the children laugh all the time, and they laugh at him when he doesn't think he's said anything funny.

He loves going to school! Turns out that he is indeed quite the character, and the children like him, laughing with him. Sometimes, the Sister laughs too. He's such a little Cajun country boy, so innocent.

Well, one day it isn't the usual. The large child that is Joseph at school turns into T-June the minute he's off the school bus. He is smothering with laughter, trying his best not to.

June says to Minou, who's starting to laugh with him, "Ya not gonna believe what Ah did today to Sister Bridget! And nobody knows anyt'in' 'bout it!"

Minou quickly stops laughing.

"Ah got finished wit' my test before tha other chil'ren, and Sister said for me to sit quietly. Ah didn't want to be quiet 'cause Ah wanted to tell her somet'in'. And Ah got kinda mad, like ya call it, boudered?

"Ah was bored, so Ah got to wonderin' if Ah could talk to her mind. Then Ah could tell her what Ah wanted to say. Ah said in her brain one time, Yoohoo, Sister Bridget.

"Mama, she looked up from her desk and said, 'Who said dat?'" Minou doesn't find anything funny now!

Now he is using his gifts for pranks! Minou pinches his fat little arm, so he gets serious right away. June knows he has done wrong. Minou is telling him, "Aww, lil boy, ya gonna make tha baby Jesus cry! Ya have gifts, not tricks to entertain ya when ya get bored! T-June, we don't want nobody else to know what ya can do!

"How many times Ah gotta tell ya! Ah don't know where ya learned dat. Not to listen. Ya just like Joe!

"Ya already in tha second grade. What tha hell ya gonna do when ya t'irteen? Okay, tell me now what happened."

T-June doesn't understand why his mama is upset. He still thinks it's funny. Baby Jesus would laugh too!

"Sister Bridget got up from her desk and was walkin' down every row, asking 'Who said dat?' She walked to tha back of tha room where tha kids who been bad sit and whacked deir desks wit' her ruler! She stared hard at Johnny. Ah guess she t'ought he done it.

"The bell rang to dismiss all of us, and we went runnin' to tha bus, and all the chil'ren were laughin' real hard at what happened. Well, Ah did feel kinda bad when dey were makin' twirly fingers on deir heads.

Sayin' 'cuckoo, cuckoo!'

"Monday, Ah'll tell her 'You so pretty' in her head so she'll feel better."

"Aw, no ya ain't! Ya gonna go tell ya papa what ya did and see if he t'inks it's so damn funny!" Minou tells him to go get ready for supper.

Butch is watching a movie, Dracula, waiting for the bishop to get there.

∞ ∞ ∞

MADAM Aucoin and the bishop have bought a big house down in Galliano, and everybody is helping them move in this weekend. The home is one of the oldest down there. It has two stories with a wraparound porch full of rockers.

The previous owner has just passed away at the age of ninety-two, Mrs. Winston Bourgeois Sr. She has left a fully furnished house of antiques and a baby grand piano. The Widow Bourgeois's children live in New York and have no time to empty the house. The Bourgeois children will never see the swamps again and good riddance.

But her children aren't complete dummies. Madam and Bishop Toussaint have spent a bunch of dollars for the house. Those two from New Orleans have a bunch of money too. They pay cash for the antiques and the baby grand piano and the huge house.

People in the area know that Madam and the Bishop have purchased the old Bourgeois house. They don't trust them yet, because the couple are really strange looking, with the Voodoo rumors being talked about up and down the bayou. Maybe they use the Voodoo to make them as rich as they are because not too many Blacks in Galliano could afford such a place.

Just something else to add to the strangeness of the family Peltier.

∞ ∞ ∞

OF course, everyone has heard what T-June has done at school. But he already knows what he will do. No matter what they say. He's got to make Sister Bridget feel better.

T-June brings Sister Bridget a handful of roses he picks in Flavia's yard. Her prize roses! Monday morning finds them in a vase of water on the Sister's desk. Sister laughs because she knows all about Flavia and her roses.

When the day is almost over for the tired little second graders, Joseph decides it is time to speak to her mind.

You so pretty.

Sister Bridget is writing on the board when she turns to the class, dropping the chalk. "Who said that to me? Who told me I was pretty?"

She just stands there, plenty confused, asking the little children the same thing over again and again. They fly out the door as fast as their legs can carry them!

T-June feels real bad this time because they all are laughing at Sister Bridget again. He decides it would be best if he didn't say anything about this one.

No such luck.

Father Becnel comes to their house and is really upset. He knows that T-June is the cause of the problem. "Sister Bridget came to the office this afternoon, thinking she is getting dementia because she is hearing things. Joseph, what are you doing?

"This poor woman thinks it's time to retire before the dementia takes over her mind.

"I know what you did, Joseph, and it's got to stop! She was kind of pleased about somebody thinking she was pretty. Poor thing, she's never been pretty a day of her life!"

Minou and Joe, Alcide and Bertha, Madam Aucoin and Bishop Toussaint, Flavia and Father Becnel, and even Butch know what T-June has done. Everybody is quite undone with June for not listening to them, as usual.

Don't use your gifts as if they are tricks!

T-June is just in the second grade, and they are so worried that if he continues his pranks, everybody in Larose will know how special this boy is. This just cannot continue!

"Joseph Alan Thibeau Junior, what tha hell we gonna do wit' you? Ah told ya not to talk again to Sister's mind! And then ya proceed to do just what we said not to do! Ya gotta start listenin' to what we tell ya, or we all will get in trouble!

"What's so hard about ya listenin'? We still know more about t'ings dan ya have learned, lil boy! Ah'm tellin' ya right now to stop, or the next time it happens, Ah will spank ya behind!" Minou says, while shaking his shoulders.

Flavia, his nanan, begins to tell him what will happen if the government finds out.

"T-June, dey will come to get ya wit' a bunch of soldiers, and we will be fightin' dem, and somebody will get shot, and den dey will haul us all to jail! Because you'll become a secret of national security, and dey won't let us see ya again. Ya gonna be put in a cage with dem testin' ya to see everyt'in' ya can do! Do ya want dis to happen? It would be terrible!

"And by the way, ya been stealin' my roses?"

June is showing fear in what his nanan has told him. "Ah promise not to do that again to Sister Bridget. She is very nice to me, and Ah don't wanna make her leave the school. Ah promise ya, and Ah keep my promises! Ah won't fool with ya roses no more, Nanan, and Ah promise dat too!"

∞ ∞ ∞

T-JUNE has kept his word, and nothing out of the ordinary has happened. He continues to bring home all his good grades and is very excited because he will have a part in the Thanksgiving play. He's going to be the chief of the Indians! Minou and Joe are so proud of him.

Of course, everyone is there for the play, taking up a whole row of seats in the auditorium.

Joseph has the most beautiful costume on the stage. Madam has made sure of that, with the full feathered headdress going down his back and the authentic Indian apparel. Minou lets him use the beautiful shell necklace that belonged to her great-pawpaw.

He stands out from the other children. He's big, and he is very striking on the stage.

Joseph's lines are coming up, and he has the attention of the crowd. He gets up to the mike and stands there like he forgot his words.

"Mais, Mais. We come to eat dis turkey wit' ya and make tha peace wit' ya too! Come on, let's do dat boogaloo wit' each other!"

Poor T-June has gotten nervous and forgotten his lines so he reverts to the language at home!

All of the audience just breaks out laughing, and there's T-June acting up on the stage, stealing the whole show. The Sisters have a hard time getting him off the stage where the other children are waiting to say their lines.

He is busy making a war dance, boogalooing on the stage while everyone is screaming out in laughter. T-June is the honest-for-sure ham!

Everybody is hugging him, along with the family, telling him he did real good!

Sister Bridget comes to him, telling him he's stolen the show!

The whole family works with him over Thanksgiving break, trying to instill the importance of listening to what they tell him. T-June acts like he's finally come to his senses as much as a boy his age can understand. But he doesn't like it one bit!

He goes to talk with his podnah Pieyan. T-June whistles, and Pieyan comes out the trees to sit in their spot. June proceeds to tell the Bigfoot about what's going on at school.

"Goin' to school is real fun for me, but e'rybody is upset wit' me 'cause Ah kinda let one of my tricks out tha bag! Tha nun, Sister Bridget, wants to call me Joseph instead of T-June, and Ah forget sometimes to answer her. Me, Ah t'ought just talkin' to her mind would be okay, but she t'ought she was goin' cuckoo! Ah'm gettin' kinda confused 'bout all of it. What ya think, Pieyan?"

T-June is asking the Bigfoot for advice when he's never been to school, unless they got a school June doesn't know about. Pieyan reaches for his little pal so they can look at each other's eyes.

"Lil man, I know all about the schools they make little children go to every day. I don't snoop around there unless it's dark, but I just run through because I can't stand the smells all the kids have. It makes my head hurt!

"You aren't grown up like you think you are, and I know all about hiding things. I mean, take a look at me! Hiding my whole life.

"I think you need to listen hard to what your tribe tells you. Just like me, you gotta hide your stuff, or the same people who chase me will come after you!"

Well, that works on T-June. Minou shoulda sent T-June to Pieyan before school started!

∞ ∞ ∞

IT'S coming close to Christmas time, and the children are getting ready for Santa Claus. T-June and Butch are making lists of what Santa will bring them.

T-June is ready for a visit at school from Santa and his little elf helpers because he will bring presents to the good children.He knows he's been good because he keeps his promises.

The day finally comes when they will see Santa Claus. Here comes a real fat man with white hair and beard, saying, Ho Ho Ho!

They are excited because Santa comes with two real elves, not knowing they are midgets that this fake Santa hires from Thibodaux every year.

T-June has his turn to sit on Santa's lap. He's squirming around and begins to tell him what he wants for Christmas, and then June suddenly starts to laugh and pulls the beard down on the man's chest.

"Ah know ya ain't tha real Santa! You old man Boudreaux who has the vegetable stand over dere by Madam's house! Why ya playin' like ya him, you? Ya could be Santa Claus every day over dere by ya vegetables!

"Mais, ya musta put some feather pillows under ya red jacket 'cause

Ah'm gettin' ready to sneeze!"

And T-June comes out and blows snot all over Santa!

June has made all the children upset and crying and hollering, all lined up at this fake Santa, and almost lands back with the bad kids.

Old Man Boudreaux gets real mad, while the elves are rolling around the floor, killing themselves laughing. They have to get help from all the children to get back up on their tiny legs! Old Man Boudreaux says, "Ah'm gonna go stop at Bertha's house and tell ya mama what ya did! Ah hope ya get ya lil ass beat! Dis has been my second job for a long-ass time, and now Ah can't do dis no more! Sister, don't call me to come over here again!"

The formidable nun, Sister Bridget, grabs Boudreaux by his shirt, and buttons start rolling away.

All the good Catholic children go to fighting over the golden buttons, knocking each other out the way!

"Mr. Boudreaux, don't you dare bully him! Who the hell do you think you are, that you can curse on this sacred ground? And the worse yet, speaking it to a child?

"You can't quit because I already fired you! Now, take yourself off this property, and don't forget those two petite hooligans with you! I'm not paying for them!"

Sister Bridget makes the man leave all the toys and candy he's brought. The school has already paid for them! Old Man Boudreaux has been making a good living off of St. Luke's.

Sister gives two presents to Joseph because she said he is a hero! She knows he is just telling the truth, and she loves that about him.

It is the day of school break holidays when T-June slips another gift from his bag of tricks. He tries so hard, poor little thing, but it just comes so natural to him, and it feels like holding your breath underwater when he has to back off.

All the kids are enjoying cookies and punch, but he is already finished with his treats, so T-June is idle for just a small moment. He starts coloring his page of Santa Claus. He is coloring when he makes the crayon spin on the page of his Santa. He is just in his own little world and not paying attention to the rest of the class. No one sees this happen, so busy stuffing their little mouths, except for Sister Bridget. She sits at her desk with her jaw dropped in amazement!

Everybody will wind up at the dentist for lockjaw before he gets to be a man!

Sister lets the rest of the class dismiss early and asks T-June to stay behind. She comes and sits down next to his desk. Poor Joseph is T-June right now and wants to run.

"Joseph, can you do that again with your crayon? You're not in trouble. Please show me that again."

He looks at her and becomes nervous. He knows he will be in trouble at home for sure if he shows anything to Sister Bridget.

T-June tells her, "My mama and papa said not to do nuttin' Ah can do. Ah got a lot of t'ings dat dey want me not to show nobody. Ah will get in trouble wit' all my family dat's helped me grow into a good boy." Sister is listening intently to what he says.

"Joseph, what do you mean when you say 'the others?' Who else lives at your house? What other things can you do? Just show me the crayon right now. It will be only you and me. I won't tell anybody else."

T-June picks up the crayon with his mind, and the damn thing starts twirling around on the page. He then makes the crayon start coloring in the lines like he is really trying to color a pretty picture. He puts the crayon down and just stares at Sister Bridget, waiting for her to say something.

She is stunned into silence.

Sister tells him that she is coming to his house tonight with Father Becnel. T-June gets up to leave for the bus, and she is still silent.

June runs into the house after getting off the bus. The other children are wondering why he is so quiet this last day of school. He always makes them laugh every day.

"Mama, Sister Bridget is comin' here tonight wit' Father. Ah kinda made a mistake. Ah wasn't doin' nuttin' on purpose. Ah try some hard not to do my stuff, and sometimes Ah get tha farts like Ah gotta go make poopoo holdin' back."

First time Minou hears it put this way, and now she has to get the castor oil!

"She saw me twirl my crayon, but nobody else saw me do dis. Ah didn't know what to do, so Ah did it again for her 'cause she asked me to. Mama, am Ah gonna get kicked out the second grade?"

Minou gets on the phone immediately and calls everybody to come to the house. Madam Aucoin and Bishop Toussaint live there now, and Alcide and Bertha live next door, with Flavia down the road.

They are all there, waiting on this visit from Sister and Father, grabbing the liquor, glasses, cups, and whatever else you put out waiting on company. Even some hot double fudge brownies are laid out on Bertha's platter that she uses for such a gathering.

They will all try to be civil with each other, but you never know about this bunch!

Butch is at his mama's house. Irene has kicked the boyfriend dude out because she's found out that he doesn't like anything, and his dislike for even his own children finally gets to her. So, Irene kicks him to the road. Since she has had Old Man Guidry picked up by the police, she's getting some backbone. But Butch will continue to live with Minou and Joe. Irene will find another man soon. Maybe the next one will be a daddy.

Nanan tells T-June it was an accident, but she is wanting to know what else he's told Sister Bridget. Anything else?

The front door is being knocked on, and Joe opens it to Sister and Father. She is totally perplexed as to why the house is full of adults, while Father walks in like it's every day and heads for the kitchen.

Sister Bridget has heard from other people the gossip that passes all the way to Golden Meadow that Madam and the bishop practice Voodoo, and she becomes very upset, thinking Joseph has been influenced by two devil worshipers!

How could Flavia, being his nanan, let that happen to her godchild? She practices the Catholic religion so fervently.

Well, that's because she is a divorcee and is trying to buy her way into heaven!

Everyone is welcoming with coffee and brownies. Sister says no to the brownies but takes a cup of coffee. Father takes a huge cup of strong black coffee to drink with all this chocolate delight.

Sister passes up the first chair empty next to Madam and goes to where Flavia sits in a rocker; there is an identical one on the side. They aren't bosom buddies, but Sister needs a familiar face because she doesn't know any of these people.

She wonders about Father Becnel. He's always been too liberal for Sister.

Father says, "May I introduce to you Sister Bridget Richard. The good Sister teaches the second grade now, and Joseph is one of her pupils. She is a teacher of all the grades and will be principal next year at St. Luke's. We are all here because little Joseph had an accident today in Sister Bridget's room."

Alcide pipes up and says, "What he did? Peed on hisself? Mais, all of us done dat! One time Ah had to make poopoo in tha garbage can!" He laughs at himself while Pawpaw Irby is snickering in his recliner.

Everyone is sitting so nervous and tense that Madam lights up her ganja pipe!

Sister Bridget gets all straight up in her rocker, not rocking, seeing Madam light that pipe up full of cannabis, and becomes paranoid, thinking the cops will bust up in there and arrest the whole bunch and her. And Joseph is exposed to that!

Much more is at stake here. The weed is the least, so she keeps silent.

Father said, "Joseph accidentally made his crayon twirl on the paper, and Sister Bridget saw him doing this. She wanted to meet all of Joseph's family and to ask a few questions concerning Joseph."

Lawd! What will she do if she finds out about the loup-garous and the magic that is always in the air here? All that Joseph can do with his gifts? Lawd, Lawd, Lawd!

Minou and Joe, Alcide and Bertha, Madam Aucoin and Bishop Toussaint, Flavia, and Father Becnel are waiting on Sister to speak. Joseph is sitting in Joe's lap.

Sister Bridget goes to where T-June is sitting next to his parents and begins to speak. "I am in a quandary. What to ask first? I have never been so honored to have a student as brilliant as Joseph. He is reading books that are fifth-grade material, but he is so innocent that he needs to be with children his age.

"I watched as he twirled a red crayon over his page! That seems to be his favorite color. He did this twice, when I encouraged him to do it again and told him he wasn't in trouble.

"I am pleading with you to allow me the knowledge of what he can perform with any other gifts that the Good Lord has bestowed on him.

"I had a niece who passed over to heaven many years ago. She is waiting in line to be canonized by the Church of Rome for sainthood. It has been proven that indeed she performed miracles. Never in my life would I have thought that I would be witness to the growth of another saint. I believe in the supernatural wonders that our Lord provides each and every day. I know about miracles, and I am ready to learn about Joseph and his gifts.

"Please, tell me what is happening in another small part of Louisiana."

Sister Bridget is softly weeping while she pulls this large handkerchief out of her pocket. Not a dainty one, for sure. Flavia puts her arm around Sister's shoulders and pats her.

Everyone is anxiously waiting for Minou and Joe to say something!

Joe and Minou admit to T-June being able to move objects but are reluctant to say anything else at this time. They tell Sister that they would have to discuss this with the family. The not-so-stern nun has quickly recognized the bond is so strong in this home and that everyone here is raising this child. Like she has told Minou, it takes a village.

Sister Bridget and Father Becnel are leaving, but he will come back after dropping Sister off to her house with the other nuns.

She leaves wondering why the two believers of Voodoo are there and chastises Father on the way home as to why he lets Madam

Aucoin and Bishop Toussaint be a part of Joseph's upbringing! And what is he thinking, letting that woman smoke marijuana in front of Joseph?

"IT'S ILLEGAL!" Sister Bridget hollers at Father, almost making him go in the ditch!

He is so very glad to get her out of his small Toyota truck. Father gets down the road, out of sight for Sister to see, and lights up his own joint. He's got some bad nerves, so he says it really calms him down. Most times he's cool as a cucumber, so is he cucumber cool or stoned?

Everyone there has asked for a big pot of strong coffee with some whiskey in it. No one says a thing, wondering what they should reveal to this Sister.

Bertha is smoking the peace pipe with Madam, and they're talking about growing a cannabis crop back there in the swamp that Flavia just knows they've been growing. It's for the family's use because more of them are asking for a hit too!

They stay up all night discussing what they should tell and not tell. Father Becnel, back from his ride, finally says this about the woman. "Sister Bridget has my full confidence and that I was right in choosing her for Joseph. She doesn't gossip with the other nuns, always quiet about what happens in her room.

"Well, Joseph did upset her with him questioning why the black clothes! She was so outdone that she had to speak about it to Sister Lydia. She has become sort of a scientist and went back to college for her third degree, this one in Catholic law.

"She's looking for the loophole keeping Charleen from being a saint. She is an intellect of many things and is always studying something. She would never tell this to another soul.

"I know that she adores Joseph, and given the chance, Sister would be another family member that we could trust in the upbringing of this oh-so-gifted child. We don't have to tell her everything, but he would be in a good spot with Sister if he had another 'accident.'

"We can tell her that Joseph can talk with her in his mind. The poor old thing is still worried about that!"

Madam is the next to speak, and she has concerns. "I could feel this woman's hatred toward me and the bishop. She was visibly upset when I lit my pipe, but I really don't give a damn! We have been with all of you from the beginning of Monsieur Mayhem's birth and his life.

"I cannot deal with this woman's persecution of me and the bishop. It took forever for Flavia to change her mind! This sista is the one talking about 'it takes a village,' so here we are! The whole village! She has to learn how to accept us because we're not going anyplace!

"What do you intend to do about this?

Alcide and Bertha stand up and are troubled concerning Sister. Alcide does the talking. "Mais, to t'ink it all started wit' Bertha and me! If Minou wasn't so damn nosy! Y'all, we don't want nobody else to know we some goddamn werewolves!

"And to tell her he can talk wit' tha animals and dat he is friendly wit' tha Bigfoot named Pieyan? And tell her dat T-June is a healer? Just what do we keep quiet about?

"Ah don't like tha way she done treated Madam. She just like all tha nuns Ah ever met. Disapprovin' and dislikin' everyt'in'! Probably 'cause she needs a good…well, ya know what Ah'm talkin' 'bout.

"Ah say to let her in on just a few of tha things he does. 'Til she proves to us if she is needed in tha damn village!"

Flavia of course has the floor now. She has told everyone the history between her and Sister Bridget concerning her sons. No one will comment on that!

Sister and Flavia now compete with roses, entering the same competitions around the parish for the prettiest ones. Flavia doesn't know this, but Madam will be entering the contests that Flavia and Sister have had a monopoly for years.

Flavia says to the group, "Lawd, have mercy! Ah can't get away from her! She shows her disapproval of me every Sunday when Ah go up for my Communion. Ah know she is t'inkin', 'divorcee!'

"Then she joins the Lafourche Parish Garden Club 'cause she's been growin' her roses for a long time too. Boy, Ah bet she t'ought dat was real funny when T-June brought her my roses! We always get first place and runner up. Sometimes it's me, sometimes it's her.

"Ah guess we are like some enemies, too busy with bullshit to know anyt'in' good 'bout each other.

"Ah didn't know 'bout her bein' Saint Charleen's aunt. How could Ah have missed dat? It makes me feel bad 'cause Ah believe in her miracles! Ah pray to Saint Charleen every night.

"So Ah say, let her become involved wit' some of my baby's gifts. Just some, not all. She's gonna have to accept Madam and tha bishop, though. And for sure to treat me better. After all, Ah'm tha nanan!"

Everyone there is exhausted from all this. They leave, saying they'll be back tomorrow. All of them now take a potion from Madam that gives you energy and clear heads. Sort of like that old time elixir, Hadacol. Madam also offers to share her ganja.

Minou and Joe decide to wait until the end of Christmas holidays when T-June will return with both of them to school to speak with Sister Bridget. She is told the conditions of her joining the family, and she agrees to this. She dreams of becoming a martyr for St. Joseph Junior's crusade! Sister Bridget is now studying the religion of Voodoo. She is despairing, seeing the similarity in the two.

T-June now will show her how he can talk to your mind. He has to apologize to Sister for scaring her. But Little Joseph says he thinks she is pretty for true, and she smiles a big ole smile and hugs him.

T-June and Sister speak all day with one another in their minds.

Sister is delighted with what T-June can share with her. She has to go to Confession for being unkind and not tolerant, with Father Becnel on the other side of the screen!

Chapter Eight

T-June and Jolie

T-JUNE is ready for the third grade when school starts again after the summer.

He continues visiting Pieyan, the Bigfoot. Everyone has calmed down about him going into the swamps. That big old hairy monkey man will take care of him.

Minou has slowed down and is feeling this pregnancy more than she did with T-June. She suffers morning sickness and swollen ankles and the heat of the summer.

Madam Aucoin tells her she will have a baby girl, and Minou believes her. This birth is different, maybe because it is a girl. Minou is so glad that she's not as cumbersome and big as she was for T-June.

T-June also tells his mama that a baby sister is on the way. While she is brushing his hair that's never seen a pair of scissors, Minou asks him. "T-June, ya can tell tha future, huh? Mais, come on. Please tell me it ain't so? Dat's a heavy burden more dan anyt'in'! Baby, tell Mama if ya can, but don't tell me tha next t'ing dat's comin' up tha road! Just shake ya head."

T-June is kinda tickled because his mama never knows what's coming out his mouth! "No, my poor Mama, I can't do that. Not yet, anyway! I just know if I can talk with you first, in your mind. I can't talk to everybody's mind, but that's good for me! I can hear a whisper from little Caldonia, she told me."

They sure are hugging and kissing each other, with the news being good for both of them!

That's a double prediction on what the baby will be. Minou knows it to be true so she and Flavia order baby clothes, definitely pretty little girl dresses and tatted bonnets. Little tiny white leather shoes with a small pearl button. Call for them to order, on page 342, just like the pecans.

T-June tells Minou to order two of everything. T-June says, "Just in case, Mama. Just in case."

Minou and Flavia and Bertha go through the massive catalogs from JCPenney and Sears all day long.

Madam Aucoin will be buying in New Orleans.

This baby's name will be Caldonia Evette; Minou loved the days spent at the Caldonia Hotel.

Joe doesn't like the name.

The godparents will be Madam as the nanan and Bishop Toussaint as the parrain.

∞ ∞ ∞

SISTER Bridget and Joseph carry on their friendship throughout the summer. She has studied the Voodoo religion, to the delight of Madam and the bishop. Sister Bridget grudgingly admits to the similarities of her Catholicism to the rites of the Voodoo, except the dancing in Congo Square in New Orleans. She doesn't even want to think about that happening in her church!

The Sister has to accept the fact that these two are part of the village that indeed helps in T-June's upbringing. She is cordial to both Flavia and Madam, as they are to her. Never being bosom buddies, but respect is what has been given.

Everyone is accepting of the truce, and so they all continue to guide T-June in his growing up to whoever he will be.

Sister Bridget looks at this as a crusade; she's so honored to be at the beginning.

Sister asks to be transferred to teach third grade. She turns down being the principal of the school so she could continue her crusade with Joseph. She will follow him through all of his grades. Father Becnel will continue transferring her to the next grade.

T-June has many new friends in third grade. Some of the children are from his old class, but many come from the other classes of second grade. All of them remember him from the previous year because he's well known for the shenanigans he did.

Remember, he's the school's clown, sometimes not even meaning to be. T-June is just a funny little character, along with all of his top-secret secrets he keeps, with endurance taught by his tribe.

He has become very aware of a little girl sitting next to him. Jolie Stelle Theriot. She has long hair that corkscrews into what Madam refers to as dreadlocks. Her complexion is a light shade of brown, and her eyes of green are slanted with an Oriental look. Her full lips make T-June just want to kiss her, smack right on the kisser! A very beautiful little girl that stares at Joseph whenever she can. Joseph does the same.

He tells Sister Bridget in her mind that he had a dream of the girl. She just smiles because she doesn't know that his dreams come true.

T-June tries to catch up with her when the bell for recess rings. He finds her waiting on him outside the class. He reaches for her hand and says, "I'm Joseph or T-June. I have dreamed about you. Will you be my girlfriend?"

She lets him hold her hand and says to him, "My name is Jolie, and I knew I would be your best friend, and for sure I'll be your girlfriend too. I'm supposed to be with you."

T-June and Jolie become inseparable after that day in third grade. He has begun to tell Jolie everything that he is able to do. He trusts her more than anybody in his life.

Jolie takes everything he says to her quiet heart and safe place. She will never repeat what he has told her and tells him her Uncle Simon is known for his healing ways. She had never heard the word "traiteur."

Different cultures they come from, but it only makes them so much more interesting to each other. T-June and Jolie are the same shade of skin.

The tremendous love they have is a lifelong love, even at this young age. T-June knows without a doubt that she has been sent to him for life.

She begins to tell him about her great-grandmother. She was a Vietnamese that met Jolie's great-grandfather on the fishing docks of New Orleans. A long line of fishermen that carry on from generation to generation.

She says her mother comes from the big city, and her family are known as Creoles. Her daddy is from around Larose, and his family has lived here for centuries.

Alcide and Joe say they know him because he is an important member of the fishing community. They both say they like him, and Alcide says, "Mais, for sure he's a good man! Me, Ah don't give a goddamn what color he is! All we fishermen see is tha blue of tha water of tha Gulf and tha color of blood if we cut ourself. We all bleed tha same color, so what tha hell!"

Jolie tells T-June some of the history that has strengthened all of the people that lived in the community she has grown up in, way down the road. The dark nights when white men would come with hoods over their faces and big horses that would trample anything in their path. Her people trying to vote and their men disappearing from their homes.

She even tells him about a great-aunt taken out of her home and raped by two of the men who come to torment. She gives birth to a son that is definitely a product of the men who rape her. That same son becomes a civil rights attorney.

T-June is so hurt for her that he starts crying, hearing about the injustice of it all. He tells her about the sad thing that happens every month of the full moon. She has never heard of a loup-garou before, but she trusts him with everything he tells her.

Jolie and T-June spend all their time with each other, both in and out of the Thibaux house and Jolie's. Minou loves the girl and knows she is the one for T-June. He has told her this, and she can only believe him.

Third grade is thrilling for the two, each one sharing in the honors of being at the top of their class. They study together and are always in each other's company.

Sister Bridget is feeling neglected by T-June, but she knows how these things are, in spite of her never having a boyfriend.

He is still being funny with the other students, and Jolie laughs the hardest when he's in his glory of being a ham. She just loves him totally with her little heart.

∞ ∞ ∞

THIS year they share the playground with Butch; they are a trio during recess. Butch loves hanging with his little brother, and he thinks that Jolie is the prettiest girl at the school. Wait until he meets Jolie's sister!

Some of Butch's classmates tease him about being with the younger kids. He tries to overlook their taunts, but he is having a rough year being in the ninth grade. He knows about the ones who smoke in the bathrooms at school, and the same boys cuss with very ugly words.

Butch is serious with his learning of the Catholic faith. He is thinking about going to the seminary that Father Becnel went to. So just that fact has caused him to become a good target to torment.

A nice cold day of autumn finds the trio on the playground during the lunch break. Butch is laughing at something T-June has told him. You remember that he is always Joseph at school but T-June when he gets home. Complications always.

Butch continues laughing with Jolie at T-June's comments when three boys from his class walk up to the trio.

"Ain't dis cute? Tha three freakin' Musketeers! What's so damn funny? Ya makin' fun of me?" the fattest of the three boys says with a sneer to Butch.

One of the boys is bald and is dirty, with leftover food on his shirt from his lunch. The last one doesn't look like he wants to be part of whatever is going to transpire. He is struggling on the fence of nonconformity. He wants to be a part of the group, but he just goes along to be liked by the other two.

The boy with the shaved head and skinny frame says to Butch, "Ah heard all about ya mama. E'rybody knows she is just an old whore and t'rew you away."

Lawd, have mercy!

Butch turns red in the face and punches Baldy in the mouth! Then the fight is on! Two against one, they think, because the other boy backs out of the situation.

They both jump on Butch, thinking they will win this with no effort. They sure don't know about T-June!

With the two on top of Butch, June makes the boy punching Butch fly up and hit the brick wall! That leaves Butch fighting the skinny one, and he punches him so hard that Baldy is laying on the ground, pleading with Butch not to hit him again.

All of the boys are brought to the principal's office. Not June and Jolie. Teachers that break up the fight think the two younger children have nothing to do with what happened. But Sister Bridget has figured out what's transpired. She begins to question Joseph in her mind, asking him what happened with the three boys and Butch.

The other children on the playground think Butch threw the boy into the brick wall. They are all pounding him on the back with glee, saying the two deserve what they got. None see what June has done, except the third boy that goes to the sidelines.

Now, he's certain he will be a good boy from now on! He's thinking he's going crazy!

The Sister has found out what has really happened because of listening to what T-June has told her. The two that fought Butch are suspended for two weeks, and the third gets detention, because he is with the others.

Sister Bridget protects the two boys of Minou's from anyone else knowing what happened. Minou and Joe are on that list.

∞ ∞ ∞

THE time has come for Minou to deliver Caldonia Evette.

They have found out that Jolie's mama is going to give birth only a few days apart from Minou.

Minou is struggling with the birthing to the point of the midwives thinking she has to go to a hospital. She cries out with another pain, and her Caldonia Evette comes into the world.

On the other side of the community, Estelle, who is Jolie's mama, gives birth two hours later and has another girl. Both girls are delivered by midwives.

The families are delighted with the news of two newborns. Madam and Flavia each have their necklaces to put on the two baby girls. Alcide says only Caldonia will wear his chain; he doesn't think the other baby will need protection from the loup-garous.

The babies both come into the world on Christmas Eve. They will become lifelong friends too, as will Estelle and Minou.

T-June receives for Christmas a baby sister, who has been nicknamed Callie, and a large computer. June loves to be on Butch's computer that his mama bought him.

Butch gets a huge chemistry set from his mama and large hip boots with other waterproof clothing from Minou and Joe.

Irene, Butch's mama, comes and brings more gifts for everybody and spends the day with them. She loves babies! Just doesn't know what to do with them after they grow up.

Everyone in June's extended family brings gifts for each other, and the Christmas weekend is blessed and joyful and peaceful.

Now New Year's Eve brings a different sight. There is a New Year's party down the bayou at the new home of Madam and the bishop. And whoever wants to come can come!

Joe and Alcide with the bishop get drunk, to everyone's delight, and Father acts like he is pretty stoned. He drinks most of the wine there!

Bishop Toussaint takes to playing the baby grand piano that sits in the parlor of his and Madam's home. Fats Domino!

Alcide is singing at the top of his lungs every word of the songs, sounding pretty doggone good! Father Becnel tries to sing along, but he has a terrible singing voice.

Estelle and Theo Theriot come too, along with their youngest daughters, Jolie being one. They dance to every New Orleans song the bishop could play. Some of their songs get down right jazzy!

The bishop is wondering how the hell can he hear horns and saxes when nobody's doing that. It's a brief thought in Bishop Toussaint's mind at that moment.

Of course, Estelle can sing like Irma Thomas.

Joe is over where the woven basket sits with his new daughter and her petite friend in it. He is singing a Cajun song to both of them.

Flavia and Sister Bridget are standing together, snapping their fingers and singing along to Fats. Minou thinks the two probably have had too much to drink too. Flavia can usually handle her whiskey. Well then, it could be secondhand smoke.

Minou is tending to the baby with Joe, and Madam Aucoin and Bertha are in Madam's kitchen making Oysters Bienville.

All is well with the family as they wait for what the New Year will bring.

∞ ∞ ∞

T-JUNE and Butch, along with Jolie, return to school after the Christmas holidays. They are eager because all three are there to learn everything they can.

Minou and Joe had quit school when they were but fifteen and are so proud of their two sons.

Coming back to school, T-June begins to feel that there are kids who don't like him. He feels this in class and on the playgrounds. They are jealous of the attention that Jolie and June get most days.

One of these jealous kids comes and shoves T-June and Jolie into the lockers. The two just overlook the incident as they think maybe the boy is in a hurry.

Butch sees what's happening while waiting for them and becomes angry, but T-June asks him not to do anything. Sometimes he has to turn the other cheek, like Father Becnel says.

Butch has become the hero of the school. He defends the underdog and smaller kids. He's gonna be a fine man!

T-June and Jolie are becoming targets for these vicious children. They whisper behind their backs when the pair walk by and continue to shove them. June knows what's being said. He finds their minds slower and easier to get in than the grownups. Usually, he'll back out quick in their minds when he finds nobody is home. He won't tell what is being said to Jolie or Butch.

He's become aware of danger. He's never been mean a day of his life. He has to be the one to figure out the situation.

Doesn't take long for that to happen. The day comes on a Friday afternoon when T-June can't refrain from doing something.

Jolie and June are waiting on the bus to arrive when suddenly he is pushed to the ground. It's a boy the same size as him, who he thinks is a friend. He tells June that he is a "nigga lover."

T-June remains on the ground and in moments, he is making the boy twirl fast-fast. He also makes him do a dance only monkeys know. The other children think that the boy is having an epileptic fit!

Some of the kids run to the office of the nurse, making her run faster than her legs can carry her. She tries her best to make him quit the monkey's dance but cannot help this kid to stop. She places a large popsicle stick in the boy's mouth, and he bites it into two and spits at the nurse!

T-June doesn't stop his mind game until getting on the bus. He turns to look at the dumbstrunk boy who has said terrible things, and the boy falls to the ground, dazed and confused.

Butch can't wait to tell Minou and Joe what has happened at school. They now ride the same afternoon bus.

He is proud of his brother T-June but doesn't realize the severity of what he's done.

Following Butch into the kitchen looking at his parent's faces, T-June knows they are very, very disappointed in him.

"What did ya do? Ah can't believe ya twirled dat kid like ya did wit' ya crayon. Ah didn't even know ya could do dat! Good t'ing dey all t'ought he was havin' a bad conniption fit! What made ya do dis to dis boy? What did he say to ya? Mais, June, what tha hell!"

T-June begins to tell his mama what had been said, and he says he just couldn't help himself. It just took him over because he was mad!

Minou tells him, if had been her to hear this, she would have punched the little bastard, him!

This incident goes unnoticed because everyone thinks the boy has had a seizure, except for Sister Bridget. She calls Minou to ask if she can come over tonight.

Lawd, Lawd, Lawd! Will this ever stop?

Sister comes over before the sun goes down on this remarkable day. She sits down at the table in the kitchen where Minou and Joe are sitting with her Joseph. Seems as though the kitchen is where things are settled with the whole family.

She begins to talk very excitedly. "Joseph, I know you caused that! How in the name of Jesus did you do this? I must know everything that you can do so I can protect you from yourself! Please tell me, because this is a miracle!

"You know, Minou and Joe, that I can be trusted by now. What are we raising? Please tell me!"

Minou and Joe begin to tell Sister Bridget the things they have witnessed since T-June's birth. This conversation lasts into the night, and she is utterly amazed at what she has been told.

She is almost completely blown away, and she asks for a large glass of water and to put some whiskey in it too. She finally has words to say.

"You tell me that he can heal too? He is a miracle walking around, and he's not even close to being grown! Yes, he will be a saint, no doubt about it! I know now why it took so many people guiding him. He needed this very special village to get him to where he is right now!

"Please know that I feel this is my calling too. I will be with you through his lifetime, if you allow me. I am so honored to be part of this young saint's life.

"My precious little boy, how confused you must be!"

T-June doesn't think he's confused. It's just been a natural thing for him, and he takes it in stride, although it has been very hard on everybody else.

He's not gonna let anyone say something bad about Jolie.

Father Becnel comes in with a slight tap on the door to join in the discussion of everything Sister Bridget has been told. He says that Sister has been put into T-June's life for a reason and that it is God's plan.

Father says again that he knew what he was doing in choosing Sister to teach the remarkable boy. She had dealt with miracles before. He's just capable of almost saying, I told you so! Tooting his Catholic horn!He says, "We have all been blessed to carry out the divine plan for your child and to raise him to the best of our abilities. I'm so thankful that you allowed Sister Bridget into Joseph's life. She will never tell this to another soul.

"But, this new gift is somewhat frightening! He has to understand that this is something else he cannot do in public or anywhere.

"Joseph! Do not begin to make people do what you have decided they should do. That is dealing with people's souls, doing something against their free will. Joseph, that would be a mortal sin! You have to see this as another gift not to be done with anybody, unless they are trying to do you harm!"

T-June is way confused now! That boy was trying to do harm to both Jolie and himself, so how is that not staying out of harm's way?

He will do bodily harm to both of those boys one day, if he doesn't nip it in the bud!

T-June tries to explain that to Father Becnel, but the Father says not to make this an argument.

He has to contain more gifts that can't be seen by the world!

T-June thinks, Wait 'til I'm all grown up! I might forget half of the stuff I can do, if they don't leave me alone!

June gets up and leaves the kitchen, slamming his bedroom door. He wakes up his baby sister, Callie, and she starts crying.

Minou and Joe are so relieved that Callie hasn't shown any signs of being different. She's just an ordinary baby, a beautiful baby girl.

T-June bouders all weekend because Father won't listen to what he's saying. He asks Minou to drive him to Jolie's house.

What a fun house Jolie lives in! Joseph loves all the people who live there too. Everyone in this family is glad to add others into their fold, as they do often.

Jolie has five sisters now since the baby was born.

Her Big Mama and Big Daddy live there too. That's what she calls her daddy's parents. She also has two cousins living there because their mama is Estelle's sister, and she was killed by their daddy. The two little cousins are darker than the rest of Jolie's family but are loved fiercely being they are two boys in a house full of girls! The two boys are older than T-June and Jolie. They like June and tease their little cousin about them being together. But since they are a few years older, the boys find they are too old to be hanging out with T-June and Jolie.

Estelle invites Minou and the baby into her warm house where you can smell the wonderful cooking and the tobacco being smoked with incense, leaving traces of a smell Minou will come to love. Patchouli.

The large house has tall ceilings with windows just as tall, like at Madam's house. The living room has many mismatched couches and chairs but lots of pillows everywhere, such different colors added. It is so inviting to anybody. Plants everywhere too.

The walls have many New Orleans paintings with vibrant colors adding to the wonderful old house, soulful and peaceful in spite of all the laughter and singing to the New Orleans music blaring. There's a bunch of soul permeating through the walls of this loving family.

T-June and Jolie have already gone to the back of the house to be alone. Butch has come too, and Minou thinks, after he takes one look at Jolie's sister, So much for being a priest!

Jolie has never told her family about what T-June has shared with her. She is the quiet sister among a boisterous bunch of girls who worry about boys and makeup and going on dates. Jolie has been the baby – until Lily comes along.

She doesn't tell her mama what has happened at school, but she knows that T-June has caused the solution.

It remains that way until Minou starts to become her mama's friend. Miss Minou will decide what she will reveal to Jolie's mama.

Both of the babies are needing to be fed. Minou and Estelle sit on the side of each other and begin to breastfeed their little girls. The babies are looking at each other while they feed. Estelle says, laughing, "Look at these two! They already know they gonna be like sistas! They watchin' each other! We decided we will name her Estelle too, but we're gonna call her Lily. That is a hoot! They're gonna be Callie and Lily, just like the flower Calla Lily."

Minou laughs with Estelle at the combination of the two names.

They begin to visit with each other and realize they will become good friends. Minou needs a girlfriend; she's never had one before.

Minou had asked if she knows of Madam Aucoin, and Estelle laughs out loud! Turns out that Estelle is Madam's third cousin. Of course! Both are famous people in the city!

So they take their babies over to Madam Aucoin's to have coffee and to talk about their days in New Orleans and the fact that Estelle has been raised going to Bishop Toussaint and Madam Aucoin's place of worship. Estelle knows the practices of Voodoo. She changed a long time ago to be Catholic because her husband's family doesn't approve of her believing in Voodoo.

Thought we settled that before!

∞ ∞ ∞

ONE cold February morning T-June arrives at Jolie's house so they can work on a project that Sister Bridget has assigned. They are in the living room laughing at Jolie's Big Mama, who is whistling and dancing in the kitchen. She does this all the time.

Joseph and Jolie notice the silence at the same time, hearing nothing coming from the kitchen. They go into the kitchen together and find Big Mama on the floor, grasping her chest.

Jolie goes screaming for her mama, and everyone is there in mere minutes. Calling 911 and trying to make her responsive. Nothing is working.

T-June sits on the floor with Big Mama but doesn't touch her. He is overwhelmed in trying to decide what to do. His natural ability comes through, and he reaches for Big Mama's hands. He is talking to her mind and rubbing her hands.

Big Mama sits up on the floor and wants to know why everybody is staring at her. They stand in disbelief as the two medical assistants come through the door. They check all of her vitals and then look up at the whole family, wondering why they've been called. Estelle says to take Big Mama to the hospital anyway.

T-June is violently ill; he throws up on the floor and asks if somebody will call his mama to come get him. Estelle and her husband are on the way to the hospital with Big Daddy.

Jolie goes with June to his house, with Minou driving faster than she should.

Everyone is called to their house. To her knowledge, T-June has never gotten ill with anything that he's done.

Minou and Joe and Alcide, Bertha and Butch, Madam Aucoin and Bishop Toussaint, Flavia and Father Becnel, Pawpaw Irby and now Sister Bridget are all there.

Did I leave somebody out?

T-June is looking pale after he finally quits vomiting. He is laying down on the sofa while Jolie sits holding his head. He knows why the whole damn village is there! He says something because everyone is looking at him, expecting him to speak.

"Mama, Big Mama had a really bad heart attack. I could feel that as I reached for her hands. I didn't know if I could help her, then I felt a strength come into my hands, and they burned. I never felt that before. Then she sat up looking at me hard. I could feel the sickness coming over me, so I didn't say anything to her. Mama, I just couldn't help myself. I was drawn to her, I couldn't help it."

Minou and Joe's house is full of silent people. The only one that isn't is saying her rosary in the corner, talking about sainthood to herself.

Sister joins Flavia in saying the rosary, and then both are talking about Saint T-June.

They all feel exhausted and want the tears to flow. What can they do about this, what can they do? Everybody is thinking about Jolie's family. This isn't hidden; they've all witnessed the healing. Who will they tell? How are they going to handle this? Will they call the newspaper?

Hearing the knocking at the door, all of them brace for the arrival of Jolie's parents with her Big Mama and Big Daddy.

No one is smiling, each knowing why.

Joe gets up and offers his recliner to Big Mama. She is the one to break the silence.

"Joseph, come sit over here by me. You saved my life, didn't you?"

Joseph is sitting next to her, and he smiles at her, saying, "Yes, ma'am. I think I did just that. You had a bad heart attack, but how are you feeling now?"

Big Mama sits straight up in the recliner and says, "You lil white boy! You tellin' me that it was you and not Jesus? You better hit your knees, boy!"

Big Mama realizes who she is talking to and gets embarrassed for her lack of manners. "Baby, I'm sorry for my ugliness. I get upset easy sometimes. I know in my heart that you healed me with the help of Jesus. You was given that gift from the Lord, Jesus Christ himself. I'm gonna take this to my grave 'cause you are way too young for this burden if everyone finds out. I know it made you sick. That was all the crud you pulled out of me.

"OH MY JESUS! SWEET MOTHER OF JESUS, MARY, BLESS THIS CHILD!

"You got to wait 'til you are a man. I also feel that you will be part of our family until I pass away to Glory. I'm gonna make everybody swear on my mama's Bible to never tell another soul!"

Estelle and her husband, Theo Theriot, are sitting holding their little Lily and begin to talk, both of them. Must be a Cajun somewhere putting his shoes where they don't belong!

"Hush now, Theo. Let me say my piece, and then you can say what you want. Please, baby."

Minou sits down by her friend, smiling and crying at the same time. Estelle is wiping her tears, telling her not to cry. "My sista. Oh, my sista! Don't you shed another one of your precious tears. Why? 'Cause you afraid of us? Oh, my sweet Jesus! You and me will be family for the rest of our lives! I wish I had a dollar for every time Joseph has told me, he's askin' for Jolie's hand in marriage! My other girls were too cuckoo to notice too much! We will never betray any of this. It stays between us and Big Mama and Big Daddy and Jolie. You know how she is silent!" Theo agrees with everything his wife has said.

Alcide and Joe with Theo go outside to the shed, talking about boats and nets and the feeling they all have sailing the Gulf of Mexico.

Minou and Estelle are feeding the babies and watching the two coo and smile at each other.

Bertha and Madam are cooking a huge gumbo with potato salad and Madam's bread to feed everyone there.

Butch is talking to Jolie's sister while surfing the channels on the TV with Bishop Toussaint. They're looking for a scary movie. The couple is sitting close to one another while the bishop just smiles.

Pawpaw Irby is sitting and listening to Flavia, Sister Bridget, and Big Mama talking about miracles and sainthood.

Father Becnel has had to leave because he has Saturday night Mass in an hour.

T-June and Jolie sit quietly on the back steps of his house. They are communicating with their minds.

Chapter Nine

Madam Aucoin's House

IT'S calm at Minou and Joe's, so it is calm at everybody else's too.

T-June is doing well at school, learning in his own way how to control his abilities. Of course, Jolie has a large calming effect on him.

It's gotten so he is called Joseph more often than T-June. Even Minou has started calling him Joseph, but he answers to both names. Confusion has the boy torn, from whatever he is called!

The baby girls are growing, and the mamas are so proud of these two little divas. Estelle and Minou like to dress them alike and pretend like they're twins. Well, they sure don't look alike, with Callie's dark hair straight and Lily's hair very nappy.

The babies continue with the bonding they have had since the birth of both.

The families are in and out of each other's homes most days, being that the friendship between Estelle and Minou is as strong as the bond between Joseph and Jolie.

The first steps of Callie and Lily are to each other, and they now hug and kiss each other all the time.

Butch has fallen in love with Jolie's sister, Katrina. They are going steady in high school and have decided to go to college together. He has forgotten all about being a priest!

Irene has a hard time accepting the mixed couple. Then she meets Estelle and Theo Theriot. Come to find out, they are related from a long time ago.

Flavia and Sister Bridget have become buddies, joining together with their roses now that they have real competition with Madam

Aucoin. It is a ferocious contest between the three. Madam is growing roses that climb all over the porch that wraps around her house. They are considered antique roses, being they were there a long time before Madam moved into her beautiful home.

Sister Bridget continues teaching Joseph, moving each grade to continue what she says is her calling. She seldom mentions the teachings of Voodoo.

Madam Aucoin comes to visit Bertha and Minou one day and tells them about the spirits that have made themselves known and comfortable in her house! "You both know I can communicate with spirits, but these haunts are not speaking with me! I get waked up almost nightly by the piano being played. Things are moved around, and I hear laughter when no one is there to laugh.

"I'm really upset because it seems as though someone is messing with my roses! I find many on the ground like they were cut! I know Flavia and Sister aren't that mean, and I can see anybody coming down my lane. I've seen no one around the house.

"The bishop and I have made the potions that have worked many times in getting rid of pesky ghosts but to no avail. The spirits seem to be oblivious to what we do. I'm beginning to doubt my abilities. Maybe I'm getting too old.

"Minou, we know that you can speak with ghosts like you did with the pirate Gaspar. Would you and Bertha come back with me to my house and see if you can find out why they're still haunting me and the bishop?"

Minou says she will definitely come. Bertha says HELL NO! Despite being a loup-garou every month, Bertha is scared of anything that pertains to the supernatural. She is still leery of her grandson, Joseph. She doesn't trust him and watches him like a hawk when he's around her. She doesn't feel that way about her little Callie; she shows a lot of love for her.

Bertha says she will stay there and take care of her tootoo while Minou is gone.

Minou goes with Madam back to her house, and they both scream in shock. There is not a single rose left on the vine! The petals have been crushed, and they float in the air and land in a pile by Minou and Madam's feet.

Madam runs to the back of her house where she has long-stemmed rose bushes. There she finds just the stems standing up with no flowers on them. Looks like an alien plant with the stalks like swords reaching for the sky.

Madam sits on the ground, crying so hard that she can't catch her breath, sobbing deeply. "How can I live with spirits so horrible that they would destroy something as beautiful as a rose? They must really hate me, and now I'm afraid of what they will do next! Aw, Minou, what we gonna do?"

Minou feels saddened and is disturbed seeing her long-time mentor in such a defeated state. Madam has taught Minou so many things, and now the shoe is on the other foot.

They walk into the house with Minou leading the way. It is as silent as the grave. That by itself is spooky. Bishop Toussaint is in New Orleans today, and they miss his playful ways and loud voice booming through the house. They both wish he would come home.

Minou is leading the way through the downstairs of the home, into the back rooms where Madam's altar is set up for her to practice her Voodoo rituals. They smell it before they see it. Every bottle of potion and elixir is broken on the shelves, with the liquids spilling all over the floor. The well-known statues of Catholic saints remain on the shelves, but not the known saints of Voodoo. They are smashed to pieces. Madam's incense sticks are broken, and Madam's stash of ganja is nowhere to be found!

Madam gets mad and is hollering for all the spirits to leave her home, saying an incantation that Minou has heard before. "Loli, Loli, Loli! Begone from here. Lolie Ma Choo, Ma Choo, Shoo Shoo, Choo, Choo! What I have petitioned will be you being gone, you hateful bastards!" They run back to the kitchen when they hear a tremendous noise. All of the cabinets have flown open, with Madam's pots and dishes flying in the air.

They can't run fast enough out the back door to keep the pots from hitting them. There's a whole lotta shakin' goin' on!

They both reach Madam's old Lincoln two-door with the fins and a paint job of shiny turquoise and a sunroof in it. Madam had the thing ordered special many years ago, a beautiful traveling car that all the old geezers love, stopping her at gas stations to talk about the Lincoln and the Ernie K-Doe cassette blaring through the opened sunroof.

Madam isn't jamming today.

Both jumping in at the same time, Madam and Minou holding on for dear life, tear out the driveway so fast that they peel out, making the gravel fly everywhere and tires screech out like at the Daytona races.

Both of them are visibly frightened when they get back to Bertha's house. Minou grabs the bottle of Crown Royal off the shelf and pours two large shots in three glasses. Bertha says, "Pour me one too! Mais, chér, Ah'm gettin' scared just lookin' at ya!"

They both are talking together, trying to tell what happened, and it doesn't take much for poor Bertha's mind to become addled. She's been that way her whole life, but being a werewolf probably doesn't help either.

After hearing what happened to Minou and Madam, Alcide and Joe can piece the story together, and they are afraid too. Should Joseph be told?

Bertha becomes the strong one and says, "Mais, goddamn sumbitch! Dey ain't no way dat dem ghosts are gonna run ya out ya house! Mais, mais, dey don't know ya Queen of tha Voodoo!! Just wait! We gonna get tha Father and tha Sister on deir asses too!

"Mais, ya and the bishop can stay here like ya used to do. For as long as it takes! Minou, ya and Joe can go back over dere by ya-selves. Try and talk wit' dem like ya did wit' Gaspar. Ah ain't goin' over dere! Me and e'rybody else will stay right here."

It is midafternoon when Joe and Minou pull up in front of Madam's home in Minou's new Jeep. Everybody has gotten a new vehicle, one of their heart's wishes. Bertha has chosen a ruby red 1965 Mustang. Yeah, you right!

They hesitate for a while before going in. Minou's not brave like she used to be. She's got a lot of responsibilities now, too many! But there's nothing wrong with her nose, being she is still very nosy!

They begin to straighten up the complete mess that they've walked into. Picking up the dishes and pots scattered across the kitchen floor. Minou is mopping, looking for any sliver of glass on the wide cypress boards that lay in every room of the house. She is washing the dishes before putting them back up where they belong.

Madam's house is always clean, neat, and orderly.

Minou and Joe hear a cry that could easily be the banshee from Ireland! They are scared out their minds! Joe runs to one bathroom while Minow runs to another. They meet in the middle of the living room where the piano starts playing a weird, out-of-key song.

Silence for a minute, then Minou and Joe hear in a voice that would scratch a chalkboard, "This is my home! Leave while you can!" Well, it's not like Minou and Joe haven't heard that before!

They reach the home of Bertha and Alcide and go straight for the liquor cabinet. They're gonna be some alcoholics before this merde ends!

Madam is insisting that they tell her what has happened! Minou reaches for Madam's pipe and says, "Dere's a mighty pissed-off ghost in ya house! Ah know dere are other haunts dere too, but dey ain't as scary as tha head honcho. Dat one is tha one causin' tha trouble. Dat one is tha one dat makes itself known in very ugly ways. Ah'm scared to death for ya two to even be in tha house. Dis t'ing ain't no pushover like Gaspar."

Madam Aucoin has known from the first day that her home is haunted. It doesn't frighten her because she and the bishop had a haunted house in the French Quarter of New Orleans. They didn't bother each other, and she has figured it would be the same in her new home.

Just sensing the presence is fine until things begin to happen. Now the spirits are ganging up to make her life miserable.

Joe says to everybody, "Mais, it makes me wonder who dey was, when dey was on tha right side of tha dirt. Got to be some local people, ya t'ink? Merde! Who tha hell knows about dese haints! Ain't no tellin' where Gaspar comes from! Mais, dis t'ing is scarier dan Gaspar ever t'ought he was! Ah got to go back 'cause Minou says so. Damn it to hell!"

Madam Aucoin is showing some defiance now about what is taking place at her house.

"I refuse to let that gang of mean spirits chase me out of my home. They must have all been bullies when they were alive! The audacity of this bunch of spirits, thinking they would get the best of me! Let's go back to the house. Minou, you and Joe come with me and the bishop. We will make a huge effort to appease these things! After what they did to my roses, I want them gone!"

They go in Madam's Lincoln, and all walk into the house as the sun is going down on this day. They turn on every light in the large home. It is quiet in the house, and they all stand in silence too.

Madam Aucoin goes to prepare for her ritual, while the bishop fixes them Bacardi and Coke to sip on. They take seats in chairs that have been placed in a circle.

Madam Aucoin stands in the center of the living room where she can turn in a circle if the piano starts playing. She stands tall with her full regalia that tells she is indeed a queen of Voodoo. Her bright, mixed-color turban, with a floor-length skirt of deep purple gauze moves around her. Big sleeves on a silver blouse hang off her shoulders; her bare feet are on the cypress floors, with ankle bracelet bells keeping a jungle beat with everyone joining in, stomping their feet.

She goes to get pedicures and manicures every week and wears bright red on both her toes and fingernails long.

Madam Aucoin has both arms covered in bracelets of gold and jewels, and they jangle, adding to the sounds of bells.

Madam finds some ganja in a button box. She has a couple of stash places. She is blowing the smoke all around her, filling the room, getting everyone buzzed.

Madam Aucoin raises both arms to the sky and begins singing a mournful song in another language.

Minou's and Joe's arms are covered in goosebumps, and they watch as Madam goes into a trance, with her head hanging down toward the floor.

She raises her head. Minou and Joe see with their own eyes that it is another Voodoo queen that looks back at them.

Madam actually cackles like a bonafide witch and scares them something awful.

Bishop Toussaint is in the back of her, in his own trance.

This other queen cackles again and begins speaking in a Caribbean accent with broken English to Minou.

"Ahh, ahh, if it ain't de petite Minou! I watch you all de time! My name is Laurette. Ha! I been knowin' 'bout you, watched you for long time. My lovely Voodooess whose body I use for these ancient spells that are for very bad people and haints. They conjure me to come.

"Well, she sure loves you plenty like de seashells on my beach, and she's got to guard that, not let somethin' happen to you tonight. Let me start with my words to banish these spirits!"

Minou and Joe are both shaking their heads in agreement, nodding yes. They can't speak a single word.

Madam is staying in the circle that the bishop has drawn on the floor. He and Minou and Joe are in the circle too.

Laurette begins talking in a language neither one has heard before. They stand by the bishop, and Minou shakes him to tell her and Joe what the hell is going on.

He says quietly, "Laurette has come to our aid! She is the saint that deals with evil and vile pranksters alive or not, that cause harm wherever they are. We call them roux-garou because they run the roads and cause trouble everywhere! She is telling the spirits that they have no choice but to appear in front of her. No spirit can ignore this incantation. It's very powerful!"

Madam is still Laurette, shaking her arms up in the air and spitting all around as she twirls. She has a bottle of elixir that she takes a sip of, then spits it out with a force.

Minou asks Joe why she keeps sipping that stuff if she already knows it tastes like crap.

Well, something is being powerful as they watch the twisting gyrating Madam as she moves inside the circle. The living room fills up with a ghostly fog. They leave the lights off as Laurette tells them to, but the fog brings a dim light.

First, they hear the piano begin to play with a lively chord, and then they hear trumpets, trombones, and horns and drums! They see a ragtag group of ghosts that are playing an old jazz tune!

Bishop starts laughing and says, "I knew I heard horns New Year's Eve! No way was I playing that good."

The spirits can be barely seen, but the fog has thinned to where you can see an outline of the band playing their music. The ghost playing the piano is a large, older woman with clothes that look like they are from the early 1900s. She is a very white old lady, with the rest of the band being nothing but colored!

They all look like they come from the same time period. At the beginning of the Jazz Era, music that is well known today.

The fog dissipates, and the band is gone.

Madam is back, wondering what had been done with her body. She asks the bishop for a beverage and gulps the Cuba Libre straight down, asking for a refill. Must be Laurette is hanging on!

All of them have witnessed the ghosts put on a show. They are baffled by the whole thing. Madam Aucoin is furious, and she says, "We are not close to being finished with this! They were told to reveal themselves as to who they are! And still even with Laurette, they didn't do what they were told! That's almost impossible, but it's known to happen when there is no belief in Voodoo.

"I still need to know why they are so cruel to me and for them to tell me why such a ragtag bunch of colored people are here with this large white woman! They are acting like some damn jackasses! Almost like they were her slaves, and I know better than that!"

They all go back to Bertha's house, and Minou is planning something with her nosy self. She and Joe tell them all goodnight, and her little head is full of plans, pretty much like the pecans!

She and Joe slip off in the early morning before the older people wake and have their coffee. They arrive at Madam's and go in through the front door. Nothing is stirring, not even a mouse!

Minou is standing, with Joe sitting on the sofa, and she says, "Okay, all ya spirits up in here, listen up. Gotta tell me who y'all are! Ah mean, who's ya mama? Who's ya daddy? Can dey make a roux? Okay, Ah was just bein' funny.

"Y'all got tha Big Kahuna on ya asses! Y'all don't want Tourette comin' back with tha whole bunch of saints really t'rowin' all of ya to tha curb, do ya? Huh? Ya just keep up with ya bullshit and see what's gonna happen!! Ah ain't gonna quit botherin' ya 'til ya do!

"Now, come on. Who's tha lady dat plays tha piano? Ah can stay here all day 'cause y'all don't scare me no more. After playin' dat music, y'all ain't scary at all! Ah got ya number!"

Here appears the piano player in all of her finery. Her long hair is done up like a Gibson girl. Her glasses hang off her face with a gold chain. She has a full bosom with a tiny waist, an hour-glass figure. Being a ghost doesn't do her justice. She is much easier to see, and she says to Minou, "What family do YOU come from? HOW DARE YOU! This has been my home since my birth, and you come here telling me what I have to do in here! You levee rats! Tell me who your family is! Can they make a roux?

"I know that woman, Madam Aucoin, is from New Orleans, and it's forbidden to do what she does in my house! Tell me first, and then I'll see if I will tell you anything!"

Minou begins talking to the ghost, telling her about the family. She starts way back, telling the ghost about the loup-garous and about T-June with all his abilities.

She tells the ghost about Madam Aucoin and Bishop Toussaint, who have been so special and helpful with T-June. She explains why her son has such an extension of people who help with the raising of him. Minou tells her about the friendship of Estelle and that they have baby girls who were born on Christmas Eve.

She even tells the spirit about Sister Bridget, who insists T-June be called Joseph!

She tells her about Gaspar the not-so-friendly ghost and how they have been able to buy their homes and land with the money they got from his hidden treasure.

Minou is tired of talking, so she tells the ghost that it's her turn to tell who she is and what she is doing with the black musicians.

The ghost says to Minou, while she is wavering in the fog, "I'm tired of all this talking! I don't know if I believe all that you have told me. It's truly bizarre and hard to comprehend this tale. Why would you lie? A tale such as this one, you couldn't make this up! I will come back tomorrow and tell you what you want to know."

Minou pleads with the spirit to continue, but she disappears into that place she needs to hide in. Minou is saying loud, "Please tell me ya won't tear up Madam's house no more! Why did ya destroy all tha roses?"

The ghost doesn't speak anymore, so Minou and Joe leave to go back to their house. They are upset as to how it turned out and so very curious, to say the least.

At her mama's house, Minou begins to tell everybody what she and Joe have done. "Dis ghost is hell, way more worse dan Gaspar was! She said dat ya house has been her home since she was born in it. Ah told her all about tha family and T-June 'cause she asked me who Ah t'ought Ah was, demandin' all dis of her. She acted like she didn't believe me! She told us to come back tomorrow and she would tell us all what we wanna know.

"Ah don't know if Ah believe her! She did say dat Voodoo was forbidden in tha city and dat she doesn't want dis practice in her home. Mais, maybe in her white world!

"We got a lotta work ahead of us. Ah did ask her not to destroy nuttin' else in tha house. Ah don't know if she heard me."

Madam says she and Bishop Toussaint are going to the courthouse to look up all the records that show the previous owners. It may be helpful in some kind of way.

It's really hard to have to wait until tomorrow, so Minou finds herself on the way to see Estelle. Callie and Lily are so glad to see each other! They have begun to talk gibberish that only they can understand.

Minou and Estelle don't keep anything from each other, so Minou tells her about the ghosts who reside in Madam's house. Estelle has built-in belief in the supernatural because she has been taught to believe.

Big Mama is listening to the talk and begins to make the sign of the cross over her bosom. She is doing fine since her healing. Big Mama seems to know a lot about hauntings and wants to put her two cents of what she knows in the mix.

"I was a lil gal when I would go with my grandmama to houses that had spirits and try to help the people living with them. She was what your people call a traiteur, but we call it HooDoo. She did a little healing, but for sure not like Joseph does! She could communicate with the dead.

"That house always had rich folk living there, so we didn't go to that side of town. We stayed where we belonged. Not like it is today, thank the good Lord.

"My grandmama would listen to her friends who worked as maids and cooks on that side of town.

They would all tell her that the house was haunted, but my grandmama was never called to come over there. She helped many of our people. She had a boarding house and she got put in the Green Book. That book was a map of where we could stay on the road when we were traveling, to be safe from all the nasty people that lived in the South.

"My child, you lucked out with that old pirate. Most haints ain't that easy to let go and move on."

Estelle begins to tell them about her grandpa from a century ago. She grew up in New Orleans and knew a lot of history. "Let me tell you this! My grandpa from a long time ago was one of the black men who started the jazz music. They used to play jazz in all the Storyville houses of ill repute, and they were legal in that part of the Quarter.

"Girl! Won't that be something if my grandpa is one of the ghosts? My little sista, I want to go with you, and so does Big Mama! She's always wanted to see the inside of that house. I already told her I would take her over there the next time I go. Well, if this ain't the perfect timing, I don't know what would be."

Minou goes home to tell Joe about what's transpired at Estelle's. He is more than happy to let them take his place. He doesn't want to miss the fishing trip he is going on with Alcide and Theo.

He doesn't like ghosts, and he tells them that. "Ah just went wit' ya 'cause Ah'm ya husband, and Ah have to watch all tha merde ya get in! Ah'm glad 'bout Gaspar 'cause we got a lot of money, but Ah'm not brave when it comes to a bunch of ghosts not wantin' to go!"

Madam says that she isn't going with them. She doesn't want to try with her Voodoo ceremony again and that maybe the three local women can communicate where she can't seem to.

They get to Madam's house, where the sun is shining brightly through the large windows and everything is picture perfect. Big Mama is looking in every room and loves the antique furniture that has been left in the house. She thinks, Lawd, if that sofa could talk!

Soon, a fog begins to twirl around their bodies, and the female ghost appears.

"What are you doing bringing in these women when I told you, just you! Now I have to know who they are! Start talking again, you little instigator, and don't tell me another one of your crazy tales!"

Minou thinks she must have been a boss when she was alive. She sure is bossy as a ghost!

Estelle and Big Mama begin to talk, unafraid of the spirits, to explain the reasons for why they are there, talking to the air because the ghost has left again.

All three are sitting on the sofa, waiting for the ghostly boss to reappear. The white woman ghost begins to form a scene with all of the other musicians joining her to play a well-known tune, The Axman's Revelry. It's said there was a killer loose in the Quarter who would take his ax and chop up people in their sleep. He wrote a message to The Times-Picayune paper saying he wouldn't visit the homes playing jazz. Every citizen of the Big Easy was playing jazz the night he said he would come.

The three women begin to laugh and clap to the jazzy tune and marvel at the sight of these long-dead people who have formed this band from the hereafter. Estelle and Big Mama start dancing to the music, and it makes the motley crew play another one.

To their surprise, all of the spirits are standing around the piano, clear as day, waiting to talk after the boss says her piece. The main spirit says, "I was as honest as I could be when I lived. I will allow you to ask who I am and why I am still here. If something else comes up, well, consider it lagniappe.

"You are the curious type and can be very devious in getting your way. It takes one to know one!

"I am Madam Consienne. I was raised in this house, and it came to me when my loving parents both died in a hurricane on Last Isle off the coast of Grand Isle and left me in the care of my grandfather. We lived in his home in New Orleans but came here for the summers.

"I was a young woman who loved being around the Quarter. I would have to slip away from the prying servants who would tell my grandfather everything, so they could get me into trouble. They were what we called uppity and didn't approve of the way I was leaning. "I don't have much energy left so I have to leave." She and the whole crew of ghosts just puff away.

"What tha hell just happened? Ah guess she t'inks Ah can come here every day and wait on her ghostly ass to finish tha story!" Minou says angrily to Estelle and Big Mama.

They leave Madam's house to go tell her what little bit they have gotten out of Madam Consienne.

Madam Aucoin wants some answers now. This ghostly matron is running the show! "The bishop and I found out there were three generations of Consiennes living in our house. Mrs. Bourgeois was the last living relative to stay there. I really don't think it is her that is haunting the place. She went straight to heaven!

"I want to go back to our home and make the spirits leave! If she hadn't been so evil to me, I could have put up with some haunting. But not now. I am going to call the whole Church of Divine Spirits down here, and then you will see what we are capable of!"

Minou asks that, before she calls on reinforcements, she let her try again to get the whole story from the crew of spirits.

She goes back to the haunted house with Estelle and Big Mama to attempt another conversation with Madam Consienne and the band.

The three women are calm and eager to hear from the rest of the ghosts playing with Madam Consienne. Minou yells out, "Listen up, all ya haints! Madam Aucoin is callin' tha whole congregation of dose holy rollers to come, and dey will make all of ya go into tha hereafter! Ah want tha rest of ya stories so maybe we can stop dis before it's too late! Laurette will appear again and finish what she started. So start talkin'!"

A flowing white fog begins to gather around the three women, and Madam Consienne and the band start playing music again. Minou tells the group to stop playing and start the story that is hidden now before it's too late!

Madam C continues to sit at the piano, gathering electric strength to be able to speak.

"I learned to play piano at an early age with a teacher of remarkable talent. I was being trained to become a concert pianist. I began to fall in love with the teacher, who was what you call a mulatto. I saw how hopeless this would be, so I went to a famous Voodoo woman. She was a granddaughter of Marie Laveau, and her potions were guaranteed to work.

"I waited on the night that would bring us together to elope. He never came. That is why I don't want any practice of Voodoo around me.

"This is during the time I became unmanageable for my grandfather and ran away permanently to the seedy part of the Quarter. I became a well-known whore for the biggest house in Storyville. I was smart with the business side and had money. I bought the whorehouse and became the madam of this very lucrative house.

"It was then when I first heard the music of jazz. We began to play together as a band that had standing room only in the house, men forgetting what they had come for.

"I repaired the distance between my grandfather and me. He never knew that I was a madam of a whorehouse! Therefore, I became very wealthy when he passed. I sold his home and the house of ill repute and moved to this home in the country.

"I never forgot the band or my true love. Still waiting for him to come right until I passed on at the age of eighty.

"I have to let the gentlemen in the band continue with the tale. I am losing strength again." Madam Consienne disappears while the band stays.

The ghost who plays the sax comes forward, gathering the power he needs to speak. "I was known as Buddy Braxton, and I played a mean sax. I became well known in the Quarter. Back then they called us Creole.

Buddy Braxton sees Estelle Theriot and recognizes her as belonging to his people. She looks exactly like his beloved wife, Shine. "Oh, my sweet Jesus! Estelle, you are a granddaughter many times over through your mama's people. You kin to the madam who lives here, but it's on the other side. It's so crazy cool to meet you! This is such an unbelievable happenin'! I wish I could hug you 'cause you are a fine lookin' woman from the Big Easy!"

The other members of the band start whistling at her but have nothing to say except that Madam C has called them in the spirit world to join her here.

Estelle and Big Mama start laughing and clapping.

Madam C reappears. "I want to speak with the witch who lives here. She is growing my roses with some kind of magic! I've seen her whispering to the roses and singing strange music too! I planted all of them. The long-stemmed ones came all the way from Texas! They never looked like that when I was growing them! It has to be with potions!"

The ghosts all agree they did enjoy the New Year's Eve party. The band of spirits joined in, playing I'm Walkin' to New Orleans, with the bishop and Alcide belting out the tune. Everybody was so pie-eyed that night, they thought it was them putting on the great concert except for the bishop.

Madam Consienne demands that Minou bring the witches back and, to Minou's great concern, the boy.

Minou has never told T-June about the serious confrontation at Madam and the bishop's home.

"What tha hell. He might do better dan any of us! Dere's got to be at least one of his abilities dat he could use!" Minou says after telling Madam Aucoin and the bishop that they have been summoned to their own damn house!

Madam Aucoin, in a fury, wants everybody to get in the cars so she can straighten out this insanely mad spirit. She already has the church congregation coming Sunday morning on two Greyhound buses!

T-June agrees to go, but not without Jolie, Minou and Joe, Madam Aucoin, Bishop Toussaint, Estelle Theriot, and Big Mama Theriot. A group of GhostBusters!

Madam Aucoin stands in her living room while everyone else sits on the sofas and high-back antique chairs. She calls out in a determined voice to the air that surrounds them, "Come forth, you hateful woman! I will call you Madam because you were notorious as one! You in the history books! You got some nerve, turning your nose up at me! You will listen to what I have to say!

"First of all, my roses grew with much care from me, no potion or whatever you thought I used. I bought the best of what is called fertilizer to feed them. I watered every day, and I did sing to them because it's been proven that plants respond to human voices!"

Madam Aucoin loves to sing Dr. John's music, along with Irma Thomas and of course, Fats Domino.

"The roses are my pride and joy, winning contests because of hard work, not because of Voodoo! How jealous you must be, and vengeance is what you used to hurt me so badly. I command you to not touch my roses again!

"The second thing you are upset with is the fact that your man didn't come and the Voodoo didn't work. I can do this for you. I have a crystal ball that is used for such occasions, like telling the future or going back into the past. We will use the ball to see if we can find out what happened with your man.

"Do you want to try? This is your last chance because, when my congregation gets here, you will have no choice but to leave my home!"

Madam Consienne becomes visible, and she appears to everybody there. Madam Aucoin has a black velvet bag from which she pulls out this beautiful clear ball and puts it on a small table in the living room. She and the ghost stand together, looking into the crystal ball.

"I will ask the question of what happened to this man in your past. What's his name?"

The spirit replies, "My beloved was Emile Verdun. He was known for his knowledge of the piano. He could have been a famous pianist if he hadn't been a mulatto."

The ball clouds up and reveals a scene that horrifies everyone in the room. It is a murder, showing two men with Madam Consienne's grandfather killing Emile Verdun with a beating and a shotgun! The murder scene has everybody upset because it is so vivid, showing the blood leaving his body while the three men laugh and kick him.

The ghost screams her ungodly howl and begins to waver in her appearance and disappears. Everyone has the frissons, making their bodies develop huge goosebumps up and down their arms. They sit in silence waiting for the spirit to reappear.

Madam Consienne reappears to the group and is still moaning over what has transpired in the mists of the ball. "I have never thought that the reason why he didn't come was because my grandfather had him murdered. I feel remorse over what I have caused. I know now that the Voodoo did indeed work.

"Please don't use your powers to make us leave! We are happy here. I will never do anything again to make you uncomfortable in this home you call your own.

"Now, will you present the boy? Buddy Braxton has something to say to him."

She has melted away while the sax player has appeared and starts smiling. He smiles a toothy grin when T-June comes to stand in front of him.

"Well, if it isn't the famous kid that lives on the bayou! We know that you have powers, lil dude. And I am so proud that you love the beautiful Jolie. I have somethin' to give you. "

The ghost reaches into the pocket of his shirt and presents a ring of tiny emeralds that covers the gold band. Buddy hands the ring to T-June and tells him, "This belonged to my wife, my true love, Shine. I want you to give this to Jolie as an engagement ring when the time comes. And it's comin' down the road. I already know this is to happen. We gonna be here for the occasion if Madam Aucoin and Bishop Toussaint allow us to stay."

∞ ∞ ∞

THE congregation shows up, but instead of what they've come for, Madam and the bishop throw a huge housewarming party, with large amounts of shrimp and crab gumbo. The food is shared with all the people who come in off the big Greyhound buses.

Men with shiny color suits and matching shoes, some have taps on their shoes. They have gigs, as they call their work, playing in the Quarter for tourists. Real good money.

The ladies are wearing huge hats that for sure match their dresses and high-heeled shoes, and lots and lots of jewelry!

They take their church seriously, with the congregation all falling out on the floor! They all carry elaborate fans to fan each other when they keel over in the spirit.

Minou has to go at least one time. You know why! She and Bertha really enjoy the service and watching people fall out like they having epileptic fits!

Alcide and Joe said they are going to smoke, but they never come back in. Just too much for them. It isn't what the family does when they go to Mass!

The party that they throw is the talk of the town of Larose. The news goes all the way to Golden Meadow. Sure enough, they are some party crashers, but nobody cares, and they have some food too.

The band of musicians, worldly and otherworldly, with the bishop playing and everyone singing, can be heard for miles. Aaron Neville shows up and plays, bringing a box full of his records to hand out.

So, to get back to the story…

The ring is shown to Jolie, and she puts the beautiful ring on her finger. Then it is put up by Minou for safekeeping.

∞ ∞ ∞

TIME has passed, and the home is very quiet these days. The two madams are sharing the care of the roses that will win in the next competition. The two are also working together also to find Emile Verdun and to call him to share the hereafter with Madam Consienne.

Madam the ghost and Madam the living both sing to the tunes of Irma Thomas.

"Time is on our side. Yes, it is."

Chapter Ten

The Cousins

MINOU talks with Estelle, if she doesn't see her, every day. How nice it is for the two of them, being like sisters to share such a friendship.

Minou has never had a close female friend before, but Estelle is so vibrant and funny and down to earth with her good common sense, Minou can't resist. There's something about those Theriot women!

Joseph is now in the seventh grade with Sister Bridget and Jolie, still inseparable and still talking with Sister in her mind.

Sister has definitely earned her spot in the family, the tribe, the posse, and for sure the village, and she's ready to walk in the desert for Joseph.

Butch and Katrina are in their second year of the college they both choose to go to, Nicholls State University. Butch is studying for his history degree, and Katrina is getting her degree in psychology. They make the dean's list every semester.

They have been together since the day they met. They are planning a wedding to take place in the summer. They live together, so they might as well. It also saves the families a lot of money. Two for the price of one!

They are good Catholics and attend Mass every Sunday, but they must be saving confession for a closer time to the wedding so they can confess just one time that they have been living in sin.

Irene, Butch's mama, spends quite a bit on the couple. She spares no expense on the two that she loves deeply.

Irene has finally found another daddy to replace Butch's papa that died tragically in the Gulf. She and Jean Breaux tie the knot when

Butch is a senior in high school. There is a huge wedding at Madam Aucoin's house, where the best music plays with extra help.

They buy one of the Cajun cottages that Minou and Joe have been renting out. Jean is a widower too, but he has no children. He loves being Butch's papa, and Butch stays with them quite often.

Monsieur Jean and Madam Irene have a life-livin' love, even though it has taken a while before they could find each other. At the right time.

Irene and Jean are having a late-in-life baby, her being all of thirty-seven and him forty-five.

Butch and Katrina are so happy for them, knowing their children will grow up with their nonc or tante!

Minou and Estelle and Irene are busy making plans for a huge wedding when Estelle brings a new set of problems for the women to work on that will not be easy to fix.

The little cousins that have come to live with the Theriots as small boys have now grown to be two militants that hate almost everything. Mohammed and Malcolm are their names, as Estelle's sister wanted names that would stand out. They surely do.

When they come to Estelle's family, they are such good little boys, two little chocolates, with their mama's eyes and their daddy's good hair. Now, they are belligerent and very defensive young teens who are mad as hell at the world, militant teens that have read all the books their namesakes have written. Now they're using these important words, all twisted around to fit their means.

You get the picture! But rightly so, any way you look at it.

Estelle and Theo are very concerned as to how this could happen. The whole family has spoiled them and loved them, and now the two can barely be talked to without causing grief. Sassy mouths both of them and their friends, who they smoke pot with, have caused Theo to be in a bitchy mood most days.

What else can you call it?

Estelle's sister was named Maybelline, and the boys' father was Laray. Their love is legendary in every neighborhood in the streets of New Orleans. There's a song sung in the Quarter all the way to

Esplanade! There's also a book that sells at Madam Aucoin's Voodoo shop.

All the money made off the music and book is being given to Laray Laverne while he rots in the New Orleans parish jail on death row for capital murder. He is guilty of shooting his common-law wife, Maybelline, in the heart in the kitchen while the toddlers are eating their Lucky Charms.

His people get the money, and they're sure not worried about the two little orphans.

∞ ∞ ∞

LARAY Laverne is unsavory, strutting his stuff, a man that's just oozing charm along with hate, earning his living doing illegal things that have him in and out of jail.

He finds Maybelline on the wrong street for him as he is far from being accepted in her neighborhood. He seduces her early, and she is pregnant with her first son in six months' time.

They are wed in St. Luke's Church of the Gospel, and Bishop Toussaint marries the two but not wanting to.

He moves her into the rundown shotgun house his parents have rented for decades in the Ninth Ward of the Big Easy. Laray puts her down without mercy in front of his mama and pop.

Laray is extremely jealous, and many times Maybelline appears with bruises and blackened eyes because he always thinks she is being unfaithful. Of course, he isn't being faithful, but that doesn't matter to chauvinist men.

At times she will wind up in Charity Hospital because of the beatings she takes. She has to have him, regardless of the other hearts she is breaking. She has to have him.

Maybelline believes in standing by her man. She loves Laray so much that he is the only thing that matters. She doesn't think about the boys and how unsafe they are, being raised by this hateful man. All that she can do is think about Laray and being with him, a more twisted kind of love that destroys everything that gets in its way.

To have to stand by and watch this tragedy unfold has Estelle walking the floors day and night, so worried for her baby sister and the babies. The family has always thought that Maybelline would wind up in prison behind Laray's doings, never about her being shot dead along with her baby girl.

Maybelline finally calls her parents to rescue, and his mama tells her, "Ya fuckin', spoiled bitch! Just 'cause tha toilet don't work right!"

Her parents have a little rent house that they give Maybelline, and there's where she dies on her clean floor.

On the morning he kills her dead, because of his insane and drug-induced mind filled with jealousy, he has just gotten home from the night before. He has been out tomcatting himself. He stinks so bad, Maybelline is ready to throw up her breakfast. She is pregnant again.

He shoots her with an illegal sawed-off shotgun that splatters her all over the kitchen along with the babies, while the boys are eating their cereal. Neither one of the boys can stomach to look at another cereal box of Lucky Charms because it sure hasn't brought them any luck.

∞ ∞ ∞

THERE are heavy fights between the Theriots and Laray's people. The Lavernes get that money every month; they waste it on booze and drugs, but they pay a heavy-hitter lawyer who represents the bonafide bad-asses! The attorney knows his clients are horrific but represents them because he makes plenty of money off the sleazy bastards because the lawyer does his job way too well and turns back out the criminal on the streets to horrify people again.

There is no way he is gonna get turned back on the streets, Laray Laverne. He gets life with no parole; best the lawyer could do.

In court, Mr. and Mrs. Laverne, his parents, are given custody of the boys, but Maybelline's family cuts up so bad and Estelle can prove what her sister's request is on a small piece of paper. They are brought to Estelle and Theo because Maybelline has said Estelle should be the one to raise them if anything ever happens.

Still the bought judge (ya think?) gives them every other weekend.

Estelle gives thanks every night for the two little boys that are hers and is relieved knowing Maybelline is in a much safer place, even though it has to take Maybelline's death to do so.

This has been a difficult time in the family, with everyone trying to help the young boys put this horrible scene behind them. So much love is given by the whole family, Theo feels they are his two sons and raises them up like Maybelline would be proud of.

They never talk about it to the boys unless one asks a question, and it is answered in a simple way.

The couple try in this fashion because it is the best way, the truth that small children can handle.

Everybody calls the two Mac and Moe because they didn't want controversy over their given names.

Estelle and Theo are being badgered by Laray's parents. They are to be allowed unsupervised visitations every other weekend.

The boys go to New Orleans every other Friday and come back so unmanageable, so hyped up with all the sugar they have been given, smart mouthed and unruly. It takes a week to settle them down, and then it's the same thing over again.

∞ ∞ ∞

THIS goes on for many years, and Estelle wants to take them back to court to try and stop the previous decision. It is not a good thing, causing the boys to be so confused about the whole thing.

One morning real early, Estelle comes to Minou's house and is so mad and cussing and crying with what she has been told this morning. Theo is in the Gulf, and she needs to talk about this serious matter.

"I have just found out that Moe and Mac have been visiting their nogood, son-of-a-bitch father in prison! Mac has told me it's been going on for years. He talks of his sperm donor being a cool dude! I can't believe this has been happening since the boys were made by the court to see their grandparents.

"I called the Lavernes this morning, and they told me it was none of my business what they do when the boys are over there!

"I have filed for another court date with a better lawyer to stop the visitations with these awful people! I know now why the boys are so unmanageable when they return from these visits. No telling what they have been told, and it seems like they believe all of their goddamn shit!

"I slapped Moe in his mouth this morning after he told me his mama deserved it!

"Minou, we don't know what to do, and it's only getting worse!"

Minou is doing her best to help Estelle while she sits and cries about the injustice that has taken place with her two nephews. She is horrified in learning that their gangster father has had influence with the upbringing of the two. She has deceived and is thinking that what her family has done in their raising of Mohammed and Macolm has been totally undone.

The friends are left with a dilemma that neither has had to deal with before. The feeling of helplessness is not a good spot to be in.

While Minou and Estelle are saying their goodbyes, the phone rings, and Minou answers the phone and hands it to Estelle.

On top of that conversation, Callie and Lily are throwing fits because neither of them is ready to say goodbye! So, Estelle is having a hard time hearing the voice on the line.

Minou picks up the terrible twosome and deposits them back in Callie's room, where they resume a game as if no time has passed since they have been playing.

Estelle is standing holding the phone in her hands. "Sista, that was the sheriff's office! That was the sheriff, Gerard Truxillo! He has both boys in custody and told me it's because he knows who we are and who they were raised by, that he found me here to go up to the police station to talk with him. The men are all on the fishing boats!"

Minou calls Bertha to come watch the girls while they go to the jailhouse to see what can be done.

Sheriff Gerard Truxillo is in his office waiting on Estelle and seems pleased to see Minou is with her friend. He knows the two families are honest, hardworking people who have never broken any law in his parish. Boy, if he only knew about the laws being broken every day!

Sheriff Truxillo, of Mexican descent, is third-generation law enforcement. His great-great-grandfather had been the sheriff of El Paso, Texas, back in the days when the law was hard to find. He shot three of a posse that came to rob the bank. By himself.

So it tells you what kind of man sits in front of the two women. He begins to tell them in the way any law enforcement would, "Mohammed and Malcolm were caught in the act of destroying property and defacing the side of a federal building. These are serious crimes being brought against these juveniles, just barely. Another year would have had them convicted as adults. It's not good, ladies. They smashed a water fountain on the courthouse lawn that's been there since the Civil War. They wrote graffiti on the side wall of the courthouse building. They wrote 'Black Power' and 'Down with Whitey' in big black paint letters."

Minou and Estelle both say, "Shit!" and "Dammit to hell!" together, and the sheriff points to a sign that says No Profanity!

"I will allow both of you to see them, but that's it. You can talk to them, but they will spend the night in jail. If y'all's men are out in the Gulf, I suggest that you call them in.

"I will talk to you tomorrow."

Estelle and Minou are led to the back of the station where the two delinquents stand in their cells with their fists in the air, hollering Power to the People!

Estelle gets so mad she tells them they could keep their little asses in jail! And they better be glad she can't put her hands on them!

∞ ∞ ∞

JOE and Alcide and Theo now fish together, and with two boats working, they have been able to open a seafood business. They are now partners and podnahs!

It doesn't take but a phone call to have them coming home. Where one goes, the other two follow.

Estelle begins talking to Theo as they dock the boat.

Minou and Bertha are waiting too. Callie and Lily, both at the same time, go running to jump in their papas' waiting arms.

Estelle is crying, telling him what has transpired with the cousins and what Moe has revealed.

"Theo, I filed papers to take those evil, good-for-nothin' Lavernes back to court, and then this stuff happened! Hellfire! They will countersue us for allowing this to happen!

"Wait 'til I tell you what the lil bastards did when we were allowed to see them! They both raised one arm up, shouting 'Black Power' and 'Power to the People!' I didn't have anything to say after that, made me want to grab both of them by their necks and squeeze some fear into them. I told them they could keep their asses in the cell! They still in jail, and the sheriff suggests that we get a lawyer!"

Theo is furious! He is a calm man with quick wit, and this is a different side never shown, but still calm with quiet fury.

All of them are shocked and serious. Alcide and Joe tell Estelle and Theo that they will have all the help they need.

Minou goes to call Madam Aucoin and Bishop Toussaint to come right away. After all, Estelle and Madam are family; they are kin. The bishop has a program through the Divine Spirit Church that helps troubled teens. Madam has got one of her potions or spells to use on the boys, Minou is sure! One spell has sure caused Joe's mama, Ethel, to be crazy in love with Minou! There's got to be something to use, like calling on Laurette to scare the bejesus out of them!

Minou calls Flavia too. She might have some pull.

Madam and the bishop arrive in the old turquoise Cadillac as soon as possible. Everyone but the Sister and Father are there at Minou's house. They're gonna hear about it and come anyway.

Bertha is cooking a big meatball spaghetti, and Big Mama is making banana pudding. She always knows where she is needed. She's the best cook out of all those women in the family, tribe, posse, or village.

Since Big Mama has come, they do each other's recipes. There's been a lot of different soul cooking in both homes because the Cajuns put their souls in everything they cook.

They want to take a vote on what they need to call themselves. Maybe just "Disciples" since they all are following St. Joseph (AKA T-June) down his little lane of true mayhem!

Bishop Toussaint takes control of the meeting of all the different minds going from nine to ninety.

"Theo and Estelle, let me tell you I have dealt with many Black teenagers incarcerated in bad conditions. Some were charged with murder. So, I know about the legalities and what they can charge a juvenile with or not. I will be with you two for the duration, and I will be there to help you through the paperwork.

"This is Madam's and my vocations. This is what we do. We have helped many, many people throughout our lives. This is what brought us here to the Bayou Lafourche. To help Minou with her and Joe's super-extraordinary child we call T-June. Bertha and Madam are lagniappe, their deep friendship.

"We soon realized how much we are needed here. We bought a home and retired to Bayou Lafourche like y'all all know. You are our chosen people, and we love you better than some of our children.

"My suggestion would be to leave those boys in that nice clean jail cell for two more days. Let's see how long it takes them to not want to follow in Laray's footsteps! Maybe they will see how good they have been treated and well taken care of.

"I've had my own dealings with Laray. Some were real bad news for a lot of people. He and Maybelline are infamous in the city, and I was the first person called to see her and the infant. I will cry every time I hear that song, and if I can, I'll turn the song off. I never will read the book! All the money that's been made on their tragic lives, but that's some people for you. Greedy and no scruples!

"That's something else you have been cheated out of. Money, that's what. Not one cent have you been given for the raising of these two wannabee gangstas!"

All the men were in agreement about letting them stay locked up. Minou and Estelle and Bertha are saying, Poor babies, Poor bébés!

Madam agrees with the men, along with Flavia.

Flavia says, "Let deir lil asses stay dere for five days! Dat's what Ah did to bot' of my boys! Well, maybe dat's why dey don't like me dat much. But Ah know tha right people to get in touch wit' for dis kind of t'ing. Ah'm callin' in favors."

Theo and Joe and Alcide and of course Bishop Toussaint go to the jail together, after three nights and days. The women are told to stay home; this is the business of men.

They don't want to go. That's why you don't hear any talking back from them!

Bishop Toussaint speaks with the sheriff, and Theo is standing on his side. The documents are drawn up to release both the boys into Theo and the bishop's custody. One call to New Orleans and the sheriff knows all about the bishop. Theo's high standing in the community is more than favorable to release the two on his good name.

They will have a court date to deal with the charges.

The local judge also calls to find out about the case. Oh, hell, yes! Flavia is as good as she said. In Louisiana, politicians always scratch each other's backs.

They drive home without a word being said. Everybody gathers at the Theriots' home to see Moe and Mac after being in jail.

The group is still divided on how to treat them, like little boys or the men they think they are.

Theo is sitting across from the juvenile delinquents. That's what he sees! He's in a position of having one knee on the floor and the other knee ready to pounce if he has to slap one of them.

"How long have you been going to see your father? I cannot believe this is the first time we have heard this, after all the years you have been with us! That's damn deceitful, and we didn't teach you that! If you can't be honest, well, not much use for a man who can't be believed or trusted.

"I have a hard time believing this crap! I just want to do bodily harm to both of you. Right now you better start talking! I want to know everything that poor excuse of a man has told you."

Mac is sitting, crying, and holding his head down. He has gotten a slap across his mouth from Estelle not that many days ago. He is feeling ashamed.

Moe is the elder, so he begins talking while the tears are flowing down his dirty face. "He's told us a lot of stuff for years. My grandparents and him told us never to say anything to y'all. Said we wouldn't be able to come back to their house if we did. She lets us eat anything we want and doesn't care what we watch on TV. No rules over there. They drink a lot of booze too. And they smoke pot. The house smells bad with empty bottles and the nasty smell because she doesn't keep her house clean like you do, Aunt Stelle.

"I'm gonna tell you what he said about you, Uncle Theo. Please don't get mad at me! He said that you are a pussy and that Aunt Stelle rules this house. Got some piss-ass job catching fish for a living. What kind of money is that, he said. Said that Aunt Stelle just makes believe that she is a Catholic but still does her Voodoo. He said he remembers her when she was wild."

Theo is icy calm and tells Mohammed to stop talking for a little while. He goes outside, and the other men follow. They take sips of cherry bounce and lighting cigarettes one after the other. Alcide steadily smokes his pipe that is clenched in his mouth.

Malcolm speaks up and begins to tell them more of the crap the boys have been told. "He told us how bad our mama was, and he killed her because she was running around on him. That baby wasn't his, he said. Told us she deserved it and our grandparents would tell us the same thing. We would come back home so confused and fearful that y'all would find out.

Y'all have never talked about them, but that's all we heard. They always talk bad about you.

"Aunt Stelle, I am so sorry about what I said. I deserved being slapped. That's not what I remembered about my mama. She loved us and was good to us. We still miss her but didn't tell that to them because they would get mad and start fussing us. They even told me that they weren't sure if I was Laray's child either. How terrible was that!

"Please, we've been so confused, and Laray encouraged us to go out and fight the system. I don't want to go back there because they wanted us to do bad things. We got in trouble and were listening to the wrong people. Now we will probably end up in jail, just like him!"

Both of these boys are frightened now and turn back into children that need comfort.

Theo isn't having any sympathy toward the boys and tells them, "You two acted like you were grown and caused much hurt to this family. We will stand by you through this serious business, but I have to have complete honesty from now on.

"You will be the ones to clean up and paint over the courthouse and repair the drinking fountain you destroyed. That will show you are trying to do the right thing, and maybe that will go better when you stand in front of the judge.

"But now, you will go pack because you will come out on the boat tomorrow morning. We are going to find out if this is a pussy job."

They go the next morning to work on the boat with Alcide and Joe and Theo. The men work them like they are truly grown up, not the kids they really are. Moe and Mac dare not complain of blisters on their hands and the exhaustion they feel when the day's work is over.

They go to bed in their filthy clothes because they are so exhausted from the day of hard labor. Theo feels it isn't his place to tell them to go take a bath!

One night Theo and Alcide and Joe offer them some straight Jack Daniels over some ice, and they gag and cough, and they feel like part of the crew. It lightens the atmosphere on the boat.

The boat stays out there for five days, and when they dock the boat, both are so glad to see everybody waiting on the crew.

First thing they do is run to the shower in the bathroom, and both jump in together! They sure don't want to wind up in showers with a bunch of perverts, they tell each other.

They sleep the whole day and wake up to gumbo full of shrimp, with everybody talking at the same time. Nobody is talking about what has happened; they're not a family to dwell on the bad. They take care of what's needed, solve the problem, and move on with the whole family as joyful as it ever has been.

Now, it's Bishop Toussaint's turn to try and save the boys from a life of crime.

He brings them to New Orleans to his large building holding everything boys need when they are on probation or parole. The building is a converted warehouse, and it houses twenty boys to live there and go to school and to settle criminal issues.

Madam Aucoin has her own building for the girls that find themselves in trouble, either for breaking the law or having a baby.

Bishop brings Mac and Moe to talk with other boys who are waiting on court dates or have already spent time behind bars. This is a rude awakening for them. They are both still in school and wanting to quit because Laray has told them school was for sissies. What an ignorant dumbass!

The bishop begins history lessons, telling them about injustices and cruelty by the White people that have made their people feel inferior for centuries. He tells them about all the courageous men and women that did stand up for their rights to be accepted as equals. Bishop tells them that these people who are in the history books now, who struggled hard but achieved their goals. Not by being vandals, he says.

Too many young people in jail have had no guidance or the love Moe and Mac have known in their lives. Bishop asks them, "Do you still think that your Uncle Theo has a lame job? Do you now know how hard he works to provide for all of you? Have you seen anything that would cause you to think that your aunt is practicing Voodoo? They both provided for you to have everything you needed or wanted. What have Laray and his parents ever given to you, besides making liars and little hoodlums out of you?"

Hell, no, they both answer concerning Uncle Theo's livelihood. Both agree they have never seen their Aunt Stelle do anything but get them up to attend Mass and try to teach them the right way.

Moe speaks up, "I remember Aunt Stelle cleaning my ears so good they got whiter! Saying our prayers with us every night. We feel safe and loved. I don't remember them Lavernes ever doing that with us."

Madam Aucoin begins to tell them about the ancient beliefs their ancestors practiced before coming across the oceans to be slaves. These beliefs are intertwined with other religions they had been made to practice, but they wanted to worship their own. The fact that it was forbidden by the slave owners, because they feared rebellions that it would cause, left the people to do it secretly.

Voodoo was feared and forbidden, though potions and elixirs and doing spells were delivered to many through backstairs where the wealthy White women were waiting.

Still like that today.

Aunt Stelle has chosen Catholicism over Voodoo, but it isn't because that ancient religion has taught her bad things. Laray has chosen crime over any belief system that would have made him a better man.

Moe and Mac are working to remedy some of the trouble they've put themselves in. They work every day, even the weekends, so they don't return to the house of Laray's parents.

Their grandparents call, and the boys refuse to talk with them.

Estelle talks with them, telling them about the trouble they have caused and says the boys will never go back again to see their father in jail. She says, "Go ahead. Take me to court! You're gonna find out what kind of people we know, to see if you ever see those boys again!

"Don't threaten me with your no-good son. What the hell is he gonna do, being locked up for the rest of his miserable life? I don't know who the hell raised you two. Poor home training all around your family! Don't call here ever again!'"

∞ ∞ ∞

MONTHS have passed as Mohammed and Malcolm continue working on restoring all they have destroyed. They are put on probation for two years with supervision from the bishop and Theo. A stipulation is added to make certain they will not hear from Laray again.

Moe and Mac do such a good job painting that the parish hires them to paint the whole courthouse! They are treated well by the people who arrested them, like they are trying to help wayward little brothers.

Bringing home paychecks makes the boys feel like they are contributing to the household. They give Estelle their money to put up for them. They will finish their schooling and maybe go to college.

Everything is calm again in the family for eight months until Theo gets a phone call from Sheriff Truxillo.

"Theo, this phone call is a very hard one to make, but it is also a very urgent one. We just got word from the Orleans Parish jail that Laray escaped this morning. He told a prison buddy that he was coming here to straighten out a bunch of people. That no one is going to keep him from seeing his boys.

"He's been spewing nothing but evil since the boys quit visiting him. All the other prisoners are backing away from him. But someone helped him.

"He also said that he would kill you and Estelle. The state troopers and the FBI both have men on the ground looking for him.

"Please, y'all stay indoors and lock up everything. Or take your family somewhere else until this is over. Leave the hunting for him to all the lawmen who are searching for him. "

That is like telling Theo nothing, because Theo calls Alcide, Joe, and the Bishop. All four know about hunting.

Estelle and her family go to Minou's to stay because Laray knows where the Theriots live. The boys are with them. That's who they want to protect.

Minou and Bertha and Madam and Estelle and Big Mama all have loaded 35s. Flavia closes the store and comes with a loaded shotgun.

Theo's papa wants a gun too, but Big Mama refuses to give him one. His eyesight is terrible, and he would be shooting somebody else!

Minou goes to tell T-June and Jolie about what is happening.

"T-June, Mama is gonna ask ya to go to tha swamps and talk to all tha animals, for sure ya friend Pieyan. Tell dem to be on tha lookout for dis bastard 'cause he's gonna have to come t'rough our swamps to stay hidden. Baby, y'all go now while it's still light."

T-June and Jolie both go to the swamps where he finds all of his furry little friends and tells them a bad man may be coming their way. He asks if they will give some kind of warning, like when Pieyan comes upon them. Scream out in their animal voices, and T-June will hear them.

June takes Jolie to the back of the swamp where the Bigfoot lives. He calls out for Pieyan, but Bigfoot doesn't respond.

Pieyan hears what T-June has said from behind some trees. He thinks it's because he has brought Jolie. She has never met Pieyan.

They are coming out from the back swamp to reach the clearing where they can sit and drink their RCs. That's when they hear all the noise animals can make when they are fearful and upset about a disturbance in their home.

T-June and Jolie walk up on the convict, standing and scratching his whole body from the piss-offed mosquitos and other flying insects that can take a bite of him. He is filthy and wearing tattered clothes that he's stolen off somebody's clothesline. The pants are short, showing his knees, and a torn shirt. He truly looks like a slave trying to run to freedom through the swamps.

Laray stares at them in disbelief and makes a move to where they stand. He has already thought that he could hold them hostage. He tells them, "I know what y'all been up to. You lil coonass got you sum coon? You'll never go back to your kind.

"You, lil nigga gal, I can tell who you for. You look just like your mama!

"Now, come over here where you can hug your uncle's neck. And I want to shake your hand, dude. You young to be out here for a lil poontang!"

Laray makes a move like he is getting ready to grab both of them. T-June takes care of that situation very quickly.

Laray is thrown back 15 feet into a large cypress tree and breaks his arm falling over a knee of the tree protruding out the water. He screams out profanity neither has ever heard and cries like a big dirty baby!

He gets up, holding his arm, not knowing what the hell has just happened to him. He screams out in pain, and he is so mad he's foaming at the mouth. He turns and goes to run because he hears noise like the posse has caught up with his ass. No such luck!

Pieyan the Bigfoot comes roaring out the swamps and grabs him! Laray screams an ungodly sound and drops to the ground in a dead faint. Pieyan smiles at T-June and runs off back to safety.

Alcide and Joe, along with the bishop, come running into the clearing where T-June and Jolie stand looking at Laray, who now is a gibberish-spouting madman. All of their guns are pointed at the miserable man who thinks he could get away with murder two more times.

Theo calls Sheriff Truxillo, and he notifies the FBI and the state troopers. All of them are there in 30 minutes.

The swamp is lit up like a LSU football game. The law enforcers are attempting to question Laray, but all he can do is point his finger toward the back of the swamps, talking like a crazy man, and telling them he's seen a monster, and it has tried to eat him!

His parents are arrested also for aiding in his escape.

The sheriff is puzzled at the group standing in front of them. Theo tells him that Laray has tried to get the two young ones for hostages and that he has had some terrible accident coming into the swamps. Maybe with an alligator?

∞ ∞ ∞

MOHAMMED and Malcolm have now both gotten their GEDs because they have quite the business painting since the courthouse building. They stay busy and have turned into businessmen that are punctual and precise in what they offer.

Bishop Toussaint helps them to turn their lives around. The young men are in counseling twice a week.

Theo with Alcide and Joe add their work ethic to the guidance of these two young men. Neither wants to go back on the fishing boat.

Laray remains in prison but no longer talks to anybody. He is permanently damaged from his venture into freedom.

The Lavernes are still in jail but are being kept from Laray. They've lost their cash cow and now don't care about the bull.

The two fine young men now get the royalties from the infamous song, which they put into their business every month.

Moe is almost ready to marry a cousin of Minou's. Her cousin's mama named her Maybelline after the song.

Chapter Eleven

A Man Finds Flavia

FLAVIA has been a contented divorcee for well over twenty years. Raising her two boys without a daddy has been hard. Flavia isn't blessed with many mothering instincts either.

Since T-June aka Joseph (aka the Saint) has been born, Flavia has found she does have motherly instincts.

Since she has never met her grandchildren, Flavia can't try the instincts out on, and they sure don't make her want to hug and kiss them. They turn their cheeks to her and blow kisses at her like she has cooties from the bayou. Calling her Grandmother, like they are so uppity. The two of them are now in their teens.

She finds out that she truly loves her godchild, T-June, so much more than she has ever felt about her two sons. It may be because they both look just like their daddy, the same man who walked up the road in broad daylight so everybody knows the loup-garou didn't get him!

She loves all the members of the village or should I say…? Nah, it ain't necessary.

She has left all of her worldly goods to T-June in an airtight will. St. Luke's Church has a considerable portion of her wealth to distribute whenever she goes to her glory. T-June gets the rest.

Maybe she will earn her spot right up next to St. Charleen! Right next to Sister Bridget, and nobody up there will remember the divorce!

She is a millionaire twice. Her people have saved every dime for generations. She doesn't talk much about her money.

Money is the last thing that T-June worries himself with. He's still the carefree Cajun boy who can just about turn water into RC Colas!

Flavia continues to call him T-June because it's what his mama named him. Never mind that Sister Bridget calls him Joseph. They still don't agree on much.

She looks pretty good for being on the back end of her fifties. She just needs to stop perming her hair! Flavia's hair is normally black, and her eyes are hazel with eyelashes still growing. A woman that towers over all her girlfriends in their own little village, helping raise T-June. Her 5 foot 9 inches of frame carries a woman with large tetons and muscular arms and legs. Carrying and unloading in her grocery store for her whole life has produced a very nice body.

Flavia just dresses like an old mawmaw, polyester pants and shirts that have seen better days. She doesn't care. She just glances at the mirror to make sure she doesn't have any dirt on her face. Her mama used to ridicule her for being so tall and never said one word to her about being pretty.

Her social skills leave a lot to be desired. She's never been the real friendly type, but she is as nosy as Minou! She finds out all about your business using very few words but don't get her started on politics or conspiracies, then she won't shut up! She dabbles in both, thinking she knows more than those elected politicians and has seen the movie JFK at least ten times.

There have been a couple of times when some brave soul has approached her for something else beside a baloney sandwich. Nobody has made it past the second date. It's been years. She just doesn't give a damn.

Minou has finally talked Flavia into letting that perm go back to the '50s! It's now her natural hair, the darkest shade of brown, with white streaks running through its waves.

Pick out some new clothes other than polyester, Minou says.

They both work together now in the store and have opened a small cafeteria with five tables in the immense building. Bertha does the cooking, and they are making a killing!

Minou has noticed that more customers are looking at Flavia, the entirely changed woman behind the counter. She has taken to wearing Levi's instead of the stretch pants and pretty blouses, because of all the attention she is getting from the women of the tribe telling what to do with herself.

She is totally oblivious to this change in the atmosphere of Mrs. Flavia's General Store. Well, it's been mostly local fellows that already know about her!

Minou is the one who visits with the customers and Bertha sometimes too. Flavia is quite content with the way it is now in her place of business.

One morning brings a stranger to Flavia's. A man as tall as Bishop Toussaint and wearing a Stetson cowboy hat, a huge shiny buckle on his Levi's, a beautiful western shirt, and boots made of alligator. Confident and friendly like a lot of Texas men are.

Minou knows the alligator skin, and you better believe she has eyed him from his cowboy hat to his pointed boots. Having to look way up being she's so small.

He tips his cowboy hat at Minou, but his eyes are totally on Flavia. She says, "How can Ah help ya, sir?"

He says, "Darlin', 'scuse me. I've almost forgotten what I came in here for 'cause you are a sight for sore eyes, miss. Tell me your name, darlin'?"

Flavia stiffens up in her usual manner and tells him, "Ah ain't nobody's darlin', mister! What in tha hell do ya want?"

The cowboy just stands there, laughing his fool head off with a laugh louder than anybody's! If he had been a fat man, his belly would be shaking! He just grins at Flavia, with her being amazed he is doing that! He is still smiling when he says, "I'm just an old cowpoke down here to buy a few horses. Hear y'all got some famous horse lines in the vicinity, and I'm lookin' for purebreds to bring back to Texas, where I'm from. I also wanted one of your lunches. That gumbo sounds good."

Flavia says, "Ah didn't ask for ya personal business. Ah do know where ya searchin' for horses. It's got a huge sign five miles down dis road, and dere's famous studs there. Quebedeaux's Horse Ranch. Ya can't miss it. Still want some gumbo?"

The cowboy looks at Flavia with a smile and says, "Well, darlin', tell me your name, and then I'll call you by your propers."

Flavia says quickly, "It's on tha goddamn sign outside! Mrs. Flavia's General Store! Ya must not be good at readin' signs! Who the hell are ya?"

He makes a big effort so all – the ladies see – in checking out her ring finger. Minou and Bertha laugh while Flavia just huffs away.

The cowboy reaches for the gumbo that Bertha has brought out to him. He sits at a table to eat while he has his eyes all over Flavia. She's bringing in boxes to unpack merchandise.

He gets up to help her, and she slaps his hands away.

Minou and Bertha are watching this like a movie!

Bertha ain't never seen no real cowboy except for the western movies she and Alcide watch. Bertha actually blushes when she brings his bowl of gumbo and he kisses her hand.

He eats that gumbo so fast and asks for another bowl. Loves the andouille sausage, he says. He finishes the second bowl and sits back and lights a pipe full of hard tobacco, putting a toothpick in his mouth at the same time.

He leans back in the chair, not being in a hurry to leave, and says, "Hot damn, that was some good gumbo, better than Ville Platte restaurants!

"My name is Stuart King, but they call me Sweet Stu. I'll be comin' this way for the next three weeks to train the horses I'm goin' to buy. Maybe longer. I'm not sure. But I'll stop here every time for some more gumbo and to look at the beautiful woman that's named Flavia."

He kisses Bertha's hand again, and she immediately tells him her name.

Minou introduces herself and begins to ask questions, of course. You know Minou, but Flavia doesn't say a word, pretending to place orders, not asking a damn thing. She's acting like she could care less about this man, but something is different about her demeanor, a shyness.

They are steadily watching this and can't wait 'til he leaves.

He is still smiling at Flavia when he tips his Stetson and swaggers out the store.

Minou can't hardly wait for Sweet Stu to walk out the door before she is questioning Flavia. "Damn, Flavia! He sure has tha hot trots for ya! Man, he couldn't take his eyes off ya! What ya gonna do if he asks ya out?"

Flavia just shrugs her shoulders and doesn't say a word.

"Live a little, Flavia! Ya ain't dead or a virgin like Sista Bridget! Why wouldn't ya be nice to dis stranger comin' from far away? Ya a fine specimen of a woman now. E'rybody sees dat, if ya don't! What tha hell would it hurt if ya did a little flirtin'?

"Holy merde, ya probably don't know tha first thing about flirtin'! How ya t'ink Ah got a husband dat adores me? Ah mean Ah always knew me and Joe would get married but him being gaga over me was 'cause of my mama. Ah watched Bertha in action. When she was younger she used her beauty to sometimes get what she needed for me and her. Dat's all a man will listen to sometimes, tha call of ya beauty."

Flavia listens to what Minou and Bertha have to say on this very exciting visit. She says, "Damn it to hell! What do Ah need from a man? Ah got plenty money, Ah do what Ah want, and Ah can say 'Kiss my ass' when dey try to tell me how to run my life!

"My son who's still alive thinks Ah'm ready for tha damn nursin' home! Ah wish Ah could see his face when he finds out Ah ain't leavin' him or dem kids who call me Grandmother one damn cent! Ah'm sure as hell not goin' to flirt wit' dat foreigner from some wildass town in Texas!"

Bertha is just busting to say something. "Mais, Flavia, all dem years and ya ain't had some? Mais, ya got cobwebs on ya coochie! Ya like a virgin. Mais, merde, ya don't have dat little stirrin' down dere for some good lovin'? Ya ain't dat old!

"Me and Alcide do some fierce lovemakin'! Ah guess being loup-garou don't hurt neither. Ya know Minou and Joe have dat kinda love too. Even Madam and tha bishop still do it!

"Oh, merde, Ah shouldna blabbed dat out!

"Anyway, mais, it's gotta bother ya! Ya just had a no-good man! Don't judge all of dem 'cause of dat bastard dat walked up tha road! Stop all dat business of being so froo-froo and find out what it feels like to have a man whose arms hold ya and kiss ya like dere ain't no tomorrow!"

Bertha has a lot to say on this topic, way more than she usually says on any subject. She said she is kinda haunt because she has a stirring herself when Sweet Stu kisses her hand!

Minou herself had quite a bit to say on the topic of love.

"Flavia, ya never had a man who loved ya and would give the world just to have ya in his arms? Ah know what, maybe Madam Aucoin can mix somet'in' up for ya, a love potion to work on just you! Ya so pretty now, and we makin' ya join the gals of our little village!

"Well, nuttin' can help Sister Bridget. It makes me sad to say dat.

"Ah mean, after ya let ya hair be 'stead of dat perm and dose ugly polyester pants. Dem jeans ya bought fit ya in all tha right places!

"Estelle showed ya how to wear a lil lipstick and some rouge on ya cheeks every day 'stead of just wearin' it to Mass! Dose eyelashes wit' mascara on dem look like dey fake!

"What good does dat do if ya only talk to Father Becnel?

"Shit! Ya got more muscles dan Joe! Sometimes ya a little manly, but men like dat too! Come on, Nanan. Talk to dat large-livin' man, struttin' his stuff, good-to-look-at cowboy Sweet Stu. Ah'm gonna sic Estelle and Madam on ya. And if dat don't work, Ah'm gonna tell T-June!"

Estelle and Madam have come in the store to visit but quickly join in on this notorious sex talk. Business is slow, and they are sitting at a table.

Madam lights her ganja pipe and proceeds to tell the bunch about everything that she has seen since she opened her Voodoo shop. "Sistas, wait 'til you hear some of my stories, but I'm not naming names!

"Back in the early '70s, I couldn't keep love potions or elixirs on my shelves! All those beautiful hippie chicks with flowers in their long hair. The young men just as pretty as the flower power young women.

A lot of the long-haired hippie dudes looked pretty much like your Jesus, with beards and long hair and sandals.

"It was one of those young men that turned me onto ganja. Boy! Did he turn me on! A young white male – with me having a huge Afro – and sexy to the point of being indecent! I was something! It was seasons of love!

"They would come in for my perfumes that I made special order. Always had patchouli scent in my concoctions. I couldn't keep up with the demands and so advertised for an assistant in perfume-making right in The Times-Picayune.

"In walks this beautiful Black man with this Afro as big as mine, so tall with sparkling green eyes, bringing me the ad out the paper. He says he is the man that I need!

"'Hell, yes,' I said. Forgot to ask him what he knew about perfumes or his credentials, not even his name!

Now, y'all know who I'm speaking about! The man of my dreams, Dr. Manly Tall! That was his name back then. Now he's the Reverend Bishop Laurent Toussaint. His family are the famous Toussaint musicians. His first cousin is Aaron Neville.

"Dr. Tall knew a lot about perfumes because his mama was a Voodoo woman too. We made a fortune together.

"He turned me every way but loose! I was just burning up with desire! He let me know in a matter of a few minutes that he was feeling the same! And Flavia, it's still the same today. I mean, not as much as we were back then, like rabbits, but pretty regular." Bertha sighs with relief.

Madam is fixing White Russians, and they all are drinking. That Kahlua can knock you cuckoo! They are all giggling and drinking one too many in the middle of the day!

They are busy cluing Flavia in on what she has missed all these years when the front door opens and Sweet Stu King walks in.

All of them stand with their mouths open. They do this often.

Bertha is blushing like a teenager! Flavia is doing her own blushing, like she has been caught talking about this man. Hell, they are all talking about this long tall drink of water!

Everybody is sizing him up.

Minou and Estelle greet him like they know him already, with Bertha fixing him a plate of crawfish stew he hadn't asked for yet.

Madam is seriously checking out his chakras and singing a tune of Etta James called At Last. She's pretty pie-eyed too.

He is a perfect gentleman, but he has a wicked sense of humor like the rest of them, except Flavia.

Sweet Stu says, "Look at all these beautiful Cajun women just enjoyin' their day! But Flavia, my darlin', you could make the sun set! You know, us cowpokes have a tender heart for sunsets."

They are so glad that they have put makeup on Flavia.

A tipsy Flavia, buzzed from secondhand ganja smoke, just starts talking with the cowboy in a decent way that the rest are very interested in.

"Well hell, ya back so soon? What about tha horses? Did ya get some?"

The storeful of these drunkass women can't hold back the laughter anymore! "Gettin' some" is what they have been talking about all afternoon!

"Flavia darlin', it's what I came to talk to you about."

Lawd! You shoulda heard the commotion. Poor Bertha, she's laughing so hard she's peeing on herself! Madam Aucoin goes to sit and falls off the chair laughing.

Sweet Stu looks confused for a minute and then he is slapping his Levi's, howling with laughter. He catches on, but so does Flavia, and she looks like she has way too much rouge on her face.

Bertha is the first one to get sober enough to say anything, and she says, "Mais, sweet baby Stu, how ya like to come eat supper tomorrow night by my house? All our men will be home in tha mornin', and dey catch plenty seafood on tha boats. How about six t'irty? E'rybody here will be dere too. Chér, Ah'm gonna call tha whole village!"

Sweet Stu smiles and says yes, ma'am, thinking, Why is she going to call the whole town? He says, "Flavia darlin', is all that land across this road yours? If it is, I'd like to rent the pasture for my horses to graze in. It looks like it's got plenty of grass, and it won't be for long. What do you say, darlin'?"

Flavia says that indeed it's her land but tells him again to quit calling her darlin'! "Ah bet ya call all tha women ya see 'darlin'! Ah'm damn straight not darlin', and Ah'm not like any woman ya ever met. Ya ain't tha first cowboy rodeo dat has strutted up in here!

"Ah will let ya graze ya horses, but it's gonna cost ya if ya have enough money. And it's only 'cause Ah love horses!"

Well, none of the women know about this!

Sweet Stu says yes, ma'am and thanks, ma'am for doing this. They shake hands because he says a handshake is as good as your word.

Flavia has done business that way herself, and she says it's been a tradition in her family for years, so don't go thinking she doesn't know about that already!

He tells all the women he will see them tomorrow night, tips his hat, and swaggers out the swinging screen doors where the sign is blinking off and on. Mrs. Flavia's General Store.

Flavia is some pissed! All of them are still laughing. and Flavia says she doesn't find anything funny. "Bertha, why tha hell did ya do dat? Ah ain't gonna go wit' someone from Texas! What's tha point?"

Minou and Estelle are asking, When did another cowboy come up in here?

Flavia's face makes that statement a lie. She is actually smiling!

Madam says she will make her famous perfume and bring a large bottle to Flavia.

Bertha is beside herself for doing the invite and is thinking that he might make Alcide kinda jealous!

The women want Flavia to go buy an outfit, kinda sexy, to wear for the next night. Minou says she ought to go to the back corner of the store, where there's an adult section with many items.

Flavia doesn't tell Minou she already has a couple of things from the back corner!

Minou says it sure worked on Joe because they came back from New Orleans with a baby on the way!

Don't worry about what Sister Bridget has to say! They can't leave her out of the village, but she's gonna have something to say.

All the women are grooming Flavia like it's a wedding or something. Estelle paints her fingernails and toes with Flaming Red. Madam brings the perfume, and everybody wants a bottle of sweet patchouli with vanilla. It has a very musky smell. Even the bishop helps with the batch.

Oh, my Gawd, save us all! The scent has the whole store smelling like patchouli!

Minou tells Flavia they are closing the store early today so they can prepare her like a sacrificial virgin.

Madam takes her shopping for an outfit that will accentuate her positives and a pair of long golden hoops to put in her ears. She settles on an off-the-shoulder blouse and a long denim skirt. Flavia says hell, no to cowboy boots.

Ooh, Lawd, what? What?

Don't forget the lovely underwear! She makes Flavia throw away her granny panties.

Bertha makes a red velvet cake for dessert. Red velvet is a mighty fine piece of fabric that helps in any act of seduction! She has been smiling all day and even asks Madam if she can have some of that perfume!

Of course, they all tell the men about what has happened, and they are waiting to see if the cowboy holds up to all their standards.

Madam has mentioned that all of his chakras are lined up strong, and he's also an old soul.

They all want to know what the hell does that even mean.

Flavia didn't have her rosary tonight, maybe thinking she is fixing to do some sinning!

Bertha and Alcide's house is rocking with swamp pop music and some good old soul tunes from New Orleans. They have provided long tables with newspapers covering them for everyone to eat at.

The screened-in porch is large enough for all of them and plenty room for dancing. Minou has put Callie and Lily to bed in the same crib.

Bertha and Alcide have boiled shrimp with plenty of andouille sausage, potatoes, corn, and with lots of garlic for this supper. They also have oysters waiting to be shucked. You know what they say about those oysters!

Everyone is on the porch, and the carport that has the tables ready for all the seasoned and boiled seafood.

Sweet Stu King comes driving up in a Black Ford Platinum King Ranch F250 truck with dually wheels on the back and front. The front of the truck has a small set of longhorns placed right on the cab.

He arrives at the time he is told to. Precisely on time.

As he gets down from the truck, with country western music blaring out the door, he smiles and tips his hat. Then he takes the hat off and reveals a head of curly red hair. All the women want to run fingers through his hair!

"Hello to all you good people, and a thank you for invitin' me to this wonderful spread full of seafood. Don't get that much of it where I'm from. We eat a lot of steaks, potatoes, and biscuits and cornbread.

"The times that I spent on the trail with a food wagon makes me so happy to do this with strangers that I hope become friends. My name is

Stu King. Just call me Sweet Stu."

He shakes hands with all the men, Pawpaw Irby too.

Pawpaw was looking hard at this cowboy, because back in the day, Texans working the oil fields would talk to the Cajuns with slurs and laugh at them. That's when the term "coonass" comes from.

Pawpaw Irby dislikes Texans. He says, Who wants to be the ass of a coon? He doesn't like the twang of how they talk and he finds them to be braggarts.

It will take some time for him to warm up to the tall cowboy. He is protective of Flavia because he has known her family for many years.

Everyone else has made Sweet Stu feel right at home, teasing him about being so sweet. He tells them that his grandpa started calling him Sweet Stu when he was three, because he was so sweet to the work hands on the ranch, helping them out with their chores. It just stayed that way for sure when he started noticing girls.

He's been a widower for many years and no children.

The seafood is good and very filling. The music continues with laughter and good conversations between the cowboy and the rest.

They have many questions for him to answer, and they discover Sweet Stu is quite the storyteller. All of the tall tales he shares are met with hard laughter and back-slapping!

You can tell without a doubt that Stu has made friends with the whole bunch. Pawpaw Irby has even warmed up to the Texan.

Stu shakes hands with T-June, telling him he is a good-looking boy with such kind eyes sparkling.

Minou and Estelle notice that he is being so respectful toward Flavia. Her excitement is slipping through her posture, and she is smiling in a way that she seldom shows to her friends.

Sweet Stu and Flavia are gravitating toward each other, and only the women are watching this transpire. The men are all tipsy, and Alcide starts dancing to the music when he grabs Bertha to dance with him.

Sweet Stu asks the crowd, "Have y'all ever heard of Willie Nelson? I'd like for y'all to hear my favorite CD of his music. It's called Stardust." He retrieves the CD from the inside of his truck.

Joe and Alcide said of course they had heard of him, then starts singing On The Road Again and an old song, Hello Walls. The CD is playing, and everybody pairs up to dance to the beautiful melodies.

Sweet Stu stands in front of Flavia and takes her hand, and she willingly goes into his arms. What Flavia knows about dancing has been wondered about, being they have never seen her do so. She seems like she has the steps figured out. Maybe she dances alone when no one is around.

You can hear a pin drop when he pulls her into his arms. The women almost sigh simultaneously at the scene. The music continues, and they stay in each other's arms, seeming like they only have eyes for each other. Everybody else has quit dancing, watching the pair.

They finally realize this and break away from each other, with Flavia being embarrassed and turning red. Sweet Stu laughs and hugs her in a bear hug that raises her off her feet!

Lawd! The group feels like they are watching an R-rated movie.

Everyone is exhausted from all the fun they've had, and it's time for saying goodnight. Father Becnel and Sister Bridget are the first to go. Father looks as if he's had too much to drink or smoke, so the Sister drives them home.

Sister has watched the scene unfold, and it seems like she has a longing in her eyes for what she has never had. Strangely, she isn't disapproving.

The women are waiting for what might happen next, and they don't have to wait long.

Sweet Stu asks Flavia if he can bring her home, and she nods yes, not saying a word to anybody.

The phones are blowing up the next morning when Minou opens the store, with Flavia nowhere in sight! The only person that isn't answering is Flavia.

The women have gathered at the store with hangovers and worries. Bertha definitely has a skip in her steps, and she is singing a Willie Nelson song. Madam and Estelle are grinning like they have already smoked some ganja this morning. Minou is worried about Flavia so you can't tell.

They all look like they got some last night!

Minou says, "Shit! What tha hell y'all t'ink is goin' on? Dammit, Ah'm 'bout to go bustin' up in her house! Crap, he might be some kinda axe murderer, and we t'rew her to tha wolves! She won't even answer her goddamn phone!"

Estelle and Madam are calming Minou down, saying this is the business of Flavia and she will tell them if she wants to.

Flavia walks in the store when they are having their noon rush in the café. At straight up 12:00. Never ever has that happened.

The girls have helped with the orders and serving the public, so Flavia just sits down at her desk, propping her feet up on the well-worn surface. Doesn't say a word to anybody.

Minou couldn't contain herself another minute. "What tha hell, Flavia? Well, just what tha hell? Ya coulda at least answered ya goddamn phone!"

Minou is acting like she's Flavia's mama! Flavia looks at her and says, "That's because Ah didn't wanna answer tha goddamn phone!"

Then they are all asking questions, and Flavia is being as tight-lipped as she usually is. She has the nerve to tell them all to quit being so damn nosy and then picks up her purse, saying she is leaving for the day.

Once again they stand there with their mouths agape! Once again. The women gathered there are all just overwhelmed with what has just taken place. They stay until Minou locks the door to the store.

All of them, that afternoon, are pondering on what took place last night. Bertha, in her mood, laughs and said, "Mais, whatcha t'ink happened? She got some!"

Flavia won't tell them about what's happening in her life. She is definitely dressing the way that says, I am Woman. Hear me roar!

∞ ∞ ∞

SWEET Stu is coming in every day and still has eyes for only Flavia, but now she is flirting back! Together, they spend time with the village people but a lot of time by themselves.

Flavia is leaving the store for Minou and the rest of the women to run daily. All of those women watch out the windows in front of the store. All try to climb on each other to get a better look.

Sweet and Flavia spend all day across the road in the pasture that is owned by Flavia. Everybody up and down the bayou is there daily to see this, this wonderful thing that is unfolding on the bayou up and down the road.

All the people living down the road had heard about this very interesting gossip, and the whole scene is stopping traffic as all the cars go slow-slow to watch this cowboy event. They stand at the barb-wire fence to see Flavia climb up on the big horses and ride like she is a professional rodeo rider.

Sister Bridget comes to the store asking if Flavia is all right. Sister says that she has missed Mass a couple of times.

What?

One Monday morning Flavia walks in with a cowboy hat on her head and a beautiful western shirt with sequins splattered down the front, with tight Levi's and displaying a huge buckle of silver. Her hair is braided down her back, with her silver loops hanging from her ears. She's wearing a brand new pair of women's alligator boots pointed high at the toe. Flavia tells them that Sweet Stu has taken her shopping at Dugas's Western Wear in Thibodaux and bought all of it for her, plus much more.

Flavia wears on her hand a huge turquoise ring that is on a band of pure silver.

These women must be tired of standing there with their mouths opened. They're catching all the flies!

Sweet Stu walks in right behind her, laughing and smiling, telling jokes to the gang of women, but Flavia is quiet. "Darlin', have you told the girls yet? You better get to steppin', darlin'! We got a long way to go before we see the sunrise!"

What do you think is happening with the women? They all say, WHAT? WHAT? WHAT? at the same time.

Flavia sits and stares at all her girlfriends there. She smiles and shows them her engagement ring and says very quiet-like, "Ah'm gettin' married."

Minou and Bertha and Madam and Estelle are jumping up and down with the news. There have been bets taken by all the men on how long it would take before they moved in together!

Then they realize the severity of the statement and sit down.

Of course, it is Minou who speaks up first.

"What tha hell, Flavia? Have y'all told T-June and all tha men? How long was it gonna take ya to gettin' around to tellin' us? And y'all are leavin' tonight? Shit on a stick! Flavia! Ah can't believe ya'd do somet'in' like dat and not tell me and Bertha? My feelings are hurt. Dis is just too nervine! What about tha store?"

All of Flavia's friends are trying to not talk at the same time and to keep the tears from running down their faces.

Madam is the next one to voice her concerns. She wants to ask if Flavia has told him why they are so tight-knit and how they all met. T-June is the reason, and how do you explain that?

"Flavia, none of us are ready for you to go riding into the sunset with a man we hardly know! Sorry, Stu, but it's the truth. Do you, Stu King, already know that Flavia has wealth? I will find that out first. Has she told you that already? I mean, we don't know a thing about you because Flavia has told us nothing. Again I ask, do you know she has money?

"I have lived in a big city my entire life, and there are many con artists that walk those streets. I presume you have already discussed this with our men, since you have spent more time with them."

Sweet Stu laughs at the accusations thrown by Madam Aucoin. He is serious for the first time and begins to talk to them in a way that a suitor would talk to a disapproving father.

"Lord Almighty, I have never been asked if I needed money! My darlin' ladies, put your minds to rest about the money. You just don't worry about her needs 'cause I got them in my back pocket. My family has the biggest ranch in all of Texas. King's Ranch has been in business for centuries, when the Lone Star State was really alone tryin' to get their freedom from the Mexicans.

"All of your men told me they had bets on us! I just wanted to shout from the biggest tree, but Flavia said I better not! I'm real sorry she hasn't shared our courtship!

"I knew there was a strong Texan woman somewhere in Flavia. I just had to come to my senses that Flavia is a mighty strong Cajun woman who has people that went west!"

Minou says, "Flavia, have ya told him all 'bout T-June?"

Sweet Stu answers for Flavia. "Oh, my brand-new family, of course she told me about the little man. I just admire all of you so much for raising' him so far and until he is grown. I know about the werewolves too. I just can't imagine this, but I'm ready to help. I know quite a bit about lassoin'. I can't wait to get T-June out there to start talkin' with some of those armadillos!"

Flavia sits down and tells Sweet Stu, "Okay, you. Ah can talk for myself.

"Look at all my sistas in tha posse! Dat's pretty funny, huh? Well, Ah know dis ain't tha time to be funny, and my heart is hurtin' right now 'cause Ah'm gonna leave all of ya.

"Ah went by dis mornin' to tell T-June at school. Sister Bridget came out tha classroom wit' him. He told me he knew already 'cause he saw it first time he shook Sweet's hand. T-June knows how to keep a damn secret! He said he loves me and will see me soon.

"Sister hugged me real tight and told me Ah would enjoy goin' to Mass at the Mexican churches. She wished me good luck and said to forget about bein' excommunicated. Take dat Host anytime Ah want to.

"Ah started cryin', and den both of us was cryin', and T-June made a joke.

"Sweet Stu has talked to tha men about dis when dey was fishin'. They all encouraged him and asked him if he was gettin' some! Y'all are some nosy about what goes on in somebody's bedroom!

"Ah didn't want to share dis wit' y'all 'cause Ah was kinda haunt. Ah have never felt dis way, and Ah wanted to keep it for myself. Ah had to be sure of what Ah was gettin' into.

"Listen, y'all. Sweet Stu is semi-retired, and he owns his own plane. We can fly here as fast as Madam can drive from New Orleans. We'll be comin' here at least once a week or when we need to come. Sweets wants to join tha posse for T-June."

Madam jumps up and says, "Why don't you just get married here? Why Texas? Why would you even think not to let us give you away? After everything we've been through together? My feelings are hurt too! Tell your family to fly over, and you have three people that can marry you here! Bishop and I and Father Becnel. We will have that covered.

"Just do it Friday morning. We can move that fast. We can have it at my house. Why run off to Texas? As if! As if!"

Well, it is in high gear from that moment on for the women. They close the store for the rest of the week, and all have assignments to take care of before the wedding.

Madam takes Flavia to get a wedding dress all the way to New Orleans, and both come back with little squinty eyes! They walk in with their arms holding many fancy bags from all the shops in the Quarter. Flavia is embarrassed when Madam shows them the fancy lingerie for her.

Minou and Estelle are decorating the house with Madam Consienne, the ghost, adding her two cents. They use bunches of magnolia flowers in the garlands of roses, with moss and ribbons going up and down the staircases.

Madam with her crystal ball is able to locate Madam Consienne's lover, and he has joined the ghostly crew of musicians taking turns on the baby grand piano!

Madam C is a different ghost now, she's so happy.

Bertha is doing the refreshments, with Sister Bridget helping with the reception and cooking like her mama taught her. There are huge pots of seafood gumbo, fried shrimp and catfish, and of course jambalaya!

Bertha makes her fabulous red velvet cakes with Sister Bridget making her sweet rice cakes.

The liquor is delivered to the house instead of the store for the reception because no telling who's coming to the celebration.

Big Mama is taking care of Callie and Lily because they are going to be flower girls. The identical dresses to be worn by the two little divas are white taffeta with long sashes of red. They are going to carry little baskets of rose petals to throw as they walk down the aisle.

The girls are told not to throw the petals all in one spot and run down the aisle.

∞ ∞ ∞

THE wedding is like out of a magazine, with Flavia walking down the staircase in a long, flowery cotton dress with a bouquet of long-stemmed roses. Flavia's hair is put up in the Gibson style, and it has little roses scattered throughout her hair. Makeup done by a professional is stunning on Flavia, making her look indeed like a young bride.

Pawpaw Irby leads her down the aisle prepared with chairs lined up on each side, and at the end Father Becnel is waiting. Pawpaw takes the place of her long-gone daddy. He cries as he gives her hand to Sweet Stu. Pawpaw tells Flavia, "Mais, bébé, ya been a good friend to me. Ah know ya from a baby in ya daddy's arms. He loved ya but hated ya mama. Ya never know.

"Ah love ya like a daughter. Don't let dem call ya no coonass, ya hear?

Watch dem Texans!"

All the girlfriends wear identical dresses as bridemaids. At this short notice, they're lucky to find matching ones. Minou, Estelle, Irene, Jolie, and Katrina walk down the aisle before the bride. These women of the posse are able to get this four-star wedding together from Monday to Saturday, moved up a day to finish everything. That is a bunch of Cajun / Creole women who know their stuff. Sweet Stu is amazed but not Flavia.

She knows what the Twisted Sistas are capable of.

Father Becnel marries them because Flavia doesn't want any Voodoo!

Champagne is flowing along with beer and wine and Southern whiskey. The food is abundant with gumbo, fried shrimp and all kinds of little cakes made out of red velvet with others bringing varieties of cakes and cookies.

The music is playing, a mixture of swamp pop, soul and of course, Willie Nelson.

Alcide asks Sister Bridget to dance, and her face lights up like a Christmas tree. What a difference a smile makes.

Bishop Toussaint begins to play piano with the two ghosts, Madam C and Etienne, adding their own versions. The jazz musicians are playing too, with Buddy playing a song for T-June and Jolie.

Even Aaron Neville and Irma Thomas show up together and cause almost a riot with all the people up and down the bayou that have come.

No invitations have been sent. The news carries from house to house up and down the bayou. Flavia is well known, and she knows everybody else's business, so the gossip is on her for a change.

T-June and Jolie are dancing like they have been doing it for years. Being the ham that he is, T-June goes to doing the alligator on the floor, and the crowd goes wild! Some of those people are scratching their heads, wondering if what they're seeing is even possible. They must be drunk!

Butch and Katrina are there with Irene and Jean. Irene's dress as a bridesmaid allows room for her large belly because she's in her eighth month. They are gonna have a little girl; it's already been spoken. Butch is ecstatic having a little sister, because he's already got a little brother, T-June.

The celebration lasts into the night. So many people are there and the free food and booze. No telling who shows up!

Flavia finally goes upstairs to change her clothes and comes down in her cowgirl ensemble for her going-away outfit.

The men of the posse are telling Sweet Stu all about being married to a Bayou Lafourche woman.

Alcide says, "Podnah, ya ain't got tha first clue! Ah sure hope ya like politics 'cause she's got one conspiracy after tha other! She's gonna find out all about dem laws ya got over dere in Texas, and podnah, she goin' to cause another Alamo!"

All of the posse are standing in the dark, watching the pair climb up in his huge truck to leave. Minou with the rest of the women in the posse are crying and waving their sorrow for their Flavia. Cans and cans of empty beer are tied behind the big Ford, making more noise than the huge truck.

Stu tells them, "We gonna hit the border of Texas just as the sun is comin' up! We got a bunch of miles to go, but we will see the sunset on my front porch. Y'all will see us soon, our posse!

Gettin' some is what makes this ole world keep some.

Chapter Twelve

Callie and Lily's Flower

IRENE Guidry Breaux is the mother of Matthew James Miller Jr. I'm talking about Butch and his mama. She was a widow too early in her life, twenty, just barely. When they married she was sixteen, just barely. It was a shotgun wedding for Irene and Matt, from Harlon, Kentucky. The good thing is that they truly love each other, and their baby boy is welcomed. Butch is named after his daddy. Matt calls him Butch because he is a terror.

She and Matt are out every weekend, dancing and having fun. He is a real nice, handsome fellow! that laughs all the time, making up for pretty little Irene's shyness.

Irene finds a babysitter down the street from where they live in Thibodaux. They are such a nice couple, they make a lot of friends.

Until the accident…

By the time that Butch turns three, they are left alone in life without the boy from Harlan, Kentucky. Irene has never met his people up in the Appalachians.

Never does Matt think, when going to the Gulf to seek his fortune, that he will die there. He is blown up in an oil rig explosion off Fourchon, Louisiana. More than a hundred workers are killed, and it is in every newspaper in the country.

Because of the reckoning, finally, of the Louisiana laws toward the oil companies with the world watching, it leaves Irene and Butch wealthy.

That is the way the boy from Kentucky makes his fortune.

Irene and Butch never lack for money, but in spite of that, she wants her man back. Irene can't imagine a life without a man.

Her women friends are looking differently at her, and so are the men. The friends take her out with them for a few Saturdays nights, but the atmosphere of fun has changed. It is one of jealousy and quiet lusting.

When one of Matt's friends knocks on her door at 1:00 in the morning, drunk and trying to kiss her, Irene calls his wife. She thinks the wife is her closest friend, and Irene wants her to know what her bastard husband is doing. It almost causes a divorce between them, and of course there are lines drawn, with the women not talking to her. The men either.

That's when Irene takes her small son and moves back down Bayou Lafourche closer to her people.

Irene, being she's been in the big city for years, has no trouble walking into a bar by herself. That's where she had met her husband, so she is searching for another one to fill his shoes.

Irene never leaves Butch alone until he is ten or so years old. He is raised to be self-sufficient, because he is the man of the house to Irene. She knows very little about raising children.

Irene has gotten to the point of loneliness and lust, that she is bringing men home from the night of her partying. She is raging in her grief.

Butch never voices his feelings until she brings home this man who starts ordering Butch around and bullying him. Irene tells him this man doesn't like children, but give her a little time and maybe she will change him.

You know the love you have is so great that it will turn your man into being truthful, kind, and faithful.

Sure. That works all the time.

Butch speaks up and says she has to make a choice. It isn't the one he thinks she will make, to ask the man to leave.

Irene's papa, Old Man Guidry, has been trying to talk her into letting him take the boy. Guidry is well aware of the money, but he doesn't even mention that, the sleazy bastard.

Irene's mama is a shy woman with a beautiful smile, the same one that's bloody and torn at times because she lives with a snake of a man who beats both of them. Her mama is from north Louisiana and that road passes Alexandria, Louisiana. That dividing line may as well be considered Yankees to the Cajuns down here on the bayou. Plus she is one of those holy rollers! She is long gone by the time Butch goes to live with his grandpa.

Irene makes a decision, like fools often do, foolhardy, not thinking about consequences.

Butch goes down the bayou to live with his Pawpaw Guidry on the houseboat that Irene had been raised on. Since her mama passed, she hasn't been back to the houseboat. Irene has no good feelings about her papa because he is mean to her and was to her mama, but he acts like he really loves Butch.

You can justify any damn thing when you're out there making a caricature of yourself.

When she finds out what her papa has done to her son, she is livid and so ashamed. Her temper drives that car to his houseboat where Irene throws open the wooden door and breaks it at the hinges.

She takes three steps onto the floor and punches her papa, knocking him out his recliner and all the way to the bayou, where he goes over the side of the walkway into the nasty water, full of guts and crap from the large catfish he is cleaning, hollering words as foul as the water!

Irene calls the Larose police, and they come down the bayou with sirens blaring, blocking the road, all five cars of them. Sheriff Truxillo puts the cuffs on Old Man Guidry and hauls his ass to jail!

And it is good night, Irene after that!

She finally comes to her senses and tells her shack-up boyfriend to hit the bricks.

This is about the time when Minou finds Butch, thanks to T-June. He becomes their second son when Irene consents to his living there. Irene is so grateful for Minou and the family but realizes Butch is where he wants to be.

∞ ∞ ∞

IRENE becomes a regular member of the tribe, visiting with Flavia and Minou. Flavia has known her, growing up on the bayou, along with her mama and papa.

Minou is younger and remembers Irene as a teenager walking down the road, going to a dance on the bayou. She always smells good when she passes by Minou sitting on Flavia's porch, because she can get the Avon lady to visit at Flavia's store.

Flavia works out a deal with the Avon lady, and she makes a little profit from her until she starts being the Avon lady herself, with Irene's help.

Minou and Irene patch up their differences, mainly Minou, because she feels some explaining needs to be done. Minou finds she really likes Irene, but Flavia is the one that takes her under the wing of her guidance, and they become better friends, picking right up from when Irene was a teen and they sold Avon together back then.

Minou has been too busy with all the quemas that lands on her young shoulders once a month.

Just like watching for the curse every month but way, way worse.

She never thinks too much more about Irene until she is shocked to see who Butch's mama is.

Irene meets Jean Breaux through some help from Alcide and Joe. He's not a drinking man, and they don't meet in a bar. So they marry when Butch is a senior in high school in a small ceremony held at Madam Aucoin's home, with Flavia as her matron of honor. Father Becnel marries them, but they jump the broom too!

∞ ∞ ∞

BUTCH and Katrina are still in school together but now married. These two have run off to Austin, Texas, and gotten hitched!

Flavia and Sweet Stu are the only witnesses of the marriage, held in a Spanish-speaking church with all the wonderful mariachi music blaring. Katrina is dressed like a Mexican maiden, and she is stunning, with her hair wild and flying in the dust.

They video the whole affair for all the posse back home.

C'est la vie, say the old folks. It just goes to show you never can tell!

Irene at first isn't impressed with Katrina, being she is Creole. Some of Irene's prejudice comes through, but she is ashamed about it. Hell, her grandpa up there in Grayson was a Knight of the Klu Klux Klan! Finding out that they are related way down the line is a quick and very real reality.

The families have been brought together because of T-June and very quickly become members of the tribe, the posse, the…Oh hell, you know what I'm talking about!

A lot of bloodlines make up the posse, family all flowing in the direction of T-June to raise him up to the best of all their abilities. After Big Mama Theriot's heart attack on the kitchen floor, T-June, along with the Baby Jesus, touches her, and she gets immediately healed.

Theo and Estelle Theriot are Jolie and Lily's mama and papa. Katrina, Butch's wife, is a daughter of theirs too. Six girls in total. Minou and Estelle have become almost inseparable too, because the two little girls – Callie and Lily – can't stand to be apart.

Madam Aucoin is a third cousin of Estelle, both from the big city of New Orleans. Of course, they visit Madam Aucoin at her beautiful house.

It takes a lot of abilities!

∞ ∞ ∞

ESTELLE and Minou now run the store for Flavia since she's turned into a cowgirl and moved to Texas with Sweet Stu. Flavia has given all her worldly goods to T-June and has an airtight will, saving nothing for her son and the two grandchildren. Flavia for sure doesn't feel guilty anymore about not giving them one silver dime. And T-June doesn't think about money at all. I mean, here's the kid that can probably turn water into Dr Pepper!

The oldest granddaughter has a very elaborate wedding, and Flavia and Sweet are invited. They fly up in Sweet's plane and stay at a very expensive hotel. They stick out at the wedding and reception like two sore thumbs, everyone greeting with fake smiles and limp handshakes.

Flavia and Sweet Stu are exceedingly wealthy, a proper 10th generation family of cattle raising. Sweet Stu King is the closest thing to royalty in the state of Texas, down-home Texas rangers with a humble beginning. Since the fight over the Alamo, a King has been involved in the Texas fight for freedom from Mexico. It's always been their motto, Stay Humble and Give.

Only another westerner could tell how much they have. The clothes that they wear, the trucks they drive, and the amount of cattle they ranch are signs of the money they have. Nothing flamboyant but how old money looks, well-worn but still good.

∞ ∞ ∞

THERE are things the village hasn't told Irene. Maybe as time rolls by she will be clued in, into the more serious side of T-June's abilities. Irene knows about some things that T-June/Joseph can do, but the monthly moon thing is kept private. He alone brings together the village/tribe/posse/disciples/followers behind the remarkable boy who might be president, saint, healer, mind reader, animal speaker, or maybe the next Jesus!

The family welcomes both Irene and Jean into the fold but not totally washed in with all of it. Yet.

Irene and Jean are told that a little girl is coming to them, and they believe it. They are getting ready for the birth of their little girl, buying everything that money can buy, with a room full of stuffed animals and murals painted on the walls. Too many damn dolls, for sure!

Irene is having the baby in the hospital because it will be a C-section. She is considered a high risk, being she is thirty-seven years old.

Everybody's waiting at Minou and Joe's for news. Flavia is with Irene and Jean. Flavia calls them on her new cell phone that Sweet insists she carry so he always knows where she is. Not in a controlling way, because that's not happening, but out of concern.

She says, "Lawd, Ah'm so happy 'bout dis phone! Dis lil girl has come wit' a head full of white curly hair and blue eyes wide open! She is very beautiful, like a lil angel. Jean's in tha lobby givin' out cigars!

"Irene is feedin' her right now. Dey gonna let her come home in two days, but y'all can come see dem! She's gonna stay at my house here. So y'all come on."

Minou and Joe are the first to go in to see Irene. Minou talks while she bunches up the pillows for the new mama. "Sista, ya just a-glowin' up here in dis bed! And look at dat beautiful nightgown. It's just too much! And dis baby don't have a mark on her, and so rosy! Well, Irene, tell me what ya gonna name her. Ya kept dat a secret from all us!"

Irene hands the beautiful white-haired baby to Minou and straightens up in the hospital bed, about as comfortable a hospital bed can be.

"My friend, dis is Flower Catherine Breaux. My mama's people are tha Flowers of Grayson, Louisiana. She was from north Louisiana, just a spot on tha way to Monroe. My grandpa was a preacher up dere in one of dose snake-handlers churches. Ah've always loved tha name and my mama."

Minou can hardly contain herself. "Do ya realize what we have now? Callie and Lily's lil Flower! Lawd, wait 'til Ah tell e'rybody! Dey gonna be wonderful sisters! Calla Lily Flower!"

Minou and Estelle bring the two little girls, Callie and Lily, to see the baby girl, Flower, in the hospital. On Christmas Eve three years ago those two had come into the world already knowing each other.

Callie has the coloring of distant ancestors, the Houmas Indians, with high cheekbones and straight black hair, but with dark blue eyes. Lily is a shade or two darker than her friend, with soft, tight curls and slanted eyes of green. The two are quite stunning and inseparable.

These two girls Bertha dearly loves, and they do no wrong.

They both very froo-froo but will tackle anything out in the yard, like the time they knock over the statue of the Blessed Mother that sits in an old porcelain tub in front of Bertha's house. They break the statue and Bertha cries, so they sit down on the side of her and cry brokenhearted with her.

Callie and Lily have huge hearts with a little attitude from all of the sistas, old and young.

Callie calls every morning to see what outfit they gonna wear that day because they see each other every day. Lily is the deciding factor of what they wear.

Somebody is always running the roads, whoever can drive them to each other. It will be a big help when they old enough to ride their matching bikes up and down the road.

Both girls are a force to be reckoned with, but we gotta put the blame where it belongs because it's Callie that gets them cross-haired with their mamas. She is just like Minou, who probably started bossing everybody around at Callie's age too.

Lily just nonchalantly follows, like it's the path she would choose anyway. It's the path Lily would go, telling the directions. Lily seems to be the brains of the two.

Irene has joined the ranks of Minou and Estelle's very busy days, raising the little spitfires, pulling the girls back from danger, and don't dare raise your voice to either one, because the other will throw a fit.

∞ ∞ ∞

IT is the second day of Irene resting at Flavia's house that Minou and Estelle bring the two little divas dressed alike. They insist on it! Being all of three years old, they insist on holding Flower together because they're big enough!

Flower is wide awake, looking at both of them and smiling at the duo, who silently smile back at her. Perhaps it is gas, but people see signs everywhere.

Now there are three identical outfits that have to be bought, just in different sizes.

The girls together can be demanding, opinionated, and are learning from the best, Madam Aucoin, Minou, Estelle, and all their little women!

Estelle and Theo ask if they could be the nanan and parrain to the beautiful Flower.

∞ ∞ ∞

THEY definitely are the trio now, and Flower is on one of their hips until she can walk. Callie and Lily never hold Flower without both holding her, and she has loved them with her little heart through the years. Flower walks to both of them with her first steps and then walks to them as they sit across from each other.

Irene is so hurt to see this, but Minou and Estelle know it would happen.

Minou gets the old bundling wrap from the cedar chest she has used for both of her children, and Estelle has a well-worn one. Of course, they have to go buy new ones, because Lily says she won't be caught dead in those old things!

∞ ∞ ∞

THE older girls turn five this year. The younger Flower is way too confident in herself and has far too much attitude for a little two-yearold. Flower is a small version of the Calla Lily sistas. She's been talking, repeating everything the little divas tell her.

The first time she raises her chubby hand to her Papa Jean and says, "Talk to tha hand," he loses it, rolling on the floor in laughter!

Older parents think everything is hilarious that their late-in-life child does.

Callie and Lily love to go exploring in the swamps behind Minou and Joe's house, with them holding each other's hands and running. That's how they tear Lily's dress.

That needs to be changed because Lily isn't going to be caught dead with that small tear. Every one of the trio insists on changing to the same outfits back at their houses. That means someone has to get in the car and go get them!

They've done it to themselves, them foolish mamas!

Callie and Lily have their fifth birthday with a huge double celebration at Madam Aucoin's antebellum home, down the road by Galliano. They love the staircase, walking down so prissy-like, not knowing the ghosts there are all watching them so they don't fall down. (When Flower is two, they have another big party, with Callie and Lily helping her unwrap all her presents.)

Madam Consienne and her band remain together from a long time ago. Lawd, if they were alive, they would be famous in the big wide-open world. They're famous in their own rights, first jazz musicians down in Storyville by the Quarter, with Madam C as the proprietor of a famous whorehouse down in Storyville. They will have to change the name of the Jazzy Jumpin' Jive Nigs because you gotta be politically correct these days, even in Louisiana.

Madam Consienne now has her long-gone suitor with her because of Madam Aucoin's crystal ball. She's much nicer.

∞ ∞ ∞

BOUNDARIES are enforced in the backyard. The girls can't go any farther than that, being they're carrying Flower with them. She just walks in front of them everywhere, trusting her big sistas to keep danger from around her.

All three girls are standing at the back fence made of cypress boards that encloses the yard. The yard has every imaginable outside toy that money could buy, several doubled at each house. Swing sets, trampolines, houses big enough for all three to get in, bikes they go riding around the yard, with Flower trying to keep up on her tricycle.

You would think that it's a fairyland these girls have, but the wooden fence is beckoning! The gate has a bell on it that rings loud and brings attention to whoever is opening it.

Callie and Lily have figured out how to escape, Lily the thinker and Callie the doer. Callie says, "Let's go see our mamas at Flavia's store! Ah want a pop rouge, and they're gonna be so proud of us being the big girls to ride our bikes to the store! What do you think, Lily?"

Madam Aucoin has made sure they speak proper English because she says the girls will be exposed to the real world and don't need ridicule from fools!

Estelle and Minou are running the restaurant at Flavia's General Store now, and they hire two young women to run the store. They have their own schedules working around Bertha's because she is the main babysitter. And Irene, of course. They have it all figured out.

We all know about best-laid plans.

The girls untie the bell off the gate, sneak the bikes out quietly, and stick Flower in Lily's big basket. They have bells on their bikes too, but they sure don't ring them going out the gate.

Bertha and Irene are inside Minou's house, drinking coffee and watching The Young and The Restless. Neither one has any worries because the girls play so good with each other, causing no trouble. No warning, no bell.

The trio are on the road, going la-la-la down the bayou to Flavia's when Lily's bike hits a rock, causing her and Flower to fall off the bike. Flower is bawling, and Lily is sobbing, and Callie is trying to get them both up without blood on their bodies or matching outfits.

This old battered pickup truck pulls to the side of the road, and the man that's driving is old and battered himself. He gets out to help the girls and smiles a toothless grin.

"Mais, Ah be goddamned if it ain't my lil granddaughter! Lemme see, bébé, if Ah can kiss ya booboo and make it bettah. Ah'm ya pawpaw, and Ah know Butch and Minou and Joe and Alcide and Bertha.

"Y'all get in my truck, and we'll put the bikes in tha back. Me, Ah gotta take y'all to tha store."

Of course, they trust the old man – he knows everybody – and they climb up in the cab, moving all his nasty mess off the seats.

Flower is happy, but Callie and Lily's senses are kinda uneasy, and they watch the road for the safety of the store and their mamas.

Old Man Guidry says, as he passes up Flavia's, "We gonna go by my house first 'cause Ah have somet'in' for ya, Flower. It won't take but a few minutes. Come on, y'all get down and help my petite fleur."

The two older girls are hesitant to walk in when Guidry slightly pushes them in the front door of his houseboat. He immediately locks the door, with him outside and Callie and Lily and Flower inside. They are steadily screaming loud, but they can't be heard, with the large motor on the houseboat making noise as its slipping out his dock.

Lawd, have mercy. Mary wept. And Jesus and T-June, please come!

Everybody watches the decrepit houseboat moving at a steady pace, heading out in Bayou Lafourche toward the swamps. At the store, people are gossiping, talking about the strange thing happening. That houseboat hadn't left the dock for thirty years.

Minou said, "Dat's a damn good t'ing. Let him go peddle his nasty ass somewhere else. Ah'm gonna call Irene to tell her tha good news!" Minou gets Irene on the phone, asking what the girls are doing.

Irene says, "Sweetie, Ah'm lookin' out tha glass doors now. Ah can see dem sleepin' in deir doll house. Dey all wrapped up in deir coats and sleepin' like some lil puppies!

"Well, Ah can give a flyin' fuck what dat old man does! Ah heard he had got out tha jail. See y'all soon!"

Irene is looking at the bundle of coats that the girls don't put on when they leave. She needs glasses. Minou and Estelle and Irene and Bertha, all of them go to wake up the girls an hour later and find empty coats, with their bikes missing.

The whole village is called, their own special one.

Everyone comes from the real-live villages up and down the bayou.

Father Becnel lets school out early, and he and Sister Bridget are almost the first to get here.

Alcide and Joe and Theo are called at their seafood business, and they come with a bunch of hard-working Cajuns to do whatever they can.

Bishop Toussaint is on the way back from New Orleans, but Madam comes quickly.

Flavia and Sweet will be here early tomorrow morning in their plane, with a posse of all his cowhands.

Butch and Katrina leave Thibodaux, coming this way soon, reaching Minou and Joe's house where they all break down in each other's arms.

The cousins, Moe and Mac, come running with their guns loaded. They bring Big Mama, but Sweet Jesus has taken Big Daddy to sing with the angels.

The neighbors begin telling them and Sheriff Truxillo about Old Man Guidry moving his houseboat fast down the bayou. Just about the same time, a call comes in from Irene's papa, the criminal who has just made parole, calling collect from some little place in the swamps that has a phone.

"Betcha ya didn't expect to talk wit' me again for tha rest of my life, huh? Ya never came to see me, even when Ah told ya Ah was born again in a letter, and den nobody showed up to get me when Ah got out! Ah had to hitchhike back to tha bayou. Now dat's a rotten way for a daughter to act like dat to ya daddy!

"Ah got tha t'ree lil girls on my houseboat way back in tha swamps. Ya won't find us 'cause Ah'm movin' all tha time all t'rough tha swamps. It's gonna take some money Ah deserve to bring dem back. Me, Ah'm gonna call collect again to tell ya where to bring tha money and take dese lil gals off my hands before Ah feed dem to tha gators!

"Mais, Flower is da prettiest one, wit' them two other lil halfbreeds dat took her on dey bikes. Ya still no good being a mama, lettin' her hang around dem two. She looks so much like ya mama, it breaks my heart! As if, as if! My lil gal is white like tha snow!

"Give me tha money, and Ah'm gonna sail to Mexico and stay dere. Mais, Ah'm gonna let y'all know." He hangs up.

The mamas are so grief-stricken, they aren't much help, crying and yelling cuss words and crying and praying and crying, cussing, and yelling. Madam Aucoin gives them all something for their nerves and rolls joints of ganja for each of them.

Sweet Stu and Flavia come early in the morning, along with all the cowpokes from Texas, to search for the babies. Each one had a big-ass holster holding their loaded guns. Two planes fly in at the same time.

The Texas Rangers are here, as well as the Louisiana National Guard. Flavia has called in favors, and every imaginable group arrives at Minou and Joe's to add to the massive hunt going on.

Sheriff Truxillo has all his deputies and has made Moe and Mac deputies right in the front yard.

T-June (Joseph) is a massive young man at thirteen, just like his papa. He is at the front of this emergency, guiding and giving orders. This might be the time when he shows abilities to the world, for sure to Lafourche Parish!

T-June tells Sweet to take him up in the air, because his stuff is kicking into high gear. Just them.

They leave a massive number of people on the ground, the swamps full of men and women yelling and guiding big hound dogs, German Shepherds, and even a few chihuahuas!

Joe and Alcide and Theo and Jean and the bishop are carrying loaded shotguns. For them, it's shoot at first sight!

Bertha and Madam and Big Mama are working hard to keep the coffee pots full and sandwiches ready to be eaten. All kinds of bottles of hard liquor are on display, with beer and Cokes in the huge ice chests that people bring.

Flavia goes inside for a few minutes with Sister Bridget and Pawpaw Irby. All three kneel, saying two rosaries.

T-June is silent for a little while in the air and then says, "Sweet! I feel them! Right over there where all the cypress trees are clumped together. You're going to have to get lower so I can do something! Look, the girls are waving and shouting from the deck! Callie is hitting the old man because he's trying to start the boat to go deeper! I'm going to stop the boat from moving." He's telling Sweet to leave and come back with more help.

He stops the boat by pointing at it. Then, T-June jumps into the back of the boat.

Old Man Guidry goes to hit him and is thrown overboard without being touched. He feels like he's gotten struck down with the Holy Spirit!

Old Man Guidry doesn't have any idea of what T-June can do, but he's gonna see more before this is through!

T-June leaves him in the water until he believes the old man will settle down. He already knows that Guidry is being visited with every sin he has committed and sees Moses with the Ten Commandments! Guidry is being baptized in the swamp waters for sure, and he is steadily praying for redemption!

The girls are in good condition, in spite of all the mosquito bites and no air-conditioning.

Flower needs to be held and comforted by a grown-up, she being an infant out there. Callie and Lily find some old rags that look clean and find some safety pins to put clean diapers on Flower, as she's forgotten all about home training.

The would-be twins are both talking at the same time. Callie of course is the mouth of the two.

"Bubba, I'm so glad you found us! We promise we aren't ever going out the backyard gate with our bikes again! Huh, Lily? We're going to make finger promises with our pinky fingers right now with Bubba!

"Mais, that is a nasty dirty man. And he didn't have any food for us to eat, just some crackers."

"And Bubba, he made Lily pee off the side of the boat! He said he didn't want 'no lil nigga' using his bathroom!

"You should have seen me! I punched him in his belly and stomped on his bad foot, and he was coughing and running around the deck holding his foot.

"Lily marched right up and went in his bathroom. It's nothing but a hole in the floor. The door just closes, but there's no lock on it."

Lily's gotta have her say in this quemas. She is quite undone with the whole thing.

"Well, Bubba, I just walked up in the front of him still crying about his foot. I told him all about himself. And then I snapped my fingers in his face! He isn't worth a bag of Elmer's Chee-Weez!

"Callie and I stayed up all night and threw dishes and pots at the old man if he tried to come in the door. He's got a lot of bites, and he's got a black eye from Callie one time when he tried to force himself in.

"I did use some words I am not supposed to say, but I was some pissed off and couldn't help myself! He never said another word to me, and he stayed outside. Flower kept putting her hand up to him and saying to talk to it.

"We made some milk from a bag of dried milk you get from the people who give you food. My sistas help over there sometimes. Callie and I like to go with them to talk to the people who need help feeding themselves."

"We mixed up some of that milk and saltine crackers because Flower was hungry and calling for her mama."

T-June can't help but laugh at the tales being told. He is some proud of these little girls. He goes out of the cabin and helps the old man out the water.

Guidry looks like he has seen the True Light of God, and he crawls in a corner of the deck, speaking to T-June in almost a whisper.

"Mon Dieu, Blessed Mother, and Holy Spirit. Oh, my sweet Jesus. Ya come back and look where ya from? Tha swamps! Me, Ah seen it all! Ah dedicate my life to ya, T-June, and Ah'm gonna live my life helpin' ya! Dat's if they let me live after all dis merde! Oh! Ah mean crap, no Ah mean poo-poo! So sorry, Saint T-June."

The old man goes to bawling with for-true real tears. Just a-sobbing, and the girls all go to him, crying with him. Soft-hearted flowers, all of them.

Boats of every kind and color surround them within 30 minutes, and Sweet lands his plane on the water.

Minou and Estelle and Irene jump out the first boat to tie up to the houseboat. Sheriff Truxillo is next, with his gun out, pointing it square on Guidry.

All three mamas gang up on Guidry, and he is beaten bad before T-June stops them.

T-June says, "Mama, it isn't the time. Take the babies, Mama, and y'all go.

"Sheriff, you trust me, I know that. Let me take Guidry back on the houseboat, and then you can do what you need to do, please, sir. We're going to be home in a couple of hours. We're going to be all right."

Minou gets in one more slap on Guidry's head before she gets in the boat. Irene won't even look at him, so ashamed and angry. She and Flower get off the houseboat she wants to burn. They don't turn, with him pleading for her to stay.

T-June starts the boat without the key, and Guidry is waiting for him to walk on the swamp water!

T-June starts the conversation by talking to the old man in his head. Guidry screams and starts crying again. He has no doubts about what's happened, and T-June calms him down. He is guiding the boat while the old man sits by him on the floor.

"Mr. Guidry, what's the name your mama gave you? Daniel? That's real nice, Daniel. That's what I will call you.

"That's one of the first things that I did when I was a baby. Talking to people in their heads. Not everybody can hear me that I do that with. But your mind has been changed, no anger left, and true love replacing all that stuff you had in there. It's wide open. No lie! Ha! I don't care what words you use, but in truth when you say anything.

"Mr. Daniel, I do a lot of things, and people are thinking they need to go to the crazy house because they don't believe the stuff they see.

"My life has been guarded and protected by all my family. It's made up of people that came into my life to help me get grown without interference of the government or by someone who would use me for their benefit.

"Tell me, Daniel, why did you demand money from us?"

Old Man Guidry is sobbing again and tries to explain himself. "Mais, Ah just want to be loved by my family, and Ah know right now, it's gonna be hard. Ah don't need no money, but it was so stupid on my part to kidnap tha babies and say what Ah did to Irene.

"Ah treated my family so bad, 'specially my good wife, who didn't stand a chance wit' me. Ah was never taught 'bout love. Ah was brought up by my papa to not trust no one, to be mean as a snake 'cause my papa was worse dan me, and he was an outlaw. Beatin' me e'ry day just to beat me!

"Ah moved my houseboat all tha way from Pierre Part to here to get away from him, but Ah stayed mean. It's all Ah been taught. Just carried him wit' me and his ugly ways.

"It's gonna be so hard for me 'cause Ah been dis way all my life! If she would just talk to me or look at me with some feelin' other dan hate me.

"Ah'm a changed man, t'anks to ya, T-June. Ah know Ah'm gonna go back to tha jail, but dey will see tha change when Ah get back home! All Ah want is to follow ya footsteps and be a help to you. Please, T-June, Ah want ya to believe me!"

T-June responds, "I truly feel your redemption. I already know you will be another to join the tribe. That's what I like to call my family. I'm asking you to be part of that family. Things will change because right now, everybody wants to kill you. I will tell you everything about me as time comes, but you have to prove yourself to many people. You will do this for me.

"I kept that a secret, because I think my tribe would have vetoed you out, not letting you join because you have been such a mean old fart. Not now, I will assure them. You need to talk with Irene yourself. That's between you and her.

"Mister…Okay, just Daniel. I know you're going to spend some time in jail, but stay on the right path even in there and help the jailbirds to be better people."

T-June drives the boat while Daniel goes inside to clean up and bathe his filthy body. They pull into his wharf, where everyone is waiting. Old Man Guidry stands with his hands up in the air, waiting for Sheriff Truxillo to put the cuffs on him. People there are hollering for the sheriff to shoot him!

Irene won't talk with him, and he drives off in the back seat of a cop car, looking back to see all the family staring back.

T-June sits down at the kitchen table and tells them what he has seen when Guidry is in the water.

He isn't pushing the issue but does take a stand on Daniel's behalf and tells them he is gonna be a part of the tribe.

They are taking this hard because they don't see the redemption and worry that T-June is making a mistake. Bishop is wanting to talk, and the tribe is listening. "I've seen worse men than him turn their lives around. I'm all about second chances, y'all know this. I will visit him in jail to see if he has truly become a better man. His alcoholism will be hard to quit in jail, but they have AA groups in there.

"I will give him a decent chance, but I won't force my decision on any of you. You have to make your own choice, and it's a hard one since Irene refuses to see him."

The girls are safe, and they say that they feel sorry for him now.

∞ ∞ ∞

FLOWER, Callie, and Lily seem unphased by their kidnapping and quickly return to being the vivacious and outspoken girls who lead their mamas a merry chase. Flower is constantly raising her hand, telling everybody to talk, to talk to it!

Callie and Lily's Flower is a duplicate of her two teachers. They are rarely seen without each other.

T-June, guided by his village and with Jolie by his side, continues to use his powers for good, with an occasional lapse into pranks to amuse Minou and Joe, Bertha and Alcide, Pawpaw Irby and even Sister Bridget. He returns to the swamps with Ruby to talk with the animals and meet with his podnah Pieyan.

But those are tales for another day.

Part Two

Chapter Thirteen

Monsieur Mayhem

THE extraordinary young man gifted with capabilities you can't hardly believe still needs his followers-disciples-posse-village to guide him because he takes life wide open and for sure not as serious as they do.

He chooses to lead himself, and what is really scary, he will act on it. Besides that, when he's driving, he claims to have all his spirits and angels fighting for their roles of being the shotgun rider in his big truck. The others are hanging on for their dear spirits in the back.

T-June Thibeau.

Lawd! If he ain't beautiful as a man of twenty-five.

He loves passionately his Jolie Stelle Theriot ever since he dreamed of her, before he started school. She loves him the same. It was love at first sight for her in the third grade, and T-June's dreams come true all the time.

Jolie has grown up to be more like her mama's side of her family. A tall, thin young lady with an outstanding, cute, perky behind, serious in her schoolwork at Loyola University in New Orleans, with round tortoiseshell glasses hiding her slanted green eyes and crazy wild hair in dreadlocks that she doesn't brush.

Jolie has done something so much out of character, but there it is, just the same. She sings at a blues club on Bourbon Street, the Bon Temps Rouler.

It gets passed on in the genes. She's got the genes of Buddy Braxton, part of the trio that haunts Madam Aucoin's house. He's also a great-great-grandfather to Jolie, and she wears the ring of her great-great-grandmother, Shine, given to her by Buddy, the ghost.

On the weekends Jolie sings, with Joseph playing his guitar along with her and singing too. She's one of those college girls who every weekend will party hardy but never ever without her T-June! A very lucrative job for both of them, although there are no money problems ever.

Nanan Flavia has that covered.

T-June – Joseph Alan Thibeau Jr. – is a replica of his papa, Joe. He's a big man, funny as shit, and will do anything you ask him, maybe a gift is needed and he goes, not hiding anything anymore.

Joseph has a thick black beard, but his round, light brown eyes, his lips, and his dimples are still the same. You still want to kiss him on those lips he's made women crazy over.

The couple has lived together near the French Quarter in the Big Easy since high school graduation. Joseph has always had a strong connection to New Orleans. Brings to mind days gone by of a similar couple, Minou and Joe, his mama and daddy.

Although they attend Mass on Sunday, sort of a habit, Joseph and Jolie both agree they don't have to have a marriage certificate. They've known this from the first time they looked at each other. Two Old Souls that have found soulmates, will never leave, and will be always together.

They can't go home on the weekends because of their gig, so everybody comes to New Orleans to see Jolie and Joseph play their music, keeping their own apartments there.

∞ ∞ ∞

FLAVIA and Sweet Stu own a large house in the city and fly in at least twice a month from Texas. They've adopted two Comanche brothers at two and three years old. Callie with Lily, the younger girls in the family, love toting them around. The boys are Grey, short for Grey Eagle, and Gerry, short for Geronimo. Full-blooded Comanche Indians with parents caught up in the addictions on the Rez, everywhere they were forced to live, the evil white man having brought the beginning, with rot-gut whiskey and tainted blankets.

Flower is the boss of them little wild Indians, now that she has someone younger to say to, Talk to tha hand!

Flavia says she's gotten another chance on her sons again, doing a much better job on these two who don't look like her ex-husband, who walked up the road in broad daylight!

And all of these babies love Nonc June!

People that know him good call him June, but in the Quarter, he's known as Monsieur Mayhem. Mr. Thibeau is used for work, or just plain Joseph. He is a top-rated social worker, the best one to come around down there ever, and works under Bishop Laurant Toussaint in his business of helping people.

Madam Alafair Aucoin and the bishop have a small house there so they can come to visit their families and not be stuck up somebody's ass. It's where they lived when they were first together during the seasons of love. They jumped the broom all those years ago, and that has been as sacred and binding as anything else.

The truth of the matter is that they've always known Monsieur Mayhem would be a tremendous force added in the neighborhoods and him thinking he could handle it all by himself. It may be that he can turn water into Dr Pepper.

You know the village thinks he can walk on that water, in the bayou, of course.

As his disciples, they give him advice when they can because he runs wide open and shines like JoJo Star, a name given at his birth by Madam Aucoin.

Madam has come back to work some, because she's bored, and the ghost Madam Consienne drives her crazy, she's so damn anal! The ghost, not Madam.

Joseph Alan Thibeau Jr. is the serious social worker all day, but at night, he is Monsieur Mayhem, who roams the streets of the Big Easy. He can't be missed, this massive man dressed like a hippy and sandals like Jesus wore, with a beard and a chest full of hair and a face so beautiful it's hard to look at him.

Playing music on the weekends gives him lots of contact with the street people. Talking to them while twirling around in their minds and will give a huge bear hug, curing them of what ails them. He brings a lot of them to the bishop.

∞ ∞ ∞

WHEN it becomes too obvious that the neighborhood is cleaning up its act with no viable answer, Monsieur Mayhem goes home with his Jolie to help the people on Bayou Lafourche, taking a well-deserved leave of absence.

T-June and Jolie's families roll out the red carpet for them when they come home, staying from one house to the other! All the little girls are gaga over June, and when Flavia and Sweet's little Indians come, it's total mayhem for the Monsieur.

T-June and Jolie love staying at Madam Aucoin and the bishop's home. The young couple entertain the ghosts, who come out in all their finery to do the same, playing music together. Madam Consienne has had her lover, Etienne Verdin, come to live with her straight out of Purgatory, and now she's a much nicer spirit. He must have been kinda bad!

Madam Aucoin has summoned up the spirit of Laurette to chill with the other spirits, Buddy Braxton and the motley crew, the Jazzy Jumpin' Jivin' Trio.

Jolie wears the beautiful emerald ring given by her great-great-grandpa, Buddy Braxton. His wife's name was Shine, just Shine. He was and is the jazz of all the jazz in New Orleans.

∞ ∞ ∞

SISTER Bridget has retired from teaching because she is the principal and administrator of all the business for the large Catholic church and school, St. Luke's. She is one of the head knockers of the disciples and follows T-June when she can, but not to New Orleans because she thinks the place is the devil's party-hardy Pontchartrain Beach! She's comes for a few weekends in the Crescent City to hear the couple's music, and that's enough for her. But she's found out that she loves piña coladas and has bought a blender for the convent of the nuns, turning all of the nuns into five o'clock drinkers!

Father Becnel is a very prestigious priest up and down the bayou, drawing many to Mass, and St. Luke's Catholic school has a waiting list. He remains the same in his appearance, but he has a dreamy look about him all the time. It's always been the same reason, because it's for his nervine condition!

Old Man Daniel Guidry has done four years in jail, and that's not long for his offenses of kidnapping, endangering minor children, and being a bona fide asshole. Irene Breaux, his daughter, has to try hard to soften her heart toward him, mainly because T-June has said Daniel is part of the followers-disciples-posse-village it has taken to raise this child, this T-June, this Joseph.

Irene visits after she is told the genuine difference in her papa, and that takes a year of convincing. He has a ministry in jail and has started AA meetings daily. Irene knows that the chances of that goodness disappearing when he gets out are great, but June has told her and her husband, Jean, she thinks he is changed for good.

Danny Guidry is the name he is known by in the jail, and that's who he is. He now lives in New Orleans at Bishop Toussaint's facilities, in a small apartment that he loves. The electricity and the bathroom are amazing, but a TV has made his life unbelievably bon temps rouler, passing a good time eating popcorn and watching cowboys. He watches all the old Western movies and is a big fan of John Wayne.

He gets paid as a counselor of sorts, like a preacher, teaching his trade to any of these young people who want to live on the bayou. His AA meetings are daily for anyone who wants to be straight and sober.

You've got to walk the walk before you can talk the talk!

Papa Danny is what he's called at home because he is so proud to be in Butch, Katrina and Flower's lives and shows pictures to everybody. Irene, Jean, and her papa are mending the fences and the houseboat still on the bayou. He's even asked Irene and Jean to go with him up to north Louisiana to meet her mama's people.

They go up to Grayson, outside of Columbia on the Ouachita River, and pull into a gravel drive in front of an immaculate old house surrounded by regal pines, making you dizzy trying to see the tops.

Irene's mama's people cry along with Irene, Jean, and Danny, so glad to see them. They cook all the mainstays of stump-jumpers: fresh vegetables, venison they shot themselves, and the golden cornbread, buttered and much better than white bread.

They try hard to boil crawfish, but they always seem to be missing something. The line starts in Alexandria, then you up there with the Yankees! They can't boil crawfish and they always have a Cajun name on the restaurant sign advertising what they do. They don't tell you Thibodeaux and Boudreaux came from Monroe or Arkansas!

∞ ∞ ∞

BUTCH, June's older brother, and Katrina, Jolie's older sister, now live around Flavia and Sweet Stu and their boys in Eagle Lake, Texas. Both are doing what they went to college for: history and psychology.

Butch teaches at a nearby school where he also teaches English to the Hispanic children, and Katrina has hung out a therapist sign.

The couple are also building their own horse ranch too. It can't compare to the King Ranch, but that's where they've discovered their love of horses.

They are expecting their first child, a daughter. Her name will be Elouise Marie Miller. They're going to call her Weedie! Adding to the Callie-Lily-Flower group, the Weed.

That's funny as shit!

Minou and Joe are raising Callie and find the job very nerve-wracking and mysterious, since she is now fifteen. Lily is the same age.

For advice, Minou relies on Estelle, who's already had a houseful of women to raise herself.

Lily is the same as she always has been, the brain with common sense, and quick to put you in your place.

Callie is also the same boisterous gal she's always been; you can't confuse her voice because it comes out a raspy drawl, loud and quick to act on something, with not an ounce of the common sense of her sistas.

Just like her mama!

Flower can't wait to be a teenager since she is right up there in the bedrooms of the fifteen-year-olds, learning shit she has no business learning! She still throws that hand up, telling you to talk to it, instead of the bird finger the other two are quick to do.

∞ ∞ ∞

IT'S the nasty part of March, all rainy and cold. June and Jolie are at home with Minou and Joe. Everyone is enjoying the fireplace burning cypress and pine. For sure old Pops is.

Pop Irby Peltier is living life as a much younger version of himself and is gonna shack up with a widow from church.

The first sign of June's abilities was toward his podnah, PawPaw Irby, who called him Atakapa! T-June went up in his pawpaw's brain the minute he held him.

Alcide and Bertha are counting the days before the full moon. As the loup-garous, they still roam their land on their monthly period. Many, many years have passed since Minou and Joe first found them trying to cross the bayou, like the Canadian Mountie calling for the Indian maiden to get to each other, across the river, shallow enough for them to walk through it. They used to howl at each other to come across, one of them.

Come to find out it is Minou's mama and her parrain. But now they are on the same side of the bayou.

There is much help for them because most of the people in their special village come to aid on that night. A few of the family still don't know about this, and it's better that way.

Old Man Danny Guidry is good with help. He had seen Alcide one time turn from loup-garou back to himself, hiding from view in the swamps. He has stayed away from Alcide since that time, tangling up like two animals when they see each other, each one wanting to mark their territories!

But Danny Guidry isn't the same dude and wants to be Alcide's friend.

"June, will you and Jolie come tonight and help?" asks Minou. "Parrain and Mama are free now and mostly romp around and run like two huge wolves racin' each other. We buy plenty meat so dey not huntin' no more. Ya see how many ribeyes Ah buy.

"It's pretty to watch, and they don't come close to us 'cause Ah still carry my Off! Spray. We keep dem on our land so dey don't run amok in our neighbors' land.

"Me and Joe, Old Danny, Estelle and Theo, and you two. It'll be fun!" Minou tells the group at nine o'clock.

Minou tells them all to get their jackets and their gear for the monthly visit to the swamps.

June has learned to tolerate the happening, never wanting to be around when it takes place. He does realize he could become loup-garou; he just won't go to that part of his brain. He is itching for a good chance to lay his hands on the Cajun werewolves, but they've both stayed at arms' length from him since he was a little boy and throwing his gifts all over the place!

It's kinda like when your hair stands up on your neck, warning something. But in a loving way.

It's midnight at the oasis. All are gathered around a huge bonfire, listening to music, drinking white Russians, and sharing tokes of some good stuff.

June watches the pair of loup-garous as they play with each other and sees the beautiful animals they become on the full moon. He won't go to that corner in his brain that says, Join us, join us!

He is standing there in the dark, away from the fire, when he sees a man and a boy.

While his son watches, the man shoots Alcide in the gut of the loup-garou as he turns slowly back into Alcide. He howls like no one has ever heard and never wants to hear again, folding into a heap of a broken man.

The neighbor stands there, screaming silently, dropping his gun as his son goes to pick it up and cocks it again.

The man, a former classmate of June's, is there with his twelve-year-old boy. They live on the side of Flavia's store. He has been a buddy to June. Pierre Dugas, known as Pete, and Rowdy Dugas, his son.

Bertha, still a loup-garou, has Pete's whole head in her mouth and biting as she turns back into Bertha.

Rowdy drops the gun and runs while Minou and Joe, with Theo and Danny, are pulling on Bertha with all their strength to stop her. When she turns back, she is still trying to kill him! Howling in despair, reaching for his throat with her teeth.

Theo and Estelle Theriot – Jolie and Lily and Katrina's parents – have never seen anything like it in their lives, I guess, but they both jump in to help.

Theo speaks out, "My podnah, my best friend, what you need me to do? Ya already know we ain't sayin' shit."

June in horror runs to both of them. Blood is pouring out of Alcide and Pete like an outdoor faucet onto the ground, soaking the clover red. Joe and Theo move them onto the palmetto mattress that's been added to for more than thirty years. Side by side, they lay looking at each other in pain and sorrow.

June, with Jolie as his assistant, puts his hands on Alcide first, and they all watch as the bullet pops out his chest. He had never done that before and is elated that he can save Alcide. Wetting his fingers, June uses his spit to close the wound.

June will do a lot of pondering later…

When Pete sees June coming for him next, he goes into a self-induced coma. His wounds are to the throat and neck area, plus a broken arm and hand, the hand that pulls the trigger. June places his hands on Pete, performing his miracles, but when June goes to his head, there is nobody home.

Bertha cannot be consoled. She constantly screams his name, howling like a pissed off wolf.

Madam Aucoin and the bishop come in their nightclothes to try and soothe the savage beast Bertha is right now, Madam taking the pain of her best friend and mournfully calling her spirits.

Rowdy comes back with his mama. She's screaming and pulling her hair out while laying across her husband, Pete, who is still in his checked-out time.

Rowdy speaks up for his mama and himself. "Miss Minou, Miss Minou! Tell me, tell me! Please tell me, Miss Minou! I know what I saw, but I don't wanna see it, believe me! Tell me and my mama what to do! We're both in some terrible shock.

"It's just us three now since Pawpaw and Mawmaw died, and I can't go home right now because I don't know what to do about my mama! I'm not even thirteen yet!"

The young man falls out sobbing, with wracking hiccups, into Minou's arms.

Estelle, the loving caretaker, takes Rowdy and Charlotte Dugas from Minou and guides both of them into Minou's house. The girls are waiting for him by the screen door.

Callie and Lily go to school with Rowdy, and they are all friends. Especially Flower, who is now closer to his age. She's had a crush forever on Rowdy.

He gets as much comfort as he can handle with the three girls, but it is a rawness of reality no amount of comfort could soothe.

∞ ∞ ∞

PART of the posse is here up in Minou and Joe's house. The doublewide trailer's been added on to twice over the years, with the whole house covered in brick and cypress. It's now a big, rambling house, with large screened-in porches all around the house, one by every bedroom sliding door. Big enough to hold a lot of people, like the five bedrooms and baths.

Rowdy's mama is Charlotte, a former schoolmate of June and Jolie. She was very timid in school, talking mostly with Jolie when she would.

Pete is very outgoing and funny. He has stood with June on anything or everything that has happened all through the years. He has watched his podnah do some strange things over the years but keeps it to himself, never wanting to open that door.

The couples have celebrated their graduation together and been to their house in the city. And vice versa. We're talking about lifelong buds.

He has been a true friend, and June is so overcome by this horrific tragedy.

Charlotte is given the bedroom that has windows on every wall and a sliding door looking out on the swamps. It is considered their sun room, old-fashioned as it sounds; it's the den that most people call it today. Very bright and sunny to take Charlotte out of her delusions and depression.

What they don't know is that that she's a regular Steel Magnolia that just can't quit weeping like the willow.

Pete just sits in PawPaw Irby's old recliner and stares at everybody, saying nothing. He does stare individually at the crew there to try to help him. That's how he is when he comes out the fantasy land he has run into with his mind.

June sits by him most of his days, rubbing his hands and speaking softly to his old podnah.

∞ ∞ ∞

FLAVIA and Sweet Stu fly in with Butch and Katrina and the two wild Comanches, Grey and Gerry.

Flavia lets them keep their hair as long as they want. She's so different now since she smokes ganja and is "gettin' sum."

Katrina is carrying lil Weedie in her belly. This baby just kicks and kicks and moves constantly. Sure makes one curious to see this little girl when she comes out.

Mrs. Flavia opens her large house and Flavia's General Mercantile and Boutique to the young ones, including the teens. She and Stu love them being there and lively, like they are with the two little Comanches.

Flavia is a changed woman in every way now that she is "gettin' sum."

Madam Aucoin and Bishop Toussaint have a party when the kids are shuffled to them. Food, music, patchouli, and ghosts. The beautiful old house on Highway 1 that is covered in vining antique roses and long-stemmed roses everywhere in the house.

Madam has found a beautiful water bong in an old head shop and finds it just right for the long stems, so she purchases one for every room.

The bishop takes over Rowdy's care, talking with him for hours, the same as when he mentored the young Butch. He takes him to New Orleans, talking the whole time in his big old Lincoln Continental; it's a two-door, turquoise, with a leaking sunroof, big tire on the back in white leather, 1975 model year, and plays cassettes.

Explaining the strangeness of all the people there to help and why, explaining the miracles that June has dealt with all his life.

Old Danny is teaching him all about a life as a trapper and fisherman. He teaches him the art of making nets, leaving the real-life fisherman's trade to Joe.

Alcide is mending slowly but makes Rowdy, Charlotte, and Pete feel at home here.

The entire posse of the women takes turns talking with Charlotte. Some sessions of one-on-one, but she seems to really perk up when it's a bunch of them. Flavia just praises the medicinal properties of smoking marijuana and "gettin' sum!" That makes Charlotte laugh real loud, this coming from Flavia, knowing who the hell is saying that. She has known Flavia her whole life.

Alcide is in his recovering bed, playing bourré with Old Danny for hours, neither wanting to fight like in the good old days.

The village has come together as they do whenever Monsieur Mayhem is involved or someone else in their (what the hell haven't we used yet?) coven!

Father Becnel and Sister Bridget come daily to say the Rosary with Charlotte and to give the last sacraments to Pete Dugas. They didn't know if he would go away to the haven in his mind and forget to breathe.

∞ ∞ ∞

THE community of Larose knows there is some trouble over there at the Peltier-Thibeau houses.

It's always mysterious, magical, life-changing, with never any money worries down on the bayou with these people. Some people are avid fans, while others stay away from whatever quemas is happening, scared and superstitious and spreading gossip like syrup.

June has had to call the place where Pete is working, telling them he's recovering from an accident in the swamps. "At my mama's house," June says.

What tha fuck?

Charlotte is a teacher at Sister Bridget's school, so the sister has taken care of that problem.

Both needi help all the time and the fewer people outside the coven who know about it, the better.

But that news spreads from one house to the other house until it reaches the Thibodaux Comet newspaper.

Rowdy goes back to school, and he and the girls are constant companions. He is showing his intelligence and street smarts that the family has always known was there already. He is silent on what has taken place in the swamps, not speaking a word of it. He is not the boy anymore that was the class clown and trouble stirrer.

Six months go by, and Joshua Silverberg, a newspaper man, knocks on the door of Minou and Joe's. Getting ready for a job change,

Joshua is moving to The Times-Picayune in New Orleans after having been in his parents' business of publishing since he was a child. His sister now runs the business.

He wants to bring his investigative story there with him, because he feels it in his bones that this story on the bayou is gigantic. He may be up for the Pulitzer Prize!

So, this big gnat lands on Minou and T-June's asses the minute she answers the door. They all will feel his bite and can't reach it to slap it off.

"Mrs. Thibeau, it's such a pleasure to meet you and your families! Here's my card. I'm Joshua Silverberg from the Comet in Thibodaux."

Minou tries not to be obvious when she wipes off her hand that he has shaken.

"I'm here to write a story about your son, Joseph, and your amazing family. You are well known up and down Bayou Lafourche. I've been gathering stories about all of you, and some are downright scary!

"If y'all would consent, I would like to tell your stories as a human interest piece, and I wouldn't add anything you wouldn't want me to. I know this is a huge story, and if I can write it, it would be your side, and many people would be interested in it.

"Please, Mrs. Thibeau, is Joseph here? Tell him, please, I want to talk with him and see how he feels about this. I would also like to see the Dugases, Pete and Charlotte and Rowdy. You've got people thinking they were killed by your family. Just to make sure."

He isn't being truthful right there, as his main reason is to investigate the disappearance of the Dugases, thinking their story will be enough, especially thinking they are being held as hostages.

Joshua is afraid to mention that first in case these people are nutcases.

This young man from Thibodaux is a stereotype of what you think of concerning newspapermen. Thin frame, almost wiry, 5 foot, 10 inches or so, cigarette hanging out his mouth and thick glasses falling down on his nose. Joshua Silverberg comes from a long line of writers, editors, publishers, and storytellers and is one of the few people of Jewish faith in the town. They go to the small synagogue in Thibodeaux and will travel to New Orleans if need be for Shabbat.

He believes the storytelling of this particular and peculiar family will be a career-changing event for him.

Monsieur Mayhem (he's in full force) walks into the living room, where his mama and Joshua are sitting. Minou serves coffee, like she's supposed to, and has gone to get Joe. She's thinking about calling everybody, even Father Becnel and Sister Bridget.

Joseph comes in and stands over Joshua and offers his hand to shake while he takes a little trip inside the man's mind. He sees a glimpse of alcoholism coming for him. Joshua's mind is chaotic but determined to write his story. Joseph drops the hand, feeling warnings but curious about the man.

"How can I help you, Mr. Silverberg? Oh, yeah, you want to see the Dugases to make sure they're living. So, come with me."

T-June leads him into the other part of the living area, where he sees Pete in a recliner with Alcide sitting close, playing Pedro with Danny. The TV station is playing Andy Griffith reruns.

Pete smiles at Joshua but doesn't say a word.

Alcide and Danny stand to shake hands with the fidgety man that has just lit another cigarette.

"Pete, can you tell me how you're doing? Lots of people are worried about you. Are you all right? Where's the rest of your family? Can you tell me?"

Pete doesn't want to talk yet and for sure not to this man, but he will when he's ready. His expressions will let you know he's still here. He lights up when Charlotte comes to him. He has a serious expression when it's Rowdy, wanting to say something to him, but when Alcide sits by him, he tears up and touches him.

T-June sits for hours and hours talking to him. It's when he's there that Pete is the most active.

Pete is wondering who the hell this man is in front of him, the one he isn't going to answer.

"Come on, Joshua. I'll take you to see Miss Charlotte. We'll have to knock hard."

June – or if you prefer, Joseph or if you prefer, Monsieur Mayhem – opens the door to Charlotte's and Pete's sitting area after knocking hard. The music is blaring New Orleans-style and swamp pop tunes. She looks up from her crocheting and turns the music down while sitting, not bothering to stand.

She's already heard most of it because Joshua has an obnoxious and loud voice.

"I am so relieved to see you and your husband doing well and alive. I was told Rowdy was at school? Oh, I'm sorry! I am Joshua Silverberg from Thibodaux, and I'm a writer for the Comet newspaper. I have many readers that want to know about what's happening down Bayou Lafourche and about y'all's disappearance."

Charlotte looks him dead in the eyes and says in her proper English teacher's voice, "Mr. Silverberg, I am well acquainted with your work. I have no idea what you are talking about. My husband and I were enjoying a bonfire with T-June and Jolie when a black cougar jumped out the swamps, attacked my husband and Mr. Peltier.

Good thing they have the antique panther rug a century old on somebody's floor, shot by an ancestor.

"Joe and Alcide began shooting but not before that cougar jumped on Alcide and Pete. It traumatized my husband and myself, so we are recuperating, being well taken care of. I had minor injuries."

June stands there listening and watches Charlotte Dugas bold-faced lie and is amazed she says a black panther while looking at the raggedy old skin. Another woman has joined the followers-disciples-posse-village-coven-sistas.

What else?

The two men walk back up to the front, and Joshua begins to tell June about the article he wants to write. June shakes his hand again and says, "Not today, buddy. I have a large family, and we discuss everything pertaining to our family. I've got your card and will call you with a decision, but for the life of me, I don't think you'll find anything special."

Monsieur Mayhem shuts the door on Joshua still talking. He doesn't like what's become clear in Joshua's mind, and there's more mayhem coming.

∞ ∞ ∞

EVERYBODY in the village is on their way.

June walks back into the room where Alcide, Danny, and Pete sit waiting. Minou goes to get Joe, and they are also there.

"Well, it's finally happened. I always knew someone would come, being nosier than my mama and nanan, and he's now coming for the story that will make him famous. I figure if we say no, it will make him even nosier and determined to write it anyway. Mama, you're going to have to call everybody to come. This is some very heavy shit!"

Minou doesn't tell him she's already done that.

Everyone in the room there stands with their mouths open when Pete gets up off the recliner, stands, and opens his mouth. "Man, Ah always knew ya was a special dude, Joseph! Ah ain't been sittin' here not payin' attention. Ah could hear everyt'in', and June, ya coulda tole me somet'in', man, Ah woulda helped ya as Ah have always been ya podnah."

Everybody gasps before Pete realizes what's just happened.

"Shit! Sumbitch! Holy Jesus! Ah can talk again! And look, Ah'm walkin'! Ooh, ooh! Ya might have to tell me to shut up! Ah'm goin' find Charlotte.

"As far as this dude comin' to write a story, he ain't gonna hear shit from me now dat we joined a new family, and we so grateful!

"Thank all of y'all for takin' care of us. And Alcide, Ah can't say how sorry Ah am for shootin' ya."

They stand and hug and kiss each other in the French styles, crying big old tears.

I don't mean French kissing. I mean on the cheeks several times.

Most of the family will be there tonight, but there will be no mention of the loup-garous to Father Becnel, Sister Bridget, and Irene and Jean Breaux, and a bunch more. All they've been told is there's been a serious accident, going along with Charlotte's straight-faced lie. Secrets in the secretive bunch already!

Alcide and Bertha want it that way.

Everyone is introduced to the Dugases, who are positively members of the peculiar tribe now. They for sure know about the werewolves.

Flavia, the political and anti-government nanan, speaks up first. "Y'all know Ah can make dis go away, ya know Ah know all tha higher-ups, and dis man will go away. Ah'll make calls in tha mornin'."

They all laugh at that. That old Flavia is still there!

Bishop Toussaint speaks up right after Flavia. "Send him to me! I can for sure give him a human rights story. Just let him see who you are in New Orleans, even touching the homeless and playing music with your wife. That's a wonderful story for him to write and enough to keep him away from the bayou.

"Hellfire, my spirits, The Times-Picayune has never written a godforsaken word about us. We have been here for twenty-five years! Come on, June, you know we could give him enough to write about."

Monsieur Mayhem stands and silences the group. Everyone wants to play their hand for the bourré pot! "He's made it very clear what he wants to write about and not something necessarily nice, not saying it but clear as day in his mind. Mr. Slick-as-Shit! This Monsieur Mayhem will show him human interest stories, just the G-rated kind. All of us will get on board to steer him in your particular community ways. We all are going to plan this, as y'all will be in the damn article too."

∞ ∞ ∞

MONSIEUR Mayhem calls Joshua Silverberg to come the following Monday, and he is banging on the door, right on time. Monsieur Mayhem laughs and says he must have been sleeping in his car outside.

He's not far from the truth. Joshua has been doing a little stalking.

"Oh, Joseph! You don't know how grateful I am for being allowed to see your people and talk to them. Y'all are highly thought of up and down the bayou, but y'all keep to yourselves. And you know how people are. They start ugly rumors if left to their own imaginations."

June is being Monsieur Mayhem, the alter ego he is when in the Big Easy. It'll be Monsieur Mayhem dealing with Joshua, being slick and streetwise too.

"I will introduce you first to my parents and my grandfather. My little sister is in school, and you will know her for sure. Minou Peltier Thibeau and Joseph Alan Thibeau Senior and Irby Peltier.

All of his family except Bertha is sitting at the kitchen table, and Joshua shakes their hands. Bertha doesn't like the dude and would rather hear what's coming out his mouth. She's busy in the kitchen but hasn't missed a word.

Joshua sits on the side of Alcide and lights up some foreign cigarette that smells like clove. Joshua takes a third cup of coffee and says, "Do y'all mind if I record these conversations so I don't miss anything?"

Monsieur M nods his head yes, and they agree to being taped.

Minou begins to talk right up close to the recorder, and Joshua laughingly tells her she can relax in her chair. It makes her nervous, and she asks Joshua for one of those clove cigarettes.

"Me and my husband, Joe, been here all of our lives. So has my mama, Bertha and my parrain, Alcide. Joe and me, well, we got married young and had a double weddin' with Mama and Parrain. We all lived off tha land 'cause we had to. My papa, Jake Peltier, was killed offshore, and we never saw any money from tha oil companies.

"Yeah, you right! We coulda sued tha bastards and won, but why? We sure don't need dat money, and dat would be greedy. Dey got tha bad luck of being tha bad-asses spillin' plenty, plenty oil and killin' tha pelicans, tha fish, and everyt'in' else. Still, dey screwed us again!

"How did we get so wealthy? Hell, dat's been a secret for a long time, but Ah really don't care anymore and believe it or not, Ah'm tired of lyin' 'bout it. Me and Joe found a pirate's treasure chest.

"Non, no outsider can go on dat property 'cause we own it, and it's got an electric fence and some strange beast is roamin' dat area, so said. Not 'cause of any treasure, ya hear me, but for my pecans!

"Joseph was born after our honeymoon in New Orleans. He has always been a special child, and we needed guidance from professionals.

"What else? Well, Ah don't know ya dat well to talk 'bout anybody else. Ah jus' gave you tha answer to a long-time mystery, so go write yo story. Ah'm finished."

Minou knows how to clean up her act, to speak without cussing when needed.

Joshua Silverberg turns to Joe and wants to ask him some questions, being so thrilled at what Minou has said.

Joe is itching to start talking. "Mais, Ah'm jus' a Cajun man who did good. Ah been followin' behind Minou Peltier's fine little ass since Ah was a real petite boy. Me and Alcide opened a seafood business wit' Theo Theriot after fishin' together for years. We got two chirren, and dey are some good, real good.

"Ah feel tha relief of dat quemas off my shoulders dat Minou jus' tole ya!

"Mais, shit! We jus' had a accident with a, how ya call it, an endangered species! We got tha rug if ya want to see. My lil podnah Pete and Alcide got tha brunt of it. Dey, Pete and Charlotte, are some good friends wit' T-June and Jolie. What else Ah don't know 'cause Ah tole ya tha important t'ings! What else ya gotta know?"

Joe sees no reason to clean up his act. What you see is what you get. He still has that inbred distrust of a stranger and seems to be going along with Charlotte's lie!

Monsieur Mayhem says, "That will be all today, buddy. We have important things to take care of. Nooo! You can't come with me today. See you next Friday." He slams the door on him.

That gnat has turned into a hungry mosquito, and it's fixing to get slapped.

∞ ∞ ∞

WHEN Joshua comes again, he wants to talk with Pete and Charlotte at their house about what has taken place that night in the swamps. It's been ten weeks since, and the couple has decided to go along with Charlotte's fabrication, as have the others, who think it is a damn good lie.

For being a good Catholic English teacher, Charlotte just lets that story slide out her mouth like she's a pro in not telling the truth. When the rest start telling the same thing, it's like it becomes the truth.

Minou has shown him the black panther rug on the floor. Thank the Lawd he doesn't look too hard because he would have seen the damn thing is a century old!

Joshua is delighted in the fact that Pete has started talking again. But when he starts talking to the reporter, Joshua is wishing he would shut up.

Pete says, "Man, what tha fuck ya doin'? Ya makin' dis whole t'ing way outta proportion. Why ya wanna come here and start crap when dere ain't none? Ah tole you everyt'in' Ah wanna say about dis, so ya can go back where ya come from, dude.

"Dese people are lifetime friends and good people dat will help ya wit' anyt'in'! Now, Ah'm t'rough!"

Charlotte has nothing to add to Pete, as she has told Joshua that she has already said to him what she wants to say.

Flavia and Sweet Stu are down here until this quemas is over. She has plenty to say. "Ah been knowin' ya mama and daddy ever since she wrote a weekly column for yo daddy! It was called 'What's New Wit' Tippy,' and Ah replied to one of her stories, and we was friends after dat.

"What is it ya t'ink ya comin' here to do? To write 'bout dese amazin' families and what dey do for tha community? Not much goin' on other dan givin' kindness and hard work! Ya sure as hell can write 'bout dat!

"Ah'm gonna tell ya somet'in' ya can take to tha bank. Ya bettah watch what ya write 'cause Ah'm T-June's nanan, and if dere is any'ing we don't like, ya can bet yo sweet ass we'll sue! We all got plenty money and time to make sure you'd have a hard time findin' a job, ya understand? Do Ah make myself clear?"

Joshua listens and records everything Flavia has told him about how T-June is so special and it has taken a village to raise him. She is so intimidating to Joshua that he can't wait to get out of Flavia's General Mercantile.

Poor lil sheltered Jewish boy.

He will have to erase some of the talk because she starts about politics, and some is downright treasonous, like throwing the Community Coffee in the bayou instead of tea and starting another revolution!

∞ ∞ ∞

MONSIEUR Mayhem takes Joshua to New Orleans to Madam and the bishop's helping center on Esplanade Avenue they have named His Divine Spirit Community Center.

Joshua Silverberg is amazed and awed at what has been accomplished here and in the thriving neighborhood of Tremé. He is so serious about writing about His Divine Spirit that the bishop and Monsieur Mayhem kind of sigh with relief, thinking that this will be the focus of his article.

Well, you know what they say about assumptions, and not the parish.

Madam Aucoin just weaves a little spell, and he listens to her in a dazed rapture. And when he listens back to the recording, it is nothing but static.

Monsieur Mayhem invites Joshua to sit that night and listen to him and Jolie perform at the bar on Bourbon, the Bon Temps Rouler. As they walk to their gig, men stop Joseph and shake his hand so vigorously with genuine happiness to see Monsieur Mayhem. Joshua is definitely curious about this and makes a mental note in his head.

Monsieur M tells him that he is their guest tonight and everything is paid for. Joshua drinks Grey Goose vodka and Sprite, and there is a steady flow to his table by the waitress who has a dyed red beehive, large set of tetons, and a short-ass skirt. She makes a killing in tips just from him that night, he who is giving off vibes he would like to take it further.

This waitress knows her customers as well as the bartender does, and she knows Joshua will be a pissy-ass drunk before the night is over. How many times she's been approached by horny men? But she always goes home to her husband and their two teenagers.

Her name is Jazzy Boudreaux, and she's from down the bayou. She has seen a lot with the families, and they always are so friendly to her, a girl who doesn't get to go home much, bringing her family fresh vegetables and deer meat. Her husband, Merlin, is from the Big Easy and has been a policeman for thirty years.

She is loyal to this bunch and starts handing him less vodka and more Sprite until he notices.

So much for that.

Joshua is enjoying the music and singing along with just about every song. When they play "Louisiana 1927," everyone in the bar stands up and sings. Joshua knows every word and sings the loudest, with tears dripping down his face.

Okay, he's maybe a crying drunk, but he sure can sing good.

Monsieur M and Jolie have to drag him out of the club and into his car, with Jolie driving. No way is he going to drive home, so they take him to the extra bedroom they have and lay him on the bed. They close the door behind them because he's still singing.

Monsieur M wakes the next morning to coffee being brewed and Joshua cooking breakfast in the same clothes he wore the night before and slept in. The kitchen has a strong smell of alcohol, along with coffee and bacon.

Monsieur sits at the table, looking up at this man who shows no signs of a leftover hangover. He should have been in bed for days!

Thinks he's the typical reporter: cynical, hard living, chasing the women and the next big story.

Joshua laughs it off, the pie-eyed drunk womanizer, and says his apologies, telling them he loved their music and if they need a promoter, he can take care of that. Joshua's brother, Jim, is in the music business.

T-June and Jolie talk all the way back to the bayou about the dude, in June's new black truck with a cab full of spirits. It certainly has been an ice-breaker and an eye-opener. The sting of the mosquito is getting deeper, with the Off! spray being looked for.

∞ ∞ ∞

JOSHUA comes the next week to talk to Father Becnel and Sister Bridget. All three will meet in the priest's office, with the religious behind desks and the newspaper man in front of them like a misguided student.

You know how Sister Bridget is, and she too has intimidated the little Jewish boy. He's having a rough time with all these women down here because he certainly is not used to strong-ass, real-to-the-bone women. It's like they see straight through him.

"Well, Mr. Silverberg, I knew your parents very well, and I was sad to hear they died within months of each other. It's just you and Jim now and your sister. He was an excellent horn-playing musician in the marching band you had in Thibodaux for all the parades.

"Your family has always been known to be ethical and truthful and wonderful newspaper people. Are you?

"I have taught Joseph since the second grade, and he is a fine example of a very intelligent boy. He was the class clown, sometimes not even knowing what everyone was laughing about. A studious student but he has continued to be a breath of fresh air as a man. Father and I are close, close friends with the families, as well as with the others who are also close. It's almost like a village.

"I have always believed he was destined to do amazing things, and he has and will continue to do so. I'm so very proud of him, and I follow him in whatever he's doing. I can't think of another thing to say, and that's all you need to know."

Father Becnel is very friendly and very calm. "Mr. Silverberg, the families Thibeau and Peltier are faithful followers in the Catholic church and attend Mass every Sunday. They are also big supporters and very generous with money to help with St. Luke's Catholic Church as well as the school. I don't think I care to elaborate any further. Maybe you will come to Mass on Sunday? The Jewish belief is not that different, other than not believing in Jesus. Nice to meet you, and have a safe trip up the bayou."

∞ ∞ ∞

JOSHUA tells Monsieur Mayhem that he's got all the material he needs for a damn good article. "Thank you so much for opening your families to me. I'll bring the final copy for y'all to see and correct anything."

Monsieur Mayhem closes the door with him on the other side and sighs with relief. He's so glad he can be T-June again.

Joshua has bought a new car that nobody knows about. Why? He's been stalking to see if he can find out something that's not so squeaky clean. He follows T-June one afternoon when he's headed for the swamp. Joshua is sneakily not far behind him, watching.

He comes up on T-June sitting on the ground, looking like he is talking to the animals. T-June laughs out loud at something that seems to be told to him, and the animals are answering him in some way. He will be silent for a minute like he can hear something, with the animals sitting in his lap, and busts out laughing again.

Joshua can't believe what he is seeing and hollers out to T-June, making the animals scatter. "Man! What the hell did I just see? You were talking to the animals like a Dr. Doolittle! Man! What the hell? You didn't tell me this, and it's a miracle! I will make you famous."

Monsieur Mayhem comes back quickly. "Damn, Joshua, why are you sneaking up on me? What the hell do you think you saw? Dude, this is very private property, and no one invited you back here. How long have you been sneaking around behind my back?"

Joshua runs into the clearing where M.M. is standing. Alcohol is just oozing out his pores. "I know what I saw, and there's no use lying about it. I saw it with my own two eyes! This is going to be front page news, and we'll get famous together."

Monsieur Mayhem stands there thinking in silence for fifteen seconds and finally says, "No. Flavia told you we will sue you if you write something we don't approve of. It was just a glare in your eyes. Now I want you to leave my property and not come back 'til we can see what you wrote."

Joshua is showing a side they haven't seen yet. He becomes a very belligerent, demanding drunk who isn't taking no for an answer. He tells Monsieur he doesn't have the right to keep this from the world and that he must insist!

Monsieur Mayhem quickly gives in, saying he's giving up telling him no; it's no use. He pauses a minute, looking like he is really thinking, and says, "You might as well see the rest. I've got something else to show you."

Monsieur is acting like he is getting excited, but the truth is he's as deadly as a water moccasin. Joshua the gnat has become a whopping big-ass mosquito that will finally be slapped hard and sprayed with Off!

Joshua stands excitedly while T-June whistles. He sure as hell doesn't want to see what comes through the trees of the swamp after the whistle.

Pieyan the bigfoot comes barreling out from the trees. He is screaming and roaring, with his arms flailing in the air, threatening Joshua and coming full speed ahead for him.

Joshua hits the ground in a dead faint and dirties his uptown, lowdown pair of designer drawers. When he awakens, T-June is standing over him, and Pieyan is standing on his side, still growling.

He pushes back as far as he can on the ground, crying for his mama.

Monsieur the streetwise dude grabs up Joshua by his collar, while Joshua is dribbling snot out his nose, and says, "Aw, aw. Mais. Oh, I thought you wanted to see what I could do. I've been friends with this bigfoot for a long damn time! You want to see some loup-garous too?

"Listen up, Mr. Inquisitive. I'm going to tell you what you're thinking right now. I have known for a long time what you were going to do. You're wishing for a drink, you're scared and rightfully so. You're going to see your brother to tell him what you found. Am I right?

"So, Joshua, you better listen to what I'm about to tell you, podnah."

Monsieur Mayhem begins to talk with Joshua in his head, and it scares the reporter straight and sober.

Pieyan has your scent now and will track you to kill you if you write anything I don't want written about. I can talk with him too. I can also suggest things to you in your mind, convincing you to do godawful acts, to the point of people thinking you are totally insane.

Hell, buddy, you've gotten to the point of losing your story and having a huge lawsuit. You also have been thinking about changing careers to be in the music business. I would suggest you do that. We will all be watching you, and a lawsuit would be the least of your worries. So, what's it gonna be?"

Minou comes running into the swamp, hollering and screaming. Pieyan isn't scared of her any more. She cooks some good deer roast for him.

"Oh, come quick, T-June! Mama is followin' ya to see what dis man is doin', and Ah heard Pieyan hollerin'. She is mad, knowin' he has no business on our land and seein' and hearin' Pieyan! Dere ain't no full moon tonight, but she is changin' into tha loup-garou. She was tryin' to get home before it happened 'cause she felt funny. Lawd! She must be goin' t'rough her change of life! Please come help us, 'cause she's comin' after ya, Joshua. You were on her mind, and now she wants to kill ya!"

Pieyan disappears into the swamp, leaving Joshua and T-June and Minou to deal with the situation that's coming. And here she comes!

The beautiful, full-figured, graying fur of the loup-garou in her regalness.

Bertha comes directly for the throat of Joshua Silverberg, and he stands in grief, knowing he has caused the whole damn thing and is about to die.

T-June stops her with a full, head-on, massive bear hug, enveloping her with his strength for five minutes. Bertha stands there naked while T-June covers her in his large coat.

She stares at her grandson and says, "T-June, my bébé, you have lifted da curse off of me. Ah can feel tha difference. Mais, Ah can't t'ink 'bout what happened. My mind is kinda cuckoo right now. But you, ya lil bastard Silvaturd, bettah git ya ass gone as fast as ya can from our property 'cause Ah can shoot real good too!"

Joshua walks ahead of the group, slowly, with his head hung down. He gets in his car – it's known now – and starts it but sits there in the dark in his car for hours.

Bertha rushes into the kitchen at Minou's, so excited to tell Alcide what has happened. The place is full of everybody, so they all learn about the miracle.

Alcide looks at her and walks out the kitchen, going to his and Joe's shop. He's feeling alone and very guarded. He doesn't want to think it's a possibility for him too. He doesn't know if he wants to stop being loup-garou.

∞ ∞ ∞

JOSHUA Silverberg comes back two months later, begging them to let him show them the masterful, powerful, spiritual, and real damn good story ready to be published.

They are all there waiting to read Joshua's finished article. Everybody has their own copy. Pete and Charlotte are there too.

He sits down at the table and takes a large sip of coffee. "Please, Joseph, know that your secrets weren't revealed and never will be by me. Never will they be spoken again by me. I cannot tell you how much this family has changed me. Your goodness has changed me into a much better man. Don't get me wrong. I don't ever want to see Pieyan again.

"I went the next night to AA and got a two-month chip last night for sobriety. I had withdrawals bad, and I dreamed of my mother tearing me a new one! I've been spraying myself silly with cologne, and I don't smell like alcohol anymore."

"I'm not taking the job at The Times-Picayune. This is going to be my swan song as a writer. I'm going with my brother, Jim, into the world of singers, musicians, and writers of music.

"I'm going to synagogue in the city too, something I had dropped for other worldly temptations."

Well, you know already that Flavia is going to be the first to talk. "Dere's nuttin' in dis story dat we would have to sue over. It's very good, tha way he wrote it. Ah'm well satisfied."

Bishop Toussaint is choked up because the biggest part of the article is about His Divine Spirit Center up on Esplanade Avenue in the city of New Orleans. He finally says, "This is the first time we have been recognized this way. He is giving The Times-Picayune his swan song. Blessed spirits are bringing the help we can use. After this hits the paper, we will see people lining up to help. Praise be to all!"

Madam Aucoin laughs out loud when she reads that Joshua has written, "Mrs. Toussaint wasn't able to make the interview."

They all laugh because Madam has told them what she did say turned out to be nothing but static on his recording. Everyone is delighted with what he's written, except Alcide because he doesn't want to read it. He has been very quiet and goes off by himself a lot, and that's not him.

Alcide walks to the back of the swamp and sits on the limb of the tree that's used frequently by T-June and all his little animal friends. He sits so sorrowful with his head between his knees and full of animal energy, wanting to turn right then into a loup-garou.

The bigfoot comes slowly into the clearing where Alcide sits. They have never been friendly with each other. Pieyan starts talking while Alcide sits there amazed. T-June has never told anyone that Pieyan talks words. They figure it is T-June speaking to Pieyan with his mind.

"Look, man, we've never been podnahs, but I know what you're feeling. I watch y'all all the time and man, that Bertha is a fine specimen of a werewolf. Wowee!"

Alcide starts growling.

"Hell, man, I didn't mean any disrespect, dude. Both of you are beautiful, and it would make me sad because I can't look like my brothers ever. You know, the humans? I could feel the difference in your woman when I watched her hang your clothes on the line to be dried. I want to do that so bad, I love it! So sorry, dude. I tend to talk a lot when I can.

"That T-June is something else! Now, I know you're trying to make a decision because it's just you now to be freed and you don't know if you want that."

Alcide is sitting there, listening to the long-winded bigfoot.

"I know all about having to hide and sometimes eating what I shouldn't. This thing you turn into has been going on for a long time. Remember when we tied up? Man, that was something! I'm sorry, we don't need to think about that.

"Is it something you want to continue, or do you want to try living without it? The freedom of your monthly change can be so intoxicating. I've been reading T-June's dictionary and learning more words. Anyway, it's just for one night? I mean, what's up with that?

"Let T-June come back here with us just to see. And if you miss your wildness, I'll come run with you, and you can be butt naked! We can be podnahs either way."

Pieyan whistles a call, and T-June is there in a short time, staring at the two. He then lets out a huge bolt of laughter.

"I absolutely love this! Two of my favorite creatures! Talking and being friendly! PawPaw and Pieyan! Oh, my podnahs. What do y'all want me to do?"

Alcide walks up to T-June, not touching him but ready to talk.

"How Ah have longed to hug ya and love on ya and never could because Ah was afraid of ya. Ah know ya can change into a loup-garou if ya want. Ah always knew ya could, but ya never paid attention to dat, some kinda way. Lawd, thank ya, Lawd! Ya could, huh? Ah'm ready for ya to try and take the curse off me."

T-June reaches Alcide, both of them crying as he pulls him into a massive hug. Alcide holds him in a loving way, touching his hair and his face.

Pieyan wants to join the hug and does.

Alcide feels the curse being lifted out of his body and turns to Pieyan, seeing a very hairy man, naked like the day he was born. Alcide wants to faint when he sees Pieyan change into that very ugly, old, bearded, naked man.

All three are standing there, looking at each other in amazement!

T-June says, after they put Alcide's jacket on the former Bigfoot, "Pieyan! I'm so sorry. Man, I didn't know I could do this! Can you live this way? Podnah, I could try hard to put you back, but I sure as hell never tried that. You couldn't resist the hugging."

The used-to-be bigfoot turns and goes back into the swamps. He for sure is upset with the changing. He has to learn how to be human.

Alcide and T-June walk back up to the house where Alcide goes to find Bertha. Both cry in each other's arms. They are cured.

∞ ∞ ∞

THE days pass slowly now for the whole changed family. Joshua Silverberg has won awards for the fantastic article, and now there is a steady line of people wanting to help at His Divine Spirit Community Center.

Joshua has become another member of the tribe that surrounds Monsieur Mayhem, and life just keeps on going on and going on and going on.

Chapter Fourteen

Callie and Lily Hollerin' at Tha Moon

LAROSE/CUT-OFF is what the sleepy little town has turned into. Two lil towns combined because of the young people coming to find more peace and security and to raise children.

Galliano will be the next slash and then Golden Meadow and one day a metropolis heading for the Gulf to the sprawling community of Fourchon.

Two-lane highways, each one way and the other. You know, DIS WAY and DAT WAY signs going in the other direction on both sides of Bayou Lafourche. Pretty much the way it is anyway, house to house to house all the way down the bayou, hardly a yard between them.

But there are newcomers hearing all the old stories, famous or infamous tales, and that depends on who's telling it.

The Peltiers, the Thibeaus, the Theriots, and Mrs. Flavia King are the wealthiest people on the bayou, and most think it's been very mysterious and speculative as to how they've become wealthy, except for Flavia. Some think it is in the outlaw way, growing marijuana and brewing moonshine and trapping endangered species.

Joshua Silverburg writes about the pirate's chest, and still it's hard to believe for most people on the bayou, but none dare to go to that property.

And so, life goes on in the smaller village that chooses to follow T-June.

∞ ∞ ∞

MINOU has had her hands full, as has Estelle, raising the two little divas, Callie and Lily. Flower's mama, Irene, is watching her like a hawk, knowing she is too smart-mouthed and too wise for her age. The two older divas have a lot to do with it.

Elouise Marie Miller, Butch and Katrina's baby, looks like a lil five-year-old Indian with some meat on her bones and hair her mama can't tame. She goes everywhere with the trio; they're willing any time to babysit because she is a trip.

Weedie is what she's called, a combination of all these little women, kind of looking like a wild weed. Funny as shit! When she comes to visit with Butch and Katrina, they all gather to laugh, with everybody in stitches. She is speaking Spanish too, and that sounds even funnier.

Flower is still trying to catch Rowdy's eye, but he isn't worried about girls, for sure not Flower. She's too young, being two years behind him. She is now thirteen. She just knows, Some day, we'll be together.

Callie and Lily are a force to be reckoned with. Both are startling in their beauty, and the charm just oozes out of both of them, when they want it to.

Both will graduate from high school in the spring. They are double valedictorians because the competition is fierce between the two, and they have had the exact grades throughout school.

Of the two, Lily is the serious one with the future planned out for herself and Callie. They will never be apart; it's what has been planted in their minds since they were babies.

Callie has prominent Native American features and dark skin with big old brown eyes and thick black hair. Lily's skin is a dark shade of coffee milk with green, slanted, almond-shaped eyes and dreadlocks she's been wearing for years.

They stand 5 foot, 7 inches each, with muscular bodies that show off their large sets of tetons and pinchable behinds.

This is the closest they will ever be, like twins. Wearing matching clothes has worn off – about five years ago when it became apparent that their styles are very different from each other. Lily is subdued in her choice of clothing; neutral, black, and few colors. She is very studious, serious, and is known for her militant views, joins all the political clubs but is well known as a young woman who takes no shit.

You got her pictured, dontcha?

Lily will scare the shit out of you with her green eyes, daring you to come any closer. She has a straight posture with a sway in her walk. She looks at you full in the eyes, and unless she cracks a smile, you won't know you're in danger. Calm but deadly. Her eyes are like a hurricane, with winds blowing fiercely, then the deadly calm with the wind coming back full force in the other direction.

Callie is the exact opposite of her sista, with a wardrobe of color galore, lots of jewelry made of turquoise, tight jeans, and cowgirl boots. She has a wicked sense of humor and loves to pull pranks on unsuspecting victims, like the time she hides and throws firecrackers on the porch where everyone is drinking coffee. Cups are broken and lots of screams and cussing! She pees on herself laughing, but nobody else thinks it's funny.

She laughs all the time but will turn to tears with a huge soft-hearted gesture to the same ones that fall for the prank to begin with. Or maybe she's laughing so hard she's crying!

Callie is prone to fall for tricks herself and tends to like the bad boys. This little Houmas gal must give off some enticing scent because the boys all follow her around like puppies. She is way far from being promiscuous. Lily would have kicked her ass! You know her; she'll fight you with punches, then turn around and strut her stuff in all her finery. Femme fatale that breaks your heart.

∞ ∞ ∞

THE graduation party is comparable to a street fair, with so many people coming in and out of Madam Aucoin's stately mansion. Laughter, music, food, presents, and buckets of beer and tears that end the party at daybreak. The band the Boogalous are showing off their popular music, not knowing they have a lot of help from the Jumpin' Jivin' Trio, the jazzy ghosts from long ago.

Callie and Lily will be following Monsieur Mayhem's magical mystery tour into the Big Easy on the Mississippi River to begin their lives. They have saved every dime for years, knowing New Orleans would be the chosen destination of their dreams.

These two have rented their own house several streets away from everybody else, put their own deposits down, furnished the place with secondhand furniture and throwaways, and rescued a half-Mastiff puppy named Couyon.

Lily is attending Xavier University in the city, majoring in political science, and working at His Divine Spirit part time. Callie is bartending at the club on Bourbon, the Bon Temps Rouler, where Monsieur Mayhem plays most nights now.

Callie isn't worried about education right now. She wants to be carefree and to experience life as she sees it. Both spend their free hours together anyway as always. Lily will study at a back table in the bar and wait for Callie until she gets off.

Callie keeps house for them, like her mama, Minou. Spotless and smells like Fabuloso on clean floors. She burns incense, patchouli, and keeps music on all the time.

Couyon the Mastiff just lays around and doesn't bite anybody, even if his name's Bite Somebody!

Both girls work together at His Divine Spirit community center on Saturday mornings. Sometimes, they go home to see Flower – and Weedie, when she's there – and spend their nights with the others in their Flower Power circle.

This particular weekend will have all four of the girls in New Orleans spending Friday night through Sunday afternoon together. Butch and Katrina, Weedie's mama and papa, are here for the time too, staying in one of the many available houses, and will carry the two younger flowers home.

All of them are helping Callie clean the bar and air it out on Saturday morning, so the shuttered doors are wide open, still inviting customers while they work. Callie doesn't turn anyone away. She will serve them drinks, and on they will go to the next bar on Bourbon.

In walks a fine specimen of a man, and all become alert to this customer, especially Lily. He is light-complected, with dreadlocks falling down to his shoulders, slim built but tall, and a smile with dimples, teeth white as snow. And a twinkle in his eyes while he asks for a beer.

"Where ya at! You lovely ladies working hard? I don't have anything to do so I will stay to help. Hand me that mop bucket because I'm good at mopping things up. My name is Toot, short for Toussaint."

He asks for five dollars in quarters, puts some New Orleans music on the jukebox, and starts dancing with the huge mop while they start laughing. Callie and Lily are laughing, while Flower is being shy but smiling.

Not little Elouise Marie Miller. Weedie is just staring at him, not cracking a grin.

Toot for sure tries to change that but to no avail.

Weedie tells them she's ready to go after she has seen all his shenanigans. They've been finished with the work, but they linger because of Toot.

Callie and Lily tell him goodbye after he promises to be back later to see Monsieur Mayhem and Jolie. He has been told that many of their people will be here too. He says he'll be delighted to meet the family of these two awesome women from the bayou.

∞ ∞ ∞

THE crowd from down the bayou is here tonight. Minou and Joe, Estelle and Theo, and Madam Aucoin and Bishop Toussaint. Bertha and Alcide are the babysitters, choosing to stay at the house where they watch the people sashay by down Esplanade.

Weedie tells Bertha as she is being bathed, "Me don't like dat dude. Mucho mojo!"

Laughing, Bertha just gets her PJs on her and lets her sit on the upstairs balcony with the rest. Weedie has been definitely trying several times to say something to Bertha, about her dislike of Toot, but no one is paying attention.

Toot comes in at the beginning of the show, greeting everybody and shaking hands. He takes the seat next to Lily, and they are having a conversation, while the three other couples sitting at the table are having déjà vu.

Bishop Toussaint is the first to speak up, knowing immediately who he is. "Toot, who are your people? I think they may be close to where we are on Esplanade. You're very familiar to me."

Callie and Lily pipe up together, "Who's ya mama? Who's ya daddy? Can ya make a roux?" Laughing while quoting a well-remembered phrase in the family and picking on Minou.

Toot stands and reaches out his hand to the standing bishop. "Sir, I'm Toussaint Laverne Junior. Just like your name, huh? My people live all over Tremé, but my pops is a barber on Rampart. He's gonna retire next year, and I'm gonna take over the shop. I'm in school right now for it."

The bishop remains standing while Estelle and Theo stand too. Estelle says, "I don't think, son, that you realize who we are. I knew you were related to Laray Laverne; the resemblance is uncanny in these lights. I'm Lily's mother, and my sister was Maybelline, Laray's wife, the one he killed. Ring any bells? I'm Estelle Theriot, the one who did her best to raise my sister's sons by this man whose family had no proper training in being human. Evil through and through.

"I can't stand to look at you anymore, so we're leaving. Family, we will see y'all back at the house."

Theo stands silent while he looks Toot in the eyes for a minute and follows his beloved.

Toot goes to leave, but at the insistence of Lily and the bishop, he sits down again, feeling like the spell has been broken for him on this wonderful day.

Jolie and Monsieur Mayhem feel the bad energy in the crowd, knowing something is happening, so they stop early, and Callie takes the rest of the night off.

Minou and Joe go back to be with their friends the Theriots, and the rest go to a 24-hour café on the corner, White Castle's.

Madam Aucoin is patting the seat by her in the large, round old booth for Toot and Lily and Callie. Bishop Toussaint orders pots of coffee and "keep the beignets coming."

Madam Aucoin speaks to Toot while hugging him. "Lil honey child! I remember you, Lil Tootie! That's what they used to call you when you were a wild three-year-old, riding your lil tricycle, tooting an old horn you found in the dump, up and down the street.

"Your mama wouldn't cut your hair because you were so pretty with all those good-hair curls! Your mother was a good spiritual woman who came to see me often. I was saddened to hear of her passing, and I was there when they had a second line for her.

"Your daddy is a hard-working and honest man, and that's because he was raised by your grandmama and auntie who saved him from his parents and Laray, his big brother. I also know that your pop was a heavy drinker and gambler. Never ever did y'all do without anything, but things would have been easier for you if he didn't gamble or drink. Is he the same?"

Toot is pushing a beignet around on a plate when Madam taps his hand to stop.

"I remember you for sure, Madam. My mama would take me for services at your church, and I still recall the time I rode my tricycle down your steps at your shop. I had to get five stitches by the doctor, and you gave me a doll. Told me to stick the pin where I hurt and it would go away, and I've used it ever since. It sits on my chifforobe in my room. And right now, I would go put that pin right by my heart."

The mood is lifted then, and everybody else starts asking questions and talking and being very nosy, finding out all about Lil Tootie Laverne.

The trademark of the village, nasal congestion of the nosy kind!

Monsieur Mayhem becomes T-June when he starts talking, after a moment rubbing Toot's shoulders. "Dude, you walked in and met the family in full force. Sure can't tell you it's not always like this. You might just run for your life after this night!

"I do know this. You are a good man with a lot of shit on your back that's not yours. Come see me at His Divine Spirit, and we'll have a long talk, even if you can't handle these beautiful young women from the bayou."

T-June speaking in favor of Toot answers the questions they all have. He is good.

While they sit talking and eating beignets, an older man walks in and, to the delight of Madam Aucoin, it is her nephew Henri Aucoin. The same young dude that has had a lot to do with starting the relationship between Minou and Madam, telling her where to find the Voodoo Shop, and the rest is major chaotic history!

Henri Aucoin now owns the Caldonia Hotel where he once worked as a pool boy and go-fer, delivering Popeyes and aloe vera lotion. He has rental property all over town and is on the city council of New Orleans. He is very handsome, very successful, very political, and very single.

Henri and Madam hug and kiss like kin do, although she sees him often. He pulls up a chair. T-June and Henri know each other well and kid each other about his being conceived at the Caldonia.

Henri shakes hands with everybody at the table until he looks at Callie. And she him. The moment is not wasted, because everyone feels the energy.

Henri breaks the silence by laughing and taking Callie up in his arms, lifting her off her feet. "I've been waiting to meet you for a long time! Caldonia! I absolutely love you and your name. And don't call me Nonc Henri!"

The other thing obvious is that little Caldonia is not wanting to let go and not crying "uncle" either.

This night will never be forgotten. We get some serious contenders, both on the same night.

It is obvious this night as to who has picked who in the romance department, and as the night progresses, four couples go their separate ways, saying goodnight and see "you in the morning!"

Lily and Toot go to her and Callie's house and don't appear until the weekend is over. Henri and Callie walk the streets until sunrise and eat breakfast together at Brennan's. Everybody else staying here is walking the floor over you (and singing that song).

Estelle and Theo are beside themselves, as are Minou and Joe, because they have no idea what has transpired the previous night with their two little flower power divas.

T-June comes that morning early and answers all their questions. It doesn't make things any better.

Estelle says, "He's a damn Laverne!"

Minou says, "He's too old for Callie!"

The other two little wilted and pissed-off flowers go home without saying goodbye. Weedie keeps saying, "Me tole ya! Me tole ya! Mucho mojo!"

∞ ∞ ∞

BOTH couples become known very quickly, but Callie is the one who makes the newspapers. Sunday morning the picture hits the front page of The Times-Picayune and has the family gathered all up in Minou and Joe's house in the city.

When Minou sees the newspaper, she sits down at the kitchen table, slamming her cup full of Mello Joy and spilling half of it.

The picture has been taken at daybreak, with Henri and Callie eating breakfast at seven o'clock in the morning.

"Goddamn sumbitch! We always t'ought it would be T-June's face on tha front page! Ah don't know what Henri is t'inkin'. Me, Ah been t'inkin' maybe he was gay! Ah mean, he was always wit' a woman, but sometimes dey hide dat. Don't want to come out tha closet for e'rybody to know deir business. Ah mean, who tha hell needs to know what happens behind closed doors? As long as dey ain't scarin' e'rybody with tha noise.

"T'ink about dat, Joe. He's old! Sumbitch! She don't listen to a word Ah say! She's jus' like you, Joe! She's jus' like you."

Estelle has stayed up all night, crying her eyes out, with Theo right on the side of her. She has already called her nephews, Mac and

Moe Theriot. Theo has adopted them so they won't carry the Laverne name. They are first cousins to Toot.

Estelle is angry now and wanting to go bust up in Lily's house and beat the shit out of both of them.

"All this time I've had peace, thinking I would never have to deal with these monstrous people again, and now the door to peace has shattered and broken off the damn hinges! I can't even think of what to do, even with T-June telling me he's good. That streak of evil runs deep in their blood, and I'm boiling over with rage!"

The bishop holds her in his arms while she cries, hiccupping through sobs.

"Baby, T-June's approval of Toot, well, he thinks if he says it, then everybody else has to get on board. T-June needs an attitude adjustment because it's not always that easy. I know Toot's people, and not all of them are like the parents who raised Laray. They're decent folk and get a lot of blame that isn't theirs.

"I can't imagine the turmoil in your and Theo's minds, and I feel you. I do. That whole incident troubles and grieves me and Alafair too, baby. Y'all have given many chances to help family turn their lives around, and you have been blessed with everybody loving you and wanting to hang out with you and your whole family. But the more you push against it, the more Lily will push back.

"Give all of this to the blessed spirits, and try to go about your business because you are letting these people live rent free in your heart."

Bishop Toussaint doesn't say anything about Henri Aucoin and Caldonia.

Henri is a fine, upstanding dude with old-fashioned values, even though he wants to ravish Callie. It's hard with her, letting him know for sure she would love to be ravished. He loves to shower her with gifts and takes her along on anything he is doing.

He buys her a new car, more dependable and classy, and every night you can find Councilman Aucoin in the Bon Temps Rouler waiting 'til Caldonia gets off work. He has made fast friends of Lily and Toot.

Back home on the bayou, the two mamas are bent out of shape and horribly nosy. They hear nothing from the grown-ass women they have raised.

∞ ∞ ∞

ANOTHER adjustment in the village follows T-June. Don't get too comfortable with the way things are, because Monsieur Mayhem will drop a dime on you in a minute.

Alcide and Bertha have become very different people, being very complacent and much quieter, behavior similar to depression or to the stages of grief. She doesn't do much cooking anymore, and Alcide seldom goes to the Gulf. They claim to be happy to be rid of the loup-garou curse, being cured, but on the full moon, they leave and stay out all night.

They go and visit poor Mr. Pieyan, the dirty old man that lives back there. You know, the bigfoot? Alcide brings the poor old man some pants so he can cover up that huge ding-a-ling. He sure doesn't want Bertha to see that!

Pieyan will seldom put on the shirt. He still pulls at the front, not enough room, and Bertha just quits replacing buttons.

He and Alcide are podnahs, but he just talks to Bertha with his head down. Pieyan doesn't want Alcide to get jealous.

Pete Dugas and Alcide are very close friends now, as are Charlotte and Bertha. Both couples are pretty well laid back.

Minou and Estelle are always together with Madam Aucoin, but she spends her days trying to help her best friend. All three have taken up crochet for something to do while they wait for the phone to ring. Afghans, scarves, slippers, and rugs are piling up in the living room because they are crocheting some fast. Bertha can't do it; it always winds up in tangles, her cussing and getting deeper in a web of her own doing.

Flavia and Sweet fly in for the weekend after the infamous one in New Orleans.

"Hellfire! Y'all know by now Ah can find out all we need to know 'bout bofe dese dudes! Ya know Ah know people! Ah'm gonna get right on it."

They all buy sinus products off the counters in bulk at Sam's, being each and every one is as nosy as hell. That definitely doesn't change in Flavia, as nosiness has always been in her genes.

They all hang around Bertha's now, trying to encourage a spark of life that has been blown out.

∞ ∞ ∞

TWO and a half months pass before the mamas hear from their little flowers, those little shitasses with their independence. Good thing, because the three mamas have bought out Walmart's yarn.

Callie calls Minou and Lily calls Estelle on the same day, in the same house, in the same room, on the same bed. Lily and Callie go in the bedroom by themselves and lock the door. You know these bayou gals don't want to miss anything about each other. There's no privacy between them; they just do what they need to do, like poopoo, and never skip a beat in their talking. You know, like Siamese twins.

Callie speaks first, with the phone on speaker. "Mama, I know y'all are all right because T-June tells me, but my life has turned upside down! I could feel your and Papa's displeasure, and I didn't want to deal with it when everything in my life is wonderful. I had to make sure if it was a battle to be fought, it was worth it.

"I know y'all have known Henri since he's been seventeen and spoken often of him with all his successes, how proud y'all were. You thought he was gay, huh, Mama? I know you. Well, he's far from that! If y'all are going to be home this weekend, all of us want to come home."

Lily takes the phone after taking a few minutes to breathe in, hold, and breathe out, amazed that it certainly works, learning that at her yoga class. "Mama, I can't hardly have this conversation, it pains me so. You and Papa have every right to your feelings, being the Lavernes were nothing but heartaches to all of you. Toot is nothing like those people, Mama. He was raised differently by his dad and mom with help from his MaDear and auntie! He wants terribly to come here and meet all of you under different circumstances and to meet Moe and Mac. We're all coming for the weekend. I love you, Mama."

∞ ∞ ∞

THE weekend can't get here soon enough for Minou and Estelle.

The couples come in two vehicles, just in case someone has to make a quick getaway. Callie's new car is a dark turquoise BMW four-door with black leather inside. Lily is driving their old car, and Toot rides in with her.

Both of these little women go to the houses they grew up in, to their mamas.

Henri and Callie come in with loaded arms, all the things they've brought from the Big Easy. Muffalettas from Central Grocery, a gallon of Hurricanes from the bar and still-warm beignets from Cafe du Monde. Everything they have learned to love that comes from New Orleans.

Henri and Caldonia (he loves to call her that) are sitting at the kitchen table across from Minou and Joe, and Henri is the first to speak up.

"We've known each other since I was seventeen, and y'all know what kind of man I made of myself. When I saw Caldonia, I saw you, Minou. I had a small crush on you, but I was mighty afraid of Joe! Y'all made such an impression on me, and to think, it's all because I sent you to my aunt!

"But the immediate connection we felt for each other couldn't be ignored by me. I fell deeply, all-consumingly in love with her. I've never felt this way before in all my years. Came close a couple of times but called it off. I know in my heart I've been waiting on Caldonia.

"Joe and Minou, I have come to ask you for the hand of your daughter in marriage. I can definitely take care of her, and she will have anything she wants or needs."

Joe reaches up in the cabinet and takes down the Crown Royal half gallon and four glasses and says, "Henri, ya got no idea what tha hell ya askin' for! Dis family ain't like de New Orleans people, fo' sure. A lot of crazy shit happens wit' us, if ya don't know dat. Lots of tha mystery and can't hardly be believed! Mais, Callie is all wrapped up in it too! Ya bettah start talkin' wit' each other.

"To top it all, podnah, ya ain't no spring chicken! Ah wonder how tha hell ya gonna keep up wit' her. Ah mean no disrespect by dat. She's been hell on wheels, her and Lily bofe! Whatcha gonna do, all of ya live together? 'Cause dem two lil girls ain't never been separated. Ya reachin' tha age where ya gonna wanna stay on tha porch, and she'll wanna run wit' tha dogs!

"Ya know, podnah, Ah love ya, and it ain't you we havin' a hard time wit'. Mais, she got a lot to tell ya, and after, ya might run fast-fast back to tha city!

"Mais, shit! What ya sayin', you wanna get married right now? Is dere somet'in' else ya ain't tellin' me?"

Joe stands up and bowls up, thinking he's got to find his shotgun.

Henri and Callie both laugh, and she says, "Papa, he's so old-fashioned he had to ask you if we could marry before carrying me to his bed. Worried about putting a ring on my finger! This man has definitely not taken advantage of your daughter. And I'm tired of waiting, truth be told! The newspapers are going nuts, trying to catch us together so they can write whatever they want about us. It's getting pretty bizarre."

Must be bad if Callie calls it bizarre after being raised by this bunch.

∞ ∞ ∞

OVER at the Theriots', things are tense, with everybody walking on those damn egg shells, going around the pink elephant in the room. Theo is being very cordial to Toot, but Estelle is cool and standoffish.

Moe and Mac have come to meet their cousin, and they hit it off right away. The resemblance of all three proves they are indeed kin.

Moe speaks up. "Man, we're glad to finally meet you after all these years of not knowing you existed, and we sure as hell will come for you to give us a fancy new haircut. We're going to be good friends with you and maybe can clean up the bad vibes, dude.

"Our mama and dad, I mean, they raised us from little boys who were traumatized and so confused. Laray even broke out from prison to get to us! I guess you've heard about what happened to him. So, they have suffered enough behind our family. Please give us some patience in accepting you with Lily. She's our baby sister."

Mac agrees with everything Moe says. They both hug Toot.

The Theriots have all their family together, along with T-June and Jolie, who have come to visit. The tension eases, and Estelle tells Toot she will give him a chance.

Toot and Lily sit together while Toot begins to tell the family, "I am so sorry how you were done that way by my grandparents and my uncle. I never even knew them, but they are still alive.

"We have news to share, and I pray you will accept me after. Mr. and Mrs. Theriot, we have come this weekend to tell you we are getting married because Lily is carrying my baby. We come asking for your blessings."

Well, that's like a bunch of firecrackers popping in the houseful of stunned people!

Estelle gets up from the sofa, walks into her bedroom, and slams the door, leaving Theo and the boys to deal with the fallout.

Lily is hugged by Theo and the cousins, but Estelle has left the building.

"Hey, y'all, that's some good news!" say Moe and Mac at the same time. "We're going to help you guys anyway we can. We've got our own painting business, and we'll come and paint for sure. Wait. Where are y'all going to live?"

T-June tells them to hush, because they all have houses in New Orleans.

Theo takes a deep breath and lights a cigarette before he can say anything. "Well, looks like y'all are gonna be together, regardless of our feelings, so I'm gonna make the best of it, and I will accept you, Toot. We have no choice. But, you better look me in the eyes right now, man to man. If you ever cause Lily any kind of grief, I'll shoot you dead.

"Now, both of you are in school, and I want completion of both your degrees, and that will earn you another notch in my belt."

Theo gets up and goes into the bedroom where Estelle sits quietly in the dark.

So, that's how the weekend goes in both houses, questions answered or not, but a lot of them.

Lily and Toot leave, with Lily and Estelle not talking.

After giving consent reluctantly, the Thibeaus and the Peltiers get down the real good crystal, and Joe goes to get several bottles of chilled Champagne from Rouse's. Minou is thinking, Ah'm gonna use tha best glasses we got so he don't think we some ignorant coonasses. Ah'm gonna put on tha dawg! And Joe, him, he bettah buy tha top shelf of Champagne!

Bertha and Alcide are there celebrating, as are Madam and the bishop. But the Theriot house is quiet, no response to the telephone ringing.

∞ ∞ ∞

CALDONIA and Henri have their wedding at St. Luke's Catholic Church, with Father Becnel crying the whole time he is marrying them. Lily and Toot stand as maid of honor and best man, Lily showing she is with child.

Flower and Weedie are the other bridesmaids, with Weedie still voicing her distaste in what her sistas have done. "I told y'all he was going to change everything! I told y'all! Mucho mojo."

Estelle still hasn't talked with Lily and for sure not to Toot.

A very large reception is held at Madam's house, with tents set up and the whole thing catered. Still in the style of Madam and the bishop, it is come one, come all.

Some of Henri's friends from the city come for the occasion, his real, close friends. All of the Aucoins from the city are there, and some of the congregation from His Divine Spirit Church, where the bishop is a high bishop (in more than one way)!

All of Madam Aucoin's daughters are there and so impressed they can't stand themselves. Wait 'til they tell everybody down Esplanade. Could have been Minou and Flavia's daughters.

The other crowd of Henri's Uptown friends are waiting on the celebration in New Orleans, in the Garden District.

Minou and Joe and Madam and the bishop and (come on, y'all; y'all know what's coming) the rest of the followers-disciples-posse-village-coven-sistas show everyone there that those from the bayou definitely know how to be bourgeois.

But then, as it gets later, the same jackasses are acting the donkey, being rude and ugly, passing out on the floor and making their wives cry. They're all the same, in the city or on the bayou.

One of Lily's older sisters gets her fill of it when this older gentleman, drunk on his ass, says, "Awww, cher petite, Ah feel like Ah'm at the Quadroon Ball!" And she promptly knocks him on his fat ass, with him folding the table on himself where a cake is sitting, dripping white frosting and strawberries all over him. There is a quick line up of Black and white men hollering at him for the rude, racist, raunchy behavior.

It could have been a lot worse, because some want to throw down on this southern white racist. The picture taken is front page news too.

A fun time had by all.

∞ ∞ ∞

LILY and Toot move into the house that the girls have shared, because Callie has moved uptown into Henri's mansion on St. Charles Avenue. Every day the sistas see each other; they must because they refuse to do otherwise. They are joined at the hip.

Lily and Toot are married by the justice of the peace, with few people making it to the ceremony. Callie and Henri are the witnesses and sign the certificate too.

Estelle and Theo are there, but the bad feelings between Lily and her mama are like the pink elephant in the room. Everybody runs into walls because they're trying not to see it. Lily's wedding, for her and Estelle, is solemn.

The other wedding that takes place at His Divine Spirit Community Center is the real celebration. They, while the family and friends are watching, jump the broom.

Toot's daddy comes, and soon he is drinking and dancing, having the best time he's had in years. When he gets a phone call, he looks disturbed and leaves.

Caldonia and Lily sit at a table together the whole time. Lily is so pregnant and can't drink or dance. They sit this one out together but tell their husbands to go have a good time.

There will be many celebrations in the future, so what's just one?

Caldonia's life is suddenly on display with all the things that socialites do, pictures being taken all the time. It is like a fairy tale that the people in New Orleans have followed since the beginning of their courtship. A young woman who works at a bar is swept up by the most eligible bachelor in the Big Easy, and the astounding fact is that she is from down in the bayou.

The fairy tale comes true.

The couples are down in the country visiting when Lily's water breaks. Lily and Toot are at Minou and Joe's when it happens, and it doesn't take long for Estelle and Theo to get there.

Toot and Mac and Moe and Henri are walking the same path used by Alcide and Joe years ago, and they are showing the way. Minus the smoking but the liquor is on the cabinet, waiting.

Lily delivers a big, healthy girl with a veil over her, and the women there gasp. No child born after T-June has had the veil. They're trying to calm Lily while Callie holds her sista. The blood keeps pouring out of Lily, and the ambulance is called to rush her to the hospital.

Estelle pushes Callie out the way and grabs her daughter and her granddaughter, and they are crying so hard together. Toot is there trying to comfort her when Estelle pushes him too.

The blood starts flowing again in the ambulance.

T-June and Jolie are there in minutes, and the cars behind them are full of everybody else.

T-June gets to her quick, before the doctors, puts his hands on Lily, and the blood stops. The amazed looks that the hospital staff all have after this happens isn't surprising to the family, but it leaves the doctors and nurses pondering what has happened, because they aren't sure about what they've seen. They've all heard about these mysterious, wealthy families, and another tale is added to the stories.

Lily is brought to her mama's house, where Estelle lets go of all the bad feelings and replaces them with happiness, seeing her new granddaughter. Her name will be Maybelline Caldonia Laverne. They want her to be named after Estelle's sister, Maybelline, the famous, beautiful woman that gave up her love and life to be with the hated, infamous Laray. And of course, Caldonia is her nanan.

It's yet to be seen what the veil means.

All is well at the Theriots' home.

∞ ∞ ∞

WHEN things get calm at the household, T-June really notices the difference in his grandparents and is there when the next full moon is upon them. He follows Bertha and Alcide into the swamps, where he finds them talking with old man Mr. Pieyan. All three of them are drinking Crown Royal and talking about the old days they miss so terribly.

T-June comes up on the huge fire they have built, and they look up at him in despair. "Oh, my beloved family! I can't stand to see all of you with so much sadness. I caused this, I think, when I changed all of you, but I thought it was what you wanted."

Poor Pieyan, he for sure didn't ask for this to happen. He doesn't like being human.

"All of you stand and join hands, go around in a circle, then put your hands on me one at a time together. I don't know what this will do, but concentration is needed."

T-June starts shaking and moaning while Bertha and Alcide and Pieyan hold on to him. And then it happens. He turns into a magnificent loup-garou.

Watching this, Bertha and Alcide turn back to werewolves and begin licking the new one that is T-June.

They hear the most terrible howl and turn to see the bigfoot that is Pieyan, again running and jumping and skipping and stomping like he used to. All little critters aren't scared of him for sure now, and they are doing the same, like Brer Rabbit.

Minou and Joe, with the Toussaints and Danny (Old Man Guidry), come running when they hear the horrifying screams from Pieyan. They witness the three loup-garous and immediately take control of the situation, doing what they've done for years, taking care of the three, with T-June being a huge black werewolf himself.

Dawn is not far off, and they all watch as the three turn back into humans. Bertha looks ten years younger, and Alcide goes to T-June immediately, not knowing what to say to him.

June walks back into the house, and Jolie follows him into the bedroom, where they stay for the rest of the day.

He's always known the creature was calling. He just wouldn't answer the phone until now.

Bertha and Alcide can't stop talking about the cure, how awful it has been, and hugging him for doing what he's done for them.

But Monsieur Mayhem won't talk with them. He goes back to New Orleans, not wanting to talk about it at all.

∞ ∞ ∞

THINGS get a little dicey back in the Big Easy; you know they would. There's always mayhem with this bunch.

Toot comes to talk with Joseph the counselor one morning early. He is disheveled like he is still in his clothes from yesterday. He has left Lily at home with the baby.

"Everything is a catastrophe! We're gonna lose everything because my dad has taken out loans against his gambling and put up his house and the barber shop as collateral. He's never been able to break this addiction, and he's gotten worse since my mama died. My grandparents and my great-aunt are in the loan shark business, and my grandma is threatening to take it all unless I pay up by the end of next week. She got out of jail and learned more nastiness up in there."

Monsieur Mayhem takes over the situation and calls a family meeting. "Well, I guess we aren't through with the Lavernes, who are up in our business again. We have to deal with this and help Toot and Lily save the barber shop and his house. Once and for all, we're going to send these people back to the gutter they crawled out of."

Henri already has undercover detectives investigating these people and sends in his men to become members of this sleazy bunch of sharks making money off the unfortunate.

Theo becomes very angry and is determined to rid his family of the sorry ass-side of the Lavernes. Of course, his partners and podnahs, Joe and Alcide, are ready to stand alongside Theo and kick some ass.

Toot calls to tell the loathsome loan lizards to come pick up their monies, to meet him and his pop at the barber shop on Rampart that night at dark. He certainly doesn't tell them that his family is coming too.

Grandma Barker (Tut Laverne) speaks up to Toot, not his dad. "Toussaint, ya sure have grown up to be the image of ya Uncle Laray! I bet that pisses off a lot of ya new family! I can't figure out why I wasn't invited to ya weddin'. I bet that was somethin' to gloat about with them bitches! Ha ha! Baby, bein' I'm ya grandma, I hate for it to come to this, but man, it's a lot of money, and your daddy knew this and just kept ignorin' us. Musta thought his mama was goin' to let him have all that money. I don't even know the dude. Shit! I wasn't ever the motherin' type! Ha ha ha, yeah!"

She watches all the family – some real familiar – walk in the front door, pull the shades down, turn the sign to closed, and lock it.

"What the fuck we got here? A real classy family reunion! Fuck you, Estelle. What the fuck you gonna do? I'm real scared. See, I'm shakin'! Ha!"

Estelle jumps on the woman with all the pent-up anger and hurt from all these years and beats the living shit out of her. Tut's men are carrying guns, but before they can pull them out, they have three loaded double-barreled shotguns pointed at their backs. They have to stand by helplessly and watch Estelle as she rips and tears the old woman into a pile of bloody crap. She does leave the woman conscious so she can hear Estelle's words.

"You will pay dearly for what you've done to my family. You sure as hell didn't think we were that powerful, did you, because we're from the bayou. Well, Laray sure found out, didn't he? So sorry you lost that cash cow. We are survivors, and nothing you've done so far has broken us. The cops are coming for you, and we will make sure you don't see daylight again!"

Theo helps his wife up and says so dead serious, "You are not getting this money, and before the cops come, we got something to show you. Get up and walk out the back door."

They all are pushed out the back door; someone has to help up the wicked grandma. Monsieur Mayhem is waiting as the large, black-furred loup-garou, snarling and hollering at the moon.

Alcide and Bertha have come to the city too and have Pieyan hiding in the large refrigerated truck. Pieyan sure doesn't want to see all the people, and the majority of them would scream for dear life and call the po-po themselves. Or the Zoo!

He has come to play his part.

The old lady screams loud, as do all her hoodlums, who are the toughest of the tough on the streets. They all have been taught superstitions, and what they see are the devils coming straight for them.

"This is what's waiting for you in our swamps if we have to ever deal with y'all's sorry asses again."

Laray's been telling them, and they've been thinking he was fucking nuts, too cuckoo!

The police come with Henri and all the marshals, the district attorney, and the mayor. This huge bust has taken a year to get the large amount of evidence they need. The undercover cop is so ready to get away from these filthy animals.

Of course, nothing ever is done legally by the sharks that set up shop on the streets of the city. The task force has been wanting to catch them in the act and has been recording all their conversations with the undercover dudes. Since most of them are three-time losers, they are getting off the streets for good.

∞ ∞ ∞

LILY gets her degree in social studies and is going back to school to be a civil rights attorney. Toot, with the help of his cousins who have made a big splash in the small pool of Tremé, turns his business into something brand new, with four chairs instead of two.

Maybelline is the hit of the nursery school at His Divine Spirit.

Monsieur Mayhem never talks to anybody about the new power he displays. They don't know if the change is permanent or if he can change at will or how the hell he's going to deal with being loup-garou.

So once a month, the swamp is all lit up and full of family that gather to watch the three werewolves and the bigfoot running loose on the Peltier/Thibeau property. They bring a lot of deer roast and big-ass T-bones for the three to chew on instead of people.

All carry Off! mosquito spray.

No one else living down there will ever venture onto that property. Something will happen for sure.

This is the day Callie tells her mama she is having a baby with Henri.

Y'all just get ready!

Chapter Fifteen

Sneakin' in Tha Dark

THE night life is the right life for all these transplants in the Big Easy from down the bayou, mostly on the weekends. You can find all the young ones down at Bon Temps Rouler on Bourbon Street.

Moe and Mac come every weekend now, staying in Estelle and Theo's house there. After all, they're Theriots too. They are finding work every day in the city. Massive restorations are going on, and Henri is finding more and more projects for them that will last for years. So, they begin to rent Estelle and Theo's house, not wanting to be just using the place.

Caldonia has found out she doesn't like being the socialite Caldonia, so Callie has quit taking phone calls and joining committees and their parties and their five o'clock drinks wherever.

The socialites have made their own conclusions. They believe you can't take the country out the country and that she chooses to be introverted. The main reason they think she's not part of the party circuit is because she isn't capable of doing the social scene and feels inadequate to them because she will never rise that far.

Many are betting between themselves that the marriage won't last another year. Many are the women Henri wasn't interested in and want another shot.

Good luck with that!

Henri and Callie hang out with the crowd from down the bayou, and except for the few photographers still trying to find out what this famous couple may be up too, they love the night life. They want to boogie.

Lily and Toot always have kin that can't wait to get their hands on Maybelline to love on her, so babysitting is never a problem. So, whenever they can join the hometown bunch, they most certainly do.

The Monsieur Mayhem Duo has quite the following now, and the bar has had to open up unused rooms to accommodate the crowds that come to hear them.

Joshua and Jim Silverberg are part of the crowd, and they want to record the duo's music and make them all famous. The Silverberg boys are talented themselves and the best kind of people to work for. They attend synagogue every week, and Joshua has picked up his chip from AA for a year of sobriety. Joshua is running an AA meeting weekly at His Divine Spirit community heathcare.

Since Henri is such a well-known man, rising in power, he has caused more young constituents to do their partying down at the club, trusting his influences.

It's just the talk of the city, drawing the crowds to the Bon Temps Rouler.

∞ ∞ ∞

LILY is back in school for the degree that will make her a top-notch lawyer; that's needed in Tremé. They've bought the house that she and Callie used to rent.

Toot's dad retires after the infamous throwdown that lands all of those unsavory Lavernes up in jail for the rest of their lives. He's quit gambling and now has a program at His Divine Spirit Community Center for helping other people caught up in the insidious addiction. He's been off the bet for two years. Bishop Toussaint welcomes all who have walked the walk and can talk the talk.

Maybelline is the love of everybody in the daycare of the center, especially Madam Aucoin. She's almost three, and she reminds everybody of her great-aunt who she is named for.

Estelle can hardly stand it, remembering her baby sister every time she sees her grandbaby Maybelline. The baby girl has sealed the bonds broken and mended the heartaches by her birth, and Toot is a treasured member of the family.

Callie is a very active nanan who buys and buys and buys everything she sees for precious, pampered, plumb little Maybelline.

Henri has gone to the bank and started her college fund.

∞ ∞ ∞

MONSIEUR Mayhem (aka T-June) is feeling the restlessness of his community, along with anger and fear. There has been a sudden rash of murders in Tremé, and they feel like the police are not trying hard enough to catch the murderer. Anger because they feel it's racial in nature, and the cops aren't worried enough about it.

Bishop Toussaint and Monsieur Mayhem go to the police department to talk with the chief about what's happening; three murders so far. The bishop does most of the talking while T-June goes meandering through the minds of the policemen involved. He knows all of them are struck with fear and keeping secrets. The big secret is how the victims all died. He doesn't believe he has the power to take care of this situation.

"We came to talk with you about what's happening in the city. Tension is rising, and the anger you can cut a knife through. The murder rate in New Orleans is atrocious and already is cutting into the tourist trade. They must be top priority because we've come to tell you that the neighborhood all the way into the Quarter is like a powder keg fixing to blow up all over the place.

"Councilman Henri Aucoin couldn't make it this morning, but he is behind us fully to solve these crimes."

Most in the neighborhood lock their doors, even in daylight, and don't take their leisurely walks at night anymore on Esplanade Avenue. Big dogs have been bought and taught to be mean.

It hasn't slowed down Bourbon Street or the rest of the Quarter in partying, however, and the gang continues to go to the club.

Moe and Mac have hit the town like hurricane Katrina. Beautiful young country men with strong work ethics, so polite and charming as hell with their accents and their smiles. Young women are vying for their cute behinds.

One night, a woman comes into the bar and changes Mac forever. She is sitting at the bar by herself and staring at Mac while he dances and drinks and laughs at what his friends are saying.

She is downright upper class, with her spiked heels of red and a sequined black dress, down to the floor, that has deep slits revealing legs of a movie star from the 1920s.

He knows she's there and is struck by the intensity of her stares. He's trying to build up the courage to speak with her when she stands, smiles, and walks out the door.

Mac questions everybody, but nobody has ever seen her before, much less knows her name. He keeps asking around about this woman, describing every detail of her but to no avail. Nobody can recall this mystery woman. Mac is starting to think he's imagined it after she doesn't come back for three weeks.

Mac's started having dreams about her, some pretty wet indeed.

He is drinking a Dixie beer when she comes back in, and he almost drops it full on the floor. Mac walks right up to her as she sits at a table. She is dressed in dark purple satin, and her hair shines the blackest, with fair skin and red, full lips.

He sits on the front side of her and says softly, "I've been waiting for you. I thought I'd dreamed you up. Please tell me who you are, and why did you come back?"

"I'm new to town, so you must be too, because I've asked a lot of questions about you. I'm sorry, but you made an impression on me I couldn't forget. I remember you, walkin' out the door."

Check out Eric Bibb, if you want to hear the rest of the song!

She speaks to him in an accent that is familiar to him but seems foreign in some way. Smiling the whitest smile he has ever seen, she says, "Hello, my beautiful one. I've come home after being gone for a long while. I was living in the Bahamas for years. My name is Claudine du Robaire, and just like you, I come from the bayou. My family has a plantation down near Golden Meadow. Perhaps you know of it? Robaire Plantation.

"I came back to this club for you."

Mac is a gone pecan.

They talk 'til almost dawn, when Claudine kisses him goodnight and again walks away, leaving him enamored, with many questions and wondering if he will see her again.

Mac calls home, asking about the plantation, and Bertha gets on the phone.

"Chér! Mais, why ya wanna know 'bout dat ole place? It's down way by tha bottom of Lafourche where it's so deep and wide. Mais, bébé, dat ain't no good place! Dey use to steal tha Houmas people to use as slaves, and we was some scared of dem! Always somet'in' evil and scary 'bout dem people. Dat big house is still dere, but nobody stays dere no more.

"Somebody must have money 'cause it's kept up, but ya can't go wit' all tha swamp trees and electric fences. NO TRESPASS! Mais, who tha hell wants to? Lawd, Ah hope it ain't you."

Now the village is on alert because Bertha can't keep that kind of question to herself.

Mac is getting obsessed with Claudine, and the gang is pretty perturbed about the whole thing. Each and every one has talked to Mac, because Claudine seems to only come once a month to the bar. He has become oblivious to everything else going on at the club and at work. He is twitterpated and determined. Mac just waits all the time for her to come, and the time she is with him, he is very exclusive. He hasn't introduced her to anybody.

One night at the club, when the Monsieur Mayhem Duo doesn't play because they are discussing contracts and such with the Silverberg brothers, Claudine walks into the bar and goes straight to Mac.

Monsieur and Jolie are finished with business, and June walks up to the table where the couple sits. It's the first time he has been so close up and personal to Claudine, because he's usually being busy making music. The skin of his body starts to rip, and he backs up and says, "You have to leave. Now."

Dead serious he is but speaking calmly.

Mac becomes irate with those words spoken to Claudine. "T-June! What the hell are you saying? For Claudine to leave? You're not making sense. Fuck! We're both going to go."

It is the last time they see him alive. He is found dead, murdered, in the Metairie Cemetery. The families are devastated.

All the village people who've raised T-June are there to stay until this shit is taken care of, filling up the houses bought in the city.

The funeral is immense, and grief-stricken Estelle has to be carried away by Toot, while Henri helps Theo.

Monsieur Mayhem knows this is not the last time he will see Mac Theriot.

∞ ∞ ∞

EVERYBODY is at Minou and Joe's house on Esplanade Avenue. All are grieving and angry, but Moe has a true breakdown of anguish and is ready to kill somebody. He can't be consoled.

Father Becnel has performed the services at the St. Thomas Catholic Church in New Orleans, where the body will be interred in their cemetery until they can bring him home, something about moving the murdered victims. Father Becnel says, "Please remember the goodness of Mac. He brought so much joy to all of us, and I don't think he would want y'all to start some vigilante posse to avenge him."

Moe stands up and says, "The hell he wouldn't! He'd be the first to pick up his gun and search for the killer."

Coroner Boudreaux has allowed T-June and the bishop to see the body of Mac Theriot before the funeral parlor comes for him. Dr. Boudreaux sits down by the body, telling them details, all the while shaking and nervous. He pours himself a large glass of whiskey and lights a cigar. He sighs heavily.

"Just like I told the sheriff before, the three murder victims were drained of blood, except for your family member. He was left with about a pint of blood still in his body. I told the sheriff it was totally bizarre and not something I see every day, much less four times. I have great fear for myself staying here with these unclaimed bodies. Shit, if they are what I think they are, we in deep shit. I told the sheriff what's been happening, and he called me a stupid, dumb-ass fool to believe in such nonsense.

"Fuck! I'm from New Orleans, and I believe in all the supernatural shit that happens here. Do you believe in vampires? You better because they all have bite marks on their necks."

The search for Claudine du Robaire is on in every corner of the city. They are calling her the Death Angel, a true female serial killer.

∞ ∞ ∞

FOUR days pass after Mac's death. During a rainy night, Mac Theriot knocks on T-June's back door.

The bishop and Madam Aucoin are there, anticipating the knock, along with Monsieur Mayhem and Jolie. They are there with clean clothes and pints of blood from the nearby hospital when Mac walks into the living room, all crazy from being buried and hunger pains he doesn't know for what.

When they give him the blood to drink, he screams out the fact that he is now vampyre! "Oh, my Lawd! Why did you let this happen to me? Now, I have no idea what to do being this way, and I must find her! She said we would be together forever. I thought she meant getting married and was saving herself for the marriage.

"She told me that we would be soulmates forever, and now she's stolen my soul forever. I can't go inside the church, much less take the host. I'm damned!"

He pauses to think.

"I know where she's at! She's at that old plantation house at the end of Bayou Lafourche. I'm going with y'all to find her. We must find her!"

When the fact hits him that he will never see daylight again, he crumples to the floor. His people who know about him have the casket picked up and brought to St. Luke's Cemetery, where he is buried with his Big Mama and Big Daddy and his infamous mother, Maybelline.

He doesn't stay put and rises to the same treatment he has gotten every night since he walks as the undead Mac Theriot.

∞ ∞ ∞

ESTELLE tells the village how strange Mac's behavior has been, even before his being murdered. She breaks down crying. Poor Joe, he's got garlic hanging around his neck, and he's pissed off at everybody.

You remember how Bertha is about the supernatural, even though she is a bona fide werewolf? She speaks up, not knowing about the vampire. "Mais, Ah talked wit' him not too long ago. He was axin' me if Ah knew 'bout dis damned place. Ah tole him nuttin' good comes from dat place, and Ah axed him why he want to know dat, but he didn't answer me."

Everyone there makes Bertha sit down to tell them what she knows about the place. "Mais, why ya makin' me talk 'bout dis shit? Alcide him, he's da one dat knows history."

So, Alcide gladly takes the role and lights his pipe, preparing his story.

"A long long time ago, dat plantation was as big as any other on tha bayou, from Donaldsonville to Grand Isle. Merde! Even Grand Isle had a plantation dat grew citrus like oranges and lemons.

"In tha history book 'bout Lafourche Parish, it says dat dey used tha poor tribe of tha Houmas to steal deir slaves. It said dey was cruel and tortured tha people unfortunate to get kidnapped. What was left of tha family died out in tha 1920s when tha flood came for e'rybody. People t'ink dat dey drowned, tha last of tha du Robaires and deir daughter.

"What's left of tha place is slowly slippin' into tha bay, but it's kept up by somebody. Nobody sees anybody dere, but some say dey see lights on in tha house.

"None of it! None of it has any good to it, tha history 'bout dat family."

Monsieur Mayhem and Bishop Toussaint are there, along with Madam Aucoin. They keep watching the sun go down on the bayou. All three make excuses as to why they have to leave and they go, hurrying to the graveyard. They are there, waiting there with clothes and blood, when Mac the vampire crawls out the grave.

Mac is very anxious and determined to find Claudine. After taking care of himself, Mac says, "When are we going? I'm ready right now! We can take your truck, T-June, since I don't know if it's legal for me to drive now. But let's get ready."

He tells them to get his brother, Moe, and T-June goes right away to fetch him.

When Moe sees him, he cries and holds his brother, and they cry together, until they notice tears of blood.

Moe freaks out when he takes a good look at Mac, so silent and so white with bloody tears dripping down his chin. He can't comprehend what has happened until the bishop explains it to him, and he freaks out again with anger and rage.

"Mac! You telling me you know where she's at? I'm going, and I'm going to stake her bitch ass. Y'all got some crucifixes and some wooden spears? Y'all have some holy water?"

When Mac says no to the stakes, Moe goes crazy for sure!

"Why in the hell not? Look what she did to you and all those other poor souls! Fuck, we're probably dealing with a whole bunch of vampires! Shit, Mac we have to kill all of those motherfuckers!"

And Moe sees the first of the new fangs on Mac!

Madam Aucoin says she knows plenty about the undead. She is well acquainted with zombies. "I'm going because we will all be protected by my spells I have conjured up. We go tonight just to see what is going on at that place. You know, casing the joint?"

By the time they get everything ready, it is 12:00. Midnight…

They walk in knee boots through the swamps until they are on the back side of the old plantation house.

Mac, with his newfound strength and deadness, raises the electric fence, with it sparking, and holds it until everybody is on the other side. That is way cool! He's wondering what else he can do.

They walk onto the porch softly, after walking up the staircase of twenty-seven steps. The house itself is immense, with five bedrooms and a large kitchen, and the living and dining areas are furnished in antiques that are priceless at today's market prices. But people won't dare try to get on the property because of the fences and superstition.

Peeking into the very tall windows, they all get a horrible view of three vampires. Two are fighting, flying in the air and hissing and pushing each other. Every one of them is witnessing Claudine at her finest.

The vigilantes make it back to the truck and speed down Highway 1 just in time for Mac to go underground, where he sleeps with the dead folk and his mama.

Moe cannot be calmed down. He is ranting and raving. "Why the hell we got to wait until the nighttime? Let's just go find their coffins and stake them in their unholy godforsaken beds. Mac doesn't need to see that. He thinks he needs Claudine, but what for? So she can show him how to kill people?"

T-June and Madam Aucoin and Bishop Toussaint and Moe Theriot and… (Lawd, I thought I was finished with that) decide to go and see if they can go in the old plantation house to locate the coffins.

And they do, all four of them.

None dare to open the lids, while Madam goes into her trance, asking for Laurette to come. And she does.

"Ha! You got yourself a mighty, mighty situation! I can help with that. I know all about zombies. Ha! Made a few myself."

Madam is doing her twirling thing, huffing and blowing and spitting all over the room, while the others are anxiously watching for the sun in the large bedroom downstairs.

Madam Aucoin comes back from her trance, and they swiftly go back up Highway 1 to safety.

"I'm going to tell you what Laurette managed to do. Though I didn't hear her, I know. She conjured a spell that would hinder them from harming us, like zombies. They will already know we were there, so we're going to go back tonight and make acquaintances with these used-to-be-alive folk."

Not all of them have the confidence that Madam Aucoin has. Moe has a makeshift stake down in his pants and under his shirt. He's carrying a rosary and holy water and a can of Off! mosquito spray, a surefire remedy that Minou and Joe have always sworn by.

They are just waiting for Mac.

"You mean you went there to kill them all? I said NO! I want to see Claudine. She has all the answers, and I still love her!"

Moe grabs Mac by the collar, and in return he gets another good look at his brother's new fangs.

Moe hollers at him while Mac has him floating in the air, his legs dangling. "What the fuck you know about love? You sure as shit weren't 'gettin' sum!' You have no clue about who she is or if she's got plans for you. Man, you were like a virgin. Let's go and get this shit over with!"

They get to the house easily this time; the gate has been left opened, like someone knows they've trespassed. They are inviting the trespassers in.

Mac goes straight to Claudine, and they hug, flitting themselves into the air. No one is prepared for that!

Madam Aucoin speaks first, with the rest standing behind her in defense mode.

"Thank you for welcoming us into your home, Monsieur and Madam du Robaire. I presume Claudine is your daughter? In my research, I found out about the 1927 flood and how everyone thought you had drowned. But that's not what happened, was it? Please let us hear your stories about what became of you."

Madam Angelique du Robaire pats the sofa for the other madam to sit. She knows this Voodoo queen has no fear of her and rightly so because Madam Aucoin has called the holy spirits to put a strong, invisible netting on all of the visitors, and she can't penetrate it. She has no desire to harm them anyway, but the same can't be said about her husband, Monsieur Beauregard du Robaire.

He stands silently, with glaring cold eyes toward all of them, especially the Black brothers and the Creole others, baring fangs to all of them. He flies up to grab Moe to kill him and gets thrown to the back of the living room. He stays where he lands, hatred coming out of him like hot water.

Angelique begins her conversation as she serves sherry in exquisite glasses too old to drink out of. "I must tell you now how glad I am that you came. I've been starving for company. Oh, no, dear. Not in that way. Goodness gracious! I'm so, so sorry.

"Well, people, it all started at the end of the war. No, I mean the War between the States, the Northern Aggression. We were celebrating Claudine's birthday, being she was eighteen and it was time for her to be finding a suitable husband. She was considered old to not be engaged at least. There were many suitors, and she didn't like any one of them.

"A new guest came in from the Bahamas. He caught her eye. He came with all his credentials, being a successful plantation owner in the Bahamas and in Louisiana. He was French, and he spoke so eloquently, we all were enamored by his manners, and his elegance was disarming. His name was Louie St. Pierre. He courted Claudine for months, showering her with jewels and flowers and a diamond engagement ring so large, it cut her finger.

"Of course she said yes.

"It happened during the night when they decided to walk the grounds of our huge plantation. We were searching for them the next morning when we came upon her lifeless body. He had murdered her in the gardens, and he was nowhere to be found.

"At this time, we had a very elaborate funeral, so grief-stricken at having to put her in the ground. Three nights passed, and she showed up, banging on the door.

"I hadn't had servants for a long while. Beauregard would fornicate with them. So, he opened the door. She was starving and went for her father's neck, and that didn't satisfy her, so she came for me. She killed us both, and then on the third night, we came back as the vampires you see now, with Claudine and Louie waiting for us.

"We have never told that to another living person.

"No one dared to come on our property, and it's been this way ever since. We fed on the now-freed slaves, and people didn't want to be part of what was happening, so scary and mysterious. We fed on the carpetbaggers who wanted to claim our house and the occasional salesmen. We have had to feed on the animals found in the swamps, because no human will come close to our place.

"Claudine wanted to find her another mate and started going to New Orleans to look for a suitable man. She had finally left Louie St. Pierre because he was way too brutal for her. She says she found her love, and she knew he would come looking for her, and now you've brought him."

Monsieur du Robaire is standing up but still at the back when he starts raving on the situation. "Never ever will I accept him into my home! She brings a nigga boy for us to approve of, and I refuse to even talk about it. I want to kill him dead, and he will wind up as pile of ashes!

"We used the Indians for slaves because I never could stand the sight of these mongoloids from Africa. We've spent all these years hiding, and now she wants to bring a nigga here to join us. I will not let this happen! I will kill him if I have the chance to do so!"

He looms over the couple, trying to strike Mac but can't because of the spell cast by Madam Aucoin.

Mac speaks up while Moe is ready to use all the things he has brought. "I wasn't a willing partner in this. I fell in love with Claudine, but when she said we would be together forever, I thought we would marry. Mister Robaire, I sure didn't want this goddam life of living only in the night, and I sure as hell don't want to be up in your house either.

"Man, you need to catch up with the times. We Black people have made many contributions to our fair country, and you don't have the right to the use of 'nigga,' and you can't vote! Much of that hatred has gone, and it has become clear to almost everybody that skin color or sexual leanings of a particular person don't matter. Nobody's business what people do when they fall in love. I've come for Claudine, and now we'll leave."

Mr. Robaire is flying up in the air and tries to attack Mac when he is knocked back by the invisible force that protects everybody. Moe comes at him with all of his vampire hunter's equipment. Robaire can't touch him, and Moe's going to kill him. He is stopped by Mac.

Everyone is in survivor mode when Madam Aucoin speaks up. "There will not be another confrontation. We have to ponder this situation. Monsieur du Robaire, Mac will not be joining you in your comfortable racist nest. We will protect him at any cost, and he will not be here for your hateful racial ravings. Claudine can come with Mac, and we will protect her as well.

"We will leave now, but know this. We know how to find you in the daylight. Don't come up the bayou looking for us. You have no idea who you'll be up against, with our very own power to truly put you back in the ground for good."

They leave in the truck with Claudine and Mac. They will be put to ground, using the same coffin.

∞ ∞ ∞

T-JUNE and the bishop with Madam call for a sit-down with the rest of the family. This is a very serious happening for the group, but what isn't? Always mayhem.

When they've all showed up for this new situation, Bishop Toussaint stands, telling of the newest quemas down the bayou. "I hope I can find the courage to tell you this. Mac Theriot is now a vampire."

The combined families start crying at the horrible news as they slowly comprehend, and they all start screaming. When they are ready to hear him, the bishop begins to tell them about the spells Madam Aucoin has conjured up that will protect all of them from the fangy bite.

"Laurette came again. You know some of y'all have met her, and she's serious business when she is conjured up. We will all be protected, but we must take extra precautions tonight because Monsieur du Robaire might be coming to claim back his daughter. He is also a vampire, and he was definitely a night rider with the Ku Klux Klan.

"His wife is a bit crazy, living in the used-to-be. She told us she is starving for company but corrected that statement. I think she is very lonely and has had to put up with his pompous, arrogant, racist ass for almost two centuries. I have no doubt she is a killer when cornered. I will explain everything when this is dealt with."

Estelle is still screaming and demands to go with them to the cemetery to see for herself if indeed Mac is a vampire. Of course, they all have to go and see for themselves too, except Joe and Bertha. These two are busy putting garlic pods all over the windows and doors, setting up loaded shotguns and silver bullets Sweet Stu has brought.

You never know what could happen, but Alcide knows for sure about silver bullets.

The St. Luke's Cemetery is full at sunset, with the whole bunch watching where they step. For sure they're not stepping on Old Man Billiot!

When Mac rises from his coffin with his arms crossed and stands in the bottom of the casket, he then turns and helps Claudine too. The village freaks out again. The bishop forgets to tell them there are two.

Father Becnel and Sister Bridget start spraying them with holy water and holding crucifixes, including the large one that hangs off of the sister's neck. Minou stops them and becomes very curious about what is going on. Flavia is right on the side of her, while Sweet Stu holds a sturdy lasso.

Madam Aucoin is not upset because she already knows this before they do and deeply believes in it. Them zombies!

They are being very cautious and barely speak to Claudine Robaire, not really knowing what to say.

Mac stands there while Estelle is hugging him and tearing at his clothes because she has a hard time believing in what he's become. She just stares at Claudine, daring her with her eyes to come any closer.

They all move swiftly back to Minou and Joe's house to prepare for what may be coming.

Two hours later, they are staring at three vampires that have flown from the Robaire Plantation to Minou's house. Angelique and Beauregard du Robaire come, along with Louie St. Pierre, who wants to reclaim Claudine as his bride. He stands in all his royalty but is ruthless in getting his way. Regal but deadly.

"Monsieurs and madams, I've come back to get her. There will be no harming of you if you just send her to me."

Mac speaks to Louie as Claudine stands on his side. "Man, what you want and what Claudine wants are two entirely different things. You don't treat women in the custom you once did anymore. If she says no, then it's no. Man, you need to get a grip and catch up with the times. Both you old-old dudes are male chauvinists, and you probably don't even know what that means.

"I don't know what the hell you think you will do to anyone standing here. You better take yourself back to the Bahamas and forget Claudine right now, or you will see the power that will be used against you."

Bishop and Monsieur Mayhem, along with Alcide, Theo, and Moe, stand side by side, together with Mac. Moe is on the other side of his brother, just itching to use his equipment on all three and maybe Claudine too.

The women are standing next to Father Becnel and Sister Bridget. They are steadily spraying the holy water on the three vampires and swinging big-ass crucifixes. They watch as the vampires keep flinching every time they get hit with the water. Father Becnel can't think of a single prayer to use in this quemas.

Not Bertha. She is not going over there by those fools but has stinky-ass garlic everywhere.

Minou and Flavia decide to move closer and are looking at their clothes. "Mais, y'all need to go shoppin' for some new clothes. Y'all fo' sure are outta date! Look what it done for Flavia! Go look at dem stores dat stay open all night by New Orleans. Mais, Ah saw a dress jus' like ya got on in tha museum over dere."

Flavia has got balls to begin with, and she starts asking questions. "Do y'all know what's been written 'bout ya in tha books 'bout Lafourche Parish? Nuttin' good! So, are y'all dose people dat made tha pages of dose books, huh? Ah heard from tha others who visited you dat ya bona fide centuries old, Klu Klux Klan members spoutin' racist remarks, and man, dat don't cut it now. Y'all pay taxes?"

Louie St. Pierre is tired of listening to this chatter and goes to where Mac and Claudine are. He flies up in the air, baring his fangs and going for Mac's throat. He is knocked away by such a force that he is addled at first. Then he tries again, and Moe drives his stake right through his heart while he is making his landing.

They all watch, even the vampires, as Louie St Pierre turns into a pile of ashes. Everybody cries at the sight.

Monsieur du Robaire and Madam Angelique both shudder but seem relieved, while the rest are hugging and patting the back of Moe Theriot, who slayed the monster.

Angelique speaks first. "Oh, my Lord, have mercy! It is such a relief to be rid of him because he was a master vampire, and he sired Claudine. At his pleasure or displeasure, she had to obey. He lost his power over Claudine when she left him. He followed her to the city and killed all those people to get her attention. We are so grateful that you freed us!

"Claudine, you can do whatever you want to do, and if that means being with Mac, I have no qualms. Your father and I are going back home because he has nothing to say at this time. He will have to work on his behavior, and if you would come again, I'll read everything that you can bring."

The vampires leave, with Claudine's father looking like he's a deflated balloon with fangs.

Alcide tells them to bring their coffins up the road because they are going to dig up Mac and Claudine and bury them on his large property. Joe and Bertha get to hollering about that decision! "What da fuck ya sayin', Alcide? Ah don' want dat on my land! Ah don' care who it is. It ain't happenin', captain."

But it does, because Minou says yes to Alcide.

∞ ∞ ∞

T-JUNE is relieved he doesn't have to turn into the loup-garou. He has been planning to tear out the throat of Louie St Pierre.

Claudine is grudgingly accepted by the family after they find out she isn't the murderer.

The couple sit and listen to the tales everyone tells about the mayhem that goes on down the bayou.

Angelique comes most nights because she is really starving from the lack of people in her life, blood or not.

The night that Monsieur du Robaire shows up it is a surprise to all, even Angelique. He has not told her he is coming.

"Thank you for letting me come in. After our last encounter, I've had to rethink everything I had been taught when I was a living man. So much has changed. It's hard to catch up on the world that we've missed. I thank you for the cable TV. If you will accept my sincere apology, Mac, we can move on with my new attitudes. What do you say, boy? Oh, crap. I did it again.

"You are welcomed at our home, and if it pleases you, we'll open the fourth coffin for you. It was purchased for Louie, but he won't need it anymore. It's hardly been used, and Claudine can use the magical things you have to make it smell good.

"Please accept my apologies, dear people, for having the manners of someone who is low born, uncouth, and racist. I had to learn, to my dismay, what the word meant. I'd never heard of such a thing.

"We are going to leave now, but if it's all right, we will continue the visits. I realized that I too have missed the company of other men."

With that said, the older couple fly back from whence they came.

Mac and Claudine will think about this revelation from her parents, but not now.

So, life has settled down for the families following T-June. Just another strange thing about those families with their mysterious and frightening ways. And now they've added real life monsters. Seems like they just roam free.

Chapter Sixteen

Dere'll be Days like Dis

THE Monsieur Mayhem Duo has hit the big time with their music since they joined the Silverberg brothers, who have recorded the band's very unusual style of playing. Because of them, the Bon Temps Rouler has become one of the places that tourists are told to go in this huge city of New Orleans.

They are hot!

Henri Aucoin runs in the election for mayor and wins with a huge majority of votes. Callie stands on the side of him, big and pregnant with their first child. Henri is up there strutting like an old rooster.

Lily has become the lawyer she went to Xavier for. She has all the business she can handle.

Little Maybelline has become a fixture in the busy office, there every day with her mama and learning everything she can. She is one smart cookie, and the intelligence is startling to anyone she meets. Maybelline will never suffer like her namesake, being taught already about minding your heart. Maybe one of the skills she will have is because of that thick veil covering her body when she was born.

You just never know about these people.

Toot Laverne is one of the top barbers in the city, with six chairs that he has a lot of fresh young barbers to occupy. They are able to keep the shop open late into the night. He does this so his cousin Mac can have his hair cut by Toot. He does this every week on account of Mac's hair just grows right back and longer, like dreads. Mac keeps up his appearance, even if he's dead.

Mac and Claudine have moved back to the city, buying an old mansion to keep their coffins in. They hang out with the gang when the sun goes down.

All of the girls are teaching Claudine about life as it is now. When she gets her first pair of blue jeans, Claudine goes twirling in the air, so pleased with how they feel. All she has in a wardrobe are gowns from the last century.

People still look at her funny because she's so damn white, and Mac just looks like he's lived on an island somewhere, with a permanent tan.

Back home, Estelle has a house full of grandchildren running her here and there for whatever they need. All her daughters are working, but two need help with their children. Roberta, the eldest, says she will never get married, and she doesn't like children. So, Estelle keeps the others' children and loves every minute.

Minou and Joe are excitedly waiting for their first grandbaby, and Minou is buying up everything needed to keep at her house for when the baby comes. Beautiful hand-crocheted blankets by the mamas. For sure, they're buying up all the baby colors of yarn at Walmart.

Henri and Caldonia don't want to know the sex of the baby, and Callie threatens her brother, T-June, with an ass-kicking if he tells anybody. Of course, he knows who's up in there. Sometimes, it's like somebody in there is singing.

The others just pester the shit out of him, and he just laughs and walks away, zipping his mouth.

Joe and Alcide are retiring, as is Theo. All three have made a killing out of fishing and now have other men and one real Cajun woman that run their business. A line of Cajun women from down the bayou are quick crab peelers that have done this their whole lives. They make a lot of money to help their husbands while they fish or trap.

∞ ∞ ∞

SWEET Stu King is killed in a bad accident on the road to Eagle Lake, Texas, riding his prized stallion that lives, bearing only brush burns on his legs. The driver is drunk, his third time driving and killing someone. They throw his ass under the jail.

A posse with lynching on their minds breaks into the jail and pulls him out the cell. They hang his ass on the nearest tree, which is in front of the century-old courthouse and with a large gazebo in the center of the street on a small piece of land. The street with the long-time merchants of Eagle Lake, Texas, goes around the large circle with the gazebo in the middle, where the old bands would play. This is a historic sight for the people since no one now alive remembers when it was done pretty regularly. There are none of those liberals in the crowd it draws, and no one takes pictures. The real victim is their beloved Sweet Stu King, so they feel it's the justice that should still be done.

After all, it's the Lone Star State of Texas, which pretty much runs its own sovereignty.

Everybody in the posse flies up for this massive funeral to be with Flavia, she being very sad but pretty stoic about the whole thing. She feels like that's what life is. She has had the most wonderful one with Stu filling her life, another chance with children and becoming very, very, very wealthy.

Flavia has had a lifetime of enough companionship, horses, and "gettin' sum" for the rest of her life. She has loved the years in her beloved Texas, but Louisiana is in her blood and it's home. Home.

If you drink enough bayou water, you can't go too far from the bayou.

A year after Stu's passing, Flavia comes home, dragging the stallion and two teenagers behind her. She has added to the store business, renaming it Mrs. Flavia's Emporium and Mercantile. She's bringing in an Uptown style of dressing to the downtown people on the bayou. She's also going to make Dugas Western Wear in Thibodaux run hard and fast for their money.

She's very proud to add the "Mrs." to her sign once again.

Still looking good for her age, Flavia brushes off any man who comes looking for her. Sweet Stu has been a perfect man, so why would she bother to replace him with these fools?

She and Sister Bridget are good buddies now, with their roses and church work. The sister probably likes Flavia better because she's no longer a divorcee but a widow.

Sister Bridget still runs the school. She is ageless in her determination to follow T-June, as she thinks it's only a matter of time before he becomes a saint. You know, Saint Junior, because all his other names have been taken up with other saints and his middle name is Alan.

That name won't fly as a saint.

Two of the nuns she is in charge of have developed a drinking problem because of her introducing piña coladas to their evening drinks.

Father Becnel sure loves the money Flavia has given over the years, but this time it's a whole lot of moola. He kisses her often, and Flavia will allow that from the holy father who stays stoned all the time.

Her boys, Grey and Gerry, have grown into fine specimens of Comanche Indian warriors. They have been warring with the native boys down here forever because all the girls want to go with them. These two are much better than Flavia's other boys.

∞ ∞ ∞

MADAM Aucoin and Bishop Toussaint are busier than ever in downtown New Orleans. Madam Aucoin has written a best-selling book that people think is a work of fiction, but truly, she's just left out names to protect the not-so-innocent.

Mac is running the night crews in his and Moe's business of doing just about everything. He's even got Claudine working with him in the nighttime, and she is flabbergasted to get her first paycheck ever. Women just didn't work in her genteel southern lady world. She is enjoying her life undead more than she did when she was alive.

These two have an arrangement with a blood bank, and a cheesy little character keeps them in a steady supply. If by chance they have no bought blood, Mac looks for an unsavory criminal on the streets, justifying it with saying, "Another bad-ass bites the dust!"

Claudine doesn't have to teach him; it comes pretty naturally.

∞ ∞ ∞

DOWN the bayou, everything is peaceful for the families, and they are getting restless with the peace. Well, you never know what's coming down the road for this bunch.

Old Danny Guidroz has become disabled from an illness he has ignored. Irene and Jean make a place for him to be comfortable in their home, and he now has his family surrounding him day and night. He gets on his knees every night, thanking the Good Lord and T-June for all the love and respect he now has.

Bertha and Alcide are two robust, healthy old-timers that still run the land as loup-garous, sometimes with T-June and Pieyan. Seems as though T-June can turn that ability off and on like the faucet in the yard.

Must be nice.

Minou and Joe have again taken up their habit of riding down the bayous in their boat. They get up early to go pick pecans at the site that has been haunted for many years. Gaspar the ghost is long gone, along with his nasty talking parrot, Pedro.

They have built a large camp where the old house stood, and everybody goes often. A huge down-the-bayou camp built up off the ground with fifteen steps and windows everywhere and all the amenities of going to the camp. Lots of bedrooms and screened-in porches with hammocks. You can really get away if you let yourself do that.

Minou and Joe are at the camp for a week, getting away from all of it for a while.

Yeah, tell it to the judge.

Minou is washing dishes, looking out the large kitchen windows that line the walls, side by side throughout the camp. All you can see until Minou lowers the blinds. She can't stand the idea that somebody or something may be looking.

She sees what she thinks is a young boy, naked as the day he was born, running around on all fours; well, he thinks they are all his legs. Minou calls Joe, and they go to investigate if it is indeed a boy and why he would be here with no clothes on and acting like a dog.

Where the hell did he come from?

They walk up on him slowly while he seems kind of confused as to why he's here himself. He looks up at them with beautiful pale green eyes and a wet, stinking body, growling at them. He doesn't say a thing to Minou and Joe, even with them sitting down next to him and asking softly for an answer.

You know Minou can't stand to not know what the hell is going on.

Joe and Minou lead him into the camp. He just follows them like a puppy; he really doesn't know anything else to do with himself. Minou finds some camp clothes in the pile that everybody leaves there and has to put the clothing on him. He allows that, just standing there while she puts jeans on him and a T-shirt. He acts like he really doesn't know how to put clothes on, scratching himself all over his body where the cloth confines him. He still doesn't speak.

He is fascinated with everything in the house and jumps when Minou puts the TV on. The boy is mesmerized watching the weatherman saying it's going to rain this week.

She fixes him a bowl of homemade vegetable soup, and he takes the hot bowl up to his mouth, ignoring the spoon, drinking it straight down, ignoring the heat. He's not bothering to chew the potatoes and carrots but starts growling when he does chew the large amount of soup meat.

They are in shock watching this, and when Joe goes to take the bowl, he growls and goes to bite him.

"Golly, mais, he was some hungry! Minou, he smells like a wet dog, so maybe you should wash him. Me, he acts like he don't like me.

Mais, ya saw him go to bite my hand. And mais! He don't wanna say nuttin'!"

Minou leads him to the bathroom and takes his clothes off again. He cocks his head like he doesn't understand what the hell she's doing. He sees the tub full of warm water with a little Avon Skin So Soft added, and he starts howling like a damn dog. He is steadily growling when Minou howls "STOP!"

Like a dog who doesn't like baths, he has to be picked up and put in the tub. He splashes water all over the bathroom trying to get out. Minou passes him a good slap, and he stops fighting, allowing her to wash his filthy body.

Sometimes, you have to do that to dogs, but you sure better not hit your children. People from the state will be all up in your business.

He leaves a tub full of muddy shit. His long hair that doesn't look like it's ever been cut is wild and tangled. She has to put some conditioner in it and tries to brush it.

He gets out and won't allow her to dry him off. He just shakes his body, spraying the walls with wetness, and tries to rub himself dry on the small rug on the floor.

"Joe! Come see dis! He acts like he was raised by a pack of dogs. Mais, he don't say shit, but he sure as hell growls and howls like he's a big pit bull. What tha shit we gonna do wit' dis child? He won't tell us his name. Merde! Maybe he can't talk like he's simple or somet'in'.

"Anyway, we gotta take him back to town and bring him to tha doctor. Mais, we have to go outside and holla to see if tha rest of his family is out dere lookin'."

Joe is such a scaredy-cat person, he doesn't like to come up with thoughts like these. "Minou, Ah hate to t'ink like dis, but what if he's one of dos aliens? Maybe he can do t'ings like T-June, and he was watchin' dogs to see how to act? T'ink 'bout it, t'ink 'bout it. What if, Minou?"

They get up to go outside, with him standing at the door, whining like he's housebroken and needs to go pee outdoors. He does just that, hiking his leg up to pee on the tree, through his clean Levi's and Batman drawers.

It's been awhile since they stood with open mouths, but they sure do at the sight of this.

∞ ∞ ∞

THEY spend most of the day hollering, hoping someone will come out the swamps to claim him. The boy seems like he wants to stay with them, so he gets in the boat with Minou and Joe. He is at the front of the boat with his head up in the air, lapping up the wind, and he begins barking and howling.

Joe almost runs the boat up on the bank of the bayou at the sound. They can't wait to get him home, so strange he is to them.

They take him to the doctor, but not before Alcide and Bertha see him. Alcide growls at him, and the boy is terrified. He is making small whimpering sounds and goes into the corner like a beat cur dog. Alcide just kills himself laughing.

"Mais, Ah jus' couldn't help it. Dis boy act like he was raised by a pack of dogs, and Ah smelled dat on him. Y'all bettah take him to tha doctor before he starts peein' on everyt'in' to mark his territory."

They take him to see the doctor but are wondering if it should be the vet.

In the meantime, Bertha gets on the phone, calling everybody to come. All of them must be on some kind of speed dial.

Dr. Harold Guillory gives him a full examination while the boy is steadily growling at him. When he goes to open the boy's mouth, he bites Dr. Guillory so hard he needs to stitch up his arm.

"Well, goddam, what the hell y'all found up in those swamps? He's in excellent health and doesn't have one single cavity in his mouth, as much as I could see before he bit me. He broke the stick in two that the nurse tried to put on his tongue. She has refused to work with him now.

"Nothing's wrong with his vocal cords. Just seems like he doesn't know how to talk.

"Y'all can take him home and start calling him Chief, like my big dog at home. I will look this up in my medical books for just what we have going on."

Might as well start calling him Chief. It's as good as anything else.

Chief runs inside like he is glad to be home but starts growling at all the people there.

Flavia says, after watching Chief knock his food off the table and proceed to eat it on the floor, "Where in tha hell y'all found him? Where tha hell are his parents? Where in tha hell? Never mind! Ah know y'all don't know shit! Well, hell! What tha shit we gonna do?"

For Flavia, that's admitting she doesn't know everything, just like Minou, because she for sure doesn't know what to do either.

Y'all better run for the hills.

Alcide speaks up after he and Chief make friends, letting Chief sniff him and his behind, ya know, like how dogs say hello. The boy curls up next to Alcide on the sofa, like a dog would do.

"Ah read 'bout wolfpacks dat steal chirren from deir mamas. It happened a coupla times down in tha swamps to lil Cajun chirren! Dey jus' t'ink dat tha wolves ate deir chirren. Thankfully, it wasn't in front of dem! But ya know, tha wolves are way gone from around here. Dey don't come here no more."

The bishop speaks next. "What Alcide says is the truth. Me and Madam have helped poor Black people dealing with this horror, and they lived in the swamps. One gentleman told me his family had lived in the swamps for almost a century. His ancestor hid in the swamp, running away from his master and slavery. He stayed there with the Houmas Indians taking him in until he became adjusted to living out there. The Houmas, like warriors, helped him to go get his family that had been left on the plantation and scared the owner and his family, staying behind the curtains on the windows.

"They were for sure showing off and making believe, because normally they were peaceful people. And he said they were very different-looking people, mixing in the blood of several beautiful Indian maidens in their lineage.

"I'm so very sorry. I definitely got off the subject. Oh, hellfire, Bertha, I forgot they're your people."

That happens a lot with the bishop, but Madam says she is working on it.

Madam finishes the story. "Actually, there is a man in New Orleans that lived through this ordeal, living among a pack of wolves until he was ten years old. He came out the woods one day, and his mama and papa hit their knees, crying that he was alive. Everybody was busy teaching him how to talk and his alphabet. It was hard for him, but he finally got everything he needed to live like a human.

"Get Monsieur Mayhem to deal with him too. You never know. We can call the man that was a wolf. He still lives in the city. Michel Melancon is his name, but we call him Mike."

Minou and Joe are sitting at the kitchen table with T-June and Jolie, who have come home that night late. Bertha is fixing a large pot of coffee and putting it on the table with the bottle of Johnny Walker Red. It's way past five o'clock, but they drink any time they want to.

Bertha laughs and says, "Mais, we gonna all turn into akyholics."

The boy is sleeping next to Alcide, who is asleep too on the sofa. T-June says, "Mama, I'm going to see what I can do tomorrow. Let them sleep. Now, y'all tell me about finding him and everything else y'all have seen with this little puppy."

They talk until three o'clock in the morning but still get up with the chickens, and it didn't seem to affect any one of them. They must have high tolerance for the booze.

T-June is up when the child wakes up with Alcide. He watches as Chief cries at the door to go out. T-June stands there with his mouth hanging open, staring. He's usually the one being stared at by others with their mouths agape.

He watches as Chief cocks up his leg and pees all over Minou's ivy growing on the tree. She's always telling him to go pee somewhere else and has her broom to hit him.

T-June goes up to Chief. At first, the boy is growling at him but stops when he feels T-June roaming around in his mind and talking with him. He gets flabbergasted knowing T-June can understand him.

Remember, T-June is a Dr. Doolittle who can talk with the animals.

Whatcha doin', huh? Whatcha doin'? Ain't had nobody talkin' to me in my head. Are ya my big brudder? Ah got lost from my mama in tha pack. Yeah, we some big, big, black wolves. And dere's fifteen of us, countin' me. We ain't been here long, but my mama tole me it's where my humans are from. Can ya talk wit' my mama like dat? Ah want her to come get me. Tha leader of tha pack has said dat Ah'm startin' to smell like humans, so he wanted me gone before Ah challenged him to be tha leader myself. So, he put us on tha wrong path on purpose.

T-June explains that his mama needs to be in front of him to talk to her, but what he will do instead is tell all his animal friends in the swamp that Chief wants to see her. He whistles for Pieyan, who comes walking very slowly toward June and Chief. He is snarling at the boy.

"What the shit are you doing with this little mongrel? The wolves are always trying to get me, and this little sumbitch bit me on my ankles."

To Chief, he says, "You better not come by me because I'm gonna bite you back."

Speaking again to T-June, he says, "I didn't tell you they were back because I didn't think they would come close to you, but they must be getting closer because of this little imp. Whistle for me if you need me. That little shit is terrible."

The family doesn't realize that the whole pack comes at night, watching for Chief to come outdoors. It really startles the Thibeaus when the howling begins, and now it's almost every night. It didn't stop the wolves from following their scents to find the house where they can really smell Chief.

∞ ∞ ∞

WHEN the family realizes what's going on, everybody wants T-June to go talk to the wolves waiting for Chief. At dusk that evening, T-June goes to the border of their property where the wolves are waiting. He walks up to them with his arms straight out, like asking for some kind of stability with the situation.

He says, "I come in peace."

The biggest one in the pack stands in front of him, questioning what is happening, and T-June immediately goes into his mind.

You human, no one has ever been able to talk from a human's mind to mine. Are you the leader of your pack?

Well, you could say that!

Where is the boy? His mama wants to see him, and since she's the top female in our pack, I brought her. Man! I'll never hear the end of it. She's very bossy and will sit on the ground when I come sniffing for a little bit. Send out the boy so she can visit because I will not allow him back in the pack. He smells too much like you. I wanted to kill him, and she beat the shit out of me.

T-June calls his mama on his new cell phone and asks her to send Chief out. The boy runs as fast as he can, like a grown wolf, to where this gigantic female wolf stands on her hind legs, jumping around.

They start roughhousing and smelling each other, and Chief snuggles with the mama who raised him.

She says, He looks well, like he's been eating, but he does smells like all of you in that house. I'll just have to bathe him a lot, and we will stay a distance from the others. Boy, you come with me now so you don't start acting like a bitch."

Chief starts to go with her, but then he says up in her head, Mama, Ah can't go wit' you. Dese people treat me good. He will kill me as soon as he gets a chance. Besides, you remember when we watched two humans turn into wannabe wolves? And tha other creature playing wit' dem? Two of dose creatures live here, and Ah like deir smells. Dey're tryin' to make me human again.

Chief – that's what everybody calls him – runs when he hears them whistling and calling him by that name. They bring him food or treats. He has learned the signal Minou gives when he needs a bath. He makes her chase him all over the yard. Only when Minou hits him does he go willingly to the bath tub. It's not a hard slap, but he acts like it does hurt, and he'll start whimpering like a puppy.

Whatcha gonna do?

He continues speaking to his wolf mother. Dis isn't tha spot where my people live. How come?

His mother tells him, The leader was giving us directions, him knowing all the time he would just drop you off anywhere but home. He wanted you to starve by yourself.

Now mind you, they're doing all this talking in their heads, but T-June is on the party line.

Chief pleads with his wolf mother to stay with him and looks at T-June, pleading with him too, like barking when he has to go pee. He's learning very slowly because some habits are hard to break, and he will revert if it's necessary to him.

T-June smiles and says, "Aw, what the hell. She can come with us." Just like him, making decisions for everybody, and you need to like it or not like it, but it's what's going t'happen because he declares it. What a pompous ass! But they have to blame it on themselves because they have made him believe he's the second coming and can walk on water too.

T-June and Chief, along with the boy's wolf mother, walk up to the back porch at Minou and Joe's house. Minou totally freaks out and stands very, very still at the sight of the big-ass she-wolf! For Minou, that's a very strange sight.

T-June goes to his mama and calms her, saying, "Chief wanted her to come with us. They would be in danger and possibly killed because the pack leader is one mean son of a bitch."

It ain't cussin' 'cause it's the truth.

"He wanted to kill Chief right on the spot. I know we can add her to the family, and I'll help take care of her."

Yeah, he won't be taking her home to New Orleans, that's for sure.

Minou fixes a big pallet in Joe and Alcide's shop for the mama wolf and Chief, gives her a large deer roast, and leaves a little lamp on for the night. The she-wolf loves the smell of fish in the shop, and she loves eating the big catfish in the waters, and it's warm because of a heater Minou leaves for her.

Chief wants to sleep with her the first night, and it's okay, but after that first night, he has to go back inside and be a human boy again.

∞ ∞ ∞

THEY name her Gertrude because she looks like a huge Viking wolf-dog. She's the best guard dog money can't buy.

Gertie walks at night along the fence line, not trusting her mate. Who knows? Maybe they jumped the log instead of the broom. It's what's called a separation, soon to be a divorce. She knows he will be back to finish the job on Chief. Mean-spirited, hateful, bastard old wolf.

Minou wonders if other men aren't raised by the wolves.

Gertie is very gentle and loves it when the children come to visit. She lays on her back so they can scratch her and brush her hair. She's not hard to live with, but Minou has to watch Chief because a lot of times he will go back to being a puppy for his other mother.

Gertie walks the perimeter for six months, a lot of it with Chief. The men all have their shotguns ready on the side of them, by the windows.

The village of St. Junior has all the villagers gaga over Gertie. Flavia orders special food for her and keeps all the bones out of the butcher department for her.

Madam and the bishop have made her a lovely turquoise collar, putting potions on it and patchouli. The smell is way too potent for their nozzles. Gertie wears it proud when she goes to New Orleans with whoever is going for the weekend.

The gang and Gertie love to sashay down Esplanade. Gertie enjoys it as much as they do. Gertie is on this large pink leash and acts like she is as prissy as she can get, like a groomed poodle in some dog show. So calm, never bothering to bark at the peons, and with her nose up in the air like she isn't a big-ass wolf but a wolfhound.

People are awed and frightened at the sight of her, but she will let anybody who is brave enough to dare pet her gorgeous mane of hair. Gertie knows how to put on the dog!

She seems to be enjoying all the human life, being pampered and loved. We can't say the same for Chief. He's having difficulty with being human, and he cusses a lot – in T-June's mind. Having both mothers correcting him, it's a pull-apart for Chief. When one corrects him, the other placates him. It's really hard on everybody trying to make him a regular little boy.

Gertie is very protective of Chief and will growl to make her presence known. She knows it's for the best for Chief to learn human ways and talk out his mouth. Gertie just can't let go because he's the only pup she has. Her mate killed her twin puppies, males both of them. He figured he could nip it in the bud, so they couldn't threaten him in the future. She has fought him tooth and fang for Chief, and it hasn't been the same for this bickering couple since.

T-June begins to show Chief how to talk and to learn his ABCs. He will say the word in Chief's mind and have him repeat it using his vocal cords, telling him how to say it.

Chief is working hard to master his talking skills, and right now he has a real deep voice, kind of guttural, but you can understand him. The voice may become lighter, but with his accent, they have to hide their faces laughing at how he says the words.

Everybody lends a hand in raising the boy, similar to what they've done for T-June, minus all his special abilities. He gets housebroken really fast, after Minou catches him shitting in the corner of the living room. You know she handles that quickly.

Now he sits at the table to eat, but he has a hard time with a fork, so he just uses a big spoon. His bath time is still a frantic episode, but Minou will pop him on the head to get a grip.

Chief loves Bertha and Alcide so much and hangs out with them as much as he can. Bertha loves on him all the time, for sure not like it was with T-June. While she had fear and distrusted her grandson, she's not that way anymore. The four of them are often together at their house. She has no qualms about Gertie, surprisingly, as she is this massive wolf that Bertha is enamored of.

Picture the werewolves in Twilight!

They all run together once a month, and sometimes T-June will join the pack of loup-garous running with a big-ass wolf and a bigfoot.

∞ ∞ ∞

AFTER seven months have passed, Gertie quits walking the perimeter of Minou and Joe's house at night. Not a situation that calls for nightly walks anymore, Gertie thinks.

Well, you know, when you let your guard down, shit happens.

These people are wide open, greeting whatever comes down the road, but they become quickly aware of what's coming. It's like sleeping with one eye open.

This is during a nighttime LSU game that has the couples down from New Orleans. Callie is big and pregnant. Lily is chasing Maybelline while eclectic conversations occur with all the different opinions, bets, and the seasonings in roux.

Flavia and Madam and the bishop start a football pool, betting on the outcome of the game, and everybody is in on it. They all are stomping the floor and screaming obscenities.

Y'all know about LSU fans!

Chief and his mama are sleeping together in the shop that has turned into a very nice lair. She has her own TV and a custom-made mattress.

During that same night, the shop is hit hard by something outside, shaking the timbers that hold it together. They are on their legs to see what has happened.

Gertie hears a very familiar howl that by itself could shatter windows. Chief looks out the curtains made by Minou and sees the large pack that has crossed the perimeter and is standing outside the shop.

The pack has grown, with other wolves and feral dogs, alarming to both Chief and his mama because the door is blocked by her ex-husband. He has his superior attitude, and he is pacing and flaunting to show all the new members who is boss.

There is a beautiful white young female at his side. It hasn't taken him long to marry his trophy wife.

Shit! This story has been told over and over and over again like a broken record.

Alcide suddenly smells the animal fragrance through the open window, and just as suddenly, the posse becomes alert too. They pause the game and put their jackets on to go outside. Kinda nippy and airish in the parish.

The bunch walk up into a bad quemas when they see the wolves and the head honcho tearing the shop down trying to get to Gertie and Chief. Not much left of the shop, but she stands there waiting. Gertie is salivating at the mouth, snarling, trying to protect Chief.

The two adult wolves are circling each other, baring fangs, with their hair standing straight up, circling and circling. The young bitch is trying her best to jump into the fight, but Gertie tells her, You better back the fuck up.

The two massive wolves are tying it up, with both standing, snarling, spitting, and biting each other and kicking the dirt into a cloud with their frenzy. When he finally gets her to the ground and goes to bite her neck off, T-June steps in, because the whole pack is coming to get some.

He gathers all his strength and points his finger at all the others saying, You better back the fuck up.

T-June proceeds to go right up in the wolf's addled mind. Dude, what the hell is wrong with you? We thought this shit was over a long time ago, and now, here you are again. What the hell does it matter? You're with a new bitch, and Gertie loves living here with Chief.

Just like human men, the male wolf has to have the last word in the process of divorce. The leader walks slowly up to T-June with an attitude and quietly speaks in T-June's mind. Man! Dude, don't you know how it looks? She disobeyed my orders and left me standing by myself and looking foolish to the rest of the pack. No female ever turns their backs on me. I could have killed her on the spot.

T-June wanders around in the wolf's head and gets real pissed off when he tells the alpha male of this pack, You don't for one minute think that I have fear of you. After all this, you still don't know about us? Y'all should have asked the creatures in our swamps, and they would tell you everything about this family. But you so arrogant. You don't stop to make friends, and your pack is full of immaturity, and they just want to fight.

No wolf of mature age wants anything to do with you, and if they do, they're coming to kill you. See, you should have made a few pals, not try to eat them, just talk. That's how I find things out, because we have a huge pipeline. Ask one of the animals about something you want to know, and it goes all the way to New York City in just a few days and then just turns around as fast with the answers.

You have an outstanding rap sheet. You have a very shitty past. You got chased out of a few packs, and you discarded several bitches with newborn puppies. You're what we call a deadbeat dad.

This wolf, who presents himself as the leader of the pack, his pompous arrogant self slow-walking like a tiger and ready to rumble, now takes an ass-whipping from Gertie. She beats him to a wood pulp in front of the pack. The male pushes his young female away. He will lick his wounds by himself. This alpha male wolf looks like a beat-down dog, hanging his head in defeat and hoping the others in his pack don't hear what T-June has said.

He could have mated with Gertie. That excites him and is worrisome.

T-June continues. Look here, you. I'm gonna call you Leroy, okay? Look, Leroy, what I can do.

T-June stands close to the wolf while he rubs his ear, and Leroy looks like he has been electrocuted, falling down.

I barely touched you, you pussy cat. Think about what I could really do to you if I was serious. I'm the only alpha man back here. Here are the terms. Twenty feet away from my borders, and you'd better howl if you even get close. It's a wonderful thing to have you guys back in the swamps, but don't start acting up in your old ways and have everybody thinking you're trash.

Leave Gertie and Chief the hell alone. She paid her dues to you. She doesn't owe you anything.

Before you leave us forever, you're going to tell me where Chief comes from so he can go back home if he wants.

Then don't let the screen door hit you in the ass. And remember, I'm the only alpha here!"

T-June goes back inside with the rest, and Gertie is brought inside for Minou to tend to her wounds. They all finish watching the game. LSU wins because this big man from down the bayou is doing his awesome coaching. They also have that Yankee helping them.

∞ ∞ ∞

THE next morning, Minou, Joe, and T-June go by boat, using the directions given by Leroy, to search for Chief's family. The boat glides into this cove where they see a ramshackle old Cajun cottage and a yard full of little children running to see who's pulled up in the boat.

Chief gets out the boat, running to where he sees all the children running to him, most of them not knowing who he is. When his human mother comes to step outside on the porch, she starts screaming, trying not to faint when she sees her firstborn son. They fall together on the ground, both knowing who each other is, wordlessly crying and sobbing, holding each other for dear life.

When Chief's papa comes running out the swamp, he drops to his knees and screams out the name Bastille! Bastille! Bastille! Bastille (aka Chief) runs to his papa's arms, still not talking that clearly, but it isn't necessary to communicate their happiness.

After the parents introduce all his brothers and sisters to him – they already know all about the brother who has been taken by wolves – they invite Minou and Joe and T-June to come inside, where Bastille's mama is cooking a huge pot of gumbo. She has to start over because she's burnt the first roux, after seeing a dream come true.

The papa lights his pipe and sits down at the large kitchen table with everybody else. "Ma name is Bastille Henri Rappolet Junya.

Bastille him is da t'ird. My wife is Megdaline Rappolet, but we jus' call her T-Mae. Y'all can call me Junya.

"How Ah can t'ank ya, Ah jus' don't know! Mais, Ah watched as dis big-ass shemale wolf grab him and de other big-ass wolf attacked me. Me, Ah had to have t'irdy-six stitches in ma arm where he bit me. Mais, Ah had to go by da doctor's in Raceland, and look see, Ah got a huge scar dat kinda made me disabled. Ah fought dat big-ass wolf for my baby son, but Ah couldn't save him, me. Mais, me and da wife caught dat depression bad and her wit' a new baby. Her mama and daddy had to come stay wit' us 'cause dey was scared Ah was gonna shoot myself and T-Mae.

"We all t'ought dat dey ate him. We had tha nightmares dat we scream out in tha night. He had jus' made two, and he was some fat. My Lawd! Mais, Ah almost caught a heart attack seein' him 'cause Ah knew right away he was Bastille."

Junya lays his head down on the table, sobbing while he holds on to Chief. There isn't a dry eye in the whole bunch, even the six children born after him. Poor things, they don't have a TV.

T-Mae sits down for a while to talk while Minou tends to the gumbo. The coffee is put on the table, along with the Southern Comfort bottle.

It's just universal with the Cajun people to offer libations to company along with the coffee.

"Oh, Gawd! Pour le mon de Bon Dieu! My prayers are answered. My baby done come home. Ah don't know what tha merde to say! T'ank ya, t'ank ya, t'ank ya! Mais, look at how big he is. Bastille, him, it's his birfday tomorrow, and he's gonna be ten. Oh, my Gawd! Y'all brung him on his birfday.

"Goddam dem sumbitch wolves! Dey took him at his second birfday party, and we all saw it. Ah was big and pregnant wit' Jude over dere, and Ah went into tha labor right den. Him and Jude was born on tha same day two years apart. Mais, 'scuse me. Ah gotta go pray by my priedieu for tha miracle He done sent us."

Minou serves everybody their gumbo while T-Mae is praying behind her bedroom door.

Junya helps serve all the other children who are lined up with their bowls. Some order to the disorder of a houseful of mouths.

It is close to dark when the Thibeaus leave in their boat and promise to return for a double birthday party. Chief – uh, Bastille – wants to stay at his mama and daddy's house with all his new pack of puppies – uh, siblings.

That evening, T-June with his mama go to feed Gertie and tell her where Chief is at for the night. Oh, Lawd. Gertie goes to howling and howling and howling at the big round moon and runs to the back where the loup-garous gather on their own property.

The mournful sounds have brought Leroy to the perimeter searching for Gertie. He's never been satisfied since she left him, so he wants to comfort her.

T-June walks back to the swamps where the wolves and the werewolves are trying to help Gertie in her anguish.

Leroy pipes up in T-June's head, Man, I couldn't help myself because she sounds like she is dying. I still love her, even after everything that's happened. Please let me stay, and for sure, please don't touch me.

T-June begins to talk to Gertie with every animal there listening. Now that T-June can turn, Bertha and Alcide can hear him too, and the rest just like the drama. Like an old-time party line with at least four listening in on your telephone conversations, if they're nosy.

Poor Ma Bell, where ya at? Everybody always knows who it is listening in. Back in the day, they used to fuss her all the time. Miss Boudreaux, put the damn phone down!

T-June says, Please, Gertie. Get ahold of yourself. He's not gone forever. I can't tell you what he's going to decide, and I have to find out if his mama and daddy want you anywhere near him. Hellfire! They would probably shoot you right now.

Stay as long as you want to, but Leroy, you best be gone at daybreak.

What a revolting development this has turned into!

T-June goes to his mama's house, so perturbed that he goes to bed to ponder the quemas started over a dirty, naked little boy.

The Thibeau family goes the next day for the huge celebration of the two brothers' birthdays. Family is called, and all of Chief's relatives come to see the miracle of his returning. It is a regular fais do-do with all crying happy, happy tears.

A huge pig is being roasted over a large wood-filled pit, and whatever you can think of in the line of fresh vegetables is on the two tables, along with pies and custards and a whole lot of pecan and peanut butter fudge.

Joe thinks to bring the ice cream maker, lots of cream, strawberries, and a massive chuck of sea salt. He is busy all day churning the stuff for all the little children, but the adults have to have some of that delicious treat too. T-June takes over after Joe says his arm is about to fall off.

The brothers and the sisters and the cousins all want to touch Jolie's dreadlocks, and everybody there is quiet, listening to the music of the Monsieur Mayhem Duo.

A fun time is had by all.

When the day is ending, Minou starts talking with T-Mae about Bastille. "Bébé, Ah'm so glad we found your baby for ya. Oh, my Lawd, tha days ya spent on ya knees prayin' and cryin' with tha grief ya felt. Ah'm so sorry for ya, bébé, but me and you and Gertie are three mamas that would grieve for ya Bastille. What do ya wanna do?"

T-Mae looks Minou in the eyes and says, "Mais, cher, who is Gertie? Dat ya mama?"

Minou asks if she can talk with her son, T-June, because she sure as hell doesn't want to be in this dogfight by herself.

After taking his last sip of coffee, T-June tries to explain the situation to Junya and T-Mae. He is thorough in telling the tale, with Joe adding his quarter's worth of sense.

You know that damn inflation!

Junya goes to throwing a hissy fit, 'til T-Mae tells him to stop.

You know, if women ran the world, no more wars. Well, probably more cat fights.

T-Mae takes over and looks like she means business. Kinda obvious who wears the pants over here.

"Junya, be quiet, and let dem talk! Ya know dey jus' some dumb animals who don't know no bettah, dem wolves. And look see, dat boy don't look like he missed too many meals, so dat shemale wolf took care of him too. It ain't all Minou. So, t'ink 'bout dat a lil bit 'til T-June gets t'rough. But Junya, Ah ain't too swift to meet dis big-ass dog, me. She might like one of tha other chirren!"

T-June has been pondering, and you know he has it all figured out, along with Joe and Minou. He takes over the rest of the conversation, but he speaks for all of them.

"We want to offer you a real good job. This way all you mamas could see Chief all the time. It's being a caretaker on a large piece of property that we have. It's down the bayou from our house, and there is a large camp on it. You have to go by boat, but y'all could live in the camp until we build you a real nice house.

"It would provide a very good paycheck, with us paying for insurance on your whole family. Hell, it would be enough for y'all to just pick the pecans we harvest every year.

"Oh, and T-Mae, he told me he likes being called Chief better than Bastille, but he didn't want to hurt y'all's feelings. We'll come back tomorrow, but we'll take Chief home tonight, if you'll let us. We can talk about this when we get back."

T-Mae is fine with that. Bastille the t'ird needs some clean clothes. His mama has nothing to put on his dirty ten-year-old body.

The night finds Chief sleeping with Gertie, and that calms down her pacing and panting.

At breakfast the next morning, Chief says what he can put together in words. "Me want to stay by you. Me feel bad, bad."

They all know he is feeling this way. They are too. They are praying Junya is going to take the job.

When they arrive at the Rappolets' house, they see total mayhem, with children running back and forth, carrying boxes to the landing full of their stuff.

Junya hollers at them, "Come on, come on! Y'all! All da way wit' Rappolet! Mais, we gettin' everyt'in' we gonna need to come wit' you."

Joe calls one of the workers at the seafood business and tells them to bring a big boat, and within three hours, the Rappolets are heading for their new home.

T-June guides the boat to the camp, bypassing Joe and Minou's house. There'll be plenty time for them to go to Minou's and see this Gertie for themselves, along with Leroy, the cause of all the quemas.

When T-June goes in the shed to see Gertie, Leroy is with her. T-June already knows what is going on between the wolves. They want to be with each other in their graying years.

T-June! T-June! Wait, wait, wait before you put your paws on me. Wait! We still love each other, and I'm a changed wolf. I left my pack so I could be with her. We can go somewhere else, but Gertie doesn't want to. Please let me stay with my Gertie.

T-June nods his head yes but not before warning Leroy that, if he turns back into the asshole alpha, he will touch him all over, and Leroy will be dead.

Days become what passes for normalcy at the houses of the disciples of T-June, who has just added nine more villagers.

There will be days like this.

Chapter Sixteen

Caldonia's

CALDONA goes into labor while they are celebrating at Henri's elaborate fancy mayoral inauguration ball. Her water breaks, running down from the stage they stand on. Everybody there is clapping at the sight, and Callie wants to go under the damn wet stage, praying no one will slip in it.

She is brought to the hospital with everyone hollering Good luck. Name it after me!

Caldonia Thibeau Aucoin – Mrs. Henri Gustave Aucoin Jr. or Callie Aucoin or just Callie – has 10 pounds of a little man with a head full of curls red as a woodpecker.

She holds her little red-headed boy, bringing him with her, and when she returns to her suite in the hospital with flowers and plants being shoved in every corner and candy enough for everybody, she checks out his toes and runs her fingers through all the hair.

Flavia has to step out because all those flowers are giving her a sinus infection.

Callie has not been told about the veil, the strongest they have seen, even stronger than T-June's. The veil has him in a cocoon like an orange butterfly and has to be cut with heavy scissors. Minou and Madam Aucoin do the cutting.

Two other babies in their village have the veil. T-June, Maybelline, and now the third. Thank the spirits he doesn't have red hair on his arms and such.

Bertha holds him, her first great-grandchild, and is simply awed with the red hair. She is twirling his hair on her big calloused fingers, loving him with her huge heart. She had never heard of this in the family, red hair. It must have been some Irishman back there somewhere, slipping into a maiden's tepee.

Henri tells them he's had many family members that had red hair with almost white skin. His ancestors, the slave women, had no telling who was forcing their seed into them during this violent act upon their innocent souls. Savage and brutal rapes, starting the women having children at young ages. Nothing racist because the Cajuns were known to do the same. It is almost inbred by men who are raping children.

The baby is quickly named Henri Gustave Aucoin the Third. The baby can be Trey or Trois, but his papa wants him to be called True after his great-grandmother's name, True Lavonia Aucoin.

T-June and Jolie come to see them, carrying candy and a big rubber plant, pushing through the door with a bunch of people to see Callie. They already know all the people gathered, and they slip by pretty much.

Henri is downstairs with the newspapers taking pictures and bragging on True, handing out huge Cuban cigars, and strutting like the cock in the barnyard.

It's good sometimes to have connections. You know, it's Louisiana.

T-June holds his nephew, being he's a brand new nonc or parrain. He busts out laughing until he falls on the floor, holding True tight the whole time.

"Oh, oh! I can't even begin to tell you what he's going to do. I'm not going to tell y'all. Lawdy, Lawdy, Miss Claudie! I'm just going to prepare y'all for what's coming up the road, just so you know. Ooh, I'm hurting from all that laughing."

Lily throws the rubber plant at him and hollers until he is out the door. They can hear him still laughing down the hall.

Henri has missed the whole thing with T-June, but he is told very quickly by the women. He sits pondering while he holds his little red-headed son. He starts laughing too.

He says, "There's something about New Orleans with you people. I truly believe it is something in the water for y'all. All I can say right now is it's hilarious.

"Hey, my little True Boy, whatcha going to do, huh? Talk to me with your little brain?"

Callie, Lily, Minou, Jolie, Estelle, Bertha, Madam, and Flavia don't think a damn thing is funny.

Madam Aucoin is steadily looking at this baby, and she makes a sign over him, not of the cross but just as powerful. She doesn't say a word, in fear of these women right now.

Awww, boy, just wait.

The papers are full of pictures and front-page articles about the new mayor and his lovely bride, Caldonia. They go nuts over True's hair of red with his high-yellow skin.

Henri and Callie have been talking about opening a restaurant where Callie will be the belle of the bar again. She misses her job, where she met interesting and friendly people, not like those fancy, frivolous, fake society women. She prefers her people from the bayou, down to earth and real.

∞ ∞ ∞

T-JUNE can't wait to get his hands on True. He is True's parrain, and he takes the job seriously, but he still laughs when he's got him. Monsieur Mayhem, as he's known in the city, spends as much time with True as he is allowed, making a damn mosquito of himself.

T-June takes him walking down by the bayou, sitting on the large pallet started with palmetto leaves by Minou and Joe when they were children. It has been added to over many years, and it just should be called a king-size mattress.

T-June has heard the story many times over the years of the bobbing fish. He knows that True is fixing to do the same exact thing as he once did. He's been hearing True talk to his mind since he first held him.

The baby makes T-June bust out laughing by himself, because the others aren't seeing or hearing anything funny. Lil True talks with T-June in a New Orleans accent like his papa.

T-June just wants to see for himself what's been so funny all these years.

In T-June's mind, True says, Parrain, just do, just do, man! Me can make it twirl in the water!

June goes down to the bank where he can throw the little red fish cork that indeed bobs under the water if you get a fish. As soon as the thing hits the water, there's a 10-pound catfish on the line. True makes the catfish come up out the water, and it's twirling high in the air, throwing bayou water all over them.

T-June just falls out on the ground, killing himself laughing.

True is clapping for himself and laughing too, sitting by his parrain in his little Huggies. He doesn't like to be pissy in his diapers, so he has taught himself how to sit on the toilet. He will play with the bidet for hours. He takes his good old time with everything. His mama banging on the bathroom door, he hollers, "I'm making number two! Don't make me nervous."

Parrain takes him to see the animals, in abundance now since the men have quit trapping. True is sitting on the ground and has the rabbits and coons and squirrels rolling around on the grass, laughing and stomping their feet like Brer Rabbit.

Pieyan doesn't show up. It would be too much for True.

His parrain sits down with him and says, "Awww, my bébé! Lil boy, you're going to be the death of me. How in hell did the old folks handle me? The spirits are laughing too, and they're all around you, watching what you're going to do next.

"You and me, we've got a big, big secret. We're not going to show your tricks to anybody right now. We have to make a pinky promise. They just aren't ready for you right now because you're about the same now as I was, and they're all getting old and might catch a heart attack.

"Full of tricks and talking with some people in your head. Be very careful with that. Go very gently to where no one has gone before. Except me."

True Aucoin is just an 18-month-old big boy. In his mind, he talks like he wants to, but he has knocked on everybody's head to see who's home.

Lawd, have mercy!

∞ ∞ ∞

CALLIE and Henri are very busy getting the restaurant opened that will be named Caldonia's.

There will be a circle like in the '40s, the floor moving slowly while you're sitting at the bar, looking at fantastic views of St. Charles Avenue. Mirrors and tropical plants with ivy growing everywhere, dim pink lights with tiny table lamps, and a large sky window on the high ceiling that can be opened. Everybody looks good under rose-colored lights, not to be confused with last drinks at the bar, with lights when anybody looks good.

There will be reservations, and it will be standing room only. Anything that is on St. Charles Avenue is high class, uptown, and expensive.

The restaurant employees are to dress in tuxedos and vintage clothing from the '20s to the '40s. Gowns that you dress up in to go to the swanky nightclubs, with the men in tuxedos, lighting the cigarette you're smoking with a five-inch ivory cigarette holder, and the women in fur coats.

Only in the movies I've seen this. God bless Hollywood with their rose-colored glasses!

Callie has bought up every piece of vintage clothing in every secondhand store around Louisiana and Texas, in every size and color. The restaurant will take care of the cleaning of these garments, and the workers are welcome to come in their own vintage apparel. She has also bought two boxes of cigarette holders for real cheap. Callie will give those clothes and the woman wearing them a real good inspection before they reach the floor. She knows what she wants.

Caldonia's is on a corner of St. Charles Avenue that once was the largest house in the middle of the other mansions, with yards meeting at the street and separated by a black iron lattice fence, low enough to jump over. Callie and Henri have bought a home with a huge backyard going into the next block in back of the property and have laid rocks on the ground for a parking area, turning cement parking down because of the location and the ambiance. Henri has discovered this while digging. It's where they used to tie horses and carriages and Model T Fords. The remnants are still there.

The finest Cajun cooks are hired, moving some out the bayou and bringing their whole families, while Callie finds houses big enough for them. The awesome soul food comes from the Creole cooks in New Orleans. What they pay is unheard of, being larger than any paycheck in their lives, with insurance and a chance to buy shares in the business.

∞ ∞ ∞

SO now, Callie definitely needs help with little True, and Monsieur Mayhem is all about taking True with him everywhere he has to go.

Bishop knows something is up with these two, and he definitely knows it's all because of True.

When Callie and Henri can find time to watch the Monsieur Mayhem Duo, they come with True.

One of the grandsons of Fats Domino, Antoine the Third, comes looking for a job and begins to play the piano in the corner. They hire him on the spot, and he does something remarkable – he brings his own old pink baby grand that was Fats' piano first.

Boy, if that piano could talk!

Now the Silverberg boys are really after them to record the music of the Trio.

One Saturday night, Callie, the mayor, and chubby little True come to watch Parrain and Taunt Jolie and Antoine. Monsieur can hear True singing in his mind loud-loud, knowing every song. Hot damn!

Besides it being in a New Orleans accent, True sounds good, just different notes from T-June. They are harmonizing.

What? Here's a new ability for both of them. Hot damn!

∞ ∞ ∞

TRUE has made it to third grade, and he's already doing things that amaze his parrain. Keeping everything on the down-low, with True wanting to talk with his parents in his mind and theirs. Monsieur just shrugs his shoulders like c'est la vie.

It goes to show you, you never can tell.

One morning at the breakfast table, while Henri is reading the paper, True speaks in his mama's head, I want some scrambled eggs, Mama.

Callie is getting ready to serve the already-scrambled eggs, and she screams and drops the pan of eggs on the floor.

Sounds like someone else we know.

Henri jumps up and goes to Callie to see if she has burned herself.

"Henri Gustave Aucoin the third! How long have you been able to talk in my head and listen to my conversations as well? Your parrain knows about this? I'm going to kill him dead! Deader than a doorknob, going to the heaven dead, in the dirt dead. That's how dead he's gonna be.

"True, do that to your papa. Go ahead, go ahead!"

When True does the same to Henri, he drops a whole cup of coffee on his white linen suit that has just come from the cleaners and hollers in amazement – and because the damn coffee has burned him.

"Shit and shinola! Boy! You have any idea how much trouble this could be for you? You can listen to everybody? Aww, shit and shinola."

The mayor calls the office, saying he has a very serious appointment taking place at his home, and he's not taking calls either.

Henri and Callie sit in the living room with True, his papa thinking this is the most important appointment he'll ever have in his life. It takes all day, but Callie and Henri have to know TODAY everything he can do, Callie wanting to strangle her big brother. She is some pissed.

True tells them they have to go to the Audubon Park Zoo because they don't have time to go to the swamps. The monkeys are good, True says, and so they walk up to the smaller monkeys' cages. He goes into the head honcho monkey's head, and the monkey goes to jumping up and down, making the noises they do while scratching their armpits and red-ass behinds and rolling around and laughing.

The one that threw crap on Joe during his honeymoon must be this monkey's great-grandpapa.

Gilbert the monkey says back to True, Hey, lil dude. Where ya at? Get back wit' ya clownin' self! Way cool, dude! I ain't ever had no human talk to me in my head. They too busy making noises like we do, trying to be wannabe monkeys. They must all be low born, and it insults us. Ya don't teach ya chirren how to behave in public? None of those little bastards come close to the right sound. Didn't know y'all could do dat, or is it just you?

Callie and Henri want to know what Gilbert the monkey says to him. And he repeats details so they will know if it's true.

Then True tells his papa that the female monkeys are all axin' for him.

You know, like the song?

Callie sees a giant ape heading toward them and grabs her family for a quick getaway. She has heard all about Joe's encounter with the nasty beast all her life. Minou has showed her the postcard picture made of Joe that circulates in Flavia's store and her little Voodoo doll that she will still use to catch Joe's attention. Minou keeps them in her chifforobe and tells her not to tell Joe!

The minute they get back from Audubon Park, Callie calls T-June and tells him to get his ass over there PRONTO!

Here comes Monsieur Mayhem, walking so proud up in their kitchen, and sits down at the table, drinking Community Coffee.

She pops him up the side of his head when he takes a sip, then he spills coffee all over his clean suit too.

He remains silent while Callie proceeds to tear him a new one, so angry at not being told everything. She knows it's going to be a gigantic problem. She speaks to T-June and doesn't mince her words.

"Why in the hell weren't we told about his capabilities? How in the hell are we going to keep this shit out of every goddam newspaper? Tell us, T-June, tell us how we will handle this. Go ahead, you're so damn smart!"

Henri is sitting with T-June while Callie is raising ten kinds of hell.

"I am so elated by what True can do. Does everyone know about this and didn't tell us? Now, that would be a true deceit from everybody. Come on, tell us what we need to know about all of this. It sure doesn't come from my side of family,

"Man, T-June, I swear New Orleans is the main factor of all this happening. Look, now there are two of you here, so there you go."

T-June begins to 'fess up to what he knows but tells them nobody else knows. He feels like everybody who has joined his village may be too old for this quemas now. He doesn't think he should tell Sister Bridget. She would become a straight-up holy fanatic, thinking there are two saints on the bayou.

T-June tells them of the veil that covered True at birth and how Minou and Madam cut the thing off True. Callie hollers at that, hitting T-June in the back of his head again.

Shit, he might catch a concussion!

He tells them that True has been talking to him in his mind since the first day he held him. T-June tells them about the time they brought True to watch them play music and how he was singing in T-June's head as loud as he could along with him, harmonizing with his lil New Orleans accent.

Another thing T-June is amazed at is the fact he knows all the words! He must have been listening in Callie's belly.

"Listen y'all, I'll be here to help with him in his growing years and teach him how to maintain around people. I will help. I know what to do. Just right now, we don't want him touching people because we don't know yet if he can heal too.

"I won't tell if you don't want me to. Nobody else knows, well, except Madam and the bishop. They're pretty attuned to it and will corner me to get the truth out of me.

"Please, Callie, don't smack me again!"

∞ ∞ ∞

BISHOP Toussaint comes to Monsieur Mayhem's office. Oh, yeah. It's Mr. Joseph at work. Poor thang, he's got that split-personality shit going on.

Anyway, the bishop sits down in Mr. Joseph's chair and begins asking him what he is hiding. "June, I feel the old vibes in the air. It feels like back in the day when we were raising you and before you came out that closet full blast as Monsieur Mayhem. I think it's all because of Henri Aucoin the third. Tell me I'm wrong. I dare you."

While True is at his Catholic school in the third grade, learning his ABCs and how to look up things on his computer, T-June begins telling the bishop, but not before Madam sits down too. They are talking about True, wondering if he can hear them down on St. Charles Avenue.

You just don't ever know.

Madam Aucoin has already put on True her chain of silver with a sacred symbol, along with Flavia's gold cross. (Alcide no longer makes his protection leather chains because everybody in the family already knows all about their business.) Not to be upstaged, Sister Bridget has a palm tree cut down and puts a leaf of that blessed sticky palm in everybody's houses on the bayou and New Orleans. She just knows the Monsieur will blow something up when the Lord finally puts a shiny halo on his head.

Father Becnel just follows along with her travels because sometimes he's too stoned to drive.

So, Madam Alafair Aucoin begins her speech. "I don't see how you will keep this a secret. If and when he does something that they aren't prepared for, they will really have a heart attack. What do Callie and Henri say about this? 'Just take it one day at a time' is pretty much what they feel about everything.

"The only one that doesn't need to be told is Sister Bridget. She would become one of those cloistered nuns who doesn't talk, and you know that's not happening. She couldn't keep her mouth shut.

"But T-June, you and the Aucoins have to go home this weekend and tell everybody what is happening. It's only fair."

∞ ∞ ∞

EVERYBODY that lives in the big city comes home for the weekend. Everybody on the bayou is waiting for the announcement of whatever they're coming down the bayou to announce.

Of course, Lily and Toot have come also, with Maybelline the second. You know those two grown women still see each other every day and talk on the phone for hours straight, going on until the wee hours. Callie has two of all the equipment that little babies have to have today.

I would have three of them in that seat, sitting behind me singing "All my exes live in Texas."

Estelle and Theo come too, waiting on Maybelline Laverne again. Now that they know everything about each other, Minou and her sistas have shared every little tidbit and have walked a mile in each other's shoes.

The women are thinking this must be about Jolie and T-June having a baby on the way, but the men not so positive. They know something is coming down the road to greet them, sighing heavily, and June just laughs all the time around True, knowing in their hearts what it is.

They go outside to talk among themselves. Minou says she already knows. "Who tha hell ya talkin' 'bout, ya big bastard? Ya think for one minute Ah don't know what to do? What tha shit, boy? And if ya think Ah'm too old, bring ya ass down here and work on tha side of me. Boy, you will be dragging in the dirt.

"Listen up, T-June, ya bettah give up ya pompous, know-it-all attitude with me. Ah ain't ever thought ya was the next Jesus or ya turn tha Kool-aid into Dr Pepper, so ya bettah bring yo sorry, hairy ass and say, 'Ah'm sorry, Mama, Ah'm sorry!'"

Joe is sitting at the table drinking a Bourbon and Coke, silently sipping until he begins big gulps. Thinking and talking to nobody but himself. "What tha shit! It's always somet'in'. We jus' can't catch a break! Sumbitch! Mais, here we go again. Ah tell her all tha time, but NOOO! It's gotta be her way. Mais, my mama ain't dat bad!"

Bertha and Alcide don't care about anything anymore. "Mais, y'all! Me and Alcide, mais, we jus' can't handle all tha drama. Dat quemas! Man, dat's what ya call tha nervine!"

Flavia for sure has something to say. "Good Gawd! Ah knew somet'in' like dis was gonna happen when ya tole me about tha veil. What in tha hell will Maybelline do is yet to be seen, but dat lil dude is 'bout tha same age as T-June was when he started doin' major t'ings! He can prob'ly heal people too.

"Here's what we should do to help. Get a buncha ex-Marine mercenaries to protect him from tha rest of tha people. Ah'll pay dem. Ya know dat Ah always felt T-June shoulda had an electric fence around y'all's property. Ya know, get some Dobermans or Mastiffs. What tha hell! Ya got two big-ass wolves!"

Lily speaks up. "It doesn't have to come with special gifts, the veil. Maybelline is not showing any of those abilities. As for me and Toot, well, we haven't noticed anything.

"We all know that she is brilliant. All of us have been flabbergasted at what she knows, and she is but eight. I'm not saying that True isn't, but I feel there's a lot of difference between those two. I think she's more on the normal spectrum."

It's yet to be seen, but Lily Laverne will probably be right. There's no blood line between her and Caldonia Aucoin. They've said they are sistas their entire lives. People have begun to believe it, and others just forgotten about it. The gaggle of women in the village have to think twice. Sometimes, they act like a bunch of quacking ducks.

They just all start laughing. The families are connected in every way possible except blood. They've chosen their family.

They have been worried about Maybelline for years, while it's True Blue they should be watching. A huge amount of worry for nothing, but now they have to be up in True's business. You see what happens in families, all up in everybody's business.

Minou and the gaggle are pleading with True to show them what he can do. True is a true ham, just like T-June, but is more a city-slicker-from-New Orleans kind of ham. He puts on this elaborate show with the music of Dr. John. He has made a tape and plays different songs for each act.

True will show each ability like he is a magician. When he starts talking in their minds, saying something funny about each one, they fall out laughing. Can't any of them answer him back.

That's different, because even Minou can't answer him. She tries and gets a busy signal.

True leads the way to the swamps in the back, the same infamous one that has held all their secrets. He brings his battery-operated cassette player and begins to play the music from Dr. Dolittle's movie soundtrack. The animals come out in droves and begin to dance with him like he is Uncle Remus.

Skippity doo da!

After all the laughing is done, walking back to the house, someone starts giggling, and then it is on again. They sure find it funny this time. That's what happens with late-in-life babies.

Flavia has got to say something, you know, and after gathering her wits, she says it. "Dat's bettah dan shows in Las Vegas, and Ah've seen a bunch of dem. Merde, he could be tha most famous magician in tha world. Why we didn't t'ink of dat before. He could be tha next Houdini. Ah know some people..."

Lily is hugging her sista, and both are crying and laughing at the same time. "Callie, baby, we will always have your back. But sista, he's funny as shit."

Henri speaks up. "He doesn't want to be a magician. He wants to play music. He's been telling me forever, he wants to be just like his parrain. We will handle this with help from all y'all. We're going to do this. Look at what y'all raised in T-June, a fine young man who is pursuing his dreams and living wide open in the city."

With that being said, everybody goes to bed, and the Aucoins go home early the next day. The mayor has to take care of his city.

The restaurant will be open in a matter of two weeks, after three years of preparations. Every detail has to be perfect, and also the neighbors are being considered on a quieter day for the workers.

Things are hectic trying to open a place on St. Charles Avenue. Henri has called in all his favors, and in return, the city council has made many things happen for the good.

Flavia calls in a few too.

Well, what ya think?

Here comes the truck with a brand-new flashing sign to put up on the front of the restaurant over the large wooden doors with intricate patterns carved out of wood always ending up in fleur de lis on the veranda. In dark blue lights, the sign with Caldonia's written in cursive letters lights up over St. Charles like a dream that dulls the senses. Subdued and sultry in the misty and mystical air of the Garden District.

All you got to say is New Orleans and two things come to mind. All the society chicks there are like little chickens in the restaurant, clucking behind the big, red-feathered rooster, Caldonia! They break their necks and almost get boiled to see who will get the first reservations.

∞ ∞ ∞

THE families are preparing for the opening night of Caldonia's. Tuxedos have been sent to the cleaners for the men. Bertha and Minou go to the back of her grandmama's cedar closet and pull out two fancy gowns from the '30s and '40s. Two they hide from Miss Callie.

Bertha and her mama have been known, back in their day, as a fun-loving Cajun-Indian pair.

As Keb Mo says, "She ain't looking for romance. She just wants to dance!"

Everybody's clothes stink of the mothballs, and Guidroz's Cleaners is very busy. If everybody in the growing village has reservations, well, they will take up the whole cleaners and cause Mr. Guidroz to have a heart attack.

True Blue is very quiet getting his tux on and his shiny shoes. He's thinking about something Maybelline has told him. He doesn't like it one bit.

Maybelline and True Blue have been best buds all their lives, sharing everything with each other. She reveals something to her bestie. "True Blue. (It's what he answers to now.) Podnah, I've got a secret kinda like yours, but no one else knows but you now. Don't you tell your mama. I have premonitions all the time, and I can feel things, maybe spirits. I mean, it's New Orleans after all, and maybe they're going to come and haunt Caldonia's. And BOO! Gotcha! Don't go tell your mama, little boy.

"Come on, baby. I was just joking! I'm going to tell you how to spell the word, and you look it up in the computer."

Maybelline protests about what her mama wants her to wear: a ruffled dress with a princess waist and a big-ass bow on the back of it. Remember Brooke Shields in that movie all about Storyville and New Orleans?

She is throwing a bona fide hissy fit. Maybelline, not Brooke.

"I am not wearing that! Who do you think would wear that? Some Baby Doll up in Storyville? Come on, Mama. You're not serious. Aw, hellfire! Then I'm not going."

Of course, she makes her mama let her wear something more appropriate for her blossoming body.

Lawd, it's a mess, everybody trying to get dressed. The ties, the corsets, the brassieres, and safety pins and perfume, the straight-up kind having to be used.

The men are complaining about that. "Shee-it! Mais, ya got me stinkin' of da stuff like Ah been in tha arms of a putain. Ah gotta open tha doors to let tha smell out. Shit! Minou, ya smell like dat woman over dere on tha corner. Oh, merde! She heard me. She walkin'…Oh, merde! She wavin' at me! She t'inks Ah want her service. Get back, y'all! Minou, go lock tha door."

Everyone is beautiful, and the atmosphere is that of the dreamy '40s in the Big Easy. Brings to mind Louie Armstrong with his horn, blowing off the Spanish veranda balcony in the Quarter, into the sultry wind of New Orleans, misty before a hurricane.

They are all there on time because they are in the city, dressing up like ladies of the night with their pimps wanting them to walk ahead of them. New Orleans ladies, sashaying down Esplanade. Our women can sure put on the dog, not looking country at all. The men are definitely not comfortable in their tuxes, but they sure are pretty! Flavia is the perfect moll doll for the swinging '40s, even wearing a full-length mink coat. She's daring someone to throw paint on her fur, and she pities the fool if they do!

Father Becnel and Sister Bridget have come for the occasion, and they both come in a little stoned. Sister Bridget has on a dress, the one she's worn forever when the occasion arises, and is keeping up with the others, sashaying up in there with the most important people in the city. The dress looks like it was bought in the '40s. She is actually pretty. A little rouge and lipstick will do it. Sister Lydia does her makeup for her, taking that huge cross off her neck, and getting her hair fixed in the latest style helps tremendously. She looks like she does this every day, but in truth, she is frightened and insecure. Her get-up as a nun is a shield against the heathens, and she feels naked.

No one has ever seen Callie looking like that, even at her wedding. She wears a full-length gown of dark blue, straight out the '40s, with sequins sewn on every part of the gown and low cut, showing her tetons. She looks like a huge diamond, her hair in a rolled-up job like a Gibson Girl. Slinky, sensual, sexy-as-hell Caldonia!

She goes to their table with a long cigarette holder in her mouth, and she takes a drag off the cigarette.

Minou speaks up first in a whisper. "Oh, my baby! Ya simply beautiful. Ya sure didn't look like dis for yo weddin'. But when in tha hell did ya start smokin'?"

Callie promptly replies to her mama, "It's just make-believe. It's not lit."

Flavia leans over the table and says, "Girl, Ah got boxes of dose things way back in some drawer from when my mama had tha store. Ah will give dem to ya for twenty-five dollahs."

And that's why she has her first dollar.

All the society women are about to bust a gut, not because of being full but at the sight of Caldonia. She's strutting around like she is the rooster of this place and they are the little chickens for a change.

Maybelline has been quiet on the way to the restaurant and immediately catches True Blue's eye when they walk in like they are in agreement with something. They are sitting together, being very quiet and alert and showing good manners. Sister Bridget starts talking with the both of them about their schools. Do they read? What do they want to be when they grow up? They are showing their good home raising, respecting their elders and saying, "yes, ma'am." Both are really talking and listening to her. There's not a smidgeon of intimidation tonight from her, drinking her piña coladas.

Callie has booked the Monsieur Mayhem Trio to play at the grand opening. The Trio begins to play, and True Blue stands up and starts singing from the table, knowing every song by heart and with a lot of soul. Monsieur Mayhem calls him up on the stand and introduces him to the crowd.

Everybody stands, clapping, a good brownie point, and because their children go to school with him. All the girls go home and tell their mamas how good he can sing, causing the little prim and proper ladies to swoon.

True's hair is not a flaming red by any means. It's almost the color of peach. Of course, he has dreadlocks, loving the way his nanan Lily wears hers. He shows a feature of his Native relatives with high cheekbones, but his eyes come from someone else because they're light green with flecks of brown. His lips full and tempting to all the young maidens and women there, and they are screaming the loudest!

He is the prettiest also.

∞ ∞ ∞

CALDONIA'S has been open for five years, with an amazing clientele. All the movie stars come here to eat their meals while on location in the city, best place in the world to make believe.

True's into the music, letting it take over. When he starts singing "Walkin' to New Orleans" and Antoine is playing that magic piano, well, they get another standing ovation. He and Jolie take the center stage, singing in perfect harmony Irma Thomas's rendition of "Wish Someone Would Care."

Maybelline is trying to get his attention. She is wishing True would pay attention to what he is singing, positioning herself where he can't miss her, and is nudging her head to the entrance, kind of pointing at two gentleman that have just walked in. Both men wear tuxedos with short coats, blending in with the upper crust of this city. Their scalps are shiny through buzzcut hair. The men keep sunglasses on, and they are heading for the bar, looking like FBI agents. They sit there, drinking for a couple of hours, when the Trio takes a well-earned break.

Maybelline grabs True while everybody else is trying to hug and praise him. True is in the ninth grade. What the hell will he be like when he's an adult? Shaking him, Maybelline whispers, "Dude, I've been trying to get your attention, but you're acting like you forgot that. Snap out of it! You're up there crooning to the girls, like nothing's going to happen. They are up in here already, and now is the time to pay close attention to what's happening."

True says to her, "Girl, Parrain and I are already on it."

The band goes back to playing. Callie has booked them for all night. True decides to jump off the platform, singing Fats' song, "A Goodhearted Man." He's moving through the restaurant, singing as he enters the bar. True is singing to everybody and stops in front of the two tuxedoed dudes.

Oh, he can feel it coming out of every pore of both of them, in their heads as well. No good, just no good.

True begins to sing Dr. John's "Right Place Wrong Time," and he is swaying and bringing the beat up and dancing like Michael Jackson. He stands in front of the dubious pair and swings his microphone, hitting one in the face, breaking his nose.

T-June is there in a second, going straight up in their heads and twirling around like it is ground meat. He makes them addled and confused as to why they are there, in the City that Care Forgot.

Two huge security guards, moonlighting from their regular jobs as the two toughest policemen in the city, come and grab them. Guns fall out of the pockets of their coats, one a sawed-off shotgun on the side, which is illegal and definitely not part of the scenery, unless you count Bonnie and Clyde.

The guards go to put the cuffs on, and the young dudes kick them in the balls. The cops both fall, hollering, knocking several people down too close for comfort.

Monsieur Mayhem goes falling backwards too, losing his concentration on the fleeing suspicious guys. Right when they get to the doors, they grab a councilman's wife and drag her with them to the waiting car, which is still running after all this time.

What in the hell?

Henri and Callie go immediately to the councilman and his three grown children. They all are frantic, in shock from what has just happened in front of them. Crying, blaming, and crying some more, the children are doing all this while the councilman stands with tears but has everything under control, like he does in his job.

Immediately, Callie is there at the table where the children are crying uncontrollably, giving hugs and comforting them and handing out her Irish linen napkins like they are Kleenex.

The councilman is steadily calling people. He's used to working under pressure. This particular councilman has always given Henri shit in the meetings. (He didn't vote for Henri Gustave Aucoin Junior for mayor.) The wife is one of those old-timers of society who snubs Callie.

He and Henri go to the side to talk with the injured security guards, who now want to catch the kidnappers and cut their balls off!

The guards begin to tell them about the well-known robbers that are called the Tuxedos. They are so elated to think they are going to catch the duo that they let their security guard senses down for a minute. Now they are pissed and kicking each other's ass, blaming each other for the failure of catching the Tuxedos.

The guards tell the group that the police station has bulletin boards full of posters of these robbers. Both guards feel responsible for letting them get away. Their captain comes and tells them not to talk with ANYBODY about this, to keep their mouths shut.

The captain proceeds to tell the men that this is the robbers' MO. Taking hostages but returning them unharmed is what they do. All the women returned just babble about how nice they are. There have been a couple of gay men kidnapped too.

They only hit places that are elite but subdued in a busy city, like off the beaten path. They case the joint, like they are waiting for someone to show up, then they go in and minutes later are out the door and speeding away with the kidnapped person, because their car is always running.

Henri and Monsieur Mayhem are happy in a way after listening to the captain, being positive and comforting the children. The councilman remains quiet. He acts like he is being so grateful as to what help they will be giving. Every meal eaten here for nothing, even breakfast, any time.

∞ ∞ ∞

THE restaurant will be closed for business until the kidnapped woman is returned. It will be the headquarters for the investigation. Caldonia and Henri give a paid vacation to their staff except for a couple to cook and clean messes made by the people who are working on the case, mostly cops who leave cans and paper and empty cups of coffee. They know most cops are messy but hope they're not the same way on their jobs.

Outside, all the ashtrays are full, and there's litter too. Callie says in no uncertain terms, NO SMOKING INSIDE!

The newspapers are all over this, another story of outrage the city is feeling. Once again, Henri and Callie make front page news. Seems as though they must be like all the other colorful characters on the streets of New Orleans.

The Tuxedos have the wife for six days and then drop her off in the Quarter to find her way home. Other than needing a change of clothes, she is in fine shape. The duo let her bathe every night with expensive shampoo and the top-of-the-line soap, and beautiful, large fluffy towels. She has someone's old clothes to wear while she's "visiting." Old clothes but nice.

She tells the police that she has been treated very well, they even call her Mrs. So-and-So and even "yes, ma'am" to her. The cooking is prepared by the older one, and it is unbelievably fine cooking. The younger one even serves her coffee, asking how she likes it and remembers how. She says that her meals are served with napkins, several forks, and a glass glass with ice cubes and a choice of beverage.

The woman feels like she's been on a vacation and is kind of guilty, but not for long.

They keep her blindfolded until they pull up in a gravel driveway leading to an old house, a large plantation home needing a paint job but otherwise still beautiful. All she sees is the house on a road where the sugar cane has once grown up to the pavement of some farm road. As far as you can see, sucrose on all four sides of the yard and across the two-lane road.

It doesn't need to be said, the kidnappers are fine hunks, and they love women. She can't tell if they are Cajun or Texan in their talk, but they are educated and read a lot. She does too while there. All of the kidnapped women say the same exact thing.

When she starts asking questions, they two answer her, speaking the truth.

This woman is up in there watching those whodunnits on cable TV and how it is done. She is one smart cookie.

All of the kidnapped women said the same exact thing. They've never been treated this well by their husbands. The women even have a choice to drink – cold drinks, iced tea, wine, beer, or doobie!

It has been asked of all of the women if they were raped. They say no.

I'm pretty sure a couple of those same women have taken one of the hunks to bed without him asking but with him telling her, "It would be a pleasure to serve you."

If the women know their names, they sure ain't tellin'! Just this most recent victim, the councilman's wife, who sings her canary head off. Justin and Scottie are their names. She wants them to feel the sting as bad as the one coming for her husband. She is a bona fide water moccasin.

Her name is, well, I won't say right now.

∞ ∞ ∞

THE bishop goes to work with the little amount of information given and starts looking into old deeds and lineage among the cane farmers all around the state.

One night, many months later in the Quarter, Monsieur Mayhem and his trusted sidekick, True Blue, are walking the streets together. True watches everything T-June does, already knowing he can do just that, but he's not old enough.

True Blue tells anybody who will listen, "I want to be just like Parrain!"

So, they are strolling the streets when True recognizes two dudes walking just as nonchalantly as they are, coming toward them. True goes immediately into Monsieur's head, and he says, I already see them. Just stay cool and act when you see me do the same thing.

The men walk past Monsieur and True like they have no idea who they are. True Blue goes into action and shocks the hell out of both of them up in their heads, jumping like they've grabbed a hot wire.

Both of those guys from who-knows-where are addled and confused again. That's real easy to do.

Monsieur Mayhem does the rest. Leading both them to a small park and making them sit down, he says LOUD LOUD in their faces (out his mouth), "Just what the hell are y'all doing? Maybe you should start registering faces when you're robbing somebody. Both of us were in the band, and it caused me to bust my head when I fell! Y'all are going to sit right there and tell me why you have to do this for a living.

"I'm not going to call the cops yet. I want to hear what you have to say, and I think I already know some of it. And listen up, you guys. We'll do worse to you if you try to escape. We will slam y'all's asses into the middle of next week."

The two kidnappers start shoving each other, each saying, "I told you! I told you!"

Being closer to their ages, True Blue says in their heads, What the shit, dudes! Somebody better start talking.

You know, words are just words, and I use them as that way to tell you choicely, they mean business! In families I know and have known, the kids get their mouths washed out with Octagon soap if you are dumb enough to say it around your mama! Today's words that are offensive to our ears are the words used to shock our mamas if said out loud, maybe causing you to get your mouth slapped. My mama almost fainted, holding her heart, when I said "fuck." I had three children at that time! You know like shit, Shit, or SHIT? I will tell you my personal favorite: fuck a duck. Sorry, I kinda digress. I wonder why?

True and Monsieur are raising three kinds of hell and loud.

One of the duo speaks up while the other lets him talk. "My name is Justin Leroux, and he's my double first cousin. Our mamas were sisters who married brothers. He's Scottie.

"Shit, I have no idea where to start, gentlemen. How much time we got? It will take a while if you want the whole story."

Monsieur orders meals delivered from Caldonia's with a six pack of cold beers, Dixie. They're looking like they've already got ahold of something else. They're still sitting in the park under dim lights with several blown out by someone's gun.

Justin begins to talk quietly. "Our people have had an old plantation house out there since the Civil War, located off the main road between Des Allemands and Raceland. Used to have a lot of cane in our family, but our father, along with his brother, wasted it all away on booze, loose women, gambling, and the banks took the rest. Over the generations our families slipped gradually into genteel old money, but there's no money any more.

"Both of our papas died young, working themselves to death on what small amount of cane we still had, and then spent it all on what I already told you.

"Our mamas had deep friendships with the women who came to help us in earlier years. They in turn helped our mamas when they needed jobs. Our mamas had very good jobs; after all, they were educated women, and the group of women and our mamas raised us to be ethical, worldly, and spiritual men who love women and music.

"Both of our mothers were killed together coming back from Mass when a man straight out of a wealthy family in the city, judge-like connected, hit them head on, outside Raceland. Although it was his third DWI, he got out of all of it with scratches and never paid a dime to us.

"Both of us were going to Tulane on the money our grandpapa had in a trust for us. We used that all up on lawyers' fees, and to put the icing on the cake, the judges and lawyers all were in cahoots. But we couldn't prove it at the time. We didn't know what to do. Being we're both smart and streetwise, it didn't take us long to figure out what happened. We had no more money other than our salaries to go after them again.

"This is what started the whole dammed thing of us being outlaws. I'm not giving you this sob story to make you feel sorry for us and us staying out of jail. Dude, don't feel sorry for us. We are severely pissed because we aren't through.

"So, we came up with a plan, and now we've got money. Our money. We have been getting revenge on every last one of those fuckers, all the way up to Tennessee. We would contact whoever had caught the attention on our bucket lists of thieves, degenerates, whoremongers, a civil servant who thought he was El Jefe. Hell, they all were bad, bad souls and had something to do with our misfortune.

"We blackmail them by kidnapping someone dear to them, in front of a large crowd of people to show it's genuine, and the victim doesn't know Jack-shit about any of it. We treat them with the manners that were taught to us by the slewful of mamas that raised us. Now, if the women are savvy and ask, well, I was taught not to lie.

"We are fascinated with women. We're both lovers, not fighters. Scottie doesn't even know how to shoot, much less carry a gun, even if it's make-believe. You saw him kinda dragging the sawed-off, and he sure as hell can't shoot it because we don't have bullets."

Justin sits back down, and Scottie stands up.

"We aren't crooks! Both of us have good jobs that allow us the weekends off, and we've been on the same jobs for five years, right when we came back from Tulane. We have no intention of robbing anyone else, just the ones we go after. All of the info about us should say somewhere that we don't do that.

"You guys caught us off guard. We were sitting there listening to your music. Then all of a sudden, you had us acting like we had a pot of red beans boiling in our heads. You" – he points at True – "popped Justin on the face with the mike. Shit, y'all broke his cute little nose. Boy, you should have seen him. He was swollen up with two black eyes."

Justin is pushing him and telling him to shut up.

"What are y'all, some kind of superheroes? I believe in all that, and I've read every Harry Potter book. I abhor any kind of violence toward our fellow human beings, and guns give me a rash."

Monsieur Mayhem takes the two brothers home, where they will be safe until he looks at the whole picture. The cops won't be called. If it's necessary to hide them more, they're going down the bayou.

∞ ∞ ∞

MONSIEUR calls home to Minou, and the whole bunch is on their way to the city. Luckily, they don't have to worry about money, and the ones still working are self-employed. So, they come running toward the quemas every time and wouldn't have it any other way.

Bishop has already looked into the Lerouxs' history after the woman – the snake, the councilman's wife, the society snob – tells the cops their first names and that it isn't far to where they kept her. He sees all the legal papers that they've signed and given away a fortune. He sees for himself how rich they were at one time. Justin has been telling the truth.

Everybody starts walking in with suitcases and recognizes the Lerouxs from Caldonia's that night.

Flavia is the one who beats everybody to the punch, of course. "Lil boys! What tha hell ya t'inkin'? Ah know ya mamas didn't raise y'all up to be no kidnappers. Ah heard on tha police band dat ya never robbed nobody, jus' kidnappin'. So, what's up wit' dat?"

If she will wait for just a minute, T-June is going to explain to everyone why these two young men are here, will be forgiven, and may be some more added to the Monsieur Mayhem's village.

The whole gang starts laughing real hard, and True Blue can't believe what he thinks is happening. He goes into T-June's brain in a second. What the hell, Parrain? You take this forgiveness shit a little too far. Man, I'm not sorry one bit for cracking in the face of that dude over there.

The Leroux brothers love being with the family, and Scottie starts right away reading T-June and Jolie's books. He totally flips when he sees their music collection on vinyl. Scottie tells them how much he enjoys their music and asks to meet Antoine Domino. Maybe he won't recognize them.

T-June calls, so excited, and tells Antoine to come to their house, that somebody is dying to meet him. He just doesn't tell him who. Scottie is so elated to meet Antoine when he walks up in the house that he immediately asks for his autograph on a T-shirt he has bought in the Quarter before they were nabbed.

Antoine for sure recognizes the brothers and looks hard at T-June and Jolie and the bishop. T-June has to catch Antoine from running out the door. Antoine's trying to get out in the most polite way he can. "My man! Don't be telling me y'all were in on this entire bullshit. Awww, awww, y'all aren't the people I was thinking y'all were. You're somebody else. Look, man, I don't want any part of this. I go to the bishop's church every weekend, and I love my wife and my life."

"Look, y'all. I don't judge anybody. I just can't be part of any Cajun Mafia. I'm sorry. I love all of y'all, but I am no snitch. I try to live a pretty righteous life, man. I got a little baby on the way."

After a few words from T-June, Antoine changes his tune. "Okay, I'm not worried. If the bishop is part of this, it must be okay."

Antoine stays and calls his wife, telling her to join them. The house is full of down-the-bayou folks, and he is having a damn good time after his bad fright, thinking the whole Cajun Mafia is here.

Scottie begs them to listen to a song he's written, borrowing T-June's guitar. Singing very well, he plays a ballad about Louisiana, and they go nuts over it. He tells them he's got a suitcase full of his writings that he keeps under his bed.

The Monsieur Mayhem Trio tells him they want to see it all, if this song is a good example.

∞ ∞ ∞

STILL undecided as to what path to take with the two Lerouxs, T-June leaves them to stay a while at Minou's house. The boys get busy doing everything that needs repairing at Alcide and Bertha's house and then build another path with bricks for Minou and Joe. This is what they do for a living, and they are damn good at it.

They make themselves at home on the bayou but have to call their boss to tell him they are on an emergency so they won't lose their jobs, not even thinking about jail.

They help in the garden, picking tomatoes, okra, mirlitons, and watermelon. They cut the grass and do what needs to be done before anybody else can do it.

Justin has taken over Bertha's kitchen, leaving her idle, sitting on her porch on the swing in the morning, drinking coffee with her mate, Alcide. Just a-swingin'. Now she gets to tend to her pot patch. She and Madam Aucoin have gotten some mighty fine cannabis, sharing with whoever indulges.

The majority of the village now indulges. Sister and Joe say they don't smoke the stuff. The poor bébés don't realize it ain't the piña coladas or the Crown Royal that's got them buzzing and wanting another drink and something to eat, laughing their couyon asses off.

Justin is cooking for the whole bunch every day, food that's familiar and some not familiar but always delicious. Even Bertha has to agree that it is definitely delicious. Hell, she's probably gotten her fill of cooking every day for the bunch and has put away her own pots. The cousins clean the kitchen as they go, and all she has to do is look, but her pots are her pride. Nobody has ever fooled with her pots.

The cousins deeply miss the family atmosphere of their mamas' houses and just lap up every bit of attention and praise, hoping the family can see they are good people just doing shady deals.

Monsieur Mayhem and Bishop Toussiant go back to the city to the police station to talk with the chief. The chief tells them, "Y'all, I'm going to tell you the strangest thing has happened. They've just disappeared, not doing their kidnapping any more. Nobody has pressed charges, not one husband or wife or boyfriend. So, wherever they went, nobody is looking for them except the two policemen that were your guards that night at Caldonia's. They've made it a top priority to catch these dudes. I've explained to them that there is no reward for their capture, but it's an obsession with them."

T-June and the bishop drive back to the bayou to tell the Leroux cousins that they are free men but to be on guard for the New Orleans policemen. So much celebration ensues, with lots of music and dancing because Scottie is a dancing fool.

Justin talks to Minou and Joe about their land. "Miss Minou and Joe, I have a question for you. We've seen the property down below with the big camp and another house for your overseer and his family. We talked at length with Junya and T-Mae, and they tell us there's an abundance of wild game and fish here, along with the pecan trees, and the wolves and what happened to their son."

You know how those Rappolets are, along with all the children putting their two cents in the conversation. Lawd! It's hard getting away from that talkative bunch, but they are simply remarkable, and their accents and morals are totally Louisiana. We love it!

Justin continues, "To get to the point, I would like to purchase an acre of land you've got back there. We prefer to be in the swamps, because we know how to build a house on it. I know y'all don't ever sell land back there, but we have grown to love all of you and want to keep helping you and being with you. What do y'all think of this?"

Minou speaks first, saying, "Mais, hell, yeah! But don't call me 'Miss' no more. Jus' Minou, okay?"

Joe is just nodding his head gleefully, saying, "It's 'bout damn time we got some help ovah here. Mais, Ah can't do dis shit no more! None of us are spring chickens."

Then, as if he has thought of something else, Joe begins to tell them about the unfriendly ghost called Gaspar and the pecans that are hollering for Minou to pick them, about how their fortune begins there with a pirate's treasure chest that Jean Lafitte has killed Gaspar over, leaving him to guard his treasure for eternity.

The Leroux boys are enthralled with the stories and the whole amazing family with all this supernatural shit.

Justin and Scottie leave for their home and lock up their old house, coming back for furniture when it's needed. They go to tell their boss they are moving to Bayou Lafourche. They have found lost relatives there, building their own house, and will put in a farm. They thank him for being so good to them and all the things he's taught them. This isn't a burnt bridge type of leaving. You just don't do this with important people in your life.

The boss has no idea how wealthy they are.

Justin and Scottie Leroux are two more people that have become part of T-June's entourage, from all walks of life. A more diverse group of people you couldn't find. It takes a village.

Chapter Seventeen

Lerouxs' Bizness

WE'VE heard about the Leroux cousins and how they become two more members of T-June's entourage. Lawd, y'all know how long the list is.

After getting their affairs in order, Justin and Scottie move to Bayou Lafourche and begin to dream about their treehouse that will have three bedrooms, large living area opening up to huge long windows and a wrap-around porch. Two complete bathrooms in their house they are so proud of, although they miss the huge claw foot tub. You can't put that up in the air, but they've found substitutes for it. The kitchen is to die for.

Justin and Scottie go to talk with the Thibeaus about the purchase of that acre of the land they have talked about, telling them money is no problem.

Minou and Joe say at the same time, "Give us a dollar, and tha land is yours."

It's an acre of swampland with beautiful old cypress trees that cannot be cut by law, moss reaching for the other trees to hang on, and big, big-ass pecan trees. They find the rest of the pecan grove with huge ancient trees surrounding, so tall you get dizzy trying to see the tops. The moss hangs so thick you could pick enough of it to make a king-size mattress just right there.

Lawd, can you imagine people having to do that? Modern times have perks. For sure, we ain't goin' dere!

Live oaks spiraling, reaching for heaven, branch out with roots making intertwining designs of nature, with startling, wonderful views of the swamps.

The boys are building their treehouse, and it's so exciting to see that everybody is there to watch and help. The Rappolet family is all out there helping and talking and helping and talking. Justin turns the boom box up and puts in earbuds, and then all are dancing while they work. He's smiling to himself because he can't hear the talk.

This magical mystery treehouse that has appeared in the trees of the swamps is quite the beauty and huge up in the trees, with twenty-five stairs going up like an elevator. Well, this house is built in no time with all the help from whoever can pick up a hammer. Lots of free labor.

Madam and the bishop come and say a blessing, and Madam conjures up Laurette. The boys know all about Madam Alafair Aucoin, but they have never seen her in action.

In the dark of the swamps, everyone is in a circle with lighted candles stuck in the ground and flames blowing with the wind. The wind is steadily blowing like a tropical storm but without the rain. Still in the dark of the night, twirling and spitting and blowing smoke up everybody's ass. All the trees are moving, with the moss swaying in the dark night, a full-blown Cajun moon trying to reach all of them, it is so big and round. The way the moon looks when it's real yellow, when you can see the face of the man in the moon.

The ganja is shared and Bacardi Rum with straight up the real deal, Mexican Coca-Cola. Madam shares a small container full of Bacardi Rum. Everybody there is to take a gulp, and then they are told to spit it out. Justin and Scottie get popped in the head by Madam because they drink straight down the rum. The cousins have to do it all over again.

Poor things!

Covered in jewelry with her Voodoo self, antique rings on her fingers and bells on her ruby red-painted toes – the big bell-ringing type handed down over centuries – Madam slumps down, her long hair falling out her turban to the ground. She comes back as this

Caribbean woman of color that lived in the 1800s in Belize named Laurette who practiced VooDoo a century ago.

Everyone in the circle is afraid to move, especially the folks new to this. Very scary; everybody is very scared shitless.

"Aww, all my people that I love! Sooo many, many I'm just meetin', but I know all about you. Look at them pretty, pretty boys! They are the ones you sent for me about? Oh, Yahweh. They are some pretty, yeah. Come see, come see me close so I can smell you. Ha ha! I even see my Alafair pick up the hammer.

"Look, my little pretty boys. You are gonna have the good life, but trouble is comin'. Be strong and take the trouble like two men would. I know some more, but I ain't tellin' no more."

And then she is gone.

Madam Aucoin comes out the trance, asking what Laurette has said. She never knows what Laurette is going to say or do.

Both the Lerouxs start talking at the same time, to tell the amazing thing they've just witnessed. Scottie is probably drunk and stoned and is dancing and raising his arms to the sky toward heaven, singing Hallelujah! They are so shocked and enchanted with Laurette. They tell her everything, so excited they are.

Junya and T-Mae have made the kids go home so they won't see this ghost, this spirit, this quemas maybe from the devil. They some nosy people from in the swamps and want to know everything and anybody's business. They try the ganja cigarette, and they start laughing at everything out there, be it animals or humans. They then run inside of their house and come out with big bags of chips, along with all the candy they can find.

I think it's called the munchies.

They are struck speechless, maybe for the first time in their lives and can't get over how much fun they have with these people. They start crying and hugging everybody, telling them, "We sure do love all y'all!"

∞ ∞ ∞

JUSTIN and Scottie are welcome additions to the entourage, staying at home in the swamps and helping everyone who has once been stars of what they can't do anymore.

Justin and Scottie refuse to go anywhere in the City that Care Forgot. They know that they haven't been forgotten. A bunch a people would still recognize them, although they have changed their appearances and let their buzzcuts grow out long. So, all visits are done in the bayou swamps.

When they need supplies from the city, everyone pitches in and goes to the city sometimes just for that, whatever they need.

The Lerouxs are kind of like hermits but not quite. They love to go dancing all over the parish. Justin and Scottie are two Cajun men who love to dance and have fun, going to every dancehall and fais do-do they can find, and soon have women chasing after them. They love Grande Isle and will spend weekends with whoever can dance the best. Not a worry in their world.

Back in the city, Callie and Henri's life is wonderful and so promising that they both give thanks on their knees, first thing in their mornings, something Henri has been taught to do. And so True Blue hits his knees before brushing his teeth.

True Blue is now sixteen and a full-time member of the Monsieur Mayhem Quartet. He graduates a year before his class. The girls are so sorry and call him all the time. True Blue will sweet talk all of them, being the smooth flirting, high-jiving trickster-for-sure dude from New Orleans.

T-June is beautiful but not like True. True's hair is in lifelong dreads, the color of light peach, green eyes being a couple shades lighter than his pop's and freckles like his mama. What a pretty, pretty boy.

He and Jolie sound amazing together, with Monsieur playing an electric guitar given to him by Jolie for Christmas five years ago, when the Lerouxs first showed up in their tuxedos. And on piano is Antoine Domino.

True is a true-blue fan of Scottie Leroux's vinyl records bought new and music by forgotten people on every spectrum of Louisiana tunes.

The Silverbergs are coming to the swamps to hear Scottie and Justin play their music and to sign them with their company, trusting what T-June told them about the cousins.

True comes to his MeMe Minou's house as much as he can. He takes the cousins to see the animals, and they are choking on their laughter, watching them dance all around.

Zippity doo dah! Zippity day!

When True shows them how he can talk with the animals, and they answer, that's when the cousins start calling him "Doo." Laughing their asses off, the cousins start asking questions, waiting to hear what True says.

He tells them his parrain used to come back here all the time to listen to them in his mind. He has had to settle disputes between the variety of animals that call this their land. Come to find out, Ruby the Racoon has some daughters that live out there. Ruby should have been called "Roux Garoux."

When True goes into the Lerouxs' minds, they feel a familiar shock, but then it opens their minds forever. Using every cuss word you can imagine, they are jumping with Brer Rabbit and his family that live in the briar patch. Yelling and dancing, they feel like they're on some kind of carnival ride up in Disneyland with this family.

They see Pieyan sneaking around back, digging in the garbage like a big bear. The old bigfoot likes their garbage because he finds half-empty beer bottles, and he drinks the leftovers.

Rappolets always have thrown stuff away, although not much, due to their expanding family. It's become almost a McDonald's for Pieyan, who likes this better than having to chase his food down.

They've been introduced to Mac and Claudine as they fly by on their property, waving as they pass by. They come by every time they visit her folks and his. They have tales to tell too. The cousins enjoy having them stop by. They find the couple enchanting but are very nervous around Claudine. She looks deadly, smiling at them while barely covering her fangs.

Oh, yeah, they know their good friends Bertha and Alcide turn to loopers once a month and are gladly part of that too. It's a party every month, back there watching the loup-garous cavort and run with the wolves.

The cousins have accepted all the eccentric ways of the families that have taken them in love and acceptance regardless. Both now believe in the supernatural in every way, every shape, and every form, sometimes seeing the underbelly of the gifts and some people not so kind. They stay busy and have added to the village, offering much-needed help, something that goes a long way.

The boys are very vague giving directions to their hidden refuge because they really don't want people to know where they live. On occasion, some young women are brave enough to come on the Peltier-Thibeau property, slipping under the fence, not knowing its history, looking for the treehouse in the swamps. Most women stop on the other side of the electric barbed wire fence, looking for the two wolves that walk the perimeter, hollering their names, and swatting mosquitoes.

Minou and Joe think this is hilarious, watching the brave and determined little girls trying not to get lost and being attacked by all the mosquitos and flying bugs. So, just one more thing added to the Mayhem Bayou.

Joe thinks it's so damn funny and kids them while slapping their backs, saying, "Mais, hot damn! Y'all got some purty lil girls chasin' y'all's asses. Me, all Ah could ever see was Minou."

∞ ∞ ∞

HENRI and Callie are very successful in the restaurant called Caldonia's, and there are reservations made sometimes for as long as three weeks trying to walk up in the place.

The workers are interesting with their vintage clothing and politeness and smiles. The waiters and waitresses bring home great paychecks, but it's the tips every night that can pay a house note, intelligent kids paying their way through college, making this restaurant very different from the other eating establishments.

We all know about those other places, be it swanky or Burger King. The waitresses in those establishments are so condescending and treat customers like they are a necessity to getting paid. They for sure don't get a tip.

At Caldonia's, they do have a good work ethic, as though they've made a new family with the other workers, and they help each other. They keep all their tips, and it's up to the waitress or waiter to share it with someone who helped them.

True Blue spends many of his nights playing his guitar for the customers, going from one table to the next, serenading them while they wait on their favorite dishes to be brought. He stands at the table of the infamous councilman and his wife, the woman who is the last victim kidnapped by the Tuxedos. They have a standing reservation every Saturday so they can watch Callie and Henri and anybody else of importance. Like two buzzards waiting on lunch.

True is picking up vibes from the two, although they act like they're glad to see him, shaking his hand and hugging and leaving lipstick traces on a cigarette in his mouth. That horny woman tries to put her tongue in his mouth, like an older woman trying to entice all the little boys. Come see, baby. I got some candy for you. She's a pervert; True isn't even old enough to vote.

He goes immediately to both of their minds.

Use it before you lose it!

What good is it if you don't use it?

Minou and Flavia have always wished they could do that, reading everybody's minds. What a way to get to the truth, if you're just plain afflicted with nasal problems.

What he hears is far from what he is seeing, changing in his mind thoughts that they are somebody other than who they pretend to be. True hears her jealousy and hatred for his mama.

The couple is very anti-Caldonia's, anti-Callie and anti-Mayor Henri and True Aucoin. They truly hate the whole family's luck, beauty, and the fact they're too nice and can't be trusted.

The wife, a former queen of the society gang, has had to step down because of Caledonia. Callie could care less about all that shit.

The councilman has never changed his loyalty or his dislike for Henri.

What's that about leopards and their spots?

They are not grateful to the Aucoins for their help and kindness. They feel like it is something for the Aucoins to lord over them and to get the councilman to change sides in the political arena. Also, it's a political ploy for more votes to keep him in the mayor's office.

You know some people are threatened by kindness because they don't have a forgiving vessel in their hearts.

The wife has carried secrets her whole life that have had her on guard forever. She has an ancestor that was a Caribbean quadroon sold on a platform built just for this purpose, in the infamous stocks of human beings being sold like horses and cattle. Stepping down off the platform so buyers could get a better look, like opening their mouths, looking at their backs for whip scars, and checking to see if they are virgins. How totally unforgivable.

It was never even thought of by these cowards of the Ku Klux Klan, and some will still deny it took place.

Fuck a duck!

The councilman is also a closet racist. Her husband the councilman doesn't know about her ancestry, and she is a basket of nerves each time she gives birth to her children. She is worried that the ancestor will leave a mark somewhere because it's happened before to her other relatives. A touch of the tarbrush. She comes from a background that is a total fabrication, and she has guarded that as well as the racial issue.

The woman has always known about her husband's indiscretions, in his personal and political careers, in the bed of a putain or a boy. She doesn't give a rat's ass about his shit, as long as she isn't involved in it. Appearances are all that matter to the cold-hearted bitch, but never does she think it's planned until the younger Leroux cousin answers her question.

Her cheating, sleazy husband has lived in hell ever since. She reminds him about keeping her out of his bullshit, every day since. The woman turns her head to his thievery. Of course, she has maxed out all the credit cards, going to the most select clothing stores. For sure, it isn't Walmart. He's got a lot more payments to his wife's tally of what he paid the Lerouxs for her ransom. All these years…

True certainly doesn't need all this crap up in his brain; it's building up. It bursts out onto the lap of the councilman's wife. Thick vomit and projectile. Literally. That woman is totally shocked at the vomit all over her designer clothes, trying to say it's all right, smiling but lying.

The councilman and his wife leave, hugging everybody but staying away from True.

His parrain has had that same thing happen to him with Big Mama Theriot, back in the day.

True goes immediately to his parents to tell them what he's learned about the councilman and his wife. He has his mama gagging, so he has to clean up first.

Callie isn't fooled one bit about the couple. The woman just tremendously oozes jealousy and dislike out her pores.

Callie talks to her own little replica of Monsieur Mayhem, her son. "True, do you think I give a minute of care about those fake women? Ha ha, you know your mama better than that. I don't care about a lot of bullshit. Take a look at who raised me. I'm a lot like your MeMe Minou. If it catches my attention and I want to know, well, I know how to do just that.

"It must be very hard on you, trying to listen to two evil minds at the same time. Well, you got sick. Parrain too, one time. Tread softly, son. You can't be listening to everybody's thoughts. I say, pick and choose.

"I already know they will send us the bill for the cleaning of that ugly, ugly dress."

Henri says to True, "Son, I already felt the vibes of these snakes but thought it was old feelings about him and me. I'm going to tell you the tale about a snake. A woman who takes in a sickly snake gets it all better. The snake turns around and bites her. When she asks why, he says, 'Because I'm a snake!' A snake is a snake is a snake. And you don't stop being one unless you are hit with the Holy Spirit.

"Remember when I asked if you could listen to everybody's thoughts? Well, True, it's time I take you to city hall."

∞ ∞ ∞

HENRI, the mayor, takes True Blue, the mind reader, to the massive building that occupies an entire floor, three stories up the elevator. The office of the mayor of New Orleans.

He tells True what minds he wants him to go into. Pretty sneaky but definitely a one up in anything the mayor needs to know.

Damn, it's just Louisiana on a smaller scale. Or maybe, that's where it starts.

True and Henri walk up in the office where everybody is clapping and hugging and putting CDs in his face to autograph, throwing him off his game. It's the first one of Monsieur Mayhem's albums.

Henri is standing next to him like a proud papa, taking in all the best wishes and congratulations. He forgets what he's brought True for.

True Blue takes himself up and down the elevator, visiting every floor, doing the same thing. He just can't concentrate.

After spending the entire day in the building, they go home, and Henri wants to know immediately about True's job snooping all day.

Henri settles down after a couple of cocktails, while Callie joins them at the exquisite antique dining table. Callie and Henri have found out, like the rest of the village, that's the place to conduct business.

Looking very serious, he tells Henri, "Man, Papa, there isn't a single person in that whole building that likes you."

Henri almost drops his cocktail on the carpet, looking so distraught with tears that True can't stand it.

"Man, that's not true. I was gaslighting you. Lawd, there are so many that are on your side, I couldn't count them. There are a few that aren't, and they stand out loud, determined to see you fail when you run again, but they sure don't act that way. A pit of vipers, for sure, man, but you can't fire them, so just know what they're about.

"Oh, and Papa? I'm not going to do that again. It stinks of deceit and snakiness, and it's terribly unethical. To get on their level? I'm not that, and you aren't either, but it sure was fun doing my little trick."

Henri says to his son, "Man, you're right. You are so right. I feel like I need a hot shower. I feel nasty. I can tell you who they are already. I don't know why I even asked you to do that, but man, we must have that ESPN going on."

You know he means ESP, right?

"I won't ask you do to that again, son. I feel ashamed."

∞ ∞ ∞

ONE night, all this time later, Justin and Scottie decide to go with the family to a special celebration at Caldonia's. The Aucoins are celebrating their anniversary and announcing the coming of another baby. Henri is strutting around like a rooster in the restaurant. He's a man who's been here a long time but has wisdom beyond his years and still can "get sum" without any help.

The Lerouxs are dressed up in suits after putting those tuxedos on the trash pile and burning them. They look entirely different from those times they've taken the law into their own hands. Back then, they both had buzzcuts in their hair and sunglasses covering their eyes. Now, their hair is long, and their bodies have muscles where they were none before. Completely different human beings.

Caldonia Aucoin just glows and seems to be more beautiful than ever. It's what is called that pregnant glow everyone sees, but then you go eight months down the road, and that same woman is big and ready to drop that load, never thinking about that damn glow.

It's almost a private affair at the restaurant because so many of the folks from the bayou have come tonight. All dressed up, acting all bougie for the rest of the patrons. Of course, there are many other tables for patrons to sit.

The councilman and his ill-mannered wife are there, smiling and hugging everybody to their faces but hiding their raw ugliness. Minou and Flavia don't give her the time of day, and Madam Aucoin just stares hard at the couple, who think they are getting away with it.

Not with this bunch. They can smell bullshit from a mile off.

They have hired the Monsieur Mayhem Band for the night, now with a drummer and a horn player, and there is standing room only in the restaurant and bar. So much noise with people talking and laughing and waiting for the band to start.

The Lerouxs sit on the same bar stools all these years later. They claim the stools are in the right spot to see the band, up close and personal. The cousins have been truly listening to the music, thinking it's too early for the councilman.

The evening is wonderful. Even Father Becnel and Sister Bridget are there, enjoying their piña coladas and their secondhand smoke.

Two men – the security guards from that infamous night – come up to the cousins and grab them so fast. No one can react quickly to the situation. That woman must have been reading their emails and has the cops on speed dial. The men no longer have jobs as guards but continue to come to the establishment, knowing well this family, just in case the Tuxedos come again to Caldonia's.

The men start rough handling them and laughing, saying they have finally caught the kidnappers of the councilman's wife.

The two handcuff the boys and are trying to lead them out the doors, watching to prevent the duo from kicking them again, when the entire village comes unglued and starts a huge ruckus to prevent just that.

Minou and Flavia are protesting loud enough for the whole restaurant to take notice of what's going on because they're up in the wannabe big men's faces (like the diners haven't already noticed).

"There is no outstanding warrant for either Justin or Scottie," says Bishop Toussaint, while he stands in front of them.

One of the cops says, "Oh, I beg to differ. The councilman is here with his wife, and they want to press charges on the two Leroux cousins for extortion and kidnapping."

They all turn to where the sleazy couple stands, who are getting ready to exit the building. No such luck.

Minou grabs the woman and Flavia the councilman, wanting to beat the shit out of them. The couple is so outdone, hollering they want to press charges on the two women for attacking them, when Minou and Flavia are doing no such thing.

But it doesn't fly.

The cops are only interested in their capture of the two criminals, so they don't pay attention to the chaos it causes. The insidious couple barely makes it out the doors before the village shows their intentions to scalp them.

You know, there's some Atakapa blood running through a few veins. The Atakapa used to be called cannibals.

Reinforcements are called for by the elated cops, who think they have solved the crimes against two innocent people. But nobody shows up. They are able to drag the two cousins out the doors while everyone is cussing and threatening them, including the mayor, who tells them they won't have their jobs tomorrow.

The bishop, T-June, True Blue, and Joe follow behind them, honking and tailing the car of the policemen driving the Lerouxs to jail. Henri leaves in his own car and beats all of them to the station. He definitely has the pull, being the mayor.

They close the restaurant and all go to Callie and Henri's beautiful house on St. Charles, a couple of blocks from the restaurant. Callie has to be taken care of because she is feeling some pain and is so upset.

"Those sons of bitches! After all we've done for them, the fucking rattlers turn around and bite all our asses. Henri will take care of this."

Everyone there is waiting for some news from the gang of vigilantes that has gone to the jail to bail out the Lerouxs. Three hours into the morning have all of the men home, including Justin and

Scottie. Everyone is clapping and crying and backslapping the cousins, while Henri goes to his beloved's bedroom and shuts the door.

"We were able to bond them out at a ridiculous amount of money. Way too big for this. But I was able to have it lowered and got them released in our custody."

The dastardly duo – the councilman and his wife –want their day in court, but it won't be theirs, as it will turn out to be.

Bishop Toussaint says, while smoking his ganja pipe, "It has definitely become a power struggle between Henri and the councilman. Neither the man nor his wife showed up at the station, but they are going to have to face us in court, if that happens. Those two water moccasins have gone back to their muddy hiding spot. They just don't know we have creatures that can bite their heads off."

Everybody goes back to the bayou so Callie can rest at her mama's house.

You know how that is, by your mama's.

The cousins go to their treehouse and stay shut up in their house for four days. Justin finally says to his younger cousin, "It's time for us to quit hiding and be the men Laurette told us to be. You get consequences for your actions. We're going to go down there with our heads held high. If we did that crime, we're going to do the time."

These two are still holding back the reasons for the kidnappings but are saving it to bring up in court, with the enormous factors on their side.

Joe is the one who speaks first. "Gawee! Mais, da shit don't never stop. We don't ever have bon chance. Shit and shinola! Mais, we gonna be wit' ya, come hell or high water. Hell! We might wind up in da jail wit' ya 'cause of all dis quemas."

Flavia of course is next. "What tha hell y'all worried 'bout? Even tha guv'nor owes me a big favor. Babies, Ah can guarantee it. Y'all ain't gonna spend one night in dat jail. What we need to do is countersue deir blown-up asses. You cousins still have tha documents dat caused tha kidnapping to begin wit'? Y'all bettah come wit' plenty to put on tha table. Y'all done got too soft! Ya bettah t'ink 'bout how y'all used to strut, pullin' dis shit off. Fight it like men. Ah'ma make some calls."

The cousins don't say a word.

Hell, the whole bunch has powerful connections up and down the bayou that can carry itself to New Orleans, causing enough quemas to make the Big Easy not too easy. Every one of those Mayhem Mafia from the bayou is putting some big-ass solutions on the table. It's all planned for the court date coming up soon. They're coming with big-ass guns.

They do, in fact, come with loaded guns, countersuing them.

∞ ∞ ∞

THE courtroom is full of reporters and photographers, this being a very sensational trial involving the mayor and several important residents of New Orleans. The sleazy snakes are there in true form, full of fakeness, with slithering tongues and grieving as innocents over the whole thing.

The judge is one of the snake's old cronies who doesn't like Henri Aucoin either. They're thinking this is a slam-dunk, but you shouldn't count your chickens.

The court comes to order with this big-ass judge stinking of cigars and fake jovial behavior.

Can you just see him?

The red forked-tongued snakes have their lawyer on his feet, asking questions of Justin and Scottie Leroux. Slamming them, and they just say, "I have the right to remain silent."

That is pissing off the lawyers, and they think they have thrown the book that will see them in jail.

As if. As if.

The Lerouxs' lawyer is from down home and has never lost a case. He asks first Justin and then Scottie what the factor is behind the kidnapping and blackmailing.

Justin answers his questions, telling the courtroom, "Scottie and myself only went after the people who did an injustice to our family.

They would also have something big to hide. We never had anything but the upmost respect for the wives, treating them like they were kin and visiting for a vacation. I don't think the women have anything bad to say about us. They may have something to hide themselves."

The female asp tries to deny it, but then she looks into Scottie's eyes and is silenced, sitting back in her chair.

What?

The lawyer from Lafourche Parish, Francis Dugas, then asks questions of Scottie. "What have you been hiding from the authorities about this law-breaking citizen of New Orleans? You are under oath."

Scottie begins to spill the beans. "Well, we remained silent about it because he paid us to be quiet. We have the right to be silent to the mayor that this particular councilman has been embezzling from the mayor's office for a long time, way before Mayor Aucoin took office there.

"We have the right to remain silent that there are several more of his employees doing the same thing.

"We have the right to remain silent about that the councilman was seeing this pretty boy and keeping him in his own apartment, before the wife was taken by us, so he knew what he had to do. And now, it isn't the same story.

"What else? We have the right to remain silent that his wife is hiding some pretty good tales herself. This quemas goes all the way to Nashville. THAT we remained silent on."

Oh, Gawd!

Court is in total mayhem at this point, and the judge can't ignore the facts without including himself. Monsieur Mayhem and True Blue don't have to do a damn thing, but they have prepared themselves for war, nonetheless.

The reporters go berserk, pushing each other out the way trying to go through the doors at the same time to write the stories that will appear on the front pages of every newspaper in the city, on Bayou Lafourche, and across the country. There is an investigation into the accusations, and they don't have to look long. It also includes the deeds and documents to prove the brazen means that have caused the

Lerouxs to lose a lot of money unlawfully to banks, to lawyers, and the people who want their land.

Justin and Scottie become wealthy again, and many people behind those schemes go to jail. You know, to the jails that house famous people, treated in the ways they are used to, with a nice bedroom (well, cell) to themselves, almost like a long vacation. Still running everything they can from jail.

Ain't this Loosiana?

∞ ∞ ∞

BACK on the bayou, Callie has to stay in bed most of the time, a very difficult pregnancy. Henri does a lot of his work from Minou and Joe's house. He keeps close tabs on what's happening in his office, giving his trusted friends the job to make sure nothing happens on their watch.

The councilman is arrested, along with his cronies, and all are given twenty-five years in the pen. The others are jailed in that infamous hotel too.

Henri has filled their positions with all supporters of his administration.

The village has heard that the woman, wife of the councilman, has to go home to her people. They also hear that she has come unglued, very much the mad hatter who's brought all kinds of hats to her poor relatives to wear for church. Her children want to hide her in a nursing home.

My, how the mighty have fallen.

Caldonia is delivered of a large, fine, black-haired baby girl. She is the replica of Minou. They will name her Minna Sue after MeMe Minou.

A wonderful time is being had on the bayou with a brand-new baby girl.

Callie has asked Scottie to be the parrain, and now they know they are true members of the followers-disciples-posse-village-coven-sistas-whatever. Flower is asked by Callie and Henri if she will be the nanan, and of course she is so excited at the request. Finally, Callie recognizes her as a full-bloomed flower.

Minna Sue gets all the attention of what's left of the Flower Power gang. Flower and Rowdy Dugas are going steady, being she's the oldest now. Their day will come.

Calm and peace are luxuries the family can't partake in. They know something else is coming down the road.

∞ ∞ ∞

JUSTIN and Scottie love the Rappolets as close neighbors. They are very talkative, and that's what they need right now. Talking, laughing, always good food. Junya and T-Mae are two realistic real people, Cajun to the bone. Both of them are truthful and have good common sense.

The Rappolets are hilarious, and you laugh at them, not because you're being mean but sincerely because they love to make you laugh, even sometimes laughing, but you don't know what's so damn funny. Good, good Cajuns with an awesome work ethic and simply stoic at what is being handed them in life.

Bastille III coming back to them after being raised by Gertie the wolf is the best thing ever happening in their lives. Their prayers are finally answered by the Good Lord. All along, they've been thinking he has been eaten by the pack of wolves.

Bastille III continues to be called Chief because he has chosen the name that Minou and Joe have given him. He lives with Minou and Joe, as he is going to school, and they have hired a school bus driver that uses his boat to transfer school children that live in the swamps. Chief excels in school, having been taught all the basics by the whole entourage. He has become very intelligent, with stealth-like behavior from being raised by wolves, being a wolf in his senses of the world.

Junya and T-Mae are so grateful for this family and are true-blue, faithful followers of the family and everyone connected.

Madam Alafair Aucoin comes often to have coffee with T-Mae. Seems as though T-Mae is going to have lessons in Voodoo training like Minou did all those years ago. It's surprising to both how some of these things are already part of T-Mae's learnings from all the women in her upbringing who have been teaching her while they knead dough. Two great-aunts that T-Mae has who are traiteurs convince Madam Aucoin she's also the real deal.

Charlotte and Pete Dugas and Rowdy, their son, have become good friends of Junya and T-Mae and all the little children. This is the family that has been introduced to the loup-garous in a tragic manner but joins the village after.

They know all about T-June because they ask a lot of questions and are right up there with Minou and Flavia in being nosy.

So, the swamps are full of people all the time but only ones that are invited, hence the electric fence and big-ass wolves guarding the fence. You still have to go by boat to get to the property, being it's five miles by boat from where Minou and Joe live. Even Alcide and Bertha now go there for their monthly howling at the moon, and the Rappolet family takes it like the laidback people they are. They invite Alcide and Bertha to spend the day and night with them before their changing. T-Mae will be there to give them their clothes when they're naked.

They have always believed in the Cajun werewolf but have never seen one in the process of turning from people you know to freaking monsters. Two of them, plus sometimes T-June too. So, on this night T-Mae makes a huge gumbo for everybody there to witness the occasion.

The werewolves love playing with the two older wolves, Gertie and Leroy, because they come too with everybody.

This life has become more normal for everyone, whatever's normal for some. This bunch isn't anywhere near the normal spectrum, and who knows what the hell is normal.

I don't think I would have anything in common with those normal people.

Minna Sue is carried from one set of arms to the other set of waiting arms. She is beloved and spoiled to the max. So far, there isn't anything happening with her like her older brother, True Blue. No signs of the strange abilities.

Thank Gawd!

∞ ∞ ∞

CALLIE brings news to the bayou that might affect all of them. She tells them about the woman that would have been on the top of her game but has fallen so far down the ladder rungs that she is forgotten by her so-called friends and can't climb back up. She has been arrested down there for stirring up trouble, and they think the insane asylum is going to be her next home. She is as crazy as the crazy gros bec loonie.

Callie continues with her gossip. "Y'all, they even had to take away her keys to her huge old Cadillac. She's been going up and down the roads trying to be the boss of all those country people. Because she was the beauty who made it big in New Orleans, those people still look up to her, even though she's left her mansion and bought a small shotgun house. Mama, I just don't trust this woman. Who the hell would warn us if she took it into her addled mind to come here?"

Minou and Bertha act like they're worried, but in truth, nothing too much bothers either one of them. They know what they have and how everybody gets involved in their shit.

T-Mae and Junya are busy making their gumbo for the evening. Alcide and Bertha are already there. They see this woman on the property just before dusk. Everybody runs out there, but she runs further into the swamp so they can't catch her. The family is alerted to be on the lookout for this woman wearing a big hat and a full-length mink coat. Nothing else on.

Justin and Scottie are preparing for a night of fun until this woman walks up on their stairs and into their house, carrying a gun. Wearing some broke-ass, red high heel shoes, with one heel completely gone, is how she presents herself, so high and mighty.

That John Wayne plane is going to crash and burn.

Both recognize her immediately, and they start talking to her in the fashion they always do, asking her politely to put the gun down. She is babbling nonsense and waving the gun in the air when she shoots one of the expensive windows out. They struggle with her for the gun and wrestle it from her hands.

Justin and Scottie have no idea how she's gotten to them, breaking through all the barriers put up for protection. She is screaming and laughing and making obscene gestures to the boys, then runs back out the door, her big hat and mink coat flapping, with her naked, floppy tetons in the wind. A truly haunted crazy woman is seen running out into the swamp.

Well, guess what happens. All this shit lands in Minou and Joe's lap, and what are they going to do?

I don't have to write another word about this bunch of mayhem.

Of course, the loup-garous are out there cavorting with the wolves while everybody is around a huge fire, smoking ganja and laughing. They don't think anything is funny when they see this woman running through the woods and begin to chase her. T-June has come to cavort too but changes back to himself. He can turn it off like that damn faucet.

The loup-garous are running after her, along with the two wolves, to no avail. They all try to catch her, but she runs faster than they can stop her, running into the deepest part of the swamp.

Oh, Gawd! She may be a haunted crazy woman dead ghost before too long. She might entice Gaspar the unfriendly ghost to come back and join her.

Fuck a duck. Them two together?

She runs so fast into the swamps. Good thing she has on her mink because of all the flying critters and briar patches and crunching pecans.

Well, the only one that hasn't made his appearance yet is about to. Pieyan the bigfoot comes walking toward her slowly, taking in her appearance and feeling her anguish. She stands and looks at Pieyan for a moment, then runs into his arms. He grabs her up and runs away with her into the deep end of the swamp.

Everyone sees this very strange sight indeed, not believing it. Some are taking pictures of this in case anyone comes to look for her or doesn't believe the happening.

T-June has one time taken Pieyan at midnight in the boat to the property five miles down the bayou. Pieyan loves it and refuses to leave, so he goes running to where the pecan trees stand in paradise. All-he-can-eat buffet. Pieyan doesn't know these critters, so he doesn't feel guilty eating them.

You know that the entire crew is there debating on what they truly need to do about the amazing happening. The village doesn't know what to do about the situation. She hasn't asked for help, so they are all just sitting in Minou's house.

Flavia for sure has her dollar to put in. "All dis time Ah almost didn't believe ya 'bout tha bigfoot 'cause it was private between ya two, and ya wouldn't lemme see him. Now ya tellin' me dat he kidnapped dis woman. What tha shit? We jus' shoot tha bastard and take her and put her in tha looney bin. It's jus' what needs to be done. He has a human bein' captured. Ah can't hardly believe right now what happened, and y'all know dat ain't me. Merde! Ah don't wanna even t'ink 'bout what he's doin' wit' her. Gawd! Lawd, Ah hope he ain't eatin' her right now."

Awww! I don't want that in my head either.

Minou begins to talk, shushing the rest. "What tha hell ya talkin' 'bout? Jus' shoot him, ya say? Dat ain't happenin', captain. He's been here forever, and he has helped us plenty. Pieyan is a true-blue friend of T-June, and he coulda eaten all of us if he had a cannibalistic bone in his giant body. We gonna let T-June handle all dis quemas!"

T-June goes to hollering and calling for Pieyan, but the bigfoot just ignores him.

T-June waits for three days for Pieyan to show up, calling for him every day after this happens. The Lerouxs and the Rappolets are searching for his lair, but they don't want to go any further without T-June being there. They aren't on a first-name basis with Pieyan. They have no idea what the bigfoot will do to them if they come up on him by accident. They know he lives here, but they don't mess with him, and he doesn't mess with them.

Leave well enough alone.

Now it's different and urgent because he's got a human woman who looks like she wants him and goes willingly.

After the fifth day, Pieyan comes out with the woman. The beauty and the beast. Pieyan and Belle (I named her!) come to the clearing where T-June has waited every day since this happened.

Pieyan tells T-June in a loud voice, "Man! You know I didn't do anything wrong. Get all those humans to leave us alone. She's got something to say to you, my Belle, and as you can see, she's calm and quiet."

Belle speaks up to T-June, wearing her fur coat and floppy-ass hat and big tetons. "I love him. He loves me more than anybody ever has. I don't want to leave him."

What a revolting development this is, as they used to say on The Life of Riley.

Gawd, I hope they don't have a baby because it would be some ugly.

T-June watches as they both go back into the swamp, with Pieyan telling him, "See you later, alligator." Then he goes back home while everybody is waiting the entire time. June speaks up because, after all, he's why they all are here.

"We're going to let them be. I heard out of Miss Belle's own mouth that she wants to stay with him. Y'all, we can't let her live out there in the elements, even though she is not a nice person. She's a human being who deserves better. So, y'all know what I'm talking about? We're going to build them a house."

No one can believe what has just come out of his mouth, and they're showing their outrage at the decision. But it's going to happen because T-June says it will, and he's not one to say no to.

Another treehouse is being built for the very unusual – to say the least – couple. They are using the Lerouxs' house plans but a little taller. Big enough for Pieyan, who's never lived anywhere but the swamps.

Minou finds out how to get ahold to Belle's sister, telling her she is being taken care of by her new boyfriend and he's building a new house just for her.

Belle's sister says, "Well, she's gone back to being high-faluting, and for sure she didn't want me in New Orleans. What's the difference?"

So, Minou has to tell Belle her sister doesn't want to see them anymore. That being taken care of, Minou and the sistas start helping Belle pick out furniture for her new home. This bunch doesn't hold grudges. They believe if you have to maintain your heart to holding onto shit, it's living rent free in your heart. Kick it out for not paying rent. They just have no time to waste on such foolishness.

Belle hasn't changed her taste for expensive items, but sometimes they aren't practical for living in the air. She loses interest after they make her change her mind.

Minou says, "Awww, no. Awww, no. She ain't havin' bettah furniture, bettah dan mine. Come on, y'all. She still has dat uppity way of lookin' at tha world and who in tha hell would be livin' wit' a bigfoot, so....Shit, she bettah take a long look at herself before she starts pointin' fingers."

The treehouse goes up fast, but it takes forever for furniture to be delivered. Then getting up a flight of steps with the damn furniture. Pieyan takes care of that in no time, carrying huge pieces under one arm and the other.

Well, they settle in the trees, and first thing you know, Pieyan is out there telling everybody, "Good morning, all you humans. Y'all are going to have to tell me your names."

What the shit?

So, now the stories go on and on and on and on…

Chapter Eighteen

The Dugases' Dilemma

CHARLOTTE Dugas has been chosen to be the principal at St. Luke's parochial high school. She is straightforward and a no-nonsense kind of gal, although she is known by the family to be an expert at telling fairy tales that are not so true. That lie saves the family in a way, and it slips out her mouth like butter.

So, it is proven to the families that she is a devout follower in T-June's entourage. Since she knows for sure about Alcide and Bertha, she is very nonchalant, and her calmness now soothes the others in all of their quemas.

Pete is bringing in more and more customers to the shop he works for, so he decides to open his own business, doing every job from the littlest to the humongous big, which takes care of all the business for the families that have changed his life forever.

Pete and Charlotte, having gone to school with Joseph (T-June) and Jolie, think the sun rises on T-June and will fight to the death for their podnah. They were the only two true-blue friends the Dugases had during school. And now as grown-ups they feel the same.

Pete and Alcide are still best buds, after the tragedy that happened on the night on the full moon. They now play a weekly game of bourré at Alcide's house with several other players for a huge pot of money on the game. They all are big gamblers in this card game and horribly aggressive when they throw down four aces. Pete will throw the cards and cuss with every hand, a Dr. Jekyll and Mr. Hyde change in his demeanor.

Rowdy Dugas, that's another story. Their only child is now a senior at St. Luke's. Flower is a sophomore there. They have been going steady for two years and are very devoted to each other. When you see one, the other is not far behind.

Irene and Jean Breaux are Flower's parents; Irene gave birth to her late in life. Flower has been a source of entertainment since she was born, and everything that happens along the way is all right with them.

It has been the Flower Power gang of Callie, Lily, and Flower, until Weedie is added to the mix. The flower power has wilted a bit since Callie and Lily have up and gotten married.

Weedie Miller is the one who has premonitions, but she doesn't come from T-June's lineage. While Butch and T-June call each other "brother," they are not kin. Weedie just has always had those premonitions. Maybelline and True have come along with them too. Now, Maybelline doesn't get it from anybody's lineage, but you throw in Madam Aucoin, and well, there you have it. A mystery solved.

Weedie had shown her ability very young, when she calls Toussaint Laverne out for being a spade. "Mucho, mucho mojo." Of course, now Weedie loves him madly, and he cuts her hair a certain way that nobody on the bayou will do to fulfill her wishes. Y'all can imagine any cut that would not be a mama and papa's wishes, but her parents believe in giving complete freedom to express who you are. Well, they sure don't know who she's going to be.

On Rowdy's graduation party night, Flower goes and finds Minou. "Miss Minou, I have to talk to you about something. I cannot tell Mama and Dad, but I'm three months pregnant. Please, even Rowdy doesn't know. I just don't know what to do."

What did I tell you?

Minou tells her to be at her house the next morning and then finds Madam in the crowd, asking her to come the next morning too.

The two older and wiser women are talking to the girl that will be a woman sooner than she needs to be. Madam Aucoin, drinking her coffee and lighting her ganja pipe, says, "Bébé, awww, so young, bébé.

Yahweh baby, I am not judging you. Ma cher, my own mama had me when she was fourteen.

"Sometimes the girls are old enough in their minds, thinking she'll take having a baby in stride. Probably because she's taken care of her siblings. A woman who is a wonderful mother, one that is born that way, with motherly genes. Some aren't, and for their own reasons, they choose to flush out the fertile happening. Absolutely no judgment there either.

"Sweet-smelling Flower, you have two things to ponder on for a few days, but I think you need to tell Rowdy."

Rowdy is a star and excels in everything he does, be it the captain of the football team or the star character in a play. He has huge scholarships from many colleges he wants to excel at too. His life is full of opportunities, but Flower's announcement will be a huge surprising surprise. He's getting the best event in his life, another star event, one he's not ready for and doesn't want.

Isn't it that way, too much of the time? One that shouldn't be a surprise, given what they been doing. Yeah.

Flower has said in no way will she abort this baby. She wants to be married and have this baby.

Of course, Rowdy stands up to his responsibility, and they have a small wedding, but it isn't a celebration. It is a duty. Not as bad as Maybelline and Laray's wedding, but it is like her duty too.

They move into Irene and Jean's house until other arrangements for a house can be made. Irene and Jean are ecstatic about the news, having another baby in their home, and they will do everything for the arrival of their grandchild. They aren't upset in the timing and don't care how old Flower is.

You know she's been a star in their home her whole life, so whatever Flower wants, Flower gets.

But Rowdy is showing another side of him, the one that feels his life is ruined. Since the time they started their romance, he's never acted in this way. He is always so tender and loving, taking Flower wherever he goes.

The village people believe that they will be together in their lives, but now there's a kink in Rowdy and Flower's plans for that life. When they move into her parents' house, Rowdy won't touch Flower at all. He tells her he's afraid that her mama and dad will hear them.

This goes on until he decides to go to Loyola University for his college education to become a star lawyer in the city. The couple then move in with Callie and Henri and True Blue and little Minna Sue in their mansion on St. Charles. Rowdy is very happy there, being he loves Louisiana history. He explores every corner and cranny of the big house.

Rowdy loves True Blue and Minna Sue, and he'll play for hours with the baby girl. Flower, seeing this, feels like he's coming back. He becomes more like he used to be, enjoying lovemaking once again, but he's still distant with Flower. She knows better, that closeness is gone.

∞ ∞ ∞

ROWDY and Flower go with the Aucoins to the Bon Temps Rouler to watch the Monsieur Mayhem Band one Saturday night. Everyone is enjoying the night except for Rowdy. He is looking like there may be someone here, because he is preoccupied watching the crowd.

He dances with Flower to a romantic tune from long ago, "Tell It Like It Is" by Art Neville. They are enjoying the dance and laughing and him pulling her closer, then all of a sudden, he decides to end the dance, leading Flower back to the table. Such a strong tie between them, but it's steadily going south.

She looks around the crowd and sees an older – like twenty-five-year-old – woman sitting at the bar staring holes in her and lusting after Rowdy.

Flower has never been someone to sit docile and is demanding to know who she is. Rowdy just blows the conversation off, saying she is someone who takes the same classes at Loyola. Well, Flower tells him she wants to meet her, calling him on his lie.

They walk together to where this beauty is sitting, staring like she is going to battle.

"Flower, this is Celeste Blanchard from Thibodaux. She's a history and Louisiana politics major. She wants to be a historical researcher and investigator for the state.

"Celeste, this is Flower, my wife. Y'all excuse me. I have to go see a man about a horse."

Every man's escape without confrontation.

Celeste laughs at that like it is her first time hearing the saying. Flower doesn't think anything is funny and comes right to the point.

"Celeste, you must be older than my husband. Just what are your plans, and do they include my husband?"

Point blank. You go, girl.

Celeste is looking very surprised. She isn't expecting anything out of Flower's mouth. You know, like being young and dumb and from the swamps.

Celeste, being the type not to beat around the sticker bush, tells her, "Since you're being so blunt with your questions, I will tell you up front. I'm coming for him, and you'll have a battle with me."

Flower should show her "the hand" and slap the Bejesus out of her. Instead, she tells Celeste, "Girl, you have no idea who I am, and if a battle is what you want, you for sure will get one. Don't take me as some country bumpkin. This is a battle you will lose."

All of this is said very quietly, while Rowdy still hasn't come back.

Flower turns and walks away from the encounter, and Celeste leaves shortly after, not saying a word to Rowdy.

All the entourage present watches this like an unfolding movie, knowing what is going down. When Rowdy returns, Flower demands he take her home, not wanting to say a thing to him about Celeste, wanting to slap the Bejesus out of him too.

This begins the tremendous turmoil in their marriage that lasts for years.

∞ ∞ ∞

ROWDY begins to stay out all night and comes sneaking in the back door, like no one knows what the shit is going on. After the fourth time he does it, Flower demands he move out, and Celeste is there, welcoming Rowdy into her spider web.

Rowdy comes to visit and to check on Flower, but she never invites him back into their bed.

The Dugases are infuriated with him, and Pete tells him he is coming to beat his ass. They are horrified at his behavior, telling him it's not how he was raised. To no avail.

When it becomes time for Flower to give birth to her son, Rowdy is there for the birthing, while Celeste waits in the lobby with all the men.

That's what you call a lot of nerve.

Rowdy comes out with the women who've witnessed the birth, strutting like the proverbial rooster, handing out cigars with blue bands on them, but he doesn't buy a bouquet of flowers for Flower.

Celeste goes to speak with Charlotte, who throws her hand out. "You better back way off."

There is a huge celebration at the home of the mayor and his wife. Henri tells Rowdy there is no way he's bringing Celeste into their home, so Rowdy chooses not to come.

Flower agrees to a legal separation, but divorce is out the question. Both of them have a Catholic upbringing, and they don't believe in divorces, the general consensus being it's a wife's duty to stand by her man. You make your bed, then lay in it, suffering for the Blessed Mother.

And using the rhythm method for birth control, looky here, all y'all. We raising good little Catholic children.

Flower comes out of her confinement with a huge bang. She has been enjoying her life separated from her husband and gets a real good job with the mayor's office. In spite of being so young, she does her job very well. Henri for sure knows what kind of person she is, even being young. Good work ethic and a smile on her face all the time. Being smarter than most of these civil servants.

She disarms even the toughest broad in the office. Other women, being old-timers, think they can push her around.

You know how it is when there's more than two women in the office. First thing you know, everybody is lining up with their cycles and some serious cat fights.

Single men are looking at her with plenty interest, like they're saying, Who is this woman and where did she come from? And now she's looking back with an interested demeanor. She is loving her full-blown, grown-up beauty and flirts back but has no intention of divorcing Rowdy.

Celeste has won the battle but hasn't fought the war. Flower just lets her think it's over, but in truth, she ain't seen nothing yet.

Flower names her son Jean (T-Jean) after her dad, and you would think he's the proud papa. She never asks Rowdy what he wants. She looks at the child being only hers, with him just being the sperm donor.

She visits the Dugases often. Flower wants Rowdy's parents to know their grandchild, because he might be the only one.

Flower has been with the family for years and is treated like family. Charlotte and Pete love Flower like the daughter they never had and are so grateful for her loyalty to them.

Rowdy can't come to their house.

They are all sitting at the kitchen table (like these people don't sit anywhere else), and Charlotte begins to talk with her. "My love, my love, never did I imagine that something like this would happen. Never, ever thinking he was capable of this. I am so angry and disappointed in my son. I don't even want to talk with him, and neither does Pete. I'm going to say something to you that I want you to know. This will be crystal clear. I want you to go out and explore the world you live in and have fun yourself."

Flavia and Irene, Flower's mama, are close friends. When Flavia comes for coffee when Flower is visiting her mama, she has to pipe up. "Flower, girl, ya need to pull up yo big lady draws and deal wit' his lil arrogant ass. Are ya gettin' chile support? Don't sit back and let him do all his shit to ya. Ya cannot take dis shit from him no more. Start dishin' out tha same treatment and see what he does den. Dat bitch t'inks she's won. Well, baby, not by a long shot. Ah done investigations into her background.

You know she did and more.

"And lemme tell ya, she sure ain't no angel. Dis is kinda her MO. Get dem when dey young and dey sowin' wild seeds and gaga over her well-seasoned body. Well, we know 'bout dat, sowing tha seeds for sure. She has affairs, bustin' up any relationship she can, and den she t'rows tha dude to tha curb, when a younger, more pliable young man comes along.

"Ya know Ah love Rowdy so much, but Ah sure as shit don't like him."

Flower and T-Jean go back to the city after getting all this pep talk from the important women in her life. She does a lot of pondering in the car while "I Will Survive" by Gloria Gaynor plays on the radio. T-Jean starts clapping and trying to sing the song. Sounds like T-Jean will be on his mama's side forever.

That Monday morning, Flower comes in to work at the mayor's office looking like a woman who's ready for whatever happens. She is beautiful.

I mean, aren't all the women that way in my stories?

She has natural blond hair and curls that flow down her back. A ponytail is how she wears her hair forever, but a change is coming, and it's coming quickly.

∞ ∞ ∞

ROWDY is living with Celeste now in her large condo and going to classes from there, as it isn't that far to campus. He leaves his brand-new truck, a graduation gift from Pete and Charlotte, for Flower to use because she needs it more. Good thing because he would have run it to the ground or wrecked it chasing behind some little floozy.

He is having second thoughts about this arrangement and misses Flower, as she is his best friend. He truly misses her younger body, although Celeste is a master in lovemaking and is constantly using her

Kama Sutra book like she is cooking from it, because she sure as hell doesn't cook.

Rowdy has gotten over the fantasy every man has dreamed, to make love to an older woman. Celeste is way too experienced and wants to do it every day or night. He is tee-totally drained.

When he visits his son and Flower, who is very cold to him and doesn't want to know about his life, he grieves the friendship gone.

Celeste drives him there and sits in the car, honking her horn if he's too long, according to her.

Rowdy is now looking at this full-grown woman Flower, who has blossomed after the birth of baby Jean. He is dying to hold her and to release all this passion he has for her.

Tough titty said the kitty, um, Flower.

Flower has definitely caught the attention of the most eligible bachelor lawyer working for the mayor. Older, he's thirty and a very handsome Creole, Jerome Anthony Mont-Pellier III. Old money he comes from, plus he's a lawyer with influence all over the state.

Jerome has fallen in love with her in a matter of a few days. He wants to devour her freshness. It's so strange to him, comparing her to the jaded and cynical women he is surrounded by.

Jerome loves Jean. He takes him to parks, the zoo and the aquarium, to every hamburger joint in the city, playgrounds, and Chuck E. Cheese. He can't believe he loves Jean so much. He doesn't care for any of the nieces or nephews he's got, and his sisters are busy sticking their noses in everybody's business and not tending to their own.

He convinces Flower he can get an annulment for her and Rowdy's marriage. He tells her it could be like Jean would be a bastard son, if they go the way of annulling the marriage, but he will take care of that by marrying her and taking Jean as his son and changing his name to Mont-Pellier right now.

Awww, shit! You know how lawyers are. It's their job to convince people.

Nobody is ready for that, and for sure, everybody has to have their hands in the pot.

"Girl, what Ah tole ya. What Ah tole ya. You a fool not to jump on dat wit' four feet, countin' Jean's. Baby, yo life will become one of luxury, wealth, and a surefire way for Jean to inherit all his money. His people are old-time rich, and he has no chirren. Girl, ya crazy in tha head if ya don't."

Who do you think said that? Yes, it's Flavia.

Bishop Toussaint stands, and the room gets quiet, even Charlotte and Pete, who are all for it. "Flower, you have no idea what you would be getting into. A family who is hard-shelled Baptist and very conservative. They have been running the city since the Civil War, and a more uppity bunch you couldn't find. They will tear you to pieces.

"It may be that he isn't close to them, but I wouldn't count on that. Every picture of him has his three sisters and his mother in it, since he is their only son and the baby of the family full of girls.

"Don't do this in retaliation, because that causes unnecessary anger and hurt, and then it becomes tit-for-tat between you and Rowdy.

"Do you love Jerome? If you have that kind of love, well, that's something else, but don't think it will be sunshine, because they will rain on you. It will be hell for you, coming from those women. I'm sure his mama and sisters already know you're coming, and they will have their claws ready."

Flavia can't shut up. "Ah wish dey would. Ah wish dey would. Dey got no idea neither who dey foolin' wit'. Baby, don't let dem bitches win, addin' to tha bitches' table one Miz Celeste. If ya love him, nuttin' will stand in y'all's way, but make sure it's love and not downright lust."

In his defense, Rowdy has always been a perfect young man, with good grades to achieve anything he goes after. Now, his grades are slipping so bad he's in danger of losing all of his scholarships. Rowdy has always been good and kind and helpful until he goes to New Orleans and runs into an honest-to-God siren. It looks like someone else has stepped into his body and out comes Mr. Hyde.

Celeste is slowly getting tired of him, and he's ready to leave her anyway but can't move back to his parents. They won't accept him, and Flower is acting like she's in a very serious relationship.

He does the next best thing. He goes to T-June and Jolie.

He is with Monsieur Mayhem when he gets the news from the front page of The Times-Picayune.

Rowdy has been there a month when Flower and Jerome announce their engagement. Now, he is frantic as to what he can do besides calling and dropping in and begging.

Seeing the paper herself, Celeste has decided she isn't through with him. She calls so excited to tell Rowdy some wonderful news. She is finally having her first baby at twenty-seven years old.

And it's his.

This boy ain't shooting duds.

This breaks Rowdy, and he isn't capable of anything, so Irene and Pete come and get him. He drops out of college, begins to drink and smoke serious pot, shut up in his old room so depressed that everybody is on a suicide watch, following every move he makes.

In the meantime, Flower and her five bridesmaids are marching closer and closer to the date. Weedie will be the bride's maid of honor along with Lily; the other three are all Jerome's sisters.

It's unbelievable how many bridal showers she has. Weedie and Lily and the female bunch of the bayou come to every one, trying to keep tabs on all the presents they can't keep up with.

Weedie says they just need to write one note, "Thanks and we all passed a good time." Print it and mass produce, handing everyone one before they walk out the door.

Weedie's mind is way out there, believe me, and somewhat – downright – scary. She is broken-hearted concerning Rowdy because she didn't see this coming, and her gift is the real deal. Love tends to make you look out of rose-colored glasses and forget to look for the real world.

Rowdy is awakened one morning by Pete and Charlotte and told to come in the living room. He just grabs his coffee.

Pete tells him to please sit and look at him. He stands over his son. "We love ya so much, and we woulda never turned ya down, even if we wanted to kill ya. But son, it's time for ya to pick up tha pieces and get it together. The courage to face down two loup-garous, ya sure made me proud when you was but thirteen. Just brazen, brave in protectin' bofe of us. Where's dat boy, son?"

Rowdy turns to go in his room, pouting and playing the victim, when Pete backhands him out of the chair into the middle of the living room floor, hollering, "Snap out of it, boy! Do ya t'ink for one minute Jean Breaux wouldn't love to come here and beat tha living shit outta ya? He has a legitimate beef to settle. Ya want me to backhand ya again?"

Rowdy can't believe this is happening. He's been spoiled by his mama and pop, getting everything he wants. Never, ever, ever has his father ever put his hands on him in anger, for sure not that first slap in his entire life. That's enough to make someone snap to reality.

After the confrontations, everybody calms down, for sure Rowdy. The family is sitting and talking about reality and steps he can take to get his family back, when someone pulls up, screeching tires and running over Charlotte's bottle tree. The driver can't seem to get themselves out the car door.

After they get Celeste out, she hits the dirt. She is some drunk and starts screaming at the top of her voice, "I see you up in there. Quit hiding and come out like a man. You think I'm going to let you get away with this? This baby is yours, and I need help because I'm so sick. I know all about you people, and I know enough to turn you into the police."

Well, guess what. Charlotte Dugas gets on the phone. The women are there in minutes, surrounding the drunk-ass Celeste. Minou and Flavia are in the lead.

Charlotte speaks very calmly to the brokedown whore, who is telling the truth or not. "You have the audacity to show up at our home? I'm going to tell you what is about to happen, and you have no say in the matter at all. Rowdy isn't leaving this yard, and we're getting ready to take you someplace."

Celeste throws up, thinking she's going to be thrown to the alligators for food.

Flavia is at her side, while Minou pushes a hidden water gun up against Celeste's ribs, saying "Get to steppin'! Ah mean bizness."

The others are peeing their draws, laughing at one of the bluffs that's been made perfect over the years.

The three women take her to the hospital, and Flavia goes to the desk, saying she wants to see the doctor. ASAP.

In no uncertain terms and in no time, the doctor opens the doors to them, and they proceed to go straight to the maternity ward, dragging the drunk who is screaming obscenities. Flavia tells the doctor they want the works checked on her, and it doesn't matter if she protests. "Ya gonna do it."

Damn, Flavia is well connected, when you can tell the doctor what to do, instead of the other way. This would be unlawful some other place, but when you're as powerful as these families, he does what is asked of him.

The doctor finally comes out to speak to the women. "Mrs. Flavia, this woman can't get pregnant. She has none of her equipment. She has had many abortions, and it caused her to have to take everything out because she was cancerous. Only thing wrong with her is she is an alcoholic and has cirrhosis of the liver. She fought us every single step, even being drunk, and I'm worried that when she goes back, we will have enormous lawsuits and may go to jail.

"A most unpleasant woman and she sure knows some mighty wicked cuss words, very inventive. Let her sleep it off, and I'll call as soon as she is sober."

The women get home and immediately start to telling the tale about the wanton woman, and they have paperwork to prove everything. They don't give a fuck about a lawsuit.

Meanwhile, back at home, Rowdy is nervous, walking the floor and contemplating what he will say to her. He truly loves Flower and their son. He's got a lot of work to do. He has to find some humility and beg for forgiveness. He is flabbergasted when told the news about Celeste. "Y'all have all saved me. I am so ashamed in how I acted, and

I beg for forgiveness. Now I have to start working on stopping a wedding."

Weedie is in the front yard taunting her as Celeste shows up in a cab the next day to get back to her car. Weedie laughingly says, "You sure as hell have lost the war. You better get off this bayou. You are so stupid, you've never met women like our bunch. We are gorillas in this fight."

Flavia says, "Woman, if ya even t'inkin' 'bout suin' us, den you'll have more trouble dan ya can imagine. Just take yo well-worn ass outta here."

The conniving Celeste gets her keys, saying nothing back, and just drives off back to where she came from.

∞ ∞ ∞

TWO days later, Rowdy is given the keys of Pete's truck. The truck is years older than the new one they've given him for high school graduation.

Rowdy pulls up at Henri and Callie's house and rings the bell for entrance. He is always welcomed there. They think he is coming to see his son.

When Rowdy sees Flower, he goes to her lips first and grabs her into his arms. "My precious Flower, I don't know how you would bloom into this ravishing beauty and be quick to take care of yourself. You've grown up better than me. But that's not what I'm pleading for. I've lost the best friend I will ever have. I'm begging for forgiveness on my knees and implore you to take me back. It's not too late. I want to be the husband who will never do anything to hurt you again. Please, baby, give me another chance."

Rowdy is crying uncontrollably, and Flower, seeing this, falls back in love with her former best friend.

They go upstairs to finish the reunion and stay for hours, while Jean runs all over the house, playing with Minna Sue and Nonc True Blue.

Flower has to go to Jerome's house to explain the situation. He is inconsolable too.

"My love, my Flower, I can't live without you and Jean. I've already put him as my heir, and of course, I've done the same thing for you. That's how sure I am, certain you love me that much too.

"Please think this through and take all the time you need to figure it out. Will you leave the one who loves you and go back to the one you love? I'm pleading with you to choose me. I'll fight him for your hand."

Flower is so upset at his reaction that she goes to bed with him too. He makes love to her like his life depends on it, very emotional and raw. He's completely trying to change her mind. Ohhh, Flower's kinda acting like she has no qualms, when she goes to bed with two men on the same day.

Talk about a whole lot of fucking for true going on.

Flower gets into the truck and drives off while Jerome is on the front porch crying out her name. The maid next door sees the whole thing while taking out the trash. She starts crying too because it is so heartbreaking, seeing this powerful man turn to mud. Something she will never forget, an epiphany in her life, seeing how the rich people deal with love in the same manner as the poor.

Rowdy moves back in the Aucoins' home and starts working on what a husband and father should do. Flower hands in her resignation and never goes back to the mayor's office. Henri takes her written document and is happy for the couple.

Jerome Mont-Pellier has stopped coming to his job and resigns too.

Everything is going like it should until two months later. Jerome Mont-Pellier puts a gun in his mouth and kills himself dead. He sees himself as a broken-down older man who can't hold on to the beautiful being of Flower.

No one sees that coming, since he is a worldly man and popular, with confidence just dripping out of every pore.

Weedie, the foreseer of things to come, says to Rowdy, "Bro, this isn't over yet. Plenty more is coming down the bayou for you and

Flower. Shame on you for causing all this quemas because you couldn't keep your pants zipped.

"Dude, you got a lot to prove to me. You think you're acting like a tiger, and now you're just a whipped puppy. If you don't believe me, well, we'll get Maybelline to tell you how the wind is blowing."

Rowdy has taken the role of being a very sheepish man who has done wrong.

When isn't it all the same shit coming down the road?

Flower really throws a bomb into the quemas when she tells Rowdy she is pregnant again. She will have this baby, regardless of who the father is.

Of course, the family is in turmoil, using the F-word, saying it's a big, big quemas. The Mont-Pelliers are having the same reaction. The eldest sister is a bona fide bitch in every way possible. She calls and tells Flower, "You little whore. Did you really believe it's the last time you would hear from us? Well, you little piss-weed, you better get ready for a fight in court. We have the police looking into everything at my baby brother's house, and we found a note saying everything is yours and your little bastard's. What did you do to get that? Probably something so obscene that I as a Christian woman would never do.

"We have found enough evidence to convict you of murder, along with your ex-husband, because you have never bothered to get married again, just shacking up. You don't even have the morals of an alley cat in heat.

"The mayor's house, no less. That goes to show you what kind of man he is. No morals, and I know he's all up in the Voodoo practices of his infamous aunt, Madam Alafair Aucoin. And she hasn't an ounce of morals."

Sanctimonious, uppity people don't know a thing about morals.

"The police will be knocking on your door any minute. And now we find out you're pregnant, and you don't know who the baby's daddy is. How lowborn can you get! You little country whore, have a nice day."

Flower thinks Jerome's sister will never shut the fuck up; she gets the distinct impression that all those Baptist, hoity-toity twisted sisters, as well as their mother, are listening to everything being said by the sister, because Flower can't get a word in. All of the sisters and the mama keep praising her in how she handles the situation.

Flavia is there at the time and redials the number because she knows the Mont-Pellier sisters are waiting for Flower to call back to beg and plead to her. Jerome's oldest sister is probably thinking Flower will beg her to stop everything, the vengeful pointing fingers and accusations of the uppity bitch trash, and listen up to her.

They for sure are after the inheritance bestowed on the people the Mont-Pelliers call "that whore and the bastard." Waiting on the news as to who this new baby is for. Then they may be coming with machine guns to take the child.

Irene and Flavia come up to New Orleans to stay until this is taken care of. The Big Easy name has been far from the truth, not being easy on anyone that has come here from Bayou Lafourche.

Flavia reaches the sister immediately, like she has just lit a cigarette, waiting. "Aww, ya crazy, dreamin' woman. Who died and made ya tha boss? You a certified dyed-in-the-wool uppity high-yellow bitch, and dat's yo own people callin' ya dat. Ya bettah go lookin' for a clue in what ya gonna deal wit' when we come for you. Ya bettah put a goddam lock on y'all's closets, 'cause Ah got as much pull as you got, and Ah'm goin' lookin' to clean dem out."

Flavia hands the phone to Irene, who says, "Don't ya ever call dis number again. Ah'll put a restrainin' order on yo ass so fast, you'll be tha one dat don't know what's goin' to be done to ya next. Read 'bout all us, lots of details, and den come wit' all tha barrels of guns ya got. If ya know dis first, ya might know what kinda people ya dealing wit'.

"Oh, by tha way, no police here will come for Flower. Ya t'ink ya got it in tha bag? Ya ain't got a clue."

That was good night, Irene!

Irene slams the phone so hard it might have lasting repercussions, causing the bitch to become hard of hearing. It's what is called "how the cow ate the cabbage."

Our women are downright invincible Cajun crusaders who aren't afraid to take anything on, like Samson and Del...no, I mean, Goliath for the underdog. They will tell you who you are dealing with and from the start, back the fuck up.

The Mont-Pelliers send the police on a wild goose chase down the bayou, thinking Flower and Rowdy with Jean are hiding in the swamps. It's the same two cops who have taken down the Tuxedo gang.

When they see the same people who have wanted to kill them, they leave quickly. "We don't want to have to deal with this bunch of coonasses.

I shudder at having to put that word down.

"We want no part of it."

They tell the Mont-Pellier family that they refuse the job. So, the Mont-Pelliers start a huge civil suit against Flower and Rowdy, unlike any that has come before in the courtrooms of New Orleans. They want the new baby's DNA right now. They are praying in church with out-loud testimony that has the congregation standing in the aisles calling for prayers to be answered right now, that it's Jerome's son.

Flower has all the Flower Power women up in there for the test. Weedie is using Mexican cuss words, daring any of his sisters to even open the door of the room.

When they find out the results, Flower is very stoic about it all, saying it's her baby, and Rowdy will love it regardless, even though it's Jerome Mont-Pellier's son.

Flavia jumps in with both barrels blasting. She is doing just what she says she is going to do, and damn if she doesn't pull out of those closets some mighty serious things and good to add to the evidence they have.

During all this quemas going on, Flower delivers a nine-pound baby boy who looks like a spitting image of Jerome. Flower names him Jerome Anthony Mont-Pellier IV. She honors the wonderful man he was, who deserved it. They will call him Tony.

Gawee!

Jerome's sisters and their mama raise three kinds of hell because of that. They believe Flower is doing that to really claim all the money and the public's sympathy to make it one of those things that gets on the front page of The Times-Picayune. This bunch of judging women wants to sweep this under the proverbial – antique – rug. To let the sordid affair of their brother having an illegitimate son from a very sordid hook-up with a "lowborn whore."

The Mont-Pelliers sure as shit should have listened to the warnings! They sure as shit should have not brought that huge civil suit against Flower.

∞ ∞ ∞

THE docket for the case is finally called, and the houses bought in New Orleans are filled to the brim with all the bayou people coming for this date. They want to show all the support they have for Flower and Rowdy. Almost filling the courtroom, leaving not too many seats for the huge crowd that comes for this.

The reporters and news channels have to use the upstairs balcony, along with the photographers taking a one-of-a-kind picture and selling it to the highest bidder.

Flavia has to be stopped before she gets to them and wreaks havoc on the whole crew.

It starts with the judge banging his gavel on his desk. Well, it could go either way at this time, being he is the closest friend to Jerome; they grew up together.

He's also a staunch supporter of Henri Aucoin.

Joe Thibeau says, "Well, ya know it could be dis way or dat way. Ya never know."

The lawyers for the Mont-Pellier family are beating the shit out of Flower and Rowdy. Just points against her for being a fallen woman, a golddigger, and for killing Jerome, holding his son as ransom.

There are many objections, but they are able to put that idea in the jury's heads before they stop.

OKAY!

Now comes the time for Flower's lawyers, the best that money could buy with Flavia's pull. They're the ones with some blinking billboards all up and down the major highways, advertising who they are.

I'm not going to name them.

The lawyers go to work on their side of the story and are ready with many questions for Flower.

Defending herself has some of the jury dabbing at their eyes. The lawyers go for the jugular veins of the above-it-all accusers. Then, when the secret is revealed, the courtroom goes wild, sending the reporters dashing out the doors with their scoops.

It is revealed to the court that the sisters know all about whores. Turns out the sisters run the biggest whorehouse in the Big Easy; their father willed it to them. They're the fourth generation in the business of selling flesh. Since Storyville was legal.

The judge is shown the note that Jerome writes before he scatters his brains all over his bed. The sisters have made up the whole thing and faked a suicide note.

Flower has the real thing; he sends it to her by FedEx the same day he shoots himself dead. Flower's lawyer says he's going to read it to the court, stating that this indeed is Jerome's writing.

"My beautiful Flower, growing in my garden for a little while.

I take Jean as my natural born son. I love him as my own.

Thank you for bringing the best gift I have ever received.

You have made them the happiest days of my life.

Please take your family back to the bayous where you will never a money problem and have the peace you

brought to me.

Something has been revealed to me this night, and in shame I will end my life for the huge amount of

shame brought on by my family.

Our father has made great strides in keeping me ignorant of the thriving whoremongers that we are.

I love you, Flower, with every beat of my heart. It's not you that has cost me anything but real love.

Live a good life, my beloved.

Jerome

Everyone in the courtroom is crying and blowing noses, including the judge and two of the lawyers for the sisters' side. The judge bangs his gavel, saying to arrest the Mont-Pellier women, every last one of them.

Come to find out, the mama has been the madam and former top whore in the Mont-Pelliers' house of ill repute, and their daddy married her.

All this money begins to be deposited in three secure safety boxes in the Bank of Larose. Nobody is questioning where this pile of money comes from. They already know.

Chapter Nineteen

Madam's Nephew's Nephew

THIS little character is named Harley Aucoin, and he is the great-nephew of Madam Aucoin's great-nephew and the son of Henri's youngest brother, Saul. Harley is an only child and has been brought up to believe he hung the moon. He is twenty years old, and all hands are on board raising this man to adulthood.

He is a sneaky, full-of-mischief, cantankerous know-it-all, all his life. Harley thinks, sadly, that he knows everything and the old folks don't know shit.

Saul, Harley's dad, is gang leader of the biggest motorcycle club in Louisiana. All of the members are successful, rich men, mostly the men that make up the 100 Black Men organizations. Their motto is, "Help the unfortunate." They all ride regally through the Big Easy, wearing black and gold, riding on huge bikes that cost plenty money and calling themselves the Saints. Never will you see this gang acting all tough and mean and causing havoc wherever they go.

The Roux Garouxs are another big and prominent motorcycle gang in New Orleans, made up of criminals, either going in or getting out the pen. Nobody can teach them the concept of being sober.

Eli St. James, their leader, has been very lax in memberships. He really doesn't care since the murder of his son.

There has been a turf war since before Harley was born between the Roux Garouxs and the Saints, starting when the gang leader's son,

Eli Junior, was killed by a gun. He was a Roux and next in line for his daddy's crown. They've never found out who shot the gun, because both gangs are told "no guns."

Since that time there's been a hard question as to who shot the boy, but the Rouxs blame the Saints, no matter what Saul Aucoin said, professing his innocence. They have hated each other since.

As Harley has grown, he's learned how to ride his dad's Fat Boy Harley. Now he is a daredevil on the same bike. What he hasn't done is something he hasn't learned about yet.

Harley is well known in the Tremé as being so confident in himself that he will try awesome, downright scary things with his stunts, all over the city, and gets paid very well. He's cocky as hell but with a grinning smile all the time that makes him a lovable character and a good person, in spite of his causing mayhem everywhere. He's been the neighborhood's problem since he was a young type because he rides down streets wide open on that big Hog, waving to all the neighbors, not paying attention to what he's doing if a bunch of girls come around. Crashes, sometimes total wipeouts, and walking away from all of it without a scratch.

His nickname is Hellbent Harley. The gang names him that because he sure behaves like he's hellbent on going there. Harley learns quickly that he didn't hang the moon, but he behaves like he's going to get the moon, as high up the air as his Fat Boy will go.

∞ ∞ ∞

HARLEY comes to visit his Auntie Alafair and the bishop at their house, speaking to the spirits who haunt this house when he walks in. Harley tells them about the ghosts who haunt his and Saul's house. He thinks it's his mama, who died giving birth to him, because he says the ghost comforts him.

Harley and his dad are faithful followers of His Divine Spirit Church where Madam Aucoin and the holy Bishop Toussaint hold services, leaning hard on the Voodoo side.

Harley is acting troubled and asks his Auntie Alafair to conjure up Laurette. He's grown up seeing her many times but never for him. Auntie gets ready for the ceremony that brings the spirit to the present. She appears quickly.

"It's the boogaloo time in your world now. Nobody knows what to do, just throw their hands into the air, like somebody is comin' to rescue them fools. Ohhh, you little man. You're like the hurricane. Blow one way, then the other. You got to make yourself calm, like the island breezes, but you stay far from them, so make believe. You gotta do this, or your brain will fall off. I know this to be true. Somebody put some heavy gris-gris on your bony little ass, and you gonna know about it soon. It's gonna be war, and you better put on the armor. That other bunch riding the monsters, they no good. Look to your papa.

"I'ma tell you the same thing I told the other boys. Pull your big man draws up because, motorcycle man, one day soon, it's gonna be caca day comin', and you already know this is gonna come. You can just bet on it!

"Now with that bein' said, you got to quit callin' me so much. I know too much of this world is gonna confuse me too much."

Madam comes back, asking what the hell Laurette says this time. Does she help him, or does she confuse the hell out of him?

He tells her everything, and Madam says, "As if! It's always something else."

∞ ∞ ∞

THERE'S a large rodeo happening in Beaumont, Texas, and the families are going to see him in the huge arena. People watching him are declaring he's the next Evel Kneivel with all the many stunts he knows.

Before his show, having nothing to do, he decides he is going to ride the biggest-ass, mean-as-the-devil bull. He's probably never seen a bouef, much less ridden the damn thing.

With everybody screaming, Don't do it! Are you crazy? Harley climbs up on the pissed-off bull's back, and the gates open, him holding on to the bull for dear life.

Mais! What the hell, you know, Harley wins the championship, beating out the professionals in riding the bull. He sure has a lot of bull in himself, so maybe that helps. In the middle of a large group of weathered cowboys, wearing his tight spandex pants and his helmet on his head, he takes the blue ribbon.

The promoters get riled because Harley isn't registered and comes out winning the contest. They've all lost a bunch of money to Harley, and they don't want to pay him the prize.

Harley is okay with that. It's just a publicity stunt.

The cowboys spit at the stunt. They tell him to stick with his bikes and don't do that again with a cowboy. The bull rider who scored the next most minutes gets the prize.

Harley starts preforming his stunts on the big Hogs, twirling around in the air and jumping over a school bus. He gets a standing ovation twice, and the crowds, mostly cowgirls, are surrounding him.

Harley goes to the back of the lot to get away from the fans, and he completes cleaning all his equipment when he's interrupted by two hoodlums wearing Roux colors.

The big dude with a bald head and a Fu Manchu beard, with big muscles showing out of his sleeveless, torn-up shirt, speaks first. "Hey, little podnah, you from New Orleans? We might be neighbors. I live on the back side of Tremé by the levee."

Same Esplanade but definitely not his neighbor.

Harley stands and tells them he has fifteen minutes to talk with them. So, the other, smaller man, full of acne scars, starts talking. "Hey, man, where ya at! We both come from the city, and so we figured we could scratch each other's backs. We'd like to transport you to wherever you go for your gigs. Looks like you're gonna have plenty. Dude, you something else.

"I know we can help each other out. We just want to move some pot, and you won't even see it. We got special-made trucks that keep everything hidden and plenty room left for all your stuff. We could even put your advertising on the truck, making it look like it's your truck.

"Whatcha say, Hellbent Harley? Think we can do a deal? We got approval for this from the Roux Garoux top dogs."

That stops Harley in midstream – a screeching red stop – and he tells them he will have to think about it.

The gang members leave without asking his full name. They are that stoned and dumb. Just make sure they have his phone number. It's all they can talk about, riding five hours back home.

Saul rides with Harley. Harley leans more on the cowboy side and has no qualms about getting a posse together. And he does just that.

∞ ∞ ∞

THE village is up in his business!

Another meeting with the families coming together as they are full-blooded members in the tribe of Monsieur Mayhem. Another war and all the braves are dancing their war dance. Damn, it sure is more of a reservation these days.

Saul and all the Saints come down on their bikes early one Saturday morning, and everyone is shaking hands, getting to know each other.

A bunch more to add to the village, you may as well say.

They all decide this is something that can't be ignored.

Saul Aucoin stands and takes the floor. "Thank you all for coming out behind us in support, but really, you don't have to be involved in this. It's going to get pretty nasty."

Who you think gets up next? Flavia just can't help herself.

"Ah'm all 'bout bustin' deir asses. We can set up tha sting and put dem back in prison. Ah'm sure dey t'ink of tha place as home. Ah'm callin' in tha Texas Rangers."

Saul and Harley are sure going to let the deed happen, not knowing if the Rouxs are aware of who he is. If not, the motorcycle gang will know shortly who they are foolish enough to be fooling with.

The thugs find him again, and Harley agrees to their proposition of hauling the dope to where he'll next perform. He doesn't have a show where he tells them he does; he just wants to get them to the spot where Louisiana State Troopers are waiting.

The troopers are hiding when the gang members drive up. The thugs start emptying the truck, but they're not taking out what Harley needs for his supposed show. They're emptying it of its illegal load. It is pure heroin, not something as harmless as weed.

They are a three-man crew, working for a while under the noses of the Rouxs and their leader, Eli St James. This isn't something the Rouxs know about, except for the man who is vying for control of the Rouxs. He sanctions it. A job not sanctified by Eli and the gang.

The two crooks pulling this job don't have a sense of what is about to take place, as they are so not attuned to anything other than murder and getting away with it. They plan to throw Harley's bike and his dead body in the back of the truck, closing it and leaving.

When one of the no-account humans doing the deed takes his gun out his pocket to shoot Harley in the back of his head without him expecting it, headlights come on, and they see the troopers in gear to take them down, with all the Saints revving their bikes with lights on the whole deal.

The one that has a gun tells him, "We gonna be out of jail before you even get back from arresting us. The Rouxs never, ever leave anyone in our gang in jail. We comin' for you with the Rouxs all behind us."

That's when a trooper pops him in the head very seriously and vigorously, telling him he's heard that threat, something else to book him on.

Harley tells the thugs, "Bring it on. You better listen when they tell you about us. You are worthless as gang members and worthless human beings. I don't think anybody's coming to bail you out. Go head, call them."

It is a week later when the head honcho of the Rouxs, Eli St. James, calls Saul. Once upon a time, they had been best friends, running the streets and getting into a lot of shit together, causing havoc on the streets. During this time, Saul picks one side and Eli picks the other side of that flipped coin, and now it looks like the friendship will never be mended.

Then comes the Big Rumble in the Jungle. Not until Eli's only son is shot dead by who knows who does the fighting stop. No one is supposed to have guns. Several members on both sides are taken to jail, along with Saul and Eli. The gangs have to be kept in separate cells because they are still fighting each other.

Saul and Eli have blamed each other all these years and haven't spoken since.

"Saul, why did y'all break the truce? You know we been bitter enemies ourselves, and I've had to restrain myself all these years. Why the hell did you do this, causin' the fuckin' state to be on our asses? And since when you got involved in the dope business? Bro, we comin' for y'all. Pick the place and time."

And he hangs up on Saul.

It's definitely on now, and the Saints pick the swamp behind Minou and Joe's house to rumble, hiring a barge to take them back there with their bikes. There will be no interruption from the police and no freaking out a bunch of people with all the bikes revving up the whole time.

The bishop knows all the men in the Saints and a few in the Roux gang, like Eli St James. He's known him since he was a boy with Saul.

Bishop Toussaint and Madam Aucoin ask for a meeting with Eli and the top dogs of his motorcycle gang. Their choice of picking where to meet is an old saloon in the middle of Chalmette, their hangout. The bishop begins to talk after he is given a cold Dixie beer. He's wondering how they've gotten their hands on this beer.

"Eli, how do you think the Saints broke the truce? Saul and the Saints were protecting their famous Hellbent Harley Aucoin, son of Saul. You must be running a crew not satisfied with your leadership, because two of your members approached him to smuggle cannabis in their van with his equipment. It turned out to be heroin. They never even asked who he was, other than Hellbent.

"Someone snitches on them, maybe a disgruntled member, unhappy with what's going on in your membership. Or maybe they know what those two are doing and wants a piece of that.

"But rest assured, it isn't the Saints that broke the peace."

Madam Aucoin speaks next. "Oh, my boys! Are you the same boys that everybody used to chase down the streets in the Quarter and loved y'all anyway? Y'all would steal something close to the front door of a tourist trap, little things that the tourists buy in the Quarter. Never getting caught. Y'all came to my house and shop many, many times, but you never stole from me. I wonder why.

"You and Saul loved each other and were like brothers. I am heartbroken because now there's a war coming between you two. And I ask, why? A battle because of what? Both you and Saul take yourselves way, way too seriously, and y'all are acting like some despots on your thrones. Over what? Please, tell me."

Eli stands, and it gets immediately quiet. He has delusions of grandeur to think he's got a handle on what's happening under his nose. "Madam and Bishop, you know we love and respect you, and I'm sure y'all are not part of this. You're trying to stop this from happening, but it's a longstanding feud between us. My next-in-line told me he saw my son shot. I have believed all these years that it was Saul Aucoin who pulled the trigger, killing my son.

"Those two members of our gang are dumb as rocks, but they swore an oath to me, never to lie to me, and to be as up front as these two can be. They said exactly what you would say, but it's their sworn truth against the Saints'. Those two don't lie."

∞ ∞ ∞

THE fight will be on the full moon, which is tomorrow night.

There are hundreds and all sizes of motorcycles coming to the country, the Saints and the Roux Garouxs driving down at the same time. People can hardly believe the two-miles-long stream of motorcycles, each gang going a little faster than the other and cutting in lines, scaring the poor people on the highway, causing mayhem, cussing with the bird finger held high and horns blowing and screeching brakes from the other drivers in their cars going down Highway 90 from New Orleans.

You reading this, you probably know right where that is. A very beat-up, four-lane highway under constant repair simply because it's trying to get back to the swamps and the Gulf from whence it came. You better be a defensive driver on that highway with a car full of spirits and angels hanging on because some people's children don't know shit from shinola about driving. My most favorite road ever in my life – and I have seen a lot of places in my lives – is and always was LA-1 from the top to the bottom, from Shreveport to Grand Isle.

The gates on the electric fences are open so the gangs can come on the property, owned and governed by the families of the Mayhem. The barge has to make four trips five miles down the bayou, putting as many bikes as it can.

The families, everyone that makes up the entourage, come together today to watch the gangs, and there isn't a single one on the long list that is pulling for the Rouxs. They all have their chairs out there, waiting for the full-full show, that's for sure.

Junya and T-Mae don't go out to see the ruckus and make sure all their little children are inside too. It is just too much for them to see all at one time. It would damage their little brains.

The moon is rising over the dark swamps, lighting up the large area where this war is supposed to take place. The battle will have hand-to-hand combat, throwing down, fists, choking, snarling spit, and just basic beating the shit out of each other.

The bikes stay in the clearing, all 300 of those Hogs and big daddies lined up in a row.

Joe is stomping his feet and cussing the whole way to the clearing. "Oooh, awww, mais, Ah'm some mad. Ah want to shit so bad on somebody's goddam parade. Ah must have a sign on my back sayin', 'Come on and kick me. Ah love it.'

"Minou, Minou, Minou! Ah've had it up to tha top of my brain wit' all dis shit. Ya gonna make me move in wit' Pieyan and dat couyan woman he has up in dere, shackin' up. Ya know, da beauty and da beast? Gawee! Merde! Mais, dat's cuckoo ma choo, Miss Belle and Pieyan. Mais, ain't dat a purty sight wit' her runnin' naked all over tha property 'cause Pieyan tole her it feels so good. Mais, wit' dose big-ass, floppy old tetons nobody wants to see.

"T-June, him, he acts like it's already his, waitin' for me to kick tha bucket. Dat's his royal ass. Mais, shit, Minou, Ah ain't goin' nowhere anytime soon, and it's gonna be fightin' to put me in tha wrong side of tha dirt. So from now on, dey gotta axe me first if dey can come back here.

"Ah'm not joking, Minou. Ah mean it. What sense is dere for us to pay dat electric bill if we gonna let all dis quemas happened back dere? Ah mean it, Minou."

Out of the crowd comes a priest, walking to the center of the battlegrounds. They are scratching their heads, both sides of the warriors. Silence takes over when Father Becnel holds his staff high with a picture of St. Columbanus, the saint for motorbikes everywhere, and speaks real loud, all dressed in his important robes with the large red hat, stoned to the bone.

"Well, gentlemen, I'm here to see if I can stop this travesty before someone gets killed on this land that for sure my family owns. If anybody wants confession, come over here. Then, I'm going to say a blessing for all of you, so get to stepping if you want to be forgiven."

The gangs think that all this is for stalling the battle, time for all the monsters on this land to appear, ready to boogie. But none is brave enough to ignore a holy man, stoned to the bone. Too, too many line up until Eli and Saul tell them to get back in their positions.

For the families that have all this at their convenience, well, it's for sure straight up fairyland.

T-June stands on the side with the bishop. Joe is pacing around and still has the nervine.

Bertha and Alcide show up for their appointment that they have every, every month. Here comes the loup-garous, the real ones, loping across the field between the two gangs, snarling at all of them and walking up on their hind legs, making them back the fuck up. The wolves, Gertie and Leroy, are here too, doing the same, dancing on their back legs too and pissing on the men.

Lo and behold, here comes Pieyan with the mad hatter Belle, still wearing that beat-up hat and nothing else. They just sashay up to the middle of the field.

What's the sense in having monsters if you can't use them to scare the shit out of anybody?

The members of both gangs are trying to run for their lives, but the wolves, Gertie and Leroy, are keeping them from doing so, walking the perimeter and snarling at whoever is brave enough to try.

There are many tears coming from all the bad-asses who think they are bad-asses but aren't. Many are so glad they've taken the time for confession, and the others are shouting for Father Becnel, "Please, oh Lawd, come back."

He's back at the house, stoned to the bone, along with drunk Joe, hiding behind closed bedroom doors with Joe's loaded shotgun. Joe has had enough. He's going to rent a room from the Leroux boys and dare anyone to come near.

Junya sneaks out and is so scared he runs back in the house, locking the doors and pulling the curtains, and he and T-Mae pray hard on the priedieu.

Never, ever has this happened before. All the swamp monsters at the same time. Pour le Mon de Bon Dieu.

Right up in the middle of this quemas, T-June decides to join his supernatural family, scaring the Bejesus out of all these city dudes and having a good time doing it. He turns right in front of everybody, tearing his shirt and pants off his body but able to keep his drawers on. He turns into this huge werewolf, black as night, with huge, snarling teeth, walking up on back legs too, strutting his stuff like he is doing the stroll with soul, boogalooing right up to the front of the two bosses to the back of the area, all the way down the field with paws reaching for them.

I sure can see him in all his glory.

Eli has turned fifty shades of white, with Saul holding his heart. T-June in wolf form walks up to them and grabs a hand of each one.

The loup-garou has to hold up Eli's body because he has straight-up fainted.

Then he turns right back into T-June, like the faucet he is. Good thing he keeps his drawers on when Saul faints.

This goes on for a while. One regains himself, then the other faints again!

Next monsters to appear are the vampires, Mac and Claudine. They just flit next to T-June, stand on his side, and a whole lot of crucifixes appear from the necks of these hard-shelled men, being held up at them. They remain to see the action, with Claudine baring her fangs wherever and at whoever is foolish enough to look at her. They for sure screaming for the Blessed Father.

Chairs are brought for Eli and Saul, with the rest of T-June's gang who will be needed in the meeting of all meetings. Talk about gangs. All the gang members are sitting on the ground, holding on to each other, no matter the colors. All are trying to defend each other.

Everyone is quiet out of respect for their leaders or just scared speechless with everything going on, for the horrors they've seen.

T-June is the first to speak. "All of us who own this property protect our endangered species. That's the reason to have electric fences on all our properties. Don't think that our monsters don't travel well. If they catch your scent, they will all get in vehicles, if need be.

"This war is going to stop tonight, and there will be no more. Y'all made the mistake of involving us on the bayou, and if we're involved, we come with everything and everybody. The purpose of all this is to let all of you know we mean business. No more fights.

"And now here comes Madam Aucoin. She has something to do for y'all that will end this war."

Madam Alafair Aucoin comes to the center of the group, dressed in her high priestess garb and carrying a black satin bag in her hands, her get-up ready for work.

Madam gives the instructions for Eli and Saul to each put one hand on the crystal ball she takes out the black satin bag. Standing close to the huge crystal, rubbing as fog appears clouding it, she says,

"We are seeking the past days, long ago between the friends who are now enemies. Show us, blessed spirits, the night of their first war."

All three of them hold the ball when it starts really fogging up, swirling, pointing and revealing that long-ago night. All three of them witness the scene that has been out of sight for Eli and Saul all these years, each blaming the other. Now they see it clearly; it's disturbing and horrifying, to say the least.

The killer of Eli's son is his right-hand man, next in line to be leader of the gang, the one who has been building up his own gang this whole time, the gang that tries to use Hellbent Harley. He has lied to Eli all these years.

So much for truth among these men.

They watch in the ball and see him stand behind trees off the field of battle and shoot Eli Jr. with an antique pistol that Eli Sr. has given his next-in-command on his birthday. The killer is trying to rid himself of his competition. Just business, nothing personal.

All three of them stand gasping at the scene that is revealed to them. All three of them turn to the gangs and spot the killer. Eli yells to restrain him.

Every one of them has witnessed the murder and betrayal.

The gangs spilt up and get ready to go in fighting, in spite of everything. They are two different gangs now, everyone picking a side. Those for Eli and Saul against the gang the killer has put together. Straight-up good versus evil.

All of T-June's tribe is ready to fight too, so add them on the good gang.

I think the whole damn bunch is wanting to go postal and let everything built up go down the drain.

Pieyan certainly does. He goes to grabbing dudes in each hand and knocking them cuckoo on their poor heads.

Some others are running for their lives from the mad hatter, Miss Belle. Some even recognize her. Belle is chasing all the men, and they are slipping and sliding, trying to get out the mud and away from the old lady who is bare-ass naked except for her hat. Pieyan has showed her how freeing it is with no clothes.

Screaming at the top of her lungs, she says, "Y'all sons of bitches, come here, come here. I'm not going to eat you. Come see me, little boys. I've got some candy for you."

When it becomes obvious who is winning with their fists and punches and kicking and scratching, the fighting stops.

And a fun time is had by all.

The leader and the two criminals who have been busted take off to the swamps, along with their evil gang, taunting and screaming that they're coming back to finish this.

They don't make it out the swamps. Gertie and Leroy and Pieyan and the loup-garous get to their throats and finish the thing themselves.

Who in the hell cares? Not me.

The silence under the full moon permeates the air surrounding the large group, causing even the animals and birds to be quiet.

Eli starts crying when he realizes he has been hating Saul all these years, blaming him for the sins of this sleazy man who he has trusted. Saul looks hard at Eli, trying to find some part of the boy he loved. They look like they are standing on the top of a cliff, waiting to see who will jump first.

Saul steps forward first, reaching out his hand to Eli. Saul and Eli hug each other, both crying about the tragedy and the loss of their friendship for many years. Not a dry eye in the bunch, everybody looking for paper towels.

Junya and T-Mae take care of that. They've got plenty of everything now that Minou takes them to Sam's.

Harley walks up next to his father and reaches for Eli's hand too. Hellbent Harley is introduced to Eli, and they hug and shake hands. Eli tells him he's watched all his shows, being proud of him too, knowing who he is.

With the help of the now-joined gangs, they throw all the bodies in the swamp water, never to be seen again. Probably all useless human beings who had someone trying to teach them lessons all their lives but who didn't listen to one of them. The alligators will eat what's left of them.

Who the hell cares? For sure not me.

Madam is heeding the call from Laurette and goes into the trance, bringing forth the old, old spirit.

"Aww, my boys are actin' like they have no sense. They've forgotten to line up for that. You have to fix this, I say right now. It looks like the good has won over the bad. That's good. You got a good start in becomin' the great, great leaders in the joining of the biggest, goodest army, the gang.

"Both of you will have babies born on the same day in the future, and it will be up to you to make sure they grow up together. The women are comin', so keep your eyes on the prize.

"I told you before, I have had enough of your time in the present. It's just gotten worse and worse. Me, I like the island for me, and days of the slaves are better than this shit. So, Alafair, don't make me come again any time soon."

Madam Aucoin immediately starts asking what Laurette has said this time. Saul and Eli start telling her and break down again, crying with joy.

The bishop calls for a blessing for the new, combined gang, and Father Becnel, hiding in the house with Joe, is called too. All the monsters go back into hiding, Pieyan having to carry his Belle because she is still hollering at the men, "Come see me, lil boy."

Harley Aucoin asks if he can put on a show about the same time the Lerouxs – Justin and Scottie – show up, having missed the whole quemas. They will become Harley's managers and road crew and podnahs, starting right then and there on the spot.

By the light of the full moon in the huge clearing, Harley begins his own magical mystery tour. Placing sparklers on every bike he has and seeing everything lit up, sparkling all around the area, well, it's magical. Flying up in the air and twirling on the land and jumping over large growths of ivies latched on to the large branches on the ground. Making it look like a large maze through the swamps.

The little Rappolet children get to see the show after the fight, and they are amazed, standing with their lil mouths open.

Joe comes back to see the show, which he absolutely loves. But being Joe, he has to find something to complain about. "Awww, bébé, Ah had me a good time. Lawd, have mercy! He sure as shit can do all dem sure-as-shit t'ings! But Ah wanna know who is comin' to put back tha field like dey found it. It for sure as shit ain't comin' out my sure-as-shit wallet."

What's left of the disgraced gang is leaving, going the long way home to ponder on the road what in the hell they've witnessed this night. Some are making themselves believe they have been given some psychedelic weed, that the whole thing is a bad trip and they've all suffered hallucinations.

Some are not that gullible, rethinking their lives, and will quit the outlaw life and sell their bikes cheap. The majority of what's left of the Rouxs has joined the other side, vowing never to talk of this again.

Everyone who has participated in the event feels it is historical. Everyone feels it's like going postal on a bunch of city slickers that can't accept the horror and the unbelievable display of monsters in the swamp.

Everyone in the families can't hardly believe it themselves.

∞ ∞ ∞

THIS land of magic and mystery has increased in inhabitants and in the freedom to be yourself, by everybody.

One of the bikers decides to write a book about the event, and it sells in the fiction category of horror, X-rated. When investigators come searching for the truth, they are met with shotguns and "no comments."

Pieyan the bigfoot goes visiting everyone because his old lady Belle wants to. T-June tells Pieyan that Belle has to put on clothes when she goes around talking to anybody who will listen, although Pieyan has the right idea of freeing yourself of the cumbersome clothes and going naked. T-June tells Pieyan that it's upsetting to humans to see this. It might make them jealous.

The Rappolet family loves to play with Pieyan when Miss Belle is visiting their mama on the porch. They all stink like skunks, Pieyan and the children, so T-Mae doesn't let them come in her sparkly clean house. It's bad enough with the dirty, disheveled, ding-a-ling Belle.

T-Mae is adding to her brood of children and gets nauseous quickly. She says it's a girl, because she is sick every time she has a daughter.

When Saul is introduced to Estelle and Theo's eldest daughter, Roberta, it is love at first sight. Saul meets Roberta while they are enjoying the music of Monsieur Mayhem's band at the Bon Temps Rouler. He's a widower who has never remarried after twenty-five years but still is in his prime.

Roberta is in her early thirties, has never married, and has never even thought about being a mother. She is a successful lawyer like her sister Lily, whose services are used by Bishop Toussaint at His Divine Spirit Church in the Big Easy. Her mama believes she is just an enlightened, modern, free woman who has made her place in the world by herself. Estelle is right.

When Saul and Roberta are married in the church and jump the broom at their reception, it is complete and very valid. Jolie is her sister's maid of honor, and Eli is the best man.

Eli and his wife, Trixie, have been married for thirty years and never had another child after the death of their only son.

Roberta becomes pregnant right away. To the delight of Trixie, she becomes with child too.

Saul and Eli joke with each other about "gettin' sum" that night of the conception. They already know their babies are coming because of Laurette's predictions.

Both infants are born on New Year's Eve at the same place, being both women come to the bayou for midwifery by the women that live there. The babies each weigh then pounds, healthy as little horses, and have a white streak in the center of their heads, with little white hair shining on their scalps of black curly hair. Madam feels it is a sign from Laurette to mark the infamous fight and redemption of souls.

Eli and Trixie have a girl, and Saul and Roberta have a boy. Their names are Precious Soul St. James and Eli Rene Aucoin, in memory of Eli's late son. Soul and Easy are what they're going be called.

Whatcha think?

Hellbent Harley becomes a famous stunt rider in a circuit of wannabe Evel Knievels, and he is the one who surpasses the famous man himself.

All three of the young men – Harley, Justin, and Scottie – are skirt chasers, loving and leaving in every town. Well, justice comes for all three. They all have to get married because their seeds are planted in very fertile soil. All three have large fais-do-dos at a big dancehall in Golden Meadow, where the girls come from. These little Cajun women have played their bourré hand and won the pot. And the trio has no idea what way-down-the-bayou women are like.

Just be terribly happy that Miss Belle is too old. Oh, my Gawd! Be terribly happy.

Babies, babies, babies everywhere! They come to be at Minou and Joe's house and are added to the families who choose to be part of Monsieur Mayhem's Magical Mystery Tour.

Chapter Twenty

'Til Tha End

THESE are the days that finally come to pass for the families, peace and contentment after all the days of following T-June and each other to handle all the quemas that comes like clockwork to their village that's now their own little town, with a sign even: Minouville.

Alcide passes with a heart attack and dies in Bertha's arms. Her heart is shattered and broken for six months, when she turns into the loup-garou for the last time, drowning the werewolf that she is, and then she joins him in the graveyard right next to PawPaw Irby, Sweet Stu, Big Daddy and Big Mama, and Pete Dugas's mama and papa.

Maybelline Laverne, Mac and Moe's mama, is reburied there too, with fresh flowers every day and candles lit by Estelle and Madam Aucoin against all things that would disturb her. Madam had been Maybelline's nanan, and Estelle is her older sister, who raised her sons up to be wonderful men, until Mac becomes a vampire.

Sometimes when Mac and Claudine come to the country, they will lay in a coffin right by his mama.

Flavia gets bad dementia, and her sons Grey and Gerry are having a very hard time keeping up with her. She no longer remembers her Buddhist son, cremated by his husband. She's lost three of her lifetime loves, starting with Sweet Stu. When Bertha and Alcide pass, it takes the rest of Flavia's reality, and she just slips into her own world that is so much more fun to make believe and doesn't hurt anymore. She'll just open whatever door is closed, and she goes up and down LA-1, walking up in people's houses and sitting at their kitchen table, waiting to be served coffee.

Horace, her last remaining son from the dude who walked out in broad daylight up Highway 1 and was never heard from again, brings his children to try to commit Flavia into a fancy nursing home for not being able to handle her affairs. They try to contest the will she has prepared, even though she isn't dead. She's written it after she and Stu get back from his daughter's wedding years ago.

Her granddaughter is being very condescending and rude to the Comanche sons Flavia has adopted with Stu. But Horace's ploy is stopped before they reach the courthouse because the two Comanche warriors, cool as cucumbers and hot as peppers, tell them in no uncertain terms to get the hell out of Dodge.

T-June's, Grey's, and Gerry's inheritance is more than $12 million – $3 million for each of them – with the other $3 million going to St Luke's.

She leaves $3 for her son and his two children.

Flavia will still put her two cents in on whatever is being talked about, telling them, "Ah got pull, ya know? Ya hear me, ya hear me? Everywhere and Ah'm gonna call tha guv'nor."

She will sit for hours, saying her rosary on Alcide and Bertha's porch, crying. She claims Sweet Stu is talking to her, as are Bertha and Alcide.

Who the hell knows?

But then she'll turn around and go into her famous store and start throwing stuff onto the floor from the shelves, saying, "All of this is cheap made, and Ah don't sell dis shit in my store. Who in tha hell will wear a hunnerd dollar blue jean and not be ashamed? Lil girl, go wash ya mout' 'cause ya smell like tha cigarette."

The brothers watch with fear as many employees run out the front screen, way before the screen door hits them in any part of their bodies, for sure their butts.

They can't keep young girls as employees because they will hide in a corner crying, they so afraid of her. The pay is very good, but you have to be able to handle Flavia. The brothers look for older women and preferably those who know her, not like the young that think she's a witch.

You go, girl, Flavia. You go!

∞ ∞ ∞

MADAM Alafair Aucoin and the righteous Bishop Laurent Toussaint are both in their 90s, acting and looking like they are sixty.

The whole village is using these concoctions that are working for them too, as well as the potion Madam uses on the bishop's addled mind. They all have seen the potions and spells and creams with that Voodoo flavor working, along with Laurette and her spells. All are the real deal against aging.

Except for Flavia. Flavia gets a rash if she even uses a potion.

Their house on the bayou has a yard full of flowers, plants, bushes and many, many roses growing wherever they want to go, causing the couple to put white rocks as paths through her yard.

You walk into the large house and you feel welcomed without a word being passed. The feeling is spiritual, calming, and smells like roses and patchouli. All her pretty bongs are used as flower vases, full of long-stemmed roses.

You will feel the ghosts, and if you're lucky, they will play their music, appearing in all their finery. Buddy Braxton lets everybody know he's here, because he will blow that horn loud and jazzy just out the blue, like Gabriel. He scares Madam's daughters terribly bad, and they get the vapors and run out the house, yelling, "Save me, save me!"

All three of those sistas have in no uncertain terms refused to come back.

Oh, well…

Madam Consienne and her lover, Emile Verdin, show up together, both playing the piano at the same time and smiling and laughing and just shining today.

I wonder if the ghosts are "gettin' sum." It would seem so.

Madam Aucoin conjures up for her almost-final Laurette visit. It takes too much out of Madam Aucoin because she is battling with the spirit who now wants to join this world.

All of Laurette's people are revolting against their masters, all up and down the Gulf Coast into the Caribbean. Too, too scary for Laurette.

Madam Alafair gets real pissed off at Laurette because she is getting stronger and wants to take over everything and tell everybody whatever she can do and say. "Laurette, you're not hitching onto my body. Who do you think you are? You're behaving like you are some body snatcher. And why in Yahweh do you insist on moving my ganja?

"Okay, we can try to send you here as a ghost. Then, you can watch way more things and you're not over my shoulders, all the time telling me I'm doing it wrong.

"I don't even know if you can do this. I've never asked you. I've just never thought about it, my mind always being somewhere else. I just don't know how this will work."

Laurette is standing on the side of Madam before she finishes her sentence, as a ghost, saying, even though she isn't dead in her world, "Well, I've been waitin' a long time for you to ask me. Lawd a-mighty, they're axing off heads with fuckin' machetes."

This is going to a big adjustment for Madam Consienne, as she's been the only woman ghost in this group of haints. She tells Madam Aucoin, "I know a putain when I see a putain. And she's a heathen enticing all the men to do Voodoo crap. I don't think she can stay here. Remember, it's my house too."

That happens sooner rather than later, actually the first night. They get into a cat fight when Madam Consienne sees Laurette casting her eyes at Emile Verdun and him looking back.

She has had to call him out of purgatory, you remember, so you never know.

Madam Aucoin goes to T-Mae and Junya's house for coffee the next morning, telling them about the homeless ghost. Madam is even thinking about dropping Laurette on the streets of New Orleans, saying she would be happy and make friends over there.

T-Mae said, "Mais, if ya don't mind, Ah'ma let Laurette live wit' us. She gonna love all my chirren, and she can tell me e'ry time she has somet'in' to say. She know all 'bout heathens. Maybe she can help raise dis bunch of heathens."

Laurette's been watching this bunch, and she likes them because they make her laugh.

Madam calls her to come for the last time. Laurette is becoming more human. She was a mulatto Voodoo queen of the Caribbean, because what she did was travel from the past to the present, a real-life crazy Voodoo queen time traveler.

Madam is thinking hard, hard about the situation.

∞ ∞ ∞

I'M sorry that I have to eliminate any of my beloved characters, but I got to make room for new ones.

Pete and Irene Breaux mourn her father, Danny Guidry, and bring the houseboat, all changed up into something beautiful. When he dies, they throw his ashes into the bayou that he loved and called his home. He's probably up with Alcide in the big bourré game in their heaven.

Irene and Jean use the boat as their camp because it's big enough now. She brings a wreath of flowers every time she comes and throws it in the bayou.

The Breauxs now have a houseful of grandchildren, and one, Tony Mont-Pellier, is a wealthy little dude. He is not treated any different, although they all have money, so…

Lives of no worries and plenty love.

Rowdy and Flower are professionals in their chosen careers, but they are wonderful parents who take time for their four boys. They produce a set of identical twin boys after Jean and Tony. Never ever do they hear again from Jerome Anthony Mont-Pellier's sisters, who are in prison along with the mama because of the quemas they've caused.

Those Mont-Pelliers don't even have names, that's how important they are.

Gone pecans.

Good riddance, y'all.

∞ ∞ ∞

TOOT and Lily Laverne have a chain of barber shops all over the city. He continues to cut hair in the original barber shop that started with his dad.

Grandma Tut Laverne, unsightly and totally evil through and through, has died alone in prison. No one claims the body, and she is buried in a pauper's grave in the prison's graveyard.

Rest her soul, but I doubt it.

Toot doesn't know what happens to get his pawpaw in trouble, but he hears Pee Wee is having a carefree life up in Angola.

Toot's daddy goes and shacks up with a woman also in recovery from gambling. She is a God-fearing woman, just like his late wife, and she has them up in Bishop Toussaint's church all the time. They both work at the Center. So do Lily and Flower.

Weedie? Well. That's another story because she has up and joined the nunnery. She sure as hell doesn't want any children. She and Sister Bridget have heated discussions about everything, especially the difference in the nuns today and when Sister was young. Weedie wears a short, light blue veil with blue jeans and boots, to Sister Bridget's dismay. She cusses like a seasoned sailor and is quick to punch the lights out of some pimp on the streets.

I don't know. Sister Bridget has been known to be pretty formidable herself, especially in her younger days as Joseph's head-knocker disciple, leading the way to sainthood.

Novice Marie (Weedie's nun name) speaks Spanish as her second language and can cuss you lower than dirt in Mexican mischief. She has never stopped talking in both languages at the same time.

Mucho, mucho mojo! I ain't the jefe.

∞ ∞ ∞

HENRI Gustave Aucoin has a huge campaign for governor of Louisiana on the Democrat Liberal party ticket, much better than the

Blue Dogs are, and wins by a landslide. He still mourns his old friend, Jerome Mont-Pellier III, the one who has committed suicide.

Bertha Mae, the next daughter he and Callie have, is a perfectly normal child without gifts, totally beautiful as a mixed girl with all sorts of blood running through her veins, making her very special looking, with the same color of hair as her brother, True. How much more beautiful can you get?

They call her MaeMae. Big blue eyes and freckles and good hair. Very studious and serious. True Blue and Bertha Mae have high cheekbones from the Natives and their great-grandma Bertha.

Callie is a wonderful First Lady of Louisiana, working for the poor and helpless women in the city of Baton Rouge. Oh, the poor society gals back in the Big Easy don't even want to hear her name spoken. Callie just can't help those women, caught up in their lives in cages.

∞ ∞ ∞

THE vampires, Mac and Claudine, have a successful business, all done in the night. Between Mac and Moe, they are millionaires.

Claudine's papa, Monsieur Beauregard du Robaire the last, goes to meet his death in the sun because he just can't accept today's views and can't make himself deal with all the mixed colors of this bunch.

The undead Angelique du Robaire comes to live in their house in the Quarter and loves to entertain and have soirees, always at six o'clock on the dot. She eats her meal of the day (and we ain't goin' there) before they visit in the night.

Angelique has sold her property to an oil company for big bucks and has the furniture brought to Mac and Claudine's house. It needs more furniture than that tomb, and heat for sure. Then, she strikes a match and watches while the old house burns away in the night. People think it's an oil rig burning.

She can finally be the belle of the ball in the fashion she was before getting bit by her daughter. She is not wearing black, either.

You go, girl!

∞ ∞ ∞

FATHER Becnel is now an archbishop in south Louisiana. Nothing has changed in his appearance except a longer ponytail and cleaner robes, but he's still stoned to the bone. Well, there's some change. He has guards and long limousines, but he still comes to pick his own pot from Bertha and Madam Aucoin's large patch of cannabis that's grown bigger every year. Everyone comes to get their medication.

The convent isn't where Sister Bridget wants to live anymore. Having to intervene on two of her nuns for alcoholism and send them to treatment just breaks her of her link to the nunnery. She doesn't want to be up in the middle of a very dysfunctional family that she may have had a part in creating. She wants to live alone for the first time since she moved into the convent at seventeen. She won't tell anybody how old she is, and they don't ask.

Sister Bridget buys a small place to retire in. It's a shotgun house with a big yard to grow her roses, right down the road from Flavia's house. Bridget thinks she bought the house, but it's really Flavia, who sells it to her for $20. They are in cahoots with each other, still trying to beat Madam Aucoin's streak of winning the prize three years in a row for her knock-out roses.

Sister says that Flavia makes more sense now, even if she's cuckoo.

Both are still looking for T-June's sainthood, or maybe he's the next coming. But they both see True in a much different light.

∞ ∞ ∞

MINOU has hit the years of menopause, and she is fighting with all she's got for it to not take over her life. She is always hot, and she and Joe fight over the thermostat. Joe says, while reaching for another blanket, "Mais, shit, Minou. Ya t'ink Ah'ma goddam popsicle? Mais, even my weenie is so cold, it's all shriveled up. Look, bébé, ya see what Ah mean?"

Minou hits him with his pillow and throws him out the room. She sure as hell doesn't want to see his weenie.

He goes to Bertha and Alcide's house. Minou and Joe have keys and keep all the utilities on.

Joe is laid up in Alcide and Bertha's bed, ready to get some sleep. All of a sudden, he hears Alcide's voice, with Bertha laughing. Poor Joe runs outside in his drawers, hollering for Minou. Scares the shit out of him because he has to run for the bathroom (as always, he's got a problem with his bowels, unlike the nasal issues) and stays up the rest of the night because he is so afraid they've followed him home.

Minou mourns her mama and parrain as much as Flavia does, and sometimes she will sit on their porch with Flavia, crying too. Minou is leaving well enough alone, staying on the porch. She doesn't want to talk with either of their ghosts. She's got all she can handle.

Madam Aucoin, Bertha's best friend for years, has gone into hiding for weeks, trying to call their spirits to Bertha's house. Now, she realizes that, because they were both loopers when they died, they are up in the place reserved for all the monsters. Maybe they're going to fight all the other monsters to get off the reservation and show up, if at all possible.

But then Madam realizes, after trying for a while, she should call them to her house. They break free from haunting their own house. Too much quemas over there at their house.

Flavia's been telling people they talk with her all the time when she's by her friend Bertha's house. Maybe that's a hallucination, or she ain't as crazy as they think.

Minou is thinking, while rocking in Bertha's old cane-back rocking chair, about how she's the one started this whole quemas, dragging Joe into the quemas that goes back to when they trapped the loup-garous in a quemas that turns out to be her mama and parrain. The rest is chaotic history.

Quemas is chaos in Cajun patois. Hoping you figured it out by now.

She sits rocking and quiet, remembering when T-June was born and how all the others have followed in her footsteps in the raising of this child that is a supernatural being.

Minou thinks about how her grown son has been a leader in everything and has become so sure of himself that now he thinks he's the boss. She's through with following behind him. That's over and done with. She has worn out the T-shirt and uses it for a dishrag.

He has brought so many characters, different in all ways, into their lives, and they all have become family and loved. People in general pick their own family because they may love their real family but not like them.

Minou contemplates all the adventures, quemas with more chaos, and takes care of everything that comes down the bayou for them to battle. Always winning in whatever situation that causes them to be saviors, soldiers, and sistas.

They for sure are the Cajun Mafia.

Minou finds it hard to believe she's the one that has started the whole thing because she is so nosy. Joseph Alan Thibeau Senior definitely didn't see all this shit up in his life. He just couldn't walk away from Minou. Still can't.

Joe has been steadfast in his falling-in-the-shitpot that Minou has him in, whatever shitpot she falls in. Joe has been forced by Minou to jump in and help, when he didn't want to. She is his life. He is a simple man, not simple in his mind, but he tries hard to offer help with less quemas. Joe may not be educated, but he is shrewd in his thinking and business dealings, and because of that, he has made them wealthy by working hard and being honest. He and Alcide have made a fortune in their business.

He is very grateful for the treasure they've found because of pecans and an unfriendly ghost named Gaspar.

His best friend, Alcide, still scares the shit out of him now, even though he's passed. He still runs away from supernatural things; he wants no part of those scary things.

But Joe can bitch with the best of those bitchers. "Mais, Minou ain't ya glad we not dealin' wit' all dat quemas dese days? But shit, it's time for me and you to be by ourselves. Mais, look all de people who live on our lands. And dey keep addin' more. To put tha icin' on tha cake, we got a crazy woman livin' wit' Pieyan.

"Ohhh, if Ah woulda been a weaker man, Ah woulda keeled over dead wit' a heart attack.

"Come on, bébé, let's see if we can still 'get sum.'"

Minou says, after slapping him in the head, "As if! As if! Ah put dat in tha attic when Ah started changin' into dis miserable woman who's hot all tha time, pissed off most of tha time, and Ah ain't wantin' to 'get sum' any time. Go away, ya dirty old man. If ya want sum so bad, go down tha road and get sum wit' an old putain. Ah dare ya! Ah dare ya! Ah will kick ya ass up and down tha bayou, makin' sure e'rybody sees it."

Okay, she told him she's pissed off, so get the hell gone. He wastes no time doing so.

∞ ∞ ∞

Y'ALL gonna have a hard time coming out to the bayou when there are no more stories. I just ain't killing no more of the village people, just in case they need to be resurrected.

Joe likes to go outside to play with the wolves and Chief Rappolet, who is out there wrestling with Gertie and Leroy. Leroy has learned to love Chief, now that he loves humans and is used to their smells. He will knock you down trying to get a hug.

They mourn Bertha in their own way, and both of the wolves lay down for days, howling out their grief.

Chief is lost for days, his podnahs Alcide and Bertha dead. You can hear him out there howling the most dreadful heartbreaking sounds. They cry in the house hearing him.

He comes back, telling them he's been at Pieyan and Belle's house, where they've helped him with his grief.

Minou and T-Mae aren't worried about him. He's lived half of his life in the woods, taking care of himself.

T-Mae is out there having more babies, two more for sure. She is a serious student of Madam Aucoin's and now can be given the title of traiteur. People come out the bayous for her remedies she combines with the teachings of Madam Aucoin and her beliefs she brings out of the swamps.

If she can't help, they call T-June. Everybody they touch comes out healthier and happier.

Madam Aucoin is shocked out her shoes when she sees Laurette, not a spirit or ghost but a real-life woman, mulatto free-born, bona fide witch from the 1800s who comes walking out her bedroom door. These women are hugging and kissing each other because they have never come face to face before. They truly love each other and seem to be the same age.

Go figure.

T-Mae is happy with the transfer because she has a real, live, built-in mawaaw who's real old but new to them. Junya and T-Mae look at her as a new mama because both of theirs have been gone to the other side.

When Belle and Pieyan visit, Laurette makes herself scarce. The Voodoo woman wants no part of them, doesn't trust either. She is downright scared of Pieyan the bigfoot but feels the same about Belle, all naked but for a hat, sitting there drinking coffee at the table, laying her huge tetons to rest on the table and scratching herself. Both stink to hog heaven.

Belle's family has never come looking for the mad woman, and Pieyan loves her and takes good care of her. She makes her own family, never remembering that she has been a snake.

∞ ∞ ∞

WELL, the Leroux cousins and Harley Aucoin are in the swamps with all their little children. Those girls sure have trapped them, but they love every minute.

All three men and their wives avoid the peculiar couple, Pieyan and Belle, like the COVID. They live behind locked windows and doors, so afraid she will come back with Pieyan some time.

The babies, Soul and Easy, and their parents, Saul and Roberta and Eli and Trixie, come to see all the relatives down on Bayou Quemas. Both men are so amazed they are new daddies and grandpas at the same time, and they all make up for the time lost being enemies.

Saul and Roberta ask Minou and Joe to be godparents to Precious Soul. They are tickled pink to be nanan and parrain, so everything Minou buys – and it's plenty – for the baby girl is pink.

Easy's parrain and nanan are Eli and Trixie, and they love him and are tickled pink too. The wives are already planning the two babies' wedding.

All the village comes to watch these babies romp and jump and have themselves a fun time. Most are related in some way and are stairsteps in age, but they all play good together.

Pieyan and Belle stand in the trees, watching and hiding and smiling, so wanting to go play themselves. Belle says to Pieyan, "I'm so sorry, Poochie, I can't have your baby. I'm just too old."

Thank the good Lawd!

∞ ∞ ∞

REMEMBER Joshua Silverberg, the reporter that changed his livelihood after his encounter with the gang? He is scared sober about what his snooping around Monsieur Mayhem (aka T-June) causes. He has gone into the music business with his brother, and they have just completed work on the Monsieur Mayhem Band's next album.

Joshua and Jim Silverberg have become well-known with a studio that records famous singers and bands coming from all over the world, mostly from Great Britain. The British bands love the laid-back attitudes of the people who threw their tea in the bayou. It is the English who threw the same people out of Nova Scotia that they try to emulate all over the world. You know, Cajuns.

The Silverbergs are able to buy what they need for their businesses and are making lots of moola! They own the Down tha Bayou Recording Studio and a publishing company named Tippy's, in honor of their mother. A remarkable musician, she played many instruments and sang like an angel. She gave them their love of music and writing. She could have published awesome work.

The used-to-be reporter Joshua wins the Hugo Award for the incredible piece of fantasy he publishes. The publishing world thinks Joshua has become one of those authors who disappears after their one book. A one-hit wonder. Then when he becomes famous in the recording business, they begin to call him a Renaissance man.

But we all know the true-blue Renaissance man is T-June.

T-June's band, Monsieur Mayhems (that's their new band name), is in sessions again, working on their third album. The first two have won them Grammys.

The cousins, Justin and Scottie Leroux, are now on their second album, because their first goes to the top of the hit parade for weeks. The Silverberg brothers are now managing the Lerouxs, and their sound is bringing back old Louisiana music, songs that have been forgotten but now sound brand new.

Everybody is making good money, including the Lerouxs, who have known hardships in their past. Their bucket once had a hole in it.

Antoine Domino III is also one of the members of the Monsieur Mayhems band, and he is wealthy. He and his wife use the money to open his own church down the street from Bishop Toussaint's church. You have to come to the Big Easy to hear the new renditions of Fats Domino music sung in spiritual words to his tunes. Antoine III has included Jesus in the mix of those they pray to.

We have two churches on lesser spectrums of religion but behaving in both just about the same, falling out in the spirit and dancing in the aisles. Sometimes, the two churches will have competitions for the best choirs between them and a few other churches.

True Blue Aucoin is successful and rich from being one of the band members, and he is definitely a man-about-town of Baton Rouge, as long as his family is there in the governor's office. True is a New Orleans dude, and he lives it up in Baton Rouge until he can return home. The girls from the Capital City love them some True Blue from the city.

He is very low key with his powers and seldom uses them unless he's with his parrain, T-June. Other than parlor tricks to enchant the ladies, he stays hidden from the world.

True's become interested in politics, and Henri and Callie are wanting him to stay and go to school at LSU to start a political education. Best, most positive way to use his ability of reading minds.

Can't you just see his campaign slogans? Vote for True Aucoin, True Blue with his promises and knows what you need all the time.

Just like his papa.

They come to the bayou as much as possible with their busy schedules. True and T-June enjoy each other's company and are so tight. True has become a grown-up podnah. The two of them cavort with all the little animals, talking and laughing and having the best time that no one else but them can experience.

True always travels with his bag of tricks for his magician act. Bless his little magical heart. He does parlor tricks with his gifts. Everyone gathers at Minou and Joe's for True's wonderful magic acts when he comes to their house. The whole bunch is crying with laughter and having to run to the bathrooms.

Nobody even lets the thought cross their minds to follow him into sainthood.

∞ ∞ ∞

BUTCH and Katrina still live in Eagle Lake, Texas. and have an amazing horse ranch, picking up from Sweet Stu's accomplishments in his legacy and taking it further, building a foundation to help the poor and the people fleeing oppression and poverty across Latin America, especially Mexico.

∞ ∞ ∞

NOW, my bébés, I'm gonna tell you about Joseph Alan Thibeau Junior's unbelievable life.

Joseph Thibeau is a famous psychologist now. This is his chosen field. But he splits two successful careers evenly. He didn't know a little gig with Jolie would turn music into this huge thing in their lives. He is now Monsieur Mayhem to the world out there, and no one out there knows a thing about T-June.

Jolie Theriot Thibeau has turned into one of the famous New Orleans ladies of soul and blues. Although her growing-up years are pious and seriously shy, she changes the minute she hits the New Orleans city limits. Jolie is earthy, and her spirituality shines through every pore of her mystical body and soul. She is a woman of the times, has money in her own right, and does what she loves, music. The genes of Buddy Braxton come out strong in Jolie, especially when she's wearing the emerald ring with diamonds that he handed her out of his ghostly pocket.

There is a huge celebration when the couple announces they will be a mama and papa in seven months. Everybody is jumping up and down, with Minou and Joe crying.

Minou says while she cries, "Awww, my one-of-a-kind son, Ah take dat back 'cause now we have True. Ah pray dis baby don't give y'all tha problems ya created when you was born! Ah, merde. Ah mean, if tha baby comes wit' gifts, well, we all are here to help now dat we know how to deal wit' it. Ya know, wearin' tha T-shirt and then usin' it for a dish rag. We old hands doin' dis. Ah mean, 'til ya moved to tha city and took back yo raisin', 'cause ya didn't want us up in ya bizness.

"But T-June, we still get drawn into quemas of ya doin's. It jus' gets bigger. Ah like it, don't get me wrong, but sometimes it's more dan we can handle.

"Ah'm sorry, June, Ah get off track easy now like tha bishop used to. Ah'm on medication for dat.

"Me and ya papa are so happy for ya. It's a wonderful announcement, and we couldn't be prouder of you two. We love ya bofe so much. Dere wouldn't be anyt'in' we wouldn't help y'all wit', as ya know.

"All of us have this sinus problem, ya know, bein' too nosy and wantin' to see what tha next day will bring, so dat's our faults too for addin' to tha quemas sometimes."

Ya think?

There are empty champagne bottles and empty whiskey bottles, ashtrays full of roaches and a few cigarettes, and empty plates all over Minou's house the next morning for her to pick up. Minou and Joe and T-June clean up because Jolie is in the bathroom, throwing up her guts. She doesn't partake in the festivities, but the sight the next morning is enough to gag anybody.

Minou's house never looked like this. Just the fact that Joe isn't bitching is a good sign.

He and Minou "get sum" the previous night. Hell! Probably everybody at the party "gets sum," except the ones who do without.

∞ ∞ ∞

THIS has been the strangest pregnancy anyone on Bayou Mayhem has witnessed yet, in all the births that have been added to the town. Jolie will have violent projectile vomiting, making you think of The Exorcist. Her feet blow up like balloons, and she's looking like she is carrying triplets. She has a voracious appetite and rashes throughout her pregnancy.

Jolie has to take maternity leave off both jobs. Doctor says she has to stay off her feet.

T-June is trying hard to help Jolie, but she isn't the sweet girl she used to be. She gets up in the morning swinging pots and pans because she can't drink coffee. It's a constant battle with everyone. She doesn't like anybody.

Jolie is running T-June ragged. He tells her not to worry about cooking. He will take care of their eating. It's too easy to find cooked food in New Orleans.

Jolie's envie is Popeyes Fried Chicken, extra spicy. Then she adds more seasoning. No wonder she has balloon feet.

Madam Aucoin and T-Mae and Laurette go to take care of her by her mama, Estelle's, house. Making potions and doing trances because Laurette's daughter has taken her mama's place. They talk every day like they are using cell phones.

Fuck a duck. They may even time travel.

It's like this baby still in Jolie's womb is telling them all with his little middle finger poking out her belly. He moves constantly and has his mama sleeping on the couch because it's a straight shot to the toilet. She is peeing every twenty-five minutes. T-June times it one night.

T-June tries desperately to help her, but Jolie reacts to everything in a negative way, wanting nothing but a big-ass joint.

Theo and Estelle are worried sick about Jolie. She has become a devil. She sure has been using inventive language, cussing like the French and Vikings. She's just this side of growling, talking in tongues, and spewing vomit, but they watch close that her head doesn't start rotating. They talk to Father Becnel about an exorcism for her.

Jolie and T-June do have their moments anticipating their baby boy, and they are tender and loving the way it is. Well, until the baby starts kicking and elbowing her.

The women are frightened but amazed when they see a little fist in her side and can identify it because of the little middle finger standing high, out by itself.

All the women come apart when they saw his foot so close to her cootchie. It looks like it will soon be sticking out her cootchie. They all knew it is hurting her terribly, because of the total nasty words coming out her mouth.

"Fuck a duck" is mild by comparison.

(My son is telling me he's gonna have to use his inheritance getting me out of jail for being a pervert, enticing all the ducks on the bayou.)

Poor Jolie, heartbroken because of this horrible pregnancy, her believing it will be wonderful because all the sistas are telling her it will pass. It gets much worse, never letting up with anything. This poor, sultry, blues singer can still belt out the blues, but she knows she is far from being sultry right now. One song she will sing every day is "Don't Ya Let Nobody Drag Your Spirit Down."

Y'all, listen to Eric Bibb. Madam C loves him as well as Keb Mo.

Poor bébé. She still has six weeks to go.

Weedie comes to visit every day. She's Sister Marie since they won't let her use Sister Weedie because there isn't a saint named that.

Behind closed doors, they will hear cussing, singing, and something sounding like punches. When the doors open, all you can see are little white beads of stuffing coming out a bean bag, but Jolie is having a better day, and the beloved sistas replace the bean bag every day.

Minou and the gang are afraid of asking who is punching the bag.

Jolie gets some sleep that night, unusual because this child isn't punching her, but she is beating the shit out of him, vicariously, of course, through that bean bag.

Flavia and Sister Bridget are sitting at the closed door, keeping themselves against the wall, steadily listening and steadily saying their rosaries and carrying bottles of holy water. A shot glass is being passed between them up against the wall, with Minou taking her turn.

Can you just see this?

Everybody in their own town comes to visit her because she's doing all of this propped up with pillows in the damn bed. Minou is saying rosaries with Sister Bridget and Flavia, and she goes to the city to His Divine Spirit every Sunday morning because she can't stand to look at either of them, Jolie or T-June.

When June comes to her for advice, she just shrugs her shoulders and walks away.

T-June is asking everybody for advice about what's been happening and rocking his world. The male critters are telling him they don't have that problem. They just leave and go to another briar patch.

He doesn't ask for Pieyan's advice because T-June doesn't want to run into the naked, stinky, mad woman wearing a droopy old straw hat with flowers wilted off the sides. And Pieyan for sure doesn't know nuttin' 'bout birthin' no babies.

T-June sits at T-Mae's kitchen table, so worn out that T-Mae takes pity on him. T-Mae tells him, "Mais, bébé, Ah ain't never seen tha like. Ah had a rough time when Bastille was took by dem wolves, dat bitch Gertie. Uh, she wanna come here and be tha boss ovah here. Dat's her happy ass. Ah don't trust tha bitch. She might take a likin' to one of my other chrirren.

"Cher, Ah wish Ah could tell ya Ah can help ya. Jolie done spit at me and holla at Laurette to get tha fuck away from her. Ah'm gonna tell ya, Ah don't know what tha shit dis baby is gonna be."

T-June goes to Joe almost in tears and sits, rolling himself a fat-ass joint. Joe tells him, "My son. Mais. Ah ain't never seen nuttin' like dat! Ah know we ain't got tha devil comin', but it sure as hell looks like dat. Ah can tell ya, you was hard to deal wit' by yourself, but Ah feel like we got another battle comin' down de road wit' dis boy.

"Mais, what ya gonna name him? Ya bettah hope it's Charlie Daniels fiddlin' and not tha devil!"

Minou finally speaks up. "Awww, Awww, Ah find tha words hard to find. And ya know for me, dat's hard. Ah ain't never seen dis before in my whole life. Ah know dere's women who have a hard pregnancy but are natural bitches. Jolie ain't never been a bitch. Ah almost believe like Estelle and Theo dat a exorcism should happen.

"But den Ah realize you tha daddy, dat yo genes are doin' battle wit' dose other genes runnin' in his blood. Bébé, Ah'm wit' ya both all tha way, but Ah don't know if Ah like dis baby. Ah love him, but dis may be tha one chile Ah'm gonna slap."

The baby decides it is time to come out after Jolie carries him ten months. The women have never seen the amount of water breaking, like a hot faucet on the jet cycle of the nozzle, like she has a weenie.

Jolie is screaming with pain, and they rush her to the hospital. The doctor tells them it is a breech birth and is going to be difficult because of this.

They all see the doctor trying to reach for the baby's foot that is indeed hanging out her cootchie. This bad boy is kicking at the doctor and pulls his foot up back in the birth canal.

The female doctor gasps and stands back at the sight.

That's when T-June speaks up for everybody, and he says to the doctor, "Doc, she won't let me near her, and I can't do anything for her. My decision is to perform a C-section because we are all ready to end this quemas. Go ahead, Doc. Knock her out."

The operating room has the women and T-June up in there in gowns and masks. All of them pitch a huge hissy fit when they're told they can't go in.

We all know they don't answer to no.

Jolie is out like a light when the doctor cuts into her abdomen, and this baby sits up in the hole, covered in thick mucus and struggling to get out the veil. He tears it open before the women can cut it, struggling to come out of his mama's stomach.

Estelle screams like the devil imp is after her and faints out cold on the floor. Flavia gets her spray bottle of holy water, trying to douse him with it, hollering, "Be gone, ya lil devil!" Minou is stunned into silence, while Madam Aucoin fans everybody with a huge fan advertising their church, steadily talking in tongues.

The eleven-pound baby props his elbows on the side of the incision and talks. Thank Gawd Jolie is still out in dreamland.

(It's 8 a.m., and this comes out my head.)

This big infant says, "Where ya at, Mama? You can call me Jude. Now Papa, help me get outta here."

All the women hit the floor, and I mean all the women. The nurses, the clean-up lady, and the doctor faint, and all are piled up on each other. What a revolting development this is.

The Life of Riley, in case you trying to place it.

T-June grabs his boy up and starts hollering at all the women on the floor to wake up and attend to Jolie. They are again professional women and finish their jobs, but the majority of them are going to retire in the next month, taking a vow of silence, never to speak of this again.

You know the HIPAA laws?

The doctor will write an article in the doctors' journal and present it at the next convention. She will be bodily removed from the podium for bringing science fiction into their serious medical discussions.

T-June allows them to cut the umbilical cord and wraps Jude up in towels and cleans him, telling him not to say a thing.

When Jolie sees her son, she starts laughing, hugging, and kissing him.

Then he says, "Where ya at?"

And she goes out back to her dreamland, which doesn't involve a talking baby only a few minutes old.

The family continues taking care of Jude and Jolie because the staff in the nursery has refused to go to their room. Too many rumors fly out that delivery room, and Voodoo is mentioned. Those women and the doctor remember the last time these people showed up birthing a baby.

'Til the end, is what I said, but I have a sneaky feeling it won't be the   last.

Part Three

Chapter Twenty-One

High Winds Soon

ALL up and down Bayou Lafourche, the lower part for sure, people have known hurricanes up close and personal.

Hurricanes come and go but not before leaving evidence they have come and gone. Leaving hardship, heartache, and horrible destruction.

The particular families we all like so much and maybe love have known many hurricanes in their lifetimes, living in the South of the South.

It's a word you learn very early in your childhood, and you never forget it.

Hurricane.

+ + + + +

Old Man Joe Thibeau is talking with his bride of how many years, Minou, while they share drinking their Mello Joy on the screened porch and reading the newspapers.

"Aww, ma lil Sweet Pea, you look nice dis mornin'. It does me so good to see ya smile. Ever so often ya need to get back to me and you. Wit' all dis quemas wit' everbody's chirren, we put each other on dat gas stove dat got a back burner. Ah mean, dey gotta come ever' Saturday and Sunday?

"And den Ah gotta haul dere asses to da property in da back. Shit, dey can afford big-ass boats, ever' single one of dem.

"Mais, why Ah gotta tell dem everyt'in'?

"Mais, at least dey bring food to feed ever'body, but Ah'm tired of Popeyes. Ah pass tha gas after ever' time Ah eat dat shit. Yo fried chicken is way bettah dan dat greasy shit.

"Mais, Ah keep waitin' for ya to pass me a slap 'cause Ah know ya smell dat.

"Oh. Look, bébé, dere's a depression in da Gulf. We got tha time to watch dat, okay, bébé?"

Poor Minou, Joe has gotten worse over the years with his bitching.

"Joseph." She calls him that when she's pissed because he's so judgmental.

"Joseph. Ya gotta LOOK for somet'in' to bitch about. Like yo worried 'bout some gas. Yo ass. Why we got dat big-ass silver tank in tha yard, for gas, right? Tha sumbitchin' t'ing is full. As if, as if.

"Ya know all dem old dudes ya laugh at? Ya just like dem, old man. Ya could tell all dis merde to tha bunch when ever'body comes, but nooo, but nooo. Ya all smiles when dey here, and then Ah catch tha merde after.

"Joseph, ya can take yo'self outside and bitch to Leroy and Gertie. Dey don't know what ya sayin' and dose bad-ass wolves love ya anyway.

"Go. Go.

"Shit, ya worse dan Ah was when Ah passed tha menopause. Mais, cher, ya t'ink men have dat?"

Minou doesn't waste a thought on the Gulf. Too much else has her attention.

∞ ∞ ∞

BISHOP Toussaint watches the Weather Channel every day. The subject is changing the names of hurricanes to include men. Why? Because we want everything they have too.

Come on. When you think about a hurricane, isn't it a woman hollering at the moon?

Hurr-icane?

The Bishop has a huge map of Louisiana on the wall in his study at his down-the-bayou home. Big enough Victorian home to house many people, if you don't mind the ghosts.

He uses every kind and color of little pins to mark all the lines leading to and out the Gulf. They even sent the bishop their little pins from the Weather Channel. He saves them for the heavy-duty women coming in the Gulf.

He's bought enough equipment for him to be able to pinpoint an accurate prediction, sometimes better than the dudes on the Weather Channel. He'll call them if he thinks they're not right.

He takes this hobby/job seriously, and he'll be on alert waiting.

He calls everybody to make sure they know and what to do to get ready.

∞ ∞ ∞

FLAVIA King now lives with her two grown sons in her big house, like it used to be. She treats them like they used to be, the two little Comanche boys, just like it used to be.

Grey and Gerry King have long, straight black hair tied with leather, wear turquoise jewelry bestowed on them by their tribe, excellent skin naturally tanned, and deadly smiles, White white teeth and dimples. Somewhere back in their genes, because Indians aren't known for their dimples.

They are able to make contact with their parents on the reservation somewhere by Eagle Lake, Texas.

Their mom and dad are both in recovery for years, and they have younger siblings.

Ohhh, their mom cries the very real tears of her mourning her two sons, never thinking she will see all her children together.

The Comanche tribe welcomes them with ceremonies and gives them the turquoise as gifts for the warriors that have returned home bearing gifts and money.

The tribe thinks it fitting indeed that a large amount of money comes from the little Indian braves out of the King's Ranch inheritance.

What goes around, comes around.

The boys have traveled the world, not a care in the world, and are eligible bachelors to the world. They are worldly and continentally known. Neither of these men cares about any of that. They just love to travel the world and make new friends, some pretty exotic and willing.

Grey and Gerry King don't take anything seriously, loving and leaving the gals on the shores waving handkerchiefs and crying in the rain.

The women from all around the world are just struck dumb and gaga at the sight of these magnificent Native American men. So many, many women have tried to make a relationship into a marriage that would be a catch in all their circles.

Good luck with that.

Grey and Gerry are so otherworldly too, slow with being stoic, and smiling all the time. Gerry is the smiler because Grey is the one with his moccasins on the dirt, not letting too many people sneak up on him.

They both come to their mama Flavia's house every weekend down the bayou. They have a beautiful home in the Garden District, their home base.

Again, not a care in the world. Until now. Their mama needs them now.

Grey is following her in the store one day, not too closely because she will turn and pass you a good slap. He's steadily picking up what she's throwing down.

Flavia will say, "Ya can't tell me nuttin'. Dis is Mrs. Flavia's General Store, and dat ain't you."

That's a sure thing. Flavia has never added her store to the inheritance that keeps being added to with more money, the store. She refuses to talk about it, saying, "If ya mind ya own bizness, den ya won't be mindin' mine."

She is causing havoc everywhere she goes, arguing about politics, sainthood, and potions she could get you under the table. Then telling everybody she has pull and tries to get everybody to smoke a joint.

Everybody that walks in the store, sometimes they turn right back around, not letting that RC Cola sign screen door hit them in the ass.

The straw that breaks the alligator's back is Flavia standing outside voting booths and trying to get the voter's vote on who she wants to see up there in the governor's house. She can finally say she's been to his house a bunch of times.

When she hits a man on the head with her heavy purse that has a loaded .357 Magnum gun in it, the man calls the cops and the poll ladies want her removed. The man has to go to the hospital, hollering he's going to sue.

She fights the po-po while they triy to put her in their car, and they are afraid of her, rightly so. They call Minou to come pick her up. The King brothers are called home to stay.

Flavia still reads her newspaper, mostly obits and who got arrested that night, but she also reads about the depression coming into the Gulf.

She tells the boys, "Listen up, boys. Y'all don't worry 'bout a t'ing. Mama's gonna take care of y'all. Ya know Ah got pull, and Ah'm gonna go call tha weatherman and see what he t'inks. Y'all don't worry."

The city slickers are trying to tell the country folk what to do about the situation.

As if, as if.

Nobody is saying "Come to our house" because we all know what Hurricane Katrina was about.

Still, they continue with advising them like renting a bunch of hotel suites north of the Louisiana Mason Dixon line: Alexandria, Monroe, and Shreveport.

∞ ∞ ∞

JOE and Pete Dugas and Junya Rappolet watch the weather intently most of their lives. All of the lives that live close to the Gulf do. It's their families, their work, and their homes that cause everyone to pay attention, like they have been taught their whole lives.

Sister Bridget is going where the village goes, to the Yankee country where Irene and Jean go to her family up around Columbia (the town, not the district). The sister will be in the car that doesn't have the Jude Dude, on purpose.

Irene has invited all to come to North Louisiana and has invited everybody to come home with her and Jean. Good thing they got some good cooks.

Damn, it's barely a tropical depression, growing into a small storm.

Be prepared, say the Girl Scouts.

Sister Marie (aka Weedie Miller) will stay to help refugees and the elderly, giving shelter to everyone, using all the money provided by Flavia to the nunnery. Flavia can be totally generous but will pick up the penny on the floor, wanting to save it.

That's why she still has that penny.

∞ ∞ ∞

T-JUNE and Jolie's son, Jude, comes into the world, talking and demanding and remarkable with his birth. It's been non-stop with the baby who tells you his name when he is born, climbing out the womb.

A code of silence appeared in the delivery room, being no one could break this and alert the world. HIPAA, you know.

The nursery is closed to this baby. Something leaks out besides the waters broken, out from behind the doors concerning his birth, and they prefer for his mama to keep him in her room.

The family is able to push the discharge early, and the doctor doesn't object. She feels like she has seen it all with the birthing of this baby and doesn't want to deliver another one.

A new one for the medical books.

When she is invited to the next doctors' medical convention to speak, she is thrown out the auditorium for this Frankenstein bullshit.

Everybody who has followed T-June to manhood knows his son will be double the trouble he was, and they are doubting their ability to follow behind this little dude, Jude. They may wind up playing the "old" card, the one stating they may be getting too old.

Jude is a talker, and boy, he doesn't shut up.

The Cajun Mafia (followers-disciples-posse-village-coven-sistas-whatever) are not expecting anything like his birth and now wish he would be silent like other babies his age. This baby can tell you he wants something to eat, when he wants to be carried, and when he needs his diaper changed.

He doesn't have too much patience. He wants what he wants and wants right now.

He will cuss like a professional cusser, and if you don't do it right then, he'll take his diaper off himself and throw the container of shit on the floor.

He can't quite walk yet, and it's an aggravation to him.

Jude doesn't like to depend on the grownups. All he needs to do is start walking, and then he can do for himself.

He's such a little smart ass, but T-June and Jolie say he's expressing himself. He's got a big Napoleon Complex.

Wait 'til he can walk, then he'll think he's not going to need anybody. He thinks so well of his little Napoleonic self.

These children, all of them, aren't being raised in the good old ways that teaches you to respect your elders, don't think you know more than them, and listen to what is being said by them, the Elders.

Big, big thing to remember: be quiet when you are being talked to and remain silent at that time.

Don't make me want to slap you.

This little man is the boss of his house. T-June and Jolie allow him to be free to do what he wants and express himself. Good thing he lives in the city because Minou has been tempted to slap his smart mouth and make him kneel on rice in the corner.

None of them knows what to do with Jude, the first of his kind, and they have backed off from following in his footsteps, for sure.

When the sister and the father come to visit Jude, he's bribed into not talking and to act like a normal baby. They really feel Sister Bridget is TOO OLD to handle this, another supernatural being. She would have a massive heart attack and keel over dead.

They don't know about Father Becnel. He's made the big times in his chosen career of priesthood. He is from humble beginnings, and he has made it all the way to the top. The humble beginnings are always a good selling point.

Most of his brother priests love his laid-back attitude and personable personality and the fact that he always has plenty of money to bring to the table.

Is it all of the above qualities or because he stays stoned all the time? Probably all; the other brothers are alcoholics.

∞ ∞ ∞

SO, everybody is watching the Gulf for a storm coming, and it's become very strong, turning into a hurricane quickly, with the name of Bertha. It's heading to their part of the world.

Everybody has been put on notice by Bishop Toussaint to get ready. You know, batten down the hatches and stay the course and get ready for Bertha.

Minou and Joe and T-June and Jolie with their brat, Estelle and Theo Theriot, and Flavia have decided to go north to Columbia, Louisiana.

They've never run from a storm before, but they look at it like it is going to be a nice visit to meet Irene's country folks.

Irene and Jean Breaux are delighted with their decision and call ahead to tell her folks that company is coming. Her people don't care about color, alone among their neighbors who fly the Confederate flag proudly and fly it close to the road, not to be missed.

It's going to be very hard on Jude, hiding his abilities from the folks that are preparing for their visit. He knows now that you have to learn to be normal around other people, just as his papa has to do. He isn't happy about this, but you never know, maybe somebody up north might have the same abilities.

Sister Bridget has decided to stay in Flavia's big house. She goes on a spending spree with nobody there and leaves her credit card on the counter, along with an itemized list of what she enjoys buying. Sister Bridget's very own shop-'til-you-drop with nobody's business but her own.

Flavia's boys are staying to make sure everything is all right, and they will end up, along with Sister Marie, helping those who cannot leave.

Everybody else will be using Madam Aucoin's sanctuary of the huge house of spirits. She tells the ghosts to remain silent, as much as they can, so as not to upset Madam's daughters, who are coming unwillingly to the house.

They better not mind the ganja.

Madam loves her three daughters, but she doesn't like them none.

T-Mae and Junya will be there with their brood but are not that worried about the whole thing. First time they've run from a storm in their lives, and going to Madam's house will be like a vacation in a swanky hotel.

T-Mae now has knowledge of how the Voodoo doll works. She loves sticking pins in it and watches one daughter scratching like a big-ass mosquito has bit her, one she can't reach to scratch.

The combination of T-Mae with Madam and Laurette are a powerful force to be reckoned with. Laurette tries to stay in the background because the daughters look at her suspiciously, knowing her but not knowing her.

The rest of the crew that live Down Below, Justin and Scottie and Harley, will batten down at Junya and T-Mae house instead of being up in the trees of their houses. Pieyan and Belle are going to tough it out in their home. Belle has no worries and will follow Pieyan like a kept woman tends to do, naked or not.

∞ ∞ ∞

HURRICANE Bertha is a category 4 storm, and she is coming full force to Lafourche Parish with all of her ba-aAss self to come and stay for a few hours, leaving nothing but quemas for days and days.

Our Bertha, Minou's mama, sure wasn't like that, unless she was the loup-garou.

Bishop tells them Bertha's winds will be coming in at 180 mph and lots of flooding, with her pushing the waters everywhere like she is throwing the big pan of water out the back door.

Oh, Lawd, it's bringing back memories of other storms that Madam C has endured all her life, with a father and husband that refuse to leave their house.

It's the day before Bertha makes landfall, and everyone heading north is preparing to leave, like the moccasin on a cypress log, sliding right out of here.

It is normally a five-hour trip, but now it's going to take more hours getting there because of the traffic of scared people driving all crazy to get gone.

The caravan of Cajuns makes it to Irene and Jean's family up in Columbia in ten hours.

Everybody in his car is telling Jude to act like a baby, please. With bribes and fingers pointed at his nose daring him, for sure MeMe Minou is warning him, itching to whip his little ass.

Poor home training.

Joe, getting out the car and stretching his legs, speaks to the first man that approaches him. "Awww, ya so nice to let us come to ya house wit' all dese people. Mais, we Irene's long-time friends, and we love her to pieces. We family, us.

"But Ah'm kinda nosy. Man, what's up wit' tha names of all dem little towns dat go from seventy to forty-five if ya blink ya eye? Some speed traps, poor t'ings, dey got to make some money some kinda way.

"Mais, Ah ain't ever heard of dat, like Uterus and Ball. What Ball? And tha best one. Dry Prong. Ha ha ha ha ha! It makes me haunt to t'ink dat.

"Mais, ya got tha Uterus and tha Dry Prong on tha road just down tha road? Somebody shoulda took care of dat by now. And mais, what's up with Hebert? Dey tole us it's called Hee-burt.

"A Lafourche River and a lake? Dat's where we from, Lafourche Parish and Bayou Lafourche.

"Mais, go figure dat."

The man turns out to be Uncle Charlie, and he shakes Joe's hand, wondering what the shit he has said, smiling at Joe the whole time. He doesn't have his hearing aids in his ears and can't understand what he's saying, the times he heard a word.

They all walk up on this large, two-story, Civil War-built house, standing in the downstairs screened porch, hugging everybody who has come to meet them.

They all are unbelieving what they've lived through coming up here, after all those winding, hilly, little one-lane gravel roads with the signs that say 55 mph.

Forget that!

Welcoming laughter and ta-tas going around the house to the road-weary bunch of Cajuns and the smells of something to eat draw them to the kitchen. Awww, you talk about good food and good company. They are so happy the families are there and roll out the red...make that the magnolia tree, blooming in the night air. Simply intoxicating with the straight up pines and the woods, their scents drifting through them, growing in the red dirt, instead of big old ancient trees that have grown in muddy swamp water.

The trees down home, pushing themselves out of the water, knees first, to help spread the Spanish moss into the next tree up against the other, the cypress tree.

In honor of.

The meal, which is served when they go into the big, old rambling house, is hot and wonderful. Pitchers of iced tea in glass gallon jugs are being put on the table. Everyone is drinking out a Ball jar full of ice and eating awesome hot, buttered cornbread, while the vegetables – small, fresh lima beans and corn on the cob – are cooking.

∞ ∞ ∞

OLD screened porches with swings and rockers and home-sewed cushions invite anybody to sit out there. The family heads to the large swings and plunks down on the big old chairs, so full from supper and smoking their own.

The matriarch chooses to sit with them out there after the baby and his mama and daddy go to bed.

Thank the Good Lawd.

Minou and Joe and Estelle and Theo are out there. Flavia has gone to bed too.

Thank the Good Lawd.

Irene's in the kitchen helping her cousin clean and dry the dishes, and Jean is mopping the big planks of the pine floor, using Pine Sol.

"Well, y'all just come hug my dirty neck. Y'all can call me MeeMaw," the old lady says, and Minou is totally not ready for that, missing the meaning behind the phrase.

Estelle does just that. She goes and hugs her, avoiding the dirty neck.

Ruby Jewel Flowers is her name, and she is as Mississippi raw-boned as they come but from Louisiana instead. A beautiful older woman with a head full of thick, shining, white hair pinned up in a large netted bun. Fair-headed at one time, glimpses of blond, a big woman in frame, not in weight. Her hands are the telltale of hard work, but her face isn't, with a broad face of little wrinkles confusing them to her age.

Rose-colored old-time frames sit on her nose, with high cheekbones telling you there's some Native blood.

A genuine kind soul and open-hearted kind of woman.

"Y'all, it does my soul so good to see all y'all people who helped bring my Irene back to my house. It's like havin' my Fancy back. I used to call Irene's mama Fancy. Her name was Sweet Kylie, because she was so purty. Beautiful young girl with flowin' blond hair, blue eyes, and freckles. She used to work at the general merchandise in downtown Columbia, and that's where your mama met your daddy, Irene."

Ruby turns to her granddaughter Irene, who joins them on the porch. Ruby is tearfully wiping her glasses on a faded full apron covering her large bosom and motioning for Irene to sit by her on the swing.

"Aw, honey, I wish you could've seen your daddy back then. He was one of those beautiful Cajun boys from somewhere down there, and when he walked up in the store where your mama worked, they wanted each other right then and there."

She stops a minute to stuff tobacco in her corn cob pipe and lights it. It doesn't take a second to smell that she is smoking ganja. They all relax then in their chairs, waiting for Ruby to continue her tale.

"I want y'all to know he was a good young man who came a-courtin' my Fancy. He had just come back from the Vietnam War, and your grandaddy loved him. They shared war stories and loved to drink that moonshine my uncle used to make. They loved to joke with each other and pull pranks, your daddy laughin' so hard.

"Grandad would call him 'Coonass.' That was before he got religion, that foolish man, your grandad. Like he knew a damn thing about snakes, and that's what got him kilt.

"I didn't go to his church with him because I didn't believe in that cow pile, and his pride was hurt bein' the preacher, you know.

"Then he becomes this fanatic ole cantankerous bastard, stickin' his hands down in a nest of vipers, shoutin' 'Holy Spirit Holy Spirit!' The Holy Spirit wasn't listenin'.

"Thank the Good Lord that's over. I paid my dues.

"Danny asked for your mama's hand, and they married in that little Catholic church on the outside of Grayson. We gave them our blessin's and watched that ole sedan go down the road.

"Oh, I'm so sorry. It still makes me cry."

Irene comforts her the best she can, because all her family knows about her mama's mistreatment by Danny later. That's too much water over that bridge, and neither one wants to carry buckets any further, her mama and her papa's business.

Ruby Jewel – MeeMaw – continues to talk with them on the porch, where they are sharing homemade wine. The wine is made from the blackberries that are in abundance up here in this neck of the state.

The Cajuns live in the bottom of the boot; on the Louisiana map, it surely looks like an old shoe.

"Well, I heard stories of all that happens in the swamps from Irene and Jean. He talks just like Irene does, now that she was raised down on the bayou. Ah, hellfire. Y'all all do talk funny. It's like we from different states, for sure."

Joe has gotta say something, you know, because Flavia is in bed and not saying anything.

"Mais, Miss MeeMaw, Ah don't mean no disrespect, but you sound funny to us too. Mais, ya talk sooo slow and twangy, just like my podnah Sweet Stu from Eagle Lake, Texas. Gawd rest his soul. Ah believe he's up dere ridin' his horse wit' Jesus. He was Flavia's husband and papa to two lil Injun brothers.

"Mais, shit, he left her a bunch of money. He owned dat Kings Ranch up in Texas, and bébé, it was old and made a lot of moola for dat family.

"Ah bet Flavia can understand ya, but good luck wit' dat 'cause we don't ever know what's comin' out her mouf. Mais, she got dat demencha now. It's worse dan ever, poor t'ing."

∞ ∞ ∞

MINOU and Estelle have their own corncob pipes, and they share each other's growth from a different garden.

They are enjoying themselves on the porch, with Joe telling MeeMaw and Uncle Charlie his favorite Thibodaux and Boudreaux jokes and sometimes having to repeat them because they don't understand what he's saying.

Irene will sometimes tell them the joke, and then they will laugh their heads off. They really like, "Guess who drowned in tha lake today? Dugas Dugas."

This big, hulking young man in overalls comes out on the porch from the back door of the house and stands there waiting for someone to say something.

We already know it will be Joe. "Mais. Hot damn. You sum big-ass boy. My name is Joe Thibeau, and dat's Minou, my wife. Dat's our family over dere, Estelle and Theo Theriot. Ever'body else went to dere beds. Ya gonna meet dem tomorrow. Mais, how yoa do? So, what's yo name, big boy?"

He smiles a big old grin with teeth missing and plops hard on the swing next to MeeMaw, his mama, swinging it hard as high as it would go, making MeeMaw slap him.

"I'm so sorry, y'all. This is my youngest son, although he aint so young anymore. This is Drake Adam Flowers, but we just call him Bubba. Bubba, where's your manners? Talk to these family members from down in the swamps."

Bubba smiles and says, "Howdy. It's good to meet you."

A man of few words, he gets up and goes into the dark of the night.

Ruby tells them after he's out of earshot, "He's different, you know. He's my special child. Not that he doesn't have all his marbles, because he's real smart. You can't tell by lookin' at him, but I taught him schoolin' here because the other children were mean to him.

"I hear you got a special child too, Minou."

To say the least, because that is something she doesn't know about.

∞ ∞ ∞

BERTHA has made landfall with 180 mph winds, and it looks like she has emptied the Gulf with all the water she's brought with her, flooding in places that hurricanes have never gone with high flood waters before, pushing Bayou Lafourche out its banks and going where it's never gone before. Leaving people stranded on rooftops to get away from the waters, waiting for somebody to come and rescue them.

That's never happened before.

Sister Marie and the King men are struggling with the large number of refugees coming to the high school for safety and forcing the big, heavy, metal doors to close behind the last stragglers and just in time.

A large oak tree comes smashing into the doors that are force-closed by many people helping. The tree slams into the door, with roots coming out the ground and breaking the windows, glass exploding everywhere and the roots trying to find somewhere to bury themselves.

They all could hear screams louder than the mighty winds of night, of those drowning and watching out the second-floor windows as their houses go floating where the current in the high water takes it. Staying in their homes, because the old belief system is intact by those who refuse to leave.

And losing their lives.

Hurricanes that come in the blackest part of night are the most bitchin' bitches, evil to the core.

Sister Marie and Grey are leading everybody to the second floor of the school because the waters are not stopping, coming into the cafeteria on the first floor where they are huddling together in the dark because, of course, the electricity goes out.

Gerry is trying to comfort the people, soothing crying babies and fussing with the alcoholics. There wouldn't be so much panic if the alcoholics would pass out. They cause more havoc being frightened and loud with their laments.

As the eye passes over them, some refugees are wanting to see how much damage is done to their properties. What the hell can they do at this point? Seriously?

We all know these people. Thinking about their livestock and the little dog forgotten or the two aunts that refused to leave.

Horror and heartache, heartache and horror.

No phones, no electricity, no gas and seeing landmarks under water have the Kings and Sister acting very calm on the outside but churning butter on the insides. They can't get out and are isolated to the rest of the community. Can't call up the northern folks and tell them shit.

Not even The Leroux brothers and Harley can call, out there in the elements.

It's the calm eye of Bertha, and you still can't see a damn thing, but don't venture out because the other side of Bertha's eye is about to slap you full force in your ass.

∞ ∞ ∞

BERTHA rages for two days, keeping the water high and not moving off the land and going where she's going next.

Well, she goes up the state, heading for north Louisiana.

The old house is shaking in the winds, the tall trees of pine swaying and throwing pine cones everywhere and bringing tornadoes right up to their doors.

At MeeMaw's neighbor down the road, it leaves a circular clothesline and takes the house.

Blessed be. MeeMaw probably has something up in her apron pocket too because they have nothing but branches to pick up.

The electricity goes out and the water system is damaged, so no clean water either, and Joe is totally outdone and speaks up the next morning.

"Mais, we run for tha first time, and look at what happens. Poor bébés, y'all got it bad too. Ah ain't nevah seen no tornado in my life, me. We ain't gotten no news, and dat's scary for sure. All dem lines are down, so we gonna be headin' home as soon as Ah can. Ah don't know if ever'body wants to leave, but Ah'm a gone pecan."

They don't hear anything from down there until late that night. Joe hadn't left yet.

Grey King is on the line. "Tante Minou, y'all stay up there if you can. Please don't bring Mama because she'll slip further into her dementia. Everyone's okay, but there's still a lot of water on the land, for sure Down Below.

"Not a thing happened to Junya and T-Mae's place, nor at Madam's house. They must have put that invisible net with their combined practices on everyone's house, because there's no damage to any of your houses, but the tree houses have serious damage. They must have forgotten to put them on their list.

"There's still people here because they have nowhere else to go. Y'all stay and don't worry. We've got it all handled.

"Weedie is awesome with help, and she has everybody laughing and in stitches because she's another one that you don't know what's coming out her mouth. I admire her so much. She just jumps right into things that need fixing and does it. Not asking for help. She is so tender with the people and especially the children. She rocks them, plays with them, and sings to them beautiful ballads in Spanish, sounding like Linda Ronstadt.

"Holy Spirit, then she turns around and is showing who raised her, you bunch of feminists. She will tell you something that will knock you out your boots, a very articulate way of cussin' in two languages.

"Please, y'all stay if you can, stay in the comfort, because I don't know when we'll have that again."

Joe gets really pissed off after that phone conversation.

"Mais, Minou. See what ah been tellin' ya? Fuck tha duck, Ah have it up to dere. Shit on a stick."

He hears that last part – shit on a stick! – come out Uncle Charlie's mouth, and he laughs so hard Charlie has to slap him in the back because he gets choked on his laughter. He's adding it to his invented and colorful cuss words.

"Dey just t'ink dey can tell me what tha shit to do. Dat Ah don't know notin. Dat's dey happy asses. Shit on a stick. We got tha biggest generator dat money could burefugy and been on by itself. Mais, at tha camp too with Junya and T-Mae's house. Dem dumbasses don't know shit from shinola.

"Mais, dat makes my hair stand up on my arms. Ah don't wanna hear anot'er t'ing come outta his mouf 'bout Weedie, uh, Sista Marie. He's up in dere, makin' a move on a goddam nun! Dat heathen don't know Jack Shit 'bout being married to tha Baby Jesus. Watch what Ah tell ya if dat ain't true.

"Me and Charlie and Jean and Theo, we gonna leave early tomorrow 'cause Charlie wants to come help wit' all da quemas. Me and Charlie and Jean and Theo feel tha same way. All dem lil bastards t'ink we too old to beat tha shit outta dem and dey know ever ting, da lil shit-asses.

"T-June needs to stay his ass up here and handle his own quemas and de big boy too, to help all y'all.

"Bébé, he makes me t'ink of Alcide – Charlie does – ever'body says dat. Ah jus' gotta learn how he talks 'cause he don't sound tha same as Alcide, but we gonna be podnahs.

"Bébé, he told me dat dere's some big-ass bucks up in dese woods, and Ah'm gonna come and get us one. Look at all dem purty deer heads mounted on tha wall."

As if Minou wants that on her walls. She's gotten Uptown.

∞ ∞ ∞

MINOU and Estelle are ready for them to go. They will handle Flavia, like they have most of their lives.

MeeMaw laughs her head off at Flavia and agrees with most of what she says.

So, the women will enjoy some women company, and it certainly isn't girl talk.

At Madam Alafair Aucoin's house, it's become unbearable for Madam, and she wants her three daughters to get up and go, anywhere else. The house is full to the brim with people and lots of babies and children, and it's those women causing all the trouble.

Madam thinks, How could I have raised these women? Maybe a touch of Laverne blood, back in the day. Everybody is related, not by choice, mixing blood with God knows who.

Those daughters can't leave during the storm and bitch to their mama the whole time. When they say it is all her fault is when Madam says for them to GO HOME. They don't have the courage to ask, Who is Laurette, kind of remembering something about her.

The ghostly Madam Consienne is furious about having to be quiet in her own house. The ghostly motley crew of horn blowers and drummers and piano players is always full of mischief and tricksters. They've taken to sneaking up on Madam's daughters and playing music to their backs, loving the way they run out of the house hollering, "Yawheh, save me" and scratching their derrieres.

You can see Madam Consienne's hand in the whole matter. She is very passive-aggressive.

∞ ∞ ∞

THE houses built in the clouds have the water up to the third step of the stairs leading to the front door. The Rappolets' house isn't flooded because it stands ten feet in the air, built in the way Cajuns like their houses, off ground that could flood any time. Most of the time safe from flooding, that's true unless the roof is blown off. Never has a flood happened before that all you could see of the house is the roof.

All of their acreage is considered high lands because they are the last lands to flood.

It is almost like a crevasse when the levee breaks and all the water from the bayou comes to claim all the high land, making it the bed once again. That's happened many times in the history of Louisiana. One day the Atchafalaya and the Mississippi rivers will combine into one hell of a massive waterway. Naming it would be a dilemma. Atchafamissippi? Missahafalaya?

It's predicted that everything below Interstate 10 will be under fifty feet of water. In fifty years, the Corps of Engineers says. It's not like everything else they do isn't fucked up.

They ought to know Cajuns by now.

Here I go again.

∞ ∞ ∞

OF course, the lights go out.

Justin and Scottie and Harley keep candles and lanterns lit all the time, hiding the stench of the swamps sometimes. Their wives love the scent of patchouli and the romantic dim lights the candles give off. They all feel more comfortable in the tree houses. They can see more.

Pieyan and Belle are a lot worse off. That poor roof is strained because of Pieyan already, so it doesn't have the timbers on too tightly, and the roof goes flying in the air, landing on a huge pecan tree, knocking all the pecans loose, green and not ready for harvest.

The weird couple (can't call them anything else) go to Scottie's new house, built for his set of twins – identical girls – and his lovely wife, who has lived on the coast all her life.

Pieyan is asking to be helped, for Miss Belle, for sure. Pieyan wouldn't have needed it, but his old lady is human, a disability.

The wives take pity on the woman and march her to bathe in the water collected in the tub for just this kind of urgency.

Pieyan wants to stay on their porch. Good thing, because he sure smells like a wet dog. They bring him the largest cup of hot coffee they can find, black like he likes it. He drinks the hot-hot coffee in one gulp, burning or not.

The boys bring him a blanket to cover him and leave him alone.

The wives, on the other hand, are amazed at the amount of dirt that comes off Miss Belle. T-Mae tries to help her bathe at least once a month, but it's putting back on the filthy clothes...because Belle insists.

T-Mae is itching to take the wilted flowered hat and throw the nasty thing in the burn pile. No telling what has happened with the mink coat.

Still, a woman can give off odors from every crease on her body. Au Naturale.

So, the wives make her scrub her privates, and they put deodorant spray all over her. They powder her behind and untangle her hair with a whole bottle of conditioner and blow her hair dry with a battery-operated hair dryer. Belle has natural waves and some curls, and she looks beautiful, the women seeing the beauty she once was.

One of their mamas has left some nice denim shorts and a plain T-shirt. Miss Belle loves them. Best labels in the clothes, and she recognizes that in her addled head, never changing her spots.

Of course, she has to join Pieyan, smelling like the perfume that is sprayed all over, with her brushed hair and even wearing lipstick and rouge, looking like she has eye shadow on with smudges on her face from the mascara. She won't let them put on mascara and proceeds to do it herself. Nothing subtle about the colors of the eye shadows.

Pieyan tells her she's beautiful, although everything is washing off as she stands in the winds and rain on the porch.

∞ ∞ ∞

UP north, the women are busy visiting and trying new crochet patterns, talking and laughing about everything.

Jolie is taking a well-earned reprieve from Jude. He's been real good. MeeMee Minou tells him so, and he's so proud of that. She has to grab him up one time up there, but in a loving way.

Minou has Jude's little face between her hands, saying, "Ya such a good bébé, you so good" and at the same time she's warning with her eyes, You bettah be a good bébé.

T-June has him walking in the woods, with Bubba showing the way to Bubba's special spot. Jude is about to explode and can't stand another minute being silent.

"Sumbitch, Papa. You know how hard it's been on me to stay quiet? Fuck a duck. I want to slap the shit out those women wanting to pinch my cheeks and legs and all of them making baby noises."

Bubba is stuck dumb and then is laughing so hard he falls over backwards on the red dirt ground and commences to coughing. Jude says to T-June to go pop him on his back. Then, the laughter starts again, and soon, they all are laughing.

Bubba takes this huge red handkerchief out his overalls pocket. It isn't too clean, but then he takes to blowing his nose, honking like a goose. And puts the nasty hanky where he pulled it out of.

Aww. Oh. Nasty.

He stays sitting on the dirt with lots of green grass growing on the hill with a view T-June had never seen before. They join him on the grass.

"Lord. Goody. Goody. Goody. I ain't never heard a little baby like him talkin'. What else does he do?

"I've got my friends who live back here, and they always come when I come to my hidey hole. But you're special, just like me. I just feel it.

"Lordy, Lordy, Miss Claudie. I ain't never seen a baby like him in the whole wide world. He take after you?

"Lord, he can cuss like Mister Nugent down the road when my hound dogs go spill his trash and gives his dog some babies. Mama said don't go sassin' him back because you have to respect your elders.

"But I know Jude does somethin' else. I can tell because I feel stuff all the time. I'm goin' to show you what I can do."

Gather 'round, all ye doubters. Lo and behold.

It must be Louisiana water because the Flowerses have never been to New Orleans. Here is this giant man-child – bigger than Joe and T-June – who's simple, but not because he doesn't think. Innocence comes out every pore, along with a look in his light blue eyes telling you, he's not from here.

Bubba lets out this sharp and piercing whistle that sounds like it comes from his gut, and all the little critters come running, even the serpents waving in the air like cobras.

Jude is in awe of the damn snakes and the whistle. "Fuck a duck. Those snakes will kill you dead. What the shit? Are you crazy? Don't start with me."

Bubba replies, "Don't ask me how I do all this. It runs in my family." When Bubba quits his belly laughing, he stays on the grass and begins to talk to the animals from his head, and they are definitely talking to him, all animated, jumping around.

June and Jude start doing the same thing, and then the critters go crazy. Here comes a massive cottonmouth ground rattler, slithering up next to the Jolly Green Giant. Bubba puts his arm down, and the snake slithers up it.

Aw, aw, aw. I got the frissons. I had to quit writing.

T-June and Jude shiver at the sight, but then they start to settle down.

Jude can't stand it. "What the hell, dude? Isn't that what killed your papa? You know that's a little too much forgiveness. I would be killing all of them."

Bubba quietly says, "This here is Ruthie Mae. She's sister to the Evil Serpent Big Bad Bruce that bit my daddy. He's still out there, but the other snakes have been lookin' for him a long time. They want to kill him because they say they got a bad rap because of him."

It becomes a party with so much conversation and dancing. T-June lets Jude take off, and he starts running; forget walking. He's loving all the little bunnies and squirrels and raccoons and little ducks waddling quacking behind their mama. He loves the little raccoons who are washing their hands in the puddles. He is trying to talk his dad into bringing a couple home.

T-June vividly remembers Ruby. He knows they couldn't handle that again.

Jude is talking his head off, laughing and running everywhere, wide open.

T-June is so glad to see this. Maybe the little baby will wear himself out and go to sleep quickly.

That little dude is a handful, even for T-June, and he can't imagine what the followers-disciples-posse-village-coven-sistas-whatever had to go through because he was an obedient child. Jude, well, most of them want to whip his little ass.

MeMe Minou now knows how Bertha and Alcide felt. You can love them, but you don't have to like them. She says he's rotten, and she dares him with her mean eyes.

They hear a loud whooping noise coming from the woods, then a loud bang on a tree. All the little critters go back to their hidey holes, and Bubba hollers back, telling them it's his friend coming.

Out of the thick wood comes this bigfoot lady with a brassiere and panties on and an old straw cowboy hat on her head, like a Queen Bee.

T-June and Jude are smothering their laughter because they don't know this female bigfoot and it may offend her. Who knows what the hell is going to happen.

What's she going to do? Hit them with her purse?

Jude finds this sight damn funny. He also thinks that Belle is scarier than Pieyan and his kind.

He's got the Sight, and he feels that, before this is over, there will be a strong competition between Belle and You Know Who.

Neither one of them has ever met a female broadfoot –she's got on some of those fluffy pink slides – dragging her humongous feet with painted toenails, and Jude is definitely going to be too wise for his years after this.

The closer she gets, they see she has big patches of rouge and big old lips painted bright red. Her eyelashes appear as though she has tried hard to put mascara on them, but it's gone all sideways because they're too long. Her face looks like she has probably shaved. And she has put her hair in pink foam rollers under the hat.

"Well, howdy. It's good to meet you. My name is Susie Q. My mama just loved that song. I watch the Grand Ole Opry with Bubba and Ruby all the time.

"Oh, mercy me. Please excuse my appearance. I didn't have time to put my dress on that Ruby Jewel made for me long time ago. I've been knowing Ruby Jewel since she was a little bitty thing. I was so glad she brought Bubba back here to meet me. Ruby thought maybe he could do something special, and she was right.

"All of us have to hide from the world we live in, for sure me and my dirty old neck. My family lives up in Oregon, where it's just too dang cold. But you know, we all run fast-fast, so it doesn't take too long to see them.

"But I haven't seen my Cajun lover in a long time. He got lost down there in the swamps. I mean, he told me he was coming back for me. He hasn't, bless his pea-picking Heart. He doesn't know a thing about his son, Pie. He left before I could tell him.

"I named him after his pappy, Pieyan. He's the reason I still get all prettied up. He loved me like that, and Ruby Jewel said, 'You get more honey from the bee that way instead of the sting.'

"Mercy me, Lord. I don't know when to shut up. I knew it was all right to come out my hidey hole.

"T-June, darlin', I don't want to mind your business, but you need to wash that baby's mouth out with the Oxygen soap. His plumb nasty mouth."

T-June and lil Jude are speechless in many, many ways.

This must be how females are for them. It's no wonder the males like to wander. Got to get away from their females if they're the same. Won't shut up and are high maintenance.

Both of them go up into her head together, telling her they're friends with Pieyan. She falls back like she's swooned (dat's true, yeah), with Bubba catching her before this massive creature hits the damn red dirt.

Suzie Q wakes up, crying tears that have washed and smeared all her heavily applied makeup, and it is running down her shaven face together like a stream.

Only after they assure her they will tell Pieyan the minute they get back does she spark back up.

T-June tells her Pieyan is shacked up with a human female, and they have a house and everything.

A house?

And she runs naked.

Suzie Q goes to swoon again, but Bubba is comforting her and telling her to muster up.

"Lord, have the mercy we all need. Hallelujah. I've found my man. What's this woman look like, and why the Sweet Baby Jesus does he live with a female human? I feel so sorry for him that he needed to keep company with a woman because there was nobody else for him to turn to.

"I pity that poor woman. He used to be some horny.

"Tell him we're coming, me and Pie. He's a grown bigfoot, as y'all call us, and looks just like his daddy."

She won't shut up, and now they have to tell Pieyan they're coming.

There seems to be common ground for all these supernatural beings being bred down south.

Zippity doo dah! Zippity day!

∞ ∞ ∞

EVERYONE picks up and leaves the north, heading for the destroyed south. Ruby Jewel, Charlie and Bubba come in his old pickup and are going to stay at Irene and Jean's house.

For sure, not Suzie Q and Pie.

Believe me, she's coming, but that's another story.

Everyone makes it home in the time it normally takes and hits the ground running. There still isn't electricity or good water, but aid comes every day in trucks loaded with ice and food and water and clothes and diapers and whatever they can throw in the trucks by the Cajun Navy.

You help your neighbors down here. It's our way.

The waters finally make it back to where the water comes from, and the water marks are unbelievable on houses and businesses and landmarks. Marks everywhere letting you know that indeed Bertha has made a pass.

Grey and Gerry and Sister Marie/Weedie are waiting with coffee and hot gumbo, where Minou and the gang head first thing. Irene and Jean go to see about their home, but MeeMaw and Bubba stay to help.

There's still people who have no place left to go, waiting on relatives to come get them. School is not open because of some damage and the refugees.

Grey is following Weedie everywhere she goes, to help her. Or that's what he says.

The men come in for a well-needed rest and are so glad to see their womenfolk. Joe pulls Minou to the back, whispering loud, "What

Ah tole ya, what Ah tole ya? Dat big-ass Injun been sniffin' behind the Sista's behind. Bébé, Ah just wanna tell him somet'in' so bad, but ya know Flavia. She be jumpin' all over my ass for fussin' wit' her baby. Aww, Ah can't hardly stand it. To watch dat.

"And Weedie, her, she's actin' like she's gonna run around on her husband, Jesus.

"Mais, what da shit is happenin' in dis world? It's fucked, fucked, fucked! Pica, Pica, Picaed."

Well, things stay the same always, regardless of what's going on around.

Minou tells Joe to quit minding everybody's business and tend to his own.

Wait 'til Flavia sees this. She's gonna have a lot to say.

∞ ∞ ∞

AT Madam and the bishop's house, things are normal for them.

NORMAL?

The daughters have left early, as soon as it is safe to return to New Orleans because this place is too haunted. The poor bébés, they can't take a joke.

T-Mae and Junya takes their brood home and say it was a pleasure to be with them in this fancy hotel.

T-Mae has something to say. "Ma cher, dem girls are so different from you. Mais, I wanna hit dem up tha back of their heads, dey so nasty to ever'body. One of dem wanted to chastise my chirren. Ah tole her, 'No way, heifer, you ain't gonna tell my chirrin nuttin'. It ain't dem bein' bad.'

"Dey wouldn't been no trouble if dey woulda been nice. Laurette had to hide tha whole time, one of dem came lookin' for her, just bein' nosy and lookin' for somet'in' to stir. Gawd, she bettah mind her own pot before she stirs in yours."

∞ ∞ ∞

T-JUNE, with Jude and Bubba, go to Down Below to check on everything there and to warn Pieyan he's got company coming.

Pieyan comes out minus Belle. She's getting her once-a-week bath.

T-June tells Jude to keep quiet, this is grownups' business.

We gonna see how long that lasts.

Pieyan falls to the ground after June tells him everything. "I never thought I would see my Sweet Pea again. Her daddy told me he would kill me if I went back. He didn't think I was good enough for her, being I came from the south. And I've got a son I never knew, that I never knew.

"She's still pretty? What's the boy look like? What the shit is gonna happen?"

Another story…

∞ ∞ ∞

WEEDIE, because that's who she is now, has left the nunnery. The couple – Weedie and Grey – goes to see his mama, who is at Minou's. Flavia takes one look at them and says, "Well, y'all took ya damn good ole time. Ah watched ya around her ever' day since we moved from Texas. Ah knew she didn't have what it takes to be a nun, sure not like Sister Bridget. Ah see ya ain't got ya veil on. Shit, Ah bet it's tha first time Jesus got divorced. Lawd, Weedie, you for sure excommunicated too.

"Oh, my Sweet Stu. Ah'm comin', just wait. Awww, Ah forget. Oh, yeah, he been dead for a long time."

Joe goes outside with Charlie, slamming the screen door hard. You know, he isn't being quiet.

"What Ah tole ya. What Ah tole you. Dey all call demself liberals, yeah, 'bout lettin' ever'body be demself and da freedom to do what dey want. Mais, me, Ah'm what ya call a Blue Dog Democrat like my papa was. Ah don't like change but shit on a stick! Mais, nevah evah dat happened since Ah been wit' Minou.

"Wait, podnah, wait. Wait 'til Ah tell ya."

Charlie and his family are staying for a long visit, and Joe is so happy. Charlie will sit for hours listening to Joe. Most times, he doesn't hear or understand, but he's fascinated with Old Man Joe.

Chapter Twenty-Two

Company's Comin'

AS Joe predicts, Grey and Weedie have a huge wedding, the best that money could buy. Joe has had a hard time accepting this because he never heard of anybody getting a divorce from Jesus.

Minou has to make him go, and his podnah Charlie sides with Minou.

The new couple leaves for their continental honeymoon that is going to be for months.

Weedie stands proudly by her man, and she'll warn all those worldly European women not to come too close. She sure as shit scares the shit out of those women, who've never been up close and personal with a full-blown woman who tells you all about yourself, calm and aloof herself.

Lots of crying in the rain, because she scares the holy hell out of the pampered little princesses who can't wait to get gone.

Flavia is some excited. She's glad and she tells everybody, "Ah don't give a rat's ass if she's kicked out that damn church. Ah wish Ah had all my money back." She tells them she's known since long time ago when her sure enough nosy self starts noticing them. Now poor darlin' Flavia is looking for a true-blue beautiful grandchild, one she can claim.

Sister Bridget visits daily. They both wish they hadn't spent so much time hating on each other.

Sister for sure has heard all about Jude, T-June's son. She's saying novenas daily with Flavia for the child because they think he's the Antichrist.

MeeMee Minou doesn't let him go around either of them. She can say what she wants, but you bettah not say a damn thing about her baby.

Meemaw Ruby and Bubba move to the south of the south and buy one of the Cajun cottages that have been in Minou's family forever. Charlie buys the shotgun house that Minou and Joe lived in when they found Gaspar the unfriendly ghost's treasure.

They all become fast friends. It's like the same two of Minou and Joe, just living in the North.

Little money is passed on the table between them, because Meemaw has sold her house to her eldest son for little money. They sure aren't worried about money.

∞ ∞ ∞

T-JUNE and Jude can't wait to bring Bubba to meet Pieyan. He can't find his way through the swamps, or he would have gone already to find the absentee father.

They take the time on a bright sunny morning to bring Bubba to meet the gang Down Below.

Oh, what a beautiful morning. Oh, what a beautiful day.

Junya and T-Mae welcome them with open arms and a pot full of coffee.

Junya is getting to be just like Joe. "Mais, hot damn. Ain't ya da sight for de sore eyes. Mais, how much ya weigh? You a big-ass boy.

"Come shake my hand. Ah'm kinda disabled wit' my back, so Ah can't hug ya, somebody big like you, cher. Come meet all my chirrin. Dey gonna love ya, even if dey gotta look up atcha. We sum short-legged lil Cajun men, but we some bad-ass."

T-Mae just hugs and hugs Bubba because he looks like a big old teddy bear in overalls and a large stiff straw garden hat with a red headband and a woodpecker feather in it.

All he needs is another big family to love, bless his little pea-pickin' heart.

Everybody knows who he has come to meet. You can't miss something like this. Everybody is up in your bizness.

Justin and Scottie greet him at their door, where Harley is also waiting. He promises Bubba to put on a show for him soon, and Bubba starts dancing to their music like George Clooney in O Brother, Where Art Thou.

He watches Harley on his TV and can't believe it's him out the TV box and real.

The whole thing gets to him, and he pulls his clean handkerchief out his pocket, honking his nose into it.

His mama says he's hurting Baby Jesus because he isn't using all the clean ones. Think about all the little children who don't have one.

He gets hugged by all of the lovely little Cajun women and all their pretty little children are amazed at the size of this man. They all say he's the Gentle Green Giant and Jolly too.

 He thinks he has never been around women and men who want to hug you all the time, but he likes it.

Justin's wife is Lola, and Scottie's wife is Emmalois and both these women are from Golden Meadow, the last spot on the road to Grand Isle. Harley's wife is Colette, and she hails from Chalmette, kin to the Halters, but she loves the country life and her two best friends.

The women are strong-ass Cajuns, keen and sometimes mean, raised up hard, but they laugh all the time. They're first cousins. Both are kin to Emile Babineaux through his wife. You remember him, don't you? The antiques dealer in New Orleans that emptied the bank of money to give to the family who found the treasure of Gaspar the unfriendly ghost by way of Jean Lafitte?

The Babineaux children are raised up right the old-fashioned way. MeMe Minou loves that.

The time has come, and the supernatural trio is waiting. Pieyan must be dragging his big feet, not wanting Belle to know and not face the music either way.

Lola and Emmalois and Colette have taken the situation over by promising Belle a bubble bath and a face with correct makeup. They tell her they've bought a new outfit for her and will curl her hair with hot rollers, dowsing her in Emerauld perfume, their signature fragrance.

∞ ∞ ∞

OKAY, it's all ready for Pieyan to meet his mate. He comes out walking very slowly, and Bubba runs and hugs his dirty neck. He isn't expecting that and just stands there, arms at his side with a surprise look, not daring to touch this man who's almost as big as himself.

Bubba begins to talk fast and excited. You know, that family is big talkers and long winded.

"Oh my Lordy, oh my Lordy. I finally get to meet you. I heard all about you from Susie Q and Pie. Well, he looks just like you.

"Poor thang, she's still waitin' on you every day to come back for her and Pie. It's been hard on her, raisin' this red-headed bigfoot up by herself because her daddy kicked them out the clan. My mama and Suzie Q grew up together as two girl youngins who were lonely.

"Just like my blessed spirit-raisin' mama, who raised me up by herself cause my daddy was bit and killed by Big Bad Bruce, the big-ass rattler. We're still looking for him. My mama says he's gonna show up one time, just wait and see. My mama says what comes around, goes around, and Ah believe her.

"My mama is back out in the house, and I know she wants to see you too. My mama says she remembers you fondly.

"My mama says to listen to your tale before I pass a judgment on you, Mama says."

Pieyan smiles, thinking back to how Suzie Q was with her chatty self and her beautiful face and remembers MeeMaw Ruby well with the little baby Bubba. She would carry notes back and forth for them, toting that big baby on her hip, just married herself to that redneck man.

Pieyan sits on the big branch that so long ago held T-June and all of these supernatural creatures who would sit to listen to Pieyan's tale.

"I never could go back. Suzie Q's daddy was her clan leader and mean as a snake. I couldn't go back up in there because he taught all of us to be mean too. The males all jumped on me and beat me bad and said they would kill me on sight if I ever came back. I loved her so bad, but I knew she wouldn't want to see me dead.

"I never knew about my son, Pie, and you were just a fat-fat baby. I used to think you would be so juicy to eat, because I was mean too. And now look at you.

"I bet that tore him a new one, her daddy having to see my son every day. He better not have mistreated my son. I'll go up there and kick all their asses.

"Bubba, when are they coming?"

Bubba says, grinning a big grin, "Any day now. She and Pie will be comin' down here and for sure company's comin'."

Here comes Belle, sashaying out the trees to find her man. Bubba watches as she approaches them.

"Golly, she's some purty. Blessed be. How did this crazy cuckoo thing happen to you? I've never seen the like. No wonder you didn't come home, Pieyan.

"Aww, Lawdy, lawdy, Miss Claudie. Wait 'til Suzie Q sees her. Lickety cricket. Bless your pea-pickin' heart."

Belle stands there flirting with all of them. What's left of a Southern belle has faded and made a parody of Belle, just downright batshit crazy. Believe me, she remembers how to flirt; she's done it her entire life to get what she wanted.

Pieyan says for T-June and Bubba to keep in touch. His brain is going crazy up in T-June's head. "Somebody better start tracking her. I'm not ready for this. The minute, you hear me, the minute Suzie comes to town, let me know."

The trio leaves and goes to the front of the property where Jude is dying to go play with all the little kids. Everybody is together in the followers-disciples-posse-village-coven-sistas-whatever of Monsieur Mayhem/Joseph/T-June/Papa.

Of course, the situation is being discussed over the blazing fire and all have brought their own, that which satisfies your soul.

Bubba goes up at the house with his mama and MeeMee Minou. Meemaw says, "Good night, and don't let the bedbugs bite."

T-Mae starts the talking, being she hangs out with Flavia. "Mais, Ah t'ought Ah'd never see dis quemas again. Junya's sister Puh got in a fight with some putain her old man was screwin' wit'. Mais, she beat tha fuck out her and her old man. Nevah took him back and married his best friend, T-Burt. Her old man was stuck wit' tha putain.

"Lawdy, Claudie. Ah pray dat don't happen agin. Can ya just see it?"

T-June is deeply disturbed with this, and he hasn't figured out what to do. Another gang war?

What a revolting development this is.

Lola, Justin's wife, speaks up next. "Mais, y'all, she ain't a bad-lookin' gal when she cleans up. Ya know, maybe they can hook her up with another bigfoot? Mais, once ya gone bigfoot, kinda hard to go back to human. Ah mean, come on, she went way on tha other side of native."

Listen to Lola. If that's not another Minou, I don't know who is.

Junya gets to put his words out there. He looks up to Joe, who isn't there to speak up. "Shit on a stick. Mais, Ah like dat, what Charlie says. Anyway, Ah don't know who dis dogfight is for, but me and mine, we gonna stay on da porch wit' dat. We gotta hep Chief get outta college. Ya can't nevah tell, it goes to show ya, ya can't nevah tell."

The two must have had fussed about it, because T-Mae shows she's pissed off by her silence.

Chief Rappolet has grown into a massive man, questing for knowledge in spite of having a rough time having to become human again. He speaks fluently four languages: Cajun English, proper English, Patois French, and Wolf. He is getting his degree in English and literature in a year with all honors. With his big frame he's still wolf-like, and dudes want no part of him.

MeeMaw and Bubba and Charlie are gonna for sure be there when the shit hits the fan. The rest will be hiding in the bushes when it happens, keeping Jude with them. He'd be right out there, for sure, up in the business of …What the hell?

Oh, yeah, he will be using foul language with his little shit-stirrer self.

Emmalois is the next to speak. Those cousins don't mince their Cajun words. "Y'all, now dat we know dere's a bunch of dem bastards, it kinda changes t'ings. Lots and lots of ground rules. Ma choo, what if dey all come? We gonna have to give dem our houses 'cause we couldn't live wit' tha stench.

Where is Joe when we need him? It's his place."

The men from Down Below are letting their wives figure out this dilemma with their plans. If they don't, well, everybody is fucked.

They saw Pieyan peeking behind a tree. He's listening to what the humans are saying 'cause it's his problem and he doesn't know what to do either.

Lola and Emmalois holler for him to join the discussion. They make room for him, and he sits down.

Belle is asleep as well as are the children, and all are oblivious to what's going on. Belle doesn't think of one thing in her mind; she's out to lunch, nobody's home.

Pieyan stands and takes the podium. "I thank our god, BooBoo, for all my new human friends and for accepting me as Belle's old man, even though I'm not a man. I never said I loved Belle. She was a wounded human that needed me. The rest is what y'all call lagniappe.

"I truly wasn't waiting for this, surprised to even find out Suzie Q's alive and kicking and bringing my son, who I didn't know I even had. I can't even think of who she's bringing with her. I had figured her dad had already given her to one of his followers.

"Now that the clan may know where I'm at, they may come to finish the job. I sure don't want that to happen because it will be a bloody mess on y'all's property, and for sure, the children don't need to see that. It'll rock their world.

"Come on, Lola and Emmalois. It's up to you to think of something, because I sure don't know."

Here comes Belle, all dressed up in her new clothes, running across the property looking for her old man or whatever he is. He goes to meet her and takes her back home.

Emmalois talks after conferring with Lola. "Mais, y'all, dat might help tha situation. Another bigfoot coming to take her off Pieyan's hands. If they come, all of us will fight, and T-June and Jude will surely rock their worlds."

∞ ∞ ∞

ANOTHER three weeks passes, and they have settled down some, thinking maybe she isn't coming.

Minou and Joe are serving coffee to MeeMaw and Charlie. Bubba's been up and gone into the swamps to visit all his newfound friends. He can't find Pieyan; he's been hollering for him.

Pieyan is hiding and keeping his hands on Belle's mouth, her thinking they're going to get kinky.

Man, I have to laugh at myself.

MeeMaw starts talking, with Charlie on the side of her, nodding his head. He's a man of few words, and Joe loves it because he gets to talk all the time now.

Lighting her corn cob pipe, MeeMaw says, "I'm so sorry to bring this trouble down here. All our supernatural beings brought this here. Iffin they would have minded their own bizness…

"Lord have mercy, Bubba is in the front like a racehorse. We can't do too much 'bout this situation unless Joe stands his ground on his land."

Aww, here comes Joe. "What Ah tole ya? What Ah said, Charlie? What Ah said? It's dat or da other. It don't matter, Ah'm always in deep shit wit' dis family. What tha fuck Ah gonna do 'bout a lot of dem monsters comin' here, it don't matter if Ah like it or not. Give me a fuckin' break."

Minou thinks for a minute, then she has her well-known come-apart. "Awww. Ah could slap tha shit right off ya face. Ah'm so tired of it bein' all 'bout you. In case ya forgot, half of everyt'in' ya got is mine. And ya bettah shut tha fuck up, or Ah'm gonna use the Voodoo on ya ass. Go to ya shop and feed tha wolves or drink a beer or bitch to tha wolves or Charlie, whoevah ya find to listen to you.

"Old Man, don't push me."

On that sunny afternoon, here comes Susie Q and redheaded Pie in the back of a pickup, getting dropped off by some cane farmer that swears to quit getting piss-ass drunk in the morning again. He thinks he's having hallucinations or he finally has the wet brain.

Most of the village is in the house. They meet Suzie Q and Pie at the back screen door.

T-June is back home in New Orleans with Jolie and Jude but says they will come when needed.

Joe takes one look at Suzie Q and falls out laughing and peeing on himself.

"Ohhh, Ah can't catch my breath. My chest is hurtin' bad. Dat's tha funniest t'ing Ah evah saw, and Mais, ya know dat's plenty.

"Mais, Ah'm so sorry, Miss Suzie Q. Mais, ya real purty for a bigfoot lady. You tha first Ah evah seen. And ya talk too. Mais, what tha shit is goin' on in tha goddamn swamps and tha rollin' hills dat's up yonder, like Charlie says, it's funny when he says it.

"Mais, what tha shit ya fixin' to do on my land? Ya brought some more shit comin' our way? You a big boy, dat's true. Ya look just like Pieyan. Ah don't know if we should wait on T-June or what?

"Mais, Ah'm gonna call his royal ass to come finish what his royal ass started."

Joe is so vocal now that Flavia isn't there to prevent that.

Minou doesn't like that.

"If ya could just listen to what ya say, you would think a couyon was talkin'. For sure, dis ain't anyt'in' we haven't already lived t'rough. Use ya brain for once. It's always you to be negative. Just t'ink good thoughts. Ain't nuttin' beat us yet.

"All of us is some strong-ass people. We all come from good stock, and we some people who act like tha crawfish shootin' tha bird at ever'body."

T-June and Jolie, carrying Jude, come in less than an hour, not coming close to the speed limit. He and Jude have already met the lovely Suzie Q, but meeting Pie is something else. He's the image of Pieyan, who must have looked like this as a youngster. Pie is a fine young bigfoot with the red hair and mannerisms like his daddy.

Jolie says hello and "how are you" to both of them but has to run inside to keep from laughing at Suzie Q and the big-ass little Pieyan Junior.

T-June and Jude and MeeMaw and Charlie and Bubba and of course Joe get in Joe's brand new, fully-equipped yacht, with people working as staff.

Lawd, he isn't messing around. He's named it The Minou. Plenty room for everybody to take the cruise five miles. Talk about GAS.

Minou don't like dat. She tried to talk some sense into him, but Lawd, he sure doesn't listen, saying it is secondhand and cheap. Yeah, big savings.

She's at home with Jolie, Estelle, Flavia, Madam Aucoin, and Irene and Charlotte Dugas.

Did I leave one of the Cajun Warrior Women out? Oh, yeah, Sister Bridget doesn't need to know this.

We already know that Minou thinks Joe is batshit crazy and likes to show off.

Pieyan meets them at the chosen place, kind of hard for Belle to get to.

Lola and Emmalois have taken her on a shopping spree paid for by T-June. The cousins can get her away for a long time, and so it shows you, they love all these people enough to put up with this woman, a wannabe bigfoot.

Pieyan sees his family and starts crying huge tears, splashing everybody there with them.

They've just watched one of the most romantic things, beating the restless and young soap opera.

Pieyan takes Suzie Q into his arms, her swooning again while he kisses her with his huge, juicy lips, spraying and crying the whole time. You can bet they are having a hard time with this, even if is romantic.

Coming up for air, Pieyan tells his Sweet Pea Suzie Q, "Oh, my darlin, my Queen Bee, Sweet Pea, I thought I would never see you again. To think I never knew about my son, no denying him.

"I have some sad news, Sweet Pea. I have to tell you, I'm living with a female human, in a house and everything. I don't love her, but I kind of like living with her. I will get rid of her, but it's going to take some time. I don't want to hurt her. She has no family and no money.

"Everybody calls her nuts to cuckoo, but I like her just fine.

"We have to come up with something because I want to be with you and Pie and not make it a problem for my people friends. Where's the clan?"

Suzie Q hates to let Pieyan go, but she can't remain quiet. "I'm just satisfied and tickled too. I can't believe what my eyes are seeing. I have been knowing about this woman. I don't know who she thinks she is. Lands sake, mixing with us. Aww, I'm sorry. That sounds like what Ruby Jewel calls racist.

"I don't want to be nosy but a female human gal? I mean, well, you know what I mean.

"My daddy wasn't told by me. We snuck off in the dark while the patrol was sleeping."

All of a sudden, they hear Belle hollering for Pieyan. The girls can't keep her shopping; it's like she knows something is up. You can't live with a sleazy man all those years and not have trust issues.

Suzie says, "Y'all, I have to go before she busts up in here and sees this. I'm going to find y'all tonight in the swamps. There's a lot of good places."

They get out of sight, when Belle shows up there. "Sweetheart, I've been hollering for you. I couldn't find you. What is that smell? It smells like Avon 'Mesmerize.' Who's been back here? I know you aren't running around on me, so what is it?" asks Belle with her brand-new clothes on and made up like a French Putain.

Belle, being all nosy with trust issues, she doesn't let Pieyan out her sight. Living with a sleazy man for years just intensifies her intuition, even if she's a loony bird.

Pieyan has to do everything on the sly, seeing all his human friends from up north and kissing everybody's dirty neck. He can't get away from her for too long; here she comes, yelling for him.

"Oh, what a tangled web we weave when first we practice to deceive."

∞ ∞ ∞

BELLE pretends to be sleeping one night when Pieyan slips out to meet his ex-woman or bigfoot or… and their illegitimate child. Belle follows him, being very quiet and sneaky, to a large area she knows nothing about. There sits Pieyan with this other female bigfoot around a barbeque pit, cooking deer steaks.

I mean, what the hell?

The area has big folding chairs, with a fire burning and a small stove for Pieyan's coffee. T-June has given Pieyan the grill for Christmas because he likes cooked meat now.

Awww, a humanized bigfoot, taming him into a big old man, human. He's spoiled and rotten to the core of his big steps. He doesn't know if he can go back to being this big monster that scares everybody.

He's busted.

Belle takes one look at Suzie Q and flies at her, screaming, wanting to beat her ass. Suzie Q just holds her off with one hand, holding up Belle in the air. Belle, her legs dangling and going in every direction, is screaming at the top of her lungs.

"Who are you, and what are you doing in my swamp? Pieyan, who is she? What an ugly woman."

Suzie Q throws Belle on the ground and says, "I'm his lifetime love, and I already have a son for him, and guess what, you're a ugly woman yourself. Fruity Tooty is what I'm calling you because you can't see the light of day, and you haven't for a long while.

"I'm a Christian now. I don't like to be ugly with my ways, but I mean a human woman coming after my man? Let me tell you something I haven't even told Pieyan. I'm having his baby."

The bigfoot community is thriving because their females catch quick and find out right then. They don't carry their babies but for six months. Think about how big these babies would be if they carried them in their wombs for nine months.

Pieyan is shocked out of his big feet and knows the proverbial shit is going to hit the proverbial fan.

"Aww, Sweet Pea, I thought we were too old. For true? For true?"

Suzie Q just smiles her silly little grin, nodding yes.

That fucking fan is blowing shit everywhere.

Belle runs off, brokenhearted, sobbing copious tears, real or not. In her addled brain, she's supposed to act like this because she needs to be taken care of.

Pieyan goes to run after her, but Suzie Q holds him back, saying she's more important than the Fruity Tooty.

Well, Pieyan sends Pie to make sure Belle doesn't hurt herself. He thinks she must be feeling an old feeling, being forsaken.

Pie starts walking slowly to go to where this human woman stays with his daddy, Pieyan. He's scared to death of this crazy woman. Pie thinks she must have some kind of power for his dad to shack up with her.

Pie walks up the stairs of her house and knocks on the door. Belle throws the door wide open and pulls him in, to his shock. He thinks, Oh, blessed BooBoo. She's fixing to kill me. He's shaken down his spine. She cries all over him, standing real close, and the next thing that happens is being downright scandalous.

Oh, Gawd, where does my head go? Don't even imagine it.

She's kissing him on his big old lips, holding him, and leading his hands to her breasts and telling Pie that he will take care of her now.

This teenage bigfoot, who hasn't tasted the joys of being a full-blown bigfoot, is a virgin. He is horrified when he starts responding. And the rest is distorted history.

Pie gets glad in the same drawers he was sad and scared in.

Lola and Emmalois are vivid red in their anger. The nerve of this wanton woman! Yeah, wash her filthy body, work with her hair and make her wear clothes and takes her shopping, behaving like one of the kids. Oh, that is so easy, just like dealing with their boisterous boys and bad-ass identical twin girls. Yeah.

She takes up with Pie the minute he is pulled in the door. Pieyan's son.

Fuck, it's like incest.

∞ ∞ ∞

BACK at the homestead, Pieyan and Suzie Q are adding things to make them more comfortable in their den of inequity.

All of the "village" people have come to see Pieyan and his lovely wife, bringing lots of gifts for their outside home. Minou thinks it will take ten yards of material at Walmart to make a receiving blanket.

T-June and MeeMaw are delighted with the news. MeeMaw says, "Oh, my sweet Suzie Q, you finally got your man. You've been lovin' him far so long. You're havin' his other baby. You will certainly have peace and happiness havin' this baby with Pieyan, and this little critter will grow up with a mama and daddy."

T-June doesn't think it's going to be that easy.

Pieyan asks T-June if they can set up electricity. He misses the TV and the air-conditioning.

Suzie Q does not want to live in a house. She thinks Pieyan has been ruined by these humans, but she believes she can change that.

Oh, yeah. They always change for their women, men, and bigfeets.

∞ ∞ ∞

THE menfolk are staying out of this soap opera. They've never had to deal with Belle.

Joe can't believe all the sinning going on, on his land and for sure rants about it.

Dis is tha icin' on tha goddamn cake. Minou. Minou, Minou. Mais, are ya tee-totally fuckin' blind and don't know no bettah? Mais, 'stead of it getting' bettah in our old age, we still fuckin' right up dat middle of shit Ah nevah evah wanted.

"Minou, Ah want a fuckin' divorce. Let me enjoy what's left of my life."

Minou says in front of everybody at the house, very calm before striking like the fucking snake, "Go ahead with yo plans. Ah'm sick and tee-totally tired of you too. Go see what's it gonna be like not livin' wit' me. Ah sure as hell don't wanna have to take ya to court, but Ah will if ya push me, old man. Ah want my half of everyt'in', and Ah already got a lawyer.

"Get out my face."

The atmosphere can be cut with a machete, and Joe leaves in his truck after closing the door softly, going to his yacht to stay.

No one has ever witnessed this before and doesn't know where to put themselves in Minou and Joe's house.

This is serious shit, anywhere you look.

Minou walks out the back door, heading for Down Below in the little putt-putt boat she's saved from the burnt pile.

This is definitely a revolting development.

∞ ∞ ∞

PIEYAN and Suzie Q keep waiting for Pie to show up, but he's been gone three weeks. They have no idea what's happening at his old house. Belle has Pie mesmerized and talks him out of leaving, using all her wiles and tricks he's learned to really like.

He hasn't been able to leave, staying in the house that Pieyan built. He is terribly sore. He doesn't know if he likes that.

Pieyan busts up in the house after all this time, grabbing Pie and growling maliciously at Belle, warning her to back the fuck up. Here she comes behind them, screaming and cursing, trying to make Pie turn around, showing indeed she came from trash.

Suzie Q shows up at this time, and she throws Belle into the middle of next week. Snarling at her with her five o'clock shadow, she says, "Little human girl, have you ever tangled with someone my size and pissed as a mother for what you did to my son? You better find some sense before I shred you to dog meat. I'm as serious as that heart attack Ruby had.

"You better run fast because I'm coming after you."

Belle runs as fast as her fat legs will carry her, running to T-Mae's house.

T-Mae doesn't like Belle's trashy ways, but she won't turn anyone from her door, especially someone who's shaking like a leaf.

Belle eventually returns to the house that once held Pieyan, but little does he know, Pie slips back when he can sneak away.

∞ ∞ ∞

IT does indeed get calm for a while, before the whole fucking clan of bigfoots starts showing up. As Joe has predicted...

One at a time, they taunt Pieyan and Suzie Q and Pie once they find out what the shit they've been doing down here in the sultry, sexy South.

Human woman? They've never heard of such, acting like the rednecks from where they come from. You know, they can be pretty racist.

God is supposed to not make mistakes.

Everybody is down there shooting guns and using T-June's gifts as well as Jude's, all up in their business. They do chase the invading army of bigfeet, shooting in the air to scare them off.

All are working overtime because Joe hasn't shown his face. Charlie is helping and doesn't know where his podnah's at.

All those red necks already know how Charlie shoots. He doesn't miss unless it's a warning.

This happens for a couple of weeks. Then it gets quiet totally. The birds are hiding as well as all the critters fearing for their lives, as vicious and mean as this bunch is.

T-June as well as little Jude go every day to see how they are faring. They tell the clan this is Thibeau land, and nobody is going to do a damn thing to Pieyan or Suzie Q or Pie or Belle if they know what's good for them.

Still, they hide. They know company's coming.

T-June knows there's a bunch of extra beings back there, though they stay hidden for the most part. Too many humans and stinks of them everywhere.

The bigfeet in the swamps – the Clan – have backed off from Pieyan and Suzie Q because there's always one of T-June's pack with a gun and that nasty little dude running around on his little feet using words they don't even know. They don't even show their hairy faces when Charlie's out there. He's ready to kill one of these bully bastard bigfeet.

Pieyan and T-June are sitting on their tree in their old stomping grounds, and Pieyan doesn't want to tell him what's fixing to happen.

"I pray to BooBoo that the whole ritual is not what's going to happen. Maybe her daddy won't think it's necessary to come here. Maybe the warnings would be enough. None of my brothers is talking to me, you know, with the howls and knocking on trees because we aren't close enough to talk face to face, and they won't do that.

"I'm going to have to tell you what they mean since you never asked. So, one howl is a greeting, a knock says we come to visit. You want to know how son of bitch sounds? You want to learn all the ugly things they're telling?

"You want to get hit with a boulder from the grounds of the piney woods? That's nothing to be carried by us. Their version is what everybody hears.

"Grown man T-June, I'm so sorry and hurt in my heart for this thing that's coming for us. If you want us to leave, we can do that, podnah, but they can smell me a mile off. I've got too much human scent on me, and we've hid for centuries, having humans think we are not real, so making friends with a human is punishment of death.

"They are going to kill me in the most horrid way they can. I'm sure the old bastard will see to that.

"My T-June that I've known since you was a child and you were my son, I helped raise you too, so think about all the good times we've had. The fun and adventures you've taken me on. Well, they just don't know joy and love in their lives.

"Remember me, podnah. I've lived a long time. Please help Suzie Q with our baby."

T-June hits him so hard he falls off the branch, looking surprised and shocked. Pieyan gets up slowly, dusting his dirty ass anyway. He's gone native again.

T-June makes him sit so they are eye level. "What fucking bull shit is this? If you won't sit there, I'll really make you, you believe that?

"Pieyan, when in the hell have we run from a damn thing? We are supposed to be in everything. That's why we're all Superman. All of us fight to right the wrongs. We with our combined families will have your back, as if I've got to say that.

"For good measure, I'm calling Saul Aucoin and the Saints to come too, and those others in the clan don't know about the magic that's always here in the air and ground.

"You better grab those big hairy massive balls and bigfoot up."

∞ ∞ ∞

ALL this time, Joe has been living on his yacht, The Minou, and loving every minute. He looks at it like this: he gets better treatment here because he's the captain and they are his crew, people hired to take care of every whim and listen to him when he wants to talk. His meals are cooked by the cook and put the food on his little table in front of him.

He's paying them well. He isn't worried about gas no more.

He puts up a "No Trespassing" sign and has his sailors on guard.

As if.

The wolves refuse to leave home, which is sad for him. Joe doesn't even want to think of no custody battle. No one's comes a-knocking because they're too busy preparing for the battle coming.

Joe acts like he could care less. He's minding his own business.

∞ ∞ ∞

PIEYAN tells Pie Jr. to take off a different way, a shortcut through all the land, as a scout to spy on his grandad – the Big Kahuna, Mean Muddy Melvin – to see how far he is in his travels.

He comes back a day later, telling everybody Mean Ass Melvin is a day behind him.

Pie would have followed him, but the old bigfoot is sniffing the air and starts laughing, along with the serpent wrapped around his neck, Boogeyman Big Bad-Ass Bruce. His tongue goes in and out, in and out, in and out like a squeeze box, hissing at the same time, looking like he's smelling the air.

∞ ∞ ∞

THE Saints motorcycle club, with Saul Peltier and Eli St. James, come in that night, idling their bikes when they reach the front land by the houses.

With their flags flying high, the fleur de lis in glory, they have come prepared to build a camp at the starting spot, same one that's been used for years.

They lay in wait for Melvin to show his cards. Pretty soon, he won't be playing with a full deck. The families will see to that.

Everyone but Joe is out there by a huge fire. Melvin already knows they do this, and he's so cocky it doesn't scare him. The rest of the clan is waiting for his arrival to make a gang of bloodthirsty bigfeets.

They're coming for Pieyan, Suzie Q, and Pie and the perverted madwoman, Belle. Direct orders to kill, even his daughter and her bastard son.

T-June prepares to speak to the gathering using one of his microphones with big speakers to make sure they all hear him, every last one of those primal throwbacks.

Before T-June could start, this old white abominable snowman comes out on all fours, coming at him fast, throwing vengeance to the winds and snarling teeth.

Whatcha think happened?

The monster bigfoot Melvin gets up from the ground after T-June has knocked his white behind to the dirt by just waving his hands. He goes into Melvin's head while he is swerving, poor old man.

"Listen up, you old fool. That isn't anything. You have no idea what will happen if you step into this clearing on my father's land. You have been warned."

Pieyan and Suzie Q and Pie come to the front of the clearing, standing together and proud. Pie stands tall by his father, showing the anger he's felt all these years, snarling and beating his chest.

Pieyan speaks up. "Melvin, why don't you give it a break? You've come to my territory looking for your revenge, and you will have it, but not on your terms. These people are my family, and it's our business what we do here. Try living in a house. You would love it. Between you and me, this is what it's all about, if you would admit it to the mob of vicious bigfeet you've created.

"You and me, Melvin, you and me."

They face off when Suzie Q steps between them. "Daddy, now it's me who is ashamed of you. It tears my heart to shreds to see you come in another's territory to kill us, your own kin. May BooBoo rain on your parade, because it's not going to be as easy as you make yourself believe.

"I'm carryin another one of us, and it is against our rules to hurt a pregnant female. You missed the chance to even know Pie. You ridicule him every time you see him.

Don't make me go all BooBoo on you. I'm a Christian."

When Melvin's henchmen (well, henchfeet) have Belle by the arm, bringing her into the clearing, they all gasp. They don't know it, but hell's coming, and it's bringing death.

Everybody joins in the quemas, the women trying to secure Belle when Minou and Lola are grabbed by the two bigfeet dudes who hold them still.

Hallelujah! Along comes Joe, bad talkin' Joe, fast walkin' Joe, Cajun vigilante Joe ,and By God Minou's Old Man. He runs full force into the young bigfoot holding Minou and knocks him to the ground when he proceeds to wipe his ass out with a loaded doubled-barrel shotgun and a massive hose full of bayou water from his yacht, knocking him down both ways.

Joe yells, "Who tha fuck ya t'hink ya are? Dis is MY land and ya got tha nerve to touch my woman? Dey ain't nevah been another man touch her. She's mine. Ya bettah get ya ass gone 'fore Ah kill ya myself.

"Ya heard my son, T-June, say who dis land is for. Ah'm so pissed Ah'm comin' after all ya sumbitches.

"Dat's my woman, and wait 'til she gets ahold of ya. Ya just don't know who ya grabbed."

Joe runs to Minou and starts kissing her all over, and she needs the comfort of his arms too, kissing like they are still those teenagers who started it all.

"Awww, bébé, Ah wanna come home. Ah'm gonna sell dat yacht cheap. Ah need ya, Ah need ya and T-June and ever'body who loves dis foolish old man.

"Ah heard T-June tell dem who's tha boss. It made me so proud of him."

Minou joins him in the seriously righteous anger, beating that young bigfoot to his knees and not wanting to get up.

"Dat's for grabbin' me like ya know me. Ya bully, Ah can be a bigger bully than yo ass. Ah'm gonna slap ya face for touchin' me."

Then she proceeds to punch his lights out.

The fighting is vicious between Pieyan and Melvin, and the families are stunned in awe of what they are watching. Pieyan gets the best of the old snowman until Melvin grabs a cypress tree and hits him while the snake Big Bad Bruce bites him on the shoulder.

Bubba is by Pieyan's side and grabs wicked Bruce and tears his head off, with his tail wiggling trying to find his missing head.

Pieyan takes the tree from the snowman, hitting Melvin with it to death.

∞ ∞ ∞

ALL the motorcycles start revving with bright lights to show who the winner is, and the remaining clan all drops to their knees. Several are beaten to the point of death.

It is righteous anger and justice on the side of the "Village" people, with heavy retributions to the evasive bigfeet. Everyone is waiting for instructions from Pieyan, the new head of the clan. Even the vampires Mac and Claudine are hovering and sucking some mighty heavy hot blood from these creatures, who are trying to knock the vamps away from them and their necks.

Angelique is loving it, getting her own samples. She has an ancient handkerchief, wiping her mouth like a lady should after eating her meal, the true Southern belle, centuries old.

Moe is out there somewhere, doing his share of the fighting too, waiting forever to go postal on somebody.

Belle is seen by the biggest motorcycle man, quite big with a long gray beard and wild thick hair.

She does her infamous swoon, and he is captivated. Belle is lifted up onto his Big Dog Harley lap and they drive off. He's not going to know what hit him until she starts making her moves in very unusual positions.

This biker, named Wayne, knows who she used to be and has regretted not grabbing her the last time.

Match made in heaven…but whose heaven?

Pieyan begins to talk, and everything gets quiet. "I have no qualms about Melvin's death. It needed to be done. You must pick among yourselves as to who will be the new clan leader. I don't want the job. You need to go back up north and choose well, someone who will lead you in new directions.

"Suzie Q and I want to be left alone."

The clan – or what's left of them after three are killed along with Melvin – start knocking on the trees yelling for Pie. Pie. Pie.

Pieyan looks at the replica of himself and tells him it is a deep honor to be asked by the main bigfoots in the clan. What a better choice than himself. Pie will bring leadership, showing his good home training.

The swamps are emptied the next morning.

∞ ∞ ∞

MINOU and Joe are on the yacht, honeymooning again. She figures she should enjoy some of what Joe's been praising.

Finally, the real honeymooners come home, with Gerry tagging along with his new love interest, another cousin from down the Bayou Mayhem.

Chapter Twenty-Three

The Summer of MaeMae

WE'RE talking about the second daughter of Callie and Henri Aucoin, who was born at the governor's mansion in an antique curtained tester bed and woke the whole house with her mama's screams birthing a screaming baby.

MaeMae has not been quiet since.

She is named Bertha Mae Aucoin, but they call her MaeMae.

Minna Sue is but four years older. Henri doesn't mess around.

Minna is the image of MeeMee Minou, but here comes MaeMae, looking like Bertha. MaeMae is built like Bertha; sleek, big boned and fast moving, similar to how Pieyan moves with his stride and hurrying to see what's on the other side of the swamp, fearing she won't find what she's been nosy about.

Charlotte and Pete Dugas are her nanan and parrain and are tickled pink.

∞ ∞ ∞

TWELVE years later…

True Blue is off skiing the mountains of Switzerland with his latest girlfriend and not a care in the world. He still plays with Monsieur Mayhem Band, and he is world famous.

MaeMae has caught Monsieur Mayhem's watchful eye. He always knows from the get-go when one appears a little different, with all these children swimming in the gene pool of supernatural.

He's looking hard.

MaeMae loves the way the family talks down there on the bayou, and she tries to imitate the words, but being from Baton Rouge and living in New Orleans, it's kind of hard. Nobody objects to this, but it's like she's trying to learn a foreign language, Patois French in the old Cajun way.

Duh, it is a foreign language; not even the French understand.

MaeMae has been known to cry when her parents say it's time to leave and insists she be left here on the bayou. It feels more at home than New Orleans, where she hates the noise and traffic in the city and misses the flowing waters of Bayou Lafourche. She's twelve going on twenty.

Well, T-Mae Rappolet says she could come to her house for the summer. What a better way to learn Cajun.

MaeMae throws a hissy fit when Callie says she'll have to think about this. She tells her mama she'll walk herself down there if no one can find the time to take her.

Her parents are extremely busy in the famous restaurant, Caldonia's, and they put Minou Junior – aka Minna Sue – and MaeMae to work early so they can develop good work ethics, teaching both of them to know it's not handed to you on a silver spoon and you're no better than the dishwasher. Give respect to the workers; they've earned it. Listen to their sage advice and learn. Politeness is a must.

In the summer, many, many programs are being offered all over the city. Minna is taking several offered but not MaeMae. If she goes to the bayou, MaeMae will miss everything that has been lined up by Callie, who's very pregnant. Hell, Callie is going to need all the help she can find, with baby twin boys. Some more children. She is in her eighth month of carrying twins. Callie is getting up in years to be birthing one baby, much less two. She's thirty-seven and considered a high risk.

That'll be five children – so far – for this couple, when everyone has thought Henri is too old.

Must have been saving himself.

Oh, that Henri! Henri is for sure not aging, acting like the proverbial rooster who's hanging around the chicken shack. Henri is not using the little blue pill, still "getting' sum" regular, and he thinks Callie is the most beautiful ever, even when she doesn't shave her legs.

MaeMae tells her mama, "Mama cher, I need to go home, and it's not gonna kill you to not see me for two months. Cher bébé, you're gonna live, Mama."

Callie has grown into a very aware woman. She is WOKE. She feels things, and mais, that goes with the genes. She's just aware of her daughter, and she can't put her finger on it. Something is very different about her, like Minou the first.

Callie calls T-June – her brother, her bubba, Monsieur Mayhem – to come and have coffee with her and Henri, and he comes right away but drinks a cold Dixie beer instead. He drinks his beer on ice in a glass and salted like a margarita.

"Bubba, I've got this feeling about MaeMae. I don't think any of us has had this feeling before. No one has said so. I get the Old Soul bit, but she is definitely someone else beyond just my beautiful girl. It's familiar to me, like I knew her before, because some of the things she does and says is all very déjà vu for me. I'm worried, so worried, about her. I'm afraid for her to get out my sight, and she's determined to go to the bayou for the summer.

"I wish Mama and Papa would come get her. Papa sure wouldn't put up with it by encouraging her, but you know both T-Mae and Madam Alafair. They will definitely jump on that with four feet. Oh, wait. Let's include Laurette in the mix. Six feet and oooh, oooh, I'm getting light-headed. I'm getting all flustered."

T-June is sitting there, sipping his beer, and takes a minute before he says a thing.

"Sister, I've been looking hard at her since she was born, and I agree, there's something there. What better place to be? Madam Aucoin and T-Mae and Laurette, they will all help her like they've done with everything else this family puts in front of them. I mean, how much has to happen before you realize we are a supernatural family and you've got the same genes as me? It just skipped you and waited for your True and MaeMae.

"Let her go, Sister. She will find out who she is with their help. Let her go. She's bound and determined to run her own life.

"Don't smack me, dammit. It's good stuff. It's all good."

Callie and Henri take the weekend off to take her, and they think she is going to kiss the ground, she is so glad to be there. MaeMae gets out the car, laughing and crying, and lets out a long howl that sounds pretty authentic of the wolves who hang around. She's howling and laughing up at the sky, and it brings shudders to Callie's heart, but Henri thinks she is the funniest one since Weedie Peltier King and Jude, T-June's burden. When things get serious, he laughs at it.

They take the five miles down the bayou in their boat. The city slickers have all bought boats because they've gotten word Joe isn't too happy with them always using his boat. You know, the price of gas?

It's always a spiritual experience to anyone that comes down the bayou just five miles and mostly quiet, except for the birds and the fish plopping in the boat, big-ass catfish.

MaeMae takes off running toward T-Mae and Junya and all the children waiting with their arms opened wide in greetings.

Everybody sits and visits, since Callie and Henri are here for the weekend. Bertha and Alcide's house is empty right now, so they're going to stay there for the night with MaeMae.

MaeMae is talking non-stop to T-Mae, grown-up subjects, telling all the children, counting all the children and one funny-looking chimpanzee.

MaeMae is quite the intellectual little girl. She's little, like her grandmother Minou, and has the curls her papa has. She has to be coaxed to brush it and even harder to bathe and put on clean clothes, the epitome of a tomboy and the image of Bertha at that age.

Not like Minna Sue at all. Minna is quite the Miss Priss, who loves to be fashionable and has many suitors, talking about balls and Tulane soon.

That's all of what's in her head.

Callie tells MaeMae to pay attention to T-Mae and Laurette and Madam Aucoin and use her manners. After all, this is a well-known rich kid, and she sure has been taught to not look down on people because of it.

That's not something to worry about with MaeMae. She has been working hard on her Patois French and has taught herself to be country in the middle of the city.

∞ ∞ ∞

IT'S the full moon that night, and they still gather, even though it's just the wolves and T-June when he feels the need to turn.

When Pieyan and Suzie Q come with Joey, it's berserk.

Everyone is invited tonight because the former governor has called some of their cooks to come barbeque for all of them, this new generation of followers of T-June, his peers. They're all enjoying the food, company, wine, and some real good expensive stuff Henri brought. His cannabis even has a name.

Henri pays well for their silence.

What happens Down Below stays Down Below.

As if.

T-June and Pieyan are play-acting their fighting, making the kids shriek and run. All the little kids are peeing their little pink panties and Superman drawers, laughing so hard.

Callie gets up to look for MaeMae and screams at what she has found up in a cypress grove banking the bayou. Everyone takes off running to where she is.

Oh, Lawd. They all see it. An obvious animal caught in the lily pads, but with MaeMae's clothes all around it.

T-Mae tells the children to go to the house and lock the doors.

The creature is whimpering like puppies do because it is one.

Callie and Henri help until the creature is loose. It stands on hind legs and looks at Callie, crying and crying and crying 'til the moon goes down at dawn.

Her mama and papa hold her shivering body.

Everybody hits the mud, unbelieving what they are seeing, except T-June. There stands MaeMae in all her loup-garou nakedness. She starts bawling again.

Callie goes into pains on the spot with her grand entrances into labor. She drenches the ground. She loses her water at the most wrong times. There is no time for the hospital, and Henri is there to assist in the difficult births.

She has the babies at T-Mae's, and all the children are told to stay upstairs 'til their mama calls for them. They all, even Junya, listen to T-Mae with no questions. (When Jude is there and T-Mae says she will beat his ass, Jude listens.)

What turmoil, with Callie giving birth to two and MaeMae so upset she doesn't want to be by herself.

No one is talking to her about what happened. These people have become so very nonchalant with all the supernaturals in their village, so MaeMae just goes to see the birthing, smelling like a wet dog.

The identical twin boys are born, healthy eight pounders, and they will be named Alphonse after Fats Domino and Arthur after Art Neville. Al and Art. Wait until they're older. You're not going to know who's answering, Al, Art, Al, Art, awww, Almighty shit.

Both look like True Blue, their big brother, but have hair a deeper shade of peach and are darker than True and Henri.

True is flying in tonight, driving there soon in his rented car to see his little brothers, who are twenty-three years younger.

Everyone is so excited about the babies, not so worried about MaeMae, so she leaves the house and goes to the swamps by herself.

Not for long.

T-June follows closely behind her and watches as she throws herself to the ground, having a battle with the dirt and leaves turning into mud. He sits on the side of her and takes her into his arms, knowing how she is feeling.

T-June is comforting her as he talks to her. "I've known for a while that you would be special. I know the signs. The only thing I can figure out concerning you and what's happening is this. You have Grandma Bertha Peltier's mannerism, her outlooks, her talking, her love of the bayou, and her pride of being Cajun and Houmas Indian. I think you are her reincarnation or that she's possessed you.

"You know both words. Well, good. I've heard you speak in ways that sound like Bertha straight out her mouth. Things you should know nothing about. You talk like they were your memories. Do you remember Alcide?"

MaeMae starts crying a copious amount of tears, asking what is she gonna do. She tells him, "Parrain, I'm scared. Sometimes, memories come so fast it startles me, and I don't know what to do when I start seeing where it's taken place, for sure Down Below.

"Did you see, Parrain, how fast they forgot about me after having this impossible thing happen to me? My feelings are hurt bad-bad, Parrain. I know the babies were coming and my mama needed help, but they still haven't come to see about me.

"Parrain, what the hell am I gonna do? T-Mae and Madam Alafair will help, I know this, but whoever saw a loup-garou puppy?

"So, IS it hereditary? I mean, nobody bit me, but I am not the seventh son.

"I want my mama and papa."

Poor little baby. She sits there feeling sorry for herself when half the family comes into the clearing. Her papa runs and grabs her up in his arms, while T-Mae and Madam Alafair come running. They go into a huge hug involving T-June, Henri, Madam, T-Mae and Cynthia, Chief's beloved and fiancée.

Flavia gets lost along the way, looking at all the pretty flowers and sitting down and smelling them.

Henri holds his baby girl and tells her, "Oooh, my precious girl, don't ever think we weren't watching you because there's just something about you that couldn't be explained. You have all the help you're going to need right here, and maybe you will be better adjusted at the end of summer.

"Mama thought it would come this summer because, well, because she thinks you will have your first menstrual cycle this summer.

"Please, baby, your mama is hollering for you, and it's time you meet Al and Art. Baby. You can't tell them apart."

The family's walking back when Flavia busts up in the clearing. "Where y'all been? Ah been waitin' for y'all to catch up. Okay, let's go and take care of tha problem. What IS tha problem? Why we comin' here again?

"Awww, somebody had a baby? Hot damn, it's Weedie, huh?"

MaeMae runs to her mama in bed, and Henri helps her get in the bed with the baby brothers. Callie is smothering her baby girl with kisses, and MaeMae is smothering her brothers with kisses. Then Henri gets some kind of way on the bed, and they are all kissing.

Sure a lot of smooching going on.

∞ ∞ ∞

CALLIE and Henri are staying at Bertha and Alcide's old house back for a few more days, and they ask MaeMae to stay with them until they leave to go back home.

Charlie and MeeMaw Ruby and Bubba Flowers, who own the house now, are at Irene and Jean Breaux's big Cajun cottage, Meemaw's granddaughter and her husband.

A whole lot of swapping these days.

Callie will need help with the two boys, having a difficult time herself telling them apart.

Minna Sue, MaeMae's older sister, is in New Orleans taking art classes every day and hitting Bourbon Street at night. Not in her little secular life is she worried. She calls every day but never after seven at night.

MaeMae and Callie are both changing diapers on the wrong one, which one needs burping, which tit hurts the worse, and Lawd, it scares me just to write it.

At the same time?

The nights in the house are quiet, leaving the windows open even though there is A/C. The wind at that time of the year is not hot yet, so the cool air blows. At times, you're reaching for the covers.

You sleep so good, if you don't have two infants wanting to eat you alive, not mastering the two full babies, each gobbling up the milk from their mama. Ohh…Ohh…

They know Bertha and Alcide haunt this house, but they feel nothing but goodness here. Callie thinks her MawMaw Bertha takes care of the boys at night, in her ghostly apron and kind of wet. She drowned herself as loup-garou. Thank Gawd she didn't come back as that.

The old house is peaceful for Callie and Henri, but it hasn't been the same for MaeMae. While she's sleeping, Mae gets waked up with Bertha calling her name and laughing. She sits up, and there stands the ghost of Bertha. She goes to scream when the ghost says, "Shush. Ah won't hurt ya. Bébé MaeMae, Ah ain't gonna hurt ya. Ah'm yo great-mawmaw and your Meemee Minou is my daughter. Ah love ya so much 'cause ya gave me that second chance to see that world again.

"But cher, Ah don't know how ya turned into de loup-garou. Dat don't make no sense. We gonna see 'bout dat, ya hear? Nah, Ah ain't gonna possess ya too-too much, if ya let me do dat, just ever once in a while. Ya so easy 'cause ya got ma name and all my ways already. Dat's on you.

"Ah'm gonna tell ya some secrets nobody else knows. Just be still, and Ah will tell ya, but only you."

MaeMae gets up early the next morning and is drinking coffee milk when Henri comes in the kitchen to fix his and Callie's.

"Good morning, my baby. How did you sleep? We got the best sleep last night. Even the babies didn't wake up. I'm gonna go bring some coffee to Mama. Thank you, sweet thing, for fixing it."

He doesn't stay long enough for MaeMae to answer his question, and she probably would have lied to him.

Mae Mae goes outside to call her parrain, who has gone back to New Orleans.

"Parrain, I have to tell you something, and it's scary. Mawmaw Bertha came to see me last night. She told me she has been possessing me a little, but the way I am isn't her doings. I just took after her on my own accord. She doesn't think it was her making me turn to loup-garou, but you never know about such things down here.

"I don't want her to come back. I was scared, even though she said not to be. She said it was good to be loup-garou again, even if I was a little pup.

"She told me a secret, and I can't tell anybody. 'Just go look for it' she said. She told me right where to go, and I need a shovel, and it's at Down Below.

"I don't want to go by myself, and I don't want her to come back to see if I did. Can you come, please, Parrain? I need you."

T-June comes back that afternoon.

Everyone is surprised to see him, but he tells them he's come to see the baby boys, which is part of the reason. He feels nothing supernatural about these boys, and he takes a sigh of relief.

Callie looks at him, and he tells her there is nothing but fine healthy boys who will give mayhem to them anyway. She sighs with relief.

T-June and MaeMae take the boat and go down the bayou five miles to Down Below.

Joe has put up a large homemade red sign before leaving.

No Trespassing Down Below

Everyone passing in the bayou knows about Down Below.

So, long ago, a young couple went looking for pecans on haunted ground. That started the whole damn thing.

T-June and MaeMae are looking for treasure Down Below too. They each have a shovel to dig and a metal detector so it won't be as long as it took Minou and Joe, and there's no pissed off ghost named Gaspar.

T-June wears his hip boots, as does MaeMae. Bertha has told her the tree she needs to find is in swamp water. Water comes up to their calves, and it is hard to dig because the water goes back in the hole quicker than they can dig.

It's obvious to the pair that this is some buried treasure because they are hitting something metal. The detector is just making noise, alerting them to the fact that IT'S HERE! IT'S HERE!

As they reach the large trunk buried under another giant pecan tree, they see the area fill up with fog, and four pirates come out the ground, solemn and threatening to them. They are silent and looming in their old clothes and high boots, with feathers in the wide brims of the hats. Their clothing is of better quality, of another century of pirates' attire.

It looks as though they were killed maybe a hundred years later than Gaspar. Probably by Jean Lafitte the third.

The ghosts stare straight at them and begin to moan and wail around them, like they can't communicate with the living. Downright zombie-looking and really scary.

T-June begins to tell her to put the shovel down and walk slowly back out the swamps, and he will follow.

"Blessed Spirits of the Dead, we will leave in peace now and not bother you again. We will leave now."

He is backing out from the tree, and when he slowly comes to her side, they run for the boat. They get to the docked boat without saying anything to all that come out their houses that live Down Below, very quietly solemn leaving everyone pondering what the hell has just happened.

T-June talks to MaeMae before he leaves, "MaeMae baby, you were hit with a double whammy this weekend. I don't know what we should take care of first. Don't go back there without me. Leave them alone. Bertha knows what happened, and tell her I said to please be quiet."

A lot of good that will do.

∞ ∞ ∞

BERTHA comes back that night only to MaeMae. "Don't worry 'bout dem assholes. We gonna come and mess wit' dem while ya get tha prize. Mais, dey like zombies, but we ain't gone dere as ghosts yet."

Alcide pops his head in behind Bertha, and MaeMae freaks out in shock.

"Mais, bébé MaeMae, Ah just want to ax how ya doin' 'cause ya my little great-granddaughter too, BooBoo.

"Mais, cher, Ah don't know 'bout dat werewolf shit wit' ya. Ah nevah t'ought dat was possible, but what tha hell, what Ah know? Just wanna tell ya Ah'm gonna fight for tha prize and ring that bell too."

MaeMae gets up after the visitations. She can't sleep because of the scare Alcide puts in her. She sits in the dark until sunrise, looking toward Down Below.

She decides to take the boat to where T-Mae and Junya's house is and is greeted by everyone.

T-Mae and Laurette go behind closed doors with MaeMae to listen to the reason she's there at seven o'clock in the morning.

"Madams, avec trois? I'm here this early because I got scared to death last night by both Bertha and Alcide. They came as ghosts to only me. He's never come before, and it must be real important what they want me to do."

T-Mae and Laurette are hanging onto every word that comes out her mouth, getting right up in her face like they could hear more close up.

"Wha, wha, what? Tell us, tell us. Ah'm scared now too, cher."

They talk all day, and at the end of it, she calls her mama, telling her she will spend the night. They have a lot to talk about.

T-Mae and MaeMae and Madam Aucoin and Laurette are waiting in the bedroom that Mae's going to uses for the summer. They wait for their old – dead – friends to make an appearance. No such luck.

Maybe they can't leave their old house, like they're grounded.

All the women can't show up at Bertha and Alcide's house for a sleepover. What the hell.

T-Mae comes up with a solution that they agree to: climbing through the window over the commode.

Agree to that? Aw, ladies, y'all slipping.

They put a ladder to the bathroom window very quiet like, and they have to cut the screen that was put in brand new a week ago.

Shit.

She came in through the bathroom window. Who else did that?

This bunch can't possibly be quiet climbing through a window that little. T-Mae falls in on Callie while she's sitting on the commode in the dark, peeing and dopey from lack of sleep. You see her? Absentmindedly scratching a mosquito bite, yawning and….

The horror scares the crap out of her, then everything comes apart. Lights come on, babies wake up screaming, Henri breaks a toe hitting a chair, and a fun time is had by all.

Of course, they are questioned by Callie and Henri, who finally looks as though he's pissed off too.

"What the hell are y'all doing? This is bad enough, but I would have been terrified to lose my concentration and go on the floor. What the hell is going on?"

Henri goes back to the babies, gives them their noonies, and gets back in bed, trying to keep his toe from throbbing. He figures he's going to know anyhow, just as soon be later. Nothing surprises him; quiet would be nerve-wracking.

They all go in MaeMae's bedroom and turn the lights out after a lengthy conversation answering questions. Callie doesn't believe any of it. She has to see for herself and soon does.

Here comes Bertha in this white, flowing gown, with a halo crooked on her head, playing a guitar.

"Mais, Ah been waitin' for y'all to come pass some time wit' me at my house inside 'cause y'all just sit on hat porch. Flavia comes, but y'all don't believe her. Whatsa matter? Y'all scared of me and Alcide? T'ank that good Lawd we ain't loup-garous.

"Mais, look, y'all. Ah learned how to play tha guitar 'cause Ah always wanted to, and Alcide can blow some mean horn.

"Gabriel, ya know dat Saint dat blows tha horn? Mais, he taught him hisself, him."

When the gaggle of women settles down from screaming at the shock and sudden appearance of Bertha, she speaks again. Poor Henri is behind closed doors with the pillow over his head.

"Mais, Ah'm sorry Ah left wit'out tellin' ya 'bout tha treasure me and Alcide found under dat big-ass pecan tree Down Below. Ah'm sorry dat Ah kilt myself and left ya hurtin'. Ah just didn't wanna live wit'out Alcide, and dat don't make no difference in our heaven like dey tole us we would burn in hell."

As if, as if.

"Well, we nevah got passed dem scary-scary ghosts guardin' it, and we nevah tried while we some ghosts. Maybe dey will talk wit' us now.

"We don't know what's in it, but dere's enough for MaeMae to go to school wit', Ah know dat.

"Ya gonna help her or not? Come see, Alcide. Come talk to ever'body, you. Look see, ya crushed de side of yo halo."

Alcide is wearing a white dress too, with a golden horn, and his halo is bent, fitting sideways on his head. He's wearing Jesus's used sandals.

"Mais, how ya do, y'all? Ah miss y'all, and ya don't come inside like Flavia. She fixes coffee for us, and she know Ah can't drink dat, but we play-like. Ah don't know nuttin' 'bout a loup-garou puppy. What's up wit' dat? Dat's too strange for me. Poor lil t'ing.

We gonna go help MaeMae get tha treasure. Whatcha say, cher?

Mais, Ah didn't wanna scare Callie wit' dem babies, so we just come see MaeMae, 'cause she's tha one to get it and got it, tha curse. Poor lil t'ing."

∞ ∞ ∞

WELL, of course, T-June has to be up in the midst of everything, so he's coming the following weekend. All the women have a ghost story to tell him that he takes in stride.

What's new with that?

T-June walks up in their house and sits at the old dining room table, calling for Bertha and Alcide to come to their table.

Soon enough, they make their presence known to everyone waiting. T-June busts a gut laughing at Alcide in a dress, and Alcide goes to hit him and passes his hand through him, laughing too.

"Oooh, bébés, it's so damn good to see y'all. Ah been moanin' so much to catch yo attention when ya walkin' next to tha house and ya don't hear shit. We gotta go get dat treasure even if we gotta fight dem haints," says Alcide, blowing that horn like he's in a concert with Al Hirt.

The women and Callie and T-June with Henri go to Down Below late that afternoon when things are getting darker with a chance of thunderstorms. They all carry guns and shovels and Holy Water and Off! to break the hold the forlorn ghosts have on what they're guarding.

Everyone has their own shovel and begins digging where the metal detector starts going wild.

Here comes the wretched ghosts out of the ground, solemn and throwing hatred stares at the whole bunch of people, but they stay silent while they watch as T-June and Henri pull up a large chest that isn't broken up in the time since it was buried.

The ghosts remain quiet, but the weather has turned into gust of wild wind, thick fog, and hail as the men break the heavy lock and pull up the treasure, a whole chest full of gold coins.

T-June and Henri are laughing and hollering, looking at what they've retrieved from the dirt, and the ghosts remain silent while there is a bona fide tempest of a storm.

Spooky shit, huh?

They reach T-Mae's house, fighting hard to get in the doors because of the storm that follows them home, along with the sumbitching ghosts just staring at the house.

There's gold coins rolling all over the floor, with the children trying to make them twirl while the storm rages.

Everybody is having an awesome time, throwing the coins and slipping on them on the floor until Henri and Madam Aucoin say to get serious about counting all this.

How the hell do you count solid gold coins in a wooden chest and get serious? They're trying to count it, and it's just too much for them to deal with.

Henri gets big-time serious and calls Monsieur Babineaux to come down to the bayou and help with the large stash of shiny golden coins. He's coming next week to appraise this fortune.

This time he doesn't break the bank, and it's not an emergency. How well he knows the family and the circumstance.

You don't forget shit like that…

∞ ∞ ∞

IT'S still storming on the bayou as the ghosts have started a vigil, day and night, standing and staring and waiting for something like their gold.

T-June comes back to the bayou to attempt to appease the haunting of the horrible and mournful pirate ghosts.

Bertha and Alcide, Big Mama Theriot, Danny Guidry, Sweet Stu with his golden lasso, and a couple more haints come together to have an understanding between the very different bunch of ghosts from a century ago.

They leave Maybelline Laverne alone. She has earned her rest.

Okay, a whole posse of Spirits, riding in to the rescue on white horses. A posse made up of a variety of people, alive or dead, coming to the rescue of MaeMae.

Ghost riders in the sky. You remember?

The pirates come to understand what's going to happen and fly back to the pecan tree in advance of the other ghosts.

Alcide in his ghostly apparel says to the five ghosts at the pecan tree, "Man, what's up wit' y'all not talkin' to nobody, all scary and stuff? Who ya t'ink ya was when ya wasn't dead? Not nobody important to dis family, so quit actin' all hoity toity wit' ya bad-ass selves. Tell MaeMae whatcha want. We tired of tha silent treatment. Or did dey cut ya tongues out before dey kilt ya?"

Still not saying a damn thing, they point at MaeMae, just pointing.

Mae thinks maybe they will settle for a few coins. What else?

The posse is irritated, to say the least, and Alcide throws a lightning bolt, hitting them with it.

Lawd, what else is coming out my head at seven o'clock in the morning?

They all run for cover when the posse of ghosts starts throwing lightning rods at each other, painting the gowns with different colors. They're playing fucking paintball!

Of course, no one else gets painted because it's all ghostly, but when Alcide throws a bucket of all his colors on the head honcho, he is defeated.

Saying to MaeMae, the pirate ghost finally speaks, a ghost of few words. "Give me the picture. Give me my picture."

MaeMae knows immediately what they are seeking. It's on her dresser at the house.

Madam Alafair Aucoin corners them with a dusty concoction, and they were frozen.

"Soldiers of fortune, you must speak to me as I command. What is it you seek? Tell me, I command this."

The oldest of the five long-forgotten pirates speaks in a whisper, "Madam, you have loosened my tongue after being silent since my murder. You are looking at what remains of the Delacroix brothers, silenced forever by Captain Bluebeard. Madam Aucoin, it is my pleasure, and in awe, I kiss your hand."

Then he swoops to the floor with the huge peacock feather in his velvet cap, kissing her hand and then….and then….

And then Madam Aucoin is twitterpated.

"You must know our tragic history so you can look for my family to know how they survived after we were murdered in cold blood by someone we loved and admired and worked for. He brought all of us to this swamp under the pretense of digging up what he had stolen from the Spanish, sinking the ship.

"Murder would come to his mind so quickly, in a blink of his eyes, and he murdered many of his wives because he was a whoremonger and always wanted his wives younger. Thought that was the best solution to his problem.

"I had just told Bluebeard that me and my brothers had started our own business to be legal for our families. He was greedy and wanted no competition. To be utterly evil, he laughed as I lay dying in the dug hole, taking the miniature of my beloved and our son out my jacket and throwing it in the hole, saying he was going to visit her soon.

"He made me watch as he killed my brothers. Our baby brother was only sixteen years old.

"Lord God, please tell me he died a miserable death and that Satan was waiting to pull him into the gates of hell.

"Bluebeard hooked up with an evil quadroon who practiced evil unholy Voodoo. She blew dust, and we were silenced before we died, not to scream.

"Please, madams and monsieurs, let me introduce my brothers, who haven't spoken either. I am Belizaire Delacroix. This is Jacques, Jean Paul, Phillippe, and the youngest Gabriel. We call him Gambi."

All of them do the exact gentlemanly thing that have all the women loving it and blushing and the men kind of turning their heads to smother their laughter at the archaic and dead chilvary.

Madam Aucoin says they will look for his ancestors. MaeMae has gone to the house to get the beautiful portrait of his family.

"Monsieurs, it is an honor to greet you in the spirit world. Your gallantry has been forgotten in ours. Please know we will speak with your family because they will be easy to find. I really think that MaeMae will share this wealth with them.

"You boys have an island named after you, Delacroix Isle. That's how you are remembered. Spirits will set you free to go see for yourselves."

Alcide has for sure got to have the last word. "Hello to ya, old dudes, ya haints. Mais, Ah'm happy ya started talkin' agin, even if ya dead now. Mais, cher, ya sum famous pirates now. We read 'bout you in school. Dey even made some movies 'bout y'all, and Bluebeard was Johnny Depp. Boff dem dudes is famous, Bluebeard and Johnny Depp. Mais, ya look like dem.

"We knew 'bout y'all too. Y'all's tha merry, merry band of pirates."

Belazaire had stiffened in his sheet, and they all lave for Delacroix, tangled up in blue.

∞ ∞ ∞

THE full moon is coming soon, so there's a lot of preparations for the night, seeing if MaeMae is truly loup-garou. T-June will join her, as well as the wolves and Pieyan and Suzie Q and Joey.

Joey is growing out the monkey stage and is much calmer.

The full moon is full and bright, shading the area with its light, when MaeMae makes a complete transformation. A real young loup-garou with red hair and quick to run. And boy does she.

The supers follow suit and are running wide open, trying to catch up with her.

The night is one of wonderment, jumping around on their back legs and licking each other.

A fun time is had by all.

The next night, Bertha comes by herself to talk with MaeMae. Everyone else is in bed snoring, catching up on the elusive sleep at this time.

"Ohh my bébé MaeMae, you was so purty-purty last night. Me, Ah was some proud of ya. Mais, poor baby, ya got two quemas to deal wit'. Ah'm sorry Ah worried ya. Ah just had to.

"Ah'm so glad ya help wit' dem two bébés who ya don't know who is who.

"Now ya got another treasure chest, like all dem years ago.

"Mais, one day me and Alcide went lookin' for some little pecan trees to plant in our yard, and we saw dem ghosts. Me, Ah fainted on tha spot, and Ah woke up in tha boat.

"Poor Alcide, he had to carry me, poor t'ing.

"Dey tole Alcide not to come back, and we sure didn't. Ah knew dere was a lot, and den we watched as y'all played wit' all de coins. We just knew it.

"Ah'm gonna quit hauntin' ya, but ya like me in all tha ways already, so Ah will always be wit' ya."

With that being said, she goes up in a smoke to wherever she goes.

∞ ∞ ∞

MONSIEUR Babineaux comes early in the morning to count the money and just visit some of his favorite people.

They drag the chest out, and they begin to count the huge chest of coins. Monsieur Babineaux gets lost too in counting, so amazed at the amount of coins to be counted.

The counting takes two hours, and Monsieur Babineaux asks for a double shot of whatever is available. Serious counting is concluded, and it is over five million dollars.

Lawd, have mercy and thank ya, thank ya.

The money is taken to New Orleans and put in a brand-new savings account under the guidance of Henri Aucoin. MaeMae wants to split the money with the family, but everyone disagrees with that notion.

She does demand a large portion of this wealth be shared with the Delacroix families.

The families probably have that saved anyway, and there's never been a money shortage with the family that comes from poverty and now is one of the wealthiest on Bayou Lafourche.

When Minou and Joe are told, they catch the first plane out heading home.

Chapter Twenty-Four

Louisiana Swamp Fairies

T-MAE is the first one to see them.

She likes to wander the banks of the Bayou Tranquille and says her rosary while walking and looking for treasures. She doesn't have to look far, because she finds arrowheads, driftwood, apple snail shells and one perfectly good brassiere.

She doesn't have to count her beads. It's automatic from a lifetime of holding the blessed beads and saying robotic prayers.

Lots of people swear by them, so you never know.

T-Mae is alone this morning, which is very strange indeed. Usually, one child or three is asking questions, fussing, shoving each other in the bayou, and it's always something. But still, she's rattling the beads as she's popping heads, not missing a beat.

She is not a stern mama and laughs most of the time at what they get into. Like the morning her youngest, Alcide, falls in the bayou and comes up covered with lily pads and moss.

Then the baby girls are screaming and peeing in their little pink drawers. "Dat monsta ate our brudder. Go shoot him, Mama."

Alcide Rappolet, named after the patriarch of the Thibeau family, comes out screeching because a turtle has bit his ass, and man!

So, this is a weird day in more ways than one. The skies are strangely orange-colored, like a storm is coming, but there's nothing in the Gulf.

T-Mae sits on the bank, pondering the sky, and puts down her rosary because she sees something out the corner of her eye. She turns quickly but stays sitting in total jaw-dropping shock, watching the caravan of what could only be called tee-tiny people, whole frickin' frackin' fey families of fairies. Flying and flitting around her, swooping down as she tries to swat them.

She sees the lily pads coming and snaps to reality for a second. This lily pad carries the high-falutin' fairies.

T-Mae can tell because they have on clothes of royalty, even though the clothes aren't but about five inches.

The important fairies have huge lily pads being paddled across the bayou with what looks like the court, the High Fey Council. They are waited on, while a fleet of guards surrounds them on the lily pad.

They, all women, are too, too fat to flit. All are dressed in finery and wings ,and T-Mae for sure knows that hasn't been bought at the Dollar General.

T-Mae stands to look all around and see if somebody is playing her for a couyon, then throws her stash bag and her corn pipe in the bayou. She kneels, and the lily pad boat comes right up to her on the bank.

T-Mae has to go make it bad, but she would rather mess herself than miss this hallucination.

The largest, fattest fairy on the pad plops to the ground and almost makes the lily tumble over for the weight lost.

The guards flit down to make sure her clothes don't touch the muddy ground, and she pops the humongous woman guard that has dropped her gown in just that.

The Queen, no King, just the Queen. No men, no males, only frickin' frackin' female fairies.

Mais, what's up wit' dat??

Lawd.

Poor T-Mae. She doesn't know if she's caught a concussion or dreaming, but she isn't asleep because she slaps her face. Snap out of it!

All the fairies just bust out giggling like little tinkling bells, and that's when T-Mae's bowels say, "Don't bother running."

She gets down with her face on the ground so she and the old Queen or Dame or whatever the frick frack are eye level, and the little fairy starts talking in a teeny tiny voice.

"Oh, T-Mae, we've been watching you since you got here to Down Below, as your people call it."

T-Mae passes out in fright, and when she wakes up, it's four hours later. Junya is hollering for her after the children had sore throats from screaming for two hours. She never hears them.

Ohhh, we're getting into another realm. Can we take it? Hell, yeah.

∞ ∞ ∞

T-MAE is silent and addled that night like she's been hoo-dooed. She burns the bread and puts salt instead of sugar in all the cups of coffee milk.

Junya says, "Bae, go to bed, Bae."

Now, T-Mae is a seasoned traiteur, and she can tell she has been spelled. She doesn't like that one bit. She stays up that night staring at the moon that will be full in two days. It's great fear she feels down in her bones, locking doors and windows never locked before.

Next morning, it is raining heavy, and all the little children are sleeping in and watching cartoons. Junya forbids any of those video games or nasty movies in his house that turn kids into self-destructive, perverted zombies. He says, "Ah nevah evah saw somet'in' like dat in my life, shit. Mais, font goss! Why dey mamas and papas let dat happen? Dey some scary lil chirren like dat movie wit' tha white-headed chirren wit' dem eyes dat, dat nevah blink. Ohhh, Lawd."

T-Mae hasn't been the same since the morning before. She's frantically whispering in the phone, telling Madam Aucoin to please hurry. She's there in twenty minutes, so maybe she IS the witch some levee rats call her to her back or just whisper, really.

They go on the back porch while it's still raining and pull their rockers up close. T-Mae reminds the kids to stay in the house like they are told every time Madam Alafair comes to visit.

T-Mae tells them, "She's my grown-ass friend and what we talk 'bout ain't none of ya bizness. It's grown-up people's bizness, and Ah bettah not catch ya lil asses around tha door."

After T-Mae tells Alafair Aucoin what's happened – because they're way past the "Madam" shit –Alafair speaks, after choking on a real cannabis cigarette that T-Mae is passing. That's how Junya and T-Mae smoke, straight to your head. Sure don't have any filters. Madam

Alafair says in aggravation, "How rude that was of Mabb. I know her from a long time ago when peace and love were in the air, along with the intoxicating smell of marijuana and patchouli. She and her Kingdom hung in the Quarters during the blessed hippie revolution. The hippies were seeing them around like mosquitos and loving the trip, not remembering the next day. It would have been too freaky leaky to find out they were collaborative in the Timothy Leary psychedelic trippy dippy trip.

"I'll call her right now to meet us behind Junya's shop."

They cross the back yard to the shop where Junya keeps his new boat, covered and roofed with mechanical lifts to raise the boat up and down into the bayou.

Junya can't drive the car a block, never bothered to learn. I mean, come on, y'all. Where was he raised?

Alafair steps out into the yard while it's raining, next to the dock, where she throws her umbrella into the bayou upside down like a luxury liner of boats for the fairies. She sings this haunting tune to the wind and sits back down with T-Mae to wait.

It takes a full hour of waiting before Queen Mabb rounds the bend of the bayou. The umbrella of black and gold comes swiftly in the current, and they see the fairies rolling all over the upside-down luxury liner.

Her roly-poly, Humpty Dumpty Excellency has to have a lot of help from her entourage to get her up. They grab her and the bayou flowing ship tilts, then they tumble on top of her and it is a circus of clowns, being they stand five inches tall.

The grand rescue and the grand entrance are made elegantly by Queen Mabb, with all the other royals in a straight row, some flitting.

She speaks archaic French from long ago, and well we speak bastard French or patois, how you call it? If you by chance come across a Frenchman, he won't know what you're saying to him, scratching his beret.

"Oh, my wonderful old friend Alafair, it's sooo good to see you. Girl, you haven't aged a year. How is old Laurent these days? He's still got that awesome hair? Blow him a kiss for me.

"Thank you for the wonderful gift of the boat. I've brought something for you too."

Here comes the heavy-duty, big-ass women fairy guards carrying this big bundle that has washed up on the coast. They have a hard time with fifteen fairies carrying it, a bale of marijuana. The burlap sack advertises where it's come came from, Humboldt County in Northern California.

Got to be good shit.

Alafair Aucoin makes room for Mabb to sit in her lap, but then warns the others to back tha frickin' frackin' up.

Mabb sits on a black, big-ass mushroom she's brought with her and begins to tell Alafair the reason for the upheaval of her clan of fairies hailing from Lorraine, France, centuries ago.

"You know, Madam, we come from France by way of Nova Scotia, when those English fairies kicked us out. Well, the same wizard fairy clan from England with Alfred the 10th is coming to kill my youngest son, Prince Harry. He's just a hundred years old and has stolen the king's daughter.

"He knows we are hiding them, but Gladiola wants to stay. She finds us a whole lot more fun to be around, although her clan and ours are sworn enemies.

My ex-king, Hank the 15th, will probably join King Alfred and it's his only son he wants to see killed, the nasty, nauseous old fairy. He was kicked out after I found him carrying on with a mermaid and he wants retribution for my actions cause the mermaid is now a croaking toad.

"I'm asking for permission to find a sanctuary on this land. I know it's Joe who owns it, but he is frightful. I think he would use a flyswatter and swat us to death. I'm so glad that Pieyan finally got rid of that distorted disturbed distressed human being. And T-Mae seems to run things back here, so...

"Madam T-Mae, can you make this happen?"

T-Mae plops down on the rocker, shaking her head. "Lawdy Claude, have mercy, have mercy. Ya know somet'in', Ah wish for my old house some time 'cause it nevah had no supernatural shit dere, well, except when Chief was taken by tha wolves. Aw, yeah. Dey ain't supernatural, but dey could be.

"Madam Queen Mabb, Ah gotta ax Minou 'cause she's tha boss up dere and Down Below here."

The fairies leave and go in search of Pieyan and Suzie Q and to meet their sons, Pie and Joey. They've been friends forever, but it's kind of like Pieyan and Alcide had been at first. Pieyan killed and ate quite a few before they came to a truce.

∞ ∞ ∞

MINOU and Joe buy an antebellum beach house down in the Keys and are fixing it up for the families to come.

Minou finally gets Joe to try the marijuana joint and he goes berserk with feeling good because he coughs his head off.

You cough, you get off.

Of course, he has to say something, but they aren't worried about the crew. They join the two smoking owners passing the joint.

"Mais, Minou. Dat's rude. We got plenty of tha shit. Give ever'body dere own joint. Hot damn, mais, dat's some good. What a trip, like ya say. To t'ink Ah coulda been – like ya say – high-high-high all tha time-time-time. It feels soo good.

"Let's go to tha bed, bébé. Mais, Ah got dat vibratin' bed, ya know? Just like our honeymoon, ya 'member? We ain't makin' no bébé.

"Anyway, Ah forgot what Ah was sayin'...All dis time but nooo, Ah had to be 'Old Man Joe Stupid' who wouldn't nevah change wit' tha tide.

"Minou, Minou, Minou, look over dere. Dat's dat mate dat prays on a teeny, tiny rug. Mais, what's up wit dat? Dat's so funny. Hehehehe.

"Where's da frickin' steaks? Mais, Ah'm starvin' all tha sudden.

"Minou, dey act like dey don't understand wha Ah say, den Ah laugh at dem when dey talk back. Dat's funny-funny."

He's going to be one of the talkers who doesn't shut up when stoned.

They are two beachcombers now who stay stoned and laid back most of the time, and it seems as though they aren't worried about what goes on back on Bayou Tranquille.

T-Mae calls Minou on her pink-studded rhinestone cell phone and tells her to go sit in the bathroom so Joe won't hear this quemas.

"Mais, Ah don't know how ya made it all dese years wit' all tha t'ings not supposed to be true, but dey are 'cause we know dat dey are true to tha bone. Shit on a stick.

"Awww, dat Charlie Flowers is somet'in' and funny as shit to put on a stick. Poowee.

"Lawd, ya know me. Ah gotta beat around da sack of crawfish 'fore Ah get to tha serious shit. Ah get nervine. Well, lemme tell ya, we got invaded again wit' another army.

"But bébé, ya ain't gonna believe dis. Ya sittin' on tha commode? It's a whole frickin' frackin' fairies fucked bad, and dey need another home. Wait 'til ya see how cute.

"Okay, ya know how Ah am. Madam is here, and you can talk wit' her. Ah'm gettin too nervine.

Here, Alafair, come talk wit Minou…"

Minou tells them to do whatever they feel needs to be done. She isn't any more interested in what's happening on her land, Larose, little people, little Jude, T-June, Flavia…whoever is left. The drama stays on the bayou.

When you live on an island you become an islander in all sense of the word. Margarita time anytime.

I have to take a breather. The words are coming too fast out of my fingers.

∞ ∞ ∞

SO, it lands in T-Mae and Alafair's lap of being in the wrong place at the right time.

Both of the ladies go right away to tell Mabb the decision. They've been hanging with Pieyan, who has vowed to fight with them against the English marauders.

Mabb will stay indoors at Pieyan's old house until a place is built for her.

She's had to leave her castle where she's lived her whole life. It has gotten too full of centuries of crap.

The community of fairies has settled in among the trees in large holes on the trunks of the cypress and oak or making homes under the house of Queen Mabb.

Madam Alafair and T-Mae go with Mabb to see what can be done to make her and her entourage comfortable, you know like making everything smaller and out their way when flitting. The fairies don't use the kitchen, other than for keeping their potions in the fridge and for drinking their special elixirs.

They don't use the toilet but fill the bathtubs for the cleansing of their little bodies and to scrub their wings, which get awful dirty. You never know when a turd will drop out the sky that you think is something in the air.

Everybody already knows what's supposed to be a huge battle between King Alfred the 10th with King Hank the 15th and their brave soldiering crusaders to remove King Alfred's child from Mabb's son, Prince Harry Emile, and kill all of them.

No one has ever seen anything like what's going to take place here in the sanctioned land of the humans. But the humans will be ready, like every damn time somebody has to fight between good and evil. You know who always win back here in Down Below.

T-June and Jude are going to be right up in the middle of everything, and T-June makes his appearance at court to be introduced to Queen Mabb. Until now, he didn't know they even existed because he's never seen one.

"Ohhh, the T-June has finally come to see me. We have written songs about you, the Magnificent Man who was conceived with our help."

Finally, the reason for the seasons of magic.

T-June stands gaping. You know, his mouth stays opened.

"We've been there the whole time to guard you and direct you on the path of righteous happenings. I knew you would come. It was only a matter of time. Please help us in our struggles. And pleased to meet you."

T-June contains his laughing until he leaves, trying to be serious with the real fat fairies trying to flit to be on eye level. No such luck.

"Yes, your most royal highness, of course I'll be on your side, and I already know we will win this historical battle. Now please, may I present my son to the court."

All of the fatty women swirl around Jude, touching his hair, kissing him with wee kisses. He stands frozen. His papa has said they were going to see a bunch of fairies. At a loss for words he isn't, but now it's a whole 'nother thing he isn't prepared for.

"Where you at? Man, I never knew y'all. For true. I mean, why not? Every other thing down here is supernatural and making their business everybody else's business.

"Y'all knew my great-grandma Bertha and Papa Alcide. I wish I would have known them. They went to loup-garou heaven and came back as ghosts. They haunt their house, and sometimes I go and talk with them. Well, I try, anyway. They laugh at me and don't say shit.

"But this? Man, it's going to be a humongous sight we have never seen. I'm going to help my pa."

The fairies already know about this child because they have watched him, as well as T-June, all his life. The fairies think he is the funniest human they've ever seen, and he's caused accidents among them, laughing so hard at him that they fall off logs and lily pads.

They are so proud of him. A couple of the fairies had even witnessed his birth. Songs have been written about him too, and they are risque in nature because Jude certainly is.

It's funny as hell to see this army of Mabb's battling each other in preparation for the ensuing battle. They just don't know when it will be. Pieyan is running with the fairies on his shoulders, shooting their arrows at the ones on Jude's shoulders, him cussing with a sailor's mouth because they are hitting him with tiny arrows.

Suzie Q and Pie and Joey all are carrying fairies in whatever is a good position, like Suzie's pocket and under her hat. Joey is still a little monkey but excellent in gorilla tactics. He's dangerous to anything flying, regardless. Pieyan fusses at him when he lets one land on his lip and he tries to eat the fairy.

Lola and Emmalois and Cynthia are fascinated with the magical, mysterious mini women creatures.

Their children forget to go to the bathroom when they are playing with the little mysterious mini women creatures. They're like the women Watusi warriors of ancient lore, except way, way tinier.

So, the kids are either running and peeing all the way or trying to blame the dog for the poo-poo in their little pink panties or Superman drawers.

Madam Alafair Aucoin and Marguerite (T-Mae Rappolet) are using their powers together as bona fide Voodoo priestesses, working around the clock to cover the whole area with the spell used years ago in keeping the vampires away and the vamps trying to tear it to suck their blood dry and kill them dead and then they come back.

HAHAHAHA.

So, it for sure needs to work.

∞ ∞ ∞

QUEEN Mabb has to be torn away from all the little girl children and the young girl fairies because they sit in enthralled silence while she tells them the fairy history as they prepare for war. "Raconteurs" is what they are called in France, these interesting storytellers.

"When the blessed Saint Patrick kicked the snakes out of Ireland, that was it for us. The man was just too frou-frou for me. We hid in the bottoms of old nasty ships bound for Nova Scotia with food and supplies to start a new community, and we found peace there for three hundred years.

"Then the frickin' frackin' fuckin' Anglo-Saxons, believing they had blue blood in their veins, came and wreaked our world. Englishmen needed to rule everywhere, and in conquering, they kicked us out of heaven on Earth, my beloved Nova Scotia.

"We came here in almost the same manner, but instead of fruit as their cargo, it was slaves. My ladies and I would sneak up on the women chained to the walls, surrounded by feral men, who grabbed and growled, making sure they got the majority of the food thrown through the hatch. We would blow dust to ensure a peaceful sleep for the tormented woman or put a wet rag in front of her to wash her privates.

"The men, well, we didn't do a damn thing for them. Instead, we caused their sitting places to be full of splinters. There wasn't too much royalty being captured, so no table manners. Of course, I should have felt sorry for them because they all were starving and no air to breathe.

"But it's like you humans say, 'every man for himself.' What horrid thoughts you people come up with in your daily lives, and it's always a man first.

"I must tell you this, my little girls. We are a female race, have been for centuries. There was a huge battle with my mate, King Hank, and his men against me and my girls. We beat them so bad, he took his half of the kingdom and he's living over by Fourchon now. All because he couldn't keep his tee-tiny little dick out of trouble.

"I turned this mermaid he was running behind into an old warted toad, and then the fight was on.

He's the last male to live here."

∞ ∞ ∞

T-MAE and Alafair are sneaking in to hear the history.

"I see you, T-Mae and Alafair," Mabb says.

T-Mae listens to her stories with a large amount of curiosity. She is hanging on Mabb's every word like a child with a fairy tale. "Mais, what? Ya don't have no men? How y'all have all dem girls? Whatcha do wit' tha lil boys? Shit, even Ah know ya ain't havin' no immaculate conception like tha Blessed Virgin, and Ah have a hard time even believin' dat. Ah mean it, how tha fuck ya fuck?"

She hangs with Flavia a lot. Can you tell?

Mabb just busts out laughing and tells T-Mae, "It's the next story. You jumped the gun, as humans say. What's that mean? I know all about jumping the broom.

"We lived among the natives, be it Houmas or Chitimachas or the Atakapa. We didn't live with the Atakapa for a long time because they were always trying to eat us. We were called the 'Chunees.' Translated, that means 'pretty little flying fat women who play nasty with our braves.'

"T-Mae, your great great-mawmaw used to hit me with her broom to get me off her clean porch. You know, she was a God-fearing woman, and we've always been heathens, and we sure don't fear our gods.

"Your mawmaw, T-Mae, taught us a lot of words, and she spoke only French, or whatever you call your speech.

"Alafair, we remember how your mama reacted, and it was so great. She taught me a lot, like the proper way of doing gris-gris.

"Only the traiteurs could see us, and we scared some of them bad. Sometimes, they would sit on their porches and converse, but then the ones who didn't want us around their clean porches were mean-ass bitches.

"People are letting their freak flags fly these days, and your marijuana helps bring awareness to your people. Truly, it is just a weed.

"This is what happens: we trap the trappers of fur, the crawfish catchers, people of color running from the masters, lumberjacks cutting our sacred trees, and the gamblers tossed off the paddlewheel boats for cheating. Those horrible men who came from someplace called Texas who tore up the swamps for oil and then turned around and laughed at your people, calling them 'coonass.' They are the coonasses from Texas. We didn't like them too much because they always stunk. We always went back to the Cajuns. Must be their French blood."

Ooh lala.

"We can grow to your size, and we do when they find us in the dark swamps. So, we entice them, and they don't know what hit them. We put spells on them, and sometimes, they don't want us to get up. 'Let's do it again,' they holler as we walk away.

"We spell them to begin with, and they don't remember a thing, but the man is never the same. He is forever addled and just busts out laughing when he looks out on the swamp. He loves to dance when he couldn't before.

"We are really who the Jezebel label was put on first. It's always been 'slam, bang, thank ya, ma'am' except we're the ones slamming and banging.

"The little Cajun man who wrote the song "Jolie Blon" was addled enough to write about one of our women he would dream about. As you all say, 'the rest is history.'"

I like that one.

"You two women are mystical and traiteurs and Voodoo priestesses, so you two could always see us. You, T-Mae, never looked. Too busy chasing after your brood.

"We do many things to help run this world, we are very powerful. You know we are around by the force of the winds coming from the swamps. We can change the weather. The grayness of that morning was because it's harder to see us and we can slip right through the swamps.

"We coax the flowers to bloom and the moss to turn gray.

"We teach the little birds to fly out their nest. We teach the raccoons to wash their paws and the tiny alligators not to bite everybody.

"We've always argued whether the nutria rat is a bona fide rat, so it gets heated, and we cause those big balls of fire you see in the swamps you call feu follet.

"We always dance with the big black bears by the light of the moon, but we never venture out when the loup-garous are out. They sure don't like women. Then I saw one was a woman female loup-garou and she liked us. We'd go on her porch many times, and she would give me coffee in a cap from a medicine bottle. I still use it.

"Blessed be, Bertha and Alcide.

"We do know all about the gris-gris, and we use them on people if they anger us. Alafair, your mama taught me a few new tricks. People who have the gris-gris put on them can't sing no more, have two left feet so they can't dance, and they don't think anything is funny. What worse thing could happen?

"So, I will sing you a song written about us long ago."

> Their kingdom is forever
> You hear their laughter in the night.
> Such amazing little creatures
> No two can be alike
> If your heart is full of humor
> And you laugh when you see us around
> You will have to take us home with you
> 'Cause in the magic you've been bound.
>
> Louisiana Swamp Fairies, born 1999
> Circa 2023
> In their honor, I pay tribute.

Mabb isn't finished, but she is for the day.

∞ ∞ ∞

THE female warriors come in after scouting, telling them the army of Alfred the 10th is on the march and that the two-timing King Hank has joined the massive army already coming to kill Prince Harry Emile and to carry Princess Gladiola back and stick her in their prison for treason.

His own son he's coming to kill and to bring retribution and hatred to Queen Mabb.

All right. The game is almost on. Queen Mabb comes out in total armor to meet the two men coming to kill her.

As if, as if.

The sky turns black like before a thunderstorm, and a few of the enemy are flying in ahead, shooting arrows at them. Both armies fight as fairies, not as seductive femme fatales.

Ooh, the invading army has no idea what they are heading into.

Come here, boys. We got a surprise for you.

As planned, the plan is going to work because this is the first time it's been used as a battlefield ploy to trick and confuse them. Mabb has ordered all of her fair maidens to take their clothes off and fight naked.

WHAT?

∞ ∞ ∞

T-JUNE knows everyone is prepared. At least they won't be tearing up the land.

T-June is thinking, "Let them slide so the whole armies can come in," them thinking it will be a push over. Their plans are very simple and will take care of problems once and for all.

Everybody from Down Below is on the field too but with clothes. This has the invading army totally confused and nervous. Never, ever have people been involved in the fighting of the fairy clans. Many times human wars have been rampant but have never involved the fairies. This is a total travesty because the people sure are up in this shit.

When the invading armies see they have a battlefield full of humans and a nasty-looking bigfoot family, the armies go into retreat and the women warriors are waiting for them, blocking their retreat, just daring just daring.

The girls are making the men look twice at their nakedness and that's when the sword comes out and the girls massacre them.

Keep your eyes on the prize. It's about fighting, not ogling.

Mabb sees her king trying to get to her where she stands under the house. He's screaming and full of intent. He is coming full force, intending to kill her. Suzie Q is protecting her when Joey grabs the exiled king. With one gulp he eats the despot trying to kill his queen.

That has happened many times in the reign of many kings and their queens. The kings are too dysfunctional and jealous. The queen never kills the king.

First, King Hank is cannibalized, and then King Alfred the 10th is eaten by Suzie Q.

That is the end of the war. It has lasted one full hour.

The fairy soldiers left are allowed to leave peacefully, no harm will come to them. They just need to get going and not look back.

Mabb and her girls take care of business.

Suzie Q is telling Mabb, "Queenie, dear, y'all have no idea how sweet tasting y'alls blood is. To supernaturals, it's an elixir, especially to the vamps. It's why y'all get eaten by us different little critters from the humans. I don't think the people eat you, but you never know about those creatures. They eat crawfish."

It is written in the book of Fairy Law that it is forbidden to change into humans while in combat because there would be more fucking than fighting.

∞ ∞ ∞

PRINCE Harry and Princess Gladiola will be married on the next full moon, and it will be the most magnificent happening Down Below that has ever been seen.

They have hired every band of fireflies to come for the whole night. They pay generously.

The mosquitoes and gnats and wasps are told to stay home that night under penalty of law.

Even that event doesn't draw Minou and Joe home. They are now bona fide Islanders who follow Jimmy Buffet. Joe has the hat to prove it. PARROT HEAD.

They think everybody left at home has turned real crazy or smoking some bad shit or too batshit to leave the bayou.

"Mais, as if as if dey gonna have a weddin' for a bunch of fairies. Here comes tha dude from tha crazy bin with a net. Toot toot toot. Bye bye."

Mais, who you think said that?

Callie and Henri have come with many mini sandwiches and little, small muffin pans for red velvet cake that can be cut into six slices.

Mabb tells the tale with humor. "I must betray myself. I'm the one who watched the chef in Georgia making the delight and brought it to Alafair's mama, and the rest is culinary history."

All of T-Mae and Junya's girls with MaeMae are to be the human flower girls, and they spend too much time picking wild flowers to hang everywhere, but at least they are out the way. The girls have some piss weed mistakes because they're pretty too, you know the ones that make you sneeze while you try to not shake them?

Taunte Alafair brings little headbands with ribbons and flowers trailing behind for them to wear. They look like they're going to do a lot of dances around the flagpole, in the pagan tradition.

T-June, Jude, Justin, Scottie, Hellbent Harley, and Junya all stand in line as the groomsmen. They all look like they're dancing, trying to scratch itches in the tuxedos. Emmalois, Cynthia, Colette, and Lady Dupree are the bridesmaids, all women of the men that live Down Below. You remember them, the 'old ladies as they are called that made their freedom and retribution known.

Junya and T-Mae are best man and matron of honor, you know, the ones on the altar with you.

Junya has to lead the groom out to the church after the previous night's bachelor party. He vomits his guts up by Old Man Babin's grave.

I didn't sugarcoat it. It's stark reality of getting married shivers.

The occasion is like a fairytale itself, the scene displaying the same scenes told by a favorite teacher, with illustrations so vivid that you remember your whole life. Subtle colors of purple and blues with the pink and orange surrounding around the sun, going down for the night to appear in its place. Mysterious surroundings in the dark of the moon but well lit up by the fireflies.

∞ ∞ ∞

A male fairy is sneaking around the perimeter, coming toward Mabb, and her guards go into defensive mode to protect her.

When he is recognized, he is grabbed by his little fairy arms and brought in front of Mabb. He is broken and some stinky. It's none other but her regurgitated King Hank.

"Oh, my goddess, that little bastard monkey spit me out because I was beating on the side of his stomach. He farted, and I came out free. Look at my beautiful clothes. These stains will never come out.

"I came back to tell you I was on your side, just playing like I was with Alfred.

"I can't stop thinking of you. I've ruined our lives by thinking I was the rooster hanging around the chicken shack, so to speak, and lost your love and respect. Let me come home. Treat me mean and cruel but love me. We will make this new home magnificent again.

"Please don't kill me. Let me make it up to you. I'm a changed man."

Mabb looks at him and said, "If you think you're just going to waltz on back here without consequences? You're dumber than I thought. You better think again, Monsieur Dumbshit. You've got to prove yourself before you come to my bed again."

That's been three months ago. Queen Mabb has him running errands. Things are peaceful for the new residents Down Below.

Minou and Joe, the Key West Islanders, have come home for a short visit.

When the pictures taken at the Fairy Festival are shown to Joe, he says, "Ha ha ha! You gonna have to wake up early for me to believe dat. Mais, Ah know y'all. Ya know all 'bout dem side effects. Y'all made dem pictures up. Ya can't trick me, that ole trickster Ah am. Mais, Ah know evert'in' ya do to start tha quemas."

Chapter Twenty-Five

Hey, Jude

MINOU calls Callie and tells her to bring everybody down to visit her and Joe in their huge hacienda. Anybody and everybody connected to the Cajun Mafia, by law, by blood, by sistas, by whatever means is necessary for the village to come see the Gulf side of Florida with its blue waves lapping up the shore and white sand with driftwood and shells scattered.

When we talk about the village, it's not the whole town, it's T-June followers who made their own village. It's the followers-disciples-posse-village that guides him.

Lochloosa, a small town still quaint and quiet, is where the Thibeaus have bought a beautiful old Civil War-era tropical plantation home that takes up two acres of private beach. Private and secluded is the plantation home, with definite vibes of being on a Caribbean island. Simply gorgeous, throwing you back to those days of drinking mint juleps on the verandas, smelling the exotic flowers growing wild. Minou and Joe's house has ten bedrooms, plus the yacht adds all kind of beds.

The crew are on paid vacations.

Who's coming? Callie and Henri with all five of their children, including True Blue; T-June and Jolie, with the five-year-old Jude; Estelle and Theo Theriot, cuckoo Flavia, Madam Alafair Aucoin, Bishop Laurent Toussaint, and T-Mae and Junya with their kids.

First vacation – and out-of-state at that – for Junya and T-Mae, who are so excited to go and see what the world has to offer they don't have at home.

Flavia's caretakers – Grey and Gerry, with their partners in crime, Weedie and Mary Marguerite – are going to Arizona. Gerry and Mary have had a traditional Comanche wedding on the reservation in full garb of brave and maiden. Fun time had by all.

The big question about this trip is of course Jude. What will he do? There ain't no tellin'.

Minou and Joe haven't seen their grandkids in quite a while, just talking on the phone or seeing them on her laptop screen.

Everybody is being told that the older children will keep their eyes open for whatever Jude thinks he can get away with. Let Jolie and T-June have some quiet time for themselves.

All of these families go down there in a caravan of cars and pull in together in the circle driveway that used to have horses and buggies pass through.

Minou and Joe are jumping in joy, and there is so much kissing and hugging it takes a half-hour to get in the house.

Everyone is mystified and stupified at Minou and Joe's home away from home. Minou uses some of the crew that works on the yacht to be a maid and a cook, giving them more money for that than they've ever seen for staying.

After all the hugging and kissing and gifts being given, all are ready for a nice siesta on the many hammocks, sipping or toking while relaxing.

The children can't wait to go to the beach in all their brand-new bathing suits and suntan lotions and toys, with Jude running ahead of all of them. MaeMae is hollering for him to stop, telling him she will beat his ass.

Running right into the water, he immediately goes deep into the waves and comes back up when it crests, then he goes under again.

They are all hollering for him to come back, and of course nobody tells him what to do, so he doesn't listen.

MaeMae will definitely beat his ass if he lives.

At first, MaeMae and the kids think it is a manatee coming close to him in the deep water. The closer they get, they saw it is a shark heading for Jude. The frickin' big creature pulls him under.

All the children are screaming and running to tell their parents, when all of a sudden, the shark appears again, with Jude riding on his back. Stunned and unbelieving of what they see are the mamas and the papas as the shark lands him on the sand.

Jude says, "What the fuck? Y'all know I talk with animals. It ain't any different with the animals of the sea."

Before MaeMae can grab him, MeeMee Minou has him by the ear and marches him back to the house, just daring T-June to say shit.

It's already started with the little imp.

∞ ∞ ∞

THE first night is a fais do-do, you might as well call it, with the children being sent to bed, for sure little Jude because MeeMee Minou puts him there, daring him also to say shit.

The salt air is drifting along with intoxicating smells of the ocean, the beach much, much bigger than Grand Isle. The breeze comes in through all the long windows; the windows open so you can walk through them like a door.

Everyone is relaxed and enjoying the lateness of the night with the tiki lights' flares blowing in the salty wind, bringing the intoxicating smells of very different flowers from roses.

Just as they say how nice it is, a huge moan comes from the top of the staircase built for hoops. In the fashion of little southern belles comes a young girl spirit down the stairs.

What the hell? Mais, what?

They all witness this as the ghost of a belle comes floating down the magnificent staircase built for southern steel magnolias, floating out of the large and long windows and moving toward the Gulf, shocking everybody as she disappears into the waves as the tiki lights go out in a flicker and silence takes over the night.

Junya watches this happen and turns to the bunch. "Mais, why ya don't say nuttin' to her? Ah mean, like dem spirits from Madam's house, dey talk back to ya. Mais, Minou, she come ever' night or just sometime?

"Ah know ya tried, but looks like she snooty 'cause she don't say shit, just sashays by wit'out a 'how-ya-do.' Mais, what tha fuck is up wit' dat?"

Madam Aucoin explains to the gathered, "She's what is referred to as a residual ghost, never saying anything, just always does the same, over and over again. Repeating the night she died. She comes every night at this time, two o'clock.

"Minou told me how she is, and it will take a powerful potion and dust to throw on her as she passes before she says a word."

Who do you think sneaks down those stairs, hiding in a corner, listening to everything? Everybody thinks he sleeps with one eye open, so he doesn't miss a thing.

He sees her firsthand. She has lit up in the hall and it wakes him up. The nosy little bastard, he passes his hand through her as she passes him, and it lights him up like that Christmas tree, never stopping her roll, but stopping him. It electrifies his hair, and he runs for the bathroom.

The next morning while the kids are eating beignets with fresh pineapple and watermelon. Jude touches one of the twins and shocks her. Everybody at the table sees this and thinks he's probably got some device to do that. Not thinking anything about it, to their dismay later.

Jude is pestering all the kids to finish, having no patience for anything.

Minou passes him a stare, and he runs outside to wait before she takes it further than that.

All the grown-ups are going deep-sea fishing except for T-June. Some grown-up needs to be there for guess who? And he's responsible for all of it anyway.

Everyone is enjoying the deep blue sea and the fishing, pitching the line far out into the Gulf, laughing and drinking and toking until the line jerks and Junya has a real big fish biting on his hook.

Minou is hollering for help. "Mais, Joe, Mais, Joe. Sumbitch. JOE! Y'all come help us, please, help us. Oh, my Gawd. It's a fuckin' shark. Aw, Lawd, aw, Lawdy Claude."

All of the men on board are trying to help him, but the shark is steadily pulling them in the other direction, closer to shore.

What the fuck?

Before they run aground, the shark stops, the boat motor is silent, and there is a ruckus on the side of the boat while everybody tries to get to the sides.

True Blue is trying to get into Jude's head, but the line is busy.

Jude pulls himself up onto the shark's back, holding the large fin in his hands like he is fixing to rodeo.

Jude swims the whole distance, talking to the shark named Jimmy Buffett, directing the whole damn thing.

Where in the hell is T-June?

Jude and Jimmy Buffett proceed to put on a show after Jimmy spits the hook out his mouth, twirling up in the air and diving under and coming right up and speeding in the water, with Jude not holding on, his hands up in the air.

Flavia is shaking her rosary at him and the shark, yelling "Antichrist, Antichrist. Begone, you devil's spawn!"

Minou faints; you know how scared she is of sharks. Joe is cussing and shaking his fist at Jude, who makes Jimmy Buffett bring him to shore so he can run fast-fast away.

When they pull into their slot, they all take after him.

T-June comes swaggering onto the sand and falls face first in it.

Joe grabs Jude up in a headlock, and that's how he stays. "Ya lil shit, what ya did to ya papa, huh? Ya bettah start runnin' ya mouf instead of ya lil fat feet. Ya bettah tell us."

Jude looks in the direction of his papa, so scattered-brained. "I got one of my mama's sleeping meds and put it in his Dr Pepper."

Joe goes to whip him, but instead he thinks about it for a minute and is rolling on the sand, laughing his ass off. "Mais. A chip off tha butcher block. Ya t'ink dat ain't been done before? Aw, shit on a stick. Go tell MeeMee Minou whatcha done. And ya papa."

T-June is very upset with his son, knowing he can't trust his boy. Jude thinks he's the grown-up in any situation; of course, he's raised to think his shit doesn't stink.

I mean, who else has pulled himself out his mama's womb?

Well, that's not what MeeMee Minou tells him. She shows him how the alligator eats the gros bec. She tears him a new one, and because this is his first time to be spanked, he immediately starts having an apocalyptic hissy fit.

Minou dares both of his parents to say anything, for sure, not even, BUT…

She punishes him for two days, and he better be glad Minou doesn't put him kneeling on rice. He better not EVEN open the door of his bedroom; she's wanting bad to lock him in. She takes all his electronics away and tells him to read.

Remember, Minou is scared to death of sharks, but sure likes their meat.

∞ ∞ ∞

EVERYONE stays up for the clock in the foyer to chime two o'clock in the morning. They watch the heavenly-looking ghost girl in a flowing brand new (for that time period) negligee gown come down the massive stairs again.

Up close she looks to be eighteen or close to it.

As she passes Madam and T-Mae, they both throw dust on her and she freezes right there and starts looking around at the motley crew in front of her.

She shrieks, "Begone, you pirates. Leave now."

Madam Aucoin introduces herself and T-Mae as Voodoo practitioners and brings her to the state of consciousness.

She screams again, "Oh my Lord in heaven. You Mulatto woman. I can't abide that. You, the country swamp girl. Please tell me why you did this. I'm glad to speak again, but why are all these people in my home?"

Madam tells her she needs to know why she's haunting this house and can help her cross over.

Madam and T-Mae are asking the questions, like "Who's ya mama, who's ya papa?"

"Tell us, daughter, who you were and how you came to your demise."

She begins talking in a thick southern drawl. "My name is Jamie Sue Buffett, soon to be Chaisson. His name was Russell Chaisson, and he came from a small village down there in Louisiana called Chackbay.

My parents had a large plantation of everything citrus, with free people of color and Cubans working there for a good pay. I would inherit all of my papa's wealth, including this house, as I'm an only child. We would have lived here.

"Ohhh, ohhh, it still pains me to talk about it. We were to be married in the fall of that year.

"Russell was on his way to celebrate our engagement with his fellow officers when they were ambushed by Union soldiers. My fiance and one of his good friends were killed. The one that escaped came directly to our home, where the party was already in full swing, to tell me before he told my parents and his.

"I just went into the vapors and was brought to my bed. When everyone in the house was asleep, I went down the staircase for the last time alive.

My mammy and her spouse, Remus, tried to stop me, but I clawed them bad and went into the warm waters of the Gulf to drown, not knowing I would be back every night, haunting my home. I wasn't but nineteen, so what did I know?

"In case y'all haven't noticed, Mammy and Remus haunt this house too because of me. They are very scary because they have blood dripping from where I clawed them.

"Some little child has been trying to talk with them, and he passed his hand through me. What do you teach your children these days?

"If you can take care of this situation, we would be deeply thankful. I'll tell y'all where a treasure is buried out there in all the palmetto groves if you help us, madams."

Lawd, these people and their buried treasures. They should have been Irish with all the little leprechauns running around.

Madam Aucoin has a crystal ball she carries in an emergency kit, and she shows the ghost where her love is.

Lo and behold, Russell Chaisson comes up in the ball, beckoning her into the hereafter with him.

She swiftly leaves in a white light, and in the older part of the house they watch as two more lights head for the heavens.

A sheet of lilac scented stationary comes floating out the clouds and lands at Madam's feet. The thin paper has instructions to find the treasure.

All of them start to laugh and then just fall out in hilarity, wheezing, trying to catch their breath.

Joe says, "Oh, my Gawd. Oh, my Gawd. Oh, my Gawd. Ah ain't believin' dis. Another chest buried in, of all tha places, tha palmetto dat snakes make deir nests in. And Ah guess ya want me to do dat, huh? Mais, not no but hell no. Ah don't need no more dough, and you youngins can take over dat project, but ya bettah not leave my property in despair."

∞ ∞ ∞

JUDE can't get close to anybody because the children run away from his touch. That lady ghost leaves him in despair, because the adults don't know what he has done, passing his hand through Jamie Sue.

Sneaking in the back part of the kitchen, trying to make those bloody ghosts respond, isn't a part of their repertoire.

The kids go and grab Madam Alafair Aucoin, telling her what he tells them. MaeMae finally gets her hands on him, daring him to tattle.

For Madam Alafair Aucoin to get pissed off, it takes a lot. She yanks him up by the arms, sparks flying as the two powerful people have contact.

Madam pours a whole bottle of potion, a full gallon size, onto his head, drenching him in the potions that may work overtime on his little smart ass. She says she won't do it again if he behaves for the rest of the vacation. If he doesn't, well, the whole thing will be embellished. And who are they going to believe?

The electricity leaves his body with a double dose of potion, and Madam tells him to go change his clothes without telling his parents.

You can't trick a trickster.

True Blue gets up early and wakes Jude to go with him to look for treasures in the palmetto grove. He wants time alone with the five-year-old miracle. True tells him, "Little cousin, you sure have them standing on their heads. MeeMee Minou's about to wring your little fat neck. Man, you got to take it easy on them old people. Leave Flavia alone, and don't let her put her hands on you. She would drown you dead in holy water.

"What's up with your act, dude? I mean, it's a bit of too much at five years old. You want all that bad attention? You aren't tired of being fussed at? Dude, you aren't even close to being grown, and you have to listen to your elders, for sure this bunch.

"Mon petite cousin, you have to lighten up and slow down with your bossy little ass. Listen to music, bro. It will soothe your soul.

"Listen up here. Don't go thinking you're old enough to smoke ganja. I'll whip your ass.

"Come on, bro. We're gonna find some treasure."

Dressed in hip boots and netted hats for protection from whatever is in there, Jude and True head out, both talking to the animals, telling all the critters they're coming through and to be nice.

There could have been a red blinking light as to where the treasure is; it's so obvious. There is a huge mound, not native, that just looks like an old garbage pile covered in dirt. The directions are precise; if anybody else would have gone in search of the riches, they'd have seen it.

Both cousins have brought metal detectors to graze the land with. No telling what they will find.

One detector starts beeping loud, possibly pointing a red blinking light, saying "Dig here. Dig here."

It wasn't hard to dig up at all, and there are no ghosts to pester them.

The proverbial wooden chest is in excellent condition and light as True brings it up out the hole. True breaks the lock easily, and Jude is inside immediately, with his feet sticking out the chest. He starts throwing money after money out of the chest and screaming, "Son of a bitch, we're rich, True Blue. We're goddam rich."

True is down in the chest, where jewelry and gold coins are just scattered around the bottom and a whole case of the finest Champagne hidden during Prohibition.

"Goddam, sumbitch, True, come see, come see. That money is crumbling in my fingers. What the shit?"

True jumps out the hole to go to Jude and sees the money just flying into the Gulf, falling into ashes.

He takes a hard look at the money and falls out laughing.

Jude gets pissed off at him and begins to cuss some of his favorites when True stops him with his hand in Jude's face, as if to say, "Do not say a word."

"Little man, it isn't any good. It's all Confederate money. It's worthless. Just like the Confederacy, it wound up in ashes. Why are you looking at me and pointing? What the ...?"

Jude is silently pointing at a large anaconda slowly wrapping itself around True's legs.

The snake ignores both True and Jude talking to him. Maybe he doesn't speak English.

They look at each other, and then at the same time they zap that snake into the kingdom of the dead cobras. Jude and True go to laughing and pointing their fingers at the brush of the thick canebrakes just in case.

True and Jude get the rest of the treasure in a large sack and haul the Champagne to higher ground, spending the rest of the day zapping the anacondas that are so pervasive in Florida, wearing out their welcome and heading toward the rest of the Gulf Coast.

They come home carrying the exquisite meat, a true foreign cuisine, telling the families they shot one.

Jude is one generous little dude because he gives a piece of antique jewelry to each of his little cousins and their mamas. He's going to keep the coins for his savings account, which is already full.

True ices down the Champagne. Everybody can take their own bottle.

Jude saves a ring, a beautiful ruby, and he solemnly handed it to his MeeMee Minou, with his beautiful eyes just begging for her to like him. She grabs him up in her arms, and they both are crying and stroking each other.

Awww. That makes me cry.

∞ ∞ ∞

TRUE Blue Aucoin, the famous musician, has decided he will take care of Jude for the remaining time, the least he can do.

All the other little children are jealous and upset because it is just Jude and True Blue.

Shit, he's the one always in trouble, so it definitely doesn't make sense to them in their little minds. You're supposed to get rewarded for good behavior, and he is bad, bad, bad. Mixed messages.

True and Jude are taking a stroll on downtown Cross Creek's sidewalks, greeting people and fans who had heard that the Monsieur Mayhem Band is here on vacation and wants to see them. He is signing album covers, CDs, and T-shirts, while Jude is bragging on his papa and True, telling them who he is.

Well, of course he is signing things too, as he writes like a ten-year-old.

They walk into a Cuban restaurant named Perdido and take a table, wanting Cuban sandwiches and fried plantains. They are looking at the décor, all bright colors and inviting, with warm and friendly people talking Cuban Spanish, a little different from Mexican. Cuban music is blaring out the jukebox while the waitress makes it to their table and the lights go on in Florida.

She is exquisite and has a smile that beckons True to her large lips. He is a gone pecan.

"Señors, what can I get you for your meals? We have a lovely menu to look over. In the meantime, our special drink for today is

Cuban Libre. But for you, mijo, it will be straight up Coke if you want. You'll be old enough next year, mijo, you think?"

Jude doesn't miss a thing because he is on the party line, listening to both of their brains. He feels the sexual tension and he busts out laughing,

"Well, hello, darling. I didn't catch your name. You are as beautiful as that red hibiscus flower in your hair, señorita."

Both True and the exotic beauty start laughing at him, so he continues when she comes back with the food after telling them her name is Isabel Mariana Castro.

"Honeypie, do you know who we are? We're famous. You know about the Monsieur Mayhem Band? Well, we're two of the members of that famous band. You want an autograph on something?"

Mariana is smiling at True, and he's doing the same. Jude is making noises of discontentment when she says, "No, mijo. I've never heard of you guys. You speak like you're from New Orleans, am I right? I love all music, so I'm sure I will enjoy this brand new band."

True and Jude are flabbergasted, never hearing that from nobody ever. They both ask at the same time if she will come for supper that night back at the hacienda.

She laughs a twinkly little sound that makes True want so bad to kiss her. Jude too.

Mariana said she's always wanted to see the house that makes her homesick for her home in Cuba. It is just like this tropical plantation.

She definitely says YES.

On the way back, True chastises Jude, who thinks he's grown. "Hey, little dude. What do you think you're doing, wooing her like you're grown? Don't make me get all jealous on you."

Laughing the whole time, he hugs Jude and ruffles his hair. Jude gets all puffy with indignation.

"What? You think I'm not grown enough? Well, she'll have to wait 'til I grow hair."

Ohhh, a child of five?

They rush home to tell everybody that company is coming tonight and a very important guest for True Aucoin. He tells them the very little he knows about her, but he tells everybody she will stay if he can do anything about it.

He tells them all, he's truly in love at first sight, and he believes she feels the same.

Minou tells him she already knows her.

As Isabel Mariana Castro crosses the sand to get to the house, Jude runs to her, trying his best to flirt with the ability of a five-year-old boy. All the children run to her, and Jude tries to make them leave because he's the one trying to court her, in spite of what True Blue has said.

This is one confident little dude, who's never been turned down on anything in his life.

True comes out to meet Isabel, and they only have eyes for each other, with Jude pouting and running off.

The family is sure looking up one side of Isabel and down the other. To catch True, she's got to be someone special because he's been catting around for years and never gotten caught strutting his stuff.

Minou takes her by the hands because she does know her. She and Joe often eat at the restaurant owned by her father. They hug each other, and she does the introduction, not giving True the pleasure, but he's okay with it.

There's a huge pot of seafood gumbo cooking, and Isabel has brought plantains to be fried to add to the feast.

Everyone is loving Isabel, with her contagious laugh and her heavy accent. She smiles the whole time. She's beautiful but acts as though she's not aware of it; just a breath of fresh air she is.

Isabel is telling them everything about herself and her family. "My parents came over on a boat years ago, being that Castro took everything from my father. He was a very successful lawyer and Castro's first cousin. He made his opinions about Castro very public, so anti, and had planned a takeover before the Bay of Pigs happened.

"Castro let us leave with nothing to our name to rid himself of someone who would have made a difference in his communism, even if he was kin. We all struggled, as my father couldn't practice law. We had help from other expatriates in opening the restaurant. I was a very late life baby being my mama was forty-two and my popi was almost fifty.

"My father is taking classes with me, to regain his status and for me to finish my law degree. My mother died shortly after I was born so it's just Popi and me. He never remarried."

Everyone is enthralled with her story and her lyrical speech, but Flavia can't help herself.

"Well, hell. We got ourselves some real Cubans. Tha ones who fought tha bastard Fidel. One time, we was at Key West to watch tha sun go down, and me, well, Ah hollered at tha trash he is, cussin' him lower dan an alligator. Ah don't know if Fidel heard me.

"You a fine señorita, Isabel Mariana Castro, and to think tha lowlife is a cousin to ya daddy. But let me tell ya, Ah got pull. Ya t'ink ya daddy wants some of dose fancy cigars?"

Theo and Estelle, best friends with Minou and Joe, have just been chilling, but Estelle speaks up. "You precious child, to have never known Cuba that is heaven. You know it's one of the only places that looks at Blacks as equals, and the children are absolutely beautiful from this liaison.

"I have two daughters that are lawyers, and they do real well. God bless you, Isabel Castro." And she takes her into her arms.

The Cuban señorita is welcomed with open hearts after she fries those plantains.

∞ ∞ ∞

JUDE goes off into the night by himself, feeling totally rejected. When he walks up on this gang of boys hanging out by their bonfire, he can read their minds, so he stays hidden. All of them look to be at least fourteen, with one bigger than the rest and the leader.

He hides further in the shadow of the palm trees when they spot him and start taunting him.

When he goes into the ringleader's head, he knows he'd better run. That little booger can run fast-fast, like his MeeMee Minou.

He is steadily running into a large canebrake, but they're natives, so he can't elude them for long.

Jude turns as he hears one of them scream and walks back to where they are. The leader of the pack has a gigantic anaconda halfway up his chest, and his gang is just freaking out, not knowing what to do.

Jude stands there and they all see as the snake stops squeezing the dude and turns and looks at the small boy flickering his tongue at the snake.

That lasts for a minute, looking like the two are conversing, the snake and the boy.

The very large snake gives up his prey for a better one, one that has the balls to taunt him.

Jude is slowly backing up while the evil snake keeps coming toward him, not even thinking he is slithering into a trap.

Jude is talking to the snake out loud, and the other boys fall on the ground, too afraid to move, along with the leader, way out of reach of the snake.

"Yeah, you just think you bad-ass. Wait and see who's the bad ass, and don't bother telling me your name because you ain't gonna be around long. I'm sure you heard of the two human monsters that killed all your brothers and mothers. That's me, you fat fuck."

He then turns his attention to what's in store for the nameless snake. The anaconda is acting like a cobra, his face up close and personal with Jude's.

Here's where it gets really funky.

Jude turns music on from his phone and starts playing Delbert McClinton's "The Jungle Room," and all the snakes hiding in the canebrake begin to dance. Jude is doing all the leading because the snakes don't have a choice in the matter.

The gang, who has found a new leader, is addled and befuddled at what they have witnessed so far. The old leader sees the light the minute the snake let him go.

Jude proceeds to make the snakes dance by themselves, with everyone laughing now.

Into the clearing comes four big anacondas. They quit dancing. The boys begin to scream and huddle in a circle while Jude throws the python at the other mean, evil, devil's pet.

Jude stands alone. No one is able to join him right now because they truly are scared shitless.

The prideful huge snake lunges at Jude, and he zaps him into snake hell. The other boys snap to it and are grabbing what they can to damage the other serpents, yelling the whole time like the natives.

Jude is coming behind the gang, zapping them on the path to hell.

∞ ∞ ∞

BY this time, everyone at the hacienda is screaming Jude's name, thinking the poor child has drowned. Jolie is in hysterics, screaming, and T-June is jumping in and out the Gulf, trying to read his mind under water.

Here he comes, just strutting his stuff with four more boys behind him, all carrying dead anacondas.

Lord, I've got to give my mind a rest.

They don't know what to make of the scene, but Jolie grabs him up and doesn't know if she should love on him or beat the tar out of him.

Here comes True with Isabel, and she hollers at the former leader of the pack. "Santonio Perez, what are you doing with that nasty big snake? Your mama knows where you are? Drop the damn thing."

Sammy starts telling her this amazing story, "Man, Isabel. This little dude has powers, a regular Superman. You ought to see what he can do. Tell them, Jude, tell them."

Jude stands there in silence, because True already knows what he has done. He is daring him to say another word.

The strangeness and supernaturalness of the families have been exposed right out there in full Mardi Gras colors. Isabel looks at True for an explanation, and he throws his hands up, not saying, "I don't know," but in his way, he says, "We'll talk about this later."

The boys are given hot cups of chocolate and leftover dessert of fried plantains and are sent home after leaving the snakes.

Joe tells them he will skin the snakes for them to bring home and to hang on the wall.

Everybody is waiting for Jude to get up the next morning, and Flavia gets to him first. "Ya lil Satan spawn. Ya know how long we been hidden under ever'body's noses, and ya come along and bust tha goddam closet door wide open? Ah already know ya tha Antichrist. Ya just not big enough yet. Come over here by my purse."

Jude does what she says, and she pulls her holy water out and dumps it on his head. He starts crying because he's got an eyelash stuck and she's scaring him because she hangs the rosary on his neck tight. Jude remembers what True has said, that she's gonna kill him.

"Lawd Jesus, look! He's burnin'. Tha holy water burnt him. Get thee behind me, Satan. But Ah still love ya."

T-June grabs him up, consoling him and fussing with Flavia for saying that, dumping the holy water on Jude's head and wanting to strangle him with her rosary.

MeeMee Minou holds him, comforting him, "My bébé, dontcha listen to dat. Flavia been crazy for a long, long time. You a good boy, and so what if tha world knows? Ah don't give a rat's ass if tha whole t'ing comes out. Nobody back home believes shit either."

Everybody is putting their two quarters' worth in the conversations when True and Isabel walk up into the kitchen, starving. No one says a word, putting Café Bustelo in front of her and asking, "How you like your eggs?"

She sits on the side of Jude and takes his little hands in hers. "You are the cutest thing I've ever known, and you can do what you do, well, it's a downright miracle. You were given these powers from your family and God. True explained everything last night and asked if I would stay after that. You see where I am, sitting next to you. And if you were older, True would have competition."

Jude starts crying, and she pulls him onto her lap.

"I'm sorry for thinking we could be together. So, I'll be your brother instead of your lover."

Joe tells him later, "Listen up, Jude. Ya tha best to come along yet. But cher, ya gotta slow yo roll, cool ya beans, and handle up on yo bizness like ever'body else who's got dis affliction. Ah love ya plenty-plenty, but ya gotta understand ever'body else is old, and dey can't handle dis shit no more.

"Mais, whatcha wanna do wit' ya skin? Hang it on tha wall?"

The crew of would-be pirates comes early that morning, and they hang out the rest of the day, Jude telling them Sammy is in charge while he's away.

∞ ∞ ∞

THE vacation is over after three weeks, and everyone is preparing to leave when Minou comes in the bedroom of Jude's and shuts the door.

"Bébé, we need to talk. MeeMee has had bad feelings 'bout ya for a long while 'cause ya was so damn bad. Ah always loved ya, but Ah didn't like ya 'cause you a lil smart-ass who demands his own way. Ya beginnin' to grow up, and still ya tha one who takes control of tha situations. Ya scared me bad-bad 'cause Ah always been afraid of sharks. Ask PawPaw.

"Dere's somet'in' Ah need for ya to listen good. Ya can't trick a trickster, and Ah go way back wit' dat. Ah love ya, Jude, in spite of what yo Pop and Mom did to ya."

They pile up in their vehicles ready to leave, T-June with Jude are in his pickup for a long talk home about trust and minding your elders.

Jude hears Minou say, "Hey, Jude."

And winks at him.

Chapter Twenty-Six

Isabel and True

WELL, the long-distance romance doesn't last long and has Isabel and her popi, Manny, moving to Louisiana.

True puts a rock on her finger, and they have a huge wedding planned for Christmas Eve.

He has built a beautiful house Down Below, up in the middle of all the young people raising children, and they plan for a dozen themselves. Shit, it's gonna be a subdivision before long, calling it Joseph Thibeau Sr. Down Below Gardens.

For sure, some kind of long bridge.

Jude is so glad he's part of their lives now, watching from the sidelines. He treats Isabel with a love of pureness now that he has no plans to deflower her. Jude is down there as often as his parents will let him. He's calling everybody to come get him almost every weekend. He spends as much time with the new couple as possible. He loves them as much as his little heart can carry.

Jude tells all the other children he's gonna be True's best man in the anticipated wedding coming up.

Jude struts around like he's grown, and he makes the other children fed up with his ways. They leave him alone with his cocky self. That's all right with him because he thinks he is 10 feet tall and gator proof.

True and Isabel are living in the new house with her popi, Manny Castro, and once in a while, her little cousin Sammy Perez will come stay for holidays and school breaks.

Sammy loves the little dude Jude, who he calls a miracle and will be a lifelong friend.

Oh, my Gawd. Manny Castro thinks Flavia hung the moon. First time he meets her, he is twitterpated with her, and she makes him belly laugh. She tells him right from the get-go, "Now, Manny, Ah really enjoy ya company, and ya so funny. Ya even come wit' me to say rosaries at Bertha and Alcide's porch, and ya brung ya own rosary. But mister, Ah ain't interested in no romance. No hanky-panky, ya hear me? Ah got a lot of pull 'round here."

Manny cooks for all the families and loves every minute of it, while Flavia sits in the kitchen with him. That's a relief for everyone because now they know where she's at. They sure can't trust her at the store anymore.

Grey and Gerry King, Flavia's sons, are elated that Manny Castro has come into her life. She gets real angry at them for trying to control her, and ugly words are spoken, causing everyone to nurse hurt feelings.

Flavia does not give a shit whose feet she tramples on.

She sure loves the idea that both her daughter-in-laws are having their first babies, considered late-in-life pregnancies, as both are in their thirties.

Weedie King, the former Sister Marie, and Mary Marguerite from way down the bayou are having their babies here with all the old midwives.

There's no chance these babies will be supernatural beings unless….

∞ ∞ ∞

MANNY and Isabel will be certified lawyers in the fall semester, not long before the wedding.

Lawd, they gonna miss his cooking.

Isabel is teaching whoever wants to speak Spanish, and Bishop Toussaint is on the front row. He needs to speak more than a few words as he helps the Hispanic community.

True takes Isabel everywhere with him, showing off her massive engagement rock. She absolutely loves the Monsieur Mayhem Band, and she and Jolie are already like sisters who love Jude fiercely, but of course, Jolie is his mama.

Isabel is teaching Jolie a song about Cuba, "Perdido," and they harmonize perfectly, Jolie already knowing how to sing it in Spanish.

The men are in shock, and True grabs her up in his arms, asking why she hasn't told him she sings like Linda Ronstadt.

Then the band starts playing the tune, and it can knock your socks off. Says Jude, "Fuck a duck, Papa. Whatcha have going on around here? That's the prettiest song I've heard in years."

Spoken like the true five-year-old he is.

Isabel joins the band, bringing with her many popular Cuban melodies and Jolie loving it. True sure does and Fats as well. They tour up until the time of the wedding, but Isabel leaves a month before them to prepare for this wonderful, massive ceremony blending the two cultures together in a big way.

Jude stays with the family when his parents are touring.

Isabel has chosen ten bridesmaids, including all the women Down Below and her best friend and two cousins.

You figure it out…

Jude is going to be best man, so Isabel asks a little cousin of hers, Juanita Cruz, to be her maid of honor and match up with Jude.

Juanita comes walking through the gravel and the rocks, carrying her little shoes, and Jude drops to his little fat knees, saying "I knew it, O knew it. Blessed Spirit, you sent her to me. Just like I saw." Never telling anyone his dream.

He runs to her, and she begins to run toward him, looking like Bo Derek did; instead, she has thick black braids and her little feet hurt.

"Oh, my señorita, I've been waiting on you. I saw you in a dream. Come, I have something for you."

Before she greets everybody, Jude takes her hand, and they run off together to his room. He locks the door. They sit together on the bed, him realizing he's just a child and can't do shit, the horny little bastard.

Jude has all the respect for Juanita as he does for her big cousin and softly puts a small box in her hands. "I saved this from the treasure we found and shared all of it except for some gold coins and this ring that's going to be too big. I bought an eighteen-carat chain to wear 'til you can wear it on your finger.

"Juanita Cruz, will you marry me when I'm eighteen and you too? I already knew how old you are and what you looked like. I've been dreaming of you since I came back from Florida. Well, will you?"

A chip off his papa's shoulders.

The little couple walk into the kitchen, with everyone greeting Juanita. Jude makes her show her gift, telling the bunch they are getting married.

First, he's got to ask for her hand from Manny since her popi isn't there.

Jude introduces her to all his cousins, and they like her, much better than they do him.

The family is going to ask questions.

Minou asks Jude, trying not to laugh, "Bébé, you been savin' dat ring all dis time 'cause ya saw dis lil gurl in yo dreams? Just like ya papa, jus' like him."

Joe ruffles his hair and says, "Mais, dat's my boy, huh? Ya papa tole me and MeeMee dat he saw ya mama in a dream too, an look at dem now. Two okra seeds, Ah tell ya, just like two okra seeds. Ya gonna be wit' ya lil señorita, Ah got no doubts in my head."

The families hug and kiss Juanita, and she just smiles and giggles. Her family acts the same way.

∞ ∞ ∞

WHILE the band is traveling, True Blue himself begins to tell Isabel all – I mean ALL – of what he's capable of. The band is there to support him with all his details.

He and T-June are doing parlor tricks for the rest of the band and Isabel, and she is laughing big old belly laughs. Just a few funny tricks at the start; don't want to send her running.

True Blue doesn't venture into her head out of respect for his love, but that doesn't mean Monsieur Jude isn't sneaking up in both their heads. He isn't selective in what he blurts out, and his little ass will be in trouble again.

Isabel is getting a choir together of all the little children to sing a song at their wedding, so of course, Jude and his señorita join. One of the little ones of Junya and T-Mae's sings his little heart out but never in the right key.

Isabel is trying to pick out where it's coming from, and Jude says, "T-bébé, man, you sound like a frog. I mean, maybe you can lip sync? And Josie, you're following behind him, so you're off too."

That statement gets him kicked off the choir for good.

Large packages start arriving daily at their home – UPS has a boat – with presents from all over Florida and other states, but several come from Cuba.

It keeps the women opening them, and now that Jude is choir-free, he's up in the middle of it all opening too. He opens one small package with a leather box inside. Jude pulls out an old gun.

You know he doesn't half-ass anything, so he's showing it to all the ladies. Isabel looks as though she has seen a ghost.

They are steadily yelling at him, pointing it here and there, before Isabel grabs him and takes the antique pistol from him.

"Jude, you need to go find something else to do. Don't say a word about this. I mean it. If you do, you won't be best man."

Isabel sits down while all the women gather, trying to get her to breathe. They are asking if they should call True. She says absolutely not.

She tells them after getting her wind back, "This is a warning from a group I use to participate in, Patriots for Cuba. We were a militant group that caused Fidel havoc in every way we could. The organization had a plane, and we would bombard the island with food, shoes, and pamphlets, warning Castro that we were coming.

"It's a lifelong commitment to this group that I had been pulling away from because they were beginning to be violent. The top general in this was my lover, Enrique Sterling. I left him and the group, but he's been trying hard to get me back.

"When the gun is presented, it means you are a traitor. It is he who sent the gun as an ultimatum. I'm wondering now who told him I was getting married. There's a large community of ex-patriots, so there's no telling. I just pray he doesn't come here. Please don't tell True."

Not sharing this information with True is going to be a big problem later on.

∞ ∞ ∞

MINOU and Joe arrive two weeks out from the wedding, bearing gifts and fruit and Sammy Cruz. He has come to be with his best podnah, Jude Thibeau. Sammy already knows Juanita and they're good friends, so the trio goes in search of anything they can find for the day. Callie and Henri are having the celebrations, showers, or otherwise for the couple at the famous restaurant Caldonia's. Callie and Henri have their five children up in the restaurant doing their jobs, even the twins folding napkins.

The twin boys you can't tell apart are Al and Art Aucoin, and they seem to be perfectly normal, no supernatural shit. Sassy little critters and full of the canaille.

Minna Sue is in college, and MaeMae is struggling in high school. She is just not interested in learning what's in those old books.

Of course, True is already playing music when they open Caldonia's.

Well, the age difference between Callie and Henri sure hasn't stopped anything.

All the houses in their village are full of people coming in for the wedding, which is two days away.

The band makes it home that week, and everyone is preparing for their roles in the massive production. True can't wait to hold his señorita and tell her about the tour. Then, she tells him everything that's been going on since she came home to prepare, but not about the gun.

All the cousins, aunts, uncles, and friends coming for Isabel are lively, colorful, and helpful, talking Spanish constantly, assuming everyone there can speak it. It's a hilarious mixture of women talking, cooking, mending, and just general mayhem.

The two cultures are definitely alike; even the dancing is similar. When the Cubans start doing the chicken dance for them, all the women join in, and the house is rocking.

The wedding ceremony and High Mass are going to be said by Bishop Becnel, who got his spiritual quest started right here in St. Luke's Catholic Church.

Seems like ages ago when T-June made himself known to Father Becnel and Sister Bridget, who has followed her Saint Mayhem his whole life.

The reception will be in Down Below, Louisiana.

Madam Aucoin and Bishop Toussaint will be there to officiate the jumping of the broom and to speak to the Spirits, if necessary.

The night before the wedding after the rehearsal dinner, True is asking Isabel if she wants to change her mind and run off instead.

She is feeling guilty and wants to tell True what's bothering her. "I have something to tell you, and it may be you that runs in the other direction.

"I used to belong to a very militant group when I was a young woman, and the leader was my lover, Enrique Sterling. He sent to me through UPS last week a package, and in it was the gun that is passed from one patriot to another to make that person snap to reality, make them feel guilty. Whoever has the gun has to keep it until it's needed again. If you don't come back, you are a traitor.

"I have no clue who told him where I am. I haven't seen him in a good eight years, but he hasn't given up on me to stand by him.

"I waited for the right moment to tell you. So much else has been going on since you came off tour."

True listens to every word in silence, and when she finishes, he pulls her up into his arms. "Baby, you just don't know us that well.

We're always waiting for something to come down the road, and we've handled every bit of it.

"You think he has the gall to come uninvited? I pity the fool if he does with all the powerful people we have in this village. He just doesn't know."

∞ ∞ ∞

EVERYBODY is running around trying to find things misplaced that are needed for this morning. Clothes scattered and shoes missing a partner and "who's got the mascara and rouge?" is the stuff being hollered for, but everybody gets to church on time.

The men waiting to leave after hours of aggravation and yelling are all ready with the help of the women they're yelling at.

Such a solemn occasion in the church but not with the groomsmen. They are sneaking drinks from a flask and occasional tokes, waiting on the bridesmaids to come down the aisle dressed so colorfully with tropical flowers and bright ribbons.

None of them feel too spry this morning because of the bachelor party and the bachelorette party, minus the couple that caused this.

After everyone else comes down the aisle, here comes Juanita with a white dress on and a huge red sash and a small hibiscus flower in her French-braided hair, simply a vision.

Jude is standing so proud in his little tuxedo, and he reaches for Juanita and puts a huge wet kiss on her little lips. Juanita reaches to slap him, and he jumps back, falling over a big bouquet arrangement and knocking it down. Here's Jude.

When Bishop Becnel comes to the altar, all solemn and serious, Flavia stands up and hollers at him, "Hey Father, where ya been? It's so good to see ya, hot damn. Man, look at all tha people here. Ya got a full-ass church today. Look at dem robes ya wearin'. Hah! Ya didn't buy dat at Flavia's.

"Quit, quit pullin' on me. Ah don't wanna be quiet. Ah got pull, ya lil bastards."

As Grey and Gerry try to make her sit down, it's only when Manny takes her hand that she sits quietly next to him.

For almost two hours the Mass lasts. A couple of groomsmen have to flee the sanctity of the church to throw up in the bushes outside.

A fun time is had by all.

The reception is getting ready to start, with tents put up everywhere and catered food along with special dishes made by all the women. Iced down Champagne and an open bar make the groomsmen want a hair of the dog that bit them. Bloody Mary Time.

Madam Aucoin and the Bishop are waiting with the pumped-up broom all decorated, ready to hang on the wall after.

So many people Down Below in all kinds of boats, hitching rides and yelling in the wind that there is a traffic jam in the bayou of boats trying to dock. Way too many people making noise and walking all over the place have caused Pieyan and Suzie Q to go to an uncharted area of the swamps to get away before someone sees them. Joey is with them because we sure don't need for him to be up in the trees.

Joe is in his cups and has to say something. "Mais, Minou, look at all tha people here. Shit, Ah t'ought tha Mass would nevah end, Mais, dat's too-too much. We left tha yacht over dere by our house in Florida, and good t'ing. Ah don't want no asshole scratchin' it.

"Mais, it's gonna be a mess back here. Shit, it looks like tha firemen's fair wit' tha mud dey make wit' tha beer spillin' and shit. Who's gonna clean dis shit up?"

Same old-same old Joe.

The dance floors are full, three built on wooden platforms, and everybody is just finishing the chicken dance when an old Cuban song the band begins to play, "Guantanamera."

Someone taps Isabel on her shoulder. She turns, laughing, into the face of Enrique Sterling in camouflage and a black beret.

"Chiquita, you remember this song? It was our favorite, remember, Chiquita?"

He tries to take her in his arms still in her wedding dress. She knees him in the balls.

They tell me that hurts bad-bad.

True walks up to him and says to his back, "It's time for you to leave, sir." All the men surround True for backup.

"Aw, I beg to differ, Patron, but I plan to stay for a while." Enrique says this while he sits at a table nursing his sore balls. This man has been tortured, so what's a little kick in his cojones by an ex-lover?

Into the tent comes an army of military power, all holding AK-47s, not quite pointing yet but aiming to kill.

Isabel runs to True's side and starts being very vocal. "What the hell do you think you're doing? How dare you! After all these years you have gotten worse instead of better. When I left you, I left no doubt that it would be for good, so what do you want? You know me. Why do you dishonor my holy marriage? Leave now. Someone is calling the police as I speak."

The whole army cocks their guns, laughing as they did so. They want the police to come; it's part of the plan.

Enrique jumps on top of a table full of plates and glasses, and he knocks all of it on the floor with the butt of his rifle. "I'm here to proclaim every Cuban here will pay sales taxes on all the money you threw away to come to this horrendous mating. You call yourself Cuban, but you turned American with all the greed of a Yankee. I am shaming you.

"Pull out your cards and cash and jewelry. It's all going to the cause of liberating Cuba."

Enrique staggers as the table starts jumping up and down hard while he looks for stability of a chair. He falls to the ground, and then he's jiggling on the floor and scratching himself like a monkey.

The army tries to shoot, but their guns are jammed. Madam Aucoin has taken care of that way before they've aimed at anything.

T-June and True have him bouncing like a red ball, back and forth between them, and he lets out a bloodcurdling scream. This is another kind of torture.

They drop him, and his whole army goes to retreat when Pieyan and SuzieQ bust up in the reception, scaring the shit out of everybody, running for cover and boats. They have been sneaking on the fringes, seeing if there is any more Champagne when they see the men with guns, so they are defending their land too.

The army can't even surrender, they are so frightened, worse way worse than fighting Fidel. A fucking pair of monsters!

What the mierda?

They are running in every direction when Enrique grabs Jude for protection, never thinking this child is a supernatural creature, like the rest of the shit shown to him tonight. He thinks that they are a coven of witches and Voodoo queens who can command monsters, so this child will be his escape before the police show up.

They can't have a shootout like planned; their guns don't work.

Hey Jude, don't let me down.

Jude jumps right up into the militant mind of the fool, and Enrique starts singing "God Bless America" and can't figure out why he does that.

Jude then tells him loud in his head, "Hands up in the air," and they all raise their hands to the command.

The police come very late to the scene because they've had to get old man DarDar up out of bed to use his boat. All the boats in the area were already rented to the guests at the reception, and they ain't cooperating.

Everyone left at the reception is silent on what has taken place. These people are all leery of authority, coming from their background, and refuse to say anything – good, bad, or the ugly.

Everything for miles around is minus boats rented to the guests and the po-po want to act all huffy and puffy for the silent treatment they receive.

Don't worry. The cops get tipped a generous deal for their Christmas party going on at the station.

True sits down at the table, after the guns are hidden and everyone left is silenced, to talk with Enrique. "Hey, man, what the shit is this about? Robbing your people just like Fidel does? Half of these people here are your relatives. Do you hate them that much for making a way in America? You're not being fair, dude. They have worked hard.

"You are an educated man, Isabel tells me, a professor of political science, and you got your education here in the USA and have lived well yourself. What have you done besides being a professor of conflict?

"Tell me what you think is going on here? It's a place full of mystery and unusual people indeed. I'm one of them. What did you accomplish that you came here for? To cause Isabel to change her mind? You sure could have done a better job at it, and you're way, way too late.

"We are in love, we sing together in our music, and we are truly, truly soulmates. Dude, you didn't have that with her. She left when you thought violence was the answer, and now you're robbing people at gunpoint. What the fuck, dude?

"It's Christmas morning, and we will have the celebration here. Y'all are going to sit down to dinner with us to participate in the wondrous time of Christ's birthday. We are going to break bread with each other this Christmas day."

Isabel grudgingly agrees. She really doesn't want to be in Enrique's presence, but it's a holy day and forgiveness will be on the main menu.

Everyone is getting the dinner ready early in the morning, and they don't know what to do with a bunch of militant men, other than ask what they want for breakfast and serve coffee to them still in their soldier costumes.

Watching all the children open their gifts from Papa Noel, the men from the failed plot are missing their families who are celebrating without them.

True goes outside to smoke his pipe, sitting on the porch, when Enrique sits on the side of him. "I can't find the words for your kindness after all the tragedy I caused on your and Isabel's special day. For this fiasco, I will never forgive myself. Shame is not a feeling I'm accustomed to, and now I feel the hotness of it on my face and in my eyes, tearing up all the time. You will probably not see me again and are probably glad. But before we leave, please let me speak to Isabel. I know she doesn't do anything she doesn't want to, so man to man, please help me a little with that, I beg you."

True goes to speak with his wife of less than 24 hours, asking her to go to speak to her old lover.

That's pretty strange, if you ask me.

She raises her voice at him, telling him no, then True says, "My beautiful wife, please don't keep that anger inside of you. There must have been something good about him for you to have stayed with him. Try finding some compassion for Enrique because he's deeply sorry for what he did. Let him go home with a little dignity. You will never forget this, but not giving him the time to speak with you, to go back to his people and his army with nothing, is not you."

Isabel insists True be with her while she's listening to whatever Enrique may come up with to say. The militant sits next to her, wanting badly to touch her.

"I wish we could go back to the days when we were so gung-ho about being the best patriots, trying to call attention to ourselves. We couldn't in Cuba because you have a place with no freedom of speech. Here you do, and we have made a lot of noise exercising that right. But now, we are referred to as a hoodlum gang that got kicked out of Cuba.

"I'm so very shamed to have done this to you, chiquita. I have caused you to have no good feelings about me for the rest of your life. Never ever did I want this to happen. I still love you, chiquita, with my heart and soul. When I heard you were marrying a gringo, I went crazy with a broken heart and anger at all our people going to the rich white man's wedding with you as his bride.

"Never did I think you would marry someone else, and a rich gringo to put the fin on us.

"I wish you everything you deserve that is happiness and peace and many children. I will leave now, and I'm sorry I'm the reason for all this happening on your wedding. I love you, Isabel, and always will."

Enrique turns to leave quietly. Isabel stops him with a sincere hug. He grabs her as if this will be the last time he will get the warmth against him.

It is.

"I forgive you, Enrique. You still have a place in my heart that will always be there."

∞ ∞ ∞

EVERYONE is gone two days after Christmas, and the village is a ton lighter. The days are spent playing catch-up after days of partying until New Year's, which will see another party.

Some of these party-hardy crazy Cubans are coming back for the New Year's Eve party. In whatever language, they will pass a good time. Juanita's parents are coming back for the celebration and for sure bringing her. She loves Jude with all her little-girl heart.

New Year's Eve has the small couple out roaming the land Down Below because she wants to see Pieyan and SuzieQ again and talk with them.

Pieyan has never felt easy around Jude. He's too much of a child who believes the world is his oyster and should be slurped off the shell. Suzie Q says his mouth is not ever clean with the words that come out of it.

But in a loving way.

They are so kind to Juanita and Jude and put them on their shoulders to walk around the swamps, a perfect way to tour the exotic and mysteriousness of South Louisiana's many, many swamps. Goes to show you, a place full of supernatural and mystical presence that everybody feels like they are in the clouds as the houses are. Pieyan doesn't see the need to hide anymore, for sure after Belle and SuzieQ and Pie and then Joey. This was their place first and then here comes all the humans!

After being gone most of the day, Jude and Juanita bring the small boat back to the docks at the house and they go in for something to eat. The duo has been out galavanting all day and they some hungry for red beans and rice MeeMee Minou has made this morning, with thin slices of onions, cucumbers, and tomatoes for a salad that comes fresh right out the garden.

It is getting dark, almost time for the party that night with all the out-of-town guests for the most part. The village loves to party with them.

Isabel is sitting on True's lap, laughing wickedly as True says nasty things in her head. True has now blocked little Jude with a busy signal so he can't listen to either of them. Jude certainly doesn't care, his head is full of Juanita.

Flavia is busy dancing the tango with Manny Castro, who is a popular lawyer among his people and the Cajuns now. They travel together to go to Florida when it's necessary, and he watches her as she travels from one realm to another, like a light switch. He finds her fascinating, and he's safety and security for her.

A group of old timers, older Cajuns with the older Cuban men, are discussing what has taken place at the wedding, and you know, since this is his house, Joe's saying something first.

"Mais, Ah didn't know what to do, me. Ah ain't never had an army up in my face wit' loaded big-ass guns ready to shoot my old ass. Ah knew my boys was gonna take care of tha situation, shit, no doubt. Mais, but it was tha best reception Ah been to in my life. A good time passed by all. Happy, happy New Year, but ya bettah not try to kiss me, non."

T-June and Jolie are dancing instead of playing music, although they are called to the floor to sing "Louisiana 1927."

Jude and Juanita are dancing too, and when he tries to steal a kiss, she shoves him. He never quits aggravating the shit out of her.

It's countdown, and the clock strikes one time. Everybody is kissing everybody, so Juanita lets him kiss her cheek, and he moves to her mouth so fast. She slaps him.

Jude is proud of the fingerprints on his face. He is strutting.

Whispering in her ear, he says he has something to show her, and she follows into his bedroom. "My little chiquita banana, I love-love you, and I want you to do something for me. Will you show me yours? I'm going to show you mine."

Well, it was goodnight, Irene, after that. Juanita gives him a huge black eye.

That horny little bastard.

Right after the New Year's bells ring and everyone is toasting each other, one of the Cuban men is yelling to put the TV on.

"We have breaking news coming in from Cuba. There was an assassination attempt on Fidel Castro in his palace this New Year's morning. The assassin was killed by his guards. His name was Enrique Sterling, the leader of the group "Patriots for Cuba" based here in our country. He was a resident of Miami, where he was a professor of political science at Miami State. Enrique Sterling has become a hero in the eyes of his people.

"His army was captured, and they were brought to the infamous jail cells of Havana.

"In Miami, there are celebrations everywhere, with guns being shot and bonfires reaching for Cuba."

Isabel is being very stoic about the tragic news. "His death is just what he had tried to accomplish in a big way. He left the game and followed his own rules. God bless his precious soul."

She goes in their bedroom alone and shuts the door.

Jude comes down for breakfast the next morning with the biggest shiner anyone had ever seen.

He wouldn't tell them anything.

Characters:

THE PELTIER/THIBEAU FAMILY

Minna Sue Peltier Thibeau [Minou] – Joe Thibeau's wife; called MeMe Minou by her grandchildren

Jake Peltier – Minou's papa, killed in an oil rig accident

PawPaw Irby – Irby Peltier, Minou's grandfather [pawpaw]

MawMaw Dardar – Minou's maternal grandmother

Bertha Dardar Peltier – Minou's mama; called MaeMae by her great-grandchildren

Alcide Peltier – Jake's brother; Bertha's husband; Minou's parrain (godfather)

Ethel Thibeau – Joe's mama

Joseph Alan Thibeau Junior [T-June and Monsieur Mayhem] – Minou and Joe's son; Jolie Theriot's husband

Caldonia [Callie] Evette Thibeau Aucoin – Minou and Joe's daughter; T-June's sister; Henri Aucoin's wife

Jude Thibeau – T-June and Jolie's son

THE THERIOT FAMILY

Jolie Theriot Thibeau – Estelle and Theo's daughter; Lily's sister; T-June's wife

Estelle Theriot – Katrina, Roberta, Lily and Jolie's mama; Theo's wife

Theo Theriot – Katrina, Roberta, Lily and Jolie's papa; Estelle's husband; Joe's business partner

Estelle (Lily) Theriot – Katrina, Roberta and Jolie's baby sister; Estelle and Theo's daughter; Toot's wife and Maybelline Toussaint's mother

Malcolm (Mac) Laverne Theriot – Estelle's nephew raised by Estelle and Theo; vampire; Moe's brother

Mohammed (Moe) Laverne Theriot – Estelle's nephew raised by Estelle and Theo; Mac's brother

Katrina Theriot Miller – Roberta, Lily and Jolie's older sister; Estelle and Theo's daughter; Butch's wife

Big Mama Theriot – Theo's mother; Jolie's granmother

Roberta Theriot Aucoin – Katrina, Lily and Jolie's sister; Estelle and Theo's oldest daughter; Saul Aucoin's second wife

Lady Dupree – Moe's wife

Maybelline and Laray Laverne – Estelle's sister and brother-in-law; parents of Malcolm and Mohammed

Big Daddy Jolie's grandfather

THE GUIDRY/BREAUX FAMILY

Butch – Matthew Miller Junior; a young boy that Minou and Joe take into their home

Irene Guidry – Butch's mama

Daniel Guidry – Butch's grandpa; usually called Old Man Guidry

Matt Miller – Butch's father

Jean Breaux – Butch's stepfather

Flower Catherine Breaux – Butch's half-sister

Matthew Miller Junior [Butch]; Irene's son; Katrina's husband

Irene Guidry – Old Man Guidry's daughter; Butch's mama

Daniel (Old Man) Guidry – Irene's daddy; Butch's grandfather

Jean Breaux – Butch's stepfather

Flower Catherine Breaux Dugas – Butch's half-sister; Rowdy Dugas's wife

Elouise Marie Miller [Weedie and Sister Marie] –Butch and Katrina's daughter

Jerome Anthony Mont-Pellier IV [Tony] – son of Flower and Jerome Mont-Pellier III

Ruby Jewel Flowers (MeeMaw) – Irene's grandmother

Kylie Flowers (Fancy) – Irene's mother

Drake Adam Flowers [Bubba] – MeeMaw's youngest son

Uncle Charlie – MeeMaw's brother

THE AUCOIN/TOUSSAINT FAMILY

Madam Alafair Aucoin – Voodoo practitioner from New Orleans; wife of Bishop Toussaint; aunt of Henri Aucoin and Saul Aucoin

Bishop Laurant Toussaint [Dr. Manly Tall] – Madam Aucoin's husband; head of the His Divine Spirit Congregational Church and His Divine Spirit Community Center

Henri Gustave Aucoin – great-nephew of Madam Aucoin; married to Caldonia Thibeau; mayor of New Orleans

Saul Aucoin – Madam's nephew; motorcycle gang leader; Roberta Theriot's husband

Eli Rene Aucoin [Easy] – Saul and Roberta's son

Harley Aucoin [Hellbent Harley] – son of Saul Aucoin, Henri's brother; Madam Aucoin's great-nephew

Henri Gustave Aucoin III (True Blue) – Henri and Callie's son; a musician

Minna Sue – Henri and Callie's oldest daughter

Alphonse (Al) Aucoin – Henri and Callie's son; Art's twin brother

Art Aucoin – Henri and Callie's son; Al's twin brother

MRS. FLAVIA'S FAMILY

Flavia King [Mrs. Flavia] – proprietor of Mrs. Flavia's Emporium and Mercantile; T-June's nanan

Stephen – Flavia's oldest son from her first husband

Horace – Flavia's youngest son from her first husband

Stuart King [Sweet Stu] – Texas horse rancher; Flavia's second husband

Grey Eagle King [Grey] – Flavia and Stu's adopted son; Comanche; Gerry's brother

Geronimo King [Gerry] – Flavia and Stu's adopted son; Comanche; Grey's brother

Elouise Marie Miller King [Weedie] –wife of Grey King; former Sister Mari

Mary Marguerite Callais – Gerry's girlfriend

THE DUGAS FAMILY

Pierre Dugas [Pete] – former classmate of T-June's; Charlotte's husband; father to Rowdy

Charlotte Dugas – former classmate of T-June's; school teacher; Pete's wife; Rowdy's mother

Rowdy Dugas – Pete and Charlotte's son

Jean Dugas [T-Jean] – son of Rowdy and Flower

THE RAPPOLET FAMILY

Bastille Henri Rappolet III [Chief] – wolf boy found in the swamp; son of Junya and T-Mae

Bastille Henri Rappolet Jr. [Junya] – T-Mae's husband; Chief's papa

Megdaline Rappolet [T-Mae] – Junya's wife; Chief's mama

Jude Rappolet – one of Chief's brothers

Alcide Rappolet – one of Junya and T-Mae's many children

Puh – Junya's sister

T-Burt – Puh's husband

THE ROBAIRE FAMILY (Vampires)

Claudine du Robaire – Mac's lover

Madam Angelique du Robaire – Claudine's mother

Monsieur Beauregard du Robaire – Claudine's father

Louie St. Pierre – French plantation owner from the Bahamas

THE LAVERNE FAMILY

Maybelline Laverne – Estelle's sister; mama of Mac and Moe

Toussaint Laverne [Toot] – nephew of Laray Laverne; Lily's husband

Maybelline Caldonia Laverne – Lily and Toot's daughter; Estelle and Theo's granddaughter

Laray Laverne – Maybelline's husband; Mac and Moe's daddy

Loretta Laverne [Tut] – Laray's mama

Louie Laverne [PeeWee]– Laray's daddy

THE LEROUXS

Justin Leroux – one of the Tuxedos; cousins who live in the swamps near the Thibeaus

Scottie Leroux – one of the Tuxedos; cousins who live in the swamps near the Thibeaus

THE CLERGY

Father Becnel – St. Luke's Parish priest

Sister Bridget Richard – T-June's teacher at St. Luke's school

Sister Lydia – a teacher at St. Luke's school from Peru

THE SILVERBERGS

Joshua Silverberg – Jim's brother; newspaper reporter and music producer

Jim Silverberg – Joshua's brother; a music producer

THE SPIRITS

Laurette – Caribbean Voodoo spirit conjured by Madam

Madam Consienne – spirit who lives in Madam Aucoin's home; leads a band of musical ghosts

Buddy Braxton –ghost of a jazz musician who inhabits Madam Aucoin's house

Shine – Buddy's wife

Emile Verdun – Madam Consienne's lover and music teacher

Jamie Sue Buffett – a spirit who lives in Minou and Joe's Florida home

Russell Chaisson – Jamie's intended

Mammy and Remus – two spirits who haunt the Florida home of Jamie Sue Buffett

MOTORCYCLE GANGS

Saints – good guy motorcycle gang

Roux Garouxs – not-so-good-guy motorcycle gang

Eli St. James – leader of the Roux Garouxs

Trixie St. James – Eli's wife

Precious Soul St. James [aka Soul] – Eli and Trixie's daughter

Eli St. James Jr. – Eli's son

THE SWAMP and THE MENAGERIE

Gaspar – a pirate's ghost

Pedro – Gaspar's parrot

Pieyan – a bigfoot

Suzie Q – Pieyan's mate; a bigfoot

Pie – Pieyan and Suzie's first son

Joseph (Joey) – Pieyan and Suzie's second son

Belle – former councilman's wife, now with Pieyan

Ruby – T-June's long-ago pet raccoon

Couyon – Callie and Lily's half-Mastiff

Gilbert –monkey at the zoo

Gertrude (Gertie) –wolf mother of Chief

Leroy – the wolf alpha male

Ruthie Mae – a north Louisiana snake

Evil Serpent Big Bad Bruce – a north Louisiana snake

Mean Muddy Melvin – Suzie Q's dad; a bigfoot

PIRATES (Ghosts)

Belizaire Delacroix – pirate ghost who seeks Bluebeard's treasure

Jacques Delacroix – Belizaire's brother

Jean Paul Delacroix – Belizaire's brother

Phillippe Delacroix – Belizaire's brother

Gabriel Delacroix (Gambi) – Belizaire's brother

FAIRIES

Mabb – queen of a fairy clan; a friend of Madam Aucoin's

Prince Harry Emile– Mabb's son

Alfred the 10th – king of an English fairy clan

Gladiola – Alfred's daughter

Hank the 15th – king of a fairy clan

OTHERS

Marie Leveau – a Voodoo priestess in New Orleans in the 1800s

Clifton – PawPaw Irby's friend, lost to the loup-garou

Monsieur Babineaux – a New Orleans antique dealer

Gerard Truxillo – sheriff

Laurence Michel Jr. – a New Orleans cab driver from Galliano, Louisiana Henri Aucoin – a waiter at the Hotel Caldonia in New Orleans; great-nephew of Madam Aucoin

Mrs. Winston Bourgeois Sr. – previous owner of Madam Aucoin's house

Old Man Boudreaux – St. Luke's school Santa Claus

Charleen – Sister's Bridget's niece, thought to be a candidate for sainthood

Jazzy Boudreaux – waitress at the Bon Temps Rouler; from the bayou

Merlin Boudreaux – Jazzy's husband; a New Orleans cop

Dr. Boudreaux – the coroner

Dr. Harold Guillory – veterinarian

Michel Melancon [Mike] – former wolf boy

Francis Dugas – the Lerouxs' lawyer

Celeste Blanchard – girlfriend of Rowdy Dugas

Jerome Anthony Mont-Pellier III – lawyer in the mayor's office; old friend of Henri Aucoin

Antoine Domino III – piano player in T-June's Band

Mr. Guidroz – owner of Guidroz's Cleaners

Colette Chassion from Chauvin Emmalois

Isabel Mariana Castro – waitress at the Perdido restaurant in Cross Creek; a native Cuban

Santonio Perez (Sammy) – former leader of a young gang in Florida; Isabel's cousin

Manny Castro – Isabel's popi

Juanita Cruz – Isabel's cousin and maid of honor

Enrique Sterling – Isabel's former lover and head of Patriots for Cuba

Old Man DarDar – boat owner

Eli St. James – leader of the Roux Garouxs

∞   ∞   ∞

Glossary

Bébé – baby

Bon chance – French for "good luck"

Bouder – pouting; put out

Bouef – French for beef

Bourré – card game

Canaille – mischievous

C'est la vie – French for "such is life"

Cher – a term of endearment

Choupic – a fish found in lakes, ponds and slow-moving rivers; also called a mudfish or bowfin

Comment ça va – how are you?

Couyon – fool

Fais do-do – a public dance; literally translated as "go to sleep"

Feu follet – marsh fire or crazy fire

Fin – Spanish for end

Font goss! – literally "You're kidding"

Frisson – goosebumps

Gris-gris – a talisman, amulet, voodoo charm, spell or incantation believed capable of warding off evil and bringing good luck to oneself or of bringing misfortune to another, according to Merriam-Webster

Gros bec – yellow-crowned night heron; translated as "big beak"

Haint – spirit

Haunt – afraid; "haunted"

Laissez-nous tranquille – leave us alone

Lagniappe – a little something extra

Loup-garou – a Cajun werewolf; sometimes called roux-garou

Mais – a conjunction; "but"

Merde – shit

Mon Dieu – French for "My God!"

Nanan – godmother

Nervine – anxious; nerves on edge

Pain perdu – literally, "lost bread;" French toast

Parrain – godfather

Pouldeau – mud hen

Pour le Mon de Bon Dieu – French for "for God's sake"

Priedieu – a prayer desk or kneeler

Puta – Spanish for prostitute

Putain – prostitute

Quel dommage – what a pity

Quemas – chaos

Rougarou – an alternative pronunciation and spelling of loup-garou

Tasso – smoked, spiced, cured meat, made from the hog's shoulder

Tante and nonc – French for aunt and uncle

Ta-ta – thank you

Tetons – breasts

Tootoo – a term of endearment

Traiteur – a Cajun healer

Tarte a la bouillié – literally, "burnt milk tart;" a traditional Cajun custard pie

Pronunciation Guide

Alcide – Al SEED

Atakapa – Ah TACK ah paw

Aucoin – O kwan

Chér – SHA

Chitimachas – Chit ti MAH chas

Dugas – DOO gahs

Hebert – A bear

Houmas – HOO mus

Lafourche – La FOOSH

Madam – Ma DAHM

Minou – Mee NU

Pieyan – Py YAHN

Peltier – PEL shay

Thibeau – TEE bo

Truxillo – Tru HEE yo

www.ingramcontent.com/pod-product-compliance
Lightning Source LLC
Chambersburg PA
CBHW021327310726
48971CB00001B/16